THE WITCH
AND THE
WORLDBREAKER

ASHES OF ISKARA: BOOK 1

Jonathan Wurst

ISBN (paperback): 978-1-968157-00-5
ISBN (e-book): 978-1-968157-02-9

First edition

Cover Art and Typography by J Caleb Design

Maps and Symbols by Jonathan Wurst

To my mom and dad, who never told me what I couldn't be...

THE KNOWN WORLD
CHARTED IN THE YEAR 425
VESHDA
TRAVA
HAVATA
YARVORE
ACRONUS BADLANDS
VELD
SELLBROOK
ISKARA
ROTHVALE
FELLGROVE
STELLEST
WEST DESERT
NELLBOROUGH
STONEPORT
ASHEN PLAINS
HAUNTED BAY
DAWNGALE
BASTIL
LASTRAIA
ATA
MERVOS
SKYVIEW
RED COVEN
D
MERVAIA
ESHGAR
IBAN
IDENE
ESHGAR
TRELLDAS
PAKSHA

N
W E
S
EXIM
ALVEG
SVIDAR
NESA
THRASDE
KAHI
OKAI
KA OASIS
EAST DESERT
DREL
CAALD
MIN
MAGMA
FIELDS
YZDAL
BYRNN
REDSCALE
ARGUS
LEGEND
VILLAGE
CITY
CAPITAL
BORDER
FOREST
MOUNTAINS
CANYON
LAKE
VOLCANO
WALL

CONTENTS

Part 1 - Fires of Nellborough 1

Part 2 - The Red Coven's Blade 79

Part 3 - The Hero of Ata..121

Part 4 - The Beast of the Eastern Plains 209

Part 5 - The Forgotten Mountain 249

Part 6 - The Godslayer's Sword 331

Part 7 - The Eye of the Storm 479

Part 8 - Sisters...537

PART 1

FIRES OF NELLBOROUGH

CHAPTER 1

A WARM BREEZE AGITATED THE ENDLESS purple flowers around Chinelo. The delicate blossoms swayed on their pale gray stems, rising and falling in gentle waves across the serene countryside. He lifted his gaze west toward the wind, watching the blooms move in a calming, comforting rhythm. The Ashen Plains were vast, empty, and hauntingly beautiful.

A sweet aroma filled the air, piercing the scent of smoke from his campfire. Beyond the expanse of gray and purple, he could just barely see the mountain peaks that marked the western edge of the kingdom of Iskara. Soon, the summer sun would descend behind those mountains.

The embers of his fire smoldered and crackled, sending up a swarm of bright sparks. He jumped, and his suit of armor rattled. His heart pounded, but it quickly returned to its usual tempo.

He sighed. He should have been over this by now.

He ran his hand through his curly black hair. It had already been eight months, but fires still seemed to disquiet him. Thankfully, this fire had reached the end of its usefulness, and it was about due for a proper smothering. He withdrew four freshly severed dragon horns from the cinders, and after a quick dousing, he stowed the first of them in his pack.

Chinelo's stomach growled. His food had run out that morning, or, more accurately, it had been devoured by the former bearer of those horns, one of the black dragons that occupied the Ashen Plains. He turned the last horn in his hand. Its curved surface shone in the sun, gleaming like ivory. He gripped it tightly before stuffing it into his bag with the other three.

He donned his helmet, lowering the visor over his eyes. Grabbing a handful of dirt from the faint path, he smothered the remnants of his fire. With night approaching, he needed to hurry east if he was going to sleep in a proper bed and eat a decent meal. He hoped the amber trees he saw ahead indicated that he was close to his destination.

Chinelo lifted his pack and hurried onwards. Loaded with provisions, clothing, and a sleeping pad, his pack weighed heavily on his shoulders. Combined with his armor, the load was grueling to carry. Fortunately, Chinelo had heard promising reports of his destination, the merchant village of Nellborough, and, thanks to the dragon, his pack was certainly lighter than on the previous day.

He continued onwards, marching towards the forest. Nellborough was nearly equidistant from the capitals of Iskara and its neighboring nations, making it the perfect place to buy and sell goods such as the dragon horns bouncing around in his pack. The sizeable sum they would yield would cover food and lodging until he found a more consistent source of income, hopefully in a role that would put his sword skills to good use.

The road veered into the forest. Chinelo looked back once more over the Ashen Plains. He had entered several days earlier, and while the journey had been tedious, his time in the mesmerizing expanse of flowers had calmed his mind and given him time to plan his future moves.

The wind's direction shifted, bringing with it an ominous cloud bank from the north. Chinelo continued his walk at an even swifter pace. The last thing he wanted was to get caught in an unknown forest at night in the rain.

The path weaved left and right around trees, rocks, decaying logs, and masses of vines and underbrush. In some areas, the brush was cut along the edges of the path. Clearly, someone was maintaining the road, which was a good sign that he was nearing the town. On his right Chinelo passed a carved stone arch that had been claimed by crawling ivy. He halted, eyeing the strange structure while he sipped from his flask. In neat columns lining the arch, runes of an unknown ancient language were etched. The arch's corners and edges were rough and jagged, eroded by eons of wind and rain.

Breathing deeply, Chinelo took in the many scents of the golden forest. The earth beneath his feet had a strong comforting smell. The aromas of leaves, wild onions, herbs, and pollen all weaved into a mischievous biting odor. The cool fragrance of rain drifted through the air, an ever-present reminder of the impending downpour and his need for shelter.

Walking ahead, Chinelo reached a fork in the path. An empty wooden signpost was haphazardly staked into the ground. The path was well traveled in both directions with rows upon rows of footprints overlapping each other. Two clear sets of tracks were visible traversing the intersection from the right path down the left path. Chinelo searched the ground around the post. Surely the sign must have fallen off and landed nearby. After a few minutes of digging through leaves, Chinelo noticed that twinkling blue lights had begun to fill the air. Flareflies.

At the sight of the insects, Chinelo let out an exasperated sigh. Night drew ever closer. Rising from the ground, he listened intently, hoping that the sounds of the village would penetrate the dense forest. His keen ears were only met with the chirping of crickets, the rustling of leaves, the light pitter-patter of woodland creatures scurrying through the undergrowth, and...

A voice.

Softly, in the distance someone was speaking. The village was close! Chinelo turned left toward the voice and raced ahead, his enormous pack shifting and rattling as he moved. Twigs and leaves crunched under his heavy steps. He pushed aside the brush, resulting in light pings and swishes as branches collided with his metal armor. Again, he heard the voice, only louder, closer. The path swerved around a large tree, and Chinelo found himself in a small clearing, face to face with...

Her.

About ten paces in front of Chinelo stood a young woman brandishing an ornate wooden staff in his direction. Rich tassels hung from a large gold ring at the staff's head, and a swirling orb of glowing blue vapor hovered within. She appeared to be close to Chinelo's age, likely in her mid-twenties. Her copper hair fell in a shimmering cascade, ending just above her slim shoulders, aside from two unruly tresses that hung below her collarbones. She was poised in a stance reminiscent of a frightened cat, equally fearful and intimidating.

Through a pair of rimless spectacles, she studied Chinelo with a piercing, wary gaze. Her round eyes, a deep blue like lapis, moved subtly, tracking every minute move Chinelo made. Her skin was fair, far lighter than Chinelo's, and freckles adorned her pale face and exposed forearms. Her loose green shirt and frayed skirt fluttered with a passing breeze.

"Don't come any closer," she commanded, shifting in her leather boots. There was an intensity to her voice that invoked an undeniable urge to obey. Chinelo stood over a head taller than her, yet he felt a faint flicker of unease dancing in his chest. As he stepped back, he wondered if he was acting in response to her fear, his own, or a combination of the two.

"I'm sorry. I didn't mean to startle you."

The woman's eyes darted down to Chinelo's side. The furrow in her brow deepened.

"If you touch that I will burn you where you stand."

Chinelo looked down. He had instinctively moved his right hand to the hilt of his sword. Raising both hands in a gesture of surrender, he recognized the source of his unconscious fear. Her staff and her threat had made that all too clear.

"You're a witch."

The woman slightly lowered her staff. "Yes. And what are you?"

"I'm a knight from Eshgar. I'm traveling to Nellborough to find work. I heard your voice and thought I was nearing the town."

The woman raised an eyebrow. Though his armor and accent would corroborate his claim that he hailed from Eshgar, her expression of doubt and distrust refused to vanish.

"Why have you been following me?"

"I—I haven't?" Chinelo replied.

"I've heard you, sensed you. You've been tailing me since I entered the forest. I will admit, you are skilled at masking your footsteps, but the voices of the forest don't lie. Frogs, crickets, birds, they all flee or fall silent when approached by a threat. I've witnessed that silence. I've sensed you!"

"I'm wearing full plate armor and an overloaded pack. I couldn't sneak up on anything even if I wanted to."

Eshgarian armor was distinctly regal, ornamented with gold trim across the arms and legs and blue cloth about the waist. It was meant to inspire and protect the knights that wore it. They were to be shining beacons of honor protecting their kin and country from any threat. Stealth had no place in a knight's skillset, and it was never a consideration in their armor's design. The many overlapping plates rattled together with every step. Sneaking in such armor was quite impossible.

The woman blinked twice before a wave of realization crossed her face. She relaxed and leaned against her staff with short sigh of relief. "Please forgive me. I'm a bit jumpy today. I've suspected that someone has been following me ever since I entered the forest. I was hoping that coming to this clearing would draw them out into the open. I'm very sorry for threatening you."

Now at ease, she abandoned her pointed tone. Her softened voice carried her words like a gentle flowing brook. She looked at the sky, analyzing the progress of the approaching storm clouds, now blazing a brilliant orange from the setting sun.

"You said you were traveling to Nellborough?" she asked, throwing him a quick glance.

"That's correct. I'm low on food and need a place to stay for the night. If you could—" Chinelo paused. While he was intent on reaching the town before dark, he didn't want to leave this woman alone if she was being followed.

"I'm afraid you're going the wrong way," the woman said. "It'll take you at least an hour to get to town from here, so making it there by nightfall is going to be impossible. Also, I would *not* want to be caught out in that storm."

"I see. Are you not going in that direction? I could accompany you if you are still worried about being followed. I'm well practiced with a sword."

"Oh, I've just come from there myself," the woman replied, adjusting her staff's position in the dirt. "I do appreciate the offer though. It is so very kind."

She looked again to the sky, tugging lightly on the hem of her glove. The corner of her mouth turned down in an almost imperceptible frown. She seemed to be concentrating, as if turning an idea over in her head.

"Would you... walk with me?" she asked with a hint of uncertainty in her voice.

"What?"

"Would you walk with me?"

"To where?"

"My cottage. As you said, I am still worried about being followed. And as I said, you'll never make it to town before dark. Sending someone into the forest at night during a storm would be disgraceful. I couldn't do that."

"How about this? I can guide you to the town tomorrow. I'm expecting a delivery there, so I was planning on returning anyways. See?" she asked with a smile, cocking her head. "This will work for both of us."

Chinelo paused. Her offer was tempting, and her melodic inflections were unexpectedly disarming. "I wouldn't want to impose upon you."

"Nonsense! I would enjoy the company."

Chinelo looked down, considering his options. He was exhausted and famished. The possibility of a roof over his head was incredibly difficult to decline. A low rumble of thunder echoed from the clouds above, and his stomach responded with a similar rumble.

"Very well," he said, removing his helmet. "I suppose I should introduce myself. My kin call me Chinelo. It would please me if you would as well," he said with a bow. Although he had been away from his home for the better part of the year, Chinelo still employed the traditional Eshgarian greeting.

"It is a pleasure to meet you, Chinelo," the woman said with a curtsy. "You may call me Isobel." Isobel reached down to pick up an open satchel from the grass. "Just let me gather my things, and we can be off."

Her nimble hands glided over the soft grass and gathered sachets of herbs, wrapped parcels of bread and cured meat, and vials of vibrant colorful liquids. Within moments she collected the spilled contents and returned them to their home.

Chinelo looked around the clearing. The path extended across the space, and protruding through the lush green carpet were more stone shards like the structure he saw in the forest. They too were etched with strange arrays of symbols. With a start, he remembered what drew him there: Isobel's voice.

"Isobel, if you are alone, who is it that you were talking to?"

"Oh! He's around here somewhere," Isobel chimed. "I told him to hide when I heard you approaching. He's probably preoccupied with a grasshopper or something—the little scamp. Mort! You can come out now."

A tuft of grass near Isobel's feet rustled. A large green bullfrog leapt onto the path and produced a loud, grating croak.

"There he is!"

Isobel extended her hand to the frog. It hopped onto her hand then waddled its fat, bulbous body up to her shoulder. From his perch, Mort surveyed the clearing before staring at Chinelo with black, unblinking eyes. Like a king on his throne, he wished to know who dared to enter his presence.

"You were talking to a frog?"

Isobel looked up. "Yes, of course. Do you expect me to sing to him?"

Chinelo was not convinced that the amphibian wouldn't enjoy that experience. Quite frankly, he was not convinced *he* wouldn't enjoy the experience, either.

Chinelo approached Isobel to help her gather the last of her belongings. He reached down and picked up a heavy tome that rested on a cluster of clover. It was bound in dragon-wing hide, and it bore characters and figures Chinelo did not recognize, though their similarity to the runes on the stone shards that littered the clearing could not be denied. Chinelo had seen a similar tome before, clutched in the hands of a witch who had been found during his early days as a knight.

"Ah, my spell-book! Thank you." Isobel hung the book at her waist, grabbed her staff, and gracefully stood. "Come! Let's go!"

Isobel set off down the trail towards the opposite end of the clearing. She entered the tree cover, looking over her shoulder as Chinelo toddled after her, his large pack shifting rather awkwardly on his shoulders. The thick foliage shaded the path well, with only a few traces of the waning sunlight piercing the golden canopy above.

Chinelo's pack swayed as he walked, snagging on nearby branches. His firm, deliberate gait and rattling equipment drowned out Isobel's gentle footfalls. Every few steps, Isobel glanced furtively at the knight, moving her gaze across his weathered armor, lingering on his sword's worn hilt, occasionally looking at his heavy pack swinging side to side. Once or twice, he thought he caught her studying his face. She appeared to be attempting to inspect her new companion rather sneakily, but such efforts were about as successful as any Chinelo might have made at stealth.

Eventually she stopped and stared down at the path ahead. She occasionally touched her chin with her gloved hand, as if she was lost in deep thought. In those moments, Chinelo became acutely aware of a growing stillness surrounding them. He shivered. Every rustle of every leaf put him on edge. There was a palpable tension in the dead air. Even with the oncoming storm, the wind had almost stopped entirely. Though he was ordinarily content to walk in silence, he felt he should say something to distract from the strange pressure that seemed to follow them. He cleared his throat.

Isobel apparently had the same thought. "So, Chinelo! Tell me about yourself," she said. "You mentioned you are looking for work in Nellborough? I'm very well acquainted with the townsfolk there. Perhaps I could point you to the right person?"

"Oh, that would be helpful. Right now, I'm looking for somewhere to settle, at least temporarily. I was working in Lastraia as an apprentice carpenter for a while before I came here, but it didn't really feel like it could be home for me."

"Oh? Why is that?"

"Well, my accent is pretty pronounced, and Eshgarians aren't readily welcomed in any town in Mervos, given our two countries' histories. The wounds from the war haven't fully healed yet. Most of the people in Lastraia were pleasant, but the odd few were enough to ruin the experience for me. I hoped I would have better luck here in Iskara."

"Well, you'll love it here. The people in Nellborough are so very friendly," Isobel gushed. "If you're looking for a carpentry job, I could introduce you to Griggs. I've been a customer of his for years, and he's always looking for help. Or you could talk to Valk! She's a close friend, and she repairs wagons and carts for the merchants who come through town. Just maybe stay away from the Rothvale Trade Guild. Those capital types... let's just say I have had better conversations with toads than I've had with them. Oh! No offense, Mort."

Chinelo stifled a smile as the frog croaked. Fortunately for Isobel, it seemed that Mort would look past the insult this one time.

"I was actually considering a hunting or guard job," Chinelo said. "Need to keep my sword skills sharp. I'm probably more accustomed to that line of work anyways."

"Well, there's not much to hunt around here, I'm afraid. Unless you count ash dragons, but we haven't had anyone who could kill one of those for five or six years. Very unpleasant creatures."

"Oh. That shouldn't be an issue. I killed one earlier today."

Isobel sharply turned her head. "You *killed* an ash dragon?"

"Yes."

"Without magic?"

"That's correct."

"Hmmm." She tapped her chin. "I don't know if I believe that."

"I did."

"No. You're making that up."

"I have the horns in my bag to prove it," he proclaimed, patting his pack.

"You probably just found those."

"What? On the ground? In a giant flower field? You think I just found them?"

"That seems like the most reasonable explanation."

Chinelo paused and looked at Isobel. In the fading twilight, a sly grin appeared on her face.

"Are—are you teasing me?"

"Maybe..." she chimed playfully before skipping ahead a few paces. "I do hope you scrubbed those horns down. Ash dragons have a very strong sense of smell and a very unfortunate habit of immolating anything with even a hint of dragon blood. I'd prefer for my house not to get burned down."

"Oh, of course. I scorched the ends of them," Chinelo said, reaching for the lantern he kept on his belt. "Speaking of fire, do you happen to have a flint kit in that satchel of yours? Mine is at the bottom of my pack."

"Oh no. Don't need one. Hold the lantern over here."

Isobel stopped walking and turned to face Chinelo. She extended her left hand and tensed. Chinelo looked at her outstretched forefinger, his eyebrows pulling together as he tried to understand what she was doing.

She whispered in a foreign, unfamiliar language. She spoke gently, with soft, almost musical inflections that somehow shook Chinelo to his core.

"Icht vasht."

With a flash, a single golden flame emanated from her gloved finger, lighting Isobel's face. Chinelo flinched at the sudden light, gripping the handle of the lantern tighter. Isobel touched the flame to the oil-soaked wick before releasing it. Her flame vanished as quickly as it appeared, leaving the two companions illuminated only by the growing light within the lantern and the blue twinkling of flareflies.

"See? Magic." Isobel smiled proudly before continuing her walk down the path, leaving Chinelo blinking behind her. He stared at the undulating flame, a playful dancer held captive within the lanterns cage. After a moment, he realized where his left hand had gone—straight to the handle of his sword. He took a deep breath, forced a smile, and followed his companion.

"So, umm, Isobel," he cleared his throat, trying to mask any wavering in his voice. "What kind of work do you do? I assume with skills like that you must be the local arsonist?"

"Oh, nothing nearly that exciting," she said with a toss of her hair. "I mostly make practical magical devices to sell to the merchants and potions for the village doctor. I dabble in the occasional enchantment if the blacksmith ever needs to add variety to his wares. But if I ever get bored, I'll definitely consider arson."

"So, you can do more than make fire?"

Isobel turned her head. "Of course, I can do more than make fire!" she exclaimed. She almost sounded offended at the question. "Anyone who knows the basics of esht flow can do more than that. I guarantee I could have you making more than just fire after only one day of training."

"Oh, I can't use magic."

"Nonsense! Anyone can use magic."

"Is that so?" Chinelo asked incredulously.

Isobel giggled. "I'm not teasing you this time, silly. Magic is inherent to all living things. Most nations either never adopted or have forgotten the Ancient Arts, so people think it's some esoteric practice restricted to old dusty hags. In reality, it's just another part of life."

Chinelo hesitated a moment. "Would you be willing to teach me?"

"It would be an honor," Isobel said, before stopping abruptly. "Oh! Here we are!"

Chinelo looked ahead.

His lantern illuminated a quaint cottage with walls of timber and plastered wattle. Above the steep shingled roof rose the crooked silhouette of a stone chimney. Isobel ascended the steps and produced a key from within her satchel before unlocking the heavy oak door. As she entered, she pressed her hand against an intricately runed glyph inscribed on the interior wall. About the room's perimeter, several candles mounted in sconces sparked to life, casting an inviting warm glow through the windows and open door.

Before entering the house, Chinelo paused on the doorstep. While their conversation may have distracted him, he could not ignore the shadowy silence in the woods, stalking their every move. The hair on his neck stood on end. He turned, scanning the dark, twisting trees for any signs of life. As raindrops began to patter across the treetops, he once again instinctively touched his sword hilt. The shadows and darkness seemed to move and swirl, shrouding their secrets from his watchful eyes. He stepped toward the trees, searching for the source of his trepidation.

Isobel leaned cheerfully against the doorframe. "Aren't you going to come in?"

"Yes..." he replied slowly, releasing his grip on his sword. "Sorry, I thought I heard something."

Isobel peeked over his shoulder, squinting into the darkness. As Chinelo entered the house, she firmly locked the door behind him.

CHAPTER 2

"WELCOME!" ISOBEL SAID, "YOU'LL HAVE TO pardon the mess. I don't often have visitors, so I'm admittedly a bit under prepared."

Chinelo surveyed the cozy interior. It was messy, yet comfortable. To his right, fur mats were placed around a low table. Spreading across the back wall was a wide work desk supporting bookshelves of acacia wood. The dark shelves were populated with dusty books, sparkling flasks of vibrant liquids, and strange devices for mixing and catalyzing chemicals. Vines sprouted from clay pots on top of the shelf, hanging far down the sides.

Sheets of parchment marked with scribbles, sketches, and complex glyphs were scattered chaotically round the desk, and several open volumes littered the floor. On the far corner of the desk stood a mortar, pestle, and a couple oil burners coated in a thin film of soot. Most notably, a tray of leaves, grasses, and moss was placed at the edge of the desk, and Mort had graced the tray with his corpulent presence.

Isobel's cheeks flushed as Chinelo's fascinated gaze lingered on her workspace. "And that is the mess you'll have to pardon. You really must give me more notice the next time you call."

Chinelo turned his attention elsewhere as Isobel entered the adjoining kitchen to unload her satchel.

"I'm sure you're tired, so please unload your pack and sit. I'll have dinner cooking shortly," Isobel said, gesturing to a chair in front of the table upon which she had released the contents of her satchel.

Chinelo deposited his pack in a corner near the door and began the arduous task of removing his armor. Eshgarian armor was light, giving him an ample range of motion to reach the many clasps and ties used to fasten his armor over his gambeson. He deposited his armor beside his pack, leaving him wearing only a snug sleeveless shirt and a pair of loose trousers, typical Eshgarian attire. Chinelo turned from the corner and was met by Mort's judgmental stare. The bullfrog clearly did not approve of Chinelo's bare shoulders.

As Chinelo took his seat at the table, Isobel chopped several vegetables she had drawn from the cupboards. She had removed her gloves, revealing a pair of elaborate runed sigils tattooed on the backs of her hands. She hummed softly, bobbing her head side to side.

"Is there anything I can do to help?" Chinelo asked, watching her face intently.

"Oh no. I'll have this ready to cook in just a moment. I would love to hear more about your journey, though. You mentioned you were in Lastraia only a few months?"

"That's right. I left Eshgar around eight months ago. I originally went east. Crossing the mountains did not sound like it would be a pleasant experience in the winter."

"Oh?" Isobel gathered a handful of sliced sausages and dropped them into her frying pan. "I was under the impression that Eshgar was still hot in the winter."

"Well, it's not exactly cold." Chinelo leaned forward in his chair, eyeing the food in front of him. "But, when you're at the higher elevations, temperatures can drop quite low. It's manageable with a well provisioned caravan, but on foot it's not ideal."

"So, you went through Mervos then?"

"Correct," Chinelo replied. "I visited the capital, Mervaia, and stayed there several weeks. Good food there. The innkeeper where I was staying was kind enough to cover my room and board if I helped around his tavern. Though, most of the time I was just warding off the more... undesirable clientele."

"Undesirable?"

"Violently inebriated or violently obtuse."

"Ah." Isobel nodded.

"After the winter passed, I moved on to Lastraia and stayed there several months. You've already heard that part of the story. I did have an encounter with bandits outside the town wall, so that was... exciting."

"Bandits?" Isobel exclaimed. "What happened?"

"Well," Chinelo remarked, resting his chin in his hand. "I got some decent sparring practice. I'll spare you some of the more unpleasant details of that encounter but suffice to say that they found very comfortable beds in the local infirmary."

"We get bandits occasionally as well," Isobel said, placing her knife on the table. "Since Nellborough is so far from the capital, the Interior Guard and Royal Garrison don't frequently station here. Most often we must fend for ourselves. I will admit, not having the strict regulations of some of the more central towns has its benefits, though. I've heard that life closer to Rothvale can be restrictive, especially for those of my occupation."

Chinelo looked up. "Have you been involved in any of those incidents?"

Isobel chuckled as she drizzled a rich yellow oil into an iron frying pan. "You could say that, yes."

"Oh?"

"It's nothing really. I'm not all that skilled at fighting, but most raiders don't know that. Throw around a little fire and ice and they tend to go running." She opened a sachet of herbs and shook it in a circle over her cooking pan, garnishing the dinner with small green flakes. "I have a few more ostentatious spells for any that choose to remain."

Thinking back to their meeting in the forest, Chinelo had no doubt that Isobel could be terrifying when she wanted to be. He had only ever seen one witch prior to meeting her, but that single experience had taught him that a witch's magic was truly something to fear.

"Chinelo, would you mind loading the fireplace? There should be some wood on the floor." Isobel pointed to a stone fireplace recessed into the right wall of the kitchen. Chinelo knelt by the hearth and piled wood onto the grate in a neat row. Soon after, Isobel squatted beside him and placed her cooking pan—now filled with chopped vegetables, sliced sausages, and dried spices—on an iron grill above the grate.

Isobel looked at him, bouncing up and down on her toes. "Want to see me use magic again?"

"Please, by all means."

Isobel hovered her palm over the firewood. "Icht vasht'ra!"

A brilliant stream of flame erupted from her hand, igniting the dry wood instantly. Chinelo flinched at the flames, averting his gaze.

"And now we wait," Isobel said. She dropped to a seat with a satisfied sigh. "I'm so very excited for you to try this. My mother used to cook this for me all the time after she and I first met. It's become a family staple."

"*After* you met your mother?"

"Yes."

"So, your mother didn't raise you?"

"Oh no!" She waved her hand. "I lived with a coven of witches until I turned fifteen. My sister Iva raised me up to that point, but after that I left to find my mother, which led me here! That was—oh—probably ten years ago now."

"I see." Chinelo's brow furrowed slightly. "I didn't know that was how covens worked."

Isobel's face clouded. She adjusted her spectacles nervously. "Well, normally it's not. I just—well—perhaps that story is best for another time..."

"I see. Sorry to bring that up."

The two sat before the hearth in silence, staring into the radiant blaze. The dish had begun to softly sizzle, projecting a savory aroma of fennel and garlic.

"So, what is your mother like?" asked Chinelo.

"Oh, she was just divine!" Isobel gushed. "She had red hair just like me, and she was a master at using magic. Some of the spells she crafted were just unfathomably beautiful. This one here on my hand—we made it together. Took us two whole weeks to figure it out."

Isobel held her left hand before Chinelo, turning it elegantly to allow him to see the tattoo that was printed upon her skin. Though he could not decipher the symbols, the spiral glyph certainly looked impressive.

"She and my father actually built this house after they had me," Isobel said, leaning back. Her lips formed a wistful smile. "I would have loved to have seen that sight—the two of them together. She used to tell me so many amazing stories about how they met and got secretly married and fought the Elder Mothers of the Red Coven. Well, the way she told it, she did most of the fighting, but he was always there with her."

"Are they...?"

"Oh, she passed on about five years ago, and I never got to meet him, unfortunately."

"Oh. I'm sorry. I know that must have been hard. That, experience—it's not exactly foreign to me." Chinelo turned away. He had not intended to steer the conversation in such a somber direction. Mort glowered in his direction and descended from his perch to the wooden floor with a resounding splat.

"Please, don't be," Isobel said, dismissing his concerns with her hand. "It's all in the past. Tell me about your family! Do they still live in Eshgar?" She placed her hands in her lap and leaned towards him eagerly.

"My parents and brother did," Chinelo's voice wavered. "But they were killed eight months ago."

Isobel gasped and covered her mouth. "Chinelo, I'm so sorry."

Chinelo shrugged.

Isobel paused. "Do you want to talk about it?"

The corners of Chinelo's mouth quivered as a lump formed in his throat. "Not right now, no. It's still a little hard to put into words. You probably understand."

Chinelo stared at the embers and gray charred wood that had fallen beneath the fire. Isobel looked down at her crossed legs and fidgeted. Her jaw clenched but she remained silent. Chinelo's mouth turned down. Memories he had hoped so desperately to forget reared their hideous burned faces within his mind.

"*CROOOOOOOOOAAAAAK!*"

Isobel let out a short, surprised yelp. Mort had shambled his rotund body between the two, leaving a glistening trail across the floor.

Chinelo laughed deeply. "Does he always do that?"

"Why, you would not believe! Just when I've started to drift to sleep, he'll let out the most guttural, visceral bellow you've ever heard, and then he'll pretend like he doesn't know what he's doing. But he does. I know he does. He's a devious, conniving villain, and for that, I've banished him to the downstairs at night."

Mort did not accept his exile willingly. Many times, he had attempted to scale the stairs leading to Isobel's bedroom, and many times he had ultimately become distracted by the sounds of chirping crickets outside the kitchen window. Mort climbed into Isobel's outstretched hand, frowning intensely.

"So, what is *he* going to eat for dinner?" Chinelo inquired.

"Oh, that's right! I haven't fed him yet." Isobel leapt to her feet. Mort's eyes bulged, and he croaked in surprise at the sudden movement.

She retrieved a jar of tangled, writhing worms from her satchel. Depositing Mort on his tray, she set several worms before his gleaming gaze. The beast was grateful for this bountiful feast; his banishment would temporarily be forgiven.

Isobel returned to the kitchen and set out several clay bowls and wooden spoons on the table. Chinelo wandered back to the living room and watched Mort ravenously devour his dinner. It was a horrific sight. The creature was merciless. Over the crackling fire, the sizzling meal, and the unspeakable sounds of Mort's hideous mastication, Chinelo heard the steady drone of rain and an odd drumming from above. He looked up. To his surprise, a wide, gaping hole was scorched through the ceiling. Above his head, he faintly heard the splashes of the falling raindrops on an improvised tarpaulin, the source of the mysterious drumming.

"Isobel?" Chinelo called.

"That's my name."

"There is a hole in your ceiling," Chinelo said, pointing to the charred planks.

"That's correct."

"How did that happen?"

Isobel glanced across the room at Chinelo before looking back to the meal she had been stirring. Her narrow chin jutted forward. "I don't see how that is important."

"It's burned all the way through the second story."

"Yes. I noticed."

Chinelo stared at her with a puzzled expression. "Are you planning to fix it?"

"No..." she replied timidly.

"Would you like me to fix it?"

"Oh, would you?" Isobel clasped her hands together. "That would be so very kind of you! I've asked Griggs so many times to come out here to repair it, but he keeps refusing because he 'has too many customers in town' or 'doesn't want to get lost in the forest' or 'doesn't take pleasure in the company of bullfrogs'. I was going to pay him handsomely, too. Honestly, it's unbelievable. For all these years I've been one of his most loyal customers. Maybe he's still angry about my rejection of his proposal. Though, I frankly don't understand why he expected a different outcome. He was so—what was the word you used earlier—*obtuse* about it."

Chinelo raised his eyebrows and paused. "I imagine that would be part of it, yes. At any rate, I would be happy to repair it."

"And I would be immensely grateful to you."

"Do you have any nails?"

"No..." Isobel's timid tone returned from its brief absence.

"Do you have a hammer?"

"No..."

"Surely you have an ax or saw?"

"Now *those* I do have."

"All right, in the morning we can take a look at the damage, and I can start assessing what we'll need to buy from town." Chinelo returned to the kitchen.

"Perfect! We'll go after the rain has stopped!" Isobel exclaimed. "And while you are working on that, you are of course welcome to stay in the second bedroom here."

"You don't have to do that, Isobel. Tonight is already more than enough. I'm sure there's an inn I can stay at in town. Hosting a complete stranger for so long isn't something I'd ever impose upon someone."

"Nonsense!" she replied, wrapping her hand in a thick cloth. "I can't have you using all your time and energy walking to and from town every day. And besides, the Nellborough Inn is exorbitantly expensive. You can just stay at the brand-new, just opened Valeria Inn. You will be our first customer! It will be lovely!"

"Very well. Though I'm surprised you trust me so readily."

Isobel laughed. "Well, you've seen what I did to the firewood. I'm sure you wouldn't want to anger the village arsonist."

Chinelo smiled. His dilemmas of employment and lodging now solved, he was free to consider his true objective: finding a place to call home. Perhaps their morning excursion to the village would yield progress toward that goal as well.

He looked towards Mort. Licking the last remnants of his meal from his amphibian jowls, the frog glared in his direction. He clearly did not approve of this interloper in his kingdom. His throne would not be usurped.

Isobel removed the iron pan from the fire and rested it on a thick cloth on the table. With her hands on her hips, she admired her work. The charred vegetables and meat emitted a fragrant steam that filled the kitchen. "Well, shall we?"

Sunlight washed over Isobel. Gradually its warm touch drew her from her slumber. She felt its gentle hand reaching for her, tempting her to open her eyes. She refused. She shifted, turning her back to the window to shade her face from the light.

In her waking moments, her pleasant memories of the previous night and the abstractions of her dreams mixed in a swirling bloom. Her talk with Chinelo lingered in her mind. They had discussed the many sights Chinelo had seen on his journey to her home. Beautiful canyons, majestic mountains, gleaming seas, lavender plains. She longed to see such sights. She was there, splashing in the pristine water. She was there, marveling at the towering peaks. She was there, peering over the infinite cliffs. She was there, wading through the endless flowers. Her mother with her, her auburn hair shining in the wind. Isobel touched her outstretched hand as a loving smile spread across her mother's face. Then, like a whisper, she was gone.

Isobel nestled beneath her blanket. She had told Chinelo of her sister Iva, the witch that had raised her from her early infancy and instructed her in the Ancient Arts. In her dreams, Isobel was in Iva's strong arms again. Though they had been apart for so long, she was held as if she was a child again, wrapped in Iva's soft green cloak. Iva's orchid perfume enveloped Isobel, and her jet-black hair was as dark as night. Isobel rested in the embrace. She was safe. She was home. Isobel looked to Iva's face. She reached for it and touched her cheek. She felt nothing, as if her hand passed through mist.

Isobel opened her eyes. She was alone.

She sat up and yawned, stretching her arms and back. How long had it been since she had seen her sister? Ten years already? Oh, the reprimands Iva would have given her if she had been there last night. Requesting the help of a stranger, inviting him into her home, letting him rest mere steps from her room all because someone might have been following her? Ridiculous! Ridiculous and irresponsible! Still, for the entire walk home, she had not been able to shake the sense of dread that had fallen upon her in the market. Something about the wind, the trees, the leaves was just off.

She had seen it in the merchants' eyes. Their normally welcoming faces were clouded with a strange distrust. She had felt it as she left the gate. The guards' typically friendly calls were replaced with harsh disapproving glares. She had sensed it as she walked beneath the trees. Sounds that should have been present were missing, and sounds that were usually absent seemed to follow her, just out of sight.

Isobel shook her head. Yes. She knew she made the right choice, despite what Iva might say. Her curious guest from Eshgar was warm and amiable, and she had felt at ease since the moment they set off into the forest. Besides, she hadn't noticed any talismans or inscriptions on his person, and Eshgar's culture had a notable aversion to the Ancient Arts. Even Iva would agree that he would be no threat for a well-versed witch such as herself. Besides, their rather unusual encounter had solved a problem that had been plaguing her for weeks, that of the burned hole in her roof.

Her bare feet alighted on the cold floor. Walking to the window, she passed her open diary on her desk and glanced down at the page. She had nearly fallen asleep writing the events of the previous day in the worn book, resulting in handwriting that fluctuated from a neat small script to a loose flowing scrawl. Isobel picked up her glasses from beside her diary and read the date: 433, 12, 15. The final month of the year was already halfway done. Soon, the autumn equinox would arrive, and with it the new year would come.

She looked out the window at the forest below. The golden leaves twinkled from the night's rain. As she scanned the forest floor, her gaze halted on the well behind her house. Her day had begun, and it was time to commence the morning chores. Her first order of business was to draw water from the well to replenish her supplies of bathing and drinking water.

Isobel donned a pair of loose tan trousers and a cotton shirt before exiting her bedroom. She gingerly walked down the hallway, carefully placing her steps on the few boards that didn't creak to avoid waking her guest. As she passed his bedroom door, she heard muffled snoring. She smiled. He had looked so exhausted during the night. His kind eyes had been clouded by an unmistakable weariness, something which Isobel attributed to his long journey. At a consistent pace, the trek to Iskara's border with Mervos would have taken almost a fortnight, and Lastraia was another two-day's journey beyond that. That was far more walking than she ever wanted to do alone, at least not again.

She stepped over the charred hole in the floor and descended the stairs to the kitchen. Lacing her boots, she eyed the sleeping mass of flesh on her work desk. Mort would not be pleased if she left the house without him, but Isobel was confident he would prefer to have his beauty sleep. As she opened the door, she grabbed a wooden bucket from beside her staff.

She skipped down the stone steps and inhaled deeply, tasting the fresh morning air. The damp smell of rain lingered. The trail had transformed into mud, and her feet sank into the ground, leaving shallow footprints behind her. The birds sang light, cheerful tunes in the treetops, fluttering from branch to branch. The crickets had become silent with the bright morning sun, but the occasional scamper of a squirrel could be heard in the distance. The sounds of the forest were like old friends to Isobel. For all her life, she could always rely on the welcoming birdsongs to lift her spirits.

Isobel arrived at the well and hooked the bucket on the rope and pulley. She lowered the bucket down the well's shaft and listened for the rush of water filling it. Her bucket was small, and consequently she expected to take several trips to and from the house to fully refill the water she had used the previous day.

She would have to ask Chinelo for assistance in the future once he had rested more. Perhaps she should purchase a larger bucket while they were in town. She struggled to lift her pail when it was filled, but she was quite confident that his brawny arms could handle the increased load. Perhaps he could even lift two.

Behind her a twig snapped, piercing the stillness of the morning. Isobel turned.

"Oh, you're up! I'm sorry. I didn't mean to wake—"

A shining silver blade cut through the air, narrowly missing Isobel's chest. She staggered, falling back to the ground. Before her stood not Chinelo but a stranger wielding a thin gleaming rapier. He was clad not in Eshgarian armor but in the battle gown of the Iskaran Interior Guard.

The birds had fallen silent.

CHAPTER 3

ISOBEL'S BODY FROZE. HER HEART SEIZED, gripped in the iron grasp of terror. She didn't think, didn't move, didn't breathe. She had no weapon, no staff, nothing. She was alone. The stranger stood above her, his slender rapier gleaming in the morning light. An ominous, hideous symbol was branded into his cheek. Isobel's instincts screamed from within.

... run...

The stranger raised his sword.

Run.

His grip tightened.

RUN!

Like a striking viper, his sword fell toward its target.

Isobel reached within, focusing her attention beneath her pounding heart. She felt a tingling, churning ocean of energy: her esht. She shifted her focus to her shoulder, ignoring all other sensations in her body. Her esht followed. It flowed like a racing torrent into her shoulder muscles, down the fibers of her bicep, along the tendons in her forearm, and finally into her outstretched palm where it accumulated in a raging tempest waiting to burst forth. With her shouted words, she imbued her esht with meaning, a command that the world must obey.

"ICHT VASHT'RA!"

Fire burst from Isobel's hand, igniting the brush around her. The stranger screamed horrifically; his robes lit aflame. Isobel rolled and leapt to her feet, twirling in a raging vortex. She ran, her escape masked by the blaze. Her feet beat upon the dirt, a panicked rhythm of retreat. An earsplitting ring sounded from behind her. A bright light pierced the air, impacting the ground beneath her feet.

The earth cracked, then shattered, launching Isobel against a nearby tree. The wood splintered as the wind was forced from her lungs. She crashed to the ground. Her desperate breath grated in her throat. Over the ringing in her ears, she heard footsteps—close, fast footsteps barreling toward her. She gasped, trying to form words. She needed to run. She needed to hide. She needed to shroud herself. She struck her palm against the tree, sending esht down her arm.

"Sono diaa, fet va sone!"

The tree's trunk ruptured, ejecting a thick cloud of vapor. Isobel dug her hands into the ground, scrambling forward. There was a sharp *thunk* as the blade thrust into the tree behind her. Covered in dirt and mud she hobbled to her feet and bolted ahead. She turned and watched in shock as the cloud of mist dissipated in a rush of wind. Her pursuer stood menacingly, his blade protruding from the frayed tree trunk. Pressed between the fingers of his left hand was a small slip of parchment covered in runes. He was a mage.

As he tugged at his embedded blade, he discarded the slip and drew another from an open pouch on his hip. Isobel heard the same high-pitched ring and channeled her esht into the tattoo on the back of her outstretched left hand, filling the spiral of runes with energy. A blue light flashed, forming a glowing circular barrier. Her opponent's spell crashed into the barrier, instantly fizzling and sputtering into oblivion. The mage raised an eyebrow, eyeing her defense before dropping the talisman.

Isobel glanced at her opponent's blade, still protruding from the tree. Her mind raced, frantically considering her options. Spells! What spells could she use? Sigils of healing and nullification were marked on her hands, but in a fight, how useful would they be? Her staff contained numerous powerful spells, ready to fly at the slightest word, but she had absent-mindedly left it in her cottage. She could improvise incantations, but her voice rang hollow in her throat.

The mage struggled with his sword. He was stationary, vulnerable. She only needed a single, solid attack. She dispelled her barrier and dashed forward, her muddy fingers clenched into tight fists. She was determined. She would defeat him. She would win. With a yell, she wildly swung at the mage's face, putting all her strength behind a single, focused punch.

Her knuckles cracked and crunched from the impact, sending a reverberation of pain ricocheting through her bones. She felt every fiber, every nerve, every tendon wailing in a chorus of agony. She staggered back, hunching over her throbbing hand. The mage sneered and struck her with the back of his hand. She stumbled and fell, landing on her arm. The mage's blade caught the corner of her shirt and pinned it to the earth. Isobel scrambled to her feet, tearing the hem in the process. Her face and hand ached. The drum of her heart intensified the pain with every pulse.

She raised her arms in a defensive stance. She was close, too close. Her reckless attack had left her exposed to his newly freed blade. She had to stun him. She had to immobilize him to create distance.

The mage twirled his blade and thrust it forward, aiming for her heart. Isobel twisted and slammed her left arm into the side of the blade, its razor-sharp edge slicing her skin as she deflected the strike. She winced and smashed her right palm into her opponent's chest.

"BELEKT FAI!"

A crack of thunder shook the forest. Startled birds flew from the trees.

The mage's body convulsed, shocked by the blast of lightning from Isobel's hand. He fell to the ground with a heavy thud, and Isobel stepped back as hot blood trickled down her left arm. She circled around him and fled toward her house.

She ran.

The man roared in anger and hurled a stone that bashed into Isobel's shoulder. She stumbled, barely maintaining her footing as her shoulder throbbed. Flinging her arm out behind her, she projected her barrier. A flurry of spells and magic blasts tore through the earth and collided with her barrier, once again fading to nothing.

If she could reach her cottage, she could reach her staff. If she could reach her staff, she could win. Heavy footsteps approached from behind.

The man tackled her, and they tumbled in a heap. Isobel felt a dozen pricks of pain as rocks, twigs, and thorns tore at her clothes and skin. An immovable weight pressed down on her frame as her face scraped the dirt. She opened her eyes. She was pinned face down on the ground beneath the raging man above her. She tried to flail her arms to fight, but her hands refused to move. Her right arm was restrained beneath his knee, and her left arm was wrenched into the mud by his cruel hand. She kicked and struggled fruitlessly.

Paper rustled.

A cold pang of terror spread in her chest. The man was drawing another talisman. She needed to escape. She needed to move. She needed a force—a great force to launch him from her back. She accumulated her esht between her shoulder blades. Straining to speak, she whispered an incantation.

"Belekt tra'vasht."

An explosion threw the man high into the air, releasing Isobel from his crushing grip. She jumped to her feet, shifted her esht to her hands, and pushed them to the ground.

"Vo aia, li hath'de limtre."

The man's body crashed into the muddy forest floor. Roots burst from the ground around him and thrashed, trapping him in a web of wood and vines. Isobel stood and panted heavily. The man squirmed and turned under the roots, tearing them from the earth. They would only restrain him briefly. She had a small window of opportunity that would soon close.

"ISOBEL!" a voice shouted from the hilltop where her house stood. She turned and saw Chinelo racing down towards her with sword and staff in hand. His half-buttoned shirt flapped in the wind as his bare feet splashed in the muddy trail.

"Chinelo! My staff! Throw me my staff!"

Chinelo hurled Isobel's staff, flinging it to her feet. She grabbed and twirled it, pointing its ornate head at her pursuer. Her esht tingled within her, rushing from her hand, through the staff's wooden shaft, and into the glowing orb at its head. It halted, surrounded by the many spells she had etched within the staff's spell-core, waiting to be guided to the appropriate one. She spoke a single resolute word.

"Inferno."

A bright light flashed before her. A raging tornado of flame erupted to the sky, illuminating the shaded forest. She shielded her eyes from the blinding glow. Isobel's nose wrinkled, assaulted by the abrasive stench of smoke, burning leaves, and scorched flesh. Chinelo approached Isobel cautiously and stood at her side, drawing his sword to strike her target.

Isobel flourished her staff and gave a second command. "Extinguish!"

A wave of wind rushed from her staff, and the flames vanished. Where her target had been constrained was only a pile of charred roots and smoldering earth. She scanned her surroundings and saw the man fleeing deeper into the forest with his tattered battle robe burning and flapping in the wind over his red-hot chain mail. He staggered and limped, groaning with every labored step. Her body relaxed.

Chinelo stepped forward to pursue her foe. Isobel caught his sleeve with her trembling hand.

"Wait!" she said. "Don't. He's a mage."

"I should go after him," Chinelo said. "He might come back."

"No. Please... please don't leave me." Her hands shook. She dropped her staff and fell to her knees, panting in short, erratic breaths.

"Isobel! Are you all right?"

She ran her muddy fingers through her tangled hair. "He was going to kill me. Why? Why would he try to kill me? Why would the Interior Guard try to kill me?"

Chinelo stabbed his sword into the ground and knelt beside her. "Hey. You're not alone."

Isobel turned and looked at him. His face was a deep sable, and his angular jawline was framed by a thin layer of stubble that matched his short curly black hair. His soft hickory eyes were slightly upturned, and the suggestion of laugh lines had begun to crease their outer edges, though his current expression was clouded with intense concern.

"Did... did I wake you?" she said.

Chinelo exhaled, flashing a weak smile above his slightly dimpled chin. "A little bit."

"Oh. I'm very sorry."

"I'm surprised *that* is what worries you."

Isobel exhaled through her nose. "Yes, I suppose it is a bit silly, all things considered."

Chinelo offered his hand. She took it, and together they stood. Isobel covered the gash on her arm with her right hand and tensed in concentration. The wound closed and faded, leaving only a smooth scar in its place. She tried to wipe away the blood that stuck to her skin, however she only smeared it further.

"You can heal?" Chinelo asked.

"To a degree, yes."

"Incredible."

"It's nothing, really," Isobel said, looking down at her red fingers.

"Well, I will have to disagree there. Come on. Let's get you back to the house."

Chinelo sat at the kitchen table, whittling a small scrap of wood. He deftly maneuvered his knife, sculpting the wood into the shape of a bullfrog. He eyed Mort, who sat before him staring at the false idol Chinelo carved. Chinelo anxiously glanced at the washroom door. Isobel had been in there for a long time, and he had not heard the sound of splashing water for several minutes. He stood and tapped on the door.

"Isobel? Are you all right in there?"

After a long pause he heard the water move.

"Yes," Isobel responded quietly.

Chinelo returned to his seat. Mort scowled at the wood shavings collected in a cloth spread on the table. They were discarded from a frog that was not him, offenses to his household. Chinelo resumed his whittling, ensuring that his carving was slightly less plump than his host's cantankerous pet.

After several minutes, Isobel emerged from the washroom clad in a clean shirt and trousers that came to her mid-calf. She took a seat at the table and sipped from a cup Chinelo had placed there in advance, staring blankly ahead. She was covered in bruises and recently healed scrapes, and her face was battered. The scar on her left arm was slick. Chinelo slid a plate of bread in front of her, and she began to pick at the crust. After several minutes, Chinelo cleared his throat.

"Do you want to talk about it?" he coaxed.

Isobel shook her head slowly, maintaining her empty gaze.

"Is there anything else I can get you to eat?"

Isobel once again shook her head. Her eyes moved listlessly behind her spectacles.

"If it's agreeable to you, I'm going to suggest that we save the trip to Nellborough for tomorrow," Chinelo said.

Isobel paused then nodded her head several times. They sat in a silence that was only interrupted by the sound of Chinelo's knife sliding along the wood he carved. Mort looked at Isobel. The silence continued. Mort looked at Chinelo. The silence persisted. Mort looked at the wooden frog. The silence was endless.

"CROOOOOAAAAAAAAK!"

Isobel jumped in her seat.

"My word, Mort. You mustn't keep doing that!" she exclaimed. "You'll stop my heart. See, Chinelo, this is what I was talking about. He's a menace."

Chinelo smiled. Somehow, he did not believe that the amphibian was as villainous as she claimed. "He certainly has a very specific timing."

"Honestly."

Isobel reached her hand to Mort and tenderly stroked his lumpy back. For once, he seemed content, almost happy. His queen had graced him with her gentle touch.

"Chinelo?" Isobel murmured.

"Yes?"

"I need to learn how to fight."

"That may be wise. Though, from what I saw, you beat that man soundly."

Isobel looked down at her battered fists. She clenched them and winced.

"That man was what my sister called a Branded Mage," she said.

"Oh?" Chinelo leaned forward, resting his elbows on the table.

"Most of them are former criminals recruited from outside Iskara, mainly from Svidar. They've committed some offense and are forbidden from using magic in those nations. It's vile what they do to them."

"And what is that?" Chinelo asked.

"Their tongues. They brand them and remove their tongues so they can't use incantations or verbal commands. It's abominable. From what Iva said, the Archmage offers them new lives here."

Chinelo shuddered.

Isobel rested her chin on her hand. "Among the ranks of the Interior Guard, that man would have been an outsider, only able to use preapproved written magic. Branded Mages are almost exclusively employed to deal with common criminals who elude the king's garrison. However, any decent Iskaran mage that could actually speak would be far more capable than that man was. Far, far more capable." She adjusted her spectacles.

"I don't know why the Interior Guard has decided that I am to die, but if I am going to protect myself, then I need to be much better prepared."

"Well," Chinelo said, "I could teach you some of the basics of hand-to-hand combat if you like. We can consider it a fair trade. I'll teach you how to fight, and you'll teach me how to use magic, if you are still willing of course."

"That would be very kind." She leaned forward and smiled, but her smile was quickly overtaken by a spark of inspiration in her eyes.

She stood. "I have work to do!"

"Oh?"

Isobel darted to her desk and began scribbling on a sheet of parchment. She pulled several books off the shelves and flipped through their pages. "Consider this your first lesson in magic, Chinelo. You've seen me perform magic three different ways. The first, Incantation Magic, was how I lit the fire last night. It is powerful, adaptable, fluid, but incredibly slow, especially if you intend to use complex spells."

"The second, Written Magic, was how I healed my wounds today." She ran her thumb along the sigil on her hand. "It is fast since it only requires a written spell instead of a spoken one, but if you don't have any on you, then it's useless. My nullification barrier and my healing touch are the only two written spells I had on me today since they are the only tattoos I have."

"The third, Command Magic, was how I created that pillar of flame. It operates on pre-prepared spells stored in objects like my staff."

She ran her fingers through her damp hair and continued, "So, putting that all together, I made the mistake of leaving my staff in here when I went to draw water this morning. That left me with only my tattoos and any incantations I could formulate in the moment. Turns out, it's difficult to improvise when you are running for your life."

Chinelo scratched his head, "So, you're going to...?"

"Make a new tattoo, of course," Isobel said, scribbling. "I have an idea for some more offensive options. I just need to work out how it will come together. If you'll pardon me, I need to concentrate."

Chinelo moved to a mat on the living room floor and continued his whittling, watching Isobel work. For several hours she studied her tomes, writing hurried notes and adding symbols to the sheet of parchment. Eventually she crumpled the sheet and tossed it across the room, then another, and another. A pile of parchment slips accumulated.

Chinelo climbed the stairs to the second floor. He stopped and inspected the burned floorboards he had noticed the previous evening. The hole was certainly large. The damage stretched almost all the way across the walkway, with only a couple boards keeping him from falling through to the lower floor. He looked at the sloped ceiling and exhaled. The damage there was even worse. The boards were blackened and sooty, and the hole easily reached over halfway to the roof's apex. This would require extensive effort to repair.

He looked down at the hole in the floor. Isobel hunched at her workstation below, her copper hair swaying and bobbing as she looked from book to book. Whatever had burned the floor had likely originated from her desk. He returned to the downstairs, grabbed his sword, and laced his boots. Longingly looking at the door, Mort hopped beside Chinelo's feet.

"I'm going to step outside for a moment."

Isobel nodded subtly and brushed another scrap of parchment to the floor.

Chinelo shrugged and opened the door. Mort followed him outside and immediately devoured an unsuspecting cricket which had ambled onto the doorstep. After walking around the side of the house, Chinelo looked up at the roof. He would need to remove the tarpaulin to determine the damage. Beneath the water reservoir on the side of the house lay a primitive wooden ladder. Appraising the height of the roof, Chinelo stroked his chin, brushing his recently shaved stubble with his thumb. It would be best to wait for Isobel's assistance before attempting to climb to the roof.

Chinelo circled around the perimeter of the house, searching the forest and listening for any signs of life. From what he had seen, Isobel had severely burned her attacker. Returning to fight would be foolish, but it was possible that the man was not alone. After several minutes, Chinelo returned to the front of the house and sat upon the step.

It was strange. If that man was the one who was following her yesterday, why didn't he try to kill her while she was alone?

This land's customs and traditions perplexed Chinelo. He was an Eshgarian knight, a beacon of hope to the people of his kingdom. He was honor-bound to protect all. Knights were raised to value life, all life. Violence was only to be used to defend or protect. Yet here in Iskara, the Interior Guard skulked in the shadows, stalking women in the night and attacking them when they were most vulnerable. It was preposterous, disgraceful. Only a coward of a ruler would allow such a practice.

Chinelo thought back on Isobel's attacker. The mage had worn a flowing dark green robe with gold filigree around the hems. A belt adorned with leather pouches had constrained the robe at his waist. If this was the typical attire for the Interior Guard, Chinelo would need to remember its appearance.

Of course, he didn't know Isobel all that well. They had only met the night before. It was possible she did something to warrant such a sentence. Even so, he was surprised that there was no system for trials in place.

Mort plopped beside him, looking slightly fatter than before, and began a deep, droning frog song. Chinelo looked up at the canopy. Birds flitted and fluttered from branch to branch, adding their cheerful notes to Mort's chorus. The leaves above glowed a brilliant gold, lit by the lowering sun. Occasionally, the birdsong was interrupted by strange sounds from inside the house.

Based on the extent of the damage, he would need a fair number of nails if he hoped to repair Isobel's roof. Getting planks wouldn't be a problem, owing to the abundance of wood nearby. It was a forest after all. He would need to buy a hammer in town and some kind of plumb line or ruler. Beyond that...

A leaf floated down and brushed against his bare shoulder. Chinelo's stomach growled. Given the excitement of the morning, he had only eaten a small meal for breakfast. Having eaten even less, Isobel would likely be hungry once she completed her research.

Behind him, the cottage door flew open. Isobel stepped past him, holding her completed parchment talisman between her fingers. She raised her hand, and a bright cyan bolt flashed from the parchment, piercing the earth like a javelin. She nodded, then launched a second bolt at a nearby tree. The projectile shattered the bark, then splashed a glowing blue liquid to the ground. Isobel let out a frustrated huff and hurried back inside, leaving the door ajar behind her. After a few more minutes, she returned and fired a shot at the tree. The wood tore and splintered, and shining crystals, as bright as diamonds, sprouted from the tree.

"This will do," she said, before sitting on the step next to Chinelo. She let out a long, relieved sigh and folded the parchment in her hands. "The sky is pretty today."

"Yes," Chinelo replied. He looked at her, astonished at her resilience.

"Do you want to eat soon?" she asked.

"Absolutely!"

"Good. I am starving."

Chinelo leaned forward. "Since you were so kind to cook dinner last night, how about I cook today? Based on what I saw in your kitchen, I think I should have everything I need to make one of Eshgar's famous crimson potato stews, or at least a very close approximation."

"That would be lovely. I'll never refuse someone cooking for me. Though, I do hope you will let me help."

"Hmmm. I think I can allow that."

CHAPTER 4

DARKNESS. SMOKE BILLOWED TO THE SKY, eclipsing the pale light of the moon. The dry ground burned a deep orange, propagating in waves across rubble and shattered timbers. Schools, foundries, homes, markets were all indistinguishable beneath the blanket of glowing cinders. There was no wind, no sound, no life, only the rising columns of smoke reaching like clawed hands to rend the stars from their celestial seats.

Within it all stood the obelisk. Its smooth gray surface, cut from a stone far more ancient than civilization itself, was unmarred by soot. He stood before it. It called to him, breathing without breath. Below his feet, he felt a heartbeat, inviting him to join his kin beneath the embers. Then, it was gone, nothing more than a fleeting memory.

"Chinelo?"

Chinelo lifted his gaze from the path and saw Isobel's concerned face before him, shaded from the morning sun by a wide brimmed hat with a pointed crown. She wore a simple blue dress that hung loosely about her slender figure, complemented by her black gloves.

"Are you all right, friend?" Isobel asked, tilting her head. "You stopped walking, and you have the oddest expression about your face."

"Oh, yes. I'm sorry, Isobel. I was... distracted," Chinelo replied.

Isobel frowned, narrowing her eyes. After a moment, her frown transformed into a playful smile. "Well. Let's be on our way then. A lady of my exquisitely fair complexion will burn in the sun like this. Or something of that nature. I'm sure you understand."

Chinelo chuckled. "I hope that a lady of your exquisite amicability will pardon the indiscretion."

She smirked and flourished her staff before resuming her walk down the road to Nellborough. Mort shuffled his slippery frog feet on Isobel's shoulder, glaring at Chinelo. He would *not* pardon the indiscretion.

The road transitioned from golden forest to idyllic hill country. A warm breeze agitated the grass, and in the distance the pointed rooftops of farmhouses and barns poked above the knolls. Chinelo's sword rattled in its sheath as he walked beside Isobel. Without his travel supplies filling his pack or armor weighing on his body, he felt light and airy, as if he could float into the cloudless azure sky.

"So how far out are we from the town?" Chinelo inquired.

"Ask me again once we reach the top of that hill," Isobel replied, pointing at the next rise ahead.

As they crested the hill, she ran to its apex, her hair and dress flowing in the rising wind. She pointed her staff to the land below. "*That* is Nellborough."

A grand town stretched across the countryside. The road snaked through the few remaining hills and entered the village to form its single main street. Countless buildings topped with rooftops of red, dark blue, and brown were arranged in tight rows and alleys that twisted chaotically about the town's outskirts. Farmland extended beyond, and tiny woolen specks dotted the surrounding hills. Seemingly at random, shattered stone ruins were scattered across the countryside, rising to various heights.

The mischievous wind carried a feast of smells to the hilltop. Roasted herbs, soft sawdust, and sweet perfumes invited them to enter the town. Even at the early hour, Chinelo could see the streets populated by merchants in colorful garb, townsfolk in muted work clothes, and guardsmen in shining armor. The roads at Nellborough's four cardinal gates bustled as the market came to life.

"So how far out are we from the town?" Chinelo asked with a grin.

"Oh, stop."

At the west gate, several guards congregated around a makeshift table covered in small painted trinkets. As Isobel and Chinelo passed their post, one, a gruff man who's face and body were not unlike those of a sleepy fighting dog, raised his head to look in their direction. His gaze hovered on Isobel for a moment, and his jowls twisted into a disapproving frown. His and Chinelo's eyes met, and he squinted, inspecting the newcomer to his town.

Isobel hastened her steps to pass through the gate from the dirt road to the brick paved street. The guard shrugged and turned back to his diversions on the table.

"That's Trallo, captain of the guard here," Isobel shuddered. "He scares me."

"He didn't say anything about my sword."

"Many people who pass through are armed. It's not uncommon."

Chinelo cocked his head. "They don't have to register them?"

"What? No. Why would we do that?"

Chinelo withheld his next remark, looking at the ground in perplexion. Iskaran customs were very different from those back home.

As they neared the western edge of the grand market, the clamoring crowds pressed in upon Isobel and Chinelo, crashing against them like ocean waves in a storm. Stooped elders, temperamental spinsters, grizzled farmers, and dusty urchins all bustled and shouted into the open merchant stalls, bartering for goods displayed on tapestries. Isobel reached her gloved hand back and found Chinelo's, pulling him through the tight crowd.

Suddenly, they were in a sprawling open square, gasping for air as if they had risen from beneath the surface of a turbulent sea. The plaza was much more orderly than the streets they had braved. Storefronts and shops were arranged about the edges of the square, and wheeled carts were arrayed in rows at its heart.

"What was all that back there?" Chinelo asked.

"The morning markets." Isobel spun on her toe to face him. Mort clung to her shoulder, trying to maintain his perch. "Merchants place their most 'desirable' wares on the outskirts of the square to try to attract customers before they've spent all their crescents. Once a few people gather, everyone else wants to know what the merchants are selling. It turns into a bidding war, regardless of the value of what's being sold. Fortunately for you, I know where to find legitimate quality."

"Now please correct me if I misremember," she continued, "but you said we needed to buy nails, a hammer, pitch, a plumb line, and a measuring rod?"

"That covers most of it for the roof, yes. I'd also like to sell my dragon horns if possible."

"We can start with those. I'm sure the smithy would love to craft those into spears or daggers. Dragon bone weapons are very popular these days, especially among the rich, from what I've heard. He'll also have the hammer and nails you need." Isobel pointed across the plaza to the southeast corner. "Do you see that stone structure there? The foundry is beneath that, and two doors down is the carpenter's shop. Between the two, you should be able to find everything you need. Just keep a tally of the expenses, and I'll pay you back."

"Are you not joining me?"

"I will. I will. Just not quite yet," she said. "I have some matters of my own to attend to. If I have not found you by the time you've finished, wait for me in the center of the square." Isobel gave a small wave and disappeared into the crowd with Mort riding proudly on her shoulder, reveling in the fact that the usurper had been abandoned.

Chinelo looked around the marketplace, taking in the many sights and sounds. The buildings were tall, built of stone and timber with walls of whitewashed plaster. Flowers adorned the open windows that overlooked the square, and several of those windows were occupied by curious faces watching the throng below. Wheeled carts were decorated with vibrant drapes and striped shades, many of which Chinelo recognized as the colors of the neighboring regions.

He hurried across the square. As he approached the smithy's shop, a large stone ruin loomed above him. It was massive, towering high above the square and casting a long shadow that reached beyond the town center. Jagged offshoots sprung from the side like torn branches, and birds rested on the many ledges. Beneath the shadow of one of these ledges was the smithy's foundry. Chinelo entered and immediately felt the distant heat of the furnace against his face. The interior was lined with numerous weapons. Swords, halberds, axes, spears, polearms, and even some unusually elaborate bladed instruments hung from racks nailed to the wooden walls. Small price tags hung from braided strings on their handles.

Chinelo wandered through the shop, appreciating the skillfully crafted arsenal. He reached the end of the weapon racks and found a gallery of armor of varying sizes and shapes. Several men were scattered across the rooms, picking weapons and tools from the shelves and testing their balance.

"Anything catch your eye, stranger?" a gravelly voice called to Chinelo.

Chinelo turned to see a lumbering, brawny bear of a man leaning against the counter. He wore a thick, heavy apron and baggy, soot-covered trousers. His bare arms were astonishingly muscular, growing from his shoulders like two great oaks. Even more astounding was the thickness of the matted brown hair that covered his body. He was a beast, but his bearded face bore a welcoming grin.

"Not as of yet," Chinelo replied, "though I'm sure a hammer and nails would look appealing if the rest of your work indicates their quality."

The man laughed a deep guttural laugh. "I like the way you speak, stranger!" he said, extending a meaty hand which Chinelo quickly shook. "Though by the looks of you I would have guessed you would be more of the fighting type."

"Ordinarily, yes. I'm helping a friend with a project at the moment, though."

"Aye, aye, aye. Good man."

The man guided Chinelo to a far corner of the shop to a table that displayed several tools and farming instruments. "These ought to do for you. I'll get you those nails. How many do you think you'll need?"

Chinelo chuckled. "A lot."

After a brief look, he selected a sturdy hammer. He had been accurate in his assessment. The craftmanship was exquisite. He returned to the counter where the man had deposited a bag of iron nails.

"By the way, good man," the smithy said, "call me Oros."

"Greetings, Oros. My kin call me Chinelo. It would please me if you would as well," Chinelo said with a bow.

"Aye, of course, of course. You're from Eshgar, then?"

"That's correct."

"Terrible what happened down there," Oros said, shaking his head.

Chinelo tensed. "So, you've heard?"

"Aye. The merchants have been chattering about it all morning. One of them, Blithe I think was his name, recently came back from there and has been spreading the word."

"I see."

"Were you there when it happened?" Oros asked.

"I wasn't in the city, no, but I was close enough to see it. My family was not so fortunate."

"What was it? Blithe says there wasn't much of the city left behind."

"I wish I knew," Chinelo looked down.

"Aye. Well, we're lucky you made it here, good man." Oros gave Chinelo a powerful tap on the shoulder. "You've picked a wonderful town to visit. You've got a place to stay, I hope? I'd be happy to put you up for a while if needed. Always looking for an extra pair of strong arms."

"That is very kind of you, Oros. That friend I mentioned, I'm staying with her. She lives in the forest west of here."

Oros's face lit up. "Oh, that must be Miss Valeria! Lovely lady, there. She's a good soul, she is. Keeps some strange company if you ask me. Not you of course, good man."

"Oh, the frog?"

"Aye. Nasty little creature, he is." Oros's nose creased as he spoke.

Chinelo laughed.

"So how will you be paying?" Oros asked, leaning against the counter. "Your total is going to be nineteen crescents. Don't accept Eshgarian talents here, but if you've got something to trade, I'd be happy to barter, instead."

Chinelo dropped his pack and dug out the dragon horns he had been carrying. "Will these do?"

Oros's eyes widened. "Aye, good man. Those are more than adequate. Harvested these yourself, did you?"

"That is correct."

"See, I knew I judged you right as a fighter." Oros pointed a girthy finger at Chinelo. "If you and Isobel ever have a spat, you come visit your old chum, Oros."

The hulking blacksmith crouched behind the counter. "You know, I haven't gotten my hands on ash dragon horns since before Esther passed. She was quite the spitfire, that one."

"Esther?" Chinelo asked.

Oros looked up. "Aye. Isobel's late mother." He slid several coins across the counter. They were marked with a sharp crescent symbol, the insignia of Iskaran currency. "There. Now that's a fair trade, good man. That ought to last you for a while."

Chinelo filled his pack with his tools and coins. "Thank you, Oros. I look forward to doing business with you in the future."

"Aye. Hey, when you see the lady, could you give her a message for me?"

"Of course, what's that?" Chinelo asked as he donned his pack, preparing to exit the shop.

Oros scratched the back of his head, tousling his thick brown hair. "Eh, those enchanted weapons she makes for me. Tell her that I can't be selling them anymore. Some new decree from the Archmage. Heard that from the Interior Guard, I did. Unpleasant fellows, those. Tore up my whole store trying to find out where I'd gotten them."

Chinelo froze at the mention of the Interior Guard. "And what did you tell them?" he asked sternly.

"Not a word, good man. Not a word. I'd never sell out Miss Isobel to those capital types."

"How many men were there?"

"Eh, two," Oros said, stroking his curly beard. "Though one of them wasn't much of a conversationalist. Had an odd scar on his face. The other was taller than you and me, and rather scrawny. It's strange, they seemed set on the fact that a witch made them, but I don't know how they—Oh! You well, good man?"

Chinelo nodded. "I'll pass along your message, Oros. Thank you."

"Always welcome, Chinelo. Come back soon! Oh, if you're visiting the carpenter, I'd advise against mentioning Miss Valeria. That boy there, Griggs Lockrell—he's awfully sour towards her."

Chinelo nodded and left the store. His spirit was troubled. Enchanted weapons? Would that really be enough to warrant someone's death?

This kingdom... it is very strange.

Isobel weaved through the crowd as she moved away from the central square. Reaching an alleyway, she ducked out of the main street and opened a door in the side of a stone building. After descending a small flight of dusty stairs, she found herself in a wide room filled with packed bookshelves. The morning light flooded through windows near the ceiling, and the feet of villagers passed by above. She approached a small wooden counter and looked around the room.

"Umfrey?" she called.

A loud thud and a cry of pain came from beneath the counter. A tall middle-aged man awkwardly stood up, rubbing the back of his narrow head. He was thin and bony, and his gray hair and prominent nose evoked the image of a large crane lifting its head from the water.

"Oh, Bel! It's you!" he said with a mellow voice.

Isobel dropped her staff and ran around the counter. She hugged the man tightly, causing the tall crown of her hat to collide with his face.

"Now, now Bel, what's all this about?" Umfrey asked. "You know, Priscila and I were terribly worried about you yesterday. Normally you don't miss a delivery."

Isobel took a step back "Apologies. I had a bit of a scare yesterday morning."

Umfrey adjusted his crooked glasses. "Tell me about it. My, what happened to your arm?"

"The Interior Guard came to my house and tried to kill me."

"Oh, gods! Are you all right?" Umfrey's eyes widened in shock.

"I am now. A friend is staying with me, so having a second person there has made things bearable."

"Why would they try to kill you?"

Isobel shook her head. "I'm not sure. You haven't heard anything have you? Any news from Rothvale? New laws, perhaps?"

Umfrey pursed his lips in thought. "Nothing comes to mind that would affect you. Though, something strange is happening in the capital. The Rothvale Trade Guild has been ordered by the Archmage to leave Nellborough, for one thing."

"The Archmage? Why? He doesn't normally trouble himself with us. He's only even been here—what—the one time?"

"Your guess is as good as mine, Bel. It's definitely strange. Trade regulations seem out of his authority." Umfrey stroked his narrow chin in thought. "Maybe, given everything that's happened, it's because we are so close to Eshgar."

"Eshgar?" Isobel looked up with interest.

"You haven't heard?" Umfrey responded. "The whole city burned to the ground. It's completely wiped out."

Isobel gasped, covering her mouth with her hand.

"Regardless, I'll ask my connections." Umfrey jotted a note down on a pad of parchment on the counter. "Maybe you should stay away from town for now, at least until the Interior Guard leaves. You know they don't often linger here."

Isobel nodded. She looked down, reconsidering her conversations with Chinelo over the previous two days.

Umfrey reached beneath the counter and drew out a heavy book, clad in black dyed leather. "Hopefully this will raise your spirits."

"It arrived! Thank you, Umfrey! This means the world!"

"Of course, Bel. I hope it has what you are looking for."

"Miss Bel!" a small voice cried. A young girl came running from a far corner of the store. A sewn doll dangled helplessly from her chubby hand as she charged toward Isobel. Mort leapt from Isobel's shoulder onto the counter with a scowl.

"Clair!" Isobel exclaimed. She dropped to the floor and took the child in her arms. "How is my favorite bookkeeper?"

"Good," the young girl said. "Mother made me a doll because she said I was very good eating my hedge tables."

"Is that right?" Isobel looked confusedly at Umfrey, who with a tired sigh mouthed the word "vegetables." Isobel nodded. "Well, I am very proud of you for eating your 'hedge tables,' Clair. My, is this a new necklace?" Isobel marveled at the pretty star-shaped pendant that rested on the child's neck.

"Father gave it to me!" Clair said, grinning.

"Well, your father is a very generous man, now, isn't he?" Isobel smiled towards Umfrey.

"Miss Bel, are you going to stay and play with me today?" Clair asked.

Isobel ran her hand through Clair's short blonde hair. "I'm sorry, Clair, but I have a friend visiting town who is going to be so terribly lost without me. But we will play next time! You will have to tell me all about your doll. Make sure you give her a good name. Dolls always need a good name."

Clair smiled, exposing her incomplete row of white teeth. She ran across the room and began drawing on a parchment notepad.

"By the way Umfrey, do you have any tattoo ink?" Isobel asked. "The ink I have at home has run dry."

"Eh, probably. I'll check." Umfrey opened a cabinet beneath the counter and began rummaging through vials of inks and dyes. "So, who's this friend of yours, Bel?" he asked. "I didn't know you knew anyone outside of town."

"Oh, he's so very kind, Umfrey. You would love him, I'm sure. I met him a couple days ago. He's a knight from Eshgar, and he's agreed to fix my roof."

Umfrey looked up and raised an eyebrow, "Ah, finally found someone to help you there?"

Isobel turned her head defiantly. "Oh stop. He offered to do it himself, and he needed a place to stay, so we came to an agreement."

"Well, I am glad you've made a new friend. We were worried about you, given all that happened with that Lockrell boy. Regardless, I hope I get to meet him next time you visit," he said, placing a vial of black ink on the counter.

"Only if your wife is here," Isobel said with a wink, sliding a pair of coins across the counter and dropping the vial into her satchel.

"Come around in the evening and she will be."

Isobel began to gather her belongings and her frog. "I really should be going. I'm sure Chinelo is waiting for me by now. Thank you once again for the book, Umfrey."

"Before you go," Umfrey reached behind the counter and produced a bag of tightly bound bundles. "Priscila asked me to give these to you if you came by today. She knows how much you love her hand pies."

"You two really are the best. What would I do without you?"

"Gods be with you, Bel."

Isobel exited the bookstore and reentered the flowing throng on the street.

Chinelo left the carpenter's shop and began finding his way to the center of the town square. His visit to the shop had been less engaging than his time in the foundry, but he had successfully acquired the remaining items he needed for Isobel's roof. He passed by the many carts in the plaza, peeking at the textiles, spices, and oddities that were being sold. These didn't have nearly as many people crowding as the earlier streets did. Upon reaching the center of the plaza, he froze.

Before him, at the exact center of Nellborough, stood a smooth stone obelisk.

It protruded from beneath the pavement as if the town had been built around it. It was tall and rectangular with symmetrical notches carved into its corners. A hollow diamond shaped cleft cut through its center. He uneasily stepped closer and felt... *it*. The sound. The noise. The vibration. The breathless breath. The beating heart deep beneath the earth. It called to him. His chest tightened. His hands shook.

"Chinelo?" Isobel was at his side.

Chinelo gasped. His fingers were numb. Quick shallow breaths filled his lungs with cold air. He staggered back, reaching for something on which to steady himself.

Isobel grabbed his shoulder. "Hey! Talk to me. What's wrong?"

At her touch, Chinelo's breathing began to slow.

Isobel stepped in front of him and looked into his eyes. "Hey. You're not alone."

Chinelo took a deep breath. "Isobel. What is that?" he said, nodding in the direction of the obelisk.

"That? The obelisk? It's always been here. Probably left behind by the gods just like all the other ruins around here. Why?"

"There was one like that in Eshgar. It was the only thing left..." his voice quivered and broke.

Isobel softened her grip on his shoulder. "You don't have to talk about it. I already know."

Chinelo's face twisted in confusion.

"I found out this morning from a family friend. I'm so sorry, Chinelo." She hugged him gently. "Let's get you some food. Sound good? We can talk about it whenever you are ready, and not a moment before."

Chinelo nodded on her shoulder. He noticed that bystanders were eyeballing the two of them with judgmental stares. His cheeks grew hot.

"All right. I know the perfect place," Isobel said with a smile. "Let's go."

The pair weaved through the lines of merchant carts and left the square, wandering down a side street. Chinelo smelled a rich fragrance of sizzling onions and eggs drifting over the foot traffic. Then suddenly, he saw a flash of green and gold within the crowd. He pushed Isobel into a narrow alleyway and ducked in behind her.

"Ow! What are you—"

Chinelo lifted his finger in front of her lips and nodded his head toward the street. Isobel peered slowly past his shoulder. The color left her face.

An extraordinarily thin man walked past the alleyway entrance, unaware of the two hiding within. Above the crowd, his blonde hair was shaved on the sides leaving only a combed shock on the top of his head. He wore the characteristic green robes of the Interior Guard, their gold filigree shimmering in the sun. His bony hand rested upon the hilt of a long silver rapier. Hovering at the weapon's pommel was a glowing orb of red vapor. After stopping outside of the alleyway briefly, he continued his slow walk toward the central square, scanning the villagers within the crowds.

"We need to leave," Isobel whispered.

Chinelo tilted his head in acknowledgement.

She turned and pushed deeper into the alley, making her way toward the west side of town. They emerged from between buildings and dashed to another alleyway, leaping over wooden crates and stray animals hiding from the bustle. Soon, they reached the west gate. Isobel ducked behind a passing wagon to hide from the guards with Chinelo following close behind. Having left the town, they began their ascent up the rolling hills to return home.

CHAPTER 5

CHINELO BRUSHED THE SWEAT FROM HIS forehead, then shifted forward to regain his balance on the ladder. He hammered the iron nail that protruded from the shingle several times, fastening it to the newly repaired roof. He gave a nod of approval, satisfied with the quality of his work. Close to two weeks had passed since he and Isobel had visited Nellborough, and he had spent much of his time chopping trees, cutting planks, and carving shingles.

"How is it looking up there?" Isobel called from below, gripping the ladder tightly to prevent it from toppling. Her left wrist bore a new tattoo, a band of runes that wrapped around her lower forearm. She too had been busy in the days of waning summer, though her time had been mostly spent gathering provisions from the forest and refining the spell that was printed upon her arm.

"Well, we will find out when it rains," Chinelo said, beginning his descent down the ladder. "I think it should hold. We'll just have to see if the pitch sealed properly." He hopped to the ground and raised his hand to shade his eyes.

"So," Isobel beamed.

"Yes?" Chinelo looked at her with moderate apprehension.

"Can I teach you magic now?"

He shrugged. "I don't see why not. We've finished the most important part of the repairs."

"Finally! I'm so very excited about this. Come on!" Isobel grabbed Chinelo's hand and dragged him to the front of her house. He dropped his hammer as they reached the center of the clearing.

Isobel took several paces away from Chinelo.

"All right. How much do you know about magic?" she asked, planting her hands on her hips.

"Not much I'm afraid." Chinelo cocked his head. "Normally when you do it you concentrate, say some strange words, and then things happen.

You told me you can use your tattoos or your staff to cast magic differently."

"And you've never seen anyone else use magic?"

"No, I have. A witch was found in Eshgar several years ago." Chinelo shuddered. "From what I recall she did most of the same things you do, but I remember feeling oddly heavy when she was nearby."

"Ah. Esht siphoning," Isobel said, wrinkling her nose. "We can cover that later. I'm sure you know the story of the world's creation?"

Chinelo shrugged. "I mean, I've heard a few versions. In Iskara, don't people believe the Creator spoke the world into existence? I'm not sure how that's relevant."

"Why, it's the most important thing!" Isobel asserted. "Magic, quite simply, allows us to do the same things the Creator and the lesser gods did before they ascended, though on a much smaller scale. We command, and the world obeys. Such are the Ancient Arts!"

Chinelo blinked. "I see."

Isobel raised her hand from the belt at her waist and lifted three fingers. "Magic has three steps. First, you must channel your esht. Second, you must give your esht meaning. Third, you must expel your esht, allowing your commandment to take form. That is all there is to it, really. We'll start with the first step. Do you know how to channel esht?"

Chinelo shook his head. "I'm not sure what esht is, Isobel."

"I thought as much." Isobel sighed. "Most people don't. Allow me to explain. Esht is a sort of energy or substance that all living things generate. It can be thought of as a manifestation of your spirit. Humans, gods, animals, plants, everything has esht."

"I follow," Chinelo said, paying close attention to every word his teacher spoke.

"Esht tends to accumulate naturally here," Isobel said, placing her tattooed hand just below her heart. "You should be able to feel it if you concentrate."

Chinelo closed his eyes and tried to focus his senses on the area of his body she had indicated. He shook his head. "I'm sorry Isobel. I don't feel anything out of the ordinary."

Isobel touched her chin. "Hmmm, perhaps you just don't know what it feels like. I was the same. I suppose that makes sense. You wouldn't be able to name a color if you had never seen it. I should be able to help with that."

Isobel stepped forward. She drew close to Chinelo and looked deeply into his eyes. Slowly, she raised her hand and placed it on his chest. Her touch was soft, gentle, pleasant. Her lips formed a slight smile as she pressed closer. Her sapphire eyes sparkled with their magnificent blue, bordered by light wispy lashes.

Smelling the sweet fragrance of her lavender perfume, Chinelo turned his head slightly. A heat rose in his neck. He felt that he should back away, yet for some reason he didn't. "Isobel?"

Within an instant, from the point where her hand rested upon him, a powerful tingling filled his chest, overwhelming his agitated senses. It was violent, churning and flowing to every part of his body. He staggered back, then fell to the ground in a startled heap.

"What was *that*?" Chinelo exclaimed.

Isobel giggled. "*That*, my friend, was *my* esht."

"Please never do that again," Chinelo said, rising to his feet.

"Oh stop. It couldn't have been that bad. Besides, I'm sure it had the desired effect. Try again. Can you feel your esht?"

Chinelo closed his eyes, then gasped. Beneath his heart, he felt a roiling ocean. It seemed familiar, as if it had always been there, hiding from him. It was ferocious yet welcoming. Turbulent yet calming. He felt it tingling, gradually spreading in random directions.

"I feel it!" he said.

"Excellent!" Isobel said. "Now, you just need to learn to move it. Esht flows best through your muscles, and it accumulates best in areas that are sensitive to stimuli. So, your hands, fingers, eyes, you get the idea. It *can* accumulate anywhere, but those areas are the easiest."

"Esht follows your focus," she continued. "Tell me, do you feel the ground beneath your feet?"

Chinelo shifted his attention to his feet, focusing on the typically ignored sensation. Suddenly, he felt the tingling wellspring move, racing through his leg muscles and pooling in his heels.

"It moved!" he said.

"Good!" Isobel clasped her hands proudly. "Now, tell me. Do you feel the wind brushing your fingertips?"

A cool breeze drifted through the forest. Chinelo shifted his attention to his fingers, appreciating the wind's playful caress. His esht moved again, torrenting up his legs, flowing through his shoulders, and filling his hands.

"It's in my fingers!" he said. He was beginning to understand. It was so natural. His esht was not some foreign substance within his body. It was a part of him, just like any muscle, tendon, or bone. No, it *was* him.

"Perfect! You are catching on quickly." Isobel beamed. "Now, you should remember a couple things. Esht flow is dependent on your concentration. If something breaks your concentration, it could disrupt your esht. With enough practice, you'll learn how to selectively ignore certain stimuli or to focus on certain stimuli above all others. Also, your esht is finite. Though it regenerates over time, if you use it too quickly, there will be some very unpleasant consequences. Now," she ordered, pointing her finger in his direction, "push your esht through your skin."

Chinelo increased his concentration, applying pressure to the pooling esht. He stiffened his hand, trying to block out any distractions. The wellspring seemed to shrink, though he could not ascertain where it had gone. His brow furrowed.

"It's smaller," he said meekly. "I must have done something wrong."

"No! No! You just expelled it. That's perfect." Isobel smiled. "You've just learned the first and third steps of magic. Now comes the hard part."

"The hard part?"

"Right! Step two, though we've already talked about this before." Isobel once again raised her hand, pointing three fingers upwards. "There are three ways to give your esht form. First, you can imbue it with meaning by speaking in the language of the gods, the Ancient Tongue. Like this." She flicked her wrist. "Icht sono va ogo."

A swirling sphere of water formed in her hand, growing larger until she released it, letting it splash to the ground. Chinelo's eyes widened.

Isobel grinned. "Magic will always obey anything spoken in the Ancient Tongue, provided that the incantations are specific and lack ambiguity. Unclear commands can have unintended effects."

Chinelo nodded.

"Now for the second method. You can give your esht form by channeling it into spell-glyphs written in the language of the gods, the

Ancient Script. That is how my tattoos work. I've printed spells on my skin so that I can activate them quickly. Like this."

She swung her arm and a cluster of bright lights shot from her fingers into the ground below, sprouting tiny crystals.

"Of course, the same rules apply in terms of clarity. A spell that is written with errors simply won't work as intended. Obviously, written spells have the advantage of increased complexity. If you have enough time, esht, and wit, you can make a written spell do just about anything."

Chinelo nodded again. "And the third way involves your staff?"

"Right!" Isobel strode to the front wall of her house and lifted her staff from the ground. "However, that one may be a bit too complicated for you, my friend. I will give you a summary. The third way involves the use of something called a spell-core. This, right here." She pointed at the swirling orb of vapor within the staff's ornate head. "Basically, I have prepared and named spells in advance and stored them in my staff's spell-core. If I call the spell's name while providing my staff with esht, the spell-core will activate the spell for me, though it can only do one at a time, and it will only respond to my voice. Like this."

Isobel pointed her staff ahead of her, away from Chinelo. "Flood."

The orb in her staff pulsed, and a jet of water streamed forth. It splashed across the ground and soaked into the earth. Isobel relaxed, and the stream ceased. She turned to face Chinelo. "I wouldn't worry about the third method right now. I can make you a spell-core if you like, but it isn't all that useful if you are unable to speak or write in the language of the gods. For now, we'll just use the first two methods. I've drawn out several talismans for you to practice with. Harmless ones."

Chinelo rubbed his hair. "This seems rather complicated."

"Oh, don't worry about that. Leave the confusing stuff to me!" Isobel chimed. "Let's get you started with the first spell you saw me use. It's a simple one: 'Form flame.' That is a sort of staple of the coven where I grew up. They probably wouldn't like me teaching you that, but I don't live there anymore, so who's going to get mad at me? Now, channel your esht into your fingertip."

Chinelo did as she directed.

"Good. Now repeat after me, then expel your esht," Isobel said. "Icht vasht!"

Chinelo closed his eyes. "Icht vasst!"

Nothing happened. Isobel shook her head amicably.

"Careful. You must have the right pronunciation," she corrected. "It's *vasht.* Try again."

Chinelo closed his eyes again. "Icht vasht!"

He opened his eyes to see a tiny flame dancing above his finger. He grinned.

"You did it, Chinelo!" Isobel skipped to his side. "Now! Make it bigger! Give it more esht! More!"

Chinelo churned his esht, forcing more into his hand. The flame grew until it was nearly as large as his thumb. Isobel brushed against his shoulder, admiring his work, and the flame vanished into a puff of smoke.

"Oh. Sorry," he said.

"No. No. You did well. You just need to maintain your focus better," she said with a smile. "It's not bad for your first time!"

"Well, naturally. I have a masterful teacher."

"Oh stop. Flattery will get you nowhere," she said, turning to walk to her front door. She looked over her shoulder. "That's a lie. Please continue the flattery."

"So, what do I do next?" he asked.

"Aside from lighting the fire with your magic and making me another batch of your delicious stew? Simple! You practice!" Isobel stood by the doorframe. "Once you've gotten the hang of using the talismans I've made for you, I'll teach you some more words you can use."

Chinelo chuckled. "You're going to work me to the bone, aren't you?"

"Of course. How else are you going to afford that lovely bed upstairs? I am, after all, a woman of business. Or something like that. I'm sure you understand."

He smirked. It was a very comfortable bed.

"Oh!" She said, tossing her hair to the side. "Never modify an inscription that you don't understand. Those talismans—don't write on them."

"I wouldn't dare," he said with a wink. "Who am I to alter the work of a master?"

"Ah, you catch on quick. Such a good student."

She reached for the door handle. As the two entered the house, they both halted at the hideous sight that rested on the floor. Mort was furious. They had left him inside while they repaired the roof, and he did not take kindly to being without his queen. He wallowed in his anger, thick as the mucus he excreted on the floorboards. Instead of his usual frog song, he croaked a deep guttural tantrum. His eyes blazed with a righteous anger, and he cared not who heard his cries.

"Such a menace..." Isobel whispered.

"Son of a deranged ostrich!"

Isobel's clenched fist hit the desk. She groaned in frustration and slammed the black book shut. She removed her glasses and leaned forward, rubbing her eyes with one hand. Above her, Chinelo's hammering ceased. She heard the creaking stairs as he descended to the main floor of the house.

"Everything good down here?" he asked, peaking around the corner.

"No," she grumbled, returning her glasses to their usual position.

"Oh?"

"These blasted texts, they're all the same. Come look at this," she said, waving him closer. She reopened the large tome she had received from Umfrey weeks before, finding the place she had left off.

Chinelo squinted at the open page. It was covered in a scrawl of runes and symbols.

"It's this frustrating quirk these old books have. Do you see how there are these gaps throughout the text?" Isobel asked, pointing to several empty spaces between the runes.

"Of course. Are those sentence stops?"

"The Ancient Script doesn't punctuate like that. No, words are just missing."

"Missing?"

"Yes!" she exclaimed, sitting up straight. "It doesn't make any sense! And I think it's the same set of words across all the texts I've read. It's confounding!"

"How do you figure that?"

"This particular text is copied from a set of monoliths believed to be carved by the gods. It is an incredibly detailed description of their understanding of physics," Isobel explained. "Now this page here—it describes a force that draws masses together. Sound familiar?"

Chinelo's forehead wrinkled. "Gravity?"

"Yes! Exactly! Look at this phrase here. There should be a word for the force they are describing, but it's just empty. And what's more, on this page here—" she flipped several pages back in the book, "there should be a rune that means 'time.' It's describing the relationship between displacement, velocity, and acceleration, so naturally there should be some symbol here for 'time,' but, again, there's nothing. I've come across that one on several occasions. It's such an important word, too."

"And you don't know how to speak them?"

Isobel sighed. "I don't. My sister always told me that some words have been lost with the passage of time, but I assumed that was metaphorical. I didn't expect them to have just been removed from all records. These aren't the only ones missing either. Any of those books on the shelf will have at least one page that is lacking a rune or two."

She leaned forward, burying her head in her arms on the desk. Her red hair shrouded her face. "I was really hoping that this book would be the one that had what I was missing. Just another dead end."

"Do you need those words?"

She turned her head, looking up at him through her hair. "It's not so much about needing them. There are just so many ideas I would love to try that I simply cannot because I don't know enough of the language. And that's coming from someone who's basically fluent. Just imagine all the spells I could code if I truly, fully understood the words of the gods. Magic is like poetry. True masters can weave words together with grace and beauty. Imagine writing poetry but with only the vocabulary of a four-year-old."

Chinelo crouched beside her, squinting at the page. "Perhaps it's for the best. From what you've told me, magic can be dangerous if used improperly. I'm sure all kinds of disasters would happen if there were no limitations."

Isobel frowned and lifted her head. "Where's the fun in that?"

Chinelo shrugged. "I never claimed to be the fun one here. On a different topic, I've finished rebuilding the frame of the floor up there. Should not be long until I have all the planks installed."

Isobel's frown intensified. "So, you'll be leaving after that?"

"I mean, you said you'd host me here while I did the repairs. I can't keep leeching off your good will, as much as I like it here. I'm not planning on leaving Nellborough any time soon, though."

Isobel buried her head in her arms again. "I'll just have to blast another hole in the ceiling, then."

Chinelo laughed. Isobel felt it, resonating deep within her, lifting her spirits. She stifled a smile. She had grown accustomed to that infectious laugh echoing between the walls.

"So *that's* what happened," he said. "I've been trying to pry that out of you for weeks now!"

"Even I make mistakes, on occasion."

"Well, moving past your accidental property damage, there's still the issue of the Interior Guard," Chinelo mused, looking out the window. "Umfrey told me that the body of the one you fought was found in one of the barns north of town. Also, that man we saw is still searching the town. I'm concerned that it won't be long before someone points him here. Frankly, I'm surprised no one has already."

"Being the only reliable witch for hire on this side of the continent has its benefits I guess," Isobel said, sitting up slowly. "Besides, I normally don't share where I live with my clients or customers."

"That's probably wise," Chinelo pondered. "All that to say, no I'm not planning on leaving until we've sorted that out. You haven't gotten rid of me yet."

"Good." Isobel looked at Chinelo, who squatted beside her. He wore his customary sleeveless shirt and baggy trousers. His face always seemed to rest in a subtle smile, accentuated by his defined cheekbones. Though he normally allowed a small layer of stubble to grow on his jaw, on this day it was shaved clean. She had watched the exhaustion fade from his face over the weeks they had spent together, and it had been replaced with a certain brightness, a vigor and enthusiasm for life. Even when their conversations drifted to more serious topics, he always seemed to exude a contagiously cheery aura.

"Hey," she said.

"Hey."

"Have you been practicing?" she asked, placing her elbow on the table.

"Of course."

"Show me."

"Icht vasht," Chinelo said, holding his hand aloft. Five flames appeared on his fingers.

"Oh! Impressive!" Isobel's eyes lit up. "You've already figured out how to cast in multiple places. That took me a long time to learn."

Chinelo shrugged bashfully. "Have you been practicing, Isobel?"

Isobel nodded. "Every morning."

"Ready to try sparring again?"

She groaned. "Only if you go easy on me."

"I do go easy on you!"

Isobel's staff swished through the air. She tightened her grip, driving extra power into the downward swing as she directed it towards Chinelo's shoulder. He sidestepped, and her staff struck the dirt. Her arms recoiled from the impact, causing her to stagger. She had missed.

My balance still isn't right.

"Your feet are still too close," Chinelo said before swinging the wooden training sword he carried. Isobel reacted quickly, raising her staff to deflect the blow.

She adjusted the positions of her feet and thrust her staff, just missing Chinelo's stomach.

Better.

She repeated the strike, adding a step as she swung the weapon. The head brushed Chinelo's tunic.

Almost there.

Chinelo stepped forward, attacking with a flurry of swings that Isobel dodged and parried. If she struck now, he would hit her, but if she waited until he swung downwards to the right, there would be an opening on his left. That would be when she would finally land a blow.

His sword fell diagonally, and the opening appeared. She swung again, aiming for Chinelo's side.

Chinelo smiled, then caught her staff's shaft, pulling her forward and tearing it from her hands. Isobel closed her eyes and yelped as his sword hit her shoulder.

"Ow!"

"Sorry." Chinelo lowered his sword. "That was good. You're getting much better."

She rubbed her shoulder. She had learned to predict his movements and react to his swings, but a month was nothing compared to his fifteen years of knight's training.

"I still can't hit you, though."

"You'll get there. Just remember, your staff's length gives you an advantage, but it also makes it easier to catch. Don't linger too long."

Chinelo tossed her staff back to her. When she and Chinelo had first begun her training, using it as weapon seemed so wrong. It was a fine instrument, a culmination of her life's studies, and yet she now used it as a beating stick. However, after weeks of practice and a couple reinforcement spells, it almost felt right. She balanced her staff on two fingers, watching it sway back and forth.

"I really wish you would be gentler with me," Isobel said, still feeling the sting from the earlier hits. "That hurt."

Chinelo laughed.

Isobel lowered her staff. She would miss that laugh when he left. Without him, her house would be so quiet, so hollow. It was hard to believe that she had spent five years alone before they met. That time seemed so very far away. She had almost forgotten the emptiness that now threatened to return.

"Isobel!" A voice pierced the trees.

They turned to see a figure running towards them. Umfrey's wife Priscila bounded through the forest, holding her long white skirt so that it didn't catch on the underbrush.

"Priscila?" Isobel asked. "Why the rush?"

Priscila slowed and halted in front of her, breathing heavily. She was tall and a bit imposing, but in a friendly sort of way. Sweat glistened on her brow and her gray-brown hair.

"Umfrey had a meeting today with the sheriff," she said. "The Interior Guard—they've left town!"

"What?"

"They've been called back to the capital! It happened late last night. Isobel, you can come back!"

CHAPTER 6

CHINELO PAUSED AS HE CRESTED THE hill outside Nellborough's west gate. The sun had begun the early stages of its descent toward the horizon ahead. He looked back at Isobel, who walked slowly behind him, staring at the ground. She had grown quiet, too quiet. For the entirety of their morning trek to town, she had gushed and babbled about the many things she wished to do and the people she wanted to see now that it was safe to return. However, as soon as they left Umfrey's bookstore, her usually cheerful demeanor vanished.

Chinelo frowned. She had been acting strangely for the past few days. Though he had hoped that the news of the Interior Guard's withdrawal would remedy her mysterious mood, it seemed that it had only been a temporary change.

Isobel stopped behind him. "It's going to be so quiet after you leave," she said. "It's been nice, you know, having a friend around."

Chinelo's brow creased. "I thought you had friends in town, Isobel. You talked about them all morning."

"It's just that... well... how do I put this? It's just not the same!" She stomped ahead, passing Chinelo.

"Well, I still need to secure a source of income before I can find a new place to stay, Isobel," Chinelo said.

Her shoulders tensed. The wind moved the hair that hung at the back of her neck. "Chinelo, know that you'll always be welcome here. Don't feel that you have to run to the door too quickly."

"I see." Chinelo joined Isobel. "You are very generous."

"Do you remember what we talked about the other night?" Isobel asked, kicking up dirt with her boot.

"Mort's insatiable appetite?"

Isobel's troubled face softened with a small smile. "Not that, no. Though yes, I'm sure he'll be starving and incredibly angry when we get back home."

Chinelo rubbed his temple, twisting his curly hair around his finger. "Oh! We talked about some of the places in Iskara I was thinking about visiting."

"Right!" she nodded.

"Yes?" he asked.

"What if we saw them together?"

"Oh!" Chinelo said. He was not expecting *that*. "Sure. That would be fun! When?"

Isobel paused. "Now?"

"Now?" he cried.

"Well, maybe not immediately," she said. "We could take some time to make proper preparations. But autumn is perfect for traveling!" Isobel turned and twirled a lock of hair that hung below her collar. "I should have enough money saved to last us a few months, and then we can find work wherever we stay, like you did in Mervos. Mage-work is in high demand, so I'm sure we could manage. And I could keep teaching you more about magic along the way! Just imagine! Traveling the countryside! Seeing new places! Meeting new people! It would be amazing!"

Chinelo pondered the thought. "I thought you liked it here, Isobel."

"I do! But I've always wanted to see the world. I'm not saying we should leave permanently. Just perhaps until winter! We'd have my house as a home base to return to, and then during the winter you could try to get your longer-term arrangements sorted out."

Chinelo scratched his head. While it was true that he wanted to settle down soon, he couldn't deny the appeal of adventure. "Would that make you happy?"

"More than anything," Isobel replied.

He touched his chin. It was true that it would be relatively easy for him to travel at that point. He had barely unpacked since he started staying at Isobel's house, and it was not as if he had many possessions beyond his armor.

"If we're going to do this, then I'd like for us to make a clear plan on where we intend to go and how long we intend to stay. Perhaps we could work on that together over the next few days? Then we can start gathering or purchasing supplies and clothing."

Isobel bounced on her toes and beamed. "Do you really mean it? You really want to?"

Chinelo nodded. "I'm certain it would be a pleasant experience. Besides, I would be lying if I said I didn't enjoy the last month."

Isobel let out a jubilant squeal. She stepped to the peak of the hill, looking over Nellborough, and spun on her toe.

"Oh! It will be magnificent!" she exulted, outstretching her arms. "The eastern meadows, the northern mountains, the southern oceans! There's so much world for us to see!"

Chinelo looked up at her. She was silhouetted against the billowing white clouds that towered over the horizon. The town below bustled and pulsed with its typical crowds. Seeing it all at once—the peridot trees in the distance, the ivory clouds above, the sapphire sky beyond, the emerald hills below—it was like viewing a beautiful painting. It was breathtaking. But most of all, *she* was breathtaking. Her hair reflected the light of the sun, shimmering in waves. Her eyes were as blue as the sky. Her deep red tunic complemented the greens of the hills and forests. She stood before him, a picture of pure joy and grace.

Chinelo felt a stirring, building pressure in his chest. It was hot like fire, yet cold like water. It was still like a forest, yet it moved like a bird. He had felt it on so many nights before, flickering weakly before being snuffed out by shadows of fear and doubt. Yet today, it burned like a raging river—uncontrollable, unstoppable. Her kindness, her zeal, her meekness, her passion—they were overwhelming. Wherever she might go, he knew he wished to follow.

A flash.

An immense golden light appeared far behind Isobel. It quickly grew, filling the air above Nellborough. It swirled and churned before erupting into scorching orange flames. They fell upon the city, coalescing to form a furious blazing tornado. It enveloped the town, rapidly expanding beyond the walls and consuming the hills.

A rushing wave of hot air hit Chinelo's skin, and tears formed in his eyes. Isobel turned in horror to see the towering maelstrom, an impossibly tall pillar of fire that pierced the clouds above. They vanished, evaporated by the intense heat.

Isobel planted her feet on the ground and channeled a flood of esht into her left hand, projecting her protective barrier around her and Chinelo. A tsunami of flame collided with the barrier and spread around them, incinerating the grass beside the trail. A deafening crash shook the earth. The stench of smoke and ash filled her throat. Chinelo fell to the ground behind her.

"Extinguish!" Isobel yelled, slamming the end of her staff into the earth. Wind rushed from her staff, and the flames faded in a wide radius around her. She stared with wide, horrified eyes at the burning column rising from the city. And then, as quickly as it came, it disappeared, leaving behind a glowing bed of cinder scorched into the land. Fingers of smoke rose from the town, reaching to the heavens. Isobel glanced back at Chinelo, who crouched coughing on the ground. She gasped.

"Clair!"

She sprinted toward the black and orange mass that was once called Nellborough, stepping over ashes and burning brush.

She had to hurry.

She had to save them.

Chinelo's hands shook. He stared at the dirt, afraid to raise his eyes and see the landscape that spread before him. His chest tightened, as if a cold hand had clutched his heart. The fire, the blaze, the sound, the smell—it was the same as on the day Eshgar burned to the ground. The same column of flame had risen to the sky, and the same column of flame had vanished, leaving behind only a scar of what once was.

It had happened again, and, just as before, he was left behind.

Suddenly, he regained his senses.

He looked up, searching for Isobel. She was gone. He saw her in the distance, nearing the town. He had to stop her. He slung aside his pack and raced after her. His heart beat in his chest, harder, louder, stronger, as if his ribcage was going to rupture. Every instinct cried out within him, pleading with him to turn back. It did not matter. If it meant stopping her from seeing what he had witnessed eight months earlier, he would face any horror that lay ahead.

"Extinguish!" Isobel shouted, forcing esht into her staff. A path of dry earth appeared around her, breaking the flames. Every few steps, she repeated her spell.

"Isobel! Stop!" Chinelo yelled. Despite her head start, Chinelo was gaining ground. Isobel ignored his cries.

She reached the gate. The heat was intense. She accumulated a massive amount of esht in her staff and snuffed the flames, clearing a portion of the blaze. She gasped. A cruel lump formed in her throat. Beside her, the tables and chairs where the town guards often sat had been reduced to a smoldering pile of gray wood. Surrounding the heap of ashes lay five blackened corpses. They were vile, repulsive, hideous amalgamations of charred bone and bent armor.

Isobel retched.

Chinelo was at her side, panting for air.

"Isobel!" he said between labored breaths. "You can't go in there."

"But Clair! Umfrey! Priscilla!" she said. "They need my help."

"Isobel!" Chinelo grabbed her shoulder. "Don't go. The things in there—you can't unsee them. It's not worth it."

"Chinelo! They *need* me!"

Chinelo shook her. "They're gone, Isobel! I'm sorry, but they're gone! Please, don't go in there."

Tears streamed down her cheeks, mixing with soot before falling on her tunic.

"Don't—don't say that! You don't know that."

"No, Isobel. I do."

"No, you don't!" She wrenched herself free of one of his hands. He gripped ever harder on her shoulder.

"Look around! Don't you see, Isobel? Don't you understand? This is what happened to Eshgar! Nothing survived!" His chin quivered. "Please, don't go. I'm warning you. No! I'm begging you. I don't want you—I don't want you to—" his words broke.

Isobel looked down as tears pooled on the inside of her spectacles. "Let go of me," she said quietly.

Chinelo lowered his hand. She turned and entered the gate with Chinelo following.

Isobel stepped carefully over the embers that littered the pavement, searching for something, anything that resembled life. The many houses and buildings that lined the streets had collapsed, their mighty timber walls charred and fragmented. She stopped to look at one house. The doorframe had crushed a body beneath it, leaving only an outstretched ashen hand reaching for the street. In others, she saw corpses draped through the shattered windows.

She shook her head and continued onwards. Blackened figures were piled against the stone foundations of each building. Some appeared to be climbing while others clutched tiny skeletons desperately. A building beside her crumbled and fell, scattering shingles across the road before her. She stepped over the shards of burning wood and pressed on towards the central square. Every few minutes, she cast her spell to stifle the flames.

As they neared the town center, a heap of bodies lay across the road, halting their progress. Isobel ducked into a side alley, climbing over boards and stones. She rounded a bend and stopped, covering her mouth with her hand. Chinelo stood at her side and looked ahead despondently. Isobel's staff clattered to the ground.

Before them lay the remnants of Umfrey's home and bookstore. The walls had been completely pulverized by the force of the maelstrom, leaving behind only a mountain of ash and rubble. Isobel stepped forward.

Something crunched beneath her boot.

Slowly, she looked down. Her face contorted and twisted as tears flowed anew.

At her feet lay the small, cracked bones of a child, blackened and covered in thick soot. About its neck sparkled a familiar star-shaped pendant.

"No..." Isobel whispered. She fell to her knees and, with shaking gloved hands, lifted and embraced the body. She sobbed, then gasped, then wept.

Chinelo knelt beside her and laid his hand on her shoulder. Her body trembled erratically, shaken by her agonized cries.

"Why?" Isobel whimpered. "Why did this happen, Chinelo? Why would this happen?"

Chinelo gave no answer for he had none. He blinked, attempting to control the growing flood of emotions that threatened to break from within, like water bursting through a dam. He had witnessed this once before, and he had tried to forget it.

Isobel laid Clair's lifeless corpse on the ground and brushed her hands on her tunic. She wiped her eyes, but her tears would not stop. Chinelo wrapped his arm around her shoulder, and she leaned into him as she cried, letting the sorrow erupt from her soul in a heart-wrenching wail.

A loud crash sounded from behind them. Chinelo looked over his shoulder to see that a burning beam had fallen and blocked the alleyway entrance. He looked about; the walls around them creaked as the fires weakened them further.

"Isobel," he whispered, "we need to leave."

Isobel sniffled into his shirt and nodded. They pushed deeper into the alleyway, hoping to find an exit. They ducked through a tunnel of debris, winding and snaking through the ravaged buildings. Eventually, they found the town square. It sprawled before them, blanketed with cinders. The stone structure above the blacksmith's foundry was streaked black with soot. Then, he felt... *it*.

At the center of the square the obelisk stood, untouched by the fires. The ground shook in a steady rhythm, the rhythm of a beating heart. Billowing pillars of smoke climbed to the sky from the edges of the plaza.

"Do you feel that?" Chinelo asked.

"What?" Isobel's hair moved as if agitated by an unheard breath.

Chinelo winced. He once again sensed the call. It reached to him from deep within the earth, beckoning him downwards. It was voiceless yet deafening. It wanted to be free.

"Ah, so the witch shows herself." A man stepped from one of the plaza's crumbling entrances. He was tall and lean, and the shock of blonde hair on his otherwise shaved head was dotted with flakes of ash. Lit by the setting sun and the dying flames, his dark green and gold battle robe shimmered. They had seen him before on the day they first visited Nellborough. He sneered at the pair, resting his hand on the hilt of his rapier. "I'm surprised you managed to make it here. I wouldn't have guessed that this was why you were hiding in this town."

Chinelo stepped in front of Isobel. "Why are *you* here?"

"My, my, my! You say that as if we've met before, but I don't think we have." The man touched his chin.

Isobel pointed her staff at the man. "Are you responsible for this?" She demanded.

The man shrugged. "Now, witch, why would you think that?"

"Don't mock me! This was done by magic," Isobel retorted.

"This was done by a *witch's* magic," the man corrected. "Fire is a specialty of your culture. We haven't managed to learn that lost art, despite our best efforts."

Isobel's brow furrowed. That didn't make sense. Magic was not locked to a specific group or region. Chinelo was evidence of that.

"You're Eshgarian, I believe," the man continued, glancing at Chinelo. "I'd advise you to step away from that treacherous creature. I know your people don't understand the intricacies of magic, so I'll be generous and warn you. She is far more dangerous than I'm sure you realize. Just look around you. This disaster, this tragedy, it was caused by her kind."

Chinelo drew his double-edged broadsword. It flashed silver as he lowered it in front of him.

The man frowned. "Nephew!"

A wiry adolescent peaked timidly from behind him.

"Head back to camp. Inform the Archmage that the obelisk is ready," the man ordered. "I'll return once I've dealt with these two."

The youth scurried off, exiting the plaza through the eastern road.

The man drew his rapier and bowed. "Greetings. My kin call me Brennen, 29th Mage of the Interior Guard. I would be pleased if you would as well."

Chinelo scoffed at the mockery of his kingdom's customs. Isobel gripped her staff firmly. She channeled esht into her left hand, readying herself for the first attack.

With his right arm tucked behind his back, the man raised his rapier, holding it vertically. He whispered a single word. "Wind."

The red orb at the weapon's pommel swelled, and the man swung his rapier. A powerful gust of air rushed forward. Thrown back by the invisible force, Chinelo tumbled across the pavement. Isobel projected her barrier, and the air spread around her. She blinked, and the man was before her, poised to stab her heart. She twisted, and the blade grazed her side.

"Shock," she shouted, slamming the head of her staff into the man's chest. Her staff sparked and crackled, but the man glided back unscathed. His movements were fluid and smooth. He floated over the ground like a ghost. Isobel's brow furrowed. Her spell should have worked, yet it seemed to have no effect.

Brennen's eyes narrowed. "Lightning? How curious. It seems that we have been deceived." He lifted his rapier.

Isobel backstepped rapidly and issued a second command. "Fireball: Fivefold!"

Spheres of orange flame formed around Isobel's staff and flew towards her target. The man glided and weaved through the onslaught. He spun lithely and charged forward, aiming once again for Isobel's heart.

Steel fell upon steel. Chinelo's sword swung down upon the man's rapier, forcing it to the ground. Chinelo twisted his wrist and swung his sword upwards, impacting the man's lower torso. The cold metal of his sword rang as it collided with chainmail. Brennen floated back before unleashing a flurry of strikes towards Chinelo. Chinelo deflected blow after blow. The attacks were weak, but unbelievably rapid.

Isobel raised her staff, preparing to cast a spell once there was an opening. She watched in awe as Chinelo expertly parried each of the man's attacks, though he could not retaliate with a strike of his own. She looked at the ground at their feet. Chinelo's kicked up small puffs of ash and dust as he moved, but strangely, Brennen's robes agitated a large cloud, obscuring the pavement beneath him. Suddenly, Brennen extended his right arm, and, with a flash, a second rapier appeared in his hand. Isobel's eyes widened. The palm of his right hand was tattooed with an intricate glyph.

Chinelo's eyes darted upwards. The second blade gleamed as it swung for his head. He ducked. The blade swished as its razor edge cut through the air above him. Brennen twisted his left arm and swung his first rapier. It sliced deep into Chinelo's shoulder. Chinelo gritted his teeth and slashed his weapon diagonally upwards. He missed, but he had created space to get his bearings.

Isobel spotted the opening. "Flood!" A powerful stream of water shot from her staff and collided with the man, sending him flying across the village square.

"Chinelo! He's using conjuring magic!" Isobel shouted over the torrent.

Chinelo glanced at her. "I don't know what that means!"

"He can create swords! Also, there's something odd about his footwork. Keep an eye on it."

Chinelo nodded then searched the stream of water for their opponent. With a flash of steel, the man burst forth.

"Volley!" Brennen shouted.

Several rapiers appeared in midair and flew toward Isobel. She released the stream as the armaments careened in her direction. She dropped to the ground, barely avoiding the storm of blades.

Brennen shouted once more, "Volley: Sevenfold!"

A second wave flew towards her. She projected her barrier, and the blades faded as they impacted it. A third wave rained upon her.

Pain. Burning, stinging, piercing her calf. One of the darts pinned her leg to the ground. She screamed and struggled to remove the blade.

Chinelo charged at Brennen and delivered a mighty swing with his sword, slicing a portion of the battle robe from Brennen's waist. He shifted the trajectory of his weapon, maintaining its momentum. Brennen crossed his rapiers and repelled the strike. He countered, attacking with one blade and defending with the other. His movements were graceful yet erratic, controlled yet wild. He was a whirlwind of sharpened steel. Chinelo sidestepped nimbly to avoid the snakelike strikes, dancing around his opponent. He glanced down, attempting to read his footwork. The mage's boots levitated over the ground, floating freely. Rings of runes were embroidered around the soles.

So that's how he moves like that! Even so, he's going to become winded eventually if he keeps attacking like that.

Chinelo waited for the moment his opponent's movements slowed. He backed away, deflecting thrust after thrust. His arms ached. He could not keep up. He felt a sharp pain in his forearm and calf. Blood flowed hot on his skin.

Brennen's rhythm broke, and he hesitated, focusing himself before his next attack. His foot briefly touched the ground, rebalancing him. Recalling what Isobel had taught him, Chinelo surged his esht.

"Icht vasht'ra!" he shouted, expelling his energy through his blade. His sword erupted into flame, and Chinelo swung it forcefully, hurling a wave of fire at his opponent.

Brennen gasped and coiled back, brushing the flames that lit his robe. Chinelo prepared a second swing.

Brennen laughed. Chinelo hesitated.

"*Vasht,*" Brennen chuckled. "It's '*vasht*' isn't it? Oh, the Archmage will be thrilled to hear this. Thank you, Eshgarian. You've revealed what *she* wouldn't." Brennen raised his rapier skyward and grinned.

"Barrage!" Brennen shouted.

Isobel ran towards the two combatants. She had mended her wounds, though she still felt an ache from where the dart had pierced her leg. A heaviness weighed down upon her body. Extinguishing the flames, healing her injuries, and blocking Brennen's volley of blades had drained a significant portion of her esht. Using inefficient spells would be risky. Ahead of her, Chinelo struggled against his opponent. Suddenly, an array of blades appeared above him, ready to rain down upon him like hail. Isobel channeled her esht into her staff and shouted.

"NULLIFY!"

A shockwave swept from the head of her staff, disintegrating the many blades along with Brennen's second rapier. Brennen's feet hit the ground, and he stumbled. The color drained from his face. Seizing the opportunity, Chinelo spun, putting the entirety of his strength behind a single slice. His blade pierced Brennen's skin and severed his right hand. Brennen shrieked. He fell, steadying himself upon his sword.

"Icht vasht'ra," Brennen said through gritted teeth, and a blast of flame flashed from his wounded arm. Chinelo leapt back.

Isobel grimaced as the strain from her dwindling esht reserves became difficult to ignore. Her last spell had been incredibly costly.

"Chinelo!" Isobel called.

Chinelo's eyes met hers.

"Wait," she mouthed.

Isobel extended her left hand. She surged esht into the tattoo at her wrist, launching cyan lights into Brennen. Shining crystals sprouted across his body, tearing his robe and leeching his esht as they grew. Chinelo darted forward, gripping the handle of his sword with both hands. Weighed down by the massive crystalline growths, Brennen flailed ferociously at Chinelo. Isobel tossed her staff aside and ran behind him. Dropping to the ground, she slid under his thrashing blade and slammed her hand into his leg.

"Belekt fai!" she cried.

Thunder cracked. No longer separated from the ground by a cushion of air, the man's nerves and muscles were ravaged by Isobel's shock. Brennen's body seized and the rapier fell from his hand. Isobel caught its handle, and with a yell drove it into his side, piercing his chain mail. Blood spurted forth, coating her clothes and skin. Brennen groaned and began mouthing an incantation. Chinelo smashed his boot to the ground and swung his sword in a brilliant curve, rending Brennen's head cleanly from his shoulders. The 29th Mage fell to his knees and collapsed in a heap, crushing the crystals beneath him.

Isobel backed away and panted. She felt tiny pricks of pain over her entire body, signs that her esht reserves were exhausted. She glanced at Chinelo as he backed away from their fallen foe. He was wounded and bleeding, but with her esht running dry, she was unable to heal him. At least, not yet.

ᛈ

Chinelo stabbed his sword into the ground and leaned against it, breathing heavily. His head ached, and the world about him spun. Beneath his feet, he felt the dull beat coming from the obelisk. The fires continued to burn. Smoke filled the air, accumulating in a thick cloud above the town. At the center, stood the obelisk. It was just like before. However, Chinelo was not alone this time. Having finally caught his breath, he searched for something to say.

"I—we should go," he said.

Isobel nodded weakly. A single tear trickled down her cheek. She exhaled and walked toward the west, heading toward the gate through which they had first entered.

Chinelo looked down at the corpse of the man they had fought. A sickening gloom passed over him, one that always followed a kill. He knelt over Brennen's lifeless body. He had not killed someone in a long time, not since Eshgar fell.

He hesitated. Brennen had not been alone, and the youth who had accompanied him was on his way to the Archmage, the leader of the Interior Guard and the advisor to Iskara's king. Chinelo's mouth formed a tight line as a chill ran down his spine.

He and Isobel had just become the Archmage's enemies.

He knelt over the body and extended his hand, whispering an incantation. "Icht vasht'ra." Fire flared from his palm and ignited the corpse. Chinelo stood and bowed with his hand over his heart. Though they had been enemies, he could at least give the man proper Eshgarian resting rites.

He hurried after Isobel. Soon they reached the hill they had stood upon hours before. They both looked back at the town. How quickly it had transformed from a vibrant hub to a deathly field of cinders. Isobel wiped her eyes with her sleeve and sniffled. For the remainder of their return trip home, not a single word was spoken.

CHAPTER 7

CHINELO LAY ON HIS BED AND stared at the ceiling. A single candle lit the room. He was exhausted, yet he could not sleep. Every time he closed his eyes, he saw the horrible remnants of the lives that had been cut short. He thought of the jovial Oros, the studious Umfrey, the scowling Trallo. He thought of his stern mother, his doting father. He thought of his elder brother Azuka, who had taught him how to care for his sword. He thought of the friends he had made in the Knight's Academy and High University. He thought of Sade, who had stood beside him on many patrols. He thought of Kam, whom he had once loved.

All of them were gone, like ashes in the wind. What he would give to see any of them just once more.

He sighed and stood. Perhaps the night air would refresh him. He cautiously peered from his bedroom, checking for any signs of activity from the adjacent room. A light shone down the hallway from underneath Isobel's bedroom door. Apparently, she could not sleep either. He tiptoed and heard a slight rustling from within. He rapped lightly on the door.

"Isobel? Do you need anything?" he asked.

He heard an odd scuffling sound. A shadow broke the stream of light that was cast across the floor, and a sheet of paper brushed his foot. Picking up the paper, he squinted at it.

"No," was scrawled across the parchment.

"Well, I just want you to know—I—" Chinelo paused for a moment. "I just want you to know I'm here for you."

He slid the paper back under the door. The scuffling continued, and the paper was returned. Underneath the first message was written *"Thank you."*

Chinelo returned to his bedroom, passing a strange black lump at the top of the stairs. It caught his eye before moving into the light.

Mort.

Chinelo nodded his head towards his bedroom, and the frog hopped into it ahead of him. Chinelo sat down on the floor beside his odd companion. He was tired. So very tired. He began to drift in and out of sleep. His mind wandered to strange and foreign places. Memories of the past and present mixed impossibly. A light knock drew him back to lucidity.

"Chinelo?" Isobel called from the hall. "May I come in?"

Chinelo rose and opened the door. Isobel stood in the hallway in her nightgown. Though little light reached into the hall, Chinelo could see that her eyelids were burning red.

"Can we talk?" she sniffled.

"Of course." Chinelo stepped toward the bed, preparing to sit on the floor again. Isobel did not move.

"Isobel?"

She stepped slowly into the room, looking away from the light. Chinelo sat and tapped the space beside him. After a moment, she joined him and leaned against his shoulder, wrapping her arm around his. She was trembling. Mort waddled to her bare feet and stared up at her.

"Was it like this with Eshgar?" she asked in a shaky voice.

Chinelo nodded.

"How did you move on?"

Chinelo sighed. "I didn't, Isobel."

She quivered. "Then, what am I supposed to do? Th—They're gone! Everyone is gone!" Her fingernails dug into her arm. "I'll—I'll never see them again. I'll never hug them again. It's not—it's not right, Chinelo!"

"I wish I knew. But accepting the emotions you are feeling is a start. It happened. It's real. The pain. The sorrow. The regret. They're all real, Isobel."

Isobel trembled. She shook her head, moving her lips to form words. "But—" She sniffled, her face twitching as she struggled to speak. "But I don't want it to be. It's not right."

"Nor do I." He wiped his eyes.

Isobel's sniffles transitioned to sobs. She wept deeply, viscerally. Any restraint present when she entered the room had been abandoned. Chinelo sat at her side, unmoving as she wept. He knew how she felt. So little time had passed since he lost his family. Grief, pain, remorse, anger, they all burned like raging fires—uncontrollable, unstoppable. He longed to comfort her, to ease her suffering. Yet what could he say? Strangers had offered kind words and condolences when his kingdom fell. It had changed nothing. His sorrow still maintained its razor edge, and words could not dull it. And so, he said nothing, merely letting her lean on him.

The following days would be difficult. After his family died, Chinelo had fallen into intense lethargy. He recalled one day on which he had awoken and simply stared at the sky from sunrise to sunset, barely even moving from his bedding. He'd struggled to muster the energy to do anything worthwhile. The only thing that had managed to rouse him was hunger.

He ran through a mental list of things that needed to be done the next day. Preparing food, hunting game, drawing water, washing clothes, gathering vegetables. He could do all of those things while she rested. Perhaps that would provide some small comfort. It was the least he could do.

Eventually Isobel's cries gradually weakened and softened. Chinelo felt her lean into him more. She grew quiet, her slow breaths brushing against his skin. Every few minutes, she twitched. Soon, she was still.

Slowly and carefully, Chinelo lifted her in his arms and carried her to her bed. He laid her on the soft sheets and pulled her blanket over her. She sighed, then nestled into her pillows.

The candle on her desk burned low. Chinelo blew the flame, and the light faded. He returned to his bedroom but left their two doors open so that he could hear if she stirred in the night. Soon, the tender arms of sleep embraced him as well.

Chinelo's eyes fluttered open. Light filtered through the window, as the sun had just begun to rise. He rolled to his feet and stretched. Looking down, he saw Mort's frog foot protruding from underneath his bed. Isobel had warned him not to wake the creature, so he crept into the hallway. Chinelo poked his head into Isobel's room, only finding an empty bed topped with twisted blankets. From below, Chinelo heard movement. He descended the stairs. Still in her nightgown, Isobel was hunched over her workbench, writing notes in one of her many books. Her hair was messy, bent into strange shapes from her night's rest.

"Hey," Chinelo said, sitting at the kitchen table. She looked surprisingly energetic, all things considered.

Isobel looked his way and smiled. "Hey." Dark circles had formed beneath her eyes.

"Can I make you breakfast?" Chinelo offered.

"That would be lovely."

Chinelo rose and began gathering ingredients from his host's cupboards. "What are you working on?"

Isobel sighed and scratched her head. "I'm trying to understand how that man yesterday was able to conjure swords the way he did. My sister once told me about that kind of magic, but I've never seen it myself until now. I'm sure there is some trick to it. Honestly, I should have grabbed the spell-core before we left."

"Oh?"

She set her pen upon the desk and looked to the kitchen table. "I suppose I never explained that. If you break a spell-core you can read the magic inside of it. It's a strange sensation—not one I particularly enjoy—but it is very useful."

"Are you saying we should go—"

"No!" Isobel snapped, shaking her head. "I—I can't go back."

"I'm sorry. That was insensitive of me," Chinelo said quietly.

"No, it's fine. This is at least keeping my mind occupied for the moment."

He poured oil into a frying pan and placed several slices of sweet bread on top. Isobel resumed her work as Chinelo lit the fire and began cooking their meal. She soon joined him at the table, and they dined together solemnly. Midway through the meal, Mort splatted down the stairs and crawled around the floor, waiting for his own breakfast to be gifted to him.

After they had cleared the table, Isobel donned her boots and set the fat frog upon his tray. He settled down and prepared for a relaxing morning nap.

"I'm going to get some air. Would you walk with me?" Isobel asked.

Chinelo nodded and laced his own boots. They stepped out into the forest, leaving Mort behind. The sun shone down from above, casting its rays through the thick haze that filled the cool morning air. Isobel inhaled, then coughed.

The smell of smoke mixed with autumn dust was intense. The pair ventured around the back of her house and strolled down the trail that ran past the well. Isobel paused and looked down at the scorched roots she had burned so many weeks earlier. Leaves had fallen from the trees and covered much of the black scar. She shook her head and continued onwards.

Chinelo's body ached. He felt heavy, fatigued, exhausted, and his fitful sleep had done little to refresh him. It was like before, like so many months earlier when he first delved into Eshgar's burning heart. Based on how Isobel walked, he assumed she suffered as he did.

She let out a sudden sigh. "Chinelo, I refuse to accept this."

"Pardon?"

"This. All of this. I can't accept this."

Chinelo frowned. "I don't understand."

Isobel rubbed her forehead. "What happened yesterday. I reject it. This fate is not something I can allow."

"Isobel, I'm sorry, but you aren't making sense."

"I'm going to change things, Chinelo. I'll undo them. What happened yesterday—it isn't right. It's not how things should go."

"Isobel, that's how the world is. It's not fair. It doesn't care. Things happen, and we can't change them."

"Well, *I* can!"

Chinelo raised an eyebrow. "How?"

"I'm going to use magic to undo what happened. I'll do it in my town— and in yours!" she said fervently.

"Is that even possible?"

"Not yet. But it can be," she asserted. "I've been thinking about those missing words I mentioned. Two of them in particular. 'Time' and 'memory.' If I knew them, I'm sure I could do it."

"I see."

"I'm going to find the missing runes and claim them as my own. The fact that they are missing proves that they exist. Someone *must* know them."

Isobel stood silent for a moment. She squeezed her delicate hand into a tight fist. "I'll find them and take them, even if I must tear them from the Archmage himself!"

"But—"

"You heard what that man said," she continued. "The Archmage did this. *He* is our enemy. He and the entire Interior Guard. I'll stop them, Chinelo. I'll go back, and I'll stop them from ever harming our homes."

Chinelo rubbed his head. Her claims were outlandish, unreasonable, absurd. Yet he wanted to believe her. He so desperately wanted to believe her. If there was a hope for his family, a hope for his friends, a hope for her, he would be willing to cast aside his many doubts and believe her.

Isobel stepped ahead, holding her hands behind her back. "I can think of one person who might know where to start."

"Who?"

She looked over her shoulder. "My sister, Iva. Though to reach her I will have to go somewhere I'd hoped to never see again."

Chinelo cocked his head. "Is this...?"

"The Red Coven. The place where I was raised. It's a horrible place, and the journey will be long. Even if I do make it, there's a good chance the Elder Mothers or their Blades will kill me for desertion. For that reason, I would advise that you don't join me. However..." She pivoted on her toe and looked pleadingly at Chinelo. The wind rustled her gown. "Would you be willing to come with me?"

Chinelo's eyes widened as he looked upon her. She was stern yet hopeful. Afraid yet resolute. Sorrowful yet beautiful. The pressure he felt the previous day stirred. Again, its strange, contradictory, cold burning fluttered in his chest. He had lost everything—his family, his home, his friends, and the life he had hoped would grow from their ashes. Only one thing he had not lost, and she stood before him.

Wherever she might go, he knew he wished to follow.

THE END OF PART 1

PART 2

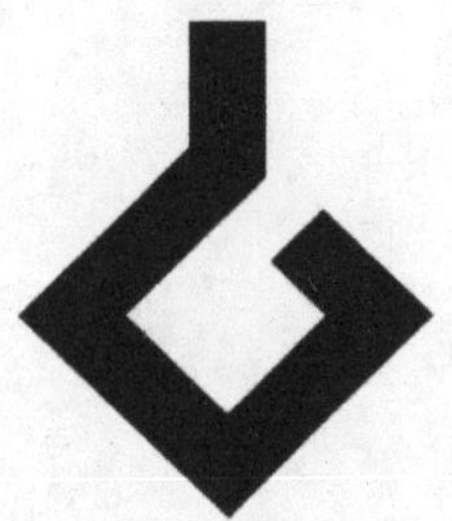

THE RED COVEN'S BLADE

CHAPTER 8

418th year, 8th month, 7th day
15 years before present day

SILENCE FELL IN THE HALLS OF the Red Coven. The young Isobel peered over the rail of her bed, searching the moonlit room for any signs of life. She heard the slow, heavy breathing of her many sleeping sisters. She smiled. Tonight would be the night she finally saw it.

She stealthily descended the ladder of her bunk and tiptoed across the wooden floor, stepping over the toys and belongings of her siblings. Reaching into the darkness with her small hands, she found the cubby where she had stored her shoes. She slid them on her bare feet, then cautiously opened the door.

A robed figure carried a candle down the hall, the dim light reflecting off a familiar gray bun. Isobel shuddered and touched the back of her hand, feeling a slight throb from a partially healed bruise. Sister Cleo would be furious if she saw her, and Isobel knew exactly what her punishment would be.

Cleo disappeared around a corner, and Isobel relaxed. She was *not* getting caught tonight. She darted into the hallway and sidled along the wall, keeping to the shadows. Her hand brushed against a doorframe. She was close. She closed her eyes and drew in a deep breath. She hated this part.

Pushing open the door, she entered a pitch-black room. The door creaked, echoing through the quiet halls.

"Icht vasht," Isobel whispered.

A tiny flame formed on her finger, lighting the darkness. Strange statues lined the walls. They were grotesquely deformed, yet vaguely human. Their arms and legs were either uncomfortably long or hideously short, and they were contorted in bizarre, monstrous poses, covering their faces with bony, clawed hands. Isobel dashed across the room. Pressing her back against the door upon exiting, she breathed a relieved sigh.

She looked around the expansive courtyard. The eaves above her were supported by carved, twisting columns. Raked gravel extended from beneath the porch upon which she stood, and three small trees grew on a circle of grass at the center of the courtyard. She had spent much time here, training and practicing in the Ancient Arts. To her left rose the pointed roof of the Temple of the Elder Mothers. It was high and steep, with curved overhangs at its edges. It dwarfed the many buildings around the outskirts of the courtyard. The moon shone down through the clear night sky. It had adopted an irregular, oblong shape, signaling that spring had reached its midpoint.

Isobel ran towards a small storage shed to her right, feeling the cool night air flowing through her long red hair. She circled around the shed's back and approached a tall, knotted tree. Its branches pressed against the wooden walls of the building, bending sharply to continue their growth. Isobel reached for a branch, then heard voices in the courtyard. She ducked behind the tree and peaked out. Two of her older sisters, Mag and Azalea, strolled across the gravel towards their barracks.

"So, I hear you're leaving with the next crew?" Azalea asked. "Where are they sending you?"

"I am! It's so exciting!" Mag replied. "I think they said Byrnn."

"Byrnn? Over in Caald, eh? I'm a bit envious of you Mag."

"Yes, I think the Mothers are hoping to add some more variety to the next generations, so off to Byrnn I go! Honestly, I was hoping for Nellborough or Yzdal, but this will do."

"Well, Yzdal is all the way on the other side of the world," Azalea said condescendingly. "Transporting an infant that far would be difficult. And as far as Nellborough goes..."

"Yes, yes. I know. No one has gone there in years..." Mag's words faded as they moved out of earshot.

Isobel waited several moments, then shivered. Her red nightgown offered little warmth. Resuming her clandestine activities, she reached for a bough and hauled herself up the tree's spiraling trunk. She stepped from limb to limb, catching her gown on several twigs. Pushing herself up with both arms, she scrambled onto the roof and began searching for the ideal spot in which to sit and watch the sky. She scurried to the front incline of the roof and halted. Before her crouched a tall dark figure wrapped in a thick cloak. The figure stood and faced her, before lifting the cloak from its head.

"You took your time," the figure said in a stern yet amiable voice. The moonlight shone on thick black tresses that were ornamented with metal rings. Her eyes were like a fox's, and they sparkled a rich jade, a color Isobel knew all too well.

"Iva! How did you know I was coming? I was so careful!" Isobel said, jutting her lip forward.

"You're not very good at keeping secrets, Isobel," Iva said, crouching back down. She held out her arm, opening her cloak. "Come on already! I've been saving this spot for you all night."

Isobel grinned gleefully and hurried to Iva's side. She leaned against her, and Iva draped her cloak around the two of them. Isobel felt Iva's muscular arm supporting her as she sat. She was safe. She was home.

"You won't tell anybody, will you, Iva?"

"Of course not, love," Iva replied. "Besides, I'm sure the Mothers will be more displeased with me for being up here than you. I'm abandoning my nightly duties for this."

Isobel snuggled up next to her sister. The ties of Iva's leather cuirass brushed against her shoulder.

"Your birthday is coming up, isn't it?" Iva asked, looking at the multitude of stars above.

Isobel nodded.

"Hard to believe it's already been ten years," Iva said. "You're getting so old."

Isobel looked up. "Well, you probably were alive when the gods ascended."

"I will push you off this roof, child," Iva retorted. "Twenty-three is still young."

Isobel backed deeper into Iva's cloak. "When is it going to start, Iva?" she asked.

Iva looked up at the moon and concentrated. She tapped Isobel's shoulder and pointed.

Lights sparkled around the irregularly shaped moon. They twinkled and scattered, streaking across the sky in brilliant white lines. At first there were only a few, then more and more, until finally the entire sky was filled with the falling stars.

"I told you it was pretty," Iva said.

Isobel nodded. "It's so pretty!" she marveled. "What are they?"

"Moonshards. They always fall around this time of year," Iva replied. Her verdant eyes reflected the moving lights in the sky. "This time they are especially beautiful. Just for you." She squeezed Isobel closer.

"Is the moon breaking?"

Iva shook her head. "The moon is shaped like a bowl, Isobel. Throughout the year the bowl fills up; then, midway through spring, it pours out."

"How can you tell? It doesn't look like a bowl."

Iva tapped the back of her neck. Wrapped in the cloak, Isobel could not see the tattoo Iva had indicated, but she had seen it many times before. Iva used it to enhance her sight, seeing impossibly far distances.

"Ohhhhhh. Can you make me one soon?" Isobel asked.

"We've been through this, Isobel. Not until you're fifteen."

"But I want one."

"So? Rules are rules. And these I will not choose to ignore."

"Where's the fun in that?" Isobel frowned and looked down.

"Oh, stop pouting, child. You'll miss the shower."

The two sat and watched the lightshow that painted the heavens. Gradually it faded, leaving only the starry sky.

"Iva?"

"Yes, love?"

"Are they going to send me away?"

Iva turned her head sharply. "Who told you they would?"

"Mag is leaving next week. Will they make me go, too? I don't want to leave you."

Iva laid her strong hand on Isobel's shoulder. "I'm not going to let that happen. When the time comes, I'll talk with the Elder Mothers. They'll listen to me."

"I want to be like you when I get my assignment. Being one of the Blades sounds so exciting. We could come and go whenever we want!"

Iva frowned. "Don't say that, Isobel. The work they have me do—it's not the kind of thing you should aspire to. It's not pleasant."

"What is it?"

"I'll explain it at some point when you're older. It's too early now."

Isobel looked at her feet and fidgeted. "Iva?"

"Hmmm?"

"Are you my real mother?"

Iva sighed. "No, Isobel. I'm not."

"Then who is? Joanne, Myrtle, and Kay all know who their mothers are. Why don't I?"

"You're asking a lot of questions tonight," Iva mused. She hesitated, clenching her jaw. Her lips turned downwards at the corners. "Some of us here don't know our real mothers, Isobel. Some of us wish we didn't. We don't choose our families, but sometimes, our families choose us." She clasped Isobel's hand in hers. "Remember that."

Isobel winced at the sudden pressure on her bruise. Iva's gaze darted down, lingering on Isobel's hand for a moment.

"How did you get that?" Iva asked slowly, letting her words hang.

Isobel pulled her hand away. The bruise was evidence of her disobedience, her failure to abide by the rules that all prospective witches must live by. It wasn't the first she had received. And like all of the others, it had been followed by a hissed warning of what would happen if she ever acknowledged its source. Isobel shuddered at the thought. "I—I bumped into something."

Iva couldn't know. She couldn't. *She* would be angry, and as soon as Iva left on the next mission, Isobel's next punishment would be far, far worse.

"I see." Iva's eyes narrowed. Isobel looked back at the sky, avoiding her sister's piercing gaze.

After a moment, Iva spoke. "You know my older sister and I used to come up here around this time of year. We'd watch the showers just like this. Honestly, you remind me of her a little."

Isobel yawned, relieved at the sudden change in subject. "Why didn't she join us?"

Iva frowned. "Esther... Esther left a long time ago, a few years before you were born."

"When is she coming back?"

Isobel felt Iva tense. "She's not coming back."

"Oh. That is sad," Isobel yawned again. She began to feel drowsy.

"I should probably get you back to your bed," Iva said, rising to her feet. "You never do well on low sleep."

Iva lifted Isobel in her arms and leapt from the roof. Her cloak spread like wings about her. Her fall slowed, cushioned by an invisible force, and she floated to the ground.

Back in her room, Isobel climbed up the ladder to return to her bunk. She buried herself beneath the sheets before poking her face out to look one last time at her sister. Iva leaned forward and kissed Isobel's forehead.

"I love you," Iva whispered.

Isobel yawned and smiled. "I love you."

Iva crept to the door and shut it silently. Isobel was once again surrounded by the sounds of her sleeping siblings.

CHAPTER 9

423rd year, 9th month, 1st day
10 years before present day

ISOBEL'S EYES FLEW OPEN. SHE GROANED and sat up in her bed, looking around her small room. She walked to her closet and began dressing herself, wincing as the folds of her shirt brushed the many bruises on her back.

Sister Cleo had beat her again. No matter what she said, no matter what she did, for some unknown reason Cleo always hated her. The last time, it was because she had spilled a potion during her alchemy lesson. The time before that, it was because she had slept too late. This time, it was because she had suggested improvements to one of Cleo's spells. Such beatings had intensified as she got older, growing far, far more frequent.

Today will be different. I'm finally fifteen. I'm finally going to become a true witch. I'm finally going to get my assignment.

Isobel slid her ring on her finger. The tiny spell-core embedded in the band glowed with its pale cyan light, the innate color of all her magical constructs. Taking a breath, Isobel entered the hall of the barracks in which she lived. Her adolescent sisters walked through the hallways, chattering about the events and gossip of the previous day. Some waved at her; others frowned and turned away. She listened to their voices as they echoed between the wooden walls.

Isobel weaved through the hall and entered the central courtyard. She crossed the gravel and sat beneath one of the three trees in the center. Closing her eyes, she listened to the familiar birdsongs. They were hopeful and joyous.

She smiled.

Yes. Today will be different.

Isobel heard her siblings walking across the courtyard to the dining hall. She didn't move, perfectly content to listen to the sounds of the forest that surrounded the compound.

"Want us to save you a seat, Isobel? For after you finish your… routine."

Isobel opened her eyes to see Joanne and Kay walking by.

"Thank you, Kay, that would be lovely," Isobel replied.

She closed her eyes again and waited for the courtyard to grow silent.

I wonder if Iva will be back today. She's been gone longer than usual.

Isobel rubbed her shoulder. She hated it when Iva was absent. Left in the care of Cleo, she was subject to her cruel wrath. She couldn't understand why Cleo despised her so much. None of her other sisters were targeted so frequently.

Maybe I can finally go with Iva on one of her missions instead of staying here.

Isobel's peace was interrupted by a loud impact against the tree. She jumped and opened her eyes.

"Child. Quit daydreaming," Cleo ordered, standing above her. Her gray hair was pulled back in a tight bun. She thumped a large, thick wand in her wrinkled hand. "You'll be late for assembly, and I do not want to remind you what the punishment for that is."

Isobel obediently stood and hurried into the dining hall.

Today will be different.

She sat quietly beside Kay as breakfast was served.

"Isobel, we need your opinion!" Joanne said, running her fingers through her long brown ponytail. "Now that I'm fifteen, where do you think they'll assign me? I hear that today is the day the next cohort gets their orders."

"I'm thinking cleaning duty," Kay quipped.

Joanne's gray eyes shot daggers at Kay, but only for a moment. "How dare you, Kay?" Kay snorted, triggering another of Joanne's glares.

Joanne continued. "Despite what my detractor thinks, I'm hoping to be one of the Elder Mothers' aides."

"So, what do you think, Isobel?" Kay asked, tossing her blonde hair.

Isobel picked at her food. She shrugged. Kay and Joanne looked at each other and raised their eyebrows in synchronization.

"How about this?" Kay said, leaning on her elbows. "What assignment do you think Joanne would be least qualified for?"

"I'm not sure," Isobel mumbled. "Joanne is good at most everything."

"Nothing? Really?" Kay said. "Normally that would have triggered one of your babbling rants. Honestly, what's gotten into you this morning?"

"Maybe she'll have more to say whenever her birthday comes around," Joanne scoffed.

Isobel felt a small lump in her throat. *They didn't remember.*

"All right, Isobel," Kay asked, "where do you want to be placed when *you* turn fifteen?"

"The Blades, like Iva," Isobel said meekly.

"You?" Joanne retorted. "Unlikely. You're far too…"

"Frail?" Kay remarked.

"I wasn't going to say that!" Joanne shoved Kay's shoulder.

Isobel looked down at her plate. She took a large bite of the bread before her, stood forcefully, and left the table.

"Isobel! Come back! We were only teasing," Joanne called. "Kay, look what you did."

Isobel exited the hall and returned to the trees.

Today will be different!

She closed her eyes. The birdsongs soothed her agitated nerves. Soon the yard around her filled with shuffling feet on the gravel. Isobel rose and fell in line with her siblings. They arranged themselves into orderly rows, facing the entrance to the Temple of the Elder Mothers. A crooked old woman, Mother Ginn, hobbled before them.

"Good morning, Daughters," she shouted in tired voice. "Why does the Red Coven live?"

The crowd chanted, "For the glory of all witches!"

"Why do you live?"

"For the glory of the Red Coven!"

"Good, good!" Ginn rubbed her hands together proudly. "Now, for today's announcements. We have assignments for a few lucky girls. Let's see…"

She put on a pair of spectacles and squinted at a small sheet of parchment.

"Ah, yes. Class 5, Joanne, come forward."

Joanne scampered beside the old woman, standing tall. She pulled a strand of her hair over her ear and looked at the crowd with an air of self-satisfaction.

"And, also from Class 5, Isobel. Come up here, child."

Isobel stepped gracefully beside Joanne. Joanne threw her a look of bewilderment.

"These young women will carry the future of our Coven," Mother Ginn continued. "Honor them, my daughters."

The crowd of young girls bowed.

"That's enough for today. Commence your morning duties." Ginn waived her gnarled hand in dismissal.

The crowd scattered, chattering amongst themselves.

"All right, you two. Let's go. This is a big day for you."

"Of course, Mother Ginn," Joanne said.

Mother Ginn led them through the doors of the temple, which slammed behind them. Isobel and Joanne followed in silence. Isobel looked about the great hall. Torches lit the wide room, casting their orange lights on painted murals. She eyed the murals. They depicted the history of the Red Coven, a history that had been taught to her repeatedly.

The first depicted a golden-haired woman, gowned in shining white. A tall, mist-shrouded figure hunched over her, offering a bright orb in its gaunt hands. Minera, the First Witch, had learned magic from the god Yvvusta.

The second depicted Minera standing over a great city. Fire, water, wind, and lightning swirled around her. She was a light guiding humanity to the future.

The third depicted her followers, the first mages, who spread across the world, giving magic to any who wished to learn. In white robes, they braved the mountains, crossed the seas, and pierced the deserts.

The fourth depicted the Fall. Cloaked in smoke, the gods stood above a fallen maiden, a golden-haired woman slain by their treacherous hands. Minera's blood soaked the earth, staining the white robes of her followers. Isobel's appreciation of the art was interrupted by Joanne's sharp tap upon her shoulder.

"Why are *you* here, Isobel?" Joanne whispered.

"It's my birthday."

"Hush, hush, Daughters," Mother Ginn reprimanded. She placed her hand on a pair of great stone doors, carved with massive runes and symbols. The doors swung open, scraping along the floor. The three entered the altar room.

Five figures robed in crimson sat in a circle of stone thrones. Torches burned around the outer edges of the room, casting ominous shadows that danced across the floor. Behind the dark figures stood a massive stone altar. It was cut from the rock, with no visible tool marks or blemishes. Nearly reaching the ceiling, it towered high above the two girls. A diamond shaped cleft ran through its center, and orange torch light flickered through.

Isobel and Joanne approached the center of the room as Mother Ginn took her seat in a vacant throne. The pair stepped onto a great seal engraved with a map of the continent. Small marks dotted the map, seemingly at random. Isobel squirmed.

"Daughters!" a loud voice called. The central figure removed her hood. Isobel recognized her cold face as that of Mother Verris. "You stand before the Elder Mothers having finally come of age to receive the title of Witch. You show great potential in the Ancient Arts, and we honor you with the privilege of serving the Red Coven."

"Joanne," a shrill voice broke from behind them. Mother Saiya lowered her hood. Her thick gray hair fell on her dark skin. "You are strong and diligent. You will make a fine witch. You shall join us as we guide the Red Coven to an even greater understanding of magic. We grant you the role of Aide to the Elders. You shall serve under Mother Verris, assisting us in our work leading the coven."

Joanne's body shook with excitement. Isobel smiled at her friend's elated face. Joanne inhaled slowly, composing herself.

"I am grateful, Mother Saiya, Mother Verris. I will serve you with my life."

Saiya smiled and leaned back.

"Isobel," a low voice called. Mother Shi stood. Her short raven hair shone in the torchlight, and proud smile appeared on her scarred face. "You are studious and beautiful. You are what we dream of when we think of our future daughters. You shall go forth, raising the next generation of witches, teaching them in the fundamental magic arts that you've mastered. We grant you the role of Caretaker. You shall serve under Sister Cleo. The two of you shall be stationed for the next seven years in Stoneport. At the time of your return, you shall bring back to us a daughter, one who will build the future of our kind!"

Isobel's heart sank. She felt a great hollowness rising within her, starting at her core and climbing through her chest. She looked down, attempting to process the words she had heard. Her hopes and dreams of becoming a master witch alongside Iva vanished, torn away by the coven's will for her future. The bruises on her back ached.

Today will be different, right?

CHAPTER 10

THE ALTAR ROOM OF THE ELDER Mothers fell silent.

"... I don't understand..." Isobel said. She felt Joanne's gaze boring into her. Mother Shi stepped forward and put her hand on Isobel's shoulder. Her dull brown eyes narrowed.

"Child, you have the great privilege of bearing the next generations of witches," Mother Shi said. "Your capacity for esht is a trait we would like to preserve. After you bear children for us, you will be free to select your next role in the Red Coven. This is a great honor."

"And if I am unable?"

"If you are unable to bear any daughters, then you must find one another way. Sister Cleo will guide you in this process. She has mentored many before you. She can help you get established and find suitors once you are of the proper age. We have no doubt that you will be desired by many men."

Isobel's fingers went numb. "You want me... to steal someone's child?"

"Though we would prefer that you pass on your bloodline to your daughters," Mother Shi replied, "we care not how you acquire an heir for us, child."

"But... that's wrong."

"Our will is absolute." Shi said, tightly gripping Isobel's shoulder. "The Red Coven must survive. Right and wrong, they do not matter." Her thumb dug into one of the bruises Isobel had received from Cleo.

Isobel paused. "I refuse."

"Refuse?" Mother Verris scoffed. "You do not have the authority to refuse our will, child. You have been selected for this role, and it is one you *will* fill."

Isobel shook off Mother Shi's hand. She caught a glimpse of Joanne's horrified face.

"I refuse! What you are asking me to do—I cannot accept it!" Isobel asserted. Her voice echoed through the chamber.

Verris stood angrily. Her hand flew from beneath her robe. She curled and tensed her tattooed fingers. A light flashed from her palm and struck Isobel. Suddenly, her body grew unbearably heavy. Her esht roiled within her, rapidly depleting.

"Iva has coddled you too long, you insolent child!" Verris shouted. "Do you think your will has any meaning? Your desires any value? Your words any merit? No! You are nothing. You insult our traditions! You insult our benevolence!"

Isobel collapsed, struggling to support herself on her hands and knees. She felt so heavy. Her esht continued to drain.

"Do you think you were not born of our traditions? Do you think your life and place in this world were not a result of our will?"

Isobel gasped. She felt a thousand needles of pain stabbing into every fiber of her being. Her esht was depleted. She screamed.

The doors of the chamber blasted open, slamming against the walls. Torches toppled and rolled across the stone floor. With billowing cloak and flashing eyes, Iva strode through the open door. Cleo followed close behind, muttering furiously.

"Mother!" Iva shouted. "Let her go!"

"Silence, Daughter! You have no say in this one's life anymore. You have clearly not taught Isobel her place in this world."

Iva touched a curved dagger that was sheathed at her hip. "Mother! Release her!"

Verris lowered her hand. Isobel's pain faded to dull fatigue.

"Iva!" Verris said, sitting back on her throne. "Have you not told her of her birth? Have you not told her of her mother?"

Iva's face became white as snow. Isobel looked up at her. "Iva?"

Mother Verris smirked deviously. "Isobel seems to be uneducated on how girls like her are brought here. Cleo, if you would..."

Cleo stood over Isobel and grabbed her shirt. She wrenched her to her feet. "Your mother was like you, child. Always so insolent. Always so disobedient. Always pretending she was innocent. She rejected her role as Caretaker, but we did not reject her child. Perhaps we should have. Perhaps it would have been better for me to leave you with that traitor.

It would have saved me so much frustration if I never had to look at you." Cleo slapped Isobel's face.

Iva's powerful, gloved fist collided with Cleo's jaw. The gray-haired woman flew across the room and crashed against the wall. Joanne peeked from behind one of the thrones.

"I told you never to touch her!" Iva roared.

"I'll do as I wish when she is under my care," Cleo replied, wiping blood from her lips. "Such is the will of the Elder Mothers."

Iva stiffened, seething with hatred for them, all of them. She lifted her left hand and pressed her middle finger against her thumb, creating a small circle. With blazing green eyes, she glared at Cleo. The muscles in her bare arm tensed. Blood coursed through the veins that snaked around her forearm.

At the sight of the gesture, Cleo's face twisted in terror. She cowered, attempting to hide behind something, anything that would protect her from Iva's furious gaze. "Please! Please! I'm sorry. Please! Forgive me!"

The Elder mothers leapt to their feet, drawing wands and daggers from beneath their robes. Spell-cores gleamed at their handles. Isobel saw something she had never witnessed in their faces before.

Terror.

"Iva!" Verris yelled, her voice sounding simultaneously wrathful and fearful. "Cease. Our will is absolute. It cannot be defied. Do not shed blood in our presence."

Iva looked at the many weapons pointed at her. Breathing slowly, she lowered her hand and clenched her fist.

"Leave us, Isobel," Verris ordered. "You will depart for Stoneport in seven days. Gather your things. Iva, you will stay. We will discuss the punishment for your behavior."

Isobel wiped her eyes. She walked despondently to the door and looked at her sister one last time. Iva did not meet her gaze, staring only at the floor. Isobel turned and exited the temple. In the empty courtyard, she returned to the tree where she had sat at the start of the day. Crossing her legs, she leaned against the trunk, careful not to irritate the bruises along her spine. The birds sang above, but this time, they could not soothe her.

——————— ⸬ ———————

Isobel dashed through the dark halls. Loaded with clothes, provisions, and books, her pack barely stayed on her slim shoulders. The wide leather straps dug into the bruises about her neck. She entered the courtyard. The moonless night was deep and dark. She hesitated, listening for the footsteps of the nightly patrols.

Silence.

She hurried to the compound's gate, keeping to the edges of the courtyard on the soft grass. As she broke from the cluster of buildings, she ran down a long dirt trail lined with torches. Reaching the inner wooden walls, Isobel pushed the doors that blocked her escape. They were incredibly heavy, and she struggled against their weight. She squeezed through a narrow opening that appeared, and the gate slammed behind her. She was almost free. A wooden archway loomed in front of her, the final obstacle. She had never passed the outer gates alone, but curiously, on this night they were left open.

She halted at the sound of a cloak flapping in the wind. Iva dropped gently to the ground ahead of her, blocking the compound's only exit.

"You took your time," Iva said solemnly, putting her hand on her hip. Her tattered cloak was wrapped around her broad shoulders, exposing her leather cuirass and gaiters.

Isobel frowned. "How did you know?"

"You're not very good at keeping secrets, Isobel," Iva replied.

"Did you tell anyone?"

"Of course not."

Isobel nodded. "Then I'll be on my way."

"Isobel, wait!" Iva sighed. "Listen, I'm sorry."

"Sorry? You're sorry? Did you know the truth all this time, Iva?"

"About your mother?" Iva ran her fingers through her hair. "I've had my suspicions."

Isobel scoffed. "You should have told me."

"Told you what? What was I supposed to say, Isobel?" Iva retorted. "That you and Esther bear a passing resemblance? That you remind me of the only person I ever loved before you? That you look like the woman who abandoned me?"

"Iva, please move. I'm leaving."

Iva crossed her arms. "Leaving, just like her."

"Are you going to stop me?"

Iva drew her dagger. "I've been ordered to kill anyone that tries to leave. Part of my new duties now that I've been demoted. No one leaves, Isobel. Not anymore."

"Fine. Do it."

"What?"

Isobel stamped forward and stared defiantly into Iva's eyes. "Go on. I'm not going to fight you. I'd rather die than endure another day of Cleo's abuse. I'd rather die than bear one of their children. I'd rather die than rip someone else's daughter from their arms."

"Isobel, please don't do this…"

"Do what? Make a choice?" Isobel said angrily. "Defy those monsters that call themselves our mothers? You certainly didn't do that. Even after all those years of promises, you never even talked to them about me, did you?"

Iva's eyes shimmered. "Please. Don't…"

Isobel shoved past her. Iva's hand clenched her dagger's handle. Her lips quivered.

"All this time," Isobel said, looking over her shoulder, "I just wanted to be with you! Was that not enough?"

"I was trying to protect you, Isobel. I didn't want you to become who I am."

"Then I guess things went exactly as you wanted."

Iva flinched and tightly shut her eyes. Tears accumulated on her dark lashes. After a long pause, she tossed aside her dagger and sighed.

"Nellborough, Isobel. Last I heard, your mother is alive in Nellborough. It's north of here. Ask for Esther Valeria. Go! Find your family, your real family."

Isobel turned, her eyes widening. Iva had crouched to the ground, burying her face in her hands. Her cloaked shoulders trembled. Isobel looked down. A great emptiness welled inside, as a lump rose in her throat.

"Goodbye, Iva," Isobel said, her voice breaking, her eyes burning. She turned and fled into the dark forest, trying to keep her tears from flowing.

Left alone, Iva fell to her knees and cried.
"Please... please don't leave me."

CHAPTER 11

434th year, 2nd month, 10th day
Present Day

CHINELO STIRRED BENEATH HIS THICK BLANKET. He flinched as a rock poked into his back. Opening his eyes, he sat up and stretched. His spine popped. Sleeping on only a blanket between him and the earth always left him stiff. Through the small gaps in the canopy of autumn leaves, he gazed up at the sky. It was a light purple, and the clouds glowed red from the approaching morning sun.

He looked to his side. The fire he had made the night before had been reduced to a small pile of cold ashes. Beyond it, Isobel lay peacefully on his sleeping pad, resting her head on her pack. In the weeks since they had left Nellborough, the previous night was the only time Chinelo had not heard her sobbing herself to sleep.

Chinelo brushed the dew from his blanket and laid it flat to dry. Silently donning his boots, he rose to his feet and untied the damp bundle of sticks he had gathered for firewood. After setting a small pot next to the wood, he held his hand over the bundle, trying to remember the phrase Isobel had used the previous morning.

"Sono diaa, axxave va ogo," he whispered.

Pure water flowed from the wood and accumulated in a hovering sphere in his hand. He released his esht, and the sphere splashed into the pot, leaving the firewood as dry as the desert. Chinelo arranged the wood on the firepit and placed the cooking grill above it. From atop Isobel's hip, Mort watched him attentively, wishing that he too could speak so that he could unleash arcane magic upon the world.

Chinelo whispered again. "Icht vasht'ra."

Fire from his hand lit the wood, and the frayed fibers and splinters at its edges cracked and popped. Chinelo smiled to himself. It was hard to believe he had lived so long without the convenience of magic. Though he had only been practicing it for a month, he had already grown accustomed to using it for everyday activities. The fact that he once thought it was evil was almost laughable. Almost.

Chinelo walked to a nearby tree and released the large sack of food he had hung after sunset. He deposited it on the ground and drew out a bag of oats, a parcel of cured meats, and a sachet of ground cinnamon. They had been fortunate enough to pass through a village several days before and had bought enough supplies to get them to their destination, the Red Coven's compound. He mixed the oats and cinnamon in the pot and placed it above the fire. He arranged the sausages in rows on the grill, and returned to his bed, waiting for their morning meal to cook.

Isobel rolled to her side, causing Mort to tumble off his perch with a frustrated croak. He hopped to Chinelo's side and pouted. He would forgive the offense, but not happily. The fire lit Isobel's face. Chinelo looked down bashfully, drawing in the dirt with a stick. Every few minutes, he stirred the pot and rotated the sausages.

Isobel moved again and leaned up on her elbow.

"Hey," she said with a smile.

"Oh! You're awake."

Isobel stretched and yawned. "Halfway there, at least." She crawled from beneath her blanket and stared blankly at the fire. "Are you ready for today?"

Chinelo shrugged. "Are you?"

"I wish." Isobel rubbed her eyes. "Believe me, the Red Coven is the last place I want to be."

"Do you want to turn around?"

She shook her head. "No. This is our best shot at reaching Iva, so... we'll just have to make the best of things."

Chinelo nodded. Over the course of several days, she had told him of her turbulent upbringing. In bits and pieces, he had learned about the strict daily routines, the strange rituals, the cultish lectures, and the grueling training she had endured. Her characteristic resilience continued to astound him.

Still, he was uncertain if the picture she had painted of her sister Iva was one to be admired. Isobel always spoke of her affectionately, but he was nonetheless apprehensive, especially considering how she left.

"Do you think your sister will help us?" Chinelo asked, stirring the pot of thickened oats.

Isobel perked up. "I think so! She's traveled much of the world and was very knowledgeable about the magic and culture of the gods when I was younger. She taught me most of what I know. As I mentioned, she basically raised me, so we were quite close. Honestly, I'm rather excited to see her again. There's so much I want to tell her about! Ten years' worth! Assuming they let us in, of course."

Chinelo frowned. Her current outlook certainly seemed more optimistic than what he had expected. He bent over a nearby stump and picked up a small bundle. Unwrapping it, he produced Isobel's spectacles and handed them to her.

"Oh! Thank you!" she said. "I suppose I won't be much use if I can't see beyond my own hands."

Chinelo scooped the oat porridge into clay cups and passed one to her.

"So, how far do we have until we get there?" he asked.

Isobel held the cup close to her face, smelling the wafting steam that fogged her glasses. The fragrance of cinnamon melded with scents of fallen leaves that permeated the forest. "That tree over there—" she nodded to her right, "I remember it from when I first left the coven. From here we should be able to make it to the compound within three, maybe four hours."

"And if Iva isn't there?"

"Well." Isobel gulped down a spoonful of the porridge. "The coven has some structures—one in particular—like the one we saw in Nellborough. So, even if Iva isn't there, we might get lucky and still find a lead on where to go next. Assuming they don't kill us first."

"You're oddly chipper about walking to our deaths."

Isobel shrugged.

Mort looked longingly at the sausages on the fire.

"Those aren't worms, frog," Chinelo said.

"Glad to see you two are finally getting along."

Chinelo chuckled. "We've been getting along for weeks now, Isobel. Isn't that right, my good lord?"

Mort glowered.

Isobel laughed. "Clearly."

Light had filled the sky by the time they finished their breakfast. The thick trees cast shadows that crisscrossed the forest floor. Withered leaves blanketed the ground. As they walked through the dense wood, Isobel listened to the birds singing in the treetops. Their songs were different from those in Nellborough. She had almost forgotten the melodies she used to listen to as a child. They still put her at ease, leaving her feeling optimistic, even hopeful. With Chinelo at her side, she was ready to face the Elder Mothers once again.

She had many questions that required answers. Why would the Archmage destroy Nellborough and Eshgar? How could he generate a spell so powerful? What were the mysterious obelisks that were left behind? Why were so many words missing from the language of the gods? How could she accomplish the impossible task of undoing the past? She only hoped that Iva might know some of the answers.

The vague trail climbed the rising forest terrain, swerving around enormous trees and boulders. Flat rocks acted as steps, assisting in their assent over the wooded hills and their descent into shaded valleys. Up and down they traveled, brushing away prickly vines and the sheer spiderwebs that clung to their faces. Soon the trail leveled and pierced the forest like an arrow. The sun shone down from above.

"Chinelo?"

"Hmmm?"

"Thank you for coming. I'm glad you're here with me," Isobel said. "I know it was a bit selfish of me to ask."

"As you have often said, 'Nonsense,'" Chinelo replied, stepping carefully over a rotting log. "The last thing I want is for you to go off and get lost in the woods out here."

"I've been the one guiding you this whole time, sir knight."

"Perhaps—Ow!"

Chinelo's boot had collided with a strange object protruding from beneath the leaves. He bent over, eyeing it curiously. It was a statue of a twisted, grotesque creature. Its lanky limbs wrapped around its gaunt body, and its giant hands covered its face.

"What is this?"

"That's a statue of one of the gods. I forget that one's name." Isobel rested her arm on Chinelo's shoulder. "Witches don't exactly have the most favorable opinion of the gods, so the statues they make of them tend to be rather unsightly."

"Ah. So, we're close, then?"

"Quite."

"Should I put on my armor now?"

"Honestly, Chinelo, I don't think armor will do you much good." Isobel said, shaking her head.

"Oh?"

"For one thing, it's not very good against the kinds of magic they teach here. For another, it might be better if we looked as unthreatening as possible. I'm not trying to start a fight we cannot win."

"I see." Chinelo shuddered.

"Come on, just a little further."

They rounded a bend. The trail was lined with many statues like the one Chinelo had seen earlier. A large fallen tree blocked the path, obscuring the forest ahead with its branches.

Isobel scratched her head. "That's odd. Normally they would have moved that out of the way."

"It looks like it's been there for a while."

Isobel shrugged. "Around or over?"

"Around."

They skirted the perimeter of the tree, walking in the shadow of its uprooted base. The root network had drawn a large chunk of earth with it, creating a shady hollow in the ground.

Isobel twirled her staff. "Well, here we are—"

She froze. Chinelo stepped beside her and gasped.

The wooden gate of the compound had been reduced to piles of splintered logs and ash. The entire archway had collapsed, leaving only a charred heap.

"It's happened here, too," Isobel said.

Chinelo scanned the walls of the compound. Further around the sides, the walls stood, untouched by the damage at the front gate. The trees surrounding the compound rose high and strong, casting long shadows below.

"I don't think this is the same thing, Isobel," he said. "At least, it's not on the same scale. Look, the walls and trees are still intact."

Isobel ran forward and climbed over the pile of blackened wood that was once the heavy doors of the compound. The inner gate, too, had been destroyed, smashed into pieces by an unknown force. She continued ahead.

"Isobel! Wait!" Chinelo shouted, attempting to keep up. His heavy pack made climbing difficult. "Not again."

When he reached her, she stood dumbfounded in an expansive courtyard. The ground was covered in a layer of scattered gravel, and tufts of grasses and weeds poked through the gaps in the stones. Three burned tree trunks stood at the center of the courtyard. The remnants of buildings lined the outskirts. The compound was empty. Isobel's gaze lingered on a small shed; its walls had splintered and buckled beneath the eaves.

She walked further into the courtyard and looked up at the shattered structure that was once called the Temple of the Elder Mothers. Now a mass of timbers and beams, it was barely recognizable as a building. The frame had fallen in on itself, and gaping holes pierced the walls.

"We're too late."

CHAPTER 12

ISOBEL STARED AT THE RUINED TEMPLE before her. It was in chaotic disarray, yet its damage was nothing compared to what she had seen in Nellborough. She frowned and kicked a stone.

"I don't understand. The Red Coven stood for hundreds of years. How could it fall like this?"

"Do you think Iva was here when this happened?" Chinelo asked.

"I don't see any bodies. Maybe she and the others escaped."

Isobel sighed. Any hope of seeing her sister that day vanished. Though, a small part of her was relieved. She had dreaded returning to the coven, afraid to revisit the site of so many unpleasant memories. She kicked another stone.

"Perhaps there's an—" Chinelo tensed. He reached for his sword.

The hair on Isobel's neck stood on end. A slight draft of air brushed her skin. Something or someone was behind them, breathing. Her heart seemed to stop. A flicker of fear danced between her lungs. She twirled her staff, swinging it behind her.

"Form: Blade."

Blue light flashed, curving around the ring at her staff's head and growing in radiant fractals. It flowed and formed an elegant, razor-thin blade fixed to the end of her staff. Though she had not yet been able to fully understand Brennen's magic, she had created a very close approximation of his techniques. With her newly crafted spell, her staff had transformed into a fearsome glaive. The blade's shining edge cut through the air.

A figure ducked beneath her swing and leapt lithely back. Long brown hair flowed from the figure's head. She was garbed in steel-trimmed leather armor, and she raised a pair of gauntlets in a defensive stance. Two glowing spell-cores were fixed at her wrists, hovering and swirling with golden mist. Her face was covered by a carved white mask, etched with twisting lines of runes and decorated with blue highlights about the eyes.

"Chinelo, she's a witch!"

Chinelo raised his sword. He shifted on his feet. Isobel braced herself, preparing to counter any attacks. Mort let out a frightened croak and recklessly leapt from Isobel's shoulder to the gravel below.

"Strength!" the figure said. Her spell-cores pulsed in response. She sprung forward, kicking gravel in a cone behind her. She dashed toward Isobel at incredible speed, punching her in the chest.

Isobel cried as the air violently left her lungs. Searing pain tore from her sternum and propagated across her body. Her bones shifted. Her muscles ached. The punch launched her across the courtyard. Coughing and gasping, she rolled to a stop in the gravel.

"Isobel!" Chinelo shouted.

He swung his sword at the masked witch, but she easily avoided his attack. She vaulted back, flying high over the ground before landing in a crashing impact. She steadied herself with her hand, then slowly stood.

"Isobel?" the witch asked, cocking her head.

Isobel leaned on her staff, supporting herself as she climbed to her feet. "Me?"

The witch lifted her mask, revealing her face. Her eyes were like a summer storm, deep and gray.

"Joanne?" Isobel exclaimed.

"You're alive?" Joanne said.

"Despite that punch, yes."

"But, how? You're supposed to be dead."

"What?" Isobel gasped.

Chinelo stepped between Isobel and Joanne, brandishing his sword.

Joanne rubbed her face, moving aside a pair of bangs that curtained her forehead.

"You can lower your blade. I won't harm you."

"It's all right, Chinelo. She's one of the ones I told you about." Isobel walked to his side.

Joanne paced back and forth, moving her fingers through her long hair. She was tall and athletic, and her jaw was sharp and square. "I don't understand." She paced faster. "We mourned for you. We carried out your resting rites. Iva, Kay, and I were distraught for months—no—years! All this time, you've been alive?"

"Yes?"

"How? Iva said she killed you."

"I beg your pardon! Iva is the one that let me leave."

Joanne rubbed her chin. Her eyes darted back and forth. She looked up and ran towards Isobel. Chinelo raised his blade. Joanne wrapped Isobel in her arms and embraced her tightly, lifting her off the ground.

"I've missed you. I've missed you so much!" Joanne said. "I'm so sorry, Isobel. I'm sorry I forgot your birthday back then. I've thought about it every day since. I'm sorry we said those things about you. I'm sorry we weren't there for you. I'm so sorry."

Isobel returned her embrace. "It's fine Joanne, really. I'm doing better now."

Joanne set Isobel back on the ground and looked down at her. "I guess you never did get any taller, did you?"

Isobel chuckled. "Not quite, no."

"I love what you've done with your hair. It suits you! Oh, and this staff. Did you make this yourself? Most impressive. That's quite the core you have in there."

Isobel looked down. "Joanne. What happened here?"

Joanne let out a long sigh. "It was awful, Isobel. I—I've never seen anything like it. So brutal, the other Blades never had a chance."

"The Interior Guard did this, I assume?"

Joanne's brow furrowed. "What? No! *Iva* did this."

Isobel recoiled. "Iva?" Her heart fell.

"It'll probably be easier to explain if I just show you," Joanne said. She walked to the entrance of the temple and crawled over the wreckage. "Come on. In here."

Isobel and Chinelo dropped their packs and followed her into the fallen temple. Light shone through the shattered ceiling, filtering through the dusty air in wide bands. Isobel gazed at the murals on the walls. They were riddled with wide, gaping holes that were perfectly circular. She stepped over a fallen timber. The torch stands scattered around the edges of the great hall were mangled and bent. Had Iva really done all of this?

She stopped and let her gaze linger on one of the murals, now pierced with holes. There was something about its depiction of the gods spreading across the continent that always unnerved her. Perhaps it was their gnarled fingers covering their faces. Perhaps it was their bony, smoke shrouded bodies contorted in uncanny positions. Perhaps it was the knowledge that they vanished in the next painting, leaving behind a wake of bloodshed and death.

She nervously walked under the great archway that led to the altar room. A chill ran down her spine as she recalled what had transpired the last time she was in that space. She gripped her staff tighter, trying to keep herself from shaking.

A strange, almost metallic smell filled the air. Fragments of stone were piled in the corners, pieces of two great doors that had been thrown off their hinges. A circle of thrones was situated at the center of the room, but they were broken and worn. Several were stained a deep, dark red in irregular patterns. Chunks of bone were scattered across the floor. Beyond the thrones was only darkness.

"Light!" Joanne shouted. A glowing orb formed above her hand and rose, casting its yellow glow about the room. The witch's altar was illuminated.

"It happened a year ago. She had just returned from a mission to Veshda, I think. She came in here, raging at the Elder Mothers. I could hear them shouting for hours. Something about 'the Source.' Eventually they called me in to escort her out, and that's when she snapped."

"Snapped?" Isobel asked.

"She killed her own mother, Isobel. No hesitation. No remorse. And she didn't even move! She just looked at her and that was it." Joanne shuddered. "The others tried to stop her, but she slaughtered them, too. It was terrifying. I ran and hid. When she emerged from the temple, all the Elder Mothers were dead." Joanne waved her hand around the room. "Iva did all this."

"I don't understand," Isobel said. "Why?"

"She always hated the Elder Mothers, Isobel. Everyone knew that. She was much more vocal about it after you died—or I guess now it's more accurate to say after you left."

"Did she say anything?"

Joanne shook her head. "Nothing all that informative. By the time she had killed the other Blades, Kay and I had already evacuated the rest of our siblings. We went back to salvage what we could, but all she said was that she had 'freed' us and that she was going to create a better world."

Isobel looked down pensively. It was true that Iva had a temper, but she had never seen her do anything like this. In Isobel's mind, Iva was always so strong, so secure, so stable. She was like a stone fortress in a storm. What had happened in the years since she left?

"Joanne?" Chinelo asked, pointing at the altar. "What is that?"

"That? Oh, that's the Altar of Fire. The Red Coven was built around it."

Isobel squinted. "It looks like... an obelisk"

Chinelo nodded solemnly.

"Obelisk? Hmmm. I suppose that's what some of the others would be called," Joanne mused.

"Others?" Chinelo turned his head sharply.

"Right!" Jonne nodded. "There are others all over the continent. Supposedly there even some off the mainland, too."

"What is it?" Isobel asked.

Joanne walked across the room and sat on an empty throne. "Ordinarily I would not be permitted to share this information, but it's not like there's anyone left to offend. The Red Coven is no more, so its secrets are no longer bound. I'll tell you what I learned as an Aide to the Elders."

"*That,*" she pointed at the stone altar, "is the origin of all magic involving fire. When she was young, Mother Ginn awakened it and was granted the secrets of flame. Or rather she was granted the words and symbols for fire."

Chinelo rubbed his chin. "Vasht?"

Joanne nodded then shot him a confused look. "Correct. I suppose Isobel has taught you that much. 'Vasht' is a word that, until you, only the Red Coven has known. For every other mage, fire magic is simply another lost piece of history."

Isobel's heart began to beat faster. "How does one awaken it?"

Joanne cocked her head and leaned on her elbow. "Well, you can't. Not anymore at least. It only had the one word in it, though I'm not sure about the others. That was part of what the Blades were investigating. If any were still alive, we could ask them. Well, any aside from Iva."

Joanne waved her hand disinterestedly. "I suppose there's some incantation that would do it. Mother Ginn never said much on the topic, for some reason. I know Mother Verris sent the Blades to find some of those, but Mother Ginn always said they should not be awakened. Not sure why. Relearning lost words doesn't seem to have a downside from my understanding."

Isobel's mind raced. This was it! This was what she was looking for! A way to finally expand the language of the gods!

"Where are the others?" Isobel asked frantically.

Joanne pointed towards Isobel's feet. Isobel and Chinelo looked down at the seal on which they stood. It was an intricate, engraved map of the continent. Old and archaic, it represented a landscape that had changed significantly over time. Chinelo stepped back and kicked a layer of dust from the seal. Strange symbols were scattered across the map in seemingly random positions. But were they random?

Isobel gasped and dropped to the ground. She ran her hands across the seal, brushing dirt from the southern peninsula. A symbol was positioned right at the center, at the location of the city of Eshgar. She moved her hand north and continued brushing the dust aside. Another symbol, directly north of Eshgar. Nellborough. She moved southeast. Another symbol. The Red Coven.

She leaned back on her heels. Her heart pounded. This was it.

Joanne's brow furrowed. She leaned on her elbow, supporting her head with a balled fist. "Why *did* you come back, Isobel?" she asked. "Why now, after ten years? Surely you didn't think they would accept you back in?"

Isobel looked up at Joanne. "My—no—our homes were destroyed. Eshgar and Nellborough are ashes. We came here hoping Iva could help us find out why."

"I see. I'm sorry to hear that," Joanne said.

"These obelisks," Chinelo said, "do you have any more information about them?"

Joanne shifted on the throne, tapping her cheek. "I suppose we could check the archives. I'm not sure what their current state is, though. I managed to snag a few of the record books from Mother Ginn's study before Iva got to them, but they are all back home in Veld. Obviously, that won't do us much good right now."

"We could also always ask Iva if we manage to track her down," Isobel chimed.

Joanne's face went pale. "This isn't what you want to hear, Isobel, but I'll say it anyways. I know you love Iva, but she's not the same person she was when we were young. Your absence—it changed her. If you do encounter her out there, I'd advise you to stay away from her."

"I'll keep that in mind."

"I'm serious, Isobel!" Joanne asserted, bolting to her feet. "When she killed the Elder Mothers, she was brutal, she was merciless, and she didn't hesitate. There were no bodies left behind. She's dangerous. I don't want you to die by her hand a second time."

Joanne walked out the temple doors, taking her glowing orb with her. Chinelo and Isobel were left in the darkness.

"Isobel?" Chinelo hesitantly touched her shoulder.

"Chinelo, there is hope for us!" Isobel looked up at him excitedly. "Your family! We can bring your family back! I need to get to work. I need to make a plan."

Isobel hurried out the door, returning moments later with her pack. She drew out a pen and began copying the map down on the back page of her spell-book. She hummed excitedly.

Chinelo looked around the dark altar room. Bloodstains, fragments of bone, shattered rock, and a faint yet unmistakable smell of death. Was this all truly done by the woman who raised Isobel?

More importantly, they certainly would not be the only ones seeking the obelisks. Would they be able to face the Archmage, the man who had destroyed their homes? Would there even be anything for them to find?

Like dark clouds in a night sky, Chinelo's doubt slowly overtook the glimmer of hope that Isobel had sparked within him.

CHAPTER 13

CHINELO PRODDED THE FIRE. ISOBEL AND Joanne sat against the burned trees at the center of the courtyard, chatting quietly. Isobel was incredibly animated, and though he could not distinguish her words, her fast voice and rapid hand motions were energetic. Joanne gazed at Isobel, nodding often.

"It's just you and me, Mort," Chinelo said, looking down at the globular creature on the log next to him. Mort blinked.

"I suppose you don't want to talk?"

Mort began one of his droning frog songs.

"Hmmm. Perhaps I'm wrong."

Mort glared at him and continued his croaking chorus.

"Perhaps not."

Chinelo rested his arms on his knees. He was surprised at how fast Isobel had dismissed Joanne's warnings about Iva. While she was copying the map in the temple, Isobel talked about Iva as if she would still be willing to help if they ever found her. He wished he shared her belief.

He didn't want to dash her hopes, but encouraging some degree of caution would be wise. He had learned that she tended to see things as they could be, not as they were. Though, as a result she didn't seem impeded by the same doubts and hesitations that clung to him.

The frog song was interrupted by stomping footsteps on the gravel. Joanne stood above him with her hands on her hips. "So!"

"Yes?"

Isobel ran up behind Joanne. "Joanne, please. I'm begging you. That's not a normal thing to ask someone."

"Are you two having a child?"

Isobel's face flushed beet-red. "JOANNE!"

Chinelo blinked twice. "I beg your pardon?"

Joanne leaned forward. "You. Her. Babies?"

Isobel looked away, shielding her face with her hand. "Please stop..." she whimpered.

Joanne raised her hands. "What? It's a fair question."

"No, it's not!" Isobel cried. "You—I—gah!" She ran back to the tree and sat with her back to it, facing away. She opened her spell-book and began scribbling notes on a notepad, huffing and puffing in frustration.

Joanne sighed. "Ahhhhhh, I've missed this."

Chinelo tilted his head. "Please tell me that isn't what you've been discussing for the last four hours."

Joanne looked down. "What? No, of course not! I just like seeing her flustered. She seems so different than when we were young, but it looks like some things haven't changed. Besides, this gives me a chance to talk to you."

She sat down beside Mort. "But seriously, are you two—"

"We're not talking about that!"

"Fine, fine. Forget I ever said anything," Joanne acquiesced. She picked up a nearby stick and poked the fire. "She told me about your family. I'm sorry about what happened."

"I appreciate that. Tell me, why were you here today, Joanne?"

"It's been a year since the day that we fled," Joanne responded. "I'd hoped to pay my respects. It's customary for us to visit the graves of the fallen annually. This is the closest thing I have to that."

"And your friend, Kay?"

"Oh, Kay is hardly what I'd call friendly. She and I live up north in Veld, now."

"That's quite far."

"You're telling me." Joanne placed her elbows on her knees. Without their armor, her arms were impressively toned. "It was a long journey across Iskara to get here. I understand why Kay didn't want to come down. This place isn't exactly one she's fond of. I'm not sure if she told you, but Isobel was treated very poorly by this dreadful hag named Cleo. When Isobel left, Cleo's wrath shifted to Kay."

"What ever happened to her?" Chinelo asked, watching Isobel becoming absorbed in her work, just as she did at home.

"Cleo? Ehhh." Joanne scratched her head and grimaced. "It was pretty grisly. Iva was certainly thorough."

"Did you tell Isobel?"

"No. I thought it would be best not to mention her. I never knew how bad it was until Kay told me. Kay's scars still haven't fully faded, and I imagine Isobel's are similar."

"That was probably wise." Chinelo nodded slowly. "So, what's life like up in Veld?"

"Ehhh, it's nice enough. Gets cold in the winters being so close to the northern ocean. It's a relatively large city, so there is plenty of activity. The countryside is a bit unforgiving, what with all the red clay, so farming is difficult."

"Oh, you're a farmer?" Chinelo asked.

"I help out on the farm, but I'm more of a deterrent than a worker. We get a lot of bandits from across the east border." Joanne looked up at the clear blue sky. "Kay works at an apothecary's store in the city. Poor thing, they hardly pay her adequately for all the work she does. If you asked my opinion, I'd say that her expertise and talents are wasted on those fools."

"Talents?"

Joanne looked over. "Right! Kay specializes in chemistry and potion magic. She's quite the genius, even if she is a bit grumpy most of the time. I suppose that's the price she must pay for holding Veld's medicinal industry on her shoulders."

"Interesting," Chinelo responded. "So then, do you two like it there?"

"We're happy enough now that we're getting settled. Adjusting to life outside the coven was difficult for her." Joanne picked up a leaf and twisted it between her fingers.

"What happened to the rest of your sisters?" Chinelo asked, poking the fire again.

"The older ones scattered. Some of them took the younger ones, some didn't. Kay and I got several of the youngest set up in good homes in Veld. They seem to be acclimating well. Having loving parents does wonders."

Chinelo nodded.

"Isobel told me of her plan to save your family and her friends," Joanne said solemnly. "Do you think she can do it?"

Chinelo looked at Isobel, sitting with her back to the tree. "I want to believe she can. Magic is not something with which I'm all that well acquainted, so I don't fully know what is and is not possible. Even so, she gives me hope. I want to believe she can do it."

Joanne didn't respond.

"Do you think her foolish?" Chinelo asked.

"Foolish? No. Naïve?" Joanne paused. "Probably. She's always been a clever one, though. If anyone could find a way, I believe it would be her. Keep her safe, will you?"

"That is my intention."

Isobel skipped over to the fire and sat beside Chinelo. "So?"

"Yes?"

"Do you want to hear my plan?" She bounced excitedly.

Joanne leaned forward so that she could see past Chinelo. "I certainly would."

Isobel looked pleadingly into Chinelo's eyes.

"Do you even have to ask, Isobel?" Chinelo said.

She grinned and opened her spell-book to the last page. She had transcribed the map of the continent with nearly perfect accuracy. She had added numerous triangles and circles to indicate villages and cities. Several of the symbols were marked with numbers.

"One of the obelisks is nearby, in Caald. There's a city here." She pointed to a circle on the southern coast. "We can stop there for a few days and recover. After we've rested in real beds, we can go here." She moved her finger to a triangle. It was beside a marker labeled with the number "1." "This is Ata, a smaller village. That will be where we find our first obelisk. After we activate it, we'll just move around the whole continent until we've found the words for time and memory, assuming no one else has already."

"May I make a suggestion?" Chinelo asked.

"Of course."

"We should try to make some money in that first city. We've used about a third of what we started with, and we're going to need warmer clothes once winter comes."

"Good idea!" Isobel nodded quickly. She marked the symbol for Iskaran crescents on the map by the city. "I can make some enchanted lamps and sell them. You can—well, you're good at everything so I'm sure you'll have no trouble."

"It looks like your second point is in Rothvale."

"Right?"

"I think we should save that for last. Dealing with the Interior Guard doesn't sound wise if we can avoid it."

Isobel nodded and made some more adjustments to her map. "We'll just skip it and go up the east coast. So, we'll go to Ata, the Eastern Plains, Kahi, Veld, then either the ones in Veshda or northwest Iskara, depending on the season."

"Joanne?" Isobel peaked around Chinelo's shoulder. "Won't you come with us? It will be grand."

Joanne shook her head. "I'm afraid I can't Isobel, as fun as that sounds. I'm sure Kay is getting lonely. Though once you've reached that fourth point near Veld you should drop by and see us. Ask for the apothecary's shop on the east wall. Kay should be easy enough to find from there."

Isobel smiled. "I'd like that. You're not leaving tonight, though, are you?"

Joanne shook her head. "No, no. I know better than to hike down these hills at night. Besides, I still need to take you through the archives."

"Right! Well, if he's willing," Isobel prodded Chinelo with her elbow, "you might have the opportunity to taste one of Chinelo's fine concoctions."

Chinelo looked up from the map. "I'm concocting what now?"

Joanne threw her head back and laughed. "Sir knight, the lady wants her dinner."

Chinelo's face lit up. "Well, fortunately for the lovely lady, I've been saving something in our provisions for a special occasion."

Isobel blew the dust off one of the tomes she had pulled from the shelves of the Elder Mothers' archives. The cloud tickled her nostrils, triggering a rather violent sneeze. At the sight of the title of the book, she let out a disappointed sigh.

A Summary of Digestion Related Magical Incantations. She cast the book aside, adding it to the growing stack of disappointments.

The archives were dim, lit only by a ring of glowing stones about their exterior. Rows and rows of shelves populated the cool room, though the entire back half of it was a charred mass of ash and soot. A scent of musty pages and smoke filled the air. Isobel pulled another book from the shelf.

"Any luck?" Joanne called from the rickety wooden ladder that descended from the trapdoor above.

Isobel groaned. "Not yet. I wish these were organized a bit better."

Joanne dropped to the stone floor and sauntered through the shelves. "Sorry about that. I inherited the reorganization project, but I never finished it before what happened. Iva's mother used to be in charge of that, and she wasn't exactly put together."

"No, Verris never gave me that impression."

Joanne began poking through the wreckage.

"How are things topside?" Isobel asked.

"Well, the soup smells amazing, but it's going to be another hour or so until it's finished. Chinelo said something about giving the ingredients time to get acquainted or something." Joanne pulled a book off a shelf.

"That's one of his sayings." She glanced over a couple pages before thumping the book shut. "Son of a biscuit! It's all just spell-coding research."

Joanne peered over her shoulder. "I thought you used to eat that stuff up."

"Biscuits?" Isobel looked up.

"No, spell-coding stuff."

Isobel pulled a strand of hair behind her ear. "I do, but it's not like I can bring all of this with me. My pack is already loaded as it is, and I can't ask Chinelo to carry more. He's already got most of our supplies in his pack."

Joanne shrugged. "Fair enough. Oh! I've got something you might like to see." Joanne pulled a thick charred book from the rubble, one that was wrapped in a sleeve of dragon-hide.

Isobel looked around Joanne's shoulder as they flipped through the book, skimming a few pages. The first several were in very poor condition, but a few of them were decipherable.

Isobel read one of the passages, moving her finger along the slanted, flowing script.

I am becoming increasingly convinced that our ancestors selected this location to build the coven's compound for a very specific reason. The walls are perfectly circular. The buildings are arranged in symmetrical patterns, with the altar at their very center. I have asked Sister Griashana for an explanation, but she has been reluctant to speak on the topic. The Elder Mothers have denied my requests for an audience. They are hiding something. I know it.

This altar, this confounded altar, seems to be the root of it all. Surely there is a purpose behind it. It does not yield to pick or hammer. It does not appear to be composed of any stone that I recognize. We practice no rituals associated with it. Surely there is a reason why it is here.

I can only assume that this structure was used for some sort of ceremony by the gods before the Cataclysm, but I am uncertain what that could be. I must consult the ancient codices for any records of it. I have heard of a repository in Veshda, my ancestor's homeland. I leave next week. May Yvvusta guide me.

Ginn, 365, 5, 17

Isobel's eyes met Joanne's.

"It's a start."

The midday sun hung in the deep blue sky, casting warm rays down upon the three travelers. They stood at a crossroads nestled among rising mountains dyed a rainbow of colors by layers of sediment. One road, running north, would lead Joanne to her home in Veld. The other, running east, would take Chinelo and Isobel into lands unknown. Ahead of them lay the nation of Caald, a realm of which Chinelo had only heard stories and rumors.

Isobel and Joanne embraced tenderly.

"I'm so glad I was able to see you," Joanne said. "I'll tell Kay about you. If your travels bring you to Veld, don't hesitate to visit."

"I won't, Joanne," Isobel replied, smiling lovingly. "Thank you for everything. Please, take care of yourself and Kay."

Joanne and Isobel separated. Joanne turned and hugged Chinelo.

"You keep her safe, or I will hunt you down."

She reached into her pocket and drew two folded slips of parchment. She pressed them into Chinelo's hand. "Some advice, to help you on your journey. Just don't overdo it. Wouldn't want you to injure yourself," she said with a wink.

She backed away and waved, before setting off down the trail at a brisk pace. Isobel leaned against Chinelo's shoulder. "What did she give you?"

"Good question." He unfolded the first slip; a series of runes were inscribed on the paper in small print. Chinelo's brow wrinkled.

"I really need to learn how to read this language," he pondered.

"Hmmm, let me see," Isobel snatched the paper away, reading it intently. "Ah! It's one of Joanne's spells. It appears to be one that enhances strength. Interesting. I suppose that would be useful for you to augment your fighting style. I imagine you'll need to regulate your esht-flow, though. This looks like it requires constant channeling to maintain. It would be good practice for you."

As Isobel slowly walked down the trail, Chinelo unfolded the other slip of parchment. He balked. Frantically, he held the parchment above his finger and summoned a flame to burn it. He dropped it on the trail and left it smoldering in the dirt.

"Chinelo, what was on the other one?" Isobel asked.

"It's probably best you don't see that one. It was a joke, and not a very good one," he replied.

"Why not? Hey! Why are you so flustered?"

The parchment curled with the spreading flame. A black line propagated across the slip, wilting it to gray ash and consuming the words Joanne had scrawled on the paper.

THE END OF PART 2

PART 3

THE HERO OF ATA

CHAPTER 14

414ᵗʰ year, 11ᵗʰ month, 30ᵗʰ day
20 years before present day

HOT. JUST LIKE ALWAYS, IT WAS hot. The sun was high, the sky was pale blue, and the air seemed to shimmer and dance. Standing beneath the sun's majesty was like staring into an open oven. It made the skin tingle and sweat. The shade was hardly much better. Though the burning pressure of the sun's light was absent, the thick air spread and filled every space, indoors or out.

It was always hot like this in Eshgar. Summer, winter, spring, fall—it made little difference. Some people even swore that Eshgar didn't have seasons. Chinelo knew that wasn't the case. You could sense the difference if you knew how to look. Or smell. The smell was easily the most notable thing that changed throughout the year. Sure, the temperature varied between warm and sultry, like a soup repeatedly being removed from its fire, but the smells, the scents—those metamorphosized like the cocooning brightmoths of east Eshgar. Winter was wet and hollow. Spring was sweet and gentle. Fall was earthy and welcoming. And summer. Summer was Chinelo's favorite. It smelled so *alive*.

Flowers bloomed across the whole city, people sweated in every street, meat sizzled on stoves and fires, spices tickled his nose from their baskets in the markets. Everything moved. Everything lived. Everything breathed.

The city churned with life in the summer. There were festivals, celebrations, games, and sports. Though, he wasn't allowed to go to very many, at least, not alone. Azuka could, but Azuka was thirteen, practically a man. Chinelo wasn't there yet, and the five years that separated him from his brother seemed eternal.

"Chinelo."

Chinelo looked up. Beside him, his mother squeezed his hand in hers.

"Come! Let's not dawdle," his mother said. Her face was stern, but her dark brown eyes were soft.

Chinelo nodded, and together they pushed through the crowds.

The streets were packed, which only made the heat more intense. A trickle of sweat worked its way down Chinelo's bare shoulder, running the length of his arm before dripping to the pavement below. He wore the typical sleeveless Eshgarian tunic bound with a belt at the waist and paired with loosing flowing trousers that bunched up at his ankles. They swished as he walked, moving air back and forth around his calves. He liked the way it felt. The movement cooled him a little, making the heat bearable.

His mother wore similar attire, though hers was more in line with women's fashion. A long, ankle length skirt of solid red hung from just above her hips, and billowing fabric was wrapped around her torso, leaving her shoulders bare, like his. Her curly dark hair was tied behind her head with a few twists hanging free. The curls were streaked with a couple wisps of silver, strands that Chinelo's mother insisted were Azuka's doing. Chinelo never really understood what she meant by that.

The buildings that framed the street were tall, multi-storied and built from sandstone. The walls were intricately decorated with carvings of animals. Most often those were lions, though hawks, camels, and other animals were not uncommon to see. Visrocs were Chinelo's personal favorite. The iron raptors with their four wings and sharp, hooked talons were always so impressive. He'd never seen one in real life, only in paintings and carvings. Supposedly they only migrated to Eshgar during the winter, soaring across the southeastern islands and roaming the coastlines for prey.

His mother tugged him along. He'd gotten distracted again. The crowds bustled around them, pressing against the pair. Chinelo's mother pulled him to the left, walking in the shadow of a large building with many columns along its walls. They had reached the center thoroughfare of Eshgar, the one that ran all the way to the queen's palace.

The street increased in incline, and Chinelo's feet began to ache. He looked up. Poking over the many dark-haired heads above him, he saw the tall spiraling towers of the palace capped with statues of roaring lionesses beneath radiant suns. How did they manage to put those up there?

Chinelo's mother veered right, and they burst from the crowd to the edge of the street. There were stanchions with ropes blocking them from going any further. The many men, women, and children all watched the street eagerly. Some looked up towards the palace's majestic arches. Others gazed down the street. There was music coming from that direction, faint trumpets and bugles.

"Ifet!" A voice called.

Chinelo recognized that voice. It belonged to his father. He searched for the source and soon found him. He was a thin man, somewhat tall but not terribly imposing. His head was bald, though a short gray beard covered the lower portion of his face. He stood between two columns on one of the nearby buildings with his full torso visible over the heads of the crowd. He waved at Chinelo and his mother, and they quickly joined him, climbing up a narrow set of stairs before stepping into a shaded alcove. It was just big enough for the three of them, and it was elevated, giving them a wide view of the street.

So, this was the spot he had been talking about the previous night. Chinelo had wondered why he left the apartment so early. Judging by how busy things were, someone else would have grabbed the spot if his father didn't. The view was excellent. Chinelo had no trouble seeing the whole district.

Chinelo's mother kissed him on the cheek. "Thank you, dear. You never disappoint."

"Are we late?" Chinelo asked.

His father grinned widely and tousled Chinelo's hair. "Your mother? Late? Never!"

Chinelo's mother released his hand and leaned against the wall, adjusting her hair tie. "How is Azuka?"

His father scratched his beard. "Nervous, but he seems to be in good spirits. It's a big day. We can't blame him."

"Did he polish his armor?" Chinelo's mother asked.

"Shiny enough to see his reflection."

"And his sword?"

"Sharpened."

His mother nodded and folded her hands in front of her, though Chinelo noticed a slight tremor in her fingers. Was she… was she worried? That didn't seem possible.

Chinelo's mother was *never* worried. She was always composed, always in control of her emotions and expressions. She expected the same from her sons. Strict adherence to decorum and form, perfect punctuality and obedience. They were to speak when spoken to, answering with clear, concise responses in voices that were neither too loud nor too quiet. They were to bow at the proper points, during introductions and farewells. They were to always thank those that treated them with kindness and respect, and they were never permitted to lash out at those that did not. Chinelo knew this, as did his elder brother. Why would his mother be worried about Azuka breaking form?

Sure, Azuka could be a little brash from time to time, but nothing bad ever happened from it. He made sure of that. Yes, there was nothing to worry about. So, why *was* she worried?

"What about his hair?" Chinelo asked, thinking that a joke might ease the tension.

Chinelo's mother balked. "His *hair?*"

Chinelo shrugged. "It looked funny."

His mother gave him a flat look. His father laughed. It seemed Chinelo's ploy had worked, just not on the intended target.

"I just hope he doesn't forget to—" Chinelo's mother started.

"He'll do fine, Ifet."

Chinelo's mother nodded firmly, and her face became like steel. Her posture straightened, her shoulders dropped back slightly, and she held her hands in front of her in perfect, elegant poise.

The crowd murmured. Chinelo gazed up the palace steps. Balanced on the shoulders of four burly men in deep blue robes, a large palanquin moved from the shadows of the arches into the blazing sunlight. It was magnificent in its regalia. Four gilded posts supported a canopy that shaded its occupant from the intense sun. Gold tassels dangled from the purple fabric, rustling with every slow step of the attendants. Patterns like vines wound to the canopy's apex, ending just below the decorative sphere at the top that represented the rising sun.

Chinelo could just barely make out the palanquin's sole occupant, or at least her lower half. The queen wore a shimmering silk skirt that covered her feet, though the sides were slit up to the mid-thigh. The material was a pale ochre color with golden lace running along the hems. The rest of the queen was shrouded from his view.

His heart pounded in his chest. He rarely got to see the queen. That made each time far, far more memorable.

Dozens of attendants fanned out behind the queen. Knights in shining silver armor marched down the steps, creating a sort of living wall between the crowds and their ruler. Their polished armor sparkled, and the golden crests on their breast plates seemed as bright as the sun above. Deep green plumes decorated the tops of their helms, protruding from a small hole behind the spiked crest on the knights' foreheads. The helms were rounded on the sides, widening towards the bottom. Visors with horizontal slats shaded the knights' eyes, but their chins were left exposed.

The knights drew their swords, the customary weapon for members of the Order, and grasped them with both hands in front of them, bending their elbows so that the hilts were a mere handbreadth from their chests. They turned the flats of the blade forward, then all stamped their right foot in unison, creating a cloud clatter. The crowd fell silent. Then, the trumpets sounded.

Chinelo whirled around. A large procession marched towards the palace, coming from all the way at the far end of the street. Five more knights walked at its head, with several others marching with long navy standards that fluttered in the breeze. Like the palace's architecture and the knights' armor, the regal banners were adorned with the crest of Eshgar, the emblem of a lioness beneath the rising sun.

While the edges of the procession were populated by knights, its core was clearly far, far younger. Pages, all thirteen years of age, marched in their ceremonial garb. They wore small metal caps that covered the cheeks and nose but left the eyes and lower half of the face completely open. The pages did not wear full plate. Instead, their forearms, shoulders, and shins were covered in lighter armor. Short swords hung at their belts, lighter versions of the glistening broadswords carried by their escorts.

Chinelo's brother was somewhere in there. Chinelo shaded his eyes and squinted, trying to identify his brother by his distinctive longer locks. He was unsuccessful. Aside from the variations in heights and builds, the pages all looked roughly the same. Azuka was supposed to be somewhere near the front. He'd gone on and on about how lucky he was to be so close to the queen.

Chinelo's father snapped his fingers and pointed. "There's our boy," he said with a wide smile.

Chinelo followed where his father pointed. He gasped. Azuka wasn't *near* the front. He was *at* the front, the first of the pages standing before the queen. His mother flinched. Her fingers clenched on themselves tightly.

The trumpets fell silent.

The crowd turned back towards the palanquin, which had been lowered to the ground. Attendants pulled back the fabric curtains, and the queen rose from her seat, stepping onto the stone stairway and into the light.

Queen Evali was a bit shorter than her attendants. Though, that wasn't terribly surprising. She wasn't that much older than Azuka, perhaps not even fifteen. She had not been queen for long. Chinelo vaguely remembered her coronation from two years prior. Something had happened to the last queen, Mide the Valiant. He could not remember what.

The queen stood before the crowd, surveying them with her chin slightly tilted upwards. Thick tight curls as black as night spread over her shoulders. They swayed slightly as she turned her head. The spiked sun on her elegant golden diadem flashed as she moved, sparkling like the winding bands that adorned her bare upper arms and wrists. Her ochre dress shimmered, and the sun shone across her reddish-brown skin. She was radiant, almost seeming to glow.

Chinelo glanced down. He always felt weird when he looked at her. He didn't quite understand why. His heart felt funny. His cheeks seemed to grow hot, and his hands kind of tingled. It was a strange sensation—one he'd refrained from mentioning to his parents. He'd told Azuka, who'd merely laughed and teased him about it. What had he said?

"You've got a crush on the queen?"

No. Chinelo did not have a crush on her. That would be silly. Girls were weird. He looked back up at her. No! He absolutely did not have a crush on her. It didn't matter how pretty she might be.

The queen suddenly extended her arm out to the right, opening her delicate hand. One of her handmaids knelt beside her, resting a long, slender sword in her palms. The queen took it without looking, flourishing it and pointing it to the sun. Any remaining murmurs stilled, so that all that could be heard was the wind.

"People of Eshgar!" Queen Evali said. Her voice carried well. It was firm and commanding. "Your presence honors me." She twirled the sword and bowed her head.

She *was* pretty.

Chinelo felt a forceful tap on his back. He started, looking side to side. Everyone in the crowd bowed in response. Everyone, that is, except Chinelo. His mother grunted and gestured with her shoulder for him to join. He did so, thankfully just before the man in front of him began to stand up straight. That would have been bad.

Queen Evali continued speaking. "Today, we welcome these young men and women into the ranks of the Order of the Sun." She waved her free hand in the direction of the procession. "They may not yet be heroes, but they have shown great bravery in their first years of training. Our kingdom relies on such bravery. Honor them. Welcome them with open arms. Cheer for their victories. Nurture them in their defeats. Join me, as we declare them our next knights of Eshgar!"

The crowd cheered. Chinelo's parents clapped their hands, and he followed suit. The queen continued her speech, but Chinelo lost interest quickly.

Something caught his eye, a shadow moving across the edge of the roof of one of the nearby buildings. He cocked his head. It looked like a person was peeking over the edge. Now *that* was an excellent spot to view the ceremony, even better than the one his father had found. If only they had thought of that.

Chinelo scanned the other rooftops. No one else appeared. Maybe it was harder to get up there than it seemed. The building didn't look terribly easy to climb on this side, but there were normally scaffolds on the backs for emergency exits.

The shadow moved. Chinelo timidly raised a hand to his chest and waved. His mother quickly patted it, signaling him to stand still. That was probably not the proper thing of him to do. He turned his attention back to the crowd.

"Debare Ishen," the queen said.

One of the pages stepped forwards, bending to one knee. Chinelo sighed. This was the slow part. One-by-one the pages would be called. At least Azuka was in the front. They wouldn't have to wait long for the important part, not that they could leave afterwards. One did not leave a ceremony before it concluded.

The queen tapped the boy's head with her sword. "I grant you the rank of squire."

The boy nodded and retreated, walking down the steps with a proud grin on his face.

Chinelo laughed to himself. *Silly.* The boy had forgotten the proper response. You were supposed tap your heart with your fist to indicate your allegiance. The queen smirked. It seemed she was also amused by the indiscretion. Though, based on the twinkle in her brown eyes, it did not look like she minded all that much.

"Akuada Rel." She called another page, a girl this time. The procedure repeated, but the girl actually remembered to respond.

Chinelo tapped his chin. The queen was calling them all by name, but she did not have a list or reference book. Did she know all of their names? How could she remember them all?

He looked up at the shadow. The figure held into something, a strange, curved staff or rod of some sort. It seemed to be fumbling with something else.

"Azuka Ide."

Chinelo's heart skipped. It was his brother's turn. He watched as his brother ascended the steps, knelt before the queen, and bowed his head. It was time. It was finally time. His brother was going to be a squire!

Chinelo's mother tensed. Her hands were clasped tightly in front of her, and her jaw clenched. His father rested a tender hand on her shoulder, and she seemed to relax a little.

The queen gently tapped Azuka's head with the blade. "I grant you the rank of squire."

Azuka placed his hand over his heart and stood. Chinelo's mother let out a relieved sigh. Azuka turned and descended the steps, letting out a breath of his own and looking at the sky. Then, he stopped. His gaze darted to the roof of a nearby building, the one where the shadow was.

"What is he doing?" his mother hissed.

Chinelo looked up. The shadow had stood, and it was holding something, drawing something back. Was that a *bow*?

Steel scraped as a sword left its sheath. Azuka clasped his short sword and dashed up the stairs taking them two at a time. The knights around the queen suddenly flew into motion, pointing their broadswords at Azuka. He leapt the final steps, shoved the startled queen to the side then whirled around, swinging his blade in a half-circle.

Wood cracked, and metal struck stone.

A broken arrow bounced down the stairs, tumbling to a stop. Somehow, Azuka had *deflected* the shot. The crowd screamed. The street erupted into chaos as onlookers ran, covering their heads. Chinelo looked up at the shadow, which was fumbling with what he guessed was another arrow.

"Up there!" he shouted, pointing at the shadow.

"The rooftop!" Azuka bellowed, his voice cracking at the last syllable.

The knights around him turned, and several drew bows of their own. The shadow ducked behind the lip of the roof, making a quick retreat. An alarm bell rang, which would summon more of the knights from their patrols across the city. Whoever that figure was, they would be found.

Attendants escorted the queen back into the palace, and several of her guards followed. Chinelo's mother grabbed his arm, and his father guided them from their perch into an alleyway. They would be safe from the rushing crowd there. They knelt behind a large crate, and his father occasionally peeked over it. Once, Chinelo peered around the edge as well, catching a quick glimpse of the knights and pages guarding the entrance to the palace. Azuka was still up there somewhere.

"Mother, what's going to happen?" Chinelo said.

His mother shushed him sternly, cocking her head to listen and glancing at the tops of the two buildings they sat between.

"We wait," his father said. The wiry man squatted before Chinelo. "Once things calm down, we'll find Azuka."

Chinelo nodded. Azuka. The image of his brother defending—no—saving the queen lingered in Chinelo's mind. He stood, resolute and focused with hands on his sword, his eyes shrewd, and his back to those he protected. That day, Azuka was a hero.

Chinelo pressed his back against the alley wall. Could he be that way some day? Could he be a hero? Perhaps. There was only one way to find out. In that moment, he knew what he wanted to become. He would walk the path his brother walked, the path of a knight.

CHAPTER 15

434th year, 3rd month, 1st day
Present Day

ISOBEL SAT ON A ROCKY OUTCROPPING, overlooking the land far below. The sky's deep cobalt hue was fading with the approaching sun. She shivered. Though winter had not yet arrived, the mornings were brisk. She pulled her cloak tighter around her shoulders.

Leaning forward, she peered at the crags beneath her. They were mottled and dappled, as if one of the gods had splattered blue and white paints on them at random. They rose and fell in sharp edges and were scarred by winding crevices. Far below her, she saw a slight movement. An agile mountain deer leapt from crag to crag before stopping and nibbling on a bundle of cliff-grass. Bats flew in swarming clusters, flapping and diving erratically. Even further beyond them lay the seaside city of Dawngale.

It sprawled across the shoreline, curving around the perimeter of the bay far below. Twinkling lights appeared, encouraged by the approaching sun. Rows and rows of whitewashed buildings spread from the coast, rising in waves over the surrounding foothills. Their red clay rooftops contrasted with the speckled cliffs nearby. Great stone citadels and temples dotted the cityscape, towering above the white houses and shops in round spires. From a dark cave in the hillside ran a grand aqueduct that cut through the center of the city with smaller ducts spreading like roots through the alleyways and side streets.

The city was split. Though most of it rested in the foothills, an imposing stone fortress sat on an island at the center of the bay. A single tower climbed high above the fortress, and a great blaze shone from its apex. Isobel could faintly see lines of red-brown docks with small bobbing shapes at the shore below the fortress: boats and shuttles to ferry the population between the two districts. Of course, those boats were mostly empty given how early it was.

A breeze carried the salty ocean air to where Isobel sat. This was her first time seeing the sea. All her life she had heard of the infinite blue expanse that surrounded the continent, but never once had she ventured so far from the heartland that she could view it for herself. Thin lines of white froth were lit by the morning glow from the horizon, mirroring the curving waves of painted buildings above the shore.

Looking to the horizon, Isobel was filled with an overwhelming sense of peace and wonder. What lay beyond the magnificent seas? From the maps she had seen, she recalled that there were volcanic islands much further south, but were they really so far that she couldn't even see them? And what lay beyond those? The maps only showed so much.

Isobel's gaze shifted to the east. Beyond the city was the nation of Caald, the land that hid the first obelisk she sought. The grassy hills rose and fell along the border of Iskara, but they ended abruptly, cut off by a great stone wall that snaked toward the horizon. It was incredibly high, casting a shadow over the eastern edge of Dawngale, and its light gray stone construction matched that of the island fortress. Beyond the great wall lay barren, rocky terrain. It was black and desolate, broken up by feathery streams of white vapor rising from cracks in the ground. The land was ominous yet somehow beautiful. Centuries of lava flow had shaped it into a curving obsidian wasteland, calm and quiet like the ocean beyond the bay.

With anticipation, Isobel looked at a distant mountain that was framed by a golden corona. A brilliant light broke from the east, illuminating the dark flatlands and reflecting off the white buildings in Dawngale. The sun had finally begun its ascent across the heavens, shining so brightly that Isobel's eyes hurt. Looking down, she watched the light move across the waking city. The sea shimmered in a brilliant sapphire blue, sparkling with each wave and ripple. Tiny specks marched like ants between the white buildings. Isobel basked in the warm morning light, taking in the beauty of the sunrise.

She stood and picked up her staff, preparing to return to camp. Using her staff as support, she climbed down the rocky steps below her. Her legs were sore, though they seemed to recover from the non-stop walking much more quickly than when she and Chinelo had started their journey. She still did not understand how he was able to move with such vigor throughout the day, though.

Isobel pointed her staff ahead of her and issued a command. "Guide."

A wispy trail of pale blue light appeared, shooting straight through the sparse trees. She had placed a talisman in her pack at the camp, and the blue line connected her staff to that talisman. She followed the trail through the tall grass, pondering the events of the previous months.

Something had puzzled her for a long time about the catastrophe that had hit Nellborough. She had been able to protect herself and Chinelo using her nullification barrier, which only affected spells or enchanted items. Against anything else it was useless. The flames had not been able to pierce her defense, which meant that they must have been the result of magic. But how could someone cast a spell so large?

Magic, like all things, had rules and limitations. Esht was used to manifest the effects of spells, and as the intensity or size of those spells increased, so did the cost. Creating a small flame was trivial, but creating a blaze, even one the size of a house, was incredibly taxing on the individual. Generating one the size of an entire town shouldn't have been possible. Isobel's "Inferno" spell consumed nearly a fifth of her esht, and it was only sufficient to cover a small area. And her esht reserves were quite a bit larger than what was considered typical. An incredibly large number of mages would be needed to execute such a technique, enough to make an army.

She set her jaw. The Archmage would have access to such an army, the Interior Guard. But why would he demolish Eshgar and Nellborough? It was clear that he wanted the obelisks and their hidden magic, but why did the towns have to fall? Why would he do such a thing?

She had seen him only once, during a rather public visit to the Rothvale Trade Guild before her mother had passed on. She did not remember much about him, just a fleeting image of his imposing figure, silver hair, and regal crimson robes. Her mother had warned her to keep her distance from him and the Interior Guard in general, owing to their history of conflict with the few remaining covens.

Most accounts of Archmage Harlyle were shrouded in mystery. Some regarded him with an almost religious level of respect. Others spoke of him as a politician. He was second only to the king, and as Iskara's foremost mage and leader of the Interior Guard, he provided valuable council to the monarchy.

Though, that raised another question: had the attack been planned by the Iskaran king or the Archmage? Attacking foreign city-states could be vaguely justified as an act of military strategy, but attacking a town within the kingdom? That didn't seem logical.

Then there was the final issue. The attack used flame. Based on Joanne's explanation, Mother Ginn had been the one who had discovered the word for fire, "*Vasht.*" Ginn's journal was marked with the year 365, almost seventy years ago. Based on that, fire could only have been utilized in mage-craft for less than a century. So how had the Archmage used that word?

The Red Coven was isolated from society, only interacting with civilization through small groups that secretly integrated into cities. Witches were indoctrinated from birth to never reveal the secrets of the coven. Isobel and her mother before her were likely the only witches who had defied that.

Isobel stepped over a log, crushing the fallen leaves with every step. The only person she had taught the word for fire was Chinelo. Had her mother taught anyone, perhaps someone who had joined the Interior Guard? Esther had mentioned trying to train the townsfolk from Nellborough in the Ancient Arts, but she never disclosed if any had actually learned that technique. The only one Isobel knew about was Umfrey, and his knowledge of magic had been rudimentary.

Isobel ducked under a branch. She felt a slight tug as her shirt caught on a twig. She carefully untangled her clothing, then continued, following the thin line of blue.

Perhaps Mother Ginn had shared the word for fire with the other covens. Isobel had heard that the Elder Mothers occasionally exchanged information with the Obsidian Order in the east or the Sisters of the Serpent in the far north. Had those covens been raided by the Interior Guard?

The first covens formed nearly two centuries earlier to ensure that witches were protected in the Mage Wars. They had scattered and insulated themselves in the far reaches of the continent, passing on their understanding of magic to the next generations. Few survived the following century. Blamed for the many disasters and catastrophes that had shaken the world during the wars, witches were brutally hunted by both mages and mage-killers alike. Only the most cunning, most isolated, or most ruthless had endured.

Isobel shook her head. She needed more information. She had hoped that Mother Ginn's logbook would provide something she could work with, but most of the accounts were just of Ginn's preparations for her journey to her homeland.

If only Iva was here, she would know what to do.

Would she? If Joanne could be believed, Iva disappeared a year earlier after annihilating the Red Coven in a single night. What happened in the ten years Isobel was gone?

The line from Isobel's staff grew brighter. She was close. A startled shout reached her ears. Isobel ran, breaking through the tall grass and stepping onto the patch of earth she and Chinelo had used as a camp. Chinelo sat on the ground, half covered by his blanket, holding a crumpled slip of parchment in his hands. Mort struggled on his back in Chinelo's lap, producing an awful, otherworldly groaning as he thrashed his plump, stubby legs.

"Isobel?" Chinelo looked up at her with wide eyes.

"Chinelo?"

"Did you put Mort on my chest this morning?"

Isobel cocked her head. "Why of course. How else was I going to keep the note I wrote you from blowing away?"

Chinelo looked down at the paper in his hand. Isobel peered over his shoulder, looking at her hastily written words from earlier that morning.

I'm going to watch the sunrise. I'll be back after dawn.

Chinelo rubbed his eyes. Mort finally regained his balance. He glared up at Chinelo, seething at the rude awakening he had received.

"Why didn't you put it on the ground?" Chinelo asked.

"Why would I do that? Mort doesn't like sleeping on the ground."

"No," Chinelo sighed. "The note!"

"You might not have seen it."

Chinelo opened his mouth, but hesitated, pressing his knuckle against his lips. Isobel sat down beside him, smiling happily. His deep brown eyes had softened, though he still appeared to be a bit disoriented. He scratched at the beard that had begun to grow across his cheek. Isobel tilted her head. She had intended to discuss her thoughts from her walk to the camp, but perhaps they could wait. Her concerns seemed to have drifted far away.

"So, how did you sleep?" she asked.

"Sublimely up until the last five minutes."

"Good! I'm glad."

Chinelo yawned. "And you?"

Isobel shrugged. "Well enough. Something woke me up maybe an hour or two ago. Probably Mort kicking. The little villain."

"I wonder what that's like," Chinelo said wryly.

Mort hopped off his lap and waddled to Isobel's knee, dragging his bulbous belly through the dry dirt. Isobel stroked his back lightly, moving her finger along two stripes that ran parallel to his spine.

"How was the sunrise?" Chinelo asked.

"Oh, it was the most beautiful thing I've ever seen!" Isobel gushed. "The sun lit the sky like a great painting. So many magnificent colors! I would have loved to watch it with you, but you looked so peaceful, I thought it best not to wake you. Not that I was looking or anything. I'm sure you understand." She fidgeted with one of her longer locks of hair.

"Oh, and the city!" she continued. "It's so quaint and inviting. It's built in layers on the foothills. It must be so very wonderous to walk through the streets. Then there's the ocean! I've never seen anything like it. It's so much water all in one place! It's so calming, so pristine. Please, please, we must go see it! I want to splash in it, to experience what the water feels like. I've heard it's salty. Does that mean it's scratchy? Does it taste bad? Do people drink it? So many questions. Oh! And if there's water, there must be fish! I've never had saltwater fish before. Can we try some while we're there? I'm sure it's delightful. Think of it! The food comes pre-salted! It must keep so well."

Chinelo blinked. "Isobel, we're going to be in the city for several days. I'm sure we'll have ample opportunities to try the food while we rest and find short-term work."

Isobel bounced subtly, attempting to contain her enthusiasm. "And the ocean?"

"Do you even have to ask?"

She shot to her feet. "Magnificent!" She reached down and grabbed Chinelo's hands, dragging him up with her. "Come on! Let's get ready to go!"

Chinelo groaned. "I've only been awake a few minutes. Give me a moment to get my bearings."

Isobel released his hands, and he fell with a thud. "Very well. I'll prepare breakfast."

"You don't want to wait to eat until we arrive?" Chinelo rubbed his posterior where he had landed.

Isobel shook her head. "From what I saw this morning, it will take us a few hours to get down the mountain."

"Ah! Yes, that would be quite a long trip with your stomach growling."

Isobel shot him a look. "It's not that loud."

Her stomach rumbled, triggering a startled jump from Mort. Chinelo raised an eyebrow.

Isobel looked away. "It's not *normally* that loud."

"I don't know, Isobel. If I didn't feed you before bed, I don't see how any of us would sleep. Though, I suppose it would keep the bears away."

Isobel's cheeks flushed. "It really isn't that bad."

Her stomach roared. Chinelo smirked.

"Well," Isobel said, smiling slyly, "if you want to talk about repelling bears, I'm sure your snoring would do the trick."

Chinelo looked up, his brown eyes flashing in an expression of horror. "Oh no. Do I keep you awake at night?"

Isobel laughed. "Not because of that, no. Fortunately for you, I can sleep through most anything when it comes to noise. It's an acquired skill from sharing a room with fifteen sisters."

Chinelo sighed in relief. "Had me worried there."

"I assure you, there is no need to worry. I wouldn't hold it against you either way, though."

"So, do you remember the plan for our stay here?" Chinelo asked as he climbed down the rocky trail that led towards Dawngale's main road.

"Locate an inn. Take a bath. Find work. Eat!" Isobel responded, carefully placing her foot on the sharp stone.

Chinelo laughed. "And also buy clothes and supplies. I'd like to start with the clothes so we have a fresh set to change into after we bathe."

"Right. And then we eat!"

"I like the way you think. What are you going to need to make those—what did you call them?"

Isobel hopped from a smaller boulder to the ground. Her baggy trousers fluttered as she fell. "Enchanted lamps?"

"Ah. Yes."

"Typically, I only need lanterns. I should have enough metallic ink to handle the inscriptions. Normally I work with a vendor to enchant their products at their store. Most will pay handsomely for the service, at least in my experience."

"And what do they do?" Chinelo asked.

"Oh! Did you never see any back home?"

Chinelo shook his head.

"It's rather simple, actually," Isobel said, speaking rapidly. "I create a binding inscription to store a portion of my esht within the lantern in such a way that it becomes self-sustaining. I then use an activation inscription to produce the desired effect. Typically, I just create one that projects a glowing orb—like the one Joanne used—whenever the cage of the lantern is touched. That typically doesn't require much esht to maintain, so as long as I make the generation rate of the enchantment high enough, it will never go out. See? Simple!"

Chinelo blinked. "Why didn't you have one of those at home?"

"Well, I did, but this one time there was this translation codex for sale in the market, and I was short on crescents, so I traded it for that. By that point I already had several spells in my staff that did the same thing. Never saw the need to replace it."

"And do they sell well?"

"Oh, you would not believe it! And at very high prices."

Chinelo nodded. "Good. Then we should be in a favorable position heading into winter."

"You're going to try to go on some hunting jobs, right?" Isobel walked cheerfully by his side. "You will be careful, won't you?"

"Of course. You have nothing to fear. Assuming they have that kind of work here. Nellborough had a decent sized bounty board at the hunter's guild, so hopefully this will be the same. I'll only go on a couple, and only on the safer ones, don't you worry."

"Good." She glanced down at his empty hand swinging at his side. She clenched her fist and skipped forward, shaking her head.

The pair reached the main road and turned to the south, approaching the north gate of Dawngale. They paused, staring at the beautiful architecture of the sprawling city that spread out below them. Something about the sounds, the smells, the sights seemed to draw up a curious urge in Isobel's mind. She once again shook her head, dismissing it.

"I can't wait to sleep in a proper bed," Chinelo said, rubbing his back.

"I can't wait to take a proper bath," Isobel said with a longing sigh.

"Well, shall we?" Chinelo nodded towards the city.

CHAPTER 16

CHINELO SLID A THIN RAZOR ACROSS his cheek, shaving away his beard and letting the hairs fall into the sink. The inn he and Isobel had found was incredibly luxurious. His room even had a mirror and running water. He turned a valve and watched his black hair wash down the drain. Such a marvel.

A knock came from the door behind him. It connected to an adjacent room, one that Isobel had reserved for herself. Chinelo walked across the room, sinking his bare feet into the plush crimson carpet. He opened the door, and Isobel fluttered through.

"Ahhhh, it's lovely to be clean again," Isobel said whimsically, hopping on the bed and crossing her legs. Clad in a freshly purchased shirt and trousers, she had washed away the dirt and grime accumulated during their journey. Though, Chinelo was quite confused why she had chosen to buy a more open, sleeveless shirt given how cool the weather was becoming. It did not align with the winter coats and pants they had purchased, nor did it match her standard pragmatic attire. Still, he had to admit, she wore it very well.

"Everything is so soft here. Chinelo! Have you tried lying on the carpet? It's so comfortable, you could sleep on it!"

Chinelo chuckled. "If the bed proves too posh, I'll certainly shift to the floor."

She cocked her head and watched him shave. "You're not keeping the beard?"

"Too itchy. Plus, it's not really my usual style."

"Oh," Isobel said quietly, looking down at her hands.

Chinelo glanced back at her in the mirror. There she was, acting strange again. His gaze lingered on her shoulder. Another new tattoo had appeared. It was a complex circular glyph, with over fifty tiny runes spiraling around some kind of schematic that resembled a knife, with lines connecting from the glyph's outer ring to the central diagram.

"What does that one do?" Chinelo asked, pointing at her shoulder with his razor. If there was one thing that consistently improved Isobel's mood, he had learned that it was asking her to explain magic.

"Oh this?" Isobel hovered her right hand over her shoulder. Light formed around the glyph, and a glowing hilt appeared, protruding from her skin. Isobel grasped it and swung it. She held a small dagger in her hand that emanated an otherworldly light. "I finally figured out weapon conjuring!"

"When did you have time for that?"

"Well, I'd been thinking about it for a while, but the actual tattoo I made while you were hunting last week. I got bored waiting around camp. Mort isn't the best conversationalist."

A faint croak echoed from her room. Was that a hint of disdain Chinelo heard?

"I've been thinking," Chinelo said.

"Oh? Have you now?" Isobel fidgeted with the blade. She grabbed its tip and bent it, shattering it into a thousand tiny sparkles.

"If you are willing, I think I would like to get one—a tattoo, like yours."

Isobel jumped to her feet. "Wait really? You would?"

Chinelo nodded.

Isobel began pacing back and forth. "Oh! This is so exciting! What do you want it to do? Where do you want it? Have you had one before? You know they hurt, right? If you want, I can make you a spell for it if you give me a brief description of the effects."

"That one Joanne gave me. I'd like to try something like that."

"Oh."

Chinelo looked back at her. She had stopped pacing. "Is that not all right?" he asked.

Isobel shrugged, looking down. "No, no it's fine. I just thought you might want to try one of mine first. Sorry, it's not a problem. It was a silly thought."

Chinelo looked in the mirror. He felt a slight heat rising in his neck. His shoulders tensed. "I'm sorry. I didn't mean it like that."

"Please don't be. I…"

"No, I recognize that wasn't considerate of me. I'm sorry, Isobel. I didn't intend to hurt your feelings."

Isobel stared at the floor. "Can I make you a better version of it?"

"Hmmm?"

"The spell. Can I make you a better version of it? I've been thinking about its effects. It's good, very good, but it would leave you with several critical weaknesses. For one thing it multiplies your strength without increasing your resistance to impact or force. So, if you aren't careful, you could break your bones just by swinging your sword too hard. Also, it requires a constant flow of esht, which would mean if your concentration broke mid-fight, your strength would be gone, too. You typically breathe and refocus between strikes when you are fighting. I could work that into the spell, so you don't have to constantly channel it. All that to say, I think I could make you a better version of it, or at least one that is more suited to you."

Chinelo walked over to her and paused. After a moment he placed his hand on her shoulder. She jumped slightly and looked up at him.

"Hey," he said. "Will you forgive me?"

Isobel nodded and smiled.

"I would be honored if you made your own version," he said. "I trust that it would be a masterpiece."

Isobel's face flushed slightly. She looked away. "Have you thought about where you want it?"

"I was thinking along my back right about here." Chinelo rubbed his trapezius.

As she glanced back, Isobel's cheeks turned a more vibrant red. "I—that shouldn't be difficult. It's a good spot, too. Your muscles are—I mean—it's close to your heart so the esht doesn't have very far to go. We should probably wait until you've had a chance to try out my version before we make it permanent. I'm sure you understand. I'll—I'll get started working on it."

Isobel hurried back into her room leaving a bewildered Chinelo standing alone on the carpet. Sometimes, many times, her behavior baffled him, especially in the last few weeks. He peeked through the open connecting door. Isobel was already scribbling on a sheet of parchment torn from one of her many notebooks.

"You don't want to go explore the town first?" Chinelo asked, leaning against the doorframe.

"Maybe in a little while after you've finished cleaning up. I want to at least get an outline of this while I'm thinking about it."

Chinelo nodded, noting the musical quality that had returned to her voice. He returned to his room and finished shaving. The pile of dirty clothes deposited in the corner of the room caught his eye. Isobel would likely want more than a few minutes, and he hardly wanted to interrupt her while she was absorbed in her work.

"I think I'll wash my clothes while you're working on that," he called.

"Sounds good! The talisman for that is in the front pocket of my pack."

Chinelo nodded, gathered his clothes, retrieved the cleaning talisman, and exited the room, locking the door behind him.

The bay spread wide to the south. Isobel sat at a table overlooking the city docks, watching the many fishermen and dockhands loading and unloading cargo and nets. The docks lined the entire shoreline, leaving only a few patches of sharp rocks between. Her dreams of visiting the beach would have to wait, unfortunately. She inhaled, smelling the briny ocean air, the pungent fish, and the husky smoke of the torches that lit the dining area where she and Chinelo sat.

She cut into the wide strip of seared mackerel that lay on her plate. The steaming fish released a delectable fragrance of lemon, paprika, and garlic. It tasted even better than it smelled. She bobbed her head as she ate the fish, dancing to an unheard tune in her head. Across from her, Chinelo continued with his own meal which looked equally ravishing—a platter of grilled shrimp dyed orange by rich, peppery seasonings. They had been fortunate to find a restaurant with such reasonable prices.

"So, what do you think?" he asked.

Isobel swallowed her current bite, the rich taste lingering in her mouth. "Oh, it's fantastic. It's like the fish we had back in Nellborough but somehow less fishy. So, ten times better! I'm a bit surprised that it's not completely saturated with salt, though. I would have expected it to have more of a bite to it given that it spent its entire life soaking in the stuff."

Chinelo chuckled. "I don't think that's how that works, Isobel."

"Clearly. And yours?"

"Exactly what I was hoping for. Want to try?"

"Oh, may I? You wouldn't mind? I've never had shellfish before."

"That's partially why I picked it."

Isobel smiled as Chinelo slid the plate across the table. He really was quite a sweetheart. Throughout their journey, he'd shown her every kindness and consideration, even giving up his own sleeping mat so that she might not toss and turn in her sleep. And there didn't seem to be any ulterior motive behind such actions. He really was just that kind.

Her fork darted downwards, impaling one of the small, unsuspecting shrimps. She popped it in her mouth with much enthusiasm. It did not disappoint.

"You're too good for this world, Chinelo. Far too good."

Chinelo laughed and gazed out over the bay, the sunlight illuminating his dark eyes. My, how they caught the light. Isobel found herself staring, but she forced her attention back to her food as he cleared his throat.

"Do you think three days will be enough time?" Chinelo asked.

Isobel nodded, wiping her mouth with a cloth napkin. "I think so. I'd like to keep up the momentum from the last month, but I recognize that rest is very necessary right now. I'm not sure about you, but my legs have been especially sore for the last week or two, so I'd like to give enough time for that to remedy itself."

Chinelo nodded.

"This will give us time to enjoy the city life," Isobel said. "We didn't really have much of a chance to explore Nellborough together before..." her words trailed off. The corners of her mouth turned down. She shook her head. "At any rate, let's enjoy ourselves."

Yes, that was what they should do. No looking back, only forward. In a few days they would resume their journey to Ata, and they would find their first obelisk.

After they finished their meal, the pair walked down the steep street towards the bay. Beyond the stone fortress at the bay's center, the sea glittered against the violet sky. The sun was setting. Couples and families passed by, talking and laughing as they browsed the shops and stands that would soon be closing with the approaching night. Isobel walked merrily beside Chinelo, bouncing on her toes with every step. She looked around the city with wonder, taking in the many sites. The white buildings were pristine and clean. Stray cats leapt from rooftop to rooftop, watching the crowd below. Trees sprouted from small enclosures nestled in the sides of buildings, breaking up the endless walls of white.

A husband and wife leaned out of a nearby window. They smiled and pointed towards the bay. The man wrapped his arm around his wife's shoulder, pulling her closer. Isobel smiled.

Two youths skipped towards the dock, holding hands as they descended the sloped street. Pausing to look at the sea, the boy leaned over and kissed the girl on the cheek. She giggled and pulled him down the stairs to the docks.

An old man and woman passed by, walking in the opposite direction. They leaned against each other, smiling from their wrinkled faces. Their canes tapped on the paving stones, and their gnarled hands were interlocked between them. They looked so happy, so content.

Isobel looked over her shoulder and watched them hobble up to a higher level of the city. The man whispered something into the woman's ear, and she laughed. Something moved within Isobel. Was it a longing, an appreciation, a vicarious contentedness? Would she be like them one day? Her smile faded.

She turned back and caught up with Chinelo, who had stopped at a small plaza overlooking the docks. He was silhouetted against the coast, standing so strong and firm. Strangely, Isobel felt an undeniable pull drawing her closer to him. It wasn't a new sensation, but it was much more acute that evening.

"Do you see that?" Chinelo pointed at the fortress. "They're lighting the beacon for the night."

Isobel didn't look. She glanced down at his hand, hanging at his hip beside her. She clenched her fist. Her heart pounded. Her arms quivered. Should she? No. He wouldn't like it. But still, she felt the pull. Could she resist?

Should she resist?

Slowly, she moved her hand and placed it in his, clasping it gently. Chinelo jumped. He looked down, then back up at Isobel's face. She felt her cheeks grow hot.

"I'm sorry. I..." She released his hand and let hers fall to her hip. She stepped away. Stupid! How could I be so—

Chinelo caught her hand and pulled it back. She felt his fingers lacing between hers, drawing her back to his side. It felt so natural, so perfect, as if their hands had always been meant to fit together. Suddenly, there was a strange sensation. It spread from her fingers and propagated all the way across her body. It left her lightheaded, but somehow not. His hand was rough, yet gentle. Strong, yet comforting. Deep within her, she sensed a trembling. Had her heart always done that?

"Isobel, look." He nodded towards the sea. His eyes were soft, dark, and kind. With great effort, she turned away to face the bay. She gasped.

The lighthouse shone, and behind it, the sky was a brilliant rainbow of colors. From the horizon, it was a deep orange and purple, moving up into a ribbon of yellow, and finally transitioning into a great expanse of deep blue above. The brightest stars revealed themselves across the heavens, twinkling and dancing.

Everything around her seemed to vanish, leaving only her, Chinelo, and the sky.

"Beautiful," she marveled.

Chinelo nodded in agreement.

Curiously, he wasn't staring at the sky.

CHAPTER 17

CHINELO BRACED HIMSELF AS THE CART in which he sat bounced over a bump in the road. His armor rattled at the sudden jolt. It had been a long time since he had worn his armor and feeling it on his body was like reuniting with an old friend—a moderately uncomfortable friend, but a friend, nonetheless. He had to admit, having a second set of hands to assist with the clasps and fastenings made putting on the armor a much more pleasant experience than usual. Isobel had been remarkably eager to help him that morning, not that he was complaining.

They had talked late into the night, and given the events of the previous day, he felt that he was getting to know her all over again. He sensed an odd but welcome warmth in his chest, one that had formed when her hand first held his and one that refused to leave. Needless to say, he was in an incredibly good mood that overcast day.

"How much are they paying you for this job, stranger?" a gruff voice called over the clattering cartwheels and the clopping hooves on the road.

Chinelo looked up. Across from him sat a lean, wiry man whose head was draped with an unkempt mat of thin blonde hair. The tangle noticeably contradicted the meticulously maintained mustache below his hooked nose. A large scar cut down his clean-shaven cheek.

"He has a name, Fenn," another man spoke. Glassow, a short stocky boulder of a man, sat next to Fenn. He looked young, likely in his late twenties, but his long wavy hair had already begun to form grey streaks. Everything about him was round and sturdy.

Fenn scoffed.

"Forgive this rascal, Chinelo," Glassow said. "He's a still bitter that the magistrate wouldn't let our crew take this job alone."

"More people means less money. It's simple math," Fenn retorted in his gravelly voice.

Chinelo heard a light chuckle from beside him. Haru, an older woman, leaned back against the cart railing, crossing her arms and closing her one good eye. Her skin was leathery and marred by a network of scars. Over her eye she wore a strip of cloth that was knotted below her snow-white ponytail. She had occasionally interjected some light guffaws, but aside from that she had not said much during the trip. She was clad in thin, light armor plates with a crimson cape around her neck.

"I apologize, Fenn. I didn't realize I wasn't supposed to take this job. I thought it was still open," Chinelo said.

"That's because *someone* forgot to mark it as claimed." Fenn shot a sour look at Glassow.

Glassow shrugged. "The guild assessor said it was at least a four-man job. Don't get mad at me."

Chinelo stroked his chin. "Why four, though?"

"You haven't heard about this one?" Glassow said eagerly, rolling his body forward.

Chinelo shook his head. "I thought it was just a boar hunt. Is it not?"

Glassow's mouth spread in a devious grin. "It's not just a boar, friend. It's a vile, evil, vicious beast. It's been attacking and eating travelers on the road towards Rothvale. It'll eat anything. Horses, dogs, men, bones. It leaves nothing behind."

Fenn scoffed. "A pig is still a pig, and I do love a good slice of bacon."

Haru chuckled once more.

"Hmmm," Chinelo said, looking down. "I don't think my… companion would be happy if she knew I was on such a dangerous mission."

"You hear that, driver? The knight wants to turn around!" Fenn shouted.

The driver, a young adolescent, turned his head. "Magistrate said no turning around. Kill the beast, and I'll haul you back."

Haru leaned forward. "So, you fancy a woman?" Her voice was low but had a silky smoothness to it.

"That is an accurate description, yes." Chinelo smiled.

"I'll be sure to get you back safe to her. Listen for my calls. My arrow strikes true. Do not impede its flight."

Fenn watched the exchange condescendingly. "Haru, what's gotten into you? Already warming up to this stranger? You've been caustic towards me for the past five years, but here you are, pouring honey on an outsider."

Haru looked at him and frowned. "This man is no scoundrel."

Fenn sneered.

"Ahhh, I'd love to find a woman someday," Glassow mused, rolling back onto his elbow. "Saw one this morning in the market. Just the prettiest thing. There she was, shining like a goddess in the morning light." He sighed.

"Goddesses are hideous," Haru said.

"Oh, not this again!" exclaimed Glassow. "You know what I mean! Think of the teachings of Nakam. He describes the goddesses as fair maidens, descending from the clouds to bring light to our lives."

"Religion is folly, Glassow," Haru said. "Only truth matters."

"So, you've told me. And what proof of this truth do you have?" Glassow rolled forward.

"Magic," Haru said proudly, leaning back and crossing her arms once more.

"Yes, yes. We *know*." Fenn rolled his eyes. "Care to teach us any of that fancy mystic jargon?"

"I do not give torches to children," Haru said, closing her eye.

Glassow shrugged. "Magic is forbidden by Nakam. I have no need. The goddesses smile upon me. I shall return triumphant and claim that maiden as my own."

Chinelo raised an eyebrow.

"Your attitude towards women is why none accept you," Haru chided.

"Oh, you know what I mean, Haru!" Glassow looked up. "Honestly, I preferred it when you were silent."

Chinelo looked down at the cart's floor. He wasn't keen to participate in an argument among strangers, regardless of how amusing it might be. The cart hit another bump, and a quiver of arrows slid past Chinelo's feet. The shaft of each was inscribed with runes. Chinelo eyed Haru's attire, searching for a spell-core hanging in her armor. Finding none, he peaked beneath the seat. Haru's longbow was hidden in the shadow of the bench on which they sat. It, too, was inscribed with runes.

"Haru, do you not use a spell-core?" Chinelo asked.

Haru perked up. "You practice the Ancient Arts?"

"Only a little. The woman I mentioned, she has been teaching me."

Fenn frowned.

"A fellow mage." Haru smiled. "To answer your question, no. Magical devices of that nature are beyond my knowledge." She leaned back against the railing.

The cart lurched to a stop. The driver turned back.

"This is as far as I go. Return here once you've completed the mission. You have until sundown."

Fenn leapt from the cart and landed with a loud thud. He discarded his cloak, stripping to his bare torso. His toned chest was carpeted in a thin layer of blonde fuzz. From the back of the cart, he grabbed a menacing war-scythe. Glassow climbed from the cart and hastily grabbed a heavy hammer. Haru, with her bow in hand and quiver over her shoulder, jumped and landed on her toes. Gathering his sword and shield, Chinelo followed.

"All, to me," Haru commanded. She extended her hand and chanted a long incantation in the Ancient Tongue. With two fingers, she touched each of the hunter's foreheads, finishing with Chinelo's.

"Listen for my calls," Haru said before turning and walking up the slope of a nearby hill. She stopped and sniffed the air. She continued, scanning the foothills with her eye. Her gaze paused on a nearby ruin that rose above the hills, a stone column resembling a broken spear.

"What was that?" Chinelo whispered to Glassow.

"A protection spell, of sorts."

"I thought you were against magic."

Glassow shrugged. "Perhaps Haru is one of the goddesses that smile upon me."

Fenn shoved past Chinelo. "Try to keep up, stranger. Or don't. I'd prefer if the bounty was split across three and not four."

Reaching the crest of another hill, Haru halted. She pointed ahead at a neighboring hill. Strangely, the grass that grew along its surface was much darker than the surrounding hills. It was almost black. Haru turned and ran, climbing up the nearby ruin. She crouched on the rough stone at its peak and nocked an arrow to her bow.

"Here we go," Fenn said, cracking his neck.

Chinelo felt a slight rumbling beneath his feet. He gasped. The dark hill before him moved. It bristled and rolled. Four massive hooves slammed against the earth. Legs like tree trunks ended in enormous shoulders and haunches of pure, feral muscle. The hill turned, revealing a hideous face. It was a boar, and a gargantuan one at that. Its glaring eyes gleamed red. Steam puffed from its girthy snout. Its tusks were like great ivory aspens, curving from the beast's jaws and ending in sharp points. A strip of bright orange fur rose from the creature's arched spine like fire on a mountain ridge.

Chinelo drew his sword and gripped the handle of his shield. The beast growled, watching the hunters with its crimson eyes. Suddenly, Chinelo heard Haru's voice. It was soft yet close.

"Fenn, to the left. Glassow, circle right. Chinelo, center. Keep it still as I prepare my shot."

"Haru?" Chinelo said, looking over his shoulder. She was barely visible from atop the ruin far behind him.

"Focus!" Fenn shouted.

Chinelo turned and faced the massive beast. He approached it with caution, holding his shield before him. Fenn pointed his polearm at the creature, drawing near to its side. Glassow stepped forward slowly, preparing to swing his hammer.

The boar lurched ahead, charging at Chinelo. It roared, swinging its tusks up and down. Chinelo leapt to the side, feeling a powerful rush of wind as the beast tore past him. Rolling to his feet, he turned to face the monster.

"Still! Keep it still," Haru's voice whispered in his ear.

The beast barreled forward, moving like an avalanche towards Chinelo. He thought of the words that had served him well throughout his journey, some of the first words Isobel had taught him.

"Icht vasht'ra!"

Chinelo's sword lit aflame. The beast reared on its hind legs, squealing in fear at the sight of the fire.

A blur shot by Chinelo's side. Fenn dove beneath the boar. Chinelo saw a flash of steel. Fenn's shining blade slashed all four of the beast's legs in a single bloody strike. The great boar roared and stomped its feet around Fenn. He scurried beneath it, dodging the heavy hooves.

Another blur passed by Chinelo. Glassow, with a powerful yell, swung his hammer, striking the creature in the jaw with a booming crack. Its face rippled and recoiled. Fenn and Glassow unleashed a flurry of strikes from both sides as Chinelo watched, waiving his blazing blade in the beast's face.

"Shot ready," Haru whispered.

Fenn and Glassow dashed away, putting distance between themselves and the dazed beast. It shook its head and growled. Then...

A light.

It moved like lightning and crashed like thunder. Piercing the boar's shoulder, it tore through its body before shattering the ground behind it. Haru's arrow had struck its target. The beast squealed and kicked.

"Preparing the next shot," Haru whispered.

Chinelo dashed ahead, swinging his sword. He struck the beast's right foreleg and ducked, narrowly avoiding its tusk. Twisting, he slashed the creature's chin, triggering an additional squeal from his target. Blood spattered across the ground. He bobbed up and down, dodging under the heavy tusks and striking in a chaotic rhythm.

Fenn charged and leapt towards the creature. In midair, he twisted and stabbed his scythe, using his weight to force the blade deep into the thick muscles on the boar's side. He mounted the beast and began pulling on his polearm's shaft to expand the wound he had inflicted. The boar bent and ran, with Fenn desperately clinging to his imbedded weapon. A sudden, violent buck flung him away. With a loud thud he landed in a heap on the ground, coughing and gasping for air.

"My protection has been expended for you, Fenn," Haru whispered.

Fenn scoffed.

Glassow yelled and ran at the creature, rumbling towards it like a crashing boulder. He held his hammer high above him, preparing to deliver a devastating blow. The boar twisted its head, hitting the stocky man with its tusk. Glassow flew back and tumbled across the ground.

"Glassow, use caution," Haru ordered. "You are no longer protected. Please refrain from announcing your attacks."

The boar panted, producing a stream of vapor from its nostrils. It looked from Fenn to Glassow, before finally settling on Chinelo. It lurched forward.

Chinelo dropped his shield. He channeled esht into the spell Isobel had painted across his back, accumulating strength. As the boar neared him, he shifted his esht to his empty outstretched hand and shouted.

"BELEKT TRA'VASHT!"

An explosion released from his hand, startling the boar. It hesitated, attempting to halt its charge. Chinelo capitalized on the opening. Fueled by the small amount of power he had stored, he dashed forward and slashed his broadsword. With his multiplied strength, his blade cleanly sheared one of the tusks from the boar's mouth. Sidestepping around the raging mountain of muscle, Chinelo stabbed his sword deep into the beast's leg, plunging it all the way to its hilt.

"Shot ready, stand clear."

Chinelo tugged at his sword, but it refused to budge. His strength was depleted. Panicking, he released his grip from his weapon, leaving it imbedded in the animal's monstrous hide. The creature ducked its head. Haru's second shot cut through the air, penetrating the animal's gleaming right eye. It roared in rage.

"Apologies," Haru whispered with a slight hint of frustration. "I must have missed its heart. Preparing the third shot."

"Bah, what are you doing Haru?" Fenn yelled. "Useless."

Chinelo focused his esht into his back, accumulating more strength. Without his weapon, he could only rely on his magic and his two hands.

"You and I both are fools," Fenn said, scowling. "Leaving our weapons in our target was an amateur mistake. Well, good luck, stranger. This is where I finish." Fenn put his hands behind his head and walked away nonchalantly.

Chinelo ignored the comment and continued concentrating esht into his back. More, he channeled more. His body grew light. He channeled more. He felt his strength overflow. He channeled more! Has armor felt weightless.

He had been right. Isobel's spell was a masterpiece. He felt that he could topple a mountain.

"Glassow!" Chinelo shouted. "Distract it!"

Glassow nodded and yelled. The disoriented boar swung its head wildly, attempting to find the source of the noise. Glassow moved within the blind spot from its destroyed eye and slammed his hammer into its jaw. The boar's head recoiled. It bucked and swung its tusk into Glassow, launching him.

Chinelo winced.

Glassow was hurt, but he had created the distraction he needed. Chinelo sprinted towards the boar. He bounded over the ground, driven by the wellspring of strength Isobel's spell had granted him. He raised his hands and grabbed the boar's tusk, using it to swing onto its head. Jamming his hands between the tusk and beast's foul maw, he pressed outwards, gripping the boar's head with his thighs. Over the giant hog's bucking and screaming, he heard a faint cracking, then a tear. The tusk began to budge. Chinelo gritted his teeth and pushed even harder. With a horrific rip, he tore the tusk from the creature's face, leaving a gaping wound.

Leaping from the monster's head, Chinelo twisted and landed on the ground. He grabbed the broken tusk and smashed it into the boar's cheek, shattering it in the process. Fragments of ivory fell to the ground.

"Chinelo, kindly step to your left," Haru whispered.

Chinelo leaned to the side. A bolt of light shot through the boar's forehead. Its body convulsed as the arrow flew down its spine before blasting out of its back and rupturing the ground behind it. The boar collapsed in a cloud of dust and dirt.

"Target has been slain," Haru whispered.

Chinelo let out a long sigh of relief. His body ached. His arms and legs had mysteriously grown heavy.

Glassow limped over to the fallen monster and kicked its side. "That's what you get, you stupid pig! You were foolish to challenge the might of Glassow."

Chinelo felt a hand on his shoulder. Fenn stood at his side. "Impressive work, Chinelo. Not sure how you managed to do that," he gestured toward the carcass, "but you have my respect."

Haru joined the crew and looked at her work. She nodded in approval.

"So! Care to join us for drinks when we get back?" Fenn elbowed Chinelo. "Celebration is a requirement in this business."

Chinelo smiled. "I should probably return to the inn to check on my companion, but perhaps I could bring her after?"

Haru stepped forward. "Please, do!"

"You're allowing another woman to join us?" Fenn inquired, raising an eyebrow.

"Of course. Where else shall I find reasonable conversation?"

Haru winked, or at least Chinelo thought it was a wink. Her eyepatch made that unclear, but the expression had felt like a wink.

"It's settled then!" Fenn said. "To the Dusty Dog!"

Isobel bent over her diary, scribbling down the events of the previous few days. After her nighttime conversation with Chinelo, she had gotten to bed much later than usual and had skipped her customary diary session. The pen felt heavy in her hand. Having spent almost all of her esht enchanting lanterns that day, her body was fatigued. As much as she hated to admit it, she would need to prioritize sleeping over chatting that evening.

After writing the date at the top of the page, she set the pen down and leaned back in her chair. She raised her hand above her and opened it, staring at its back. She still felt it, the sensation of his fingers between hers. She closed her eyes and smiled, clasping her hands to her chest.

From within the sink, Mort watched her solemnly. She'd attended to his every need as was expected of her, but still, her split focus disturbed him. The usurper must be dealt with.

She glanced at the window. The sun was getting low in the sky. Where was he? He'd left at the same time as her, but even after the full day, he was absent. Was he all right? Had something gone wrong with the hunt?

She shook her head. She'd witnessed his skill before. She knew he was perfectly capable of taking care of himself, even without the assistance of magic.

A light clattering came from the adjacent room. Isobel sat up. On bare feet she walked across the carpet and peaked through Chinelo's door. He struggled to undo the clasps of his armor. She smiled, silently watching him. After a few moments she cleared her throat.

"Oh! Isobel!" Chinelo started. "You're back already."

Isobel leaned against the door frame and nodded. "How did it—oh my, is that blood?"

Chinelo's breastplate had spatters of red across it. "Pig's blood, yes. Sorry. I guess I missed a few patches when I was scrubbing down."

"So, you've taken up butchering?"

"Not quite. Just boar riding."

"I'm sure that must have been quite the sight. One that I am sorry to have missed," Isobel said as she stepped into the room. "So, how was it actually?"

"Well, the crew I was working with certainly had some colorful characters."

"Oh?" Isobel began assisting with the fasteners of his armor. "Tell me about them."

"I have another idea. Want to meet them?"

Isobel looked up and cocked her head. "Meet them?"

Chinelo nodded and flashed a quick smile. "They've invited us for drinks. Both of us."

"I'd love to," Isobel said. She struggled with a particularly stubborn buckle. "Though I won't be drinking much. Have to save money, after all."

"I... I don't think we will need to worry about money for a while, Isobel."

"Oh?" Isobel loosened the straps fastening Chinelo's pauldrons. "How much was the bounty?"

"Five thousand crescents."

"Five thousand! I thought you said it was a pig."

"It was a very big pig."

"I'm going to need to sell more lanterns to keep up with that."

Chinelo dropped his gauntlets and began working on the breastplate. "How'd your day go?"

Isobel sighed. "Not quite as well as I'd hoped. The vendor I found wasn't very enthused about working with me, but I managed to persuade her."

"You *can* be very persuasive." Chinelo winked.

"Oh, stop." Isobel removed Chinelo's breastplate and set it on the floor. "We only managed to sell a couple of the lamps I made, and she refused to list them at the price I suggested. Still, two hundred isn't the worst haul. I just wish she would have listened to me more."

"I'm sorry it didn't go as well as you hoped. Though, on the bright side, two hundred will at least cover the inn fees and food for a few more days."

"Right." Isobel added his gaiters to the growing pile of armor. "There, all finished."

She sprung to her feet and looked up at him expectantly.

Chinelo stretched and sighed. "I am in intense need of a bath now, so I'm going to visit the washroom before we go." He gathered a change of clothes from his pack and hurried out the door, leaving a slightly disappointed Isobel behind.

CHAPTER 18

ISOBEL'S THROAT BURNED. SHE COUGHED, RUBBING her neck and wrinkling her nose. Her sinuses filled with a pungent vapor emitted by the drink that scorched its way down her esophagus.

"Absolutely not," she said, smacking her lips in disgust. She reached for her cup of water and downed it, attempting to wash away the harsh aftertaste. She slid the tankard back to Haru, who sat chuckling beside her. "You drink that? And you enjoy it?"

Haru merely smiled and took a large swig from the flagon.

"Wait, wait. Chinelo, you must try this!" Isobel said, tapping his arm.

Haru slid her tankard to Chinelo. He lifted it and took an apprehensive sip. The corners of his mouth shot downwards, and his face contorted. He gulped down the swill and gasped.

"That has quite—" He coughed. "Quite the bite to it. Wow." His eyes watered. He slid the drink back to Haru.

Fenn let out the loud laugh he had been pretending to contain. The occupants of the other tables at the Dusty Dog looked at him with minor hints of disgust. "Well, call me surprised. After that display with the pig, I would have thought you could handle a man's drink, Chinelo."

Chinelo shrugged. "We do not often drink in my homeland. It's a tradition that never carried over to the southern peninsula."

The Dusty Dog lived up to half of its name. Lit by lanterns of frosted glass and a large central fireplace, it was dingy and dark. Customers huddled around circular wooden tables on humble oak stools, sipping from tankards of various spirits. Large kegs were stored against a back wall, arranged in a honeycomb pattern that was topped with a thick layer of dust.

A single brunette waitress scurried back and forth, splashing frothy cups of liquor, and balancing large trays of minced eggplant and braised meat on her arms. She was short, even shorter than Isobel, and her billowing skirt swished as she hurried between the tables. The entire establishment was permeated by the strong scent of fermented citrus, the rich smell of sizzling pork, and a noticeable hint of body odor. Not a dog was in sight, much to Isobel's disappointment.

Glassow had arrived very late, and his face was mottled in a variety of colors. Purple and green from the bruises, yellow from the drink that dribbled down his chin, and most notably, a rising wave of red creeping across his round cheeks. He sat across the table, fidgeting with his short round fingers. He had not said much, instead muttering to himself and gradually growing more and more flushed. Fenn, on the other hand, had not stopped yapping with much-exaggerated accounts of their hunting quest.

"So, anyways, this fellow—" Fenn slapped Chinelo on the shoulder. "He charges like a madman at the boar and punches it between the eyes. Then he grabs its tusk, rips it clean off its face, bludgeons it into a paste, and proceeds to skewer it and cook it on a spit. Funniest thing I've ever seen."

Isobel raised an eyebrow and glanced at Chinelo. He shook his head.

Fenn continued, "And now they're serving the meat here! Better eat up Bella and Chella! It's not getting any fresher than this."

"Chella?" Glassow scoffed.

"Yeah, Chinelo! Chella. You know I always give my closest friends nicknames? Eh, Glassy?"

Glassow rolled his eyes.

"This morning, Fenn, I would have thought that you hated me," Chinelo commented.

"Hated you?" Fenn looked flabbergasted. "You wound me, dear friend! I just didn't know how impressive you would be. No, no. You're a man's man, and I respect a man's man. In fact, you should join us on our next hunt! Do you approve, Haru?"

Haru nodded. "I'd be curious to see Isobel in action, myself. It's always a pleasure to witness the work of a fellow mage."

"Oh, I'm no fighter," Isobel demurred. "But I appreciate the sentiment."

"I'm pretty sure you could have killed that boar all on your own," Chinelo said, giving her hand a light squeeze beneath the table.

Isobel blushed.

Fenn took a heavy swig from his drink. "Now let me tell you about the time Glassy got his hammer stuck up a—"

Haru bolted upright. "My tankard has gone dry. Care to join me at the bar, Isobel?"

"I'd love to."

The two left the table and weaved through the disorganized tavern, finally reaching the bar on the far side of the establishment. Their feet left footprints on the dusty floor. Fenn looked after them. His cheery expression wilted.

Ψ

Glassow slammed his hand on the table. "Chinelo! How dare you?"

Chinelo raised his eyebrows and leaned on his elbow.

Glassow muttered something beneath his breath and continued. "You didn't tell me she was that... that... gorgeous!"

"You never asked."

"By Nakam! I need to find someone like that." Glassow sighed and took a sip from his cup.

"Ehhhh. She's not really *my* type," Fenn said, leaning against the table. "I prefer a woman with a bit more—ahem—volume. You know what I mean? Eh, Chella?" He elbowed Chinelo in the ribs.

"Thank you for your opinion on the topic, Fenn," Chinelo replied flatly. "I'm sure the entire tavern would love to hear about it."

The waitress dropped a steaming tray of braised pork shoulder onto the table. "These two causing you trouble, friend?"

Glassow perked up in his seat. "Oh, we would never! My Sefiya, you look ravishing today."

"And you look like you lost a fight," she jabbed.

Fenn let out a booming laugh. "He did actually! Let me tell you all about it!"

"Always a pleasure, gentlemen!" Sefiya hurried back to the kitchen. Fenn wilted even more. Even his mustache seemed to droop in dismay.

Glassow let out a melancholy sigh. "One day, perhaps she'll notice me. One day."

Fenn began voraciously cutting the slab of meat into slices. Chinelo deposited a small cut onto his plate and looked over his shoulder at the bar. Haru and Isobel were locked in conversation. Isobel's lips moved rapidly, and she motioned and gestured with her hands as Haru nodded. They would be a while.

"So, what's the next hunt?" Chinelo asked, taking a bite of the meat.

Glassow grinned and leaned forward. "One of the nobles wants a magmaw skull for his foyer. He's contracted us to acquire one."

"What is a magmaw?"

Fenn laughed. "Monsters over in Caald. They're big stone lizards."

Glassow's sly smile turned into a devious smirk. "They're massive and very ill-tempered. They eat lava, Chinelo."

"And you intend to kill one?" Chinelo asked.

"I intend to slaughter one." Glassow's eyes flickered wickedly.

Chinelo shuddered. Perhaps there were multiple reasons why women didn't accept Glassow.

"Fenn! Is that you?" a deep voice called from the tavern entryway.

"Barlow!" Fenn replied. "Good to see you! Come! Come! Sit!" He waived his hand to the empty seats.

"Oh! Talia! You're here, too!" Glassow said with sudden enthusiasm.

A man sat at the table in Haru's seat. His peaked bald head reflected the light of the fireplace, and his short black beard was groomed neatly on his chin. Beside him sat a young woman with long blonde braided hair. They were dressed in long robes, robes of dark green with gold filigree, robes of the Interior Guard.

Haru leaned against the bar and sipped her drink. "You'll have to pardon the company I keep. Those two are good souls, but they aren't known for their manners."

"Oh, it's fine Haru. They are very amusing," Isobel chimed. "I've enjoyed hearing Fenn's tall tales. I'm not sure what to make of Glassow, though."

"He doesn't do well around women, especially ones he finds attractive." Haru shook her head. "Try as I might, that man never learns."

"I've encountered the type," Isobel chuckled, thinking back to her experiences in her early years in Nellborough.

"So, you and Chinelo are travelling to Caald?" Haru asked.

Isobel nodded. "We have business in Ata."

"Ah, my hometown."

"Really?" Isobel clasped her hands. "Tell me about it!"

Haru looked at the ceiling. "Not much to tell. It's small, but it's home. Good people. They lead a hard life, dealing with the lava fields. They are not used to outsiders. Remember that."

"Good to know."

"And your home?" Haru said. "Why did you leave it?"

Isobel looked away. "Do you always ask such questions?"

"If it seems worthwhile."

Isobel rubbed the tattoo on her wrist. "If it's all right, I'm not terribly enthused to talk about that right now. Chinelo and I—our journey did not begin under pleasant circumstances." She shook her head. "No. Let's just enjoy the night."

Haru nodded. "Your companion tells me you know magic. Judging by those tattoos, you must be quite skilled."

"Oh, I'm hardly all that! Just a simple scholar. And you? What do you specialize in?"

Haru smiled. "Protection, for my companions. I've studied other applications, as well, but protection is my preference. What is yours?"

"Hmmm. I've never really thought about it." Isobel shrugged. "I suppose nullification. Though, that's mostly inherited from my mother. I've not really found another Aspect I favor yet. I just enjoy trying new things."

"Nullification? I've not heard of such a technique."

Isobel's face lit up. "Oh! It's surprisingly simple. It functions on a similar principle to esht siphoning if you are familiar with that. Instead of pulling formless external esht toward you, you scatter formed esht in random directions. Think of it like blowing on a dandelion. It starts as a flower, but then the seeds scatter, and it is no longer a flower. If you structure your spell properly, you can use that to disrupt any active spells and effectively cancel them. Though, it's a rather draining process, unfortunately. I'm sure you understand."

Haru smiled. "Clever. So, how did you learn of the Ancient Arts?"

Isobel looked down. "I was born into it, in a sense. It's a long story, but I was raised by witches. That's the origin of it, at least. The rest is owed more to my own curiosity. What about you?"

Haru sighed and closed her eye. "When you've lived as long as I have, you will have had many opportunities to see and learn strange things. My husband was one of those strange things. Perhaps I am now."

Isobel cocked her head. "I don't follow."

"He and I were self-taught." Haru opened her eye and looked at Isobel. "Though our time in the Interior Guard provided ample resources for study."

Isobel's stomach twisted. Instinctively, she moved away from Haru. "You... you were in the Interior Guard?"

"Before you were born. You need not fear me."

Isobel looked down. She rubbed the scar she had received from the Branded Mage's blade.

Haru sipped her drink. "When the current Archmage took command of the Interior Guard, I left. My husband did not."

Isobel's breath caught in her throat. The Archmage, her enemy. She needed information about him.

"The Archmage. What is he like?"

Haru's face grew cold. "He is a scoundrel. A very clever scoundrel who has the charisma and eloquence to hide his nature, but a scoundrel, nevertheless. He promised so much, yet he trampled so many. His lust for knowledge twisted the Interior Guard into its current state."

"Do you think..." Isobel said, "do you think he would go so far as to destroy a country for knowledge?"

Haru raised an eyebrow. "That is an odd and very telling question, Isobel. You suspect that he is responsible for Eshgar?"

"I... I didn't say that."

"Young lady, your companion wears Eshgarian armor, but he does not travel with other knights. News travels slowly, but even we have heard of what happened there. It is not difficult to draw conclusions."

Isobel looked down at her trousers.

Haru frowned. "Archmage Harlyle is an insatiable man who would stop at nothing to increase his own power and knowledge. He is exceptionally versed in the Ancient Arts, and he leverages that for his own gain. He is subject only to the king, and the king is a coward. You would be wise not to make an enemy of him. That is the answer I will give."

Isobel clenched her fist. It was a little late for that.

Haru glanced down. Her frown deepened. She cleared her throat.

"Your companion seemed to know a few very unique tricks," Haru noted. She placed her tankard on the bar counter and crossed her arms. "I assume that the fire and strength enhancement were learned from your teachings?"

Isobel smiled. So, he *had* tried her spell. "Yes, in a sense. Was the spell that obvious?"

"No man can just casually tear the tusks off of beast like that."

"Oh! So that part of the story was real."

Haru chuckled. "I would be curious to know how you managed to teach him to use fire. I never could translate that word."

"Well, that's supposedly a coven secret, but—Oh!"

Chinelo's hand was on her shoulder.

"Isobel," he hissed, "we need to leave."

Isobel tilted her head. "Leave? Why? Haru and I were enjoying ourselves."

"The Interior Guard is here."

Isobel's stomach lurched. Haru scowled and glared across the room at the table where Fenn, Glassow, and three guardsmen sat laughing over one of Fenn's rambunctious tales.

"There's more," Chinelo said, his dark eyes darting back to the table. "They're going to Ata in two days. I think—I think they are trying to find the obelisk."

Haru flung the door of her small stone house open. Torch light from the streetlamps flooded past the doorframe, dimly illuminating the space.

While they ran through the dark streets of Dawngale, Chinelo had informed Haru and Isobel of the conversation he heard at the table.

Barlow and two other guardsmen planned to visit Ata in search of an ancient artifact. Chinelo had been fortunate that Fenn was so well trusted by the guardsmen.

"Candle! There!" Haru pointed in the darkness.

Isobel conjured a flame on her finger and lit the candle. From a small cupboard, Haru produced a tattered, empty sack. She filled it with food from her pantry, snatching items from the shelves and tossing them into the bag.

Isobel ran her fingers through her hair and exhaled a long anxious breath. She was trembling. Chinelo peaked out the door and watched the streets. They had not been followed.

Haru spoke. "You can reach Ata by two different routes. Either skirt the wall along the main highway or climb the breach and cross the flatlands."

Chinelo joined Isobel. She had dropped to a squatting position and was holding her temples with her hands.

"Which way is faster?" he asked.

Haru tied the bag and placed it on the counter. "Climbing the breach. It cuts off at least two days, though you must cross the lava fields. In the daylight, those are quite safe, but at night they are treacherous. The Interior Guard will be unable to go that way. They travel with horse-drawn wagons."

Chinelo touched his chin. "That will give us four days."

"Gah!" Isobel said. "I should have known they would already be searching for more. I'd hoped they were moving north instead of east."

"If we can activate the obelisk before them, perhaps they won't strike the town," Chinelo said. He placed his hand on her shaking shoulder. "Remember? They investigated Nellborough for weeks before the blast."

"We can hope," Isobel murmured. "Assuming I can learn how to activate it in time."

Haru handed Chinelo the bag she had filled. "This is not much, but it should last you a few days. Food is scarce on the lava fields. Unfortunately, I only have enough for the two of you. I will gather provisions in the morning and follow."

She opened a box and drew out several paper slips. "This is ko, the currency of Caald. In Ata, they do not accept crescents."

"Thank you, Haru! You've done so much for us!" Isobel held Haru's wrinkled hand gently. "I wish there was some way we could repay you."

"Live. That is all I ask. You will reach the breach within a few hours. I'd advise you wait to climb it until there is light," Haru said. She whispered a long incantation beneath her breath and touched Isobel's forehead with two fingers. "Go! You are protected."

CHAPTER 19

THE LIGHTS OF DAWNGALE HAD VANISHED, consumed by the shadow of the great wall that loomed beside the road. Isobel walked swiftly, attempting to keep up with Chinelo's pace. She was exhausted. Her body was plagued by the fatigue of esht drain, and her legs were still sore from the months of walking. She felt Mort hanging onto her shoulder, and even he seemed to weigh her down.

Ahead, Chinelo's armor jostled and shone as it swung from his pack, reflecting the light of the lantern she had fastened to her staff. How did he move so quickly? Had he been holding back this whole time, walking at a pace she could handle? She panted, straining under her load.

Still, she was driven to push forward, driven by her desire to save the people of Ata, driven by her goal to reverse fate, driven by the hopes she tried so desperately to cultivate and the fears she tried so desperately to ignore.

The lantern flickered and went dark. Chinelo stopped.

"Out of oil?" he asked.

"Yes. Sorry, I must have forgotten to check it before we left. I'll make a light for us so that we can replenish it."

Isobel concentrated, trying to channel the last remnants of her esht into her staff. She winced. Stabbing pain afflicted her entire body, as if thousands of nails were being driven into her skin. Pushing further would have permanent consequences.

"Mort," Isobel said, gritting her teeth, "I need your assistance."

From the point where Mort sat upon her shoulder, Isobel felt a spreading tingling sensation. Esht flowed into her. It moved down her body, accumulating beneath her heart. Harnessing the energy, she gave a command. "Light!"

A glowing orb formed from her staff and hovered above her. Isobel dropped her pack, producing a small flask of oil to refill the lantern.

"I'll hold off on lighting it until my light goes out," Isobel said. "It will save us some oil that way."

Chinelo fidgeted on his feet.

Oil slowly filled the lantern's reservoir and soaked into the wick. After a moment, Isobel stopped up the flask and returned it to her pack.

"Ready!"

Chinelo resumed his pace.

How did he move so quickly? He should have been tired from his hunt earlier in the day. Was he using her spell to give himself strength? No. He had scrubbed the paint from his shoulders when he bathed. Isobel panted and forced herself forward.

The moon was shrouded by clouds. A few stars twinkled in the gaps in the cloud cover, but most of the sky was an inky black void. Isobel could faintly see trees, hills, and other strange shapes beyond her light's radius. To her right, there was only the dark shape of the wall. While in Dawngale, she had not truly grasped how tall it would be, but at its foot, she felt so small, as if she were some ant creeping along the side of a castle. It reached high, so high that the very sky seemed to rest upon it.

She had heard stories of ruins and structures such as these, told to her by her mother. Esther had said that the gods once ruled the continent, building great cities and citadels from which they oversaw their realms. In the depictions Isobel had seen, the gods were great lumbering titans cloaked in smoke and mist. She had always imagined that those depictions were exaggerations. No living creature could be that large. The wall contradicted that assumption. Isobel shuddered.

The gods had vanished, leaving behind only vestiges of their magic and ruins of their civilizations. If they still walked the continent, would they have stopped the destruction of Eshgar? Could they undo the end of Nellborough? Would they prevent the impending doom of Ata?

Isobel's toe collided with a stone that was imbedded deep in the ground. She suppressed a faint cry and stumbled. Chinelo continued on. How did he move so quickly?

"Chinelo! I need a moment to catch my breath."

Chinelo stopped and turned. The light illuminated his worried face.

"Do you want to stop for the night?"

"No. No. Just give me a moment. I'm struggling to match your pace."

Chinelo stepped closer. "I apologize. I haven't been paying attention."

Isobel leaned against her staff. "You've done nothing wrong. I understand we need to cover ground quickly. My legs are just shorter than yours, and I'm still very fatigued from today."

"Ah. Would you like to lead going forward?"

Isobel shook her head. "I like having you in front. It makes me feel safe."

Chinelo smiled. "Very well, then I will aim to walk at a more comfortable pace."

Isobel nodded in assent. She was grateful she was not alone.

The ground shook. Isobel looked up. A nearby shape moved in the darkness, emitting a faint growling that was slowly growing louder. Chinelo stepped in front of her.

"Isobel. What is the word for launch?"

"Launch?" Isobel asked nervously.

"In the Ancient Tongue."

"Fet."

Chinelo nodded. He outstretched his arm, forcing his palm toward the noise.

"Icht vasht'ra va ogo iv fet!"

Flame burst from his hand and curled, forming itself into a tight sphere. It grew, expanding into a raging fireball. Chinelo relaxed his forearm, and the sphere flew from his hand, piercing the darkness. It crashed into the hill, creating a burst of light that revealed the startled form of a great wild boar. It squealed and ran away, fleeing in terror from Chinelo's flame.

Isobel looked at him proudly. She thought through his words in her head. *Form flames as a sphere and launch.* Her face beamed.

"I'm impressed! You've learned!"

"I've been taught very well."

"I never taught you that specific incantation, though. That's one that I normally trigger with my staff."

Chinelo shrugged. "I'm beginning to understand how the words fit together. I just rearranged what I already knew."

"Exactly! That's what magic is! Rearranging what you know in new ways! It's like poetry!"

Chinelo nodded. He fidgeted, shifting on his feet. He wished to continue onwards. It was obvious to Isobel. She shook herself. "I'm ready, Chinelo."

He set off again but at a slower pace. Isobel's light flickered out. He sighed.

"I'm sorry," she said. "I'll light the lantern now."

Isobel lowered her staff and hovered her finger over the wick. She focused, trying to gather any esht she had left. Her pain returned. She groaned. A wave of exhaustion washed over her. She heard Chinelo shuffling on his feet ahead of her, anxious to continue.

"Chinelo, are..." she paused. "Are you mad at me?"

Chinelo turned around sharply. "What? Why would I be mad at you?"

"I can't keep up with your pace, and I keep slowing us down. You sighed and... you sounded annoyed."

"Isobel, I'm not mad at you. Stressed, yes, but given the circumstances that seems appropriate."

She heard him draw close to her. His figure was barely visible in the dark.

"Would you tell me if you were mad?" she whispered.

"I would."

"Could you... hold my hand again?"

"If you want me to." He found her hand in the darkness. His touch soothed her just as the birdsongs once did. She closed her eyes.

"What would you like me to do, Isobel?" Chinelo asked. "I can listen. I can talk."

"Could you light the lantern this time?" Isobel asked.

"Anything for you." He conjured a flame on his finger and lit the lantern.

Chinelo suddenly winced and released his hand.

"I'm sorry," Isobel said. "I didn't know you were already low, too."

"Oh, that's what was going on?" Chinelo said, shaking out his hand. "I was wondering why that last spell was so uncomfortable."

"You're likely fatigued from esht depletion. We both are."

"We should stop soon."

Isobel nodded. Soon, they rounded a sharp bend in the wall and halted as a shard of stone stood in their path.

"The wall! It's broken up there." Chinelo pointed.

Isobel looked up. A jagged crack extended down the wall. The damaged stone was rough with many edges and outcroppings that rose like stairs toward a gaping hole near the wall's apex. The lantern cast strange, terrifying shadows up the wall. They looked like great insects waiting to pounce on unsuspecting prey. They had reached the breach.

Chinelo appraised the wall. "We should be able to climb that, but certainly not tonight. Let's set up camp here."

Isobel had already dropped her pack. Together, they laid out their bedding beneath the stone shard. They built no fire, for they had neither the energy to gather firewood nor the will to dig out a flint kit from their packs. Isobel extinguished the lantern, and they were left alone, huddled in the darkness.

Isobel wrapped herself tightly in her blanket. She wished she could go back to the city. The two days they spent there had been pleasant. Things almost felt normal. She wanted just one more day to pretend that she wasn't burdened with the weight of her friends' deaths. She wanted just one more day to pretend that she didn't fear for her life. She wanted just one more day to pretend that she wasn't constantly physically and mentally exhausted. She had been walking for so long. The long days, the sleepless nights, when would they end?

Things had been good. She had been happy living with Chinelo. She had been happy dreaming about traveling together. She had been happy when he agreed to see the world with her. She had been happy knowing that no matter how far she went, she would always have the people in Nellborough to welcome her home. Why did things have to change?

She squeezed her eyes shut. She was being selfish. Thousands of lives had been lost, and here she was, thinking about childish fantasies. Even when she was happy, Chinelo had been carrying the burden she now carried. Before her, he too had been happy in Eshgar. Was it selfish of her to want to go back to a time when she was content while he suffered? He had stayed with her out of convenience. He needed a bed, and she had provided it. He needed work, and she had provided it. And now, he needed hope, and she provided it.

If all that were gone, would he stay? If they were able to reverse fate and undo what had happened, would he have a need for her anymore?

Would anyone? Would she be alone again? She had been alone when her mother had died. She had been alone when she left the Red Coven. She had been alone when Iva departed on missions. She didn't want to be alone again. The thought of that haunting silence, that relentless emptiness frightened her.

She closed her eyes even tighter. She was being childish. Hundreds more were going to die soon, and she was worried about herself.

Would he truly care for her, knowing she was selfish?

A lump rose in her throat. Her body shook as she tried to suppress a sob. She sniffled. She felt a cold chill as a single teardrop ran down her cheek.

She felt Chinelo's hand tap against her shoulder. She jumped.

"Isobel, are you all right?"

She paused. "Yes." Her voice wavered.

"You're sobbing."

"I—" she brushed her cheek with her fingers. "I—" the words would not come. She sat up and pressed her hands to her eyes. Why couldn't she stop crying?

She heard a scuffling beside her. His strong arm wrapped around her shoulders, drawing her closer.

"Hey. You're not alone," Chinelo whispered.

"Please... please don't leave."

"I won't. I promise."

Rain began to fall, pattering on the dirt beyond the shelter.

Chinelo woke before sunrise. The rain had stopped, leaving only damp earth and dense fog behind. Against the fog was Isobel's silhouette, seated on a rock that was mysteriously dry. Mort squatted on the ground beneath the stone, surveying his new kingdom regally. Chinelo crawled from his bed and joined her.

"I'm not letting them die," Isobel said. Her voice was low, determined, and... angry? "They've taken enough. These people will not be next. I'll claim the obelisks' power, and I will stop the Archmage and his Interior Guard."

Chinelo nodded. She rarely spoke like this, but when she did, he felt that the very world would obey.

"*We* will," he corrected.

Isobel leaned against him. Not heavily, but just enough so that he could feel she was there.

"We must climb," she said. "I'll make a path."

She stood and turned to face the breach. It shimmered and dripped from the water it had accumulated during the storm. She outstretched her hand towards the wall.

"SONO GEST, ECHT SONE!"

Chinelo watched as the water that fell from the breach instantly became mist, blanketing the surface.

Isobel extended both hands toward the breach.

"BELEKT FULRECH!"

The vapor was pushed skyward by a powerful blast of wind from Isobel's hands. Hit by the gust, Chinelo staggered. The rough crack that was the breach was dry. It rose high above them, broken into a series of ledges.

After eating, Isobel drew a small brush and vial of paint from her pack. She had used it once before to paint the enhancement spell on Chinelo's shoulders.

"Extend your arm."

Chinelo did as he was told. Isobel painted runes on his forearm. She nodded, then painted the same runes on her own arm.

"What are those, Isobel?" Chinelo asked.

"Strength multiplication, like the one I made for you earlier. I imagine climbing will be difficult with our gear. Just remember it's in a different location than it was yesterday. It's a bit chilly out, so I'm not about to ask you to disrobe while I paint this on you. Plus, your pack straps would probably smudge the paint and that would make it useless."

Chinelo nodded. He carefully donned his pack, threading his arm through the strap slowly to avoid smearing the inscription. Isobel called to Mort, who begrudgingly came hopping to her side. He did not appreciate his morning sunbathing being interrupted.

"I'm sorry Mort, but it's probably best if you hide in my pack for now," Isobel said, softly petting the frog's back.

Mort scowled.

"Just think of how great the nap will be!" Isobel opened her hand.

Mort grumpily crawled onto her palm. She made a small nest for him out of a folded shirt and deposited him at the top of her pack, covering him with the wide leather flap used to close it. After securing her staff to her pack, she and Chinelo approached the wall. Their destination, the great crack above, was no short climb away.

Chinelo searched for handholds and footholds. Finding a small crevice with his fingers, he hauled himself off the ground before stumbling and falling back. His forearms ached. He channeled esht into the spell on his arm and tried again. He managed to stay on the wall and climbed up to a nearby ledge. Isobel followed, but at a much quicker pace.

They climbed in stages, one after the other, moving from broken ledge to broken ledge. The climb was tedious, especially with their loaded packs. Boots were not meant for climbing, and the footing was difficult and unsteady. Many times, Chinelo lost his footing and nearly fell, hanging on only by the power Isobel had granted him. His fingertips burned, irritated by the rough stone edges he used as handholds. His callouses ached as they pressed against his skin. His forearms were painfully tense. Reaching a wide outcropping, he sat back and shook out his hands. Isobel joined him and stared up at the crack. They were close. She had barely broken a sweat.

"Isobel, are you a climber?" Chinelo panted.

She shook her head. "I've climbed trees before, but never anything like this."

"Well, you're handling this impressively well. Putting me to shame."

"I am a lot lighter than you. And the magic helps."

She looked down at her palms. "The rock does seem to have some unfortunate effects on my skin. My hands have gone raw."

"Raw? Shouldn't Haru's spell protect against that?"

Isobel shook her head. "Not from what I heard her say. It's worded to protect against impacts and similar injuries. Abrasions like this are exempt, probably so that it holds when it actually needs to."

Pressing her palms together, she closed her eyes. After a moment, she released them. "There! All better!"

Isobel looked down at the route they had followed. She cocked her head. "It's strange. The outer surface would suggest that this wall was formed from unbroken stone, but the broken bits look more like fragmented blocks."

"How is that so strange?"

Isobel turned to face him. "Stone must be cut. Making stone blocks of this size with the level of precision necessary to hide all seams wouldn't be possible even with modern equipment."

"I never knew you were so fascinated with stonework." ,

Isobel flushed and turned away. "I—back in Nellborough, when I first moved there, I was courted by the son of a stone mason. He liked to talk about his work. A lot." Mort croaked from within the pack with a noticeable note of displeasure.

"Ah." Chinelo nodded.

"He was nice, but a little dense. That was a long time ago, though."

"Was this the one that proposed to you?" Chinelo inquired.

Isobel shook her head. "No, no. That was Griggs. His father is—I mean—was the sheriff."

"You never did explain that story." Chinelo scratched his head. "You said you rejected him?"

"Yes. It was very strange. No idea what he was thinking."

"You weren't a couple?" Chinelo asked.

"He seemed to think we were." Isobel looked back up at the crack. "I suppose a lot of people did."

Chinelo made a slight noise in acknowledgment and adjusted the ties of his boots.

"It's a shame, really," Isobel said. "I thought we could have remained friends..."

"Sometimes that's hard—being around people you once loved. It can be difficult, even if you don't want it to be." Chinelo looked down. Memories of Kam creeped into his mind. He shook his head. He didn't want to think about her.

Isobel seemed to have similar thoughts. "Let's not speak of the past."

Chinelo drew in a deep nervous breath. She was right. Their future was what mattered. Some things had been left unsaid, and he wanted to ensure that they did not remain that way. "This may be inappropriate, given our current circumstances," Chinelo said, "and this may not even be the right wording—I'm not totally familiar with the customs of your country..." He hesitated.

Isobel looked down. "Yes?"

"I'm sorry. The absurdity of asking this on a cliffside is not lost on me, but are we—I mean—do you want to—could we court each other?"

Isobel didn't answer, but she did smile.

Chinelo scratched the back of his neck. Pressure built in his chest. "Sorry, I know there's a lot going on right now. Perhaps I'm confused, but I thought—"

"I'd like that, Chinelo. That would make me very happy. It won't be in the traditional method, of course, but let's try, as best we can."

Chinelo felt the pressure ease. "Good. Sorry. I didn't want you to wonder about how I felt about you. You know how it is. Communicating intentions is important."

Isobel squatted and grabbed both his hands, her face beaming. "Thank you."

Another displeased squawk sounded from Isobel's pack. Unlike her, Mort was not "very happy." Isobel rolled her eyes. "Such a villain. He just has to ruin the moment. Well! Shall we continue?"

Chinelo stood, preparing for the next pitch of the climb. He accumulated strength, then began his ascent. He somehow felt a little bit lighter than before. He climbed, crimping and pinching on the torn rock. Nearing the edge of the breach, he twisted his body to reach a handhold and hauled himself into the crack. It stretched cleanly through the stone wall, and the blue sky was visible on the other side. Chinelo turned and lowered his hand, assisting Isobel with the final push.

"We made it!" Isobel said cheerfully.

They traversed the large crack before stopping to look over the foreign land beyond. The ground below was black, an endless field of igneous rock with steam vents that shot towering pillars of vapor into the sky. Strange brown piles of stone were scattered across the plains. It was beautiful but barren.

"Are you ready?" Isobel asked.

Chinelo took a deep breath and shook out his arms "As ready as I'll ever be."

Isobel nodded and began her descent. Chinelo accumulated his strength and followed, slowly climbing the steep stone wall towards the dark land below.

CHAPTER 20

THE TERRAIN WAS DESOLATE, LIFELESS, AND unwelcoming. Streaks of pure white calcium ran over the solidified lava rock. The wind blew vapor from a nearby steam vent, carrying with it the unpleasant stench of sulfur. Small tufts of coarse grass rustled with the passing breezes. This was Caald.

Isobel stepped carefully over sharp shards of obsidian and pumice, following the faint path that cut across the land. They had been walking for several hours, and the sun was reaching its apex. Though the weather had cooled significantly with autumn's final days, the ground radiated heat. Isobel had removed her coat and stored it in her pack much earlier and in the process had returned Mort to his rightful throne upon her shoulder. Chinelo walked beside her, picking his way over the rough rock and stone. He was smiling, and there was a noticeable spring in his step. Isobel was not much different.

They passed one of the strange brown rock mounds she had seen from the breach. Isobel eyed it curiously. What was it? It was a different color than the rest of the black landscape. The stones seemed to be separate but somehow connected. If they were not so pressed for time, she would have gone closer to investigate. She shrugged and looked ahead, shading her eyes from the sun with her hand.

The path stretched to the horizon. It did not turn, it did not bend, it merely rose and fell over the waves of lava rock. Beyond it, there was only the pale blue sky. Even the wall disappeared below the horizon, far off in the distance. The land was unbelievable vast. Far to the southwest she saw great plumes of gray smoke rising to the sky and mingling with the clouds. The lava must have originated from somewhere, and the plumes likely marked the source.

Her stomach growled.

"Want to eat soon?" Chinelo asked.

"Is it that obvious?"

Chinelo sent her a mischievous look. "Let's stop at that stone pile ahead."

They halted near one of the strange formations. A ridge of brown rock curved from the mound. Sitting on the ridge, Chinelo untied his armor from his pack, giving access to the flap at the top. He set the armor to the side and drew forth Haru's supply bag.

"Isobel, I've always wondered something," Chinelo said after sipping from his flask. "You can create water with your esht, right?"

"That's correct. Though create isn't quite the right word." Isobel dug through the bag and found a large chunk of bread.

"So, why don't we drink that?"

"Have you ever tried drinking your own spit?"

Chinelo laughed. "Why would I do that?"

"Exactly. The result of drinking something you generated with magic is similar."

"Ah."

Isobel tossed him a piece of bread. It was not the heartiest of meals, but it would keep them going for a few more hours. "It was a good idea though. Using magic to gather water works well enough. I suppose you've already seen that."

"That water you draw from the earth, is it clean?"

"Of course!" Isobel said between bites. "The spell only affects water, so anything dissolved in it gets left behind. I'm surprised you're only asking this now. I've been refilling our flasks that way for months."

Chinelo shrugged. "I just never really thought about it."

The ground shook. Chinelo felt a deep rumbling from behind him. Isobel kicked up her staff and leapt to her feet in a single fluid motion. She adopted her signature cat-like stance, brandishing her staff towards the noise. Mort scurried behind a stone and peeked out nervously.

Chinelo jumped up and reached for his sword.

"Chinelo! Wait!" Isobel said. "Don't move. It's behind you."

Chinelo's heart pounded in his chest. *It?*

He felt a wave of hot air against his back. The ground shook again. There was a great scraping sound, like that of boulder dragging across gravel. Stones clattered together. Slowly, Chinelo turned his head and peaked over his shoulder. He saw it.

An eye.

It was enormous and glowing like the heart of a forge, bulging from a rocky, reptilian face. A scaly eyelid blinked over it. Teeth, wide and flat like millstones, lined the creature's menacing jaws. Its smokey breath hit Chinelo's skin like the air of a furnace. It growled, or rather it rumbled, producing a sound like an earthquake from deep within its girthy throat.

Chinelo clenched his fist, digging his nails into his skin. The creature was watching him, but perhaps, if he didn't move it wouldn't feel threatened.

It roared like an erupting volcano. It felt threatened.

Chinelo ran forward and drew his sword, turning around to face the beast. It was a great lizard covered in brown stone shards and jagged scales. It had short stubby legs that it used to drag its heavy body across the ground, creating the scraping sound he had heard earlier. Along its spine was a gaping crack that glowed orange from within. Its face was wide and bulky, and the crack along its body extended through its forehead, ending right above its protruding snout. From its lipless jaws lava fell and splattered along the ground, steaming and solidifying into igneous rock.

Recalling Glassow and Fenn's description, Chinelo whispered a single word. "Magmaw."

"What?" Isobel asked, pointing her staff at the beast as it circled them, swinging its tail behind it.

"It's called a magmaw. It eats lava."

"I think it wants to eat a lot more than lava right now."

The beast roared and rumbled forward. The pair scattered, and Isobel swung her staff, shouting a command. "Volley!"

Metal spikes formed in the air then shot towards the creature. They clanged as they bounced off its hide, barely even scratching the stone plates. Chinelo tried to find a weak point. None presented itself. Aside from the crack along its spine, its armor seemed impenetrable, and neither he nor his sword would be able to withstand the heat of its body.

The beast opened its mouth and dragged itself forward, crashing towards Isobel. Hot lava glowed from within its jaws.

"Flood."

Water shot from her staff directly into the beast's mouth, instantly evaporating into a cloud of steam. Isobel darted to the side, narrowly avoiding the disoriented lizard. There was a strange crunching, the sound of the beast's jaws smacking to break apart the solidified lava.

"We need to run, Isobel!" Chinelo said, slinging his pack over his shoulder and grabbing hers in his hand. Isobel nodded and plucked Mort from the ground. With her frog in one hand and her staff in the other she sprinted, running along the trail.

Chinelo ran ahead of her, jostling their packs. He looked back over his shoulder. The magmaw thrashed in the cloud of vapor. Orange lights sparked from the smoke, falling to the earth and creating puddles of glowing lava. Suddenly the beast shot out of the mist, sliding on its belly at great speed, leaving behind a trail of magma. Something metallic crunched underneath it, though he could not see what it was. Propelling itself with its short sturdy legs, the magmaw barreled closer and closer, opening its mouth wide to catch Isobel in its jaws.

"Isobel! Behind you!"

Isobel squatted and enhanced her strength with the spell on her arm. She vaulted high over the beast, completely avoiding its lunge. Her eyes widened. The ground beneath her was coated in a layer of lava. Her mind raced. She gripped onto Mort tightly as his fat frog legs flailed.

"Flood!" she shouted again. Water streamed from her staff, crashing into the ground below. Vapor swirled around her as she fell and landed on the wet earth.

"Wind!" she commanded, channeling esht into her staff and swinging it in a half circle. A gust of air cleared the vapor. The beast had already turned around and was preparing another of its charging slides.

A sphere of water crashed into its face, splashing over its nose and into the crack on its forehead. Chinelo had dropped both his and Isobel's packs, and he was whispering an incantation. Another sphere of water formed in his hand then splashed across the beast's head. The magmaw roared and shook its head, turning to hide its face from Chinelo.

Isobel raised an eyebrow. Was it that simple? Had her first guess been correct? She accumulated strength briefly, then channeled it into another powerful jump. Mort squawked as she flew from the ground. She twirled her staff and pointed it at the crack that ran down the beast's back. Magma burned within.

"Water Shot!"

A large sphere of water, as wide as she was tall, formed in front of Isobel's staff and flew into the magmaw's back. The lizard bellowed as another cloud of vapor erupted to the sky. Slowly, its eyes, mouth, and back ceased to glow. Isobel landed with a thud and steadied herself with her staff.

The magmaw's movements became sluggish and eventually halted. Its head drooped to the ground and landed with a loud crash.

Isobel frowned. "Is it dead?"

Chinelo shook his head and carried her pack to her, stepping carefully on the slick wet ground. "I don't think so. It sounds like it's still breathing."

"Good. We probably startled it," Isobel said. "The poor thing was just napping, and you went and sat on it."

"Sat on it?"

"Yes! You were sitting on its tail!"

"Oh!" Chinelo said. "Sorry, magmaw."

Chinelo frowned. He hastily looked at his pack.

"What is it?" Isobel asked.

"My armor!"

Chinelo broke into a quick sprint, hurrying back towards where they had sat moments before. He hopped over jagged rocks until a streak of glowing magma came into view. Directly at the center lay what was left of his amor, a deformed and bent mass that vaguely resembled the suit he once wore. The cloth about the waist and joints had lit aflame, and very little of it remained.

He felt a sudden oppressive gloom weighing down on him. His armor had been like a friend, the one thing that linked him back to his homeland. It was crushed and burned to ashes, just like everything else had been. He took a deep breath, trying to ignore the lump in his throat.

Isobel caught up and panted. "Oh, good you found... it."

Chinelo dropped to his knees and stared at the hot stone, feeling its intense heat on his face. He put his head in his hands.

"Chinelo? What's wrong?"

Chinelo gestured towards the slowly solidifying lava rock. "My armor," he said weakly.

"Oh."

Chinelo stared blankly ahead.

Isobel sat down beside him. "Do you want us to try to get it repaired?"

Chinelo looked at the decorative markings as they melted away. The cloth was gone. The regalia was gone.

"No. It's beyond that, I'm afraid. It's not—it's not important." Chinelo sighed and lifted himself to his feet. A quick tug from Isobel stopped him.

"It *is* important, though," she said. "It's important to you, so it's important to me. Do you want to try?"

Chinelo rubbed his forehead and closed his eyes. Much had changed since he left Eshgar. He had traveled across the land of his enemies. He had become close with a witch, someone who would have been shunned in Eshgar. He had learned to practice magic, an art feared by his countrymen. He had witnessed another city fall to the same evil that afflicted his home.

He no longer protected the queen. He no longer protected his country. He no longer protected his family. He no longer held to the Oath.

"Chinelo?" Her gentle voice brought him back.

"I am a knight of Eshgar no longer," he said. "I do not know what that makes me, but I will continue."

"Maybe that just makes you Chinelo." Isobel squeezed his hand softly. "And maybe that's not so bad."

Chinelo squeezed her hand in return. There was still one person he could protect, one person he would protect at any cost. If he could no longer be Eshgar's knight, he would be hers.

Isobel leaned against his shoulder, watching the clouds move across the clear blue sky. Soon, Chinelo stood and let out a long sigh. "Let's go."

CHAPTER 21

THE SUN WAS SETTING. IN THE distance, Chinelo saw rooftops and small wisps of smoke rising over the horizon as he and Isobel approached Ata. They had crossed the barren wasteland at an impressive pace, though as Haru predicted, their food was running very low. They had long since drunk the last of their water, surviving only on what Isobel was able to pull from the earth or purify from puddles of rain. Their nights had not been restful. Magmaws, while normally dormant in the daytime, were active after sunset. They moved in the darkness with eyes shining like lanterns. Though they never attacked unprovoked, they were rarely far away.

Chinelo yawned. He was ready for a good night's sleep and a good bath after they activated the obelisk. *If* they could activate it.

Isobel walked ahead with Mort in his usual position on her shoulder. She had been silent for several hours, staring pensively at the ground. Chinelo watched her, and she suddenly broke that silence.

"I'm worried, Chinelo."

"Oh? Why is that?" he asked, walking faster to stay by her side.

"What if I can't activate the obelisk? Joanne said that Mother Ginn didn't share the method, so what if it requires some hidden magic that I do not know? Or what if it uses words that I've never seen before? What if it does not contain either of the words we need?"

"Well, that may be true, but we won't know until we try."

"I suppose," she grumbled.

"Since we're arriving at night, we can always try several things. None of the townsfolk should be awake, so we shouldn't be interrupted. Maybe we'll stumble across the method through trial and error."

"Perhaps."

She did not seem convinced.

"Hey! You're smart. I'm sure you will be able to work it out."

That remark drew a smile from her.

"I'm glad you think so. Hopefully the obelisk will be near the town center, like the one in Nellborough. It would be convenient if it was at least easy to find."

Soon, darkness fell. The town ahead was lit only by torches along the streets and candles from within the stone buildings. Eventually, even the buildings darkened. At the edge of the village, Chinelo and Isobel crossed a bridge over a rushing stream. It wrapped around the village and connected to a similar stream from the opposite side at the south. Chinelo glanced down at the babbling water.

I suppose this is how they keep the magmaws out.

Entering the village, Chinelo and Isobel walked solemnly through the streets. They moved their way toward the town's center, attempting to make as little noise as possible. The houses were dark, made of rough stone blocks with thatched roofs. The streets were unpaved. Instead, they were composed of the same rock as the landscape Isobel and Chinelo had crossed, worn down by years of foot traffic. Scents of smoke and cooking fires lingered in the air. The town slept peacefully, unaware of the two travelers.

Chinelo felt a steady pulsing beneath his feet. It shook him to his core, resonating with his own heartbeat. As they pushed deeper into the village, the pulse intensified.

Thump thump.

They rounded a bend and found themselves in a small plaza at the heart of the town. The plaza was lined with shoddy carts and vacant booths. In the day, the square would likely be very active, but at night it was as still as the grave.

Thump thump.

Chinelo looked up. At the center of the square stood a great stone structure. It was tall and wide, and a diamond shaped cleft ran through its center. Its upper surface was perfectly flat, like that of an altar. Ridges ran up and down its surface, and its corners tapered outwards, extending diagonally toward the ground and sky.

THUMP THUMP.

They had found the obelisk.

Chinelo's hands went numb. His breath became shallow and rapid. His face felt cold. The world turned around him.

Isobel caught his hand in hers.

"Hey. Are you all right?" she asked.

Chinelo took a deep breath. He crouched to the ground and touched the earth, focusing on different sensations. He felt the rough stone brushing against his fingers. He felt the cool night air on his skin. He felt his pack weighing down on his shoulders. He felt sweat accumulating on his back. He felt her hand gently clasping his.

"Chinelo, talk to me," Isobel said. She crouched beside him. "Do we need to turn back?"

Chinelo took a deep breath and shook his head. "No. Sorry. This happens sometimes. Thank you."

"I'm sorry for asking you to do this."

"No, Isobel, don't be. I thought this would have passed by now, this panic."

"How often does this happen?" she asked, setting her staff on the ground and reaching for his other hand. Mort looked down from her shoulder at him. He almost looked concerned.

Chinelo shrugged. "I'm not sure. Sometimes, I can feel it coming, and normally I'm able to bring myself back before it hits. The intensity isn't usually this great or this sudden. I suppose we haven't been near one of these obelisks in a while, though."

"You never mentioned that." She looked perplexed.

"No. I—I didn't want you to worry," Chinelo said, looking down.

She squeezed his hand. "I'm here for you, all right? You can tell me about these things. I won't think less of you."

Chinelo did not raise his eyes to meet hers. There was more to it than that. How could he protect her if he himself needed her support? Burying his thoughts within him, he stood.

"Let's activate the obelisk."

The two dropped their packs against one of the buildings. Isobel placed Mort on top of hers, and he quickly settled down and closed his eyes to sleep. Together, she and Chinelo approached the obelisk.

"So, what is your plan?" Chinelo asked.

Isobel took a deep breath. "I'm not sure. I have thought of a few different phrases that might activate it. I suppose I'll just start with a simple one. 'Activate.'"

She extended her hand and pressed it against the obelisk's surface. She closed her eyes and focused.

"Vulges!"

Nothing happened.

"Feliacht, vulges!"

Nothing happened. Isobel frowned.

"Feliacht'ra gest, vulges!"

Nothing happened. Isobel sighed.

"I suppose it wouldn't be that easy."

Chinelo touched the obelisk. He still felt the faint pulsing. It called to him, begging him to reach it beneath the earth.

"What did you try?" he asked.

Isobel touched her chin. "'Activate', 'Structure activate,' and 'Structures nearby, activate.' I'll check my notes and see if there's anything I'm forgetting."

Isobel ran to her pack and drew out a book. She hurried back and dropped to the ground. With her staff, she summoned a light and flipped through the pages. At regular intervals, she reached out and touched the obelisk, chanted an incantation, and continued digging through her notes. Chinelo circled the structure, searching for any clues or hints that might be carved into its smooth surface. There was nothing.

The moon shone brightly in the clear sky. Stars twinkled in a beautiful arching pattern above them. The constellations were different from those he once saw in Eshgar.

Isobel slammed her book closed. "Son of a stick! Nothing is working!"

Chinelo sat down beside her. The thumping shook his body. "Joanne didn't give any other hints?"

"No! She just said that Mother Ginn activated the obelisk back at the Red Coven. She didn't say how. Ugh! Why can't I figure this out?"

Chinelo scratched his head. "You've only tried incantations involving 'activate?'"

Isobel crossed her arms. "Mostly."

"Perhaps we're approaching this the wrong way."

Isobel's brow furrowed. "What do you mean?"

"For one thing, whenever I'm near one of these, I feel this deep thumping. It's like a heartbeat."

Isobel cocked her head. "That's... odd."

"The other thing that confuses me is that I could have sworn Joanne didn't say 'activate.' She said 'awaken.'"

"How does that make sense? It's a bunch of stone," Isobel said.

"Perhaps it's not just stone. Perhaps it's somehow alive. Or something inside of it is alive."

Isobel shrugged. "It's worth a shot. We've already been out here for a while, so I'm open to new ideas."

"You'll figure it out! I have faith in you!"

Encouraged by his words, Isobel stood and stretched. "I'm going to try that second theory of yours. That makes the most sense to me. So, all I have to do is say something along the lines of 'All that is within, awaken.' If your theory is true, that should do the trick."

"All right! Let's see it!" Chinelo jumped to his feet and wrapped his arm around her shoulder.

Isobel reached out her hand and touched the obelisk. Her hair shifted, as if moved by an unheard breath.

"Gra ter o diaa, troshte!"

The ground rumbled, then stopped. A pale blue light flowed from the earth into the obelisk, rising in grid-like lines up its surface before stopping at the diamond shaped cleft at its center. They reappeared further up the altar, moving vertically and turning in sharp corners. A small blue light appeared at the center of the cleft, hovering in midair. It swirled and grew, expanding like billowing clouds until it formed a levitating sphere of radiant mist.

A smile spread rapidly across Isobel's surprised face. She hopped excitedly and looked at Chinelo.

"It worked, Chinelo! It really worked!" She turned back to face the obelisk, staring at the swirling orb above her head. "Now we just need to—" The color left her face. Her smile disappeared as quickly as it came, leaving only an expression of pure terror.

Chinelo looked up to the top of the obelisk. His breath froze in his lungs. Something was perched above them.

It squatted upon the obelisk, gripping the stone edge with a pair of hideous clawed feet. Its short legs were nearly skinless, and the red muscles that wound around its bones were covered in a tangle of tendrils and veins. Fibers and sinew hung from its frame, writhing erratically. In contrast to its muscular legs, its body was gaunt and emaciated, a black skeleton covered with mere scraps of tissue holding it together.

Its exposed ribcage was slick like oil, and within it, entrails and viscera hung loosely. Its skeleton seemed to merge and combine with the flesh along its withered shoulders, and arteries shot in and out of its skin like threads in a tapestry. It wrapped itself in a pair of long bony arms, covering its face with grotesquely large, bony hands. The skin of its arms seemed to move and shimmer, as if a thousand serpents coiled within.

It was a contorted abomination, vaguely resembling something that could be called human, but compressed and extended in ways that were unnatural and frightening. Though it was hunched, it stood nearly five times the height of the companions at the obelisk's base.

Slowly, the creature unwound its arms, stretching them out wider, wider, wider, until the elongated claws at its fingertips nearly touched the ground below the obelisk. Chinelo looked up expecting to see some monstrous, horrific face snarling down upon him, only, there was no face. Instead of a head, the creature had a massive stone symbol grafted onto its bloody stump of a neck, held in place by wriggling tendrils of flesh. It was of the same material as the obelisk, and its shape was a single vertical line with two wide, horizontal lines intersecting its lower half.

The creature breathed, and air whistled from an open hole in its throat. The lungs behind its ribs expanded and contracted, and its heart beat loudly.

Thump thump.

Isobel covered her mouth. Chinelo's breath hung in his throat. He wanted to look away, but somehow, he couldn't.

Thump thump.

The creature moved its lanky arms, resting its palms on the obelisk's edges. Its elbows were bent high above the stone cross it had in place of a head. It inhaled and then let out a deafening, mouthless screech. By sheer force of will, Chinelo remained still.

Isobel stumbled and fell on her back.

The creature's head turned sharply as if it had somehow seen her movement with its eyeless, faceless head. It leapt from the altar and crashed to the ground. It crawled on all fours, bending its emaciated spine and moving its head near the ground, drawing closer and closer to where Isobel huddled. Chinelo slowly drew his sword.

Isobel's heart pounded. She sat on the ground, frozen in terror. She could hear it behind her, breathing, crawling closer, towering over her. She could feel a slight puff of air moving her hair. She could smell the vile scent of iron and rotting flesh. She squeezed her eyes shut.

A slash! The sound of a blade tearing sinew.

The creature let out a loud shriek, and, pushing off its hands, it leapt into the air and vanished with a flash.

Isobel jumped to her feet and picked up her staff. Chinelo ran to her side.

"Where did it go?" she asked.

"I—I don't know," he panted.

"We can't let that... *thing*... hurt the villagers," Isobel said.

Standing back-to-back, they spun in circles, waiting for the beast to reappear.

Another flash.

"Up!" Chinelo shouted. The two jumped apart as the beast slammed into the ground where they had stood. It furiously clawed the air around it, shrieking madly.

Isobel's feet skidded and caught the rocky ground. She twirled her staff and channeled her esht.

"Fireball!"

The creature turned its head and dashed towards her, wailing as her spell blasted into its squirming skin. It did not stop, swinging its long arms in a wide sweep and slashing its hand directly into Isobel's side. She felt the air leave her lungs as she was thrown headlong into a nearby building. The world spun around her.

She gasped for air. She expected pain but was surprised to discover that she had remained unharmed. Haru's protection had not faded. She looked up at the beast, but it no longer seemed interested in her. Instead, it shambled about the square, dragging its claws along the ground and moving its head rapidly in random directions.

"Icht vasht'ra!" Chinelo said, lighting his sword ablaze. The beast turned its head towards him and dashed forward, smashing its clawed fists into the ground. A rush of air brushed Chinelo's skin. He dove and slashed at both of its legs, burning the muscles around the wounds. Ducking between its legs and behind it, Chinelo turned around. The wounds he had inflicted sprouted squirming tendrils that intertwined and bound them closed.

Chinelo's heart pounded. Its wounds had healed.

Instinctively, he channeled esht into his back, expecting to find the painted spell that would grant him strength. It rushed in a tingling surge from his heart into his shoulder muscles but found no inscription to give it form.

The creature lurched and spun around, swinging its hand downwards upon him. It flattened him to the ground.

"Chinelo!" Isobel cried. She pointed her staff toward the creature. "Volley: Twofold!"

Metal spikes cut through the air into the creature's body. It flailed its arms, attempting to block the stabbing darts.

"Form: Blade!" Isobel's staff transformed into her mighty glaive, and she dashed ahead. The creature slung its arm towards her. She gripped her staff with both hands, unleashing a powerful strike into the monster's palm, halting its attack. Her blade caught its skin, shaking her body. She twisted and weaved between its legs, striking while dodging its long, flailing arms.

Chinelo shook himself and rose to his feet. He, too, remained unscathed, though based on what Haru had said, he would no longer be protected. He watched in awe as Isobel danced around the enormous figure, cutting its flesh with her staff's magical blade.

"Bekekt, tra'fai!" she shouted.

Lightning released from her outstretched hand, coursing through the beast's body. She slashed its thigh. Black blood spurted, creating an inky slick puddle on the ground. The beast's hand swung downwards. Isobel ducked below the slashing claws and slammed her hand into the bloody pool.

"Sono natte va gralles'ra!"

Frozen spikes erupted from the ground, impaling the beast's legs and arms. It screamed from its severed windpipe. Isobel raised her staff and ran forward, severing the tendons along the monster's groin. She spun around, extinguished her blade, and pointed her staff at the beast.

"Inferno!"

Light flashed, and a raging tornado of flame formed, rising to the sky. The beast flailed its arms madly as its body burned. The smell was horrific. It was rotten, repulsive, oppressive. Chinelo's nose wrinkled. From within the blaze, the beast unleashed a pained cry and vanished in a flash.

"Isobel! Chinelo shouted. "Haru's protection spell only works once! Be careful!"

Isobel gasped. Her face went pale.

Another flash. The beast reappeared across the square and charged towards Isobel. Her eyes widened. It appeared to have no injuries, despite her relentless assault.

Chinelo accumulated esht in his hand and began chanting an incantation.

"Icht vasht'ra—" he hesitated.

The monster stopped moving. It turned its head towards him. Clawing the earth, it launched itself upwards, hurtling in his direction. Chinelo ducked and ran, narrowly avoiding the creature's impact. Dirt, pebbles, and shards of rock struck his arms, creating tiny, stinging cuts.

Isobel watched the creature approach Chinelo. She had to stop it or at least slow it down. Fire had not worked, but perhaps she could weaken it another way. She thought of the tattoo on her left wrist. Her spell would drain the esht of anything it struck and use it to generate large, cumbersome crystals. Esht fatigue affected all things, even if they had no idea how to use magic. Such a spell *would* slow the creature. She raised her hand.

Cyan lights blasted from her tattoo and flew like javelins toward the creature's back. They pierced its skin, forming crystals larger than she could have imagined. They grew and twinkled in the moonlight, creating towering structures far larger than the beast itself.

Such esht! Were its reserves unlimited? Something like that should not have been possible!

The monster screeched and tore at its own body, rending the crystals from its skin. It was a hideous display. The creature's long claws mutilated its flesh, but the wounds closed faster than they had formed. With a feral roar the fiend grasped the two final crystalline masses, and crushed them, sending a shower of sharp shards down upon the square.

Isobel ducked and covered her head with her arms. Her skin stung as the crystals rained down upon her.

Chinelo watched the beast closely. It turned towards Isobel and began looking around, searching for her. It seemed to be distracted easily, focusing on its current attacker and not its previous one, regardless of how close they might be. Chinelo shouted.

The creature did not acknowledge it.

He channeled esht into his sword. The monster turned its head and slashed at him. He blocked the attack with his sword but was knocked off his feet. He tumbled and rolled, feeling a jolt of pain with every impact. He released his esht. The creature looked around frantically.

Isobel ran towards him, passing by the obelisk. The monster looked up and then vanished, reappearing on top of the obelisk and clawing at the ground below it. Its claw cut a gash into Isobel's back. She screamed and fell.

The rocky ground was rough against her cheek. Her arms burned and stung from the many abrasions that covered them. Her back throbbed from the wound that plowed down from her shoulder blade to her spine. She lifted her right hand, straining to maneuver it into a position where she could heal the wound. Suddenly, she heard a dull, ominous scraping.

"Isobel! Wait!" Chinelo shouted.

Isobel looked up at him. He seemed to be concentrating, focusing, as if he was preparing to cast a spell. Only, he did not speak an incantation.

She rolled to her side and looked up. The monster had lifted its hand and was moving its head in Chinelo's direction. Beside her, the obelisk's light surged and the swirling orb at its center pulsed. The creature disappeared. Her eyes widened.

Could it be? No! That was absurd.

Chinelo released his esht and leapt back. The creature reappeared directly over where he stood, traveling almost instantly from its perch on the obelisk to the air above his head.

Slowly, he reached to the ground and grabbed a stone. He focused esht into the stone and hurled it across the square.

The beast shrieked and chased it, trying to catch it with its long slender fingers.

"Now! Isobel! Heal, now!"

Isobel urgently channeled esht into her healing tattoo. The wound on her back healed. She leapt to her feet, kicked up her staff, then tried to run towards Chinelo. She stumbled. Her body was heavy. Her esht was running out.

"Wait!" He gestured for her to halt. He eyed the monster, which had begun aimlessly wandering the square, moving its head erratically, looking from house to house. "Walk very slowly towards me."

Chinelo and Isobel approached each other, taking one labored step after another.

"Why didn't it see us?" Isobel asked. "It attacked me when I moved."

"I don't think it really sees, Isobel," Chinelo responded. "Or rather, it only seems to respond when *esht* moves quickly."

Isobel's eyes widened.

"So, when you threw that stone..."

"Right! I forced my esht into it."

"Clever, but that means if any of the villagers start moving about, it will detect their esht moving unless they walk incredibly slowly."

"What's more, I'm not sure how we can kill this thing." Chinelo shook his head. "Its flesh seems to regenerate, and it doesn't care about fire."

A light flickered in a house across the square. A silhouette passed by the window and a man peaked out the door. The creature's head perked up. The obelisk pulsed, and the monster vanished, reappearing above the man's house.

"NO!" Isobel shouted.

Before her eyes, the monster slashed its claws through the man's body, cleaving him into four bloody pieces. It scooped up the gory viscera and shoved them into its chest. Its ribs opened like a set of mandibles and crunched down upon the body. Muscle and skin grew about the creature's spine.

More lights flickered. The beast disappeared in a flash, then reappeared. It slaughtered and consumed another villager. And another. And another.

Isobel clenched her fist. Her stomach twisted within her. She whispered something beneath her breath.

"Isobel! Don't!" Chinelo cried. "It will see you!"

Isobel ignored him. She continued her incantation. Her body grew light. The fatigue faded. Her muscles grew taut. She felt strength flowing throughout her entire being.

A scream rang out through the night. Townsfolk gathered at the edges of the square, then turned and ran in horror at the sight of the bloody beast. The monster lifted its head from its current victim. It dropped from the shattered house on which it stood and crawled towards the crowds.

Isobel sprinted forward, moving at a blistering pace.

"Form: Sword!"

Her staff flashed, and blue light grew and spread in lines from its head, connecting to form an enormous, double-edged blade. It was nearly twice the length of her body, and she was only able to carry it with the assistance of her multiplied strength. She ran toward the beast, crouched, then leapt high into the air, soaring above the town. She spun her staff, gripping it firmly in both hands above her head. The wind whistled through her hair. She fell upon the creature, and with a yell she swung her blade.

It slammed against the ground, shattering the stone. The creature screeched and held its hand over the bloody stump where its arm had once been attached. Tendrils, like vines, erupted from its shoulder, writhing and flailing. They moved toward its severed arm. Then...

A light.

It flew like a falcon and tore through the monster's leg. A voice whispered in Isobel's ear.

"Sorry I took so long. Glad you're both still alive."

"Haru?" Isobel said.

"Pay attention! Preparing second shot."

Isobel felt a sharp pain in her ankle. She had landed off-balance during her previous attack, and her ankle was likely sprained. She clenched her hand into a fist then looked at the obelisk. From a distance, the swirling orb at its center looked much smaller. It looked much more familiar. She glanced down at her staff. The spell-core that hovered at its tip swirled with blue mist.

"It's a spell-core," Isobel whispered.

The obelisk pulsed. The creature shrieked and disappeared. It reappeared on top of the obelisk which began to glow and shine brightly. The tendrils on the beast's wounded shoulder twisted and coiled together, forming bone. The skin spread over them, crawling down the bone like a legion of beetles.

She muttered. "If it's using it as a spell-core, then all we need to do is destroy it."

Chinelo watched in horror as the beast's arm fully regrew. He glanced at Isobel. She seemed to be mumbling to herself. The beast began searching the town for additional prey. It hopped from the altar and scurried across the ground. Chinelo surged his esht, forcing it to his hand.

The monster halted.

"Chinelo! Keep it distracted!" Isobel shouted.

Chinelo nodded. He reached down, grabbed another stone, filled it with esht, and hurled it across the square. Only, this time it did not chase it. This time it stared at *him*.

His blood turned cold. However, he did not flinch. He would protect her.

The beast lurched forward, racing towards him with gleaming claws outstretched. Chinelo steeled his soul, gripping his sword with both hands and tensing his legs. He would not falter!

A blur raced across the square. A deafening crunch rang out as a heavy hammer slammed into the monster's hand.

"Take that, foul creature!" Glassow shouted. He pounded the monster's claws relentlessly, and the cracks from his hammer strikes echoed through the square.

The monster lifted its other hand. From a nearby alleyway, a figure bolted into the light. A flash of silver cut through the air. Fenn twirled his war scythe, cleaving the monster's hand cleanly from its wrist. He sent Chinelo a proud smirk, then continued his assault.

Chinelo yelled and joined them, sending streams of flame from his sword. The monster hunched over, shrieking and wailing at its assailants.

Isobel ran forward, charging at the obelisk. The hunters' distraction had been exactly what she needed. With every step her ankle screamed out in agony. The monster turned its head and moved towards her.

Fenn and Glassow dove to its sides, relentlessly swinging at its ankles.

A second light crashed into the creature. It shrieked.

"Preparing third shot," Haru whispered.

Isobel crouched. "Form: Spear."

A thousand needles of pain stabbed into her. She gritted her teeth, ignoring the pain.

Using the last of her accumulated strength, she jumped, flying and falling toward the obelisk. She twirled her staff and pointed its magically formed edge at the glowing orb at the obelisk's center. Gripping it with both hands, she fell and plunged her blade deep inside.

Behind her, she heard a deafening cry from the monster. The core ruptured and exploded in a flood of blue mist. It surrounded her, consumed her, blinded her. Words, knowledge, symbols, sounds flooded into her mind. Years of study passed within seconds. She understood. She could transcend the laws of space. She could move without motion. She could be in two places. Both, then one. She closed her eyes. A word echoed through her mind.

"HOMVELCHT."

Then, she fell.

CHAPTER 22

ISOBEL GROANED. HER MUSCLES ACHED. SHE was lying on her back. Was that a hand cradling her head?

Her ankle throbbed. A strange weight pressed down on her abdomen. What were those noises? Rustling, murmuring, chattering, stomping. Feet against stone. Voices overlapping into an unintelligible droning. Her body shook.

"ISOBEL!"

She opened her eyes. The sky was blue. The sun had risen. She squinted. Chinelo leaned over her, holding her in his arms.

"Hey."

"Thank all that is good!" he said in relief. "I was so worried."

"What happened?"

"You defeated it, Isobel," Chinelo said. "You killed that monster."

Isobel blinked and turned her head. Haru stood above her, smiling from her wrinkled cheeks. Her snow-white hair fluttered in the wind. Behind her were Fenn and Glassow, two proud grins spreading across their faces.

"Why does everything hurt?" Isobel asked with a groan. She felt oddly groggy.

"You fell," Haru replied. "You hit the ground pretty hard."

"You were barely breathing, Isobel," Chinelo said. "I was worried."

"I'm sorry."

Chinelo smiled. "I'm just glad you're all right."

Isobel looked up at him. "Chinelo, we were right. I've learned something, something incredible."

Chinelo's face brightened. "You can tell me all about it, but first, there's someone here who is very worried about you, too." He nodded toward Isobel's hip.

Isobel slowly sat up.

She felt a movement from her abdomen. Mort stared up at her from her lap, blinking his bulging eyes. He croaked. Isobel reached down and tenderly petted his back.

"Sorry for worrying you, Mort."

"You should apologize to me, too, then," Haru said. "You two were on the brink there."

"Aye, it's a good thing we got here when we did," Fenn added, dropping to a squat and giving Chinelo a slap on the back. "My, what a story this will make."

Glassow pressed his hands on his hips and looked at the sky, his long hair falling on his shoulders. "Yes, to think we'd be hunting *that*."

A breeze whistled through the rip in the back of Isobel's shirt, sending a chill down her spine. She looked around. She and her four companions were huddled at the base of the obelisk, and behind them were the shattered remains of the beast's head. They were surrounded by a crowd in a wide circle. They stood at a distance, muttering and murmuring to themselves. Isobel scanned their faces. Some regarded her with gazes of awe and wonder. Others cringed at her in fear. Holding Mort in her hands, she tried to stand. Chinelo pushed against her back, assisting her to her feet.

She winced, and her leg buckled. She felt Chinelo's hand supporting her shoulder. A sharp pain throbbed from her ankle.

"Haru, would you grab my staff? Something seems to have happened to my leg."

Haru reached behind her and passed Isobel her staff. After placing Mort on her shoulder, Isobel leaned against it and forced herself to stand. The crowd murmured. A man stepped forward and knelt before Isobel. He was old and wrinkled, and his thin white hair grew in a ring around his bald head.

"Strangers. We are grateful to you. We wish to thank you."

Isobel didn't respond. The words hung in her throat.

"Please! Strangers! Let us thank you!"

Haru elbowed Isobel in the ribs. "You saved these people. Say something."

"I—" Isobel's stomach rumbled. "Would you—could you point us to somewhere we could eat?"

The man jumped to his feet. "Roh! Provide our guests with food. Give them anything they ask for."

"Oh, please," Isobel said, "we are happy to pay for—"

Haru's hand was on her shoulder. She shook her head.

A young boy appeared from the crowd. "This way! You are welcome in our home!"

He grabbed Isobel's hand and pulled her forward. The crowd broke. Isobel hobbled behind the boy as the others followed.

As she limped through the crowd, Isobel listened to their murmuring voices.

"... savior..."

"... witch..."

"... hero..."

"... Minera..."

"... goddess..."

Then she heard a cry, a wail, a wretched scream. She turned her head. Beyond the crowd stood a shattered, crumbling building. A man knelt on the ground, bending over a bloody heap. He sobbed, staring down at the unrecognizable viscera.

Isobel felt sick. The boy tugged her hand and pulled her from the square into a side street. Her hunger had left her.

Chinelo entered the house in which he and Isobel had been resting. Since Ata was rarely visited by travelers, it had no inn. Instead, Lenah, the village's head, had opened a section of his spacious home for Isobel and Chinelo, hosting them as they rested from their long journey. Chinelo's pack was filled with food that he had collected at the market that morning. Against his many protests, the villagers insisted on giving him anything he wished to buy for free. Chinelo looked about the kitchen. Neither Lenah nor his wife were in the house.

Chinelo opened the pack and produced two small bundles wrapped in thin parchment. A faint smell of ginger and pepper wafted to his nostrils. Grabbing two flasks of water, he carried the food down a short stone hallway. He stopped at a curtained doorway.

"Isobel? May I come in? I brought lunch."

"Please," Isobel responded.

Chinelo pushed aside the curtain and entered the room. Isobel sat on a layer of blankets on the floor. Her ankle was propped up on a stack of pillows, and it was wrapped in rune covered bandages. She had been using a cooling spell to assist with the recovery from her injuries. She sat with her spell-book in her lap and papers scattered around her.

"How's the ankle today?" Chinelo asked.

"Still sprained."

"Why don't you heal it?" Chinelo said, squatting down and placing their flasks beside Isobel's bed.

"I can't. My spell mends cuts and scrapes. Doesn't do much for sprains or internal injuries."

"Ah."

Chinelo sat on the floor beside her and handed her one of the wrapped bundles. He glanced at her face. It was clouded, and she seemed to be avoiding his gaze. It seemed that her somber mood from the previous day had not changed.

She unwrapped the bundle to reveal her meal. It consisted of seared chicken, onions, and a strange, grass-like leaf wrapped in a thin layer of flattened bread. Isobel took a bite and stared down at her lap.

"So," Chinelo said after chewing his first bite.

"Hmmm?"

"Do you want to talk about it?"

Isobel looked away. "Talk about what?"

Chinelo sighed. "Something is troubling you."

"Chinelo," Isobel said, "how many died?"

Chinelo blinked. "What?"

"The villagers. How many died?"

"Isobel, I'm not sure that's—"

"Chinelo!" Isobel asserted. "Tell me!"

He sighed. "Ten."

Isobel's face went pale. She let out a labored, erratic, sigh.

"I'm sorry, Isobel."

"Ten? Ten died, because of me?" She ran her fingers through her hair. "This wasn't supposed to go like this. I was trying to save them."

Chinelo set his food down and placed his hand on her shoulder. He leaned in. "And you did. There are two hundred people in this village. If you had not killed that... *thing*... then all two hundred would likely be dead by now."

Isobel looked up. "But if I hadn't awakened that monster..."

"Then all two hundred of the people in this town would have died," Chinelo said. "Remember why we came here."

"But... those ten." Isobel said. Her voice cracked. "They didn't deserve this."

"You didn't know what would happen."

She balled her hands into fists and slammed them down on her blanket. "And that absolves me of guilt? That makes this somehow excusable? Those people say I'm a hero, but I'm the one who put them in danger!"

"Remember why we came here, Isobel. The Interior Guard is coming. If we didn't—"

"I was trying to save everyone, though!"

Chinelo shifted his position, turning around so he faced her directly. "Then, let's save them."

She looked up. Her eyes were watery.

"I'm upset, too. These people died, and... I—we weren't able to save them. However, remember what you told me, that morning after the fire? You said you would undo things, and I still believe you will."

Isobel opened her mouth but said nothing.

"There's something you haven't told me," Chinelo said. "What did you learn when you broke the obelisk's core?"

Isobel removed her glasses and wiped her eyes. Her expression hardened. "It's possible."

"What?"

"Turning back time. It's possible," Isobel said. "I learned a new word. It isn't one of the two we need, but I know now that we can do it. We just have to keep searching until we find the correct words."

"Then," Chinelo said after a pause, "let's continue. We'll find the words for time and memory. We'll turn back time and save them. I haven't given up yet. I haven't stopped believing in you. And neither should you."

Isobel smiled. "Could you move a little bit closer? Down this way?" She gestured beside her.

"Sure. If that's what you want." Chinelo shimmied across the floor until his hips touched her thigh. She leaned forward and wrapped her arms around him, drawing him into a tender embrace.

"Thank you," she whispered into his chest. Chinelo felt a slight trembling from her. They sat there for several minutes, holding each other close.

"Still..." she released him and leaned back. "We are probably going to have to kill more of those creatures if we want to have a chance at finding the right word."

Chinelo nodded. "So, our next destination is the Eastern Plains, then?"

"Right. Though, I'm going to need time to recover from my injuries. That may give us time to prepare better for winter and to watch for the Interior Guard here," Isobel said. "If we are lucky, we may learn more about how they are involved."

"And then we can find the next one before they do."

She looked down and clenched her fist. "I'm not going to let more people die, Chinelo. Even if we can reverse time, we may not be able to succeed at our end goal. And reversing their fates doesn't make them something we can ignore. There is a good chance that we will be killed either by those monsters or by the Interior Guard. I say this because I want you to understand the risks of continuing this journey. I don't want you to feel like you can't leave. However, I know this is selfish, but will you continue to help me?"

Chinelo smiled. "Do you even need to ask?"

THE END OF PART 3

PART 4

THE BEAST OF THE EASTERN PLAINS

CHAPTER 23

423rd year, 9th month, 25th day
10 years before present day

ISOBEL DREW IN A DEEP, APPREHENSIVE breath. Before her stood a small cottage, surrounded by a dense forest. It was humble but welcoming. She had followed the instructions given to her by the couple she met in town, a tall bookkeeper named Umfrey and a kind physician named Priscila.

"Follow the west road until you reach a fork with a sign. Head up the north trail to the cottage on a hill."

This was the place. Her hands shook nervously. She had thought of this day for weeks since she left the Red Coven. Would her mother like her? Would she like her mother? Would her mother even want her?

Her stomach growled. She had rationed her food for the first leg of the trip, but her provisions had run out days before. She had no money, nor did she have anything she could sell aside from the ring she wore on her finger and the books she carried in her pack. Should she have brought anything else? Would her mother accept her if she was empty handed?

She sighed and closed her eyes. The birds sang around her, chirping in cheery arpeggios. Her heartbeat slowed. Her breath felt less shallow. She stepped up to the oak door and knocked. After a few moments, the lock clicked. The polished brass knob turned, clunking loudly. The door swung open, and Isobel looked up at the woman who stood before her.

She was tall and slim, and her voluminous auburn hair fell in waves down her back. Framed by thin laugh-lines, her eyes were a pale robin's egg blue. She was older than Isobel, likely in her late thirties or early forties. She leaned against a crooked staff that was ornamented with a golden crescent at its end. A glowing violet orb of vapor hovered within the crescent, swirling like sediment in a flooded stream. In sharp contrast to Isobel's dirty and frayed clothing, not a wrinkle nor blemish was present in the woman's attire, a tidy indigo tunic and smooth brown leggings.

The woman's brow wrinkled. She eyed Isobel curiously, her gaze lingering on Isobel's messy hair.

Isobel squirmed. She felt that she was being inspected, like the woman was evaluating if she was worthy of stepping on the doorstep. She looked down shyly and curtsied.

"Greetings. Are you Esther Valeria?"

The woman glanced down at Isobel's hand, squinting her eyes at the glowing spell-core that was embedded in her ring.

"I am," she answered in an uneasy voice. "And you are?"

"My—my name is Isobel. I—I've been told by the witch Iva that I am your daughter."

Esther's eyes widened. She gasped and blinked several times. Her blue eyes slowly filled with tears. She held her hand to her face and covered her mouth. Her staff tumbled to the floor.

Isobel found herself pulled into a deep, warm embrace.

She let out a deep breath. She was safe. She was home.

CHAPTER 24

434th year, 3rd month, 20th day
Present Day

CHINELO DUCKED INTO A DARK ALLEYWAY, standing with his back against the stone wall. His targets walked ahead, oblivious to him. He peered out. Torchlight reflected off the bald head of the man he was tailing, and it shone across the fair hair of the woman that accompanied him.

Taking a deep breath, Chinelo drew a talisman from his pocket, a thin strip of parchment. He channeled his esht into it, and all fell silent. His breath, his shirt dragging against the stone, his feet on the ground, even his heartbeat were completely noiseless. Chinelo tapped the wall. It produced no sound.

He smiled. Isobel's ingenuity never ceased to amaze him. That wasn't the only thing, but at that moment it was certainly the foremost.

He focused his attention on the skin along his shoulders. His esht rushed from his heart and into the tattoo Isobel had created for him. He felt his body grow light. Though his shoulders were still sore from the application, the spell worked perfectly. He leapt up to a nearby wall, a barrier that separated the outer portion of Ata from the inner market.

He stalked along its surface, searching the street below for his targets. At the edge of the town, the man stopped and looked over his shoulder. His black beard was barely visible in the dim light. He frowned and continued walking beyond the town's outskirts with his companion close behind. Chinelo ran across the wall and leapt, flying through the cold night air and landing silently on the volcanic soil.

The pair followed the path north. After they were a short distance from the town, the man summoned a light to illuminate the road. He said something to the woman, and she nodded in response. Chinelo remained at a distance, unfortunately a little to far to hear what was spoken between the two. Without his sword, he had to ensure that he remained unseen. He climbed onto a nearby boulder and watched the guardsmen move further and further from Ata.

Chinelo had been caught by surprise that morning. As usual, he had gone to the market and acquired food for Isobel and him to eat. He offered to pick up food for Haru, but she tended to be busy catching up with her siblings, nieces, and nephews. The other two hunters had returned to Dawngale several days earlier to prepare for their next hunt. While Chinelo had been watching the town intently for the green and gold robes of the Interior Guard, he had not expected that two of them would prance into town completely unarmored.

Chinelo should have foreseen it. Ata was a town of Caald, and as such it was not subject to Iskara's rule. The robes of the Interior Guard would not be welcomed there. Thankfully, Chinelo had not been seen by Barlow or Talia, two of the guardsmen he had encountered at the Dusty Dog.

Chinelo climbed to the top of a small rocky plateau. The landscape on the north of Ata was far more varied than that to the west. It rose and fell, and the lava rock had solidified around preexisting hills and plateaus. At the bottom of one of those hills was a light. He had found Barlow's camp.

A man huddled beside a fire. Three tents were arranged in a row, and horses were tied to a large stake embedded in the ground beside a covered wagon. Barlow and Talia entered the radius of the fire's light and sat.

"So. How'd it go?" the man asked.

Barlow groaned. "Pass me a drink first, then I'll answer."

The man tossed Barlow a flask.

"That bad?" the man said.

Barlow took a long swig. "It's empty."

"The flask? I just filled it."

"No, you idiot. The obelisk." Barlow rubbed his forehead.

The man jumped to his feet. "Empty? That—that's impossible. I didn't think anyone else knew how to activate them."

"Clearly someone does," Barlow replied. "Unless Talia has been lying to me."

Talia flinched and shied away.

"N—no. It really was empty. I—I couldn't feel it. It was silent!"

The man stroked his chin. "Do you know how recent it was?"

"No," Barlow said. "The townsfolk refused to speak about it."

Chinelo exhaled. His warnings to Lenah had not gone unheard.

"The Archmage isn't going to be happy about this, Barlow."

"Thank you, Rulk, for your insightful commentary. Honestly, I don't know how we'd get by if you didn't feel the need to impart your boundless wisdom on us whenever the wind blows."

Rulk shrugged then sipped from his flask. "Sorry."

Barlow groaned. "I'm less worried about the Archmage's reaction. He at least is tolerant towards those of us with a history of loyalty. It's that woman." He shuddered.

"I was looking forward to sleeping well tonight. Thanks for ruining that," Rulk grumbled.

"How the Archmage manages to keep that creature under control is beyond me."

"Sh—she's really not that bad," Talia said.

Barlow scoffed. "Trust me, Talia, she is."

"Well, at least we don't have to worry about Caald catching on." Rulk stroked his chin. "I'm sure they wouldn't be pleased if one of their towns suddenly disappeared, especially one that was hiding something so powerful."

"It wouldn't matter, anyways. Caald wouldn't dare retaliate."

"I've got an idea, Barlow!" Rulk said. "How about—now hear me out— how about we get Talia to tell them about the obelisk? Eh? Eh?"

Talia raised her hands in protest. "I—I—I—"

Barlow rubbed his face with his hand. "Rulk, I will feed you to the magmaws."

"Hey! If she can't complete a full sentence, she can't say anything they don't like. No offense, Talia."

Barlow frowned. "Idiot."

Talia folded her hands in her lap and looked down in shame.

"So, what's our next move?" Rulk asked.

Barlow stood. "We'll all return to the operations base and report our findings to the Archmage. He'll probably send us back to Rothvale after that. I'm sure he isn't keen on travelling in the winter."

"Well, my wife will certainly be happy to hear that," Rulk said.

Barlow nodded, and the three sat in silence. Chinelo scooted forward, trying to make sure he didn't miss any of their conversation. The wind rushed over the camp in a sudden gust, causing the fire to flicker and the tents to pull against their stakes.

"Do you wonder why we have to... you know?" Talia said.

Barlow leaned forward. "No."

"B—but if it really is dead, th—then—"

"They got lucky, Talia. You know what happens when things go south. We can't risk that."

Rulk cocked his head. "What's that? Who's 'they?'"

Barlow shifted his position, resting his elbow on his knee and sipping from his flask. "More bad news. A certain red-haired witch was spotted in the area several days ago."

Chinelo felt the blood drain from his face.

"Blast!" Rulk said. "Do you know if it's the same one from... eh? What was that town called?"

"The description matches," Barlow replied. "Slim, short, carrying a staff, and accompanied by a dark-skinned man."

"N—Nellborough," Talia said.

"What's that?" Rulk looked her way.

"The—the town." Talia frowned. "It was called Nellborough."

Rulk rolled his eyes and muttered something.

Chinelo pushed to a kneeling position, brushing his hand against a small rock. The stone fell from the hill and rolled toward the fire. His heart dropped.

Talia leapt to her feet and drew a talisman from her belt. She looked towards the hill, squinting her eyes.

"What is it?" Barlow asked.

"We are being watched," Talia said in a low voice.

Chinelo frantically reached into his pocket and grabbed a stone talisman, one half of a pair. It was time for him to flee. Better for them to be suspicious of being watched than to find him.

Forcing his esht into it, Chinelo watched the world around him compress into a single point.

Isobel paced around the room. She still felt a dull pain in her ankle, but it had faded to the point where it was barely noticeable. She ran her fingers through her hair, causing it to gradually become messier and messier. Haru sat in a chair with her arms crossed, watching Isobel amusedly with her single eye, while Mort watched her confusedly with his two eyes.

"You really ought to sit down, Isobel," Haru said.

"Fine." Isobel sat on the floor with a huff and opened one of her many notebooks. She jotted down a few words, fidgeted, then slammed it shut. "I can't take this, Haru. Why didn't you go with him?"

"Barlow would recognize me," Haru replied. "Also, if I weren't here, I'm certain you would do something rash."

Isobel grumbled beneath her breath. She once again opened her book, made a few hasty scribbles, then closed it. "What if something happens?"

"Then you will need to trust that Chinelo will handle it. I understand your worry, but Chinelo is perfectly capable of handling things. He's no fool."

Isobel looked down. Chinelo's sword rested on the ground beside her. She had planned to spend her day crafting a spell-core for it, normally a long and tiresome process. To her surprise, she had been able to craft it in a single sitting.

Spell-cores were complex magical devices, and they required a high level of skill and a massive amount of esht to forge. Typically, Isobel crafted them in stages, cycling between transferring esht to the blood sample that made up the core's base and resting until she was able to accumulate the right quantity. However, that afternoon she had been able to transfer enough esht without even feeling a hint of fatigue. The result hovered at the pommel of Chinelo's sword, a dark blue orb of mist that held a hint of the cyan typical of her magical constructs. Though, with his blood at its heart, the core would not respond to her, even if it was mostly comprised of her esht.

Isobel closed her eyes and focused on the swirling ocean of energy within her. It had changed since she pierced the monster's core, nearly tripling in capacity. Spells that would have exhausted her became effortless. With the increase in size came an increase in regeneration rate as well. She could rest for short periods and feel revitalized. It was incredible... and worrying.

She was not the first to awaken an obelisk. If the Archmage had been able to conquer the beasts within Nellborough and Eshgar's obelisks, then he would already have two cores, and his esht capacity would be even vaster. If—no—*when* she eventually had to face him, she would be at a significant disadvantage.

Isobel glanced at her bed. A stone talisman, half of a pair, rested on the blankets. Using the knowledge she had gained from the core, Isobel had inscribed the stone with a spell unlike any the world had seen for centuries. She watched the talisman, waiting for what would happen if Chinelo channeled esht into the other half of the set. She did not have to wait long.

A light flashed over Isobel's bed. Chinelo appeared and fell onto his stomach. Mort hopped away, startled by Chinelo's sudden return.

Isobel jumped up. "Oh! Finally! What happened?"

Chinelo stood and began moving his mouth, but no words could be heard. His face contorted in confusion, and he began waving his hands.

"Oh! Right!" Isobel reached down and grabbed her staff. "Nullify!"

A shockwave passed over the room, and Chinelo gasped.

"That is a very unpleasant sensation." He rubbed his jaw.

"I guess that means your idea worked," Haru said, rising from her chair.

Chinelo nodded. "Like a dream. Same with that travel spell. I will say, that was a strange sensation, too. It's like the world shrunk and then expanded."

Isobel giggled. "It definitely takes some getting used to."

"So, what did you learn?" Haru said.

Chinelo scratched his head. "Well, there's good news and there's bad news."

"What's the good news?" Isobel asked.

"They aren't going to attack the town. We were right. The Archmage *is* looking for the obelisks. Sounds like that campaign is halting for the winter, though."

"That will buy us some time, then," Isobel replied.

"Also, it was a good decision for you to stay indoors over the past few days, Isobel," Chinelo said.

"Oh?"

"That's the bad news. Someone must have told Barlow about you." Chinelo frowned. "They are aware that we are here, and they have made the connection that we were at Nellborough."

"That's... not good." Isobel looked down.

"You'll need to be careful as you travel," Haru interjected. "I'd recommend you spend as little time in Iskara as possible. If the Interior Guard still operates like it did when the Archmage took over, then they will likely be on the hunt for you. Rogue mages are rarely tolerated."

Isobel nodded. "I think we can make that work." She grabbed her spell-book from the floor and opened it on a table in the corner, flipping to the map on the back page. Chinelo and Haru crowded around her.

"So, my original plan was to head northeast for this second point here." Isobel pointed at a mark near the east coast of Iskara. "If we head further east, we can stay within Caald for most of the journey, though it will likely add a fair amount of time."

Haru squinted. "That would bring you through the desert. Traveling across that region in winter is risky unless you have a reliable way to stay warm without firewood."

Isobel fidgeted with her hair. "I don't see any other option if we're trying to stay outside of Iskara. If we can make it to—what's this town called?"

"Ka Oasis," Haru said.

"Right! If we can make it to Ka Oasis, then we can stop there for a while. We should reach the next obelisk by the start of spring. Hopefully that will have one of the two words we need."

Chinelo glanced at the closet. A thick coat hung from an iron bar, a coat that they had purchased in preparation for winter. "Could we inscribe our clothing with warming spells? Then we wouldn't have to worry about the cold. Would that work?"

Isobel beamed. "That's genius. I could paint them with a similar spell to the one I use to heat water back home, then set them up so that they are self-sustaining. I can probably have those ready in... hmmm... two, maybe three days. That's such a clever application!"

"Will your ankle be able to handle the walk at that point?" Chinelo asked.

"I think so, if we walk slowly," Isobel said. "If need be, we can always stop in Drel to rest. That's a decent sized city. Haru, I assume you aren't coming with us?"

Haru shook her head. "No. I am leaving in the morning for Dawngale. My next hunt contract is due soon, and I'm not going to leave Fenn and Glassow on their own for that."

"Oh. So, this will be goodbye, then," Isobel said with noticeable sadness.

"I'm afraid so, my friend."

Isobel hugged Haru tightly. Haru gasped in surprise.

"Thank you, Haru. I'll miss you."

"I—I will miss you both as well. Should your travels bring you back to Dawngale, then come and find me. I—I ought to be going now. Old bones like mine need their rest." Haru turned and walked toward the door, stopping to look over her shoulder. "Chinelo, try not to worry her too much."

Chinelo nodded. "Don't miss those shots of yours."

"I would never." She disappeared through the curtain.

"She left so abruptly," Isobel said after a long pause.

"Well, it is late," Chinelo said. "Maybe she doesn't enjoy goodbyes."

Isobel yawned. "I suppose. We should probably rest, too."

"Agreed," Chinelo looked down.

"Right," Isobel said after another long pause.

"I—I guess I'll be going, then," Chinelo said. He nervously shifted his weight from one foot to the other.

Isobel fidgeted with her hair.

Chinelo glanced at her furtively.

Isobel stared at the floor.

"Well, goodnight." Chinelo turned and walked to the door.

"Goodnight," Isobel said in a low voice, trying to hide her disappointment. She closed her spell book, running her fingers across the rough cover. She sighed. *Maybe next time...*

CHAPTER 25

THE DESERT WIND WAS COLD AGAINST Chinelo's cheek. Snowflakes accumulated on the short beard that had grown over the two months since he and Isobel left Ata. Ordinarily he would have preferred to shave it once it started itching, but Isobel had been very encouraging about him trying a new look. He rubbed his hands together, and the warm fabric of his woolen gloves caught on his calloused skin. His coat hung to his knees, and though it was heavy, its imbued warmth had been much appreciated during the journey.

He squinted his eyes. The setting sun cast a bright light across the snow dusting the red wasteland. He'd seen deserts before. Southern Eshgar was much like a desert, and he had seen the peaks of dunes before entering the Ashen Plains months earlier. However, he had never witnessed a desert like this.

It was dry and rocky, and the shallow hills were dotted with coarse gray bushes. Towering crimson stone spires pointed to the sky, and wide flat buttes were capped with a thin layer of white snow. In the distance an ancient stone citadel poked over the horizon. Though it stood tall, it had long since begun to crumble, battered by centuries of wind.

He turned north. Several spires stood nearby. They were eerie, and in the fading light they resembled hooded figures cloaked in crimson. A particularly tall spire overshadowed the rest. He looked up to its peak, searching for his companion.

A flash.

Isobel appeared beside him, bundled in her thick coat. She shook the snow off her shoulders, then stooped to pick up a stone talisman from the ground.

"How did it look from up there?" Chinelo asked.

Isobel removed her hood, releasing her flowing hair. It too had grown since the start of their journey, falling just below her shoulders in a wavy cascade.

"I think we are close. Off to the north it looks like the rough terrain ends and the grasslands begin. I think I could see a road in the distance, so that's a good sign."

"Ah. So, we are probably already back in Iskara, then?"

"As best I can tell." She reached down for her pack and opened the flap, revealing a large bundle on top of her belongings. Chinelo peered over her shoulder as she carefully unwound it. He could just barely see the tip of Mort's snout poking from within the bundle.

"Still hibernating," Isobel said with a sigh.

"Is the treatment you applied working?" he asked.

She looked up. "It appears so. The talisman seems to be keeping his skin moist, so he should be in excellent health once spring arrives, though probably not in excellent temper."

"Well then, he'd be his normal self. The little grump lump," Chinelo said, resting his hands on his knees.

"He is not a grump lump!" Isobel cried.

Chinelo smirked and raised his eyebrows

"Fine. But he's a cute grump lump," Isobel said, closing her pack and lifting it to her shoulders. "Let's get moving. I'm sorely in need of a good night's rest. I think I saw a cave up ahead where we can set up the tent."

"Sounds like a good plan, great keeper of the grump lump."

Isobel rolled her eyes. "Oh, stop."

The cave was shallow but well sheltered. Chinelo checked the floor for evidence of any animals. Aside from some old ashes, he found nothing. He glanced at the cave's ceiling which was covered in patches of soot.

Their tent was not large, but it was cozy. They could just fit their bedding and packs inside, but the confined space helped the air within to stay warm while they slept. After eating, they huddled within, using one of Isobel's magically summoned lights to see in the darkness. Isobel scribbled in a notebook while Chinelo watched happily from beneath his blanket.

"What's going in the diary tonight?" Chinelo asked slyly.

Isobel shot him a look. "You know it's not the same if I tell you."

"Just wanted to make sure you only had nice things to say about me."

"Nice try. But you will not break me, Chinelo. A girl must have her secrets."

Chinelo smirked. He rolled to his back and put his hands behind his head. He'd never been one for camping. Who would have thought that he would spend over a year of his life on the road?

He frowned. It had already been fourteen months since Eshgar was destroyed. The pangs of grief were still present, but they had long since dulled, only reappearing on lonely, quiet nights.

It was strange. He missed his homeland. He missed his family. He missed his friends. That aching, that longing to see them again drove him forward. But somehow, this new life had become like home. Traveling the kingdoms, seeing the world, journeying across the continent, that was home.

He glanced to the side. Isobel proudly closed her diary and opened her spell-book. She scribbled in it, another piece of her nightly ritual. She was incredibly disciplined, practicing spell-coding regardless of how tired she was. It was this discipline that had rapidly expanded both of their magical arsenals.

Chinelo rolled onto his arm. "So, what does this one do?"

"Oh, the spell? Basically, it would let me melt metals and then solidify them in new shapes. I'm not sure exactly how useful that would be, but I imagine it would look impressive. It's kind of an offshoot of fire magic, but it uses a conjugation of fire which means heat. So instead of something like *'Vasht'* or *'Vasht'ra'* it would be based on *'Ba'vasht.'*"

"So could you use that to control metals?"

"In a sense, though I'm sure you remember that the details of how they would be controlled have to be defined before the spell is cast."

"Ah. Right."

Isobel leaned forward, resting her elbows on her knees. "Have you thought about any spells you would like in your spell-core?"

Chinelo scratched his head. "Beyond what's already there? Do you think it would be possible to make one that would increase my sword's range? That could be useful."

"Oh, of course! That would be easy. Think about the activation conditions for that. I'll consider some options for the specifics, but that—" she yawned "—that shouldn't be a problem."

Chinelo sat up, folding his blanket down to his knees. "Want to call it a night?"

"It would probably be a good idea. Really hit a wall there all of a sudden." She yawned again. Her eyes twitched.

Chinelo squatted on his knees and hugged her. "Goodnight, Isobel."

Isobel wrapped her arms around his neck. "Goodnight, Chinelo. Sleep well."

Isobel inspected the map she had drawn in her spell-book. She glanced up, surveying the flat, grassy plains in which she stood. "It should be around here somewhere."

"Good," Chinelo responded. "Are you ready?"

"As ready as one can be. Slaying one of those... *things*... is a bit of a daunting task."

"We can do this," Chinelo said, laying his hand on her shoulder. "We know how they see. We know how they die, and we are better prepared than before."

Isobel nodded. She hung her spell-book back on her hip. "The good news is that this time we aren't going to have to fight inside a town."

"There's one nearby, right?"

"Yes, but assuming the obelisk is where it is supposed to be, we should be pretty far from it."

Chinelo cracked his neck and stretched his broad shoulders. "Good."

"I'm going to take a look and see if I can find it." Isobel dropped her pack and drew two stones from her pockets. She surged esht into a tattoo on the right of her abdomen. Her strength grew. She dropped one of the stones. Then, with a mighty throw, she hurled the other straight up into the air. It flew until it was no longer visible.

"See you in a few!" Isobel dug her hands into her pockets and found two additional stones. Clasping one in each hand, she channeled esht into her left. The world around her imploded into a single point, then exploded in a brilliant display of color. She was in the sky, drawn to the stone she had launched.

She fell, and the ground far below her began to grow more detailed. She turned her head, rapidly surveying the land. She would only have a few seconds.

Grass. Everything was grass. It shimmered in muted green waves as its color slowly returned with the coming spring. Then, she saw it. A small gray mound. The wind rushed by her ears. Her stomach seemed to hang within her, resisting her descent towards the rapidly approaching earth. She channeled her esht into her right hand, and everything vanished.

With a thud, she appeared on the ground, and the stone she threw fell at her feet. She pointed in the direction of the gray mound. "That way."

They gathered their belongings and continued, plunging deeper and deeper into Iskara's expansive eastern grasslands. Their journey had been slow, monotonous, and challenging. Caald's harsh landscape protected it from invaders, but it made travel difficult. The lush flatlands of Iskara were welcoming, belying the dark secrets they held. Though they were far from the eastern coast, the faint scent of the sea still drifted over the plains. The open fields presented few obstacles to the ocean wind.

"We need to remember something," Isobel said, raising a finger. "The last one was able to vanish and reappear because it was bound to 'homvelcht.' We should assume that this one will be bound to a different word. Our priority will be to draw it from the obelisk."

"Right. I can keep it distracted like I did last time."

"Good!" Isobel replied. "Once it's far enough away, I'll use my travel stones to vanish to the obelisk. Then I'll destroy its core!"

"Sounds like a plan."

"For safety, I should probably go ahead and apply protection." Isobel channeled esht into a tattoo on the left of her abdomen. She touched Chinelo's forehead, protecting him in an invisible barrier, then applied the barrier to herself. "That will only work once, but if all goes well, we won't need it."

Chinelo touched his sword's hilt. The dark blue spell-core at its pommel hovered and swirled. He had learned several incantations and was already beginning to grasp the rules and syntax of the Ancient Tongue, though its written form was still a mystery to him. With Isobel's help, he had filled his sword with pre-prepared spells, several of which were of his own design.

He would use them. He would keep her safe. This time, he would ensure she wasn't hurt.

A gray mass poked above a small rise in the ground. Isobel ran forward, cresting the hill. She stopped. Chinelo's brow furrowed. Ordinarily he would have felt the pulsing once the obelisk was visible, but the ground was oddly silent. He joined Isobel's side.

"That's not good," she said.

The obelisk, or rather, the obelisk's remnants lay shattered on the ground. Judging by the size of the pieces, it had been significantly larger than the others they had seen. Chinelo descended the hill and approached the broken structure. Something crunched beneath his boot. Looking down, he gasped. On the ground were fragments of a sun-bleached human skull. He circled the ruin and soon found several other bones along with a few chunks of rusty armor. Whoever activated the obelisk had not been fortunate in the ensuing battle.

Isobel remained on the hill, leaning on her staff.

"This looks like the right spot, Isobel. I think it was activated a while ago, though."

"How long?" she asked.

"It's difficult to say. There are a lot of bones down here, and they are heavily bleached. So, the earliest we are looking at is a month ago. The rust on the armor would indicate it was even earlier than that. Probably several months or a year."

"The last one's body evaporated when it died, but the head remained."

Chinelo looked around. "Right, but there's not one here."

"I have a hunch." Isobel planted her staff firmly on the ground in front of her. "First, none of those fragments have the signature diamond shaped hole that all the obelisks have had. Second, look at those depressions in the ground."

Chinelo squinted. The grass seemed to be growing in inconsistent lengths, almost as if the ground wasn't fully smooth. There was a pattern.

"Hmmm. I didn't notice those. They look almost like..."

"Footprints! And big ones at that. Now, I have an idea, but I'm not sure it will work." Isobel closed her eyes. "Douse: Esht"

Hundreds of glowing wisps erupted from her staff, gradually forming distinct lines. They flowed from its tip, pointing in numerous directions. Chinelo glanced down. One was flowing directly into his chest, entering his body right below his heart. He glanced at Isobel. She had a similar line, only it was much thicker and pointed from the staff into her arm.

He looked around. Every blade of grass had its own glowing wisp that connected it with the staff's head. Isobel moved her staff. All the lines moved. Thicker lines pointed off to random locations in the distance, likely connecting to small rodents and creatures that hid within the tall grass.

"What are you doing, Isobel?"

"Searching for esht, though I don't have the range I need yet."

The lines intensified. Suddenly, a brilliant array of wisps burst from her staff and flew off into the distance beyond the horizon to the east. There were thousands of them, and they all moved subtly. Chinelo cocked his head. There was one that seemed particularly pronounced, like Isobel's, but brighter.

"That's the town," Isobel said. "Still not what I'm looking for."

An incredibly thick line erupted from her staff. It flew beyond the horizon, heading north.

"There!" Isobel exclaimed.

"Our target?" Chinelo asked.

"Hopefully." She ran in the direction of the light.

Chinelo followed, jostling his heavy pack in the process.

"Isobel, will the townsfolk be able to see those lights?"

"Probably. I may have given them a bit of a scare."

Chinelo glanced at the thick line that ran towards the town. "I think you should deactivate it, Isobel. Call this my hunch."

Isobel nodded. The lines vanished. She ran faster.

They crossed the fields, following the enormous trail of footprints. They pushed through the thick grass, leaving a wake of depressed foliage behind them. Small rodents, covered in brown and white spots, scurried out of their way, squeaking and chattering as they found new hiding places in the grass.

The ground rose. Isobel and Chinelo no longer ran on flat earth but scrambled instead up a rolling hill. They reached its peak. Chinelo heard a low rumbling. Ahead of them, he saw a large stone structure. It resembled a fortress but one that had been shattered by some great impact and hastily reassembled. He barely had time to look at it before Isobel took off running again, flying down the hill at incredible speed.

They neared the fortress. The rumbling continued. It was low and uneven, shaking the ground in short bursts. Something hard hit Chinelo in the face. Looking over his shoulder, he saw an odd shape hovering above the grass. Was that a pebble?

"Ow!" Isobel cried. She halted.

Pebbles, stones, tufts of grass, and dirt hovered over the field at various heights, moving gently in the wind. Isobel reached out and touched one of the stones, giving it a push. It floated away, colliding with other objects and causing them to bounce in wild directions.

Chinelo glanced at Isobel. The ends of her hair curled up, pointing towards the sky so that they no longer rested on her shoulders.

Isobel swung her staff. "Wind!" A powerful gust of air blasted from her staff and pushed the debris away. It caused a ripple in the grass, and it expanded around them in a wide circle, clearing a path. The rumbling continued.

Isobel walked slowly through the grass. Her feet kicked up dust that seemed to hover in the air indefinitely. She fixed her eyes on the fortress. Something was off. It seemed still from a distance, but as they drew close, it almost looked like it had moved. The rumbling ceased.

"Douse: Esht."

A thick line flew towards the fortress. Suddenly, it moved again, turning in their direction. A large pillar rose from the earth and slammed down, shaking the ground. Chinelo gasped.

"We need to drop our packs. Quickly!"

It wasn't a fortress. It was a beast, like the one they had seen in Ata, only covered in broken fragments of stone. It moved like an enormous ape, supporting itself on its muscular legs and the knuckles of its massive clawed right hand. Its entire left forearm was a single pillar of stone, held to its bicep by tendrils of flesh and sinew. Red glowing lines ran down its surface in a grid-like pattern, ending in a giant stone hand. Like the creature of Ata, it had no proper head. Instead, its neck ended in something that resembled a round stone table supported by a single column beneath it.

It crawled forward, shaking the earth beneath Isobel's feet. If she didn't move her esht, it wouldn't be able to see either her or Chinelo. So why? Why did it keep crawling towards them? It drew closer and closer. Isobel's chest suddenly felt light. Why was it so big? The creature in Ata was already colossal, but this one was something beyond that entirely.

"Isobel!" Chinelo said. "Why is it still moving towards us?"

"I—I don't know. It shouldn't be able to see us."

The beast halted and moved its faceless stone head. It groaned, then emitted a low guttural growl from its trachea. A pulse of red light spread across its body, moving from its chest to its extremities. The whole earth shook. Isobel and Chinelo were launched off their feet and flew into the air. Isobel winced and braced for the impact of the ground, but it didn't come. She floated weightlessly, spinning and tumbling. Around her, numerous stones floated. What was going on? Why didn't they fall? She twisted her body, trying to face the beast.

It stood there motionless, silently watching them float off the ground. It raised its massive stone arm above its head. Isobel's eyes widened. The beast had torn the spell-core from the obelisk and fixed it to its chest, surrounding it in a crude cage of stone. It pulsed red as the creature slammed its stone fist to the ground.

Isobel fell. It was sudden. It was violent. It was as if her weight had increased by a factor of twenty. Her vision went blurry, and her back collided with the ground. She felt a sharp pain at the base of her skull. The wind left her lungs, and everything went black.

CHINELO WAS NOT A COMPLICATED MAN. He saw the world as it was, not as it could be. And as he saw it, any opponent, either man or beast, could be slain by his sword. It was a simple viewpoint, but he had trusted it on numerous occasions, and it had rarely betrayed him.

That was before her, before Isobel. She had introduced him to a world beyond anything he had imagined. A world of magic and monsters. A world of gods and mages. A world where even fate could be defied. Isobel saw the world as it could be, not as it was. She had hope, and hope was contagious.

However, the world he had grown to love threatened to end, for as he stood from the ground, pushing against the heavy weight of his own body, he saw her lying motionless. A pool of blood slowly accumulated around her, shining in a deep crimson.

He screamed her name, but she didn't respond. The ground shook. He turned and faced the colossus that thundered towards him, a beast of stone and sinew. Against such a foe, his sword seemed like a mere toy.

A storm surged inside of him. Rage and fear, affection and hate, a selfish urge to run and a selfless desire to protect. They swirled and mixed, combining in an indecipherable tempest. He gripped his sword's hilt. He was not a complicated man. He would fight the world as it was.

He had accumulated strength before the impact, and he had been fortunate enough to be oriented so that he fell feet first. Even so, the crash had shaken his whole body. He should have been protected. Isobel had replicated Haru's spell, but somehow, it had been useless both to him and to her. His mind raced.

The pebbles! They had run headlong into stones that levitated from the beast's strange power. Their protection broke before they were even near the beast.

The monster ambled forward, pointing its head toward the ground where Isobel lay.

Why? It didn't make sense. The other creature had only attacked when esht moved, lashing out like a wild raging animal. Yet this one—it moved with purpose. It moved with chilling intelligence.

Chinelo surged his esht, channeling it to his extremities and back into his core. He circled the monster to draw it away from Isobel's body. The beast turned its head, tracking his movements, then looked away disinterestedly. It continued its slow crawl toward Isobel.

Chinelo grunted, and with multiplied strength, he leapt forward, dashing towards the creature's right side. Attacking would have no lasting effect on the beast, but a distraction was all he needed, something to buy him time to formulate a plan. The beast's glowing core pulsed, and Chinelo felt his body become weightless. He gave a slight push on his toe and floated above the monster's titanic form.

He was unbound by gravity, floating through the air with what momentum he had when he left the ground. It was disorienting. From above, Chinelo looked down on the beast's back, covered in stone plates like the rest of its body. Dark flesh showed through the gaps in the improvised armor, and there was a noticeably large gap directly behind the creature's head, presumably to allow its neck to move. Chinelo twirled his blade and pointed it at the creature. He knew exactly how to exploit such a weak point.

"Fireball: Threefold!"

Orbs of flame appeared and fell upon the creature. Two crashed into the stone plates, but one hit its mark, burning the skinless muscle in the creature's neck. It roared, droning in a deep guttural cry. Chinelo felt the weight return to his body, and he fell, plummeting towards the creature below. He twisted, pointing his feet downwards. With a great thud, he landed on the monster's back, using his accumulated strength to withstand the landing. The creature turned its head, trying to find the gnat that had dared to strike it.

Chinelo crouched and gripped the edge of the plate on which he stood, steadying himself against the slow lurching motions. Cold, oily tendrils brushed against his fingers. He gripped tighter, and the stone's rough edges dug into the skin of his hand. He raised his sword, pointing its shining tip towards the exposed muscles on the monster's neck. He drew in a breath, forcing esht into his sword's handle.

"Freeze!"

He thrust the blade deep into the monster's neck. Blood spurted and froze into an icy black bloom. His position had been awkward, and he'd not been able to generate much force behind his blow, but the added frozen blades that sprouted from the creature's veins would make his attack devastating.

The monster lurched and cried. Chinelo felt a sudden pull, as if he was falling into the sky. His hand slipped, but he managed to withdraw his blade from the monster's neck before he floated away. He gasped. The ground was so far below. A fall would be dangerous if not deadly. He needed a way to move. He needed a way to combat the weightlessness.

The few words he knew flowed through his head.

"Icht"—to form. *"Belekt"*—to release. *"Sono"*—water. *"Fulrech"*—wind.

How would those help? Magic formed from esht, but there was a small distance between the point from where it exited the body and the point where the spell was conjured. It was like vapor from a boiling kettle, only becoming visible after a short gap. Spells rarely affected the caster unless they were specifically crafted to do so. Fire did not burn the skin. Water did not cause clothes to become damp. Force did not recoil back on the caster. However, there might be a way.

Chinelo bent his left thumb and pointed it into the heel of his hand. He accumulated esht into his thumb, then uttered a command.

"Belekt fulrech!"

Wind burst from his thumb and into his palm. It was strong and rough, and it spread like water pouring into a spoon, blasting outwards from his hand. Ordinarily, such a current of air would be inadequate to move him, but without gravity's pull, he spun and descended toward the ground in a chaotic spiral. His movement was dizzying and difficult to control, but he had closed the distance between him and the grass. He swung his arm, blasting the wind beneath him, causing him to gradually slow.

Out of the corner of his eye, he saw the creature raise its stone arm. A wave of red light passed over it, and its massive stone fist slammed against the dirt. Chinelo plummeted. He landed and rolled to his feet, using the last of his multiplied strength to withstand his increased weight. He dashed forward. He had to bring the creature down. It had stopped moving towards Isobel, but ultimately, his attacks had merely annoyed it. He needed to strike the core in its chest.

He sprinted beneath the creature's legs. Its ankles were almost as high as Chinelo's shoulders, so reaching them would have been difficult, were he not prepared.

The creature slowly moved its arm and reached for him, attempting to grab him with its immense clawed hand. Chinelo rushed past the creature's ankles and spun on his toes, skidding to a stop. He surged his esht, forcing it into his sword where it accumulated in the pommel, awaiting his command. He glanced from one leg to the other. The right was coated in a layer of stone. The left, however, was completely exposed.

"Extend!" Chinelo shouted. He swung his sword. Cut grass fluttered around him. Blood spurted from a grisly gash torn by an invisible edge, an extension of Chinelo's sword.

The creature groaned and leaned forward. With the tendon in its heel severed, it struggled to support its enormous weight. Already, the wound began to close, knitting itself shut with a network of writhing fibers and squirming appendages, but the monster's momentum could not be stopped. It toppled forward, and Chinelo saw a flash of red light. The beast's spell-core was in view, and with his extended blade, it was within range. He lunged forward, thrusting his sword in the direction of the core.

Impact.

Steel on stone. Blade on rock. His sword vibrated, sending the shock of the blow through Chinelo's arm and into his shoulder. His strike had missed.

He glanced up. No! It had been blocked!

The creature covered its core with its hand, protecting it with a layer of stone that was bound to the back.

Chinelo leapt back. This beast, this abomination, exhibited none of the ferocity of the previous one. The last monster was wild and feral, but this one was cold and deliberate. It knew its strengths. It knew its weaknesses. Chinelo's mind raced. What was different? Its head was composed of the same stone. It lacked eyes, ears, and a mouth, but somehow it seemed to recognize its surroundings.

Had he been wrong? Did they see by some other means than tracking esht movement? Or was this beast merely more cognizant than the last? Based on what Chinelo had seen at the broken obelisk, this monster had been awakened months ago. The one they fought in Ata had been awake for mere moments. Was this how these beasts truly behaved? Was the manic flailing of the previous one the result of it being disoriented, like a man awoken by an attacker in the night? Or perhaps was it a product of the environment, a village of hundreds of esht sources?

Chinelo shook his head. He did not have answers. The world was as it was. He would do as he always did. He would adapt.

The beast turned its head back to Isobel's motionless body. It crawled forward, crashing its knuckles into the grass and dragging its heavy stone arm. Chinelo ran, bounding through the tall grass like a lion chasing its prey. The beast turned its head towards him, and a dull rumbling escaped from its throat. Once again, Chinelo was weightless. His footsteps pushed him from the ground. However, he had a solution for that problem.

"Belekt fulrech!"

He twisted and pointed his arm behind him, expelling a jet of air from his hand. He flew forward, spiraling over the monster's back. Then, it moved. It braced itself on its right hand and raised its mighty stone arm, preparing to slam it to the ground and send Chinelo plummeting into the earth. Chinelo moved his arm, changing the direction of his flight, directing his trajectory straight for the beast's left elbow.

"Extend!"

He slashed his blade, driving it into the tissue above the monster's elbow. His sword flashed in the sunlight, shining like the crescent moon as it cleaved through the exposed red flesh. A stream of black blood erupted and hung weightlessly in the air, then fell. The cut had been deep. The monster groaned.

Chinelo landed on his feet and slid to a stop. The monster's stone arm dangled from the severed tissue. The cut had not fully sundered the appendage, but it had devastated the muscles. The weight of the stone column did the rest. Chinelo winced as he heard a horrific tearing, like wood splitting from a tree trunk. The stone column fell, ripping from the monster's arm and crashing to the ground in a turbulent cloud of dust.

Chinelo rushed forward. The creature roared in pain. Tendrils erupted from the grisly wound on its arm, writhing and coiling toward the stone column. Chinelo planted his feet and gripped his sword with both hands.

"Fire!"

A column of flame shot from his sword, billowing and blooming in a brilliant blaze. It expanded as it flew and ignited the wriggling tendrils that sprouted from the beast's arm. The monster screeched, lifting its hand from the ground. It would only be a moment before it toppled. Without the support of either of its arms, the beast's massive weight would drive it to the earth. That would be Chinelo's chance to deliver the lethal blow.

Something hit Chinelo's side, knocking the wind from his lungs. His stream of flame flickered out. He felt crushed, pressed in on all sides by some great oppressive force. He looked down. The monster had grabbed him in its enormous hand. He had been wrong. Without the weight of its stone arm, the beast did not need additional support to balance itself.

Chinelo hacked at the monster's girthy fingers. The grip tightened. Something within him broke. He screamed. In his agony, his sword fell from his hand and stabbed into the ground far below him.

Chinelo grew sick. His entire body felt only pain. His head fell back. He saw the inverted horizon, a green wave that bordered the pale blue sky. There was something else: shapes, figures. Many of them. Were those people in the distance? The edges of his vision blurred.

Isobel opened her eyes. Why was the sky so bright? Why was it so fuzzy? She squinted and slowly sat up. Her head throbbed, like a hundred hammers were slamming an iron band around her skull. She reached up and rubbed the back of her head. She felt something warm and sticky. Blood, and a lot of it.

Frantically, she covered her wound with her right hand and channeled esht into it. The gash closed and healed, but the pain in her head did not dissipate. She squeezed her eyes shut. Why did everything hurt so much? Why did her stomach rebel against her, sending a wave of nausea into her throat? She attempted to stand. The world spun. Why did the ground shift? Why was the grass so loud?

A scream pierced the air, driving a sharp pain through her skull. Isobel grabbed her head and pressed her hands into it. Why was there so much noise? She opened her eyes. Another scream. She winced. That voice. It was familiar.

She looked up. Chinelo was clutched in the hand of the monster, and it was drawing him towards a gaping maw in its chest. Its stone armor had moved away to reveal the beast's jaws, and at their center hovered the monster's spell-core, surrounded by a shell of stone and flailing tentacles.

"NO!" she shouted.

She ran. Her feet pounded on the grass, inflicting another hammer strike on her head with every step. She ignored the pain. Chinelo was about to die, and she refused to let that happen. She had previously dropped her staff, but that did not matter. She had prepared a precaution for such an event—a spell tattooed around her right wrist. She channeled her esht into it, and her staff flashed to her hand, drawn by the power of the monster she had slain. She shifted her esht, moving it to her left abdomen. She was protected. She moved her esht again, forcing it into her right abdomen. She was strengthened.

"Form: Sword!"

The monster lifted its head as if startled. Isobel leapt and hit the ground beneath it. The monster groaned, and its core flashed. Isobel felt her body grow light, as if gravity no longer affected her. She pushed off the ground with a great surge of strength, flying directly upwards. Her blade swung in a fearsome circle. With a yell she cut cleanly through the beast's wrist, triggering an enraged roar from the monster. Free from its grip, Chinelo pushed away from the floating hand and tumbled weightlessly through the air.

Isobel's head throbbed. Light was overwhelming. She gritted her teeth. She would not be stopped. Without gravity, she ascended, flying towards the sky. She twisted and dug her hand into her pocket, finding one of the two travel stones she kept there. She hurled it straight down, then grabbed the other stone. After a moment, she channeled her esht into it, and the world collapsed around her.

She reappeared beneath the monster and glanced up. The maw in its chest closed, and the stone plates returned to their protective positions. Suddenly, her weight returned. Her sword fell to the ground, knocking her off balance. A strange noise sounded from behind her. Squishing, tearing, and popping. She looked over her shoulder. The monster had regrown its hand, and it was reaching for her. She stumbled and ran between its legs.

Her stomach twisted. She turned around and steadied herself on her staff, trying not to vomit. She looked up. The beast raised its stone arm. On the other side, she saw Chinelo brace himself against his sword.

The beast slammed its stone hand into the ground and a wave of red light surged through the column. Isobel felt the skin on her face stretch and pull downwards, sagging as if she had suddenly aged. Her body was heavy. Her ankle gave out and she stumbled to her knee. The dull ache from the sprain returned. She felt lightheaded. The force did not subside. She shifted and braced herself with her arm. The force pushed down on her. Her vision grew blurry. Thinking quickly, she surged as much esht as she could muster into her staff and uttered a command.

"Nullify!"

A shockwave blasted from her staff. The weight ceased, though it was replaced by fatigue. She had spent too much esht, sending her spell over a much larger area than necessary. Without her increased reserves, she would have been completely drained.

The monster turned and faced her, cocking its head.

Chinelo felt an intense sting coming from his side, and it stabbed into him with every breath. He looked up. The monster was crawling around Isobel, keeping a considerable distance between them. Something had changed in its posture. Its back was arched. It seemed to be trying to make itself look large. Did it feel threatened? Isobel stepped back and fired a torrent of magical attacks at the beast.

He shook his head. He needed it to expose its core. He ran. If he could sever its hand again, it would not be able to cover the core. The beast groaned. His body grew weightless once more.

Isobel floated off the ground. She hesitated. The beast was watching her, waiting for her to nullify its spell. Instead, she pointed her staff at the beast.

"Volley!"

Shining blades formed in front of her staff and shot toward the beast's core. It shifted, deflecting them off its armored chest. It raised its stone arm. Isobel's eyes widened. She was too far off the ground. She had no way of preventing the attack before it hit. If only she could move.

Chinelo shot across her field of vision and slashed through the monster's left arm. It grew limp and gravity returned. Isobel landed on her feet and ran forward. While the monster was distracted, perhaps she could hit the core.

Chinelo watched as Isobel hurried toward the beast, preparing to strike. In horror, he saw the monster snatch her from the ground. Her staff was knocked away.

"Isobel!"

She pushed against the monster's fingers, but they refused to budge. The creature's chest opened to reveal its hideous gaping maw. Within it, organs, viscera, and entrails pulsed and wriggled, and at their center hovered the beast's core.

Chinelo extended his blade and charged forward. He had to free her from the monster's grip.

"Wait!" she shouted. "Stay back!"

Chinelo halted. He didn't understand. She was going to be consumed. He had to save her!

"NO!"

"Chinelo! Trust me!"

Chinelo panicked. His heart felt cold. His lungs felt hollow. His fingers grew numb. She was going to die. He had to protect her! Why did she refuse?

Isobel exhaled. *This* was her chance. She would only have one opportunity to strike. The beast was intelligent, but so was she. It thought it had won, but she knew the truth.

Isobel hovered her hand over her right shoulder and channeled her esht into her tattoo. The hilt of a dagger appeared.

Slowly, the beast drew her to its jaws. They were revolting. They were sickening. Squirming tendrils sprouted from the slick entrails within. They grew and reached for her, developing rows of teeth. Isobel pulled on the hilt and her dagger fully formed. Then, as the beast's mandibles closed around her, she yelled and plunged her dagger into its core. Red mist erupted, filling her vision with brilliant eddies of crimson. The creature roared.

Words, shapes, colors, and phrases suddenly rushed into her mind. Knowledge of the universe, of the forces that bound the planets, of that which drew all to the heart of the world was suddenly hers. Gravity would bend to her will. As her esht swelled, a single word echoed through her soul.

"GARIASHEQ!"

CHAPTER 27

CHINELO GROANED AS HE LIFTED THE enormous shard of rock and hurled it to the side. The beast had fallen screeching and melting into a pool of thick black oil that rapidly evaporated into noxious vapor. The numerous stone chunks fused to its body had crumbled and collapsed in a pile. He tore at it, flinging smaller stones to the side and using all the strength he could summon to lift the larger pieces. At the heart of the pile, he hoped to find Isobel.

The pile slowly shrunk, and he hurled a large section of rock over his shoulder. He gasped. There she was, lying on her back. She had been lucky. The stone armor on the monster's chest had fallen around her, creating a cavity of air that prevented her from being crushed by the larger plates on its back. Chinelo hooked his arms under her shoulders and gently dragged her from the pile into a soft patch of grass. He laid her on the ground and pressed his ear to her chest. Her heart thumped quietly. He let out a relieved sigh and knelt beside her.

She looked peaceful. Her light lashes rested upon her cheeks behind her spectacles. He chuckled. How did she manage to keep those from flying off her face? Though, as he leaned closer, he caught a glimpse of what he thought might be the method: a delicate inscription running down the rims on each side of her face. She really did think of everything.

Her chest rose and fell with each quiet breath. Small insects alighted on her face, but Chinelo quickly warded them off with a swipe of his hand. The moments became minutes, piling upon each other for the better part of an hour.

The wind rustled the grass around Chinelo, and as it did, a feeling arose in his chest, an intense longing and worry. On multiple occasions during the battle, he had thought that he would lose her. He had felt powerless to protect her, just as he had been when his kingdom fell. But he couldn't lose her.

He *couldn't.*

If she was gone, what would he have left? He needed to grow stronger, to become the knight he was meant to be. He needed to ensure that no matter where she went, she would be safe.

He needed to tell her how he truly felt.

He treasured his time with her, but there was a part of him that was always scared around her—scared that something would happen to her, scared that something would separate the two of them, scared that she would be taken from his life, just like everyone else had been. He had done his best to quiet those fears, but they had never truly faded. He held her hand in his. Today, he *would* overcome his fears.

Chinelo paused. Was he really thinking about this now? It seemed silly, but somehow, it was all that would occupy his mind.

A shadow moved across the grass. Chinelo's head popped up. He released Isobel's hand and leapt to his feet, turning around rapidly. He was not alone.

There were close to twenty men and women dressed in the green robes of the Interior Guard. Chinelo drew his sword and faced the crowd before him. His heart thumped in his chest. He had never fought so many mages before; however, he would do what he must to protect Isobel, no matter the cost.

At the front of the crowd, two figures stood. One, a man, was dressed in a robe like that of the guardsmen around him, only the shimmering fabric was a deep crimson with silver filigree. His regal clothing curved around his broad shoulders, flowing down his arms and ending just above his laced fingers.

On his right hand he wore many rings, each with a tiny glowing spell-core. His left hand was inked with complex tattoos that were partially hidden by his sleeve. He had no rapier like the guardsmen that surrounded him. His gray hair and beard were combed but slightly unkempt, tousled by the wind. A proud smirk showed from beneath the mustache that flowed into his beard.

The other figure, a tall woman in a black leather cuirass and armored boots, stood slightly behind. Her complexion was fawn with a subtle olive undertone, and she wore a strip of thin, slightly translucent cloth over her eyes. Her arms were muscular and bare, aside from a pair of gauntlets and a tattered green cloak that was bundled over her shoulders.

Her dark, wavy hair was tied back into a thick ponytail, but two longer tresses framed her face, ending in ornamental silver rings.

The front row of soldiers drew their shining silver rapiers. Some had gleaming spell-cores at their pommels like Chinelo's sword did. Others were held in the hands of Branded Mages.

"Stay back!" Chinelo shouted.

"Sheath your blade, young man," the bearded man called out in a deep voice. His tone was commanding but somehow jovial. "This is not a fight you can win." He took a step forward. "Now. Kneel."

Chinelo raised an eyebrow. He tightened his grip on his sword.

"So disrespectful. Don't you agree?" The man looked over his shoulder at the woman. She gave no response.

He shrugged. "No matter." The man unclasped his hands and raised his left. "Kneel!" He flicked his wrist and curled his fingers.

Chinelo's scowl intensified. Why would he—

He was on his knees, and his sword had fallen to the ground. His body had moved on its own. He tried to move his arms, but they were frozen.

Isobel's eyes flew open, and she bolted upright. Her head throbbed, drawing forth an intense feeling of motion sickness. Her whole body felt wrong. It was as if her sense of balance had been muddled or shifted. She pressed her hands against her forehead. The point of impact, a point just above the transition from her neck to her skull, seemed to radiate ripples of dull pain around her face. Her ears, her eyes, her brain, all ached with an intensity she never thought was possible.

She heard footfalls and the rustling of cloth in the wind. She looked up. A single figure stood above her. It was a woman, one who was in her late thirties and whose face was framed by voluminous jet-black hair. Isobel's eyes widened. Her heart leapt. It had been so long, yet here she was.

"Iva?"

CHAPTER 28

ISOBEL CLIMBED TO HER FEET. A powerful pulse of pain shot through her head, triggering another accompanying surge of nausea. She winced but continued and embraced Iva, wrapping her arms below her shoulders.

"Iva! I've missed you so much! I—" Isobel leaned back. Iva was tense and did not reciprocate the embrace. "Iva?"

Iva frowned and looked down at her. "So. It really was you."

Isobel stepped back. "What?"

Iva rubbed her forehead and sighed. "I was hoping it wasn't. I was really hoping it wasn't. What a mess you've gotten yourself into."

"Iva? I—I don't understand." Her brow furrowed. "Why—wait why are you wearing a veil?"

"That is for your protection, child," a deep voice called from behind her.

Isobel turned and gasped. An array of rapiers, held in the hands of guardsmen, was pointed at her. At the company's head stood a man. *Him.*

Archmage Harlyle.

He was just as she recalled: a tall, muscular man in his sixties, robes of deep crimson, warm tan skin, hair of pale gray. It was him. It was the Archmage, her enemy, and kneeling on the ground beside him was Chinelo. His face was pointed towards the dirt, and the Archmage's claw-like hand hovered over his head.

"Isobel," Chinelo rasped in a voice that was barely audible, "run!"

The rage that had smoldered within her for months erupted. Without a moment's hesitation, Isobel launched a volley of spells from her wrist. The Archmage smirked and raised his hand, swatting away the shots like flies. Several ricocheted into the mages behind him, sending them tumbling to the ground as crystals burst from their bodies. Isobel summoned her staff and pointed it at him, surging all of her esht in her anger.

Iva moved like lightning. She wrenched Isobel's staff from her hand and swung it at Isobel's legs, knocking her off her feet.

"Don't," Iva said. "Don't fight him."

"Well, well," the Archmage sneered. "Isn't she a feisty one?"

Isobel groaned and sat up. "Iva? Why are you with *him*?"

"That doesn't matter," Iva responded. "*Don't* fight him."

"But he's killed hundreds of thousands!"

The Archmage stepped forward, still pointing his hand at Chinelo. "Child, your accusation wounds me. I would never do such a thing. I am a man of the kingdom. I am the protector of this land. I would never harm my people like that." He waved his free hand extravagantly while sneering. "No. No. No, child. If you are looking for someone to blame, then direct your wrath at my irritable companion."

"Quiet, Harlyle!" Iva growled.

The Archmage laughed wickedly. "You see, child? Irritable. But it seems most witches are. You've certainly demonstrated similar behavior toward two of my favorite mages. Surely, Brennen and Elgacht didn't deserve such brutal treatments."

Isobel's mind raced. Her eyes widened. "Iva? What does he mean?"

Iva frowned and looked away.

"Wait. Was it you?" Isobel demanded. "*You* destroyed those towns?"

Iva's shoulders tensed. Her frown deepened. "And if I did?"

Isobel felt lightheaded. The world spun around her. "Why? Why would you? How could you?"

Iva crouched before her. Faintly, through the thin fabric of the blindfold, Isobel could discern the shape of Iva's eyes.

"I'm creating a better world," Iva said.

"I—I don't understand."

"You've seen them, haven't you, Isobel? You've seen those abominations that sleep beneath the obelisks. They are beasts, monsters, false deities. They stole the magic that was ours. They dangled the right to control our fates in front of us then took it for themselves. They slaughtered our ancestors and left us to rot. I'll kill them, Isobel. I'll kill them, and in doing so I'll mend what they broke."

"But Nellborough, Eshgar—" Tears streamed down Isobel's face.

Iva's voice swelled in intensity. "Think, Isobel! Think of how much better our lives could have been if we could choose our own fates. Think about how different things could have been if you and I could have chosen the circumstances of our upbringings. We never would have been abused. We would never would have been abandoned. We could have been together."

"But all those people..." Isobel's eyes stung.

"Unfortunate but necessary sacrifices. Do you know what happens when those fiends consume enough esht? They grow. They learn. They regain their lost senses of self. They become unstoppable." Iva stood and crossed her arms. "I merely remove that possibility."

"So, you just slaughter entire countries?" Isobel shouted. Her vision blurred. "My friends were there, Iva. You killed them! His family was there, Iva! You killed them!"

"Yes, and had we not, they would have been devoured. It won't matter, Isobel. You don't understand now, but you will. Once I have fixed the world, you'll see that I was right."

The Archmage laughed, clearly enjoying the display that unfolded before him. Chinelo stirred. It wasn't much, but his arm moved slowly towards the Archmage's leg. The Archmage looked down in surprise.

"Oh? You're able to resist? Interesting."

He flicked his hand and Chinelo flew back, landing on his back and sliding across the ground with a groan.

"CHINELO!" Isobel shouted. She tried to stand, but her head throbbed even more.

"Lady Iva," the Archmage said sardonically, "this has all been very entertaining, but would you just get on with it?"

Iva scowled down at Isobel. "Have you found the Source yet?"

Isobel stared up at her. "What?"

"The word for the Source—have you found it?" Iva demanded, her voice growing louder.

Isobel answered without thinking. "N—no?"

Iva sighed. "Thank Yvvusta."

The Archmage's mustached twitched, his forehead wrinkling as he stared at Isobel. "How many has she consumed?"

Iva glanced down, squinting. "Two, if I had to guess."

The Archmage winced. "That *is* a problem. Ah, well, it's nothing we can't overcome." He snapped his fingers and strode toward Isobel. With a sudden movement, he grabbed her by the neck and hoisted her up in front of him. Her esht instantly depleted, leaving her with only an overwhelming inundation of pain.

"Oh my! You *do* have an abundance of esht." The Archmage looked over his shoulder. "Iva, do you have this much all the time?"

Iva looked back and forth between them, her mouth slightly open in shock. Isobel kicked and flailed, batting at the air with her feet. The grip tightened around her throat.

"I'm sorry, child," he said. "I'm sure you are a talented mage, but we can't have you running around collecting what we need, now can we?"

Isobel coughed and struggled to breathe. Everything hurt.

With a yell Chinelo ran towards them. He was halted by a slight movement of the Archmage's hand. Falling face first into the dirt, he let out a pained grunt.

Isobel choked and clawed at the Archmage's arm. She felt an overwhelming pressure, as if her head was going to explode. Her vision distorted. She gasped for air, but the Archmage's grip was iron. Her attempts to scream only resulted in a dull grating from her throat. Chinelo strained to look upwards, watching in horror as Isobel thrashed and slowly weakened.

"That's enough, Harlyle," Iva said.

Isobel extended her hand towards Iva in desperation. Her fingers moved feebly.

"Harlyle!" Iva said. "We don't need to kill her! I'll—I'll handle it."

The Archmage did not listen. He only smiled.

"HARLYLE!"

Iva tore cloth from her face and held her left hand in front of her, creating a small ring with her middle finger and thumb. The Archmage frowned, then released Isobel, who tumbled to the ground and landed in a limp heap. She coughed and gagged.

"Always so difficult," he scoffed. "You know she killed my men, don't you, witch?"

"I'll do far worse if you touch her again!" Iva snapped.

The Archmage rolled his eyes, and after one last disgusted look towards Isobel, he turned and walked away, rejoining his group of guardsmen. "Interior Guard! Sheath your blades." He looked over his shoulder. "We will discuss this later, witch."

Isobel heaved and coughed. Her extremities had gone numb, and the sudden surge of air into her lungs felt as if it were going to rupture her chest. Her eyes burned.

Iva crouched down in front of Isobel.

"Isobel. Leave Iskara. There are no obelisks in Svidar. Go there. I am not certain what you hope to accomplish, but you should abandon your quest. Forget about the gods. Forget about their power. Forget about the Source. If you continue, you will die. Run. Rest. Live. Love. When all this ends, I'll find you. And when that happens, you won't have abandoned me anymore."

Isobel's voice rasped quietly, scraping out unintelligible sounds.

"I am sorry things turned out this way, but I won't ask for your forgiveness. You will understand once this is over." Iva stood and tied the veil over her eyes. "Leave Iskara, Isobel. Consider this a warning."

She picked up Isobel's staff from where it had fallen. "I'll be taking this." She reached into the ring at the staff's head, wrapping her fingers around its core. She strained, and the staff shook. With a sudden tug, Iva pulled the core free. She tossed the empty staff before Isobel. With the core in her hand, she followed the Archmage, who had already crested a nearby hill.

After some time, Chinelo felt his muscles relax. He finally had control of his body. He crawled to his feet and ran to Isobel's side. With every breath he took, the pain in his ribs stabbed into him once more. Isobel had not moved. She only stared vacantly into the grass with rivulets of tears rolling down her cheeks. Ghastly bruises had formed on her neck.

Chinelo helped her to sit up. "Hey. Hey. Talk to me, Isobel."

Isobel's lips moved, but they only produced a silent whisper. She looked up at him sadly.

"I've got you. You're safe now," Chinelo said.

She turned her head to look over the field. They were once again alone. Chinelo reached down and grasped her hand. Her fingers barely moved.

"I'm sorry, Isobel. I—I—" his voice broke.

Isobel's body shook. She sniffled. She pulled her hand away from his and wrapped her arms over his shoulders, staring blankly into the horizon.

THE END OF PART 4

PART 5

THE FORGOTTEN MOUNTAIN

CHAPTER 29

Ⴐ

426th year, 12th month, 6th day
8 years before present day

CHINELO RUSHED DOWN THE SHADOWY STREETS with a cavalcade of fellow knights. Their armor rattled with each hurried step, and the clattering and clanging overlapped into a constant metallic drone. They raced towards Eshgar's southernmost residential district, the home of over a third of Eshgar's citizens. Sleepy faces peered out of the windows of the tall sandstone insulae that lined the streets

Another group of knights appeared from a side street. Chinelo spied a familiar set of locks protruding from one of the knights' helmets.

"Azuka!" He called as he joined his older brother's side.

"Oh! Chinelo! You're here, too?" Azuka replied. His face was wide and firm, with a well-defined jaw and a beard that was cut short.

"What are we chasing?" Chinelo asked. "The commander didn't say much."

Azuka shook his head. "A child has been abducted."

Chinelo gasped.

They burst into a wide plaza and fanned out. A collective murmuring rose from the knights. Soon, Chinelo and Azuka saw why. Surrounding the central statue of Sila the Pure was a wide circle of collapsed knights, many of which lay groaning on the pavement. Chinelo and Azuka eyed the bodies strewn across the plaza.

"Knight!" Azuka shook one of the fallen. "What happened?"

The knight answered in a slow, labored voice, one that Chinelo recognized.

"Witch..." Sade said.

Chinelo's heart seized. He had heard of witches before, dark creatures that channeled an ancient and arcane power to bend the laws of nature to their will. They congregated in covens, plotting and scheming to use their forbidden magic against those that once oppressed them. They had long since been purged from Eshgar, though rumors persisted that they lingered in the neighboring nations. He shuddered.

"Speak, knight!" Azuka ordered. His voice was low and resolute. "Where did they go?"

Sade pointed his shaky hand to the south of the plaza.

"The gate!" Azuka scrambled forward.

Chinelo took a step to follow, but he felt a tug on his hand. Sade removed his helmet.

"Chinelo, she has a child. You have to save her!" Sade whispered.

"I will. I'll be back soon, my friend."

Chinelo hurried after Azuka. He caught up to the company of knights, his feet hammering against the pavement. He looked up. A dark figure, cloaked in gray wisps of cloth, leapt from rooftop to rooftop ahead, a flitting shadow in the darkness.

"Azuka! There!" Chinelo pointed with his sword.

Several of the knights halted and drew their curved longbows.

"Wait!" Chinelo shouted. "She has a—"

Twang!

A torrent of arrows flew from the taut bowstrings. They sang as they sailed through the summer night. Chinelo heard a faint cry, and the cloaked figure fell to the streets below. It stood and hobbled ahead, urgently moving towards the southern gate. The knights drew closer, and as they did, Chinelo was able to perceive the figure in greater detail. She was hunched over a bundle, moving with a pronounced limp, a result of the arrow protruding from her leg. In her hand was a strange, leatherbound book covered in mysterious symbols. On its spine was a tiny glowing mass of something. Was that mist? Or a gemstone?

Chinelo's brow furrowed. Witches were supposed to be devilish creatures that could transcend the limits of their bodies and souls. He had always imagined them as imposing, but the one that fled before him was disarmingly frail.

"Halt, witch!" Azuka called.

He pointed his sword in her direction, and the knights circled around her, blocking any exit routes.

The woman turned frantically, and her dense curls swayed as she moved. Her brown eyes flashed in terror. Chinelo gasped. She was young, no more than twenty. Could this woman, barely older than a girl, really be something so terrifying?

"Please! I can't go back!" the woman pleaded. "You don't know—you don't know what they'll do to me!" The babbling cry of an infant escaped from the bundle she held.

"You're Eshgarian?" Azuka asked.

The woman nodded. Azuka stepped forward resolutely, without even a hint of fear in his posture. He was strong, brave, and devoted to his queen, everything Chinelo wished he could one day be.

"You must know the sentence for child abduction," Azuka continued, his sword gleaming in the night.

The witch exhaled rapid, panicked breaths. "Please! I don't want to hurt anyone. This—this is my daughter."

Azuka lowered his sword. "Then there will be no harm in returning with us. If the child is yours, you are free to do as you please."

"No! No! No! NO! I can't! I can't. They'll find me. They'll take her!" Her face suddenly turned cold. Her dark skin grew pallid. "Forgive me."

Chinelo felt the hair on his neck stand on end. There was a look in her eyes, one that he had only seen in the eyes of cornered beasts.

"SIPHON!" the witch shouted.

The grimoire's mass of light pulsed, and Chinelo suddenly felt incredibly heavy. His whole body ached as if he had been running for hours and hours. Several of the surrounding knights stumbled and fell. Chinelo shifted his feet to steady himself.

The witch muttered in an unknown language. She pronounced the syllables with a guttural, sorrowful inflection. Wheels of flame appeared and hovered around her, spinning in wide circles. Chinelo instinctively ducked as one of the blazing armaments flew over his head, an action that was driven not by thought or calculation but by pure fear. Several of his comrades were not as fortunate. They cried in pain as they were burned by the attack.

With a yell, Azuka leapt over and slid under the rings. He was unstoppable, the very sound of his steps seemed to ward off danger. He drew closer and closer to the witch. His movements were slow, hampered by the strange fatigue that Chinelo felt, but like always, he was undeterred. The hero Chinelo first saw twelve years earlier had returned.

"Three!" the witch shouted. Her book pulsed again.

Shadows of the witch, three smokey images, leapt from her position. Flaming blades appeared in their hands and they dashed towards Azuka. He blocked the first with an adroit shove of his buckler, and he drove his sword through the second before kicking the third with his boot. They vanished like mist in the wind.

"Seven!"

More shadows separated from the witch. They spread out and moved in erratic patterns, slashing the air wildly. The knights shied away from their burning blades, but Azuka fought on. Again and again he slew the phantoms, and again and again the witch summoned more.

Chinelo blocked a phantom from striking Azuka's back. He noticed patterns in their movements. They looked like the witch, but they lacked her limp, and they didn't vary their movements based on Chinelo and Azuka's approach.

"Thanks!" Azuka grunted as he warded off another attack.

"I've got your back!" Chinelo exhaled before slashing a stray phantom.

Azuka was a force of nature, a fearless storm of unyielding valor. In sharp contrast, Chinelo's heart pounded, his body screamed at him to run, but he fought on. Together, the two brothers faced the dark conjurations of their mysterious foe. One slashed at shadows, the other defended from spectral blades. When one faltered, the other was there to press them onwards. When one became reckless, the other covered his back.

Chinelo yelled and slayed another of the phantoms, its hazy form dissipating into a thin puff of smoke. The witch cowered against the heavy gate. The pair drew closer. She summoned more phantoms, but they too fell. She staggered back, gripping her book tighter.

"Legion!"

Suddenly, the oppressive weight on Chinelo's body increased. He groaned. Azuka's breath hissed through his clenched teeth. Hundreds of phantoms appeared, all overlapping and moving randomly. The two knights were driven back. In a desperate attempt, Azuka loosened his shield and hurled it at the witch. It pierced the cloud of smokey shadows, striking her in the head with a loud crack. She cried and fell, and as she did, so too did Azuka. One of the infernal blades had penetrated a gap in his armor.

"Azuka!" Chinelo cried. His brother had fallen. *Azuka* had fallen. That—that wasn't possible.

"Chinelo! Do what you must!" Azuka said. "Don't worry about me. Hurry!"

The witch lay in a heap, extending her shaky hand towards the crying, swaddled child. Chinelo stepped forward and kicked aside the heavy tome she dropped. A fire burned within him, rage and hatred toward this vile creature. She had harmed his comrades. She had harmed his own brother. And now, she was helpless.

Helpless.

All his anger faded when he saw her face. He stood over the witch, staring down at the petrified young woman. There was no malice in those eyes. There was only a longing, a desire for relief. She was frightened and in pain. He recognized that look. It was the same as the one the queen had made when Azuka saved her so many years ago. It was a look of helplessness, a look of powerlessness. Her life was not in her own hands.

"Please!" she whimpered. "Forgive me."

Chinelo held his sword over her. She was an enemy of Eshgar. She was a *witch*. She deserved the blade. Any retribution brought by its edge was undoubtedly warranted.

"Kill her!" Azuka shouted.

"Please... I—I don't want to die. Please let me go."

Chinelo glanced down at her leg. The arrow had torn a gruesome wound into her calf. Blood trickled across the paving stones. Her clothes were tattered and torn, barely even fit to be called rags. He'd seen people in such scraps before. Beggars, vagrants, and orphans, while rare, still existed in Eshgar. Though most people led lives of comfort under the queen's watchful eyes, the forgotten few clawed for the crumbs that fell from the table. Their lives were hard, painful, lonely. He'd seen that in their eyes. He saw it in hers, too.

"Chinelo! Do it!"

The witch pleaded, "Please! I had to! They made me!"

This *wasn't* right. There were laws. There were rules. There were protections for all, even criminals. Even one such as her. Even a witch.

"Chinelo!"

Chinelo shook his head. "No."

"What?" Both Azuka and the witch looked at him in shock.

"She is defenseless. We are bound by the Oath to give her asylum until trial."

"She's a witch, Chinelo!"

"She's one of us." Chinelo looked over his shoulder at his fallen comrades.

"She abducted a child!" Azuka shouted.

"Then, we must give her trial." He looked back. "What is your name?"

The witch responded. "M—Myrtle."

"Full name."

"Just... Myrtle..."

"Myrtle, you are suspected of violating the law of Queen Evali of Eshgar. You will be subject to trial before the queen, and you will be held in custody until your trial."

"No one will be able to find me, then? I'll be safe?"

Chinelo extended his hand. "Yes."

The witch sighed in relief and reached for his hand. "Thank you. Thank you—"

A sword plunged through her chest. Azuka stood over the witch and removed his blade.

"No!" Chinelo shouted. The woman collapsed into a pool of blood.

"Pathetic," Azuka scoffed towards Chinelo.

Chinelo stood dumbfounded. A tear trickled from the woman's lifeless eyes and diluted the crimson pool in which she lay. Azuka wiped his sword and sheathed it.

"By the queen, Azuka! What were you thinking?"

Azuka held his hand over the wound in his side, applying pressure to stop the bleeding. "You saw what she did to our comrades. I just saved your life."

"What about the Oath?"

"The Oath says that we must protect our kingdom. I have done just that."

Azuka frowned and stooped to pick up the fallen infant, cradling it in his free arm.

Chinelo stared down at the woman—no—the girl's lifeless body. In a moment, everything seemed to shatter. Azuka stopped by Chinelo's side, giving him a sour and disappointed look. Chinelo tensed, clenching his fists. They were Eshgarian knights. They were supposed to be heroes. But killing someone helpless? Ignoring pleas for protection? That wasn't something a hero did.

"She could have—"

"Don't even start," Azuka snapped. "We are knights. We have a duty to our kingdom. I have done my duty. If you won't do the same, then what even are you?"

The knights around them slowly rose to their feet. They followed Azuka out from the square, leaving Chinelo standing alone in the darkness, staring down at that witch's lifeless body. That single question rang through his mind.

What was he really?

CHAPTER 30

433ʳᵈ year, 4ᵗʰ month, 2ⁿᵈ day
One year before present day

CHINELO, SADE, AND AZUKA SAT ON a small rise that overlooked the great city of Eshgar in the distance. It shone like gold in the afternoon sun, and the lush fields around it shimmered in the balmy wind. Chinelo tried to rub his shoulder, but his armor made that incredibly difficult. He knew the many bruises that covered his torso were completely inaccessible.

Azuka wiped his sword and sheathed it, letting out a long sigh. "Hard to believe they made it this close this time."

"You're telling me," Sade replied, scrubbing at a particularly stubborn splatter of blood on his shield. "Though, I guess this is what happens when the Border Guard abandons their posts."

Azuka scoffed. "Dishonorable louts."

Chinelo looked down at his sword. It too was covered in a thin red film, but after a few minutes of cleaning, that was no longer an issue.

"You really saved our skin back there, Chinelo," Azuka said, patting him on the back. "Fighting five assassins at once? That's the stuff they write ballads about."

"It's nothing," Chinelo said. "Just doing my duty."

Knowing his comrades and kingdom were safe was enough for him. He didn't need any praise. This was what he lived for, his reason for being. That was what it meant to be a knight, and a knight was who he was. Protecting his kin and country was just expected. Though, he did appreciate the proud smile that spread across Azuka's face. He didn't get those often anymore. Not since that day.

The three of them were dispatched to investigate rumors of Mervosian mercenaries crossing the border. Such rumors were not uncommon, but they were rarely true. That day, however, had proven otherwise. They had found a small village ransacked, and they chased the brigands responsible for almost an hour, ending their pursuit in a bloody brawl.

"Well, I'll be sure to give you glowing praise when we report to the queen." Sade punched him in the shoulder. "Mr. Hero of Eshgar. Azuka might have to finally give up his title."

"Ow!" Chinelo said. "Come on! I've got bruises there."

Azuka laughed and stood. "At least the title stays in the family. Well, shall we? We've got quite the walk to get back home."

Sade groaned. He began limping back to the main road. "Might as well!"

Chinelo followed. It would be at least two hours until they reached Eshgar's outer walls. However, short journeys with Azuka and Sade were rarely unpleasant, even if he and Azuka sometimes argued. Things had never been the same since that night seven years earlier. There was constant friction between the two. Though infrequent, their arguments always seemed inevitable, as if pressure had been building for months and needed to be released. Those arguments were typically short lived. Not since that one incident had they really, truly fought.

The road was shaded by wide spreading trees, and the many sandstone outcroppings and rises shielded them from the wind. Not that the wind was bad. Winters in Eshgar were very comfortable, rarely even approaching what could be called cool.

The road curved around a small outcropping of rock, and they once again faced the city. Azuka stopped and sighed. "She's a beauty."

Chinelo nodded.

Sade kept walking. "Well, let's appreciate that beauty up close."

A sudden pulse shook the ground. Chinelo flinched. His head throbbed.

The other two turned. "You all right?"

Chinelo shook his head. "Did—did you two feel that?"

Sade and Azuka locked eyes and shrugged. The ground shook again in two rhythmic beats.

"That! That shaking," Chinelo said. He gazed at the city. Why did he suddenly feel drawn to it? The pulsing continued.

"That might just be your legs," Azuka said. "Fatigue will do that."

The ground shook again.

"Want to stop?" Sade asked.

Chinelo paused. This wasn't his legs. He knew it. He glanced over at the rocky outcropping beside him. Maybe resting again was a good idea. No! He didn't want to inconvenience the other two. He could only imagine the looks he would receive from his brother if he sat down moments after rising.

"No. Let's keep moving," Chinelo said.

Sade and Azuka walked ahead, chattering about something Chinelo could not hear. The pulsing continued, stronger and stronger. It called to him, beckoned him, begged him to join it. Down. Down. Somewhere beneath the city it lay.

A light flashed above Eshgar.

It grew, glowing brighter and brighter until it erupted into a vortex of flame. Fire consumed the city, spreading over the surrounding countryside in an unstoppable blazing wall of destruction. Sparks and brimstone fell, billowing in a seething storm. Azuka and Sade gasped, transfixed by the approaching blaze. A cloud of dust blew over them, tearing at their armor and skin. Chinelo coughed and shielded his eyes, looking left and right for anything that might protect them. A large, crooked rock with a sizeable cleft in its side stood beside the path. Thinking quickly, Chinelo ducked behind the boulder. His heart pounded. Sweat trickled down his cheek.

"Sade! Azuka!" He screamed.

They turned, their eyes wide.

"RUN!" Chinelo yelled.

Azuka dropped his shield and broke into a terrified sprint. Sade limped behind him, struggling to cover ground. The fire approached. The air grew hot, rippling and bending around them. Chinelo extended his hand, reaching from behind his cover.

"Hurry!" he screamed.

Azuka was close. Just a little further. Just a few more steps and he could reach him! His armor rattled as he ran. He looked over his shoulder, slightly slowing his pace as the blaze drew close. Sade broke into an uneven sprint, stumbling but still moving. The light grew brighter. The flames grew closer.

Faster! Please! Faster!

Sade faltered, dropping to a knee. He turned and raised his arms in front of him, trying to shield himself.

He was gone in a second.

The fire washed over him, and Chinelo and Azuka watched in horror as his armored silhouette vanished. Azuka halted. His hands trembled. The elder brother, once unyielding, was now frozen in fear.

Chinelo yelled. His heart pounded. He scrambled to his feet, abandoning his cover. He raced forward, the oncoming blazing growing brighter and brighter as it rushed towards his brother. Just a little further. He reached out.

Azuka turned and faced Chinelo. He screamed a single word.

"Chinelo!"

The blaze overtook him.

A blast of hot air knocked Chinelo to the ground. He covered his head as the fire churned and raged. The heat was overwhelming, and scorching, howling wind buffeted him. He pressed his hands against his ears, trying to block out the sound. He squeezed his eyes shut, hunching over in a small ball.

As he huddled on the ground, waiting for death to take him, all he could think of was the images of his two comrades being consumed by the fire. They repeated, over and over. His brother's voice echoed in his mind, calling to him from the roaring wind. Then, all fell silent.

The heat dissipated. Chinelo lifted his head. The scent of smoke filled his nostrils. He coughed. His eyes burned. He scanned the land ahead of him facing away from the city. Rocks were covered in a thin layer of soot. Trees were singed, with a few of the broad canopies smoldering beneath the bright sun. Slowly, cautiously, he turned to face Eshgar, hoping that maybe, just maybe they had somehow survived. What lay before him dispelled any hope he might have had.

Devastation.

Ash and cinder, a wasteland bereft of life. All that remained of Eshgar was a black and orange scar, a bed of embers and fire. The city lay in ruins. The towers and domes that formerly rose above it had crumbled. His city, his home, once glorious, was now defiled. The cinders spread across the land, extending from the city, over the hills, and stopping in a ring mere steps away from him. If he had moved any further, the fire would have taken him. However, somehow, by some miracle, it had spared him from its blazing wrath.

Chinelo fell to his knees, letting out a grating whimper.

His gaze caught on something.

Them.

Two charred skeletons lay on the ground, covered in deformed plates of armor. His stomach turned, and the realization of what had unfolded finally hit. The city he was meant to protect, the people he loved—all of them were gone.

CHAPTER 31

434th year, 7th month, 15th day
Present day

ISOBEL AWOKE. THE NIGHT BEFORE SEEMED so very distant. Her memory was once again clouded. She had almost gotten used to the strange symptom of her condition, one that had persisted ever since her head was concussed. Still, the fog that plagued her memory was disorienting, as was the stubborn dizziness that returned when she moved. She closed her eyes and rubbed her forehead. What had she been doing the previous night?

She sat up, and a sharp stab of pain afflicted her head. She stifled a groan. She was in their tent, and Chinelo slept peacefully on his sleeping mat beside her. Light filtered through the beige fabric of the tent's wall. Morning was near. Leaning forward, Isobel found her diary in the dim light. She flipped it open and thumbed through the pages until she found the most recent entry.

434, 7, 14

We moved today, if only a little, and I suspect that we are drawing near to Nesa's border. Chinelo has been kind enough to carry my pack for I am still unable to maintain my balance. Perhaps tomorrow will be better.

Chinelo hasn't spoken much. I fear something is troubling him. I hesitate to ask, for it is possible that I already have. He alluded today to a conversation we had earlier, and I recall none of it. He seemed hurt that I would forget. I try to remember. I try so desperately. I am afraid that I have forgotten many important things. There are some things, though, that I want to forget, and yet cannot.

This affliction confuses me.

Perhaps tomorrow will be better.

Isobel let out a disappointed sigh and flipped through a few of the earlier entries. She vaguely remembered writing them, though her own brevity frustrated her. She would have to be more detailed in her entry that evening.

She slid out from her blanket and crawled to the tent's exit. Chinelo stirred but continued snoring. After lacing her boots, she exited the tent. As she stood, she felt the dull ache of her sprained ankle and the throbbing dizziness in her head. She took a deep breath to compose herself. The frigid air stung her injured throat, causing her to shiver.

The tall grass rustled around her. The eastern fields of Iskara had transformed from their muted grayish tones to the more vibrant greens that signaled winter's end. The change had been sudden and captivating. In the distance Isobel could see the majestic, snow-capped mountains at Nesa's border. They rose one after the other, obscured by clouds and haze. Crossing those mountains would carry her outside the reach of the Iskaran military, and perhaps she and Chinelo could finally have some peace while they recovered from their injuries.

Isobel looked up. The sky glowed gold with the approaching sun. She took a step, and the world suddenly rocked. She stumbled and let out a faint cry as the ground rushed toward her. The thick grass cushioned the impact, but the experience was still jarring. From behind her, she heard a frantic scuffling. Chinelo appeared from the tent.

"Isobel!" He hurried to her side and helped her sit up. "Are you hurt?"

Isobel pressed her palms to the side of the head.

"No." Her voice was raspy and hushed, and it took great effort to form even a single syllable from her stinging throat.

"Why didn't you wake me before you went out?"

Isobel looked down. "I—the fire." She coughed. "Breakfast."

Chinelo frowned. "I thought we agreed that you were going to rest today."

Isobel winced. "We—we did?"

"Yesterday, when we were eating lunch."

Isobel closed her eyes tightly. She dug deep within, trying to extract the memory. She searched, exploring her own mind as if it was some dark, unfamiliar forest. She could not find it.

"I'm sorry."

Chinelo sighed. "Yesterday you said the dizziness had gotten worse, so I thought it would be good for you to rest. We'll just stay here for today, and we can make our way across the mountains another day."

"How far?" Isobel rasped.

"When we checked the map yesterday, it looked like it was going to be another week of constant walking to the closest town."

Isobel frowned. "So, with me holding us back?"

"Probably longer."

"I—I'm sorry." She coughed.

Chinelo didn't respond. Isobel glanced up at him. His eyes were sad, and he looked away.

"Chinelo?"

Chinelo rubbed his face. "Sorry, I'll help you back into the tent. I need to start working on our food."

A lump formed in her throat. She felt Chinelo's hand under her shoulder as he slowly lifted her to her feet. They returned to the tent, and she lay back down on her sleeping pad, positioning herself so that her face was away from him.

"I'll bring your breakfast once I've finished it," Chinelo said. "I'll make something warm to help with your throat."

Isobel curled up tightly beneath her blanket and nodded. She held her breath, trying to suppress her sniffles.

"Isobel, I—" Chinelo paused. "I'll be back soon."

She heard him exit. His footsteps became softer and softer as he left to gather supplies for a fire. Then, silence. She was alone.

Days passed. Chinelo lay on his mat, unable to sleep. His body was still, but his mind was active. They had made little progress in their journey towards Nesa, and he was becoming increasingly concerned for Isobel's health. She was finally able to walk for a few minutes before needing to rest, but her ever-present confusion and forgetfulness were apparent. They needed to find a physician.

He heard a noise behind him. A sudden inhalation, one that he had grown to recognize as Isobel's attempts to hide her sobs. He rolled over and reached his hand out into the dark, extending his arm until his fingers brushed against Isobel's quivering shoulder.

"Hey. I'm here."

She jumped and sniffled. Chinelo sat up and removed his blanket.

"Hey. Hey. I've got you. It's all right." He tugged on her shoulder gently.

Isobel sat up beside him and wiped her eyes. "Sorry. I didn't mean to wake you."

"Don't worry about that." He wrapped his arm over her shoulder, and he felt her lean against him, trembling. The corners of his mouth tugged downwards. He closed his eyes tightly. Knowing she suffered was excruciating. Knowing who was responsible made it worse.

"Do you want to talk about it?" Chinelo asked.

Isobel shook her head. The same answer as always. She still refused to speak of what had happened with her sister. She pressed closer, and Chinelo winced at a sharp pain in his side. She had brushed against his injured rib.

"Chinelo? Did I hurt you?"

"It's nothing. Bruising from the fight. Nothing more."

"Oh." She paused. "I see."

She seemed to shrink in his arms. They sat together in silence. Crickets chirped. The grass rustled in the breeze. The clouds broke, and moonlight vaguely illuminated the tent. Chinelo closed his eyes. He saw a flash, a memory, a clear horrific image of Isobel being strangled before him. He tensed, but the memory was gone.

"Are you all right, Chinelo?"

Chinelo turned his head in surprise. "Me?"

Isobel nodded.

"Shouldn't I be?"

"You've seemed distant lately."

"I—" he paused.

"You can trust me, you know?" Isobel's head shifted on his chest.

Chinelo sighed. "I know, Isobel. And I do."

"Then will you tell me what is wrong? I've heard it in your voice. I've seen it in your eyes. You don't look at me like you used to. You don't talk like you used to. Even now, I can feel you shaking. It worries me."

Chinelo did not respond. How could he? He wasn't the one suffering. He wasn't the one who had come so close to death. He wasn't the one whose family had betrayed them. He did not deserve pity. After all, wasn't this his fault?

"Please, Chinelo! Is it me? Am I the problem?" Isobel pleaded.

Chinelo remained silent. He couldn't tell her. It wasn't the time or place for such things. *She* was the one hurting. She needed him, not the other way around. His pain, his guilt, they were not her burden.

"Chinelo?" Isobel said. Her voice shook. "Please... please just talk to me. I'm afraid."

"I'm sorry, Isobel." Chinelo answered with wavering inflections. "This is all my fault."

Isobel jerked back. "What?"

"All of this—your injuries, what happened—I could have prevented it."

Isobel angled her head. "I don't understand."

"I'm supposed to protect you, Isobel. I was too careless to notice our barriers fell. I was too busy daydreaming to notice the Interior Guard. And I—and I was too weak to stop them from hurting you."

"That's not right, Chinelo," Isobel whispered.

"Isn't it, though? If I'd only been better, been stronger, none of this would have happened. Instead, I couldn't even move. I just sat there, watching them kill you..." He hesitated, afraid to say the next words, afraid to admit the truth.

Moonlight streamed through the tent, briefly illuminating the space before being obscured by a passing cloud. Chinelo took a deep breath and forced those final words from his lips. "There was nothing I could do about it. I thought I was going to lose you. I couldn't stop it."

"When have I ever asked you to protect me?" Isobel asked.

"That's what I'm supposed to do!" Chinelo asserted, slightly raising his voice. "That's what you deserve. I'm supposed to keep you safe, but I couldn't. You deserve better than me, Isobel."

"Stop."

Chinelo's body shook. "I'm sorry, Isobel. Everything you're experiencing is because I'm a failure."

"Stop!" She pulled away from him.

Chinelo looked up. Her beautiful, stern face was halfway lit by the moonlight. Another cloud moved and obscured the moon, and they were once again plunged into darkness.

"Now you listen here!" she said indignantly. "*You* do not protect me! *We* protect each other! It's mutual. We're a team. What happened wasn't your fault."

"But—" Chinelo felt Isobel's finger on his lips.

"I'm not done yet!" she said. She took a deep breath. "All this talk about what I do and don't deserve—I won't hear any more of it! Do you think I'm incapable of understanding and deciding what I 'deserve'? I'll decide that, not you. All right?"

"Sorry."

"Chinelo, I—" she paused. "I don't blame you for what happened. I would never." She hugged him gently, moving her arm over his shoulder to avoid his cracked rib. "And your ability to protect me is not why I—it's not why I care about you. You do not need to protect me. Remember that, all right?"

Chinelo nodded. Her words had eased his sense of guilt, though the convictions had not fully faded. "I'm sorry. I didn't want to make this about me."

"Nonsense! I'm the one who asked. Making things about you is part of what we agreed to. At least some of the time. It's all right to express how you're feeling, especially when you are hurting."

"But you're the one who is hurt," Chinelo whispered.

"And that invalidates your own feelings?" Isobel retorted.

He did not respond.

"I don't expect you to be unbreakable, Chinelo. I hope you don't expect that of me."

"No. I don't." Chinelo looked down. "I really don't deserve you."

He felt a sudden movement. Isobel's lips pressed against his cheek. It was like a shock, a crash of lightning, a clap of thunder. His heart skipped.

"I think we will have to disagree there," she whispered. He felt her gentle breath against his skin. "Perhaps, one day, I'll be able to convince you of my perspective on the matter." She nestled into his embrace.

He sat there dumbfounded. Did she really mean that? Could she? He glanced down at her face, her tired yet peaceful face. Her eyes were shut, their soft lashes resting on her cheek. In spite of her pain, she still comforted him. *Him.* Could he ever deserve that? He did not know the answer, but he hoped that he one day might.

She was more than he had ever expected, more than he had ever imagined. Somehow, in spite of her weakness, she was still strong, far stronger than him. He held her tighter, an intense surge growing in his chest. He wouldn't lose her. He wouldn't. Not now. Not ever.

CHAPTER 32

CHINELO HAMMERED THE TENT STAKE INTO the ground, completing the final steps of setting up camp. He stood and looked over the flatlands far below. They rippled with the wind beneath the cloudy sky. Wisps of white spread across the heavens, painting the clear blue canvas with a feathery fresco. He had finally reached the first plateau in the series of rising mountains of Nesa, and the view was certainly worth the trip.

Chinelo squinted. In the fields below, he could just barely discern the structure where they had camped the previous night. It resembled a great weapon, a colossal stone sword driven halfway into the earth. From this distance, it didn't look nearly as imposing, but up close, the sheer size of it was chilling. To think that something once wielded that blade. A god, perhaps? Or something else?

The trek had been arduous, and the terrain was rough. It had been a long time since he traveled alone, and the solitary silence and monotony of it was not something he missed.

He turned and looked ahead. The dense, snowcapped trees continued to rise with the steep terrain beyond the plateau. Somewhere in those white mountains was a village, Kahi. The trail was ill-defined, but even the slight hint of a road gave him hope that he would be able to find it.

Chinelo shivered. At the higher altitude, the chill of winter stubbornly lingered. However, lighting a fire would not be wise until he brought Isobel to the camp. He pulled a travel stone from his pocket and forced his esht into it. He blinked, and he was no longer in the mountains.

Isobel jumped.

"Oh! You're back." She sat cross-legged with her back to the great stone blade, surrounded by a circle of books. "Did you find a place?"

Chinelo nodded. "I did! It's close to a small pond, so we should have plenty of water. There's also lots of trees, so firewood won't be an issue."

Isobel closed her books and piled them back into her pack.

"Excellent! Thank you so much for making the climb. I'm sorry I'm still not able to manage it just yet."

Chinelo helped her to her feet. "That is what I'm here for. Think nothing of it. How was your day down here?"

"Oh, it was very productive; you would not believe it! I made a new spell-core, and I've been experimenting with that new word I learned. Watch this!"

She hobbled with her staff, which was no longer lacking a core, to a nearby shattered chunk of stonework and pressed her palm against it.

"Awge gariasheq."

The shard lurched upwards and flew vertically into the sky. It ascended higher and higher before eventually disappearing above the clouds.

Chinelo blinked in surprise. "Well, that's something."

"Isn't it?"

"Is it going to come back down?"

"Once I release the spell, yes. We should probably stand back first."

Chinelo complied, taking a few steps away from where the rock had sat. After a moment, he saw a tiny speck in the sky plummeting down towards them. He took a few more steps back. The rock grew larger.

"Is this far enough?" he asked nervously.

"We should be fine at this distance. There's not much wind today."

The fragment fell and crashed into the ground. A startled covey of leopard quail fluttered away, flapping their speckled wings.

"See? I've figured out gravity inversion!" Isobel smiled faintly. It was the first time Chinelo had seen her do that in a long time. "Once I'm not so dizzy, just imagine what I could do with this. Think of it—flying through the clouds, floating weightlessly in the sky. We could be as free as the birds!" She gazed longingly at the fleeing quail.

"Have you learned how to control it enough for that?"

Isobel frowned. "Not quite, but I'm close. It would involve a very large and very complicated glyph. I made a few sketches of it, but it still needs a lot of work. At any rate, I have time to think about it. Until my head gets better, I won't be able to try."

Chinelo watched as she loaded her belongings back into her pack, and his expression shifted to one of concern. Her tendency to forget had not waned, though from his conversations with her, he had learned it only seemed to affect shorter-term memories. Things older than a few months did not seem to fade. "Have you written your ideas down?"

"A good scholar always does!"

"Good," he said, reaching down for Isobel's pack. "Shall we get to camp?"

Isobel crouched and grabbed a travel stone from the ground. "I'm ready when you are!"

Chinelo clasped her hand in his, and together they were pulled to the campsite.

Chinelo poked the glowing remnants of the fire. He sat alone on the rocky ground beneath the clear night sky. As spring progressed, their journey took them deeper into the mountains, and based on Isobel's map, they were nearing Kahi, their next destination and the location of a third obelisk. The village was close to Iskara's border, but it was so high in the mountains that most travelers completely avoided it. However, its proximity to an obelisk was worrying. Iskara's relationship with Nesa was tense, and he hoped that tension would ward off any attacks from Iva and the Archmage, at least for a time.

Looking up, Chinelo saw Isobel's figure silhouetted against the night sky, staring up at the moon. His brow furrowed. Normally she would be huddled in the tent recording the events of the day in her diary. He stood and slowly walked over to where she sat. At the sound of his footsteps she looked over her shoulder and smiled. With a subtle motion, she tapped the space next to her.

Chinelo sat on the log beside her, resting his elbows on his knees. He looked up at the brightly shining moon, which had shifted from its typical perfectly circular form to a strange, oblong shape. Isobel let out a melancholy sigh.

"Hey," Chinelo said, glancing to the side. "Are you doing all right?"

Isobel's mouth formed a tight line and she shrugged.

"Do you want to talk about it?"

After a long pause, she shook her head.

Chinelo nodded and looked down. He shifted his foot, kicking a pebble with his toe. Day after day, she still gave the same response.

He felt a tap on his shoulder. Isobel was pointing up at the moon. Directing his gaze to the sky, Chinelo marveled at the sight. Streaks of bright light spread across the heavens from the moon, raining in a glimmering waterfall of color. Moonshards, shining brighter than the stars.

Isobel exhaled. "We used to watch this every year when I was growing up."

"Hmmm?"

"My sister and I," she said wistfully. "We would sneak out and meet on one of the roof-tops back home to watch the moonshards fall. I would always forget to wear my coat, so she would wrap me in her cloak to keep me warm. She was so strong. I always felt safe, as if nothing could ever touch me. She was still wearing that cloak, after all these years."

"I remember one year," Isobel continued, "I think when I was twelve or thirteen, Mother Verris almost caught us outside after curfew. That was Iva's birth mother," her voice wavered for a second as she said Iva's name. The pause was brief, but it did not escape Chinelo's attention.

"We hid in the bushes, and my nightgown got all torn and dirty. I was so worried," Isobel laughed. "I was afraid that the mothers would punish me if they saw it, but the next morning I found a new gown on the foot of my bed. I don't know how Iva got it, but that was her way: always making things right."

The lights streaked across the sky, leaving trails like brilliant auroras.

Isobel chuckled again. "She used to wake me up on some summer mornings, long before the sun was up, and we'd go practice magic in the center yard, that one with all the gravel. I struggled at first in school, but she explained things in such a simple way, it became easy." Her voice faltered again.

Chinelo leaned closer and rested his hand on hers.

"I miss her." She sniffled. "I miss her so much."

"I know." Chinelo squeezed her hand.

"She would always swoop in and save me. If I was being mistreated by my sisters, Iva would be there. If I was struggling in my classes, Iva would be there. If I was lost, Iva would be there. All this time, I think I've been hoping that she still would find me, that she would swoop in and make all of our problems go away, just like she always did."

Chinelo looked furtively at her face. She sighed and wiped her eyes.

"I love her, Chinelo. I don't understand her, but I love her. It doesn't make sense. I shouldn't love her after all the things she's done. Perhaps it would be easier if I didn't. It might be less painful if I was just angry at her." She turned her head towards him. "You know? I could direct my rage at someone or something. It would be easy. I almost want it. I almost want to hate her, but I can't..."

She fell silent. She stared at the shard shower, opening her mouth before shutting it again. After several moments, she spoke.

"I *should* hate her. Her actions are irredeemable. She's become something terrible. Maybe she was always that way, and I just never saw it. But still, I can't. Instead..." she broke off.

"Instead?"

Isobel sighed. "I don't know how I feel. It's like I'm somehow hollow or empty. Sometimes I'm sad, but most of the time, when I'm able to think about things, I just don't feel anything. It's like there's an empty fog. It's formless and shapeless. I want it to become something I recognize, but I'm scared of what happens when it does. I'm scared that once I understand what I'm feeling, it will become real." She looked back up at the sky. The shard-showers began to fade, like streaks of paint washed away by rain.

"Do you hate her?" Isobel asked.

"Me?" Chinelo exclaimed in surprise. "I—I don't really understand how my feelings on the matter are relevant."

"She murdered your whole family. Of course they're relevant. And besides, you're the man that I—" she paused. "You matter to me, and so your feelings matter to me."

Chinelo looked down. At the mention of his family, he felt a deep, painful emptiness inside, and weak hidden anger flickering beneath. "I don't know, Isobel. A year ago, I probably would have. I was like what you described back then. Empty, hollow, wanting desperately for someone to blame. But now, I don't know. I suppose I've tried to replace those feelings—or at least bury them under others."

"Hmmm?"

"How do I put this? When we met last summer, I was empty. I had nothing. But then, you came along. Or I suppose from your perspective I came along," Chinelo said with a smile. "I remember you were terrifying at first, but you were also intriguing. You were kind. You were cheerful. You had a light that I wished I had. I won't say that you made me whole, because I don't think that's a healthy way of looking at things, but you brought me out of the fog. You still do. You made me happy at a time when I didn't think I ever could be."

He scratched his head. "Sorry, I kind of lost your question there. All the anger and grief I felt aren't gone, Isobel, not by any means. I miss my family. I miss my friends. I miss my home. I would do anything to get them back. Anything. Those feelings are a part of who I am. But maybe they've been joined by something stronger."

"So." He looked up at the sky. "Do I hate her? Probably. It would be impossible for me not to have some level of anger towards her. But that doesn't really matter to me anymore. Not the way you do. Stopping her, however, still does. More people are going to get hurt. I can't let that happen."

Isobel pulled her hand away from his. "More people are going to get hurt..."

"Sorry, I didn't mean to—"

"No. You're right. More people *are* going to get hurt. They'll be like you and me. I can't let that happen either. It doesn't matter who is responsible. Iva's actions don't make sense to me, but that doesn't mean we can't keep fighting. Something happened to her. Something changed her. And that just means that this time I will be the one who has to save her. Maybe that's foolish of me."

"Maybe. But, you know, that optimism is one of the many things I admire about you." Chinelo looked at her. "You still have hope, don't you? That we can go back and change things?"

"We can do it, Chinelo. I know we can." She stood and clenched her fists. "I'm not giving up. Not yet. You'll have to forgive me, though, if I'm less energetic than I formerly was."

Chinelo stood beside her. "We'll figure this out. Together. And if you ever want to talk about how you're feeling, well, you know I'll always listen."

Isobel smiled. "Well right now I'm having some very strong feelings."

"Oh? Is that good?"

She nodded. "They're the best kind."

She looked up at him and grasped both of his hands in hers. Her lips parted. She moved forward slightly, standing on her toes, bringing her face up to his. Chinelo's heart pounded. She was so near, he could feel her breath on his skin, soft, gentle, hesitant. His hands began to sweat. He slowly leaned in and...

"Croak!"

A loud squawk came from their tent. Isobel dropped to her heels and released Chinelo's hands.

"Mort?"

She ran over to the tent and dug through her bag. Chinelo stayed where he was. A shiver ran down his spine. That small space between them was replaced by a sudden gulf, one that might as well have been an ocean. He shook his head, trying to regain his wits. After a moment, he sheepishly walked to the tent.

Isobel unwrapped the hibernation bundle she had prepared for Mort. He poked his warty nose out and let out a deep bellow. The king had returned.

CHAPTER 33

ISOBEL'S EYES FLUTTERED OPEN. THE NIGHT before seemed so very distant. She sat up and rubbed her eyes. Her chest felt oddly warm. What had she been doing the previous night?

She glanced at her diary on the nightstand beside her. If she really needed to remember, she could just try reading it. She shook her head. No, she needed to remember on her own, to prove she could.

She looked around the room. It was small, with wooden walls and flooring. A humble reed mat was beneath her bed. Her *bed*? She wasn't in the tent anymore. She squeezed her eyes shut and rubbed her temples. She had to focus. She had to pierce the fog that clouded her memory.

An inn! She and Chinelo had arrived at Kahi and stopped at an inn. But what else? What was this strange warmth, this mysterious excitement she felt inside? Why did she feel so elated? Something must have happened, but she could not remember what. Everything was so blurry. Everything was so far away.

She remembered they had reserved adjacent rooms. They had talked late into the night on his bed. Then, she had returned to her room with Mort, written her daily diary entry, and gone to sleep. Nothing unusual there. She rubbed her forehead. She vaguely recalled talking with Chinelo about visiting the obelisk that day to confirm it had not been claimed already, but not much beyond that.

She kicked off the sheets and braced herself for the dizziness that always came. Summoning her staff to her hand, she stood.

"Oh?"

She felt normal. Her head did not hurt. There was no pressure, no spinning. She shifted her weight. Nothing. She took a few steps. Nothing. She spun on her toe, twirling in a circle. Nothing!

A smile broke across her face. Today would be a good day. She hurried to her pack and pulled out her winter clothes. Though spring was nearing its conclusion, Kahi was at a very high altitude, and the snow would still be present, even if more did not fall. She bundled her change of clothes and left for the washroom.

Chinelo stroked his beard, which seemed oddly thick that morning. It had long since stopped being itchy, making it much more bearable. He had to admit, it had its benefits. An extra layer against the cold air was appreciated.

He pulled a wrinkled shirt from his pack and put it on. As he was threading his arms through the sleeves, he turned his head in confusion. His hand stuck through a large hole, one that was torn just below the sleeve. When did that happen? Had it ripped in his pack? Usually, he was careful about sharp objects, but perhaps he had been careless.

Chinelo shuddered. The hair on his neck stood on end. Something was watching him. Something menacing. He slowly stood and clenched his fist. He could feel it—a presence. An enormous, oppressive presence. He spun around to see it. Mort.

Chinelo relaxed. "How did you get in here?"

Mort blinked his cold black eyes.

Chinelo shrugged. "Well, if you're in here, I'm blaming this on you." He gestured to the torn shirt.

Mort scowled at him.

"I really have missed your amiable temperament," Chinelo said dryly.

Mort turned his head. His gaze rested on a slip of paper on the floor beside him. He looked back at Chinelo with a devilish twinkle in his devious frog eyes. Chinelo raised an eyebrow.

"I don't like that look, Mort."

Isobel buttoned her shirt and ran her fingers through her hair. Should she tie it back or let it fall? The ends reached down to her chest, which was much longer than she normally liked to keep it. She wanted to cut it, but she had absent-mindedly left her hair kit back in her cottage many months before. She sighed. She would need to check with Chinelo on their current funds if she was going to buy a new kit. She wasn't about to let him use his sword to cut it. For the time being, she would leave it down.

Isobel took an apprehensive step into the hall. She shifted her weight on her ankle, testing it for any lingering pangs from her sprain. Nothing. Her mysterious elation returned. She'd felt so fatigued the night before, yet she had miraculously recovered, just in time for her birthday the next day. The only thing that remained was her foggy memory, but the nice thing about that was that she sometimes forgot that it was a problem at all.

She pranced happily down the hallway. A grizzly man turned around the corner and collided with her, causing the bag he carried to spill spectacularly across the floor.

"Oh! I'm terribly sorry!" Isobel crouched and began gathering the man's belongings.

"Ehh, no worries." The man slumped beside her and piled his clothes back in his bag. His brown-black hair was messy and disheveled, and that with his bewildered expression and slightly puffy eyes pointed to a clear fact: the man had just woken up.

"You're from out of town?" he asked after a stifled yawn.

"I am, yes!" Isobel replied cheerfully. "Just got in last night."

"Ah. Likewise. Came all the way from the northern coast. You?"

"Nellborough originally," Isobel chimed, "though I most recently came from Caald."

"Ah! Quite the journey. Impressive. Planning to stay long?"

"Possibly! My companion and I are recovering from some rather unfortunate injuries, so we thought we should rest for a while before we move on. I'm a little clumsy myself and have a tendency to stumble my way into some rather ridiculous accidents. I'm sure you understand."

The man chuckled. "Your companion—she's here, too?"

"*He* is," Isobel corrected while handing him a prickly wooden hairbrush. The man glanced down at the tattoo on her hand. He frowned.

"You're a witch?"

Isobel withdrew and pulled her sleeve over her tattoo. "I—yes."

"Ah, that's a shame."

The man shoved passed her towards the washroom.

Isobel stood up and looked after him. So, the rumors she heard were true. Witches were not readily embraced in this land. There was history involving witches here, history that traced back to the Minera, the first witch, and her feud with the gods. Isobel huffed. She really should have studied that era better when she was in the coven.

She continued down the hall, stopping beside Chinelo's door. Beneath her feet, she felt the vibrations of his heavy footsteps. She reached up to knock, then hesitated with her knuckles just barely touching the rough wooden surface.

A crash! Chinelo yelled from inside his room.

Isobel tried the handle then pounded on the door. "Chinelo!" She continued slamming her fist against the door, but it was useless. She peered through the keyhole. A figure rushed past her narrow field of vision, then something large flew after it.

Isobel's heart thumped in her chest. Her mind raced. Words, phrases, spells. She needed one that would get her through the door. She ran her fingers through her hair. The commotion continued.

"Chinelo!" she pounded on the door. "Let me in!"

She received no response, only another loud thump. She slammed her hand against the door, racking her brain for anything that would help. If only she had her travel stones.

Inspiration!

It appeared like a spark and quickly ignited a blaze of ideas. Her travel stones. She always used one to travel to the other, but the words that powered the spell didn't need to be arranged that way. She always gave the spell a specific location, but instead, she could base the spell on direction.

She channeled her esht into her chest. The rushing ocean of power within her prepared to release like water from a broken dam.

She defined the action of the spell: transportation across space.

"Homvelcht."

She described the subject of the spell: herself.

"Tor vrefden."

She announced the conditions: forward.

"Solstari!"

She released a small amount of esht. She felt it exit her body. First the required cost of using the words, then the portion that determined the distance. She did not need much, only enough to bring her past the door.

The space around her converged and then exploded. She was in Chinelo's room, surrounded by scattered furniture, clothing, and belongings. The bed was haphazardly tilted against the wall, and the mattress had slid onto the floor. No one was there.

"Chinelo!" she cried. "Where are you?"

She heard a door creak behind her, and she spun around. She channeled esht into the tattoo on her left wrist, preparing to launch a volley of spells at any threats. From within the shadow of the closet, she saw a figure—a tall, muscular figure. A chill rushed down her spine. The figure towered over her, just as the Archmage had.

"Isobel?" Chinelo peaked out of the closet.

Isobel sighed in relief. "Oh good. It's you. Are you hurt?"

"No, but only barely." Chinelo stepped out. He was wearing only his trousers.

Isobel felt a heat rising in her cheeks. "I—um—uh—what happened?" She looked away.

"Your pet tried to kill me!"

"What?" Isobel whirled around. Mort sat on the floor behind her, proudly resting his corpulent self on a small paper talisman. "Mort?" She scooped up the frog.

"Why did you leave him in here?"

"Me? I didn't! I took him with me last night."

Chinelo frowned. "Well, I certainly didn't bring him over here. You're the only person who could have done it."

"I didn't though! I promise!"

Chinelo sighed. "Isobel, I'm sorry to have to ask this, but is it possible you forgot?"

"Really? *Really?* You're going to go there?" Isobel felt the heat return to her cheeks, but from a different source. "You're using that against me?"

"I'm sorry," Chinelo said, slowly raising his hands. "That's not my intention. I'm just trying to understand what happened. Is there a chance that you left him here?"

"No! That's ridiculous. I distinctly remember bringing him with me last night, writing in my diary, then..."

"Then?"

Isobel looked down. "I—I don't remember. But I know I wouldn't bring him over here."

"You're the only person I gave a key to." Chinelo lowered his voice. It was tense, but there was little anger behind it.

Isobel winced. She had forgotten the key. If she had remembered it, then getting in would have been much easier. She shook her head. "Chinelo! I didn't bring him over here!" she asserted. "I wouldn't forget that!"

Chinelo's face clouded. "Isobel, listen," he said gently. "This isn't the first time something like this has happened. I know it's not what you want to hear, but—"

Isobel cut him off. "Wait. It's not?"

Chinelo rubbed his forehead. "Unfortunately. Conversations, names, things around camp..."

"Oh." Isobel's heart sank. He was right. The last several weeks were incredibly blurry in her mind, and recalling details required intense effort. Major events were rarely a problem, but she could barely remember what she ate within a few hours. It was infuriating.

"Still. I know I wouldn't just leave him here," she said quietly.

"I know you don't think you would," Chinelo clasped his hands together, "but could we entertain the possibility—"

"I'm not lying!" Isobel asserted. "I promise! I put him to bed like I always do. In his little nest with a worm in case he gets hungry."

"Well then how do you explain him showing up in my room this morning and magically launching furniture across the room at me?" Chinelo retorted. "Look around you! Do you think I did this?"

Isobel looked up in surprise. "I'm sorry, he did what?"

Chinelo let out an exasperated sigh and sat on the tilted mattress, resting his bare arms on his knees. "That talisman there." He pointed to the paper on the floor. "He used it. You know I can't write those symbols like you do, so it had to have been you."

"Mort? When did you learn how to use talismans?" She held the frog in front of her face.

The frog gave no reply, for he was a frog.

"Does he even know how to use esht?" Chinelo asked.

"Oh, of course!" She waved her hand dismissively. "I taught him that years ago."

Chinelo blinked. "You did what?"

"I taught him esht channeling," Isobel said.

Chinelo ran his fingers through his curly hair. "How?"

"Same way I taught you."

Chinelo blinked again and looked at the floor, his face pensive. After another long pause, he spoke. "You never thought to mention that?"

"No. Why would I do that?"

Chinelo rested his head in his hands. "Well, when he starts using talismans, it's kind of something I would like to know about, dear."

"All right, well now you know." Isobel picked up the talisman. "That definitely looks like my handwriting, but—" she felt a sudden flutter in her chest. A heat. An elation. "Wait. Did you just call me 'dear'?"

Chinelo blinked. "I—I suppose I did. Hmmm." He rubbed his chin and mused. "Just kind of slipped out. Interesting. Do you not approve?"

"No, no! I do." She waved her hands defensively, with Mort flopping around as she did. "Please, please, say it again!"

"Umm, if you insist... dear." His final word exited his lips very awkwardly.

Isobel wrinkled her nose. "Maybe we should just let it happen naturally."

Chinelo crossed his arms. "Agreed."

She sat on the bed beside him, placing a very displeased bullfrog on the edge of the mattress. She could not stop herself from smiling, and her heart refused to cease its fluttering. She placed her hands on her knees and leaned forward.

"You called me 'dear!'" she said.

Chinelo rubbed her back with his hand. "Hopefully, Mort won't be too upset if I make that a habit."

"Well, I am afraid he doesn't have much of a choice in the matter." She bent over her very incensed pet and put on the cutest voice she could. "No, you don't my little froggy friend—" She coughed. "I forgot. My voice still doesn't have the range for that."

She rubbed her throat, then stared at the floor. Something wasn't right. She didn't remember how the conversation had started. She remembered pieces. She had left her bath. She had entered the room using magic. Chinelo told her Mort had somehow used magic. But there were gaps. It was as if words on a page had been smudged.

"I'm sorry, were we talking about something before?"

Chinelo sighed. "In a manner of speaking yes, though it was more arguing than anything else, unfortunately."

"Oh." Isobel tensed. It came back to her in bits and pieces. She remembered what he had said. She remembered how she had snapped back.

"We don't need to revisit it," he said, looking away. "I don't want us to fight."

Isobel looked down. "I'm sorry."

"No, I wasn't being considerate of you. For that, I am sorry."

She leaned against his shoulder. "But, I think you were right. Clearly, I am forgetting things. I'm sorry for snapping at you."

"All is forgiven, dear."

Isobel felt another flutter of elation. She looked over at Chinelo, then quickly kissed his cheek. "Want to go see the town? We could try to at least locate the obelisk while we are at it."

"If it's with you, then I'd love to!" Chinelo placed his hand on hers. "Though I should probably clean this mess up first. And put a shirt on."

CHAPTER 34

"IT'S A LOT WARMER THAN I expected," Isobel said. "I thought there would be more snow."

"I suppose we do look a bit silly," Chinelo replied, looking down at his thick winter coat.

The village of Kahi was small and quaint, and its few steep streets were lined with narrow wood-framed buildings that had barely any space between them. They were all jammed together, with some of the larger buildings having elaborate wings that overhung the heavy curved roofs of the smaller establishments. Piles of snow clung to the shaded portions of the roofs, slowly melting and sparkling. The streets wound up the mountainside, ending in a large stone arch at the far side of the town.

"I'm going to go change into something lighter." Isobel turned on her toe and reentered the inn.

The innkeeper, a portly man with an astounding mountain of a nose, tracked her movements with his much less noteworthy eyes. He shrugged and continued counting coins on his desk. Chinelo rested his arms on the counter.

"Pardon me."

The innkeeper glanced up, then leapt to his feet. He clasped his hands in front of him and bowed, curving his spine over his monumental belly.

"May Hylarteph bless your morning, Master—?"

"Ide. Chinelo Ide."

"Of course! Master Ide! How may I help you this morning?" The man fidgeted.

"Does the weather here normally change this quickly? Last night there was still snow everywhere, but it all seems to have disappeared." Chinelo adjusted his arms on the desk, leaning lower to bring himself closer to the man's diminutive stature.

"It is rather unusual. Normally the snow melts much later. Anything else?"

Chinelo stroked his beard. "The day. Do you know the current day?"

"Of course. By my count it is the four-hundred and thirty-fourth year, the eighth month, and thirtieth day."

Chinelo nodded. One day until Isobel's birthday.

"Right. Last question. Do you know where I could find any lacquer? I'm working on a gift, and I used the last I had a couple days ago."

"Of course! At the bottom of the hill, Master Take can sell you lacquer. If you like, I can run down there myself and buy it for you. I can add it to your bill."

"Oh! That would be incredibly kind of you!" Chinelo replied. "I'd prefer for her not to see to preserve the surprise."

"Is this for Lady Ide?" The man asked, jotting down a note in a small notebook that he had produced from his within his robe.

Chinelo blushed faintly. "In a sense. Though it's Miss Valeria, actually. We are not married."

"Ah. Of course. Forgive me." The man bowed.

Chinelo dismissed the man's concern with a wave of his hand. "I should be going. She will be back soon, so I should get changed to deal with this weather."

"Of course. I thank you heartily, Master Ide. Enjoy your stay."

Chinelo nodded and returned to his room. He tossed his winter coat inside, then waited outside Isobel's room. He thought back to the innkeeper's words.

Lady Ide. He liked the sound of that.

Isobel's door creaked and she fluttered into the hallway. "Well Mort was certainly happy to see me."

"Was he now?"

"He was rather cross when I left, but the extra worms and crickets should keep him busy for a while."

Chinelo laughed. "I hope you didn't leave any talismans where he could reach them."

"Of course not!" She smiled. "All right! Let's go!" She grabbed his hand and dragged him out of the inn.

They began their climb up the steep center street towards the town's peak. As it was late in the morning, the village was alive and active, though the streets were not what anyone would call crowded. The sharp sound of metal on metal rung through the air, and it was accompanied by a peculiar scent.

"Wait! Isobel! I'm curious about something." Chinelo stopped and peeked into one of the narrow buildings, a restaurant of sorts, but one that only allowed for a few customers at a time. It was dimly lit by lanterns, and a few occupants huddled over a wide steel plate, the source of the ringing. A single cook was preparing some kind of strange dish on the metal sheet, grilling narrow, bushy leaves of some sort atop a thin wafer of batter. With one hand, he cracked an egg over the grill and spread it into a wide circle, cooking it almost instantly.

"Fascinating," Chinelo said.

"Hmmm?" Isobel looped her arm through his.

"It's some kind of local dish. Look! He's transferring the egg to the top of those leaves. Interesting. I've never thought of that combination. And is that garlic and chilies? Oh! He's flipping the whole thing over onto another wafer!"

"Want to try?" Isobel said with a twinkle in her eye.

Chinelo nodded. His mouth watered. They entered the restaurant, which was hazy with steam from the grill. The cook bowed before gesturing towards an empty pair of stools.

"May Hylarteph bless your morning. I will be with you in a moment!" The man smiled, hiding his green eyes within his wrinkled cheeks. His short dark hair was streaked with thin lines of silver.

Isobel looked down at the counter in front of her, then glanced at the other patrons. They each held a small metal spatula in their hands, and thin iron sheets lay on the counter in front of them.

"I wonder how they eat it," she mused. "There are no plates or forks."

"You know, in Eshgar we don't have forks."

"You don't?"

Chinelo shook his head. "Only spoons."

"How do you cut things then?"

"We typically prepare our food so that it does not need to be cut, but also normally the edges of the spoon are a little sharp."

Isobel leaned on her elbow. "And if you need to stick or grab something?"

"We use a smaller spoon."

Isobel laughed. "Well, I see why you make so many soups now. Oh! Look, they just scoop the food off that metal sheet. And they all share the same meal. Fascinating!"

The cook moved to Isobel and Chinelo's side of the grill. "Welcome, travelers. I'm afraid we only offer one meal here, but I hope it is to your liking. Shall I begin?"

"That would be lovely," Chinelo said.

Isobel nestled against Chinelo's arm and aimed a giddy smile at him. She turned and watched the cook begin the process of preparing their food.

"I'm so very excited for this! All the different foods have been some of my favorite parts of this journey!" Isobel said. Her stomach rumbled loudly in agreement.

Chinelo shot her a look.

"Not a word, Chinelo! Not a word."

Chinelo chuckled. "I would never."

"Ah, so he's a knight and a liar," Isobel quipped.

Chinelo watched their food slowly come together in front of him. The process was beautiful, a dance of steam and spice that produced the exquisite dish. Soon, it sat before him, begging to be consumed.

"You first!" Isobel gestured with her spatula.

Chinelo obliged and took a bite. He was blessed with an overwhelming wave of flavors combining in ways he never thought imaginable. There was a slight heat, but a subtle sweetness to balance it. There was a deep savory taste, and a bite of garlic to give it some edge.

"Exquisite," Chinelo gestured to the chef, who responded with a satisfied grin.

"I'm glad you like it, friend."

Isobel and Chinelo began to polish off their iron tray. Though Isobel's attention seemed to shift at a sudden rise in the conversation that was happening across the grill from them. She set down her spatula, and Chinelo followed her gaze.

"I'm telling you! They're just gone," one of the men said.

"Come on, Issin. How do you lose an entire herd of cattle?"

"I didn't. I put them to field last night, and this morning they were all gone."

Another man chimed in with his deep voice. "Could they have climbed the fence?"

Issin scowled. "They're too stupid for that. Except maybe Number 12. She's a clever one. Regardless, the fence would break if they thought of it. No. They've all just vanished."

"How many were there?"

"Fifteen," Issin grumbled.

One of the men, an older one with thin white hair and a long flowing mustache, frowned deeply. "Something similar happened at my farm. Half of the pigs have disappeared." He placed a hand on Issun's shoulder. "Friend, this is worrying."

Isobel tugged nervously on the hem of her glove.

"You all right?" Chinelo asked, resuming his meal.

Isobel jumped in her seat. "Oh! Sorry. Just eavesdropping when I probably shouldn't be."

Chinelo chuckled and took another bite. *By the queen, this is good!*

Isobel raised her hand. "Pardon me, mister chef?"

The cook looked up from his current task: scrubbing down the far end of the grill. "Yes? How may I help you?"

"We're both new to the area, and we've heard that there is some kind of shrine nearby. We've been traveling across the world visiting old shrines—a pilgrimage of sorts—and we were hoping you could point us toward it. I'm so very excited to see it."

The man stood up straight and folded his hands neatly in front of him. "Kahi is a religious community, madam. We have many shrines. The gods sleep in these mountains. Do you know which god it honors?"

Chinelo narrowed his eyes and glanced sideways at Isobel.

"I'm sorry. The name escapes me. I'm rather new to religion myself." Isobel tossed her hair playfully. "That's part of why we are here—to seek the truth. If it's like the others I have seen, it would be made of stone with a diamond shaped hole in the center."

"Ah! Of course!" The man's face lit up. "You seek the goddess Hylarteph, the protector of this mountain. May she bless you."

"Yes! That's her name!" Isobel snapped her fingers. "Hylarteph!"

"The goddess rests at the top of the mountain. Follow the path outside the town and ascend the sacred steps."

Isobel clasped her hands in front of her. "Thank you so much. Can you tell me about this goddess? I desperately want to know more. The ancient texts I've read are not very detailed. I'm sure you understand."

"Of course, madam!" The cook began an intensely thorough sermon about the goddess Hylarteph, queen of the mountains and sky. He ran through a variety of topics: the goddess's winged form, her position as the deity of Kahi, the proper customs for praying for her blessings, her role in the greater pantheon. Isobel listened with much fascination, nodding intently between bites.

Chinelo's mind drifted, and he soon became distracted by the other occupants of the restaurant, who had begun to stare at Isobel. Their expressions were unreadable, but something about the look in their eyes put him on edge.

"So! The goddess Hylarteph—may she bless you—she used to walk among the people here?" Isobel asked.

"Many centuries ago, yes. She would descend from her temple in the form of a maiden, adopting the shape of her worshippers to better understand them. If you are curious, there is a mural by the north gate depicting such things."

"She sounds like a loving and kind deity indeed. I've heard similar things about the god Yvvusta. He's sort of the patron deity of my sister's home."

The men at the far end of the counter suddenly looked horrified. The cook's face twisted in disgust. "My dear. Please do not speak such a vile name here."

"Oh? Forgive me," Isobel batted her eyes. "I did not know the significance."

"Hylarteph will forgive you, I am sure. Her brother's name is forbidden, for he betrayed our goddess and forced her into her eternal slumber."

The corner of Isobel's mouth turned downwards. "I understand. Thank you."

The cook relaxed. "I think you should hurry to the shrine, madam. I will pray for your enlightenment and your forgiveness."

"We should probably go." Chinelo dug into his coin pouch. "Do you take crescents here?"

The cook nodded. "We will take anything here. Hylarteph is generous and accepting of all. Five should be sufficient."

"Perfect! I'll—oh? That's odd." Chinelo pulled his hand from the pouch.

"Hmmm?" Isobel leaned forward inquisitively.

"I thought we had a lot more. Strange." Chinelo shrugged and slid five coins across the counter. "Thank you for the meal! It was exceptional!"

The pair stood and quickly left the shop.

"Not going for subtlety at all today, are we?" Chinelo asked.

"What? It got us the answers we needed," Isobel responded.

"Can't argue there. But it also got us several dirty looks."

"I hardly noticed."

"Why did you bring up that other god?"

Isobel shrugged. "It was a long shot, but I wanted to see if they recognized the name. It indicates a connection, though I am not sure what it means."

Chinelo nodded. "How did you know the name?"

"Oh! Yvvusta is basically the one god that witches actually respect. He's the one that taught the first witch how to use magic. It's a lovely story. She and the god, best of friends. Minera would visit Yvvusta and teach him about the world below, and he would instruct her in the ways of the gods. They journeyed far and wide, protecting humanity from evil. That is until the other gods murdered her."

Chinelo coughed. "That's not a very lovely story."

"No?" Isobel looked up for a second and tapped her chin. "I suppose it really isn't. Hmmm."

"At any rate, let's head up the mountain to check the shrine. Will your ankle be able to make the trip?"

"You know, that's the strange thing," she said. "It doesn't hurt at all today."

"Ah. Interesting. My ribs are also much less sore today."

They were interrupted by a commotion from one of the tiny houses at the edge of the town. A small crowd had gathered outside, clamoring around the low building. Chinelo peeked over the heads of the villagers, and Isobel hopped up and down trying to see past them. A woman was hunched in a small ball, crying on her doorstep.

"Ami! Ami! She's gone! Ami!"

A man with long dark hair rested his hand on her shoulder. "We'll find her. She can't have gone far."

Isobel jumped. "Chinelo, what's happening? I can't see."

Chinelo frowned. "From what I've gathered, either that woman's child or her pet has gone missing."

Isobel placed her hand over her mouth and gasped. "Oh no! That's terrible."

"Indeed." Chinelo tugged on her arm. "Let's go. We'll keep an eye out on our way up the mountain."

Isobel nodded and followed him toward the town's exit. She glanced at a wide stone mural beside the gate. It depicted what the cook had described, a smoke shrouded maiden descending from the mountains into the town. She squinted. The mural portrayed the maiden with skin like ash and with hair as black as night.

"Isobel," Chinelo said, "you'll have to forgive my lack of knowledge on this, but when did the gods vanish?"

Isobel scratched her head, slightly tangling her hair in the process. "That is a tricky question to answer. Most stories I've heard put it at over four centuries ago. I think many people believe that our calendar started at that point in history, but it's kind of unclear from the records that still exist. It could have been a while before that depending on how long society took to rebuild after the Cataclysm."

"Cataclysm?"

Isobel nodded then began ascending a long set of stone stairs that climbed up the mountainside. "Right. Think about it. For over a thousand years, the gods existed alongside mankind, but then they suddenly disappeared. Essentially, that would be like humans disappearing from the world right now and leaving only animals behind. The animals would take a while to adjust to no longer having anything higher on the food chain, but eventually things would stabilize. I imagine that is part of what happened after the gods left. Plus, they kind of slaughtered most of the existing mages on their way out."

"Wait! What?" Chinelo turned his head sharply.

Isobel cocked her head. "Is that not how they teach it in Eshgar? I thought everyone knew that."

"We don't really have much in our history books about gods or mages. The main thing I always heard was that mages started wars and used occultic powers."

"Well, one of those is true." Isobel shrugged. "Wait! Did you think I used occultic powers when we met?"

Chinelo laughed nervously. "Not exactly."

Isobel's eyes narrowed. "Chinelo? Is there something you want to share?"

"Didn't you think I was stalking you when we met?" Chinelo asked with a wink.

Isobel opened her mouth to respond but hesitated for a moment. "A fair point."

The stairs they climbed were steep and precarious. They were cut from clean stone, and they were bordered by dense trees that strangely had no branches for the entire lower half of their stature. At regular intervals, Isobel and Chinelo walked through carved stone archways, hundreds of them, that lined the ascending path. They reached a plateau and stopped to sip from their flasks. Through a gap in the trees, a beautiful expansive vista was visible below them. The wide curved rooftops of the village dotted the steep mountainsides, and beyond them densely packed forests completely covered the pointed peaks.

"Quite the view up here," Isobel said before taking a large gulp of water.

Chinelo nodded, though he was preoccupied with a different thought. Where was all the snow? The night before, the entire jagged ridge was blanketed in white, but on that cool afternoon, it seemed that it had almost completely vanished. Only the very tops of the sharp summits still maintained their winter adornments.

He squinted. There were odd stone shards scattered across the mountains, curving shapes covered in lines and ridges. He shrugged and then continued the ascent. His upper legs were ached, and his heart pounded in his chest. The air was thin and difficult to breathe.

"Surely we're getting close," Isobel gasped.

"I certainly hope so. The trees make it difficult to see what's ahead."

The path kept going. Stair after stair, step after step. Seconds become minutes. Minutes became hours.

"Any chance you've figured out how to fly yet, dear?" Chinelo panted.

"I wish. I'm close, but there are still some issues with the control," Isobel said between heavy breaths. "Nullifying gravity is the easy part. It's making sure you end up where you want without hurtling into the ground that is tricky. Also, as I mentioned, the way I'm planning on implementing it is with a tattoo running down most of my back. Haven't had the time for that yet."

"Ah. Well, it was a hope."

"You'd think by now we'd be more accustomed to hiking. It's kind of all we do these days—ow!" Isobel stubbed her toe on protrusion from one of the steps.

They reached another plateau. A thick fog bank was approaching from the east. It soon fell over the valley below, completely obscuring the village. Small clumps of snow were scattered across the stairway above them, a sign that they were finally nearing the end of their climb.

After rounding another bend in the path, the stairs ended. They had reached a final spacious plateau, paved with smooth polished stone. There were no trees, only broken columns of stone that resembled ancient, petrified trunks. Some of them had large, deep gashes cut into their sides.

"It's so big!" Isobel exclaimed. "I'm surprised we couldn't see this from the bottom."

Chinelo walked forward and looked around. The space was enormous, stretching out like a great hall within a palace. At the edges, there were worn walls of stone, with large gaps that at one point were likely windows. One of the columns rose above him and terminated in a broken curving arch.

"Isobel. This is a castle, or it once was."

"A big one at that. I wonder what happened to the roof. Oh! Look over there!" She pointed to the far end of the plateau. There was a wooden structure, built in the style of Kahi's beautiful architecture. Isobel ran ahead and stopped. Chinelo joined her side.

"The roof is... shattered," Isobel said quietly. She stepped forward and entered the small building. "Chinelo. Have you felt any thumping like you normally do when we are near an obelisk?"

"I haven't."

"Well, then we may have a problem." Isobel pointed to the far end of the building. There was a smooth gray pedestal, and a small square column protruded from its center. It was torn off at the top, leaving only a jagged surface behind.

"Is this one of them?" Chinelo asked. "It seems much smaller than the others."

"I'm not sure. This lines up with the map, and it is where the cook said it would be. It's also the right texture and color. I guess I can't really confirm without seeing the rest of it, but I think this *is* it."

"So then..."

Isobel shook her head. "Someone got to it before us."

"Well, that explains why the roof is so torn up." Chinelo looked up. "Whatever was here probably wasn't happy about being confined in a box."

"I suppose," Isobel touched her chin. "Want me to douse for it? Just in case?"

"I'm concerned about what would happen if suddenly all the villagers had magic lines pointing them to the mountain top. Maybe we should wait until early morning when everyone is still asleep."

"Fair point. They seemed a bit touchy. Probably shouldn't do anything that would scare them." She stretched her back and arms. "I suppose there's nothing more for us here."

"At least we don't have to worry about the village being attacked now," Chinelo observed.

"True! All right! Let's head back."

Chinelo rubbed his forehead. "Perhaps we should rest a bit first. I'm not sure I'm ready for the climb back down."

Isobel cocked her head. "Couldn't we just use a travel stone?"

Chinelo blinked. "You have one with you?"

"Of course."

"And you left one back down there?"

"Obviously."

"Oh, thank the queen! I've been dreading the descent for the whole trip."

Isobel smiled. "Lucky for you, my laziness has saved us today!"

She grabbed his hand, and they vanished from the mountaintop.

Isobel sat on the floor with her back to her bed. She scribbled excitedly on the parchment in her hands. With a final flourish of her pen, she completed the glyph and smiled proudly. Another draft of her gravity defying flight spell. But would it work?

She placed her hand on the glyph, resting each of her five fingers on small circles printed on the paper. She channeled esht into one of the circles. The paper rose from the floor and hovered beneath her hand. She shifted her flow into another of the circles. The paper moved left. She moved to a different one. The paper moved right. Her heart pounded. It was working!

She shifted her esht into her thumb. The paper floated backwards, then suddenly twisted into a tight knot before ripping itself asunder.

"Son of a leprous finch!" Isobel slammed her hand against the floor in frustration, resulting in a slight prick of pain from the impact.

Mort looked down at her from the nightstand judgmentally.

"Oh, don't give me that look, Mort!"

Mort blinked at her.

"Isn't it already past your bedtime?"

Mort made a motion with his eyes, the amphibian's equivalent of an eyeroll, and waddled to the nest Isobel had made for him beside her bed. He hunkered down, waiting for her to give him his nightly feast. Isobel produced a worm from a jar she kept in her pack and placed it on his nest. Mort devoured it with little mercy, as was his custom. Lesser beings did not deserve pity.

Isobel sat back down on the floor with her diary. She flipped to the first blank page and wrote the date at the top.

434, 8, 30. My last day of being twenty-five.

She sighed. She had told Chinelo about her birthday several months earlier, but she felt that it would have been selfish to remind him. Still, she hoped he would remember. He had not mentioned anything about it, so perhaps he really did forget.

She shook her head. There were bigger things at stake.

She began writing an account of their day, describing the events in precise detail. She recounted what she could recall: Mort using magic,

Chinelo's sudden habit of calling her "dear," their delightful breakfast, the tedious climb up the beautiful mountain, their evening trying more of the local foods. It had been a good day, even if it did not go as she originally expected. If this was all she would have to remember for this birthday, it would truly be a happy one, even if Chinelo didn't have anything planned. With a smile, she closed her diary and set it beside Mort on her nightstand. He would watch over her precious memories, even if she couldn't.

Isobel scratched an itch along her lower back. Her fingers ran across her skin, but they brushed over something unexpected, something smooth, a line of slick flesh that didn't feel right. She took off her shirt and twisted, trying to position herself so that she could see what she had felt. She could just barely see a smooth pink line wrapping around the side of her abdomen. Was that a scar? When had she gotten that? It felt like a wound healed by her magical touch. Her brow furrowed. She had trouble remembering things, but forgetting an entire gash? That seemed unlikely, even for her.

She shook her head. Everything was foggy. She walked over to her pack to retrieve her nightclothes and outfit for the next day. She dug through it and pulled out a soft tunic. It was green, one of her favorite colors and one in which she looked ravishing. This would do.

Something caught her eye. A tear, one she did not remember. She unfolded the article and put it on. The rip aligned with her scar. What was going on?

Something was not right. She thought about the events of the previous two days. When they arrived in Kahi, it was still very cold. So, what had happened to the snow? When she went to bed the night before, she had put Mort in her room. So, why was he in Chinelo's room that morning? When had she written the talisman Mort used? Where had all their money gone? Why had animals and people gone missing from the town? Why had her injuries suddenly healed? Why had she felt so elated that morning? Why couldn't she remember?

Thud!

Isobel looked toward the source of the sound. Her diary had fallen off her nightstand, and Mort stared down at it from his perch.

"Mort, must you do this now? I'm trying to think."

Isobel flipped over the book and read the date on the page. *434, 8, 30.* However, the entry was not the one she had written that night. Her eyes widened.

She flipped to the most recent page and then moved to the previous entry.

434, 8, 30

She turned back another page.

434, 8, 30

She flipped to another, and another.

434, 8, 30

434, 8, 30

434, 8, 30

Twenty entries all with the same dates. She skimmed the entries. Each one was different, each one was forgotten, but each one started with the same date. Isobel's mind raced. She grabbed her head. Her heart pounded.

She gasped. "Chinelo."

She snatched her diary and dashed to the door, frantically trying to unlock it.

A screech.

It was deafening. Isobel's head throbbed. She collapsed to her knees and pressed her hands against her ears. The pain hammered into her head, squeezing her skull. Her vision went blurry. The screech pulsed louder. Then...

Nothing.

CHAPTER 35

ISOBEL SAT UP. THE NIGHT BEFORE seemed so very distant. She rubbed her eyes and glanced at her diary on the nightstand. She shook her head. No. She didn't need it.

She looked around the room. It was small, with wooden walls and flooring and a reed mat beneath her bed. She closed her eyes tightly and pressed her fingers against her temples. What could she remember?

An inn! She and Chinelo had arrived at Kahi and stopped at an inn. But what else had happened? Everything was so blurry. She remembered they had reserved adjacent rooms. She vaguely recalled talking with Chinelo in his room, but nothing beyond that.

A slight movement from across the room drew her attention.

Mort.

He was waddling around on the floor, patrolling the room for any insects on which he could snack. Isobel smiled. It was time for her to feed him his breakfast. She kicked off the sheets and braced herself for the dizziness that always came. Summoning her staff to her hand, she stood.

She gasped. She felt normal. Her head did not hurt. There was no pressure, no spinning. Regardless of what she could or could not recall, today would be a good day, which meant that her birthday the next day would likely be good as well. She hurried to her pack and pulled out her winter clothes, along with Mort's food jar.

"Oh! It's empty?" she said. "Sorry, Mort. I'll have to find you some food in the town."

Strange. She had caught a whole knot of worms the previous day. She shrugged. As of late, her memory wasn't the most reliable, a consequence of her injuries. Perhaps she had fed him before bed. Returning to her pack she bundled her change of clothes, grabbed her gloves from where she had tossed them the night before, and approached the door, preparing to leave for the washroom.

Something caught her eye, a word scrawled by the handle.

Forget.

She cocked her head. Had she written that?

Chinelo stroked his thick dark beard, pondering how long it had gotten. This was getting out of hand. Regardless of how much Isobel praised it, he wasn't willing to keep an unkempt mat of hair dangling from his face.

He pulled his shaving kit from his pack and recited an incantation Isobel taught him. "Axxave sone va sono iv natte va ba'dargash."

The air grew dry. Water appeared above his hand and accumulated in a circular sheet before freezing into a smooth, reflective disk. Chinelo propped the disk against the wall and trimmed his beard with the improvised mirror as a guide.

After finishing, he glanced over to his pack. He had left Isobel's birthday present out to dry the night before, but strangely, it was not where he expected it to be. He dug through his pack and found a small circular parcel.

Had he forgotten that he hid the gift in his pack? As he retrieved the bundle, a small bottle tumbled out of the pack. It was a bottle of lacquer, barely half-full. Chinelo blinked twice. He thought he had run out of lacquer the night before. He remembered that he needed to find some that day if he hoped to finish the second coat.

He hurriedly unwrapped the bundle. His gift for Isobel, an ornately carved wooden bracelet decorated with depictions of singing birds, sat before him. It was complete and fully coated with a cured glossy finish. He clicked his tongue on the roof of his mouth. Perhaps he had completed the work immediately before bed.

But then, where had he gotten the lacquer?

Isobel buttoned her shirt and ran her fingers through her hair. Astoundingly, the ends reached down to her ribs, much longer than she normally liked. She tilted her head. Had it really been that long yesterday?

She frowned. She much preferred her hair to be short, but she hadn't packed her hair kit. With it being this long, it would probably be annoying to maintain. She tied it up behind her in a ponytail, leaving a few strands to hang loose on the side. Having finished her preparations, she slipped on her gloves.

The word she found lingered in her mind. *"Forget."* Why would she write that on the door? She already knew she was forgetting things. Though, if she couldn't remember writing it, maybe the reminder really was necessary. Her memory *was* concerningly foggy that morning.

She tiptoed down the hallway. A grizzly man with black-brown hair turned around the corner and collided with her, causing the bag he carried to spill spectacularly across the floor.

"Oh! Please, pardon me!" Isobel crouched and began gathering the man's belongings.

"Ehh, no worries." The man crouched beside her and piled his clothes back in his bag. "You're from out of town, I suppose?"

"I am, yes!" Isobel replied. "Got in late last night."

"Ah. Likewise. Came all the way from the northern coast. You?"

"Nellborough originally," Isobel said. "Though that was several months ago."

"Ah! Quite the journey. Impressive. Planning to stay long?"

"Possibly! My companion and I are recovering from some rather unfortunate injuries, so we thought we should rest for a while before we move on. That we might do some sightseeing, visit a few monuments, maybe try some of the local cuisine. I'm sure you understand."

The man laughed. "Your companion—she's from Nellborough, too?"

"Eshgar, actually," Isobel said while handing him a prickly wooden hairbrush. "And it's actually—"

"Eshgar?" The man gasped. "Terrible what happened down there."

"Oh, you've heard?" Isobel stood.

The man scratched the back of his neck. "Just the other day. Oh! I should introduce myself." He extended his meaty hand. "The name's Gabb."

Isobel hesitantly shook his hand. "Isobel."

"Pleasure to meet you! I'm also visiting some of the temples and shrines around town and would love to have a friend along the way. Sounds like we have a common interest there. Would you like to join me? Assuming your friend wouldn't mind?"

"Oh! That's very kind of you! I'm not sure I can, though. I'd have to discuss it with my partner to see if he'd be able to join us. We're both always looking for friends, though."

The sleepy man's face fell. "Ah. That's a shame. Well, if you change your mind, give room 5 a knock. I'll be around for a few more hours once I get cleaned up. Must prepare my lunch after all." He laughed nervously.

Isobel's face lit up. "Oh, my partner loves cooking, perhaps you two would get along. He's always so very eager to talk about it, but some of it goes over my head. I'd like to think I'm a decent cook, but the complexity of the things he makes is just so far beyond me."

"Maybe we would. Well, it was nice meeting you, Isobel!" He walked around her and waved.

"Nice to meet you, too..." Isobel stood in the hallway, a bit flabbergasted at the interaction.

Chinelo stood at the window, touching his chin as he gazed at the adjacent building. Hadn't its roof been covered in snow the previous night? He remembered an icicle falling just as he was turning in for bed, though now the roof was completely clear. And what was that odd smell? Surely that wasn't him. He'd bathed the night before.

A knock came from the opposite end of the room. Three quick raps. He turned and crossed the reed floormat, then opened the door. Isobel stood in the hallway, looking absolutely radiant.

"Oh! Good morning, dear!" Chinelo said cheerfully.

"Good morning!" Isobel chimed. "I just had—" she paused. "Wait! Did you just call me 'dear?'"

"I suppose I did. Hmmm. It just kind of slipped out. Interesting. Do you not approve?"

Isobel giggled. "No, I very much approve. Perhaps, you could say it again?" She batted her eyes.

"Right now?" Chinelo scratched his neck. "I feel like that would be a bit awkward, don't you think?"

"Bah! You're no fun." She stepped into the room and hugged him. "That's a lie you're very—" She cringed and recoiled.

"Something wrong?" Chinelo asked.

"I—I'm sorry it's just..." she looked down, sniffing the air. "Your shirt is a little... um... pungent."

Chinelo backed away. "Oh! I'm so sorry! Oh my! That's embarrassing. I must have gotten my dirty clothes mixed up. I'll—give me a moment." *Well, that solves one mystery.*

He went to the corner of the room and dug through his clothes until he found a shirt of which he approved. He tore off the first with much disgust.

"You know, I had a very unusual interaction with one of the other guests a few minutes ago," Isobel said. Chinelo looked over his shoulder. Her cheeks were bright red, and she appeared to be trying to stare holes into the floorboards.

"Oh?" Chinelo slid the new shirt on. He moved to the bed and patted a space beside him. "Unusual in what way?"

She sat and leaned against his shoulder. "Well, I bumped into this big man in the hall. He had to be two or three times my size. Enormous!" She spread her arms, trying to roughly indicate Gabb's general size.

Chinelo chuckled. "Well, you're not exactly the biggest person yourself."

"I know! But anyways. Let's say he was twice *your* size."

"That is a big man," Chinelo assented.

"Right? So, I ran into him and then he asked if we wanted to go see the temples and shrines with him."

Chinelo turned his head sharply. "With nothing before?"

Isobel waved her hand. "No, we talked a little, but it was only pleasantries."

"And he invited both of us?"

"Yes! I mentioned that I was here with you, then he asked me if I would like to go with him to see the shrines."

"Ah!" Chinelo chuckled. "I see."

"What?"

"I think he was probably just inviting *you*, dear."

Isobel pursed her lips. "Why would he do that?"

"Do you want me to explain it?"

"Well, obviously."

Chinelo waved his hand in front them, setting the scene he wished to describe. "Imagine with me, you're a lonely traveler wandering the countryside. You're a long way from home, you haven't spoken to anyone in days, and you are hoping you'll find just one friendly face."

"Then out of nowhere, this charming, gorgeous, funny redheaded woman appears in front of you. She's friendly, she's smart, she's kind—just the complete and total package. Wouldn't you want to do everything you could to ensure you talked to her again?"

Isobel leaned forward, resting her elbow on her knee and her chin on her hand. "Well, that last time that happened to me, that woman was my mother, and I immediately moved in with her. It's funny. You did almost the exact same thing with me."

"R—right..." Chinelo said. "So, you see, there's a very nice redhead, one you might want to court..."

"You're not redheaded, though."

Chinelo shook his head. "But let's say I was."

"Oh, I would normally never court a redhead!" She tapped her chin. "I'd make an exception for you, of course."

"What's wrong with redheads?" Chinelo cried.

"Well, obviously, red hair and the accompanying pale skin are recessive traits, so if two redheads get married and procreate, then their children are guaranteed to be redheads. That means you will have a whole family of redheads, and that just would look silly. Plus, those children would be doomed to a life of sunburns and old women petting their hair, and you know, I couldn't just sentence my children to that. Honestly, it's really quite simple if you think about it. There are rules for these things when you are a redhead."

Chinelo blinked. Isobel stared back at him then cocked her head.

"What were we talking about?" Isobel said. "I'm sorry, I forgot."

Chinelo sighed. "How about we just go find some breakfast?"

Isobel's eyes lit up. She jumped to her feet and hauled him off the bed. "Oh, yes! Let's go!"

CHAPTER 36

"IT'S A LOT WARMER THAN I expected," Isobel said. "I thought there would be snow."

Chinelo looked at the full green trees that had mysteriously regained all their foliage in the night. He felt himself starting to sweat within his winter coat.

"It's hot."

"It's so bizarre. I was so cold last night. I had to pull on an extra blanket," Isobel said. She took a step into the sunlight. "Now, it feels almost like summer."

Chinelo nodded and scratched his head.

"I'm going to go change into something lighter." Isobel reentered the inn.

Chinelo followed but stopped to speak with the innkeeper.

"Pardon me."

The innkeeper glanced up, then leapt to his feet. He clasped his hands in front of him and bowed deeply.

"May Hylarteph bless your morning. How may I help you, Master Ide?"

Chinelo rapped his fingers on the counter. "Does the weather here always change this quickly?"

"Typically, no."

Chinelo stroked his beard. "Do you know the current day?"

"Of course." The man once again bowed. "By my count it is the four-hundred and thirty-fourth year, the eighth month, and thirtieth day."

Chinelo frowned. So, he had not been wrong about the day. Up in the mountains, winter should have been fading at that point in the year, but there still should have been a month or two of spring before everything was warm.

The man twiddled his thumbs. "Is there something else, Master Ide?"

"Oh. No. Sorry. Just feeling a bit confused this morning. Thank you!"

"Of course. Enjoy your stay."

Chinelo returned to his room. He tossed aside his winter coat and changed from his thick tunic into one of his many sleeveless shirts, giving it a thorough sniff check before. He then reentered the hall, waiting outside Isobel's room.

Isobel's door creaked and she glided into the hallway. She too was wearing a loose sleeveless shirt, one she had purchased while they were in Dawngale and one that Chinelo very much liked.

"Well, Mort was certainly happy to see me," she exclaimed.

"Was he now?"

"I'll need to come back quickly after breakfast. I'm out of food for him, and I'm sure he will be exceedingly grumpy if I don't feed him soon."

Chinelo laughed. Isobel pranced in front of him and spun around to face him. "Shall we go?"

"Please." Chinelo moved from the wall from where he leaned to follow her. She turned, and as she did Chinelo saw something strange. Tattoos were running down her neck and across her upper back.

"Isobel? When did you get those tattoos?"

Isobel turned. "Hmmm? What tattoos?"

"The ones on your back."

She cocked her head. "I don't have any on my back."

Chinelo tapped her skin between her shoulder blades. "Right here. They run all the way between your shoulders."

Isobel craned her neck, trying to see over her shoulder. "I—I don't remember getting any tattoos. Not since we left Iskara. Bah! I can't see anything. What do they look like?"

Chinelo's brow furrowed. "Lots of symbols. I'm not really sure how to describe them. I suppose there are two circles with some runes on each of these places." He tapped just behind her arms. "Then there are lines with runes running towards your spine. Along here." He ran his finger along the lines.

Isobel shuddered.

"Sorry!" Chinelo said.

"Oh! It's no problem. That just tickles a bit."

"You've got another circle with larger symbols here." He tapped directly below her neck. "I can't see the rest of it, though there is more."

The corner of Isobel's mouth twitched. "That is very bizarre. Let's step back in my room for a moment."

They ducked inside, and she rolled up the back of her shirt. "What do you see?"

Chinelo scanned her back. The tattoos ran down the entire length, ending just above her hips. A series of circles were printed down her spine, and each had two branches that ended in additional circles on her sides. It was incredibly intricate, with hundreds of tiny runes inked in fanning patterns.

Chinelo frowned. The tattoos had been printed over faint scars. One, a long gash running diagonally up her back, Chinelo recognized from their first fight in Ata. Another, a large slit on her side, looked much more recent.

"There's a center circle here with a bunch of runes," he tapped the center of her back. "Then there are branches that end here and here." He tapped the outer runed circles.

"How many?"

Chinelo counted. "Fifteen circles in total."

"Fifteen. Interesting. You don't recognize any of the symbols?

Chinelo squinted. "Maybe a few of them, but nothing I can parse."

"Hold on! I have an idea." She ran over to her nightstand and flipped open one of her notebooks, turning through the pages until she found the one she sought. She shoved the book in Chinelo's face.

"This! Does it look like this?"

Chinelo studied the page. "It does, though it's not exactly the same from what I recall. For one thing this only has five circles instead of fifteen. Oh! This character here!" He tapped one that repeated several times in the circles. "I recognize this one."

"That is the symbol '*Gariasheq.*' It means 'gravity.'" She crouched down and ran her fingers through her hair. "Of course! Of course! Five wasn't going to be enough control points. Fifteen, though. That would give enough for precise maneuverability."

"Isobel—" Chinelo was silenced by a sudden raised finger.

"Shhh. I need a moment." Her eyes moved rapidly. "I could try it. Should I try it? I suppose I will have to. It's already here. Maybe just a little." She closed her eyes. The ends of her hair suddenly moved, floating upwards. Her eyes flew open. She looked up at Chinelo, who was growing increasingly more confused.

Isobel leapt to her feet, scampered to her pack, and dug through it, frantically throwing out her belongings. She produced several empty vials and one that only had a few drops of black ink. Her eyes widened.

"These were full yesterday. So, that means that we really did do it here," she muttered to herself. "Which means it would be Chinelo who did it. He's the only one I would trust. Which means..." She looked up at him again. Her expression was wild. "You don't remember putting this on me?"

"When would I have had time to do that? We've been traveling for weeks."

"No. No. Don't think of it like that. Do you remember it?"

"No?"

She stood up. "Did you notice anything strange today? Anything out of the ordinary? Anything you forgot?"

Chinelo scratched his head. "Now that you mention it..."

"Yes?" Isobel stepped closer.

"I noticed that I had some lacquer in my pack that I don't recall buying. Also, our coin pouch was almost empty when I checked it. And... you know about my clothing situation."

Isobel's face lit up. "Good. Good. That supports it. What else?"

"I suppose that it was odd how warm it was this morning."

Isobel nodded. "How about your hair? Did it look any different this morning? I noticed your beard is cut shorter today."

"Right. It seemed a bit longer than I prefer so I trimmed it."

Isobel nodded rapidly. "Right. Right. That makes sense," she muttered. With a sudden movement, she let down her hair. "Notice anything strange?"

"It's really long? It looks good, by the way."

"Put it together, Chinelo. Think like I have been. I want to hear you say it, to know I'm not losing my mind here."

Chinelo took a step back. "Isobel, you're not making sense. What does this have to do with the tattoo?"

"Everything! Think about it. I have a tattoo that wasn't there when we arrived. My hair is abnormally long. The weather is suddenly warm. You have things you didn't buy. Your beard was longer than you remember. There are scribbles on the wall. I'm out of worms for Mort. We're almost out of money. Think, Chinelo! What does it mean?"

Chinelo rubbed his forehead. "I don't know! It doesn't make sense."

"We're forgetting things, Chinelo! I didn't give it a second thought today because you know how foggy I've been recently, but you're forgetting things, too." Isobel ran over to her diary and opened it. She flipped to the last entry. "What day is it today?

"That's easy. 434, 8, 30."

"Then why do I have an entry for that in my diary already?"

Chinelo looked at the page. His eyes widened. Isobel flipped to another page. Then another. Then another. They all had the same date.

"It's worse than I thought," she exhaled.

"What is?"

"If this means what I think it does, then we arrived—hold on!" She thumbed through her thick diary and counted the entries. "Weeks—no—months ago!"

Chinelo reeled.

"Chinelo, something is making us forget!"

CHAPTER 37

WITH A RESOUNDING THUD, ISOBEL CLOSED her diary and let out a long sigh. She had finished reading the entries, none of which she remembered writing. They all followed roughly the same flow of events, though the accounts varied in detail. Many described her meeting with Chinelo in the mornings. On some days they would argue, on others they would not. On some days they would rest at the inn. On others they would climb the mountain to find the obelisk, and they would return after finding it destroyed.

She had gotten close a few times, writing notes about strange things happening around the town, dancing around her recent realization. Though, such entries were followed by long flowing accounts of her conversations and time with Chinelo. It was clear where her priorities were when she wrote in her diary.

Isobel sighed again and touched her lips wistfully. There was one particular night that she wished she could remember. She shook her head. She could make up for lost time once she and Chinelo had found a way to escape their predicament.

She slid her diary across the floor and opened her spell-book. Several loose pages fell out of the back, scattering like autumn leaves. She arranged the pages in a wide circle and dug out another of her notebooks. Opening it, she flipped to the back pages. Scribbles, sketches, and spell drafts were scrawled across the parchment. Though she could not recall making them, Isobel recognized her methods. The design intent of the spells was clear, and they followed a progression towards the tattoo on her back.

Mort hopped onto her foot and stared up at her with his longing amphibian eyes.

"I'm sorry, Mort," Isobel said gently. "Chinelo should be back with breakfast soon. Just a little longer." She lightly stroked his lumpy back.

Mort scowled but didn't move. He merely settled himself down to wait on her foot until Chinelo returned.

"You know, on one of these days, I wrote down that you had learned how to use magic. Anything you'd like to share with me about that?"

Mort glanced up at her then looked away.

"All right, well I'm going to keep an eye on you. I can't have you trying to hurt Chinelo."

Mort pouted. Foiled again!

Isobel continued flipping through her books. She found another spell, one that allowed her to travel through walls. Another levitated and launched objects. Others described additional forms for her staff.

The door of Isobel's room flew open and Chinelo burst inside. His arms were loaded with bags and parcels.

"Oh! You're back!" Isobel said with a bright smile.

"Sorry it took so long." Chinelo dropped his bags to the floor. "I was making some inquiries around the market."

"Did you learn anything?"

Chinelo hunched over the bags and lifted out several parcels that emanated appetizing aromas. "Not much, I'm afraid. First off, everyone I talked to remembers the days leading up to 8, 29 and 8, 30, but nothing after. Also, it seems like a lot of people are missing animals from their farms. There are a few people missing as well. It's concerning."

Isobel nodded.

Chinelo raised an eyebrow. "You don't seem surprised about that." He sat down next to her.

She shook her head. "No. I've read as much in my diary."

He handed her one of the bundles and unwrapped his. He took a large bite of his meal, a large pastry filled with a rich red paste. "So!" He gulped down his first bite. "What did you learn?"

Isobel eyed her bundle hungrily. "Quite a lot actually. It turns out most mornings follow the flow of things today, at least at first. After the first couple days, it sounds like we traveled up the mountain to see the obelisk, but someone already activated it."

"That's a bit concerning."

Isobel nodded and unwrapped her breakfast, smelling the sweet scent of the pastry.

"On one of the days Mort apparently used magic to throw some furniture at you. The little scamp."

Chinelo stared down at the frog. The creature had a devious expression on his fat face.

"I suppose I should probably offer him his meal, then." Chinelo drew out a small jar from his pocket and dumped out the writhing worms that were kept inside. Mort, in turn, attacked them with ruthless ferocity, forcing them down his throat with grotesque convulsions of his eyes.

"Let's see," Isobel mused. "About six weeks ago was when you started the tattoo you saw. Took the whole day."

Chinelo looked up. "I—I did that?"

"That's what it says. That's also what I suspected. I wouldn't trust anyone else."

Chinelo blinked and looked away.

Isobel cocked her head. "What?"

"Sorry. It's nothing."

She shrugged and took a bite of her food. "Wow! This is good. I'm not sure what it is, but I like it."

Chinelo nodded and continued to stare at the floor.

Isobel recalled what she had read. A slight heat rushed to her cheeks. "On one of the nights..." She did not finish the thought. Somehow, being so forward seemed like it would ruin the moment, were it to happen again. She hoped it would.

"Hmmm?" Chinelo wiped a smudge of red bean paste from his cheek.

"Never mind. I'll explain later. There are more important things to discuss. I've come to a few conclusions. First—" Isobel raised a finger. "Something is making us forget each day."

Chinelo nodded.

She raised another finger. "Second: the townsfolk remember things from before we got here as well, but nothing afterwards."

She raised an additional finger. "Third. Whatever is making us forget happens at night. I always write in my diary before bed, so it must be very late if I can still remember the events of the day at that point. A few entries are cut short, though. So, whatever happens is happening around midnight."

"What do you think it is?"

Isobel raised a fourth finger. "That is my final conclusion. Something like this has to be done by magic. That leaves two options. There is a mage or set of mages making us forget. That has some problems, though. A spell with that large of an area would require an insane amount of esht to power. Also, I've not written anything about mages in my diary, and I don't know what words could be used to make people forget things like this. Obviously, I don't know every word in the Ancient Tongue, but I'm semi-fluent, and words like 'memory,' 'remember,' or 'forget' are not present in any codex I've seen."

She continued. "Let's put the pieces together. Incredibly powerful magic is being performed in a way that would require very high esht. Magic is being used with words that, to my knowledge, do not exist. The village has an obelisk that has already been activated. The widespread forgetfulness started when we arrived at the village. Animals and people, all of which are large esht sources, are missing. Lastly, we both have wounds we don't recall receiving. So! What does it mean?"

Chinelo scratched his head. "Well, it sounds like you're suggesting that the obelisk creature is responsible."

Isobel snapped her fingers and pointed at him. "Exactly!"

"But if that is the case, wouldn't the townsfolk forget things from before we arrived? If it was already active, then it would be like we just appeared one day. The innkeeper remembers us arriving, though."

"That would be the case, unless we were the ones who activated it."

Chinelo leaned forward and rubbed his head. "Right. And that might also explain that scar on your side."

"So, now, we just have to find it!" Isobel said cheerfully.

"How?"

"Simple! We wait until midnight. I might have a plan for that as well, though before that I need to finish loading my staff's core."

Chinelo's head nodded forward as his body demanded sleep. He opened his eyes wide and blinked. It was late, far later than when he usually went to sleep. He groaned and stood, pacing around the empty street and yawning several times..

"Dear, I need you to sit here, remember? My barrier won't reach you over there." Isobel tapped a space on the ground beside her.

Chinelo obediently sat down and watched as the barrier from her left hand closed around him. "Sorry. Having trouble focusing."

"I can start shrieking at inconsistent intervals if that would help."

Chinelo clicked his tongue. "I don't think that will be necessary."

Isobel shrugged and looked up at the moon. "It should be almost time. Are you ready?"

"As ready as I can be." He touched his sword and scanned the streets for anything threatening.

"How about you, my little frog friend?" Isobel looked down at the sleeping heap of bullfrog in her lap. "One of these days he'll be awake."

Chinelo gazed up at the clear night sky. The stars stretched in a great celestial arch across the heavens, twinkling in bright hues. A small section of the sky was dark, likely blocked by a passing cloud.

It moved.

Chinelo tensed.

"What is it?" Isobel whispered.

"There's something in the sky."

Isobel looked up and watched the dark shape glide through the air. A small twinkle of green followed behind it. She reached for her staff and breathed out a command.

"Douse: Esht."

Cyan strands of light erupted from her staff, pointing in many directions. One, an incredibly thick one, pointed towards the mysterious twinkle.

"That's it!" she exclaimed.

Chinelo squatted on his toes and drew his sword, preparing himself for anything the dark shape might do. Isobel held her breath and focused on her barrier.

The shape moved closer and closer to the moon, until suddenly its silhouette passed in front of the silver disk. It swooped and hovered on two enormous wings, though its emaciated form was like that of a human's. A long curling tail ended in a strange mass from which the green light shone.

It screeched.

Isobel clutched her head.

"Gah! What is that?" Chinelo leaned forward and covered his ears. The shrill screeching continued, filling his whole head.

"Hold steady!" Isobel yelled.

The screech suddenly stopped, and the creature dove, swooping and plummeting towards the village streets. It flapped its massive wings and crashed into the earth, standing on two gaunt legs. Relative to the other beasts they had slain, the creature was small, standing at about three times Isobel's height. Its body was barely more than a skeleton, with strips of crimson flesh running along its sides and legs. Its bony arms ended in a pair of leathery wings that stretched the full span of the street. A coiling tail squirmed behind it, ending in a knotted mass of stone and flesh that glowed green from its shining core.

Isobel and Chinelo sprung to their feet, each grabbing their weapon. The winged beast turned its head, a smooth stone line with curved points coming from its sides. With intense ferocity, it lurched forward.

CHAPTER 38

ISOBEL DUCKED BENEATH THE BEAST. IT flapped the leathery wings it had in place of arms and thrashed at her with its clawed feet. The air rushed around her as she dodged the fearsome talon strikes.

"Form: Blade!"

Isobel slashed her glaive at the creature's ankles. The sharpened edge sang as it swung through the air, but a sudden forceful flap from the monster's wings propelled the beast skyward. Isobel breathed heavily. Though she had struggled against the creature, she had been unable to land a single blow. She heard the pounding of Chinelo's footsteps as he rushed past her.

"Project!" Chinelo shouted. He swung his sword in a flurry of slashes. The air above him distorted, bending and shimmering like the desert horizon as barely perceivable arcs flew from his sword.

The beast shrieked. Blood erupted from its shoulder, a fountain of pure black that was silhouetted against the silver moon. With a bellow, the monster dove, plummeting toward the two travelers. It spread its wings just above the pavement, gliding over the ground at blistering speed.

Isobel accumulated strength and vaulted over the monster's assault, twisting and turning as she fell back to the ground. Her feet slammed against the earth, and she forced a torrent of esht into her staff.

She heard a deep cry. Chinelo had not managed to evade the monster's dive and had been sent careening across the pavement into a nearby wall.

A fire burned within Isobel, an intense rage that demanded retaliation. She shouted a command.

"Inferno!"

A light flashed from her staff. The beast erupted into a churning tower of orange flames, illuminating the entire street with its brilliant blaze.

The monster screamed with its mouthless cry. From within the fire, Isobel saw a faint pulse of green light. Her heart lurched. Instinctively, she projected her barrier just as the monster emitted a second piercing scream.

The beast leapt to the sky and flew away, erratically fluttering as the flames burned its writhing flesh.

Isobel ran to where Chinelo lay. "Chinelo! Are you hurt?"

"Isobel?" He looked around blinking and squinting. "Where are we? Why is it night?"

Isobel's dropped to a squat. "What is the last thing you remember?"

Chinelo rubbed his head. "We were in your room. You had a strange tattoo. Ow, why does everything hurt?"

"Listen closely. We're fighting one of those monsters. It can make you forget things. It flew away, and I am going to chase after it. I need you to follow me on the ground. Understand?"

Chinelo nodded.

Isobel stood. With a groan, Chinelo joined her. She pointed to the sky at a burning orange speck in the distance. "There. See?"

"How are you going to go after it? It's so far."

Isobel took a deep breath and channeled esht toward the central circle on her back.

"I'm going to fly."

With those few words, she crouched, preparing herself to jump. She expelled her esht and became weightless. Then, she pushed herself off the ground and soared.

It was a strange sensation, moving without gravity. She flew along a straight line, propelled only by her initial push. The air rushed through her hair, causing her ponytail to flutter behind her. The night was cool, and she felt so free.

Her target was ahead of her. She would need to increase in speed if she hoped to catch it. She released her esht and suddenly felt gravity's pull drawing her back to the ground. She flew across the sky in a curved trajectory, then surged energy into the second circle on her spine. Gravity shifted, pulling her directly forward instead of down.

It was wonderous. The world seemed to move. She fell to the horizon ahead, plummeting away from the mountains behind. Gradually, she picked up speed, diving faster and faster toward her target as the wispy clouds flew past her.

Isobel shifted her esht into the center of the tattoo. She gasped. She was going too fast. She sailed past the beast, completely overshooting it. It screeched and dove towards the forest far below.

Isobel twisted and somersaulted midair before directing her fall after the monster. She accelerated toward the ground, then reversed the direction of gravity, slowing herself slightly. With a minor shift in her flow, she redirected her trajectory to be level with the treetops. Rolling and weaving between the tallest trees, she followed the beast's flight. She slowly gained on it. It was close, close enough to reach with one of her many spells. She pointed her staff at the monster.

"Stone Shot: Sevenfold!"

Glowing lights appeared around her staff's head and coalesced into dense stone spheres. They shot away from her, cutting through the night air like diving falcons. One tore through the monster's shoulder, and it roared in pain.

It spread its wings, abruptly slowing down. Isobel sent her esht into the fourth circle on her back, pulling her backwards to slow her flight. She floated underneath the creature and stared up at its emaciated burnt body.

"Icht vasht'ra!"

Fire burst from her hand and crashed into the monster. It flapped its wings and ascended. Isobel twisted and then flew after it, directing gravity into the sky.

It was natural. The position of her esht flow determined the direction gravity pulled. The rate of the flow determined the intensity of that pull. Though she had no memory of drafting the tattoo, using it felt as familiar as walking.

She shifted her esht to her side, causing her to climb in a wide spiraling pattern. She summoned her blade, then pulled herself toward the monster, slashing wildly. Her blade's razor edge cut through the air and pierced the flesh on the monster's side. She pulled herself to a stop, twisted, and then slashed again and again. The creature flailed its legs, trying to catch Isobel in its gnarled talons. With a sudden flap of its wings, it delivered a powerful gust of air, sending Isobel tumbling away.

The world spun around her. She lost control. Her tattoo allowed her to direct gravity's pull on her, but it was relative to the direction she was facing. With her spinning, the pull constantly changed, causing her to zigzag across the sky in an erratic spiral. She shifted her esht, causing her to float completely weightlessly. Her spiral continued. The ground was up, down, then behind, then above, then in front. Bile rose in her throat.

Something hit her, and she stopped tumbling. She felt sharp stabbing pain in her sides. The beast clutched her in one of its talons. However, with the world no longer spinning, she had finally caught her bearings. She needed to escape. The beast's claws dug deeper as it ascended higher and higher into the sky. She recalled the spells she had read from her spell-book, ones that she had no memory of writing. One of them would serve her purpose perfectly.

"Homvelcht tor vrefden solstari!"

The sky flowed into her, then suddenly exploded. She had vanished from the monster's claws and reappeared nearby, floating freely in the air.

The beast turned its head frantically, searching for its lost prey. Isobel watched the glowing mass at the end of its tail. She needed to pierce the core to slay the beast. She once again summoned her blade, and dove forwards.

She blinked. She was falling. Where was she? The sky was above her, but her staff was no longer in her hand. She felt a burning pain in her right shoulder. What had happened?

A speck in the sky grew larger and larger. The monster dove towards her with outstretched talons. Isobel channeled esht into her back and she soared out of the monster's reach. She steadied herself and hovered in the air.

Memory! The monster could affect her memories. If things suddenly changed, then she had merely been forced to forget.

Chinelo watched the sky. Isobel and the creature had disappeared behind the mountains, and he was unable to determine in which direction they had gone. He searched and searched, hoping to find the two dark figures soaring in aerial combat. He heard a loud screech from the north. He ran towards the sound, but a dark lump on the ground caught his eye. It croaked.

"Come on, Mort. We've got to find her!" Chinelo scooped up the frog and placed him on his shoulder. He accumulated strength and crouched. "Hold on tight."

Chinelo dashed forward, sprinting up the steep street toward the mountains. The trees sailed by as he carefully leapt up the steps, vaulted over rocks, and splashed through puddles of standing water that reflected the pale moon. He climbed the mountain at breakneck speed, glancing skyward.

He reached a plateau that overlooked a valley. Two shapes danced in the sky, spiraling around each other in a double helix. Light sparked from the smaller of the two shapes, blasts of fire and bolts of lightning. With a flash the speck vanished and reappeared above the larger shape, the winged form of a tailed monster. The small figure dove into the monster, causing it to plummet before swooping and fluttering upwards.

"I need to get closer," Chinelo grunted. He looked down at the hill below him. It was steep but would be manageable if he was careful. Chinelo leapt from the trail and ran down the hill. Above him, the two figures continued their deadly dance.

Another screech. Chinelo looked as the smaller figure, Isobel, fell.

He shouted her name.

Isobel blinked. She was falling again, with no memory of how she got there. The last thing she recalled was blasting a wave of flame towards the monster. Now, it once again hovered above her, moving its long snake-like tail.

Branches collided with her back, scraping and tearing at her clothes and skin. A faint cry of pain escaped her lips. Thinking quickly, she surged esht into her left side. She was protected.

The protection immediately broke as she collided with another branch. She applied the spell again and again. She hit the ground, and the wind left her lungs. Fortunately, she was otherwise unharmed. She had timed the spell right as she collided with the earth. She coughed as evergreen needles fell around her.

"Isobel!" a voice shouted. Chinelo rushed down the hill and stopped at her side.

"Chinelo," Isobel panted. She sat up and looked around.

"Are you hurt?" Chinelo asked, helping her to her feet.

Isobel looked down. Her shirt had several holes that were soaked red, and a trickle of blood ran down her arm. "A little. Nothing that can't be fixed."

She touched her wounds with her right hand, healing them one by one.

"Bah! I can't reach this one. I'll have to deal with it later."

"What happened? Why did you fall?" Chinelo said.

Isobel summoned her staff to her right hand. "This beast is clever. It makes me forget that I'm fighting it."

"Can you nullify it?"

"If I know it's coming. The problem is, I can't remember how it does it."

Chinelo scratched his head. "Can't you just apply a nullification barrier to yourself like Haru did for physical damage?"

Isobel looked up. "Chinelo. You are a genius!"

She shook her left hand and touched the wound on her right arm. She winced, then began scribbling in blood on her arm, inscribing a messy glyph below her elbow. She hovered her hand over it.

"Axxave sono."

Water accumulated in her hand, drawn out from the blood that was painted on her arm. Isobel moved her arm and let the water drop to the ground.

"I'm going to bring this thing down," she said, glaring at the sky. "I'll try to pull it back over here. If it falls..."

Chinelo nodded, touching his sword. "If it falls, I will finish it."

She crouched, preparing to leap back into the sky, encouraged by the knowledge that he would be fighting alongside her.

"Isobel!" Chinelo said. She looked back at him. "Please, be careful."

She smiled. "I will. I'll be back soon. Thank you, dear. Thank you, Mort." She surged her esht into her back and shot off into the sky.

The ground below her grew smaller and smaller. The trees became blurry. She halted herself and spun around, searching for her target. In the distance, she saw a faint green flicker. She accelerated after the beast.

It grew larger and larger, until it eventually was within reach. Isobel activated the bloody spell on her arm.

The beast turned its head and rolled to the side before releasing a piercing screech. The light at the end of its tail pulsed, but nothing happened. Isobel's memory was intact. She applied the protection again, then pointed her staff above the creature.

"Barrage!"

A hundred spikes formed over the creature and rained down upon it, tearing through its flesh. It fell, shrieking as it plummeted toward the treetops. Isobel dove after it, picking up speed.

The light in the monster's tail pulsed, and the holes in its wings and body closed, filled with wriggling threads of flesh. It spread its wings, and its fall slowed.

"Form: Hammer!"

Isobel's staff head sent out curving blue fractals that coalesced to form an enormous glowing mallet. She gripped it with both hands, and every tendon in her fingers grew taut. With a yell, she slammed her hammer into the monster's chest. A shock recoiled through her staff and across her body. The monster let out a pained groan and its wings crumpled.

It crashed into the trees, splintering the branches as it plunged to the ground. The beast collided with the earth with a loud crunch, but it quickly rolled itself to its feet and raised its wings to return to the sky.

"Form: Javelin!"

Isobel's staff shifted from a hammer to a slender pointed spear, a form she had crafted specifically for throwing. It combined the sword conjuring techniques of the mage Brennen with the force augmentation spells of the hunter Haru. She twirled it, tensed her arm, and hurled it to the earth.

A shockwave emanated from the staff as it fell like lightning, piercing the beast's wing and shattering the ground into a thousand rocky chunks. The monster screamed, then tugged at its pinned wing. It clawed at the dirt, but its wing refused to move.

Isobel landed with a thud and ran over to its thrashing tail. She summoned a knife from the tattoo on her shoulder and began furiously hacking at the flesh that had grown over the beast's core. Her blade cut through the thick tendrils like grass. The creature flicked its tail, sending Isobel flying. She shifted gravity, slowing herself in the air until she hovered just above the ground.

The monster turned its head in her direction and let out another shriek. The light in its tail pulsed again, but the spell had no effect on Isobel. The spell on her arm held fast.

The monster thrashed and clawed at its shoulder, tearing the limb from its body in a bloody display. Its tail pulsed, and tendrils began growing from the grisly wound, gradually taking the shape of another arm.

Isobel called her staff back to her hand. She had to kill it before it flew away. She shifted her gravity, launching herself toward the monster. It made a sudden movement, bringing its leg high above Isobel.

It hit her back, sending her crashing into the ground. She skidded and tumbled across the thick foliage that blanketed the mountainside. Her lungs hurt. They demanded air. She gasped and panted as breath rasped in her throat. An intense burning sensation afflicted her entire body, which had become covered in bruises and abrasions. A forceful gust of air washed over her skin. She looked up to see the beast flying from the forest back toward the town.

Isobel clawed at the ground and stood, bending over with her hands on her knees to catch her breath. In addition to many painful scrapes, she felt a faint fatigue affecting all her muscles. Even with her enormous esht reserves, she was reaching her limits.

Something brushed against her shoulders and neck. Her hair had come untied in the fight.

She clenched her fist and leapt from the ground, flying after the hideous creature. She called her staff back to her hand and accelerated. As she grew closer to the winged monstrosity, she conjured salvo after salvo of magical attacks and elemental blasts. Fire, wind, lightning, metal, all shot through the air at her target, but its flight remained unhindered. She needed to send it to the ground again.

Chinelo scrambled up the hillside, returning to the trail. Above him, the two dueling figures sailed south, heading back towards the village. A weak croak sounded in his ear.

"I know, Mort. I'm worried about her, too." Chinelo looked up. Isobel wielded her staff, shifting its form from blade to hammer to sword with every vicious strike. She vanished, then reappeared above the monster, diving downwards and thrusting her blade towards it.

"I wish there was some way we could help," Chinelo said as he stumbled down the stone steps toward the village center. Mort croaked in agreement. A light flashed above, illuminating the town as if it were day. Chinelo raised his eyes again; the beast had caught aflame and was thrashing wildly. Isobel floated at a distance, keeping clear of the beast's fearsome claws.

Chinelo leapt from the stairs and slammed into the stone pavement, poising himself into a focused stance. He reached for his sword then extended his left hand.

"Belekt tra'vasht!"

A loud explosion burst from his hand. Isobel looked down at him, then backed away from the monster. Chinelo gripped his sword hilt tightly, focusing all his strength into his arms. The veins on his forearm pulsed. His muscles tensed, and he inhaled. From the frog's perch on his shoulder, Chinelo felt a steady stream of esht. With their combined strength, Chinelo shouted a command.

"Project!"

He drew his sword from its sheath, swinging it in a wide silver arc. Responding to his command, the blade sent forth a distorted wave through the air, a curved razor that shot upwards toward the beast. He had provided it with a bountiful supply of energy, and the translucent crescent flew through the crisp night before slicing clean through the beast's thighs. Its severed legs fell, and a shower of black blood followed. It rained down upon the village, steaming and bubbling as it splashed against the heavy roof tiles and stone pavement. The monster screamed a horrific, chilling wail.

Isobel exhaled. Chinelo had created the opening she needed. She shifted her gravity, causing herself to fall toward the beast, which still flashed and screeched as its body burned. She twirled her staff.

"Extinguish!"

The flames vanished from the monster's body. It moved its head in her direction and flailed its tail to bat her away.

"Homvelcht tor vrefden solstari!"

Isobel vanished and reappeared behind the monster. She twisted, then slammed her hand into its oily black skin. She only needed two words.

"Jovachte."

Increase.

"Gariasheq."

Gravity.

The beast dropped, pulled to the ground by an irresistible force. It spread its wings, howling as their leathery membranes tore from the rushing air. Far below, it impacted the stone pavement with a resounding crunch.

The sky lightened. Morning was approaching. It was time to slay the beast.

Isobel raised her hand above her, inhaled, and delivered a final incantation. Chinelo was down there waiting. He would handle the rest.

"Icht dagas va ogo iv fet."

Chinelo and Mort looked up. Isobel hovered above the town, holding her staff behind her with eyes ablaze. Her hair floated weightlessly, shimmering and waving in the gentle breezes. She was beautiful, a maiden floating in the heavens. She was terrifying, a witch wielding arcane forces as deadly weapons.

She raised her hand upwards. Though he could not hear, Chinelo saw her lips moving. A shape formed above her, a stone sphere that rapidly grew and grew until it was more than twice her height. She swung her hand downwards, and the boulder plunged toward the earth. It crushed the beast. Its body grew limp beneath the stone.

A sudden movement caught Chinelo's eye. The beast's tail writhed, and flesh flowed like oil from the body toward the core. It accumulated, and small wriggling appendages formed along the tail's bones, lifting the tail from the ground and extending to cover the core. He gasped. The beast was re-forming itself.

Chinelo sprinted forward, pounding his feet on the pavement. With both hands, he gripped his sword and held it downwards at an angle. He leapt and swung the blade, slashing through the tail and cleaving it from the body. The tail convulsed, and the vestigial limbs flailed in their attempts to scurry away. Chinelo twirled his sword and thrust it into the tail's flesh. He ran, cutting a path directly to the core. The monster screamed, its high-pitched voice filled with rage and terror. The core pulsed, shining a brilliant green beneath him.

Chinelo adjusted his grip, grasping the handle of his blade with both hands. Then, with a mighty yell, he stabbed his sword downwards, directly into the monster's core.

Green vapor erupted and shrouded him. Words, symbols, and phrases rushed into his mind. He gained knowledge of thought, knowledge of soul, knowledge of memory.

A word echoed internally.

"CHANAVOSHTA!"

CHAPTER 39

CHINELO LAY ON THE GROUND, TIRED and exceedingly groggy. A cool breeze brushed his skin, drawing him from his slumber. He couldn't remember why he had fallen asleep, but internally, a single word reverberated in his mind.

"Chanavoshta."

It repeated, over and over. Memory. It was the gods' word for memory, one of the two words they needed to reverse time. It existed within his mind as if he had always known it. The base word, the many variations and modifications, even the symbol felt like they had been part of his vocabulary since he first learned to speak. Finally, after all this time, they had made progress towards their goal.

He stirred. The surface on which he lay was hard, bumpy, and rough. Who thought making a bed out of this was a good idea?

He felt a hand gently touch his face.

"Wake up..." Isobel's voice whispered, an intense pleading woven into her inflections. "Please, Chinelo..."

His eyes flew open. Isobel leaned over him, her worried face suddenly lighting up as he took a deep breath.

"Chinelo!" She tackled him, wrapping him in her quivering arms. "I was so worried! You were asleep for so long. Are you hurt? I can heal you. I've saved a little bit of energy in case you need it. Just... just, please tell me you're all right."

Chinelo held her close. "I'm fine, Isobel, really." He forced himself up and rested his chin on her shoulder. The heavens above were shining like a brilliant sapphire. Chinelo stared at the clear sky. It was like her eyes, so deep and blue. He was seated on the sun-touched streets of Kahi, the morning light brightly illuminating the quiet town. Several steps away, Chinelo saw the broken remnants of the fallen monster's head.

Isobel let out a sigh of relief and released him, dropping to a seat and brushing the hair away from her face. She smiled that sweet, beautiful smile that made his heart stir. She was battered and bruised, scraped and scratched. Her clothes were torn, and the edges of the frayed holes were soaked red.

"Are you well?" Chinelo asked, repositioning himself so that he knelt on one knee.

Isobel nodded emphatically. "I am. Though it seems my clothes are a bit more ventilated than I would prefer."

Chinelo chuckled. "We can get you some new ones that don't have quite so many holes."

Isobel looked into his eyes. Her face was beaming.

"What is it?" he asked.

She cocked her head. "I'm just happy to see you."

He felt a deep swelling inside, a tidal wave of emotion, rushing to burst forth. A single thought filled his mind, a single truth that he could not deny, nor could he contain. If he ever had any doubts before, those all vanished as she looked into his eyes.

He had to tell her. Still, why was he suddenly terrified?

Before he could say anything, she spoke. "What was the word you learned?"

Chinelo paused, redirecting his thoughts to the question at hand. "Memory," Chinelo said. "It's memory."

Isobel's eyes widened. Her fingers touched her lips. "That's... we did it, Chinelo! That's the first piece we need! We did it!"

"We did," Chinelo nodded and looked down. He had to tell her. He had to.

Isobel touched his hand. "Hey. Are you all right?"

Chinelo looked into her eyes. "It's like you said. I'm happy to see you, too."

He inhaled deeply and exhaled a shaky breath. It was time. He was terrified, but he knew what he had to do.

"Isobel?"

"Yes, dear?"

"There are some things I want to say to you."

"Oh! All right. I—I have a few things I'd like you to hear as well. You first."

Chinelo sighed and clenched his fist. His hands shook.

Isobel glanced down at his trembling fingers. She gripped his hand tightly in hers and leaned forward.

Chinelo breathed again. "I—I think you know I'm not the best at putting my feelings into words, but..." He paused.

"Yes?" She tilted her head. Her eyes shone.

"We've been on this journey for so long, and I know that it hasn't all been good, but I want you to know that..." he once again hesitated. Why was it so difficult to say? His body trembled.

A soft squeeze on his hand pulled him back. He looked up at her. She appeared to be slightly confused, but the fond expression had not left her face.

Chinelo took in another deep breath and drew closer. "Can I have your permission to do something?"

"Of course. Anything you want." Isobel smiled, then tilted her chin slightly forward.

Chinelo reached up and touched her hair. His heart pounded. With a single fluid motion, he leaned forward, closed his eyes, and kissed her.

It was overwhelming, a symphony of sensations both internal and external. He felt her hand touch his cheek, pulling him in tenderly. After a lingering moment of passion and intensity, they separated.

Chinelo opened his eyes. "I love you, Isobel."

Isobel's expression was exuberant. She squirmed and giggled. "You kissed me."

"I did. I hope that was all right."

"You could say that it was." She took a deep breath. "I have something important to tell you, too."

"I'm listening."

"It's a secret."

"All right."

She leaned forward and brought her lips close to his ear. He felt her warm breath on his cheek. She whispered.

"I love you, too, Chinelo. So very much."

She kissed him again.

Their first kiss had been short but passionate. Their second was long and tender. It was, however, very rudely interrupted by an incensed squawk from Isobel's side.

Isobel shot an annoyed glance down at her slimy amphibious companion. "Mort, I adore you, but you have the worst possible timing."

Chinelo laughed. "I suppose I wouldn't exactly be comfortable if I were in his position."

"Well, he needs to learn that Mom and Dad sometimes need their personal time, and he is going to have to live with it." She glanced up and blushed. "Though, it seems we have an audience of a different sort."

Chinelo looked around. A few people, residents of the village going about their morning chores, had begun to stare.

"We should probably get back to the inn," he said nervously.

"Probably. First, just one more. A quick one." Isobel tugged on his collar and kissed him a third time.

THE END OF PART 5

PART 6

THE GODSLAYER'S SWORD

CHAPTER 40

**427th year, 7th month, 25th day
8 years before present day**

THE BULLFROG LOUNGED ON THE LILY pad, surveying his small kingdom. He was a proud ruler of his pond, an emperor adorned in slime. Like the greatest of kings, he was admired by his allies and feared by his many, many foes. He kept a watchful eye on the edges of the still water, searching for any signs of movement that might indicate an invasion.

Life was slow, but it was comfortable, aside from when his belly was empty. His first few weeks out of hibernation had been busy, a frantic rampage through the reeds culling the weak who would dare stand in his field of view. Such creatures were not worthy of life. Their writhing, squirming, chirping bodies were only made to find their ends in the bullfrog's jaws.

Movement.

A water strider, an insolent, vile creature, streaked across the pond's surface. It was a fool. All who dared to disturb the clear reflection were doomed to a horrific death. That was justice.

The bullfrog slowed his breathing. He did not move. He became one with the world, blending into his environment perfectly. He could sense everything. Every breeze. Every ripple. Every rustle of every leaf.

The strider darted across the pond and slowed to a stop near the lily pad. Had it seen him? Impossible. No mere mortal could pierce the frog's camouflage. No, it was merely pondering silly things, such as how many legs it had, or how many days it was going to live.

Foolish creature. There were no days left for it to live, and soon, its legs would be separated from its succulent, appetizing body. It only needed to move a little closer.

The strider glided forward, and the bullfrog moved. He opened his mouth, shooting forth his long, flexible tongue. It hit its mark, and the strider was quickly devoured. All was once again at peace within his kingdom.

However, his cavernous belly was still empty. He had purged all of the insects from his pond, and few dared to return. If he wished to find more food, he would need to leave his lovely kingdom. Worst of all, he would have to leave his lily pad, which was very comfortable.

A rustle.

A crunch.

Something was walking in the woods. The bullfrog looked around with slight apprehension. He was not afraid, no, for what creature would dare to harm him? He was merely concerned. He soon saw the source of the sounds.

Two bipedal figures passed the pond. The bullfrog relaxed. It was merely the two humans who lived nearby. He had often seen them, an older, taller figure and a younger, more energetic figure. Their heads were topped with hair of a brilliant color, a color that would surely make for poor camouflage.

They stopped. Why would they stop? They never stopped. The smaller figure, a rather adorable female, bent over the water and dipped her hand in the pond before withdrawing her hand.

"It's still so cold."

The bullfrog never questioned his ability to understand the language of the humans. In his mind, it was only natural that he could understand all things, so an explanation was never required. He listened closely. Perhaps their words would contain secrets that would allow him to expand his domain.

The older figure, also a female, hobbled behind the younger, supporting herself on an ornate staff.

"You're avoiding the subject, Isobel," she said with a wheeze that was barely audible to the frog's drum shaped ears.

"I don't want to talk about it, Mother."

The mother let out a long sigh and sat on a nearby log.

"Come now, he couldn't have been that bad."

Isobel shot a look back at her mother. "You have no idea."

"Was the meal he fed you at least nice?"

"No! It was all burnt but somehow still squishy. It's like he overcooked all the bread, then wanted to hide that, so he just doused it in gravy."

"Well, some of us aren't as skilled as you are." The mother grinned deviously.

"Very funny, Mother. I at least know how to toast bread properly."

"And what else? What did you and Garlo talk about?" the mother coaxed.

"*I* didn't talk about much. He really missed out in that respect. Oh, the things I would say had he only listened."

"Yes, I'm sure the poor boy has no idea what he is missing."

"Exactly. I am a lovely conversationalist."

"A humble one, too." The mother's eyes twinkled.

The younger figure rolled her eyes, something the frog had never quite learned how to do, likely for lack of practice.

"Anyways, first he muttered for nearly an hour about the how he doesn't like his father, which is silly, because his father is just the kindest little man I've ever seen. Then he went on and on about how all the other girls in the village are ugly and egotistical."

The mother chuckled. "Not you, though?"

"Oh, no. What was the word he used?" She snapped her fingers a few times. "Exotic!"

The mother laughed. "Exotic?"

"Yes! I'm different, you see, because I wasn't raised here."

"What a flattering compliment."

"Right? So, of course, I tried to interject that I didn't agree with his assessment, but he wouldn't stop interrupting me. Every time I tried to express an opinion, he would just smother it with one of his own. And they were always wrong. I've never met someone who was so consistently wrong on a fundamental level."

"Do you have any examples?"

"Well, he said he sleeps in stockings."

"That's not so—"

"*Only* stockings, mother."

The mother snickered and tilted her head to the side. "I wonder how you reached that conversation topic."

"Through a winding chasm of poor opinions and outlandish claims. Did you know that twelve children is the optimal number? Because, I was unaware of such a fact, and it seems quite inconsiderate for no one to have told me until now."

"Well, he certainly has ambition," the mother said.

"I pity his future wife," Isobel said, crossing her arms. "Which is someone who I will not be. When he went to relieve himself, I left."

"Isobel!" The mother said in shock.

"What?" Isobel looked up with a bewildered expression.

"Th—that's not the ideal way, considering our family's ties to his. It's matter of decorum." The mother shook her head. "I'm sure he was confused when he returned."

Isobel shrugged. "I don't particularly care. I have no intention of speaking with him again."

"That may be, but his father is one of my most loyal business partners." The mother coughed a deep, rasping cough.

The bullfrog cocked his head. A faint smell of death reached his nostrils. Something was very wrong with that woman. He hopped from his lily pad to the bank and waddled his way around the pond. The younger of the two figures, Isobel, had nerve, and he respected nerve. His kingdom was in need of subjects, and he was convinced that she would make a lovely citizen. And, if his nose had not betrayed him, she would soon need a companion. The bullfrog had observed that humans were rarely solitary creatures.

The mother shook her head. "I'll try to smooth things over with Marcin when I see him tomorrow."

"I'm sorry, Mother."

The bullfrog crawled through the thick reeds and poked his nose out. He was directly next to Isobel's boot.

"It is all right, honey. I'm sorry I pressured you into courting him. I was hoping it would be a good experience for you."

Isobel rubbed her shoulder. "It could have been worse. I appreciate the attempt."

"Oh! It seems we have a visitor. Perhaps another suitor?" The mother chuckled and gestured towards the bullfrog's hiding place.

Isobel looked down. Her face lit up. "Oh! He's adorable!"

She scooped up the frog in her hands and held him before her face. "Look at him! He's so lumpy!"

The mother laughed. "I was joking, daughter. Please do not court that frog."

"Well, I am not! Can I keep him?"

"You are almost nineteen, darling. You do not need my permission. Just make sure you feed him well. Bullfrogs are very hungry creatures."

Isobel smiled and looked back at the frog. "Hmmm. I wonder what I should call you. Lumpy? How does that sound?"

The bullfrog scowled.

"Oh! You did *not* like that. How about a real name? Mother, what is a good boy's name?"

The mother grinned. "Garlo?"

Isobel's expression mirrored that of the frog.

The mother laughed, but that laughter became a nasty cough, once again spreading the scent of death. "Bartoss always wanted to name you Mortavel if you were a son."

"Hmmm. That seems too long for someone so stubby." Isobel looked up ponderingly, and the sunlight reflected off her spectacles.

"Mort!" she declared. "Yes, that will fit perfectly. Greetings, Mort. My name is Isobel Valeria, and I am going to feed you so many worms."

Mort did whatever frogs do instead of smiling. This arrangement would be to his liking.

CHAPTER 41

435th year, 2nd month, 5th day
Present day

THE BAG IN WHICH MORT HAD been stuffed bounced, sending him tumbling around its stinky interior. This arrangement was not to his liking.

Suddenly, his fat frog body felt weightless. He was falling. With a dull splat his bulbous belly collided with a hard surface. He shook himself. He would not forgive this abuse.

Mort wriggled his body around the bag until he found a small tear in the side. Though his magnificent corporeal form was malleable and squishy, he was far too large to squeeze himself through the hole. Peeking would have to suffice. It was a small consolation. He would get to witness his captors' final moments before they received their just deserts.

Mort's stomach rumbled. Dessert would have been appreciated before he was so rudely frog-napped.

Through the frayed hole, he saw his captor plop down on a stump next to a pitiful campfire. He was thin and wiry, a man with dark hair and green eyes, like many of the peasants Mort had seen in Nesa. A pelt of dark fur was draped over his shoulder, and he adjusted it frequently as it was just slightly too big for him. The man was not alone. Another set of eyes twinkled in the dim firelight, and far beyond Mort could see the ominous shadow of a walled city against the starlit sky.

"You're empty handed, Ei," a voice called from the darkness. Mort could just barely discern its source.

Ei shook his head. "Not so, Rasheko. I—" he flourished his arm and gestured towards Mort's bag, "—have dinner."

Rasheko leaned forward, revealing his face. He was attractive by human standards, with a well-defined jaw and gentle eyes. Mort, however, did not find the man attractive, for he was a frog.

"Dinner? You followed those two for hours and all you found was dinner? We're going to have so much dinner once the others get back. You were supposed to get valuables, Ei, valuables! Something we can sell."

"Rash, Rash, my friend and comrade, have you ever had the delight of eating grilled Nell frog legs? It's like nothing you've ever tasted." Ei smacked his lips. "Exquisite."

Mort scowled. What an insult. His legs were for admiring not eating. This man would receive his punishment in due time.

Rasheko frowned. "Please tell me you have something else."

Ei stood up and dug his hand into his pocket. "I have this." He produced a carved wooden bracelet, one decorated with etchings of birds. He tossed it over the fire, and with a flick of his wrist Rasheko caught the bracelet.

"Pretty good craftmanship." Rasheko shrugged. "This will do. Consider yourself pardoned, Ei."

Mort's jowls shot downwards in an enraged scowl. How dare those vile ruffians touch his queen's prized possession? Even if it had been gifted to her by the troublesome interloper, it was still her precious keepsake. Justice would come.

Voices murmured from the south. Two more figures approached the fire.

"Jira! Naol! How did it go?" Ei held his arms wide open, offering an embrace that was promptly ignored.

"Naol chickened out." Jira, a tall woman with short black hair, dropped a large sack on the ground. Her face was harsh, a stone effigy that was exclusively angles and corners.

"Pardon me for exercising caution!" Naol, an exceedingly short fungus of a man, waddled beside the sack. He was pudgy, but somehow scrappy at the same time—a contradiction, one which Mort did not very much like. The bullfrog's perfect proportions were not to be imitated, and this bipedal mushroom dared to make a mockery of them. He must be fixed.

"I've seen that masked creature before," Naol continued. "I don't relish the idea of getting driven into the ground like a shuttle-cart spike."

"Coward." Jira rolled her eyes. "Why did I ever marry you?"

"You didn't."

"Well, I should have, just so I could break it off right here and now."

Ei chuckled and wrapped his arms around his fellow bandits, a difficult task, considering their notable differences in height. "Friends! Cease your bickering, for tonight we dine as kings!"

Jira shoved him away. "What's gotten into you? Apple-berries and squash are hardly kingly."

Ei raised a finger. "True, true, but Nell frog legs drizzled in apple-berry juice make a fine meal."

Jira blinked. "Rash, I told you not to let him drink during raids."

Rasheko shrugged. "This is pure, unadulterated Ei."

Naol shuffled to the fire, clutching a skewer in his hand. "Rash, where's the food?"

Something sounded in the distance. A crashing, crunching sound. Footsteps approaching their location. Mort settled himself down. This was the moment. The bandits had enjoyed their final fleeting minutes of life. Justice was coming, justice in the form of a very angry witch.

The bandits all leapt to their feet and drew their weapons, a ragtag arsenal of daggers and short swords. Into the light a figure stepped, a tall, muscular figure with dark skin in a sleeveless tunic.

"Pardon me, strangers. Forgive the intrusion. Have any of you seen a large frog around here?"

Mort scowled. It was the interloper, the usurper.

The bandits twitched nervously. Ei spoke first.

"Frog?"

Chinelo nodded. "Yes, about this big."

Mort scowled even more. Chinelo's hand gestures had not accurately portrayed his majestic size.

Ei glanced at the bag. "No. Now shuffle off! We're not eager to make new friends tonight."

The insolence! That creature had lied in Mort's presence.

Chinelo rubbed his neck. "Ah. Well, have a nice evening." He turned to leave.

Mort let out a loud croak. He did not often ask for help, and that is not what this was. He was merely informing Chinelo of his location to correct the lie of that disgusting beanpole of a man.

Chinelo looked at the bag with a frown. "I'm going to need that frog back."

"No! It's my frog!" Ei shouted.

Mort began a droning frog song.

"Friend, can I just have the frog back? My partner is very grumpy tonight, and if she hears him singing like that and finds him in a bag, she will be rather difficult to reason with."

The bandits looked around at each other nervously. Rasheko opened his mouth to speak but was interrupted by the sound of footsteps racing toward their position. Mort once again adopted a pleased expression. Justice was coming. The queen would soon arrive.

A figure vaulted high into the air and slammed into the ground at the center of the camp. Mort scowled. The figure was *not* Isobel.

She was tall with long brown hair, and she was garbed in leather armor with steel trim. Most curiously, her face was covered by an intricately carved white mask.

Naol let out a frightened cry.

"She followed us! Run!" Jira bellowed.

The armored figure adopted a fighting stance, raising her heavy gauntlets in front of her. A cloud of thick fog erupted from her shoulders, completely enveloping the camp. Mort grimaced, his view obstructed. He would not be able to witness justice with his own eyes. He could, however, very clearly hear it.

Cries broke out, and with them came the crunching sounds of fists striking skin and bone. Shadows danced in the mist, fuzzy outlines of frightened combatants. They quickly fell to the masked figure's relentless assault.

Mort's bag was wrenched upwards. He was tossed around quite rudely, and he faintly heard Ei's terrified breaths.

"I just wanted a decent meal," Ei whimpered.

Mort jammed his head through the hole. The bag twisted, and he briefly caught a glimpse of the camp. The cloud of vapor hung thick in the air, but to the side Chinelo leaned lazily against a tree. Such an insufferable creature. He had not even lifted a finger in service of Mort.

The bag untwisted and Mort saw what was ahead. Ei pushed through thick grass and brush, attempting to flee the maelstrom behind him.

Mort seethed. If this continued, he would not be able to see his queen again, and that was a fate far worse than death. He resumed his frog song, though its pitch rose and fell with every bounce of his fabric prison.

"Halt!" A voice called out. Isobel's voice. Mort's spirits lifted. His queen had arrived, and her wrath would be apocalyptic.

Ei turned around and faced her. Mort looked up, and he saw his queen's graceful form. She hung in the sky, floating weightlessly above the fields. Her hair, recently cut to just above her shoulders, moved gently in the wind. She held her staff behind her, and its spell-core's shifting vapors emanated a light cyan aura.

"I believe you have what is mine," Isobel said sternly.

"The bracelet is back at the camp. I'm sorry, I didn't know it was so important!"

Isobel glared downwards and muttered something beneath her breath. Her spell-core pulsed, and tongues of flame appeared in the air around her, twisting and growing until she was surrounded by a multitude of raging fireballs. The grass moved in a shockwave beneath her, and rocks and pebbles floated from the ground, hovering menacingly around Ei.

With a squeal, Ei tossed the bag and scurried off, fleeing from the terrifying witch.

Mort heard a cry from Isobel, and the bag hung weightlessly in the air, floating like she did. Soon, he felt it rest in her gentle hand, and the neck of the bag was torn open.

"Mort!" Isobel shouted cheerfully. She stroked his back, a lovely feeling that, in Mort's experience, had no equal. "I'm sorry, friend. He must have raided our camp while I was bathing. I hope you aren't hurt."

Mort was not hurt, and though he had previously been furious at his predicament, all that had faded upon seeing his queen. Isobel pressed him against her check and nuzzled his slimy body.

"Let's head back."

She lifted him to his beautiful throne, her shoulder. Mort proudly seated himself and once again surveyed his kingdom. All was right in the world.

They returned to the bandits' camp. The thick vapor had dissipated, revealing the groaning bodies of Naol and Jira. Silhouetted against the firelight, Rasheko and the masked figure fought in a violent, pugilistic storm.

Isobel joined Chinelo's side.

"Is that who I think it is?" she asked.

Chinelo nodded. "Looks that way."

"You're not going to help?"

"I think she has it under control." He winced. "That one looked like it hurt."

The figure ducked under one of Rasheko's punches and whispered a word.

"Strength."

A gold light pulsed from her gauntlet, and she delivered an earthshaking uppercut, sending the bandit flying. He landed with a loud thud and ceased moving.

The figure shook her hands and glanced over in their direction.

"Isobel? Chinelo?" she breathed heavily.

Isobel waived. "Hello, Joanne!"

Joanne lifted her mask, revealing her face in the warm light of the fire. "You finally made it."

Isobel dropped her staff and ran to Joanne, wrapping her sister in her arms. "Sorry it took so long. We had a few mishaps on the way."

Joanne hugged Isobel, squeezing a very unhappy Mort between them. Physical contact from outsiders was rarely tolerated.

Joanne stepped back. "Welcome to Veld, I suppose. We have a bit of a bandit problem."

Isobel giggled. "I noticed."

"How are you, Chinelo?" Joanne looked past Isobel's shoulder.

"Well enough. Your lovely sister has made the journey pleasant."

"Oh, has she now?" Joanne smirked.

Mort felt a heat coming from beside him, one that he knew meant that his queen was blushing. Insolence. How dare they subject her to such embarrassment?

Chinelo bent to the ground and picked up something. He dusted it off against his tunic. "Here you go, dear."

"Oh! You found it! Thank you so much! I would have been absolutely distraught if we hadn't been able to recover this." She slid the carved bracelet over her glove and admired it. "There! It is back in its proper place."

Mort turned and saw a movement from Joanne. She leaned back behind Isobel and mouthed the word "dear" questioningly in Chinelo's direction. Chinelo shot her a knowing look, to which Joanne responded with a satisfied nod.

"I assume you're camped nearby?" Joanne said.

"Yes! Down that direction." Isobel pointed into a nearby cluster of trees. "Though it's only half set-up."

"Perfect! You can stay at my place tonight!"

Isobel's face lit up. "Really?"

"Of course! Kay and I have plenty of room. Our guest bed is very comfortable, and big enough for two!"

Mort felt a slight heat from Isobel again. "That—that would be lovely, Joanne. Thank you!"

Joanne grinned and put her hands on her hips. "You're in luck. The harvest festival is tomorrow night. You've picked the perfect time to visit."

Mort did whatever frogs do instead of smiling. Harvest festivals typically involved food, and food typically attracted flies. Yes, this arrangement would be to his liking.

CHAPTER 42

"KAY! I'M HOME!" JOANNE SHOUTED AS she barreled through the door, shaking the whole house. Isobel followed close behind, a vague sense of apprehension hovering over her.

Kay hunched over a humble wooden table. Dozens of glass jars and vials were scattered before her, and a flask of a bright pink liquid bubbled over a small burner.

"I really wish you wouldn't do that, Joanne," Kay looked up, brushing her bobbed blonde hair from her round face. "One of these days I'll—" she stopped speaking, and an expression of shock overtook her. She snuffed the burner. "Isobel?"

Isobel waved nervously. "Hello, Kay."

Kay stood and brushed off her apron. She was not particularly tall, but also not particularly short, falling somewhere between Joanne's impressive height and Isobel's much less imposing stature. As was the case with her height, most things about her could be described as falling directly between two extremes. Her dress was neither flamboyant nor austere. Her movements were neither graceful nor stiff. She was neither short nor tall, neither plump nor thin, neither muscular nor frail. She was merely Kay.

She walked across the room and stood before Isobel, looking down at her with an unreadable expression on her face. The room fell silent as tension built between the two sisters.

"Are you well?" Kay asked.

Isobel jumped at the sound. "Oh! Yes! And you?"

"I'm surviving."

"That's good, that's good." Isobel looked down. She fidgeted nervously.

Mort croaked from Chinelo's hand. He was staring longingly at Isobel's shoulder, eager to return to his perch. Chinelo had asked to hold him before their entry into the building, perhaps as an attempt to bond with the creature. It was not an appreciated attempt.

Joanne shifted on her feet, eyeing the awkward display in front of her.

"Kay!" she whispered and nodded toward Isobel, shooting Kay a displeased glare.

Kay let out a long sigh and drew Isobel into a stiff embrace, positioning her hands in such a way that she did not touch Isobel's back. "It's good to see you, sister. I'm sorry for those things I said. Will you forgive me?"

"Oh! Of course. Think nothing of it! I'm sorry I left you two without saying goodbye."

"You had your reasons, I'm sure."

Kay released her and finally smiled. "Well, now. Who is this?"

Isobel fluttered to Chinelo's side. "This is Chinelo. He's been coming with me on my journey, and he's the most amazing person I've ever met."

Chinelo balked slightly at the comment then bowed. "A pleasure to meet you, Kay."

A voice called from a far corner of the cozy living space. "And a pleasure to meet you as well!"

Joanne whirled around. "Valyx! You're still here? It's so late!"

A stocky man rose from a crooked stool in the corner. He was a sturdy and ruddy creature, a living brick that was all smiles. A bush of thick red hair topped his head, having a much darker shade than Isobel's vibrant copper locks. Unfortunately, it also had the rather undesirable effect of clashing violently with his perpetually flushed cheeks.

"Kay said she wanted some company." He shrugged. "I'm company."

Kay sighed. "Valyx, it's probably time for you to leave now. Joanne is right. It is rather late."

Valyx nodded cheerfully. "Still good to meet at the fountain tomorrow for the festival?"

"Of course," Kay said with a slight wave of her hand towards the door.

Valyx wrapped one of his thick arms around Kay's shoulders and squeezed her to his side. He nodded jubilantly at Chinelo and Isobel, winked at Joanne, then rumbled his way out the door.

"So!" Joanne clapped her hands. "Tell us all about your journey. It's been almost a year now, I think, since I saw you last."

Isobel scratched her head. "That will take some time."

Joanne smiled. "Well, we have all night. Kay and I are both off work tomorrow for the festival. Have a seat."

"I am curious to hear how things have been," Kay agreed. "Joanne gave me an account when she first returned, but I'm sure she left out some details."

"I would never."

"You definitely would."

Isobel and Chinelo sat on one of the two faded couches that adorned the living space. Chinelo wrapped his arm around Isobel, and she began a rather winding and convoluted account of their journey, babbling late into the night.

Chinelo unrolled his sleeping mat on the floor in the guest room and let out a loud yawn. He and Isobel had quarreled amiably over who would sleep in the soft bed, and he had ultimately won, convincing her that she needed the bed the most. He himself was surprised at his victory. Isobel could be unbelievably stubborn when she wanted to be.

"So!" Joanne peeked into the room. "How are those babies coming along?"

"By the queen, Joanne! Don't start that again!"

Joanne shrugged and leaned against the doorframe, holding a stack of books under her arm. "You're sleeping on the floor?"

"I am. It's what we're comfortable with."

She cocked her head. "You men confuse me."

"You don't say?"

"But seriously, are—"

Chinelo glared at her.

"So touchy." Joanne raised her hand. "I just want to know when I'll be an aunt."

"Are you two even blood related?"

Joanne shook her head and entered the room, dropping the books beside Isobel's pack. "Of course not. But I want nieces and nephews and you're my best shot at it. Now." She smacked her hands together twice.

"Get to work. Go get married or… whatever normal people do. That's normal, right?"

Chinelo sighed. "Yes, Joanne. Most people marry before having children, if they have them at all."

"Still can't get over that."

Chinelo raised an eyebrow.

"Oh, don't give me that look," Joanne said. "I'm not judging you for how you were raised. This is all quite the adjustment for some of us." Her back slid down the wall, bringing her to a seat on the floor. "I just want a couple nieces. That's all I'm asking for."

"Don't you have any faith in Kay?"

Joanne scratched her head. "Ehh, Kay is an odd one. She tends to prefer the more solitary life."

"Valyx seemed pretty enamored with her."

"Maybe. I don't think that's the kind of relationship they have, but clearly, I'm no expert. I only first spoke to a man a year and a half ago."

Chinelo blinked. Joanne gave him a flat look.

"Do you think it was wise to leave Isobel and Kay alone together?" Chinelo asked. "Things seemed tense."

Joanne let out a long sigh. "I think it needed to happen. Those two share more than most, for better or for worse."

Chinelo looked up. "You're referring to…"

"Cleo."

"Ah." Chinelo nodded.

"Kay did not take the news of Isobel being alive in the way I expected. I imagine her feelings toward her are complicated, given what happened after she left."

"I see."

Joanne scratched her shoulder. "I think some things need to be said between those two, some things I cannot be present for. I imagine that is why Kay asked me to come keep you company."

Chinelo nodded and sat on the bed. "So, how have you been?"

Joanne's face brightened, and she joined him, hopping onto the bed and landing with a bounce. "Good, good. Work on the farm has been busy. Those bandits we caught tonight have been making the duke's life rather disagreeable for some time now. Other than that, I've taken up some hobbies. I used to dance when I was younger, and I've been teaching some of the local children. They are picking up quickly. And you?"

"Well, you've heard most of the story already."

Joanne crossed her arms. "I heard Isobel's story with your interjections on the areas she forgot. How you're doing I haven't heard as much about."

Chinelo nodded in understanding. "I'm surviving, to quote Kay. It hasn't been easy, but we are making good progress. Some days are definitely harder than others. She's been through so much, and it's been difficult to watch at times. The good days have been very good, though. She is a blessing."

"And her plan?"

"She tells me it will work."

Joanne narrowed her eyes. "Do you still believe her?"

"I do."

Joanne looked down, her eyes moving side to side. She pursed her lips contemplatively, then spoke. "I've searched for the obelisk here, by the way."

Chinelo looked at her in surprise.

"It's not in the city," Joanne said. "Of that I am confident."

"That makes sense, the position on the map was west of Veld not on top of it."

"If it was here, believe me, Kay and I would have left long ago," Joanne responded. "I passed one of the towns that was... affected."

"Oh no. What did you find?"

"Ashes."

Chinelo bent over and pressed his head into his hands, muttering beneath his breath.

"I suppose you two have been out of touch for a while now, but word has come of others in similar situations."

Chinelo felt heavy.

"How many?"

Joanne scratched her neck. "At least five, not including Nellborough or Eshgar. I heard one in Veshda, two in Mervos, and two in Iskara."

Chinelo shuddered. "By the queen..."

He stared somberly at the floor. Memories resurfaced, images of things he had driven down and held at bay for almost two years. There would be others. Others like his brother. Others like his family. Others like him, returning home to find only ruin and decay left in dark scars on the earth. A lump formed in his throat.

"Hey." Joanne rested her hand on his shoulder. "You're doing the best you can. This isn't your fault, friend."

Chinelo pondered her statement, joining words in his head to form his response. "It seems that is inadequate in this situation."

Joanne retracted her hand and folded it in her lap. They stared at the floor silently, until the sound of laughter drifted from the living area into the hallway outside the guest room. Chinelo heard Isobel's hastened voice rising cheerfully, though he could not discern the specific words. He let out a pained sigh.

"I suppose they've worked things out." Joanne said.

After a few minutes, Isobel peered into the room, with Mort hanging onto her shoulder.

"Kay is off to bed, Joanne, so I think it is time for us as well," Isobel chimed.

"Then, that's my signal! Goodnight, you two!"

Chinelo nodded solemnly and began his preparations for bed. Soon, he and Isobel were huddled beneath their blankets, lit only by the shaded moonlight coming through the window.

"How did things go with Kay?" Chinelo whispered.

Isobel sighed. "They went well. It was a lot to process, though."

"I see."

"What did you and Joanne talk about?"

Chinelo opened his mouth but hesitated. "Perhaps we should discuss it tomorrow. It's already pretty late."

"Good idea. I'd probably not give you any chance to sleep if we started talking now."

The sound of rustling sheets and blankets reached Chinelo's ears. He looked up and saw Isobel's shadowy figure peering over the bed.

"Hey!" She said. Her smile was vaguely visible in the darkness.

"Hey?"

"I love you."

Chinelo's heart skipped, fluttering like a bird ascending in the sky.

"I love you," he responded.

Isobel made a slight noise, an entreat that Chinelo had grown to recognize from their many nights in the tent. He sat up and kissed her. She let out a long, satisfied sigh, snuggled under her covers, and whispered a final word.

"Goodnight."

Chinelo forced a smile. "Goodnight, love."

He pulled his blanket over his shoulder and waited for sleep to come. Its approach, however, was repelled by a heavy weight of guilt that lingered over him.

CHAPTER 43

ISOBEL'S SPIRIT SOARED. SHE STOOD ATOP Veld's high stone wall, overlooking the bustling city and taking in the many smells and clamoring sounds. Veld was easily the largest city she had ever visited, a thriving spired metropolis built on reclaimed ruins of the ancients. The walls themselves were in fact vestiges of an era long since passed, though they had been maintained extraordinarily well considering their age. Throngs flowed in out of the gates, swirling and churning around the buildings like water breaking around rocks in a stream.

The architecture of the city was eclectic, an incongruous amalgamation of pointed stone towers and sturdy wooden buildings built onto those great structures. In some places, entire neighborhoods and markets existed on the flatter rooftops of the ruins, and communities thrived both on the ground level and at the apexes of the towers. It was a wonderous sight. No matter where Isobel looked, there was life and activity.

At the heart of the city stood a colossal castle, one that was larger than the entirety of Nellborough. Every corner, every edge, and every line were adorned with swirling gold patterns resembling vines and leaves. Its many parapets and rises were crowned with spreading trees of brilliant orange and gold hues, shading the castle with their vibrant autumn leaves.

The city below bloomed with the same colors, ornamented with waving banners and flags to celebrate the fall harvest, though the decorations were also present on top of the walls. Music sounded faintly from the streets, overlapping in melodies that were played on lutes and psalteries, flutes and tambourines.

An updraft rose from the streets and rushed over the walls, carrying with it the rich scents of the many harvest treats that were being sold below. Cinnamon and apple-berries, buttersquash and beef, pumpkin and cloves, all weaving a welcoming warm aroma that blanketed the city like a thick felt coat.

Isobel saw it all and took it all in, savoring every joyous song, every majestic sight, and every inviting scent. On her left shoulder, Mort stared over the town with wide glistening eyes. There was so much for him to rule.

She was drawn out of her enraptured trance by a hand on her right shoulder.

"So, what do you think?" Joanne asked with a proud smile.

"It's so big!" Isobel marveled.

"Isobel! Come look at this!" Chinelo called from the wall's edge wall.

Isobel hurried to his side and looked across the countryside beyond the city. Orchards and farms stretched far to the west, arranged in neatly rowed plots of land. Tiny specks, farmhands and workers, moved in the fields, picking apple-berries and hauling grain. The fields were broken by patches of forest, deep crimson clusters of maple and Iskaran ironwood.

Further beyond, Isobel could faintly see shapes stuck in the ground. Some were long and slender like spears, and others were wide and stout like clubs or bludgeons. One caught her eye, a massive rectangle protruding diagonally from the field. Its peak was capped by a wide cross and a long thin shaft. It was a colossal sword, far larger than any of the similar armaments she had seen during her journey. The blade had a curious pointed hole midway down its length.

"Wow. That's a big one," Isobel said.

"It is!" Valyx said, rumbling up beside her and leaning against the wall's barrier. "That out there is Ozhath's Battlefield. It's a pretty popular tourist attraction. Apparently, if you believe the myths, the gods once had an incredible battle there for what is now the duke's castle. Those swords and spears are all that remain. They're massive and all made of stone!"

"Incredible." Isobel shuddered. Imagining something big enough to wield such an enormous weapon was truly chilling. She shook her head and looked north. A glistening lake stretched across the land, sparkling in the golden sun.

She glanced at Chinelo. He was still looking over the fields. Something had seemed off about him that morning. She wasn't certain of what. She at least recognized the signs. The slight hesitation before he smiled. The lower pitch of his voice. The shifting of his eyes when she looked at him. Yes. Something *was* off. If only she knew what.

Valyx continued, drawing her attention back to the west. "The way the story goes is that Ozhath, the god of destruction, wandered the land and waged war against mankind and the gods just for the sport of it. Well, the queen of Veld got sick of that and decided to put a stop to Ozhath's rampage, taking on his entire army on her own. But Ozhath wouldn't go down without a fight, no. They fought out on that battlefield, until he finally fell. At least, that's if you believe the myths."

"He doesn't sound very agreeable," Isobel said, touching her chin.

Valyx laughed. "No, he doesn't."

"Well, now that you've seen the city and heard Valyx's tall tales, what would you like to do today?" Joanne pressed her hands on her hips. The claret dress she wore rustled in the wind as her hair whipped over her tattooed shoulders. "The proper celebration begins this evening, but the activities run the whole day!"

"Hmmm, Chinelo?" Isobel glanced his way.

Chinelo blinked twice. The clouded look about his face vanished, and he grinned. "I think you know what I want to do today, dear."

Isobel smiled. Had she been wrong? "Joanne, what is the best food they serve during the festival?"

Joanne opened her mouth to speak.

"Apple-berry fritters," Kay interjected. "No contest. Valyx, what was that place we went to last year called?"

Valyx's face lit up. "Oh! Frann's Fritters? Frann normally sets up in the West District. So, down that way. Let's go!" He thundered over to a wooden platform, a lift that was moved by a series of pulleys and winches. It quickly took them down into the pulsing streets of Veld.

Frann, the owner of Frann's Fritters, was a hunched old woman with more forehead than face. She scuttled around the humble tent in which she prepared her famous fritters, scurrying back and forth between bowls of seasoned flour, trays of fresh apple-berries, and shimmering vats of cooking oil. She crafted her fritters with the care of a master artisan and the attention of a painter, and her work exuded the passion she poured into it. That radiant passion, or perhaps the strong scent, attracted a lengthy queue.

Isobel excitedly bounced on her toes as she and her four companions approached the tent. Her rumbling stomach was not audible over the crowds, thankfully. She looked back. Chinelo and Joanne were chatting about something. He looked cheerful. Yes. She must have been wrong.

A rise in the conversation in front of her drew her attention.

"The original ones are the best, and that's a fact," Valyx declared.

"Valyx, what happened to your sense of taste? The ones with cheese are clearly superior. You've gotten almost as bad as Joanne."

Joanne was too busy chattering with Chinelo to notice the remark.

"Kay, only a fool would cover up Frann's genius with cheese."

"Frann is the one who puts cheese on them!"

"Kay, let's approach this from the perspective of an idealized society."

Kay rubbed her forehead. "Not this again."

Valyx raised a finger. "Society is like a fritter. It has a backbone of flour, a sweet smattering of cinnamon and sugar, and, bringing it all together, the succulent apple-berries."

Kay blinked. "That is going to require a more thorough explanation."

"Well, you see, you are an apple-berry," Valyx proclaimed. "You—"

"Look great on a dinner plate?" Kay interjected.

"No! No! Well—" he looked to the sky meditatively. "Maybe. But no, you bring the flavor."

"Cheese has flavor."

"Yes, but it's the wrong flavor!" Valyx's face turned even redder. "Apple-berries such as you should be allowed to shine amongst the masses of flour, not be snuffed out beneath the slime of the cheese."

Kay stared at him long and hard. The corners of her mouth twitched slightly, as if she was suppressing a laugh. "So, which one of us is the cinnamon?"

Valyx touched his chin. "That's easy. Joanne."

Joanne looked up. "I'm what now?"

Kay hushed her with a wave of her hand. "All right, and which one is the sugar?"

"Isobel, naturally. She seems sweet." Valyx shot a knowing glance at Chinelo, who promptly nodded in agreement.

"The oil?" Kay continued.

"Mort, I suppose." Valyx shrugged.

Isobel giggled but felt an enraged aura from her shoulder.

"And the flour?" Kay began to smirk.

"Well, by process of elimination, Chinelo." Valyx shot a much sorrier look at Chinelo.

Kay's smile stretched across her face. "That means you're the cheese."

"You villainess!" Valyx said jovially. "You vile woman! I trusted you! To think you would lay such a devious trap for little old me. Unbelievable."

By that point Kay and Valyx had reached the front of the line.

Frann's daughter, who also possessed the same monolithic forehead, pointed cheerily at the menu, a small painted canvas with the three varieties of Frann's Fritters portrayed in skillful brushwork.

Kay shot Valyx a mischievous look, then turned to the young woman. "I'll have one with cheese please. This joker will have the traditional."

At the mention of the cheese, Valyx wrung his hands in displeasure.

"Oh stop. I like cheese," Kay said.

Isobel leaned over to Chinelo. "Don't worry, I don't think you're flour."

"Well, I'd certainly hope not. Have you decided which one you want?"

"It's difficult. I feel I shouldn't deviate from the basics until I've tried them, but I am curious about the other two flavors. The one with salt intrigues me."

Chinelo smiled. "Well, I'm dying to try all three, myself."

He produced a few Iskaran crescents and dropped them in Frann's overflowing coinbox. "We'll do one of each."

"You are the best," Isobel chimed. "Definitely not flour."

They sat around a wooden table that was shaded by bright orange awnings. Isobel hungrily held the first fritter, a crispy fried mass that looked like solidified bliss on a stick. She took a small bite, and her eyes flew open.

It was amazing! A crunchy exterior shell contrasted by a warm gooey center that dripped rich apple-berry juice. It was sweet and homey, with a tickle of cinnamon dancing with a bite of tang. They waltzed together, two distinct flavors beautifully performing on a saccharine stage.

"You must try this, Chinelo." She swapped to the second fritter, one with salt, and took another bite. The waltz transformed into a chorus of senses, picking up speed. Somehow, the sweetness was amplified, and the tanginess was reduced, held at bay the crunchy salt crystals.

Chinelo was already enraptured by the first fritter when Isobel shoved the second into his hand. She took a bite of the third. The chorus was silenced, resting before the quiet savory ballet that the cheese brought. The performance was magnificent, and Isobel's stomach demanded an encore.

She squirmed happily. "I'm so glad we came here."

Valyx looked disapprovingly at the cheese laced fritter. "The witch has gotten to you with her wiles."

Kay rolled her eyes.

"I'm a witch myself, good sir," Isobel chided. "We are resistant to each other's wiles."

"Have you considered, Valyx, that the food is in fact just that good?" Chinelo said between bites.

"Have you considered, Chinelo, that the witch has gotten to you with her wiles?" Valyx's eyes twinkled.

"I never contradicted that, my friend. Isobel can wile away all she wants, and I shall be content."

"I do not wile," Isobel interjected between bites. "I scheme. They are not the same."

Valyx glanced at Joanne. "What's your take on the matter, Joanne?"

Joanne wiped a dribble of juice from her cheek and licked it off her finger. "Kay wiles. Isobel schemes. Chinelo plans. Valyx whines."

Valyx shook his head. "No, no. What is your opinion of the fritters? Surely, you can see reason. Surely, you understand that the original is superior."

Kay smirked. "Yes, Joanne, we'd all love to know which type you got. You were the last one of us to order so I didn't catch it."

Joanne grinned and held up the dripping mass she had been chewing. "Mine has salt *and* extra cheese."

Valyx let out a displeased howl.

"What? I couldn't decide which to get, so I got all three at once."

Valyx stood to his feet and slammed his hands against the table dramatically.

"You four are irredeemable."

Kay pulled him back to his seat beside her. "Shut up and quit pretending you don't like us."

Valyx let out a huff. "We have about seven hours until the merriment starts tonight, and gods smite me if I don't culture the four of you properly by the time the evening is over. Hurry up. We have more to see."

Isobel exhaled. How nice it was to be around friends like this. Joanne and Kay had made quite the happy life for themselves since Iva destroyed the coven. It was almost like...

No. She didn't want to think about that. There was too much to do that day to worry about such things.

The sun had long since set, but Veld still shone brightly, lit by countless fires through every plaza and every square. The plaza where Chinelo walked was incredibly active as the crowds bustled around the roaring bonfire at its center. He pushed his way through the clamor, searching for the friends he had quickly made that day.

He saw Joanne, Kay, and Valyx sitting at a table, laughing and sipping their drinks. He frowned; Isobel was not in sight. He whirled around, searching the edges of the plaza until he saw her hunched on a set of stairs that climbed up to the roof of one of the tall stone structures.

He hurried up the stairs. She was bent over, resting her chin in her hands and her elbows on her knees as she watched the festivities below.

"Hey there, gorgeous!" Chinelo said as he took a seat beside her.

She smiled and looked down. "Hey there, handsome." Her smile quickly faded.

Chinelo leaned forward. "You all right, dear?"

"I am. Just a little tired from the day."

"Makes sense. It has been a long one."

She leaned against his shoulder. "And a very, very good one."

Chinelo glanced to his side. Mort was napping on the step beside her, also exhausted from their long day of exploring the city, trying local treats, and participating in the many games and shows that took place during the harvest festival. Not that he did any of those things. However, governing his expanding domain clearly required great mental effort.

They watched the fire for several minutes.

"And you?" Isobel asked.

"What?"

"Are you doing all right?"

Chinelo pondered the question. He had every right to be content. The day had been pleasant. He was tired, but somehow energized, as if he had gotten a taste of what life could be again. Or what it once was.

"I'd say so."

Those words hurt. The doubt from the previous night hung over him. He hadn't told Isobel about his conversation with Joanne. He'd brushed off her questions that morning, and he'd refrained from mentioning it for the duration of the day, though the topic would not leave his thoughts. However, was now really the time to have this conversation? It seemed cruel to tell her. The revelation of Iva's actions had upended her whole world. He didn't want to make that worse. He couldn't.

"Chinelo?"

He jumped. "Yes, dear?"

"Do you think we are wrong for what we are trying to do?"

Chinelo turned his head sharply. "What do you mean?"

Isobel sighed and nodded towards her sisters. "Look at how happy they are."

Chinelo looked down. Joanne and Kay were laughing as Valyx danced around the fire, hopping up and down from one foot to the other.

"They wouldn't be here if Iva had not destroyed the Red Coven."

Chinelo nodded. "Right. Though I fail to see your point, I'm afraid."

"If we turn back time, this life they have will be lost. All the good times and good memories will vanish as if they never happened. Even today won't exist." She moved her feet up a step, hugging her knees to her chest.

Chinelo frowned. "What are you suggesting?"

"I don't know." She sighed. "I'm confused. All this time I've been focusing on bringing everyone back, I never even stopped to consider that the world had moved on. Maybe it's time that I do as well."

"Isobel, what about all we've done?"

Isobel took off her spectacles and rubbed her eyes. "I don't know, Chinelo. But can you really look me in the eye and tell me that our happiness is worth more than theirs?"

Chinelo looked down. "It's not about *our* happiness, though. What about the hundreds of thousands that have died? Are their lives not worth it?"

Isobel bent her head forward. "But they're dead."

Her words stabbed deep into Chinelo's soul. "We're talking about my family, here, Isobel. She killed them, and she's not going to stop." He again recalled Joanne's words from the previous night. He hesitated. He didn't want to tell her.

"I know! I know! I'm just so confused." Isobel lowered her hand. "We have to stop her, but I don't know how. We don't know what her goals are. We don't know what she is planning. We don't even know why she's doing it. How are we supposed to stop someone we don't understand?"

Chinelo did not respond.

"This is the kind of life I want, Chinelo. I want to have friends. I want to have family. I want to relish every waking moment, and I want to do it with you. What if that life is here, and we just didn't know it until now?

Chinelo still didn't respond. He turned her words over in his head, trying to understand how to answer.

"Is this not the life you want?" Isobel asked.

Chinelo sighed. He was torn. He longed to see his family again. He longed to see his friends. He longed for the knowledge that their pain had vanished. But he also longed for her to be by his side. He wasn't willing to abandon either of those desires. After a long pause, he said a few quiet words.

"I want a life with you."

Isobel shivered.

"But I *can't* give up on my family. Are you asking me to do that?"

"No." Isobel sighed. "I just—I'm so confused!" She looked up and pressed her fingers against her temples. "I've been going over it in my head. If we succeed, the Joanne and Kay we know here disappear. If we don't succeed, then our friends and family stay dead. How am I supposed to pick between those? How am I supposed to make a decision like that?"

Chinelo watched Valyx dancing around the fire, gesturing for Joanne and Kay to join him. Kay lifted a defensive hand, but Joanne scampered forward and joined Valyx, hopping behind him while clapping to the rising music.

"How long have you been thinking about this?" Chinelo asked.

Isobel shifted. "Since this morning."

"I see."

Chinelo glanced to his side. Isobel's mouth was pressed into a tight line, and the corners twitched. Her eyes glistened as a single tear ran down her cheek.

He wrapped his arm around her and whispered.

"I'm sorry."

She sniffled and nodded.

"I'm just so tired, Chinelo. I just want to rest. Maybe she gave up. Maybe she couldn't find the other obelisks. Maybe—"

"And if she hasn't?" Chinelo said.

"But we don't know that!" Isobel exclaimed. "We don't, Chinelo. What if she found whatever she was looking for already?"

Chinelo shifted uncomfortably. "And if we do know that?" He turned his head.

"Do we?" Isobel asked. She was staring at him with a confused expression on her face.

Chinelo averted his gaze and nodded slowly.

"Tell me!" There was a sudden edge to her voice.

"She hasn't stopped, Isobel. She's destroyed five more cities."

"How do you know that?"

"Joanne told me."

Isobel's eyes flashed. "When?"

Chinelo looked at his feet and responded in a low voice. "Last night."

Isobel exhaled and ran her hand through her hair. "*That's* what you were talking about? And you didn't tell me? This whole day you've known, and you didn't tell me?"

"I—I'm sorry. I—I didn't want to hurt you."

"Chinelo, we talked about this!" Isobel said, raising her voice slightly. "So, that's why you were acting strangely today. I was racking my brain trying to figure out what was wrong. Why didn't you just tell me?"

"I'm sorry," he clenched his fists. "I wanted to protect—"

She stood up with a groan. "Why do people keep saying that? Why does everyone keep treating me like I'm some fragile little child? You're all the same! First Iva, now you!"

Chinelo recoiled, horrified at being associated with that name, even more horrified at such an association coming from Isobel. The flickering light of the pyre at the center of the plaza drew back images of the fires that had ravaged his home, fires that consumed his brother before his very eyes, fires that Iva had set.

Isobel looked down. She was furious. That was obvious from her face. That anger quickly faded as an expression of shock overtook her.

"Chinelo, I—I'm sorry. I shouldn't have said that."

"No. You are right to be angry." He stood and turned, descending the steps. He felt dazed, and his chest grew tight, as if it were going to rupture. Is that what she thought of him? That he was like *her*?

Isobel caught his hand in hers. "Wait!"

Chinelo looked back. He only met her gaze for a moment. Guilt, anger, and shame overtook him. He needed to run. He needed to get away from that fire, the fire at the heart of the square, the fire in her eyes.

"Please," Isobel said. "Please don't go."

Chinelo's heart pounded. "I—I'm sorry... I..."

What was he trying to say? The words wouldn't form. They wouldn't connect. He withdrew his hand and fled down the stairs.

Isobel watched him duck out of the plaza. A lump formed in her throat.

Stupid. How could I be so stupid? Why do I always do this?

She collapsed on the stairs, bunching her knees up in front of her. A steady stream of tears tricked down her cheeks. Why did it have to go like this? Why did things always go like this?

She rested her forehead against her knees and sniffled, having completely forgotten her anger from moments before. That had vanished, replaced by fear. A fear she'd hurt him. A fear that he'd leave. A fear that'd she been right. They left. They always left. Her mother had left. Umfrey and Priscila had left. This time, it was her fault. She had hurt him.

The song ended and another started. Smoke drifted to her, causing her already irritated eyes to burn even more. She heard sounds. Dancing men and women, laughing children, footsteps approaching. She ignored them, thinking only of Chinelo's horrified face when those awful words left her lips.

"Hey," a voice said.

Isobel jerked up and hastily wiped her eyes. Kay stood a step down, bending over her.

"What happened?" Kay said. "Where's Chinelo?"

Isobel sobbed. "I messed up, Kay. I messed up."

Kay's normally cold face softened. She sighed and sat beside Isobel. "Talk to me."

"I got mad, and I said something awful, and... and..." She wiped her eyes again. *Blast these tears!*

Kay passed a handkerchief to her. "Well, I suppose we all do that from time to time. How bad was it?"

Isobel blew her nose. She gave a muddled account of their conversation and eventual argument. Kay nodded as she spoke, listening to each word intently. After Isobel finished, she let out a long breath.

"Well, sounds like you both need to apologize."

Isobel nodded. "I really messed up, Kay."

"Happens to the best of us." Kay stared at the fire, watching Joanne and Valyx trot around the plaza with four small children in tow. "I actually wanted to talk to you about something, if you don't mind. Not to change the subject, but it's important, and it might solve one of the things ailing you."

Isobel turned her head, growing concerned. "What is it?"

"Joanne and I have been talking," Kay said slowly. "I have some questions about this plan of yours, specifically the spell you are planning on using to reverse time."

"What?" Isobel asked. How was that relevant?

"The spell. How would it work? You said that you needed the word for 'time' to do it, but what would the rest of it be?"

Isobel pulled her hair behind her ears, sitting up straighter. "Umm, at the moment, I'm thinking of structuring it so that time is reversed for the entire world while maintaining the memory of the caster and whoever they touch. I'm not sure how much esht that will drain, but that is the tentative plan."

"I assume the drain could be shared with anyone you touch?" Kay said, an odd expression on her face. "So, the esht cost wouldn't be as taxing."

"Umm, probably."

"Hmmm." Kay nodded with a slight smile. "Good. Then, we're going to help you."

Isobel turned suddenly. "What?"

"It's simple really. Iva needs to be stopped, and we can do something about it. What other choice is there?" Kay said, her face brightening. "You really ought to rely on your family a bit more. Always doing things on your own."

Isobel sat there, dumbfounded. Joanne and Kay. If they helped her, if they were there when she cast the final spell, the spell to reverse time, then the lives they had wouldn't be lost. They wouldn't vanish. They'd go back with her!

Kay raised her finger. "Now, keep in mind that I still have terrible esht reserves, but my potions and elixirs should serve you well. Joanne is Joanne so I'm sure you have an idea of how she could help. That overachiever."

Isobel looked back at the square. Joanne danced far below, suddenly stopping and waving at the two. Kay gave her a small wave back.

"Kay... this is... I don't know what to say. Thank you!"

Kay chuckled. "A thank you is adequate, I believe."

Isobel looked at her sister, her dear, long-lost younger sister. She leaned over and wrapped her arms around her shoulders. Kay let out a displeased exhalation.

"Isobel, I appreciate the gesture, but I would prefer if you don't."

Isobel recoiled. "Right! I'm so sorry! I forgot."

Kay's amiable expression soon returned. "Anyways, we'll start by helping you find the obelisk here. You said you were searching tomorrow? We'll join you for that. Who knows? It could be fun!"

Isobel nodded. They weren't alone anymore. Not anymore.

The music suddenly changed, adopting a familiar cadence. Isobel perked up. "Hold on. Is that what I think it is?"

"A jig? Yes, I believe so!"

Isobel sighed. "It's been so long since I've danced to one."

"Isobel!" Joanne called from the bottom of the stairs. "Get your cute rump down here!"

Isobel rose, then hesitated.

"Something wrong?" Kay stood beside her.

"Chinelo. I—he probably doesn't want to talk to me right now, but... I need to."

"Ehh, you two can talk after," Kay said. "Besides, a quick dance should help with that redness about the eyes."

Isobel nodded, then with a determined huff, she descended the stairs.

CHAPTER 44

CHINELO LEANED AGAINST A STONE WALL, staring up at the starry sky visible between the rooftops above him.

By the queen. I really made a mess out of things this time.

He let out a long sight. She didn't mean what she said. He knew it. He shouldn't have left like he did. He was the one in the wrong, hiding things from the woman he loved when she was nothing but honest with him.

Disgraceful. Utterly disgraceful.

Yet, when he saw her face, when he heard that name, when he felt the heat of the fire, every instinct demanded that he run. What a failure he was. Just like always, no matter who or what he tried to be, he still could not abandon his natural tendency to stumble—or race—headlong into failure. And just like always, his failure had gotten her hurt.

The stars twinkled above. The night was cool, and a faint breeze drifted through the empty street. He could still hear the sounds of dancing and celebrating coming from the square nearby. He needed to go back. However, was he really ready to face her knowing what he had done? How could he?

"Ah! There you are!" a cheerful voice called.

Chinelo turned his head and pushed away from the wall. Kay walked down the street with a fat and sleepy frog balancing on her hand.

"Been looking all over for you."

"Sorry," Chinelo said. "Needed some air."

"Well, I hope you got enough, because I've got something you need to see."

"And what's that?"

Kay grinned mischievously. "A witch's dance!" She turned and gestured towards the square.

Chinelo sighed and followed. Once they reached the square, Kay found a table and waved him over. He glanced back to the stairway where he and Isobel had fought. She was gone.

He joined Kay at the table, facing the pyre. The music was bright and airy, and a crowd was gathering around two dancing figures.

His eyes grew wide. Isobel and Joanne were dancing at the plaza's heart.

Their boots tapped across the pavement. Their dance was energetic and lively, primarily consisting of quick movements of the feet and subtle flourishes of their arms and hands. The tapping of their toes matched the rhythm of the jig that was being played on stringed instruments and small drums.

Their feet bounced up and down, moving over each other at a rapid pace while emanating a sound like rhythmic hail falling on a rooftop. They tapped three times in front, once in back. Three times in front, once in back, then a kick behind, all within barely more than a second.

"So, this is traditionally done wearing special shoes with hardened soles," Kay said to Chinelo. "Obviously neither of those two have them today, so the sound isn't quite what it is supposed to be. It's intended to be a loud pop instead of a tapping scuff."

Chinelo and Mort watched the two dancing before the firelight. Isobel and Joanne exchanged smiles and laughed as they stumbled over the complex movements, occasionally missing a beat or becoming unbalanced. Soon, their mistakes became less frequent as they moved with the rising melodies. Joanne waved her long skirt around, adding its fluid motion to her dance. Clad in trousers and a tunic, Isobel accentuated her movements with elegant flicks of her wrists. Chinelo was awestruck.

"I had no idea she could do this," he exhaled.

"Oh? She never told you?" Kay answered. "That's actually how Joanne and Isobel first became close. They started when they were very young, maybe three or four years old."

Chinelo shook his head. "You're not joining them?"

"Oh, gods, no," Kay waved her hand. "I unfortunately do not possess that talent. Plus, I have something else that requires my attention."

Valyx attempted to join the two dancing witches, and in doing so he flailed around madly like some flightless bird attempting to ascend to the skies. The result, of course, was even more laughter from Joanne and Isobel.

"Do they dance in Eshgar?" Kay asked, crossing her arms and leaning on her elbows. Her face was illuminated orange by the raging bonfire.

"We did, yes," Chinelo smiled. "The preferred form was called a Ga-Shide. It was always done with a partner. I'm not the best at it myself, however."

"You should teach her. I think she would enjoy that."

Chinelo froze. The thought had never occurred to him. Would she even want to after their argument? "I... I don't know. She's probably upset at me tonight."

"Perhaps. Perhaps not."

"I made mess of things."

"Seems to be a trend these days."

Chinelo nodded. He needed to apologize, but he wasn't sure exactly how to approach that.

"You two should talk, you know," Kay said. "Whatever it is you need to say to her, she'll listen."

He shook his head. "What could I even say? I hid things from her, things she needed to know."

Kay studied his face. "Do you love her?"

"Of course!" he said indignantly. "I would die for her."

"Well." Kay smiled. "How about you start with that? Maybe leave out the dying part. You could always preface it with an apology. That might be good."

The music changed. One of the musicians, a fiddler, had suddenly become much more animated in his performance. His resonant notes rose and fell, fluttering high before drifting down in a bouncing descent.

"Oh! Watch closely. This is the best part." Kay leaned forward.

Isobel and Joanne's mouths moved, and their feet kicked high in front of them before slamming down into a burst of blue flame. The growing crowd let out a gasp. With every tap of their toes, sparks of light leapt forth, flowers of fire that bloomed and vanished within an instant. Valyx balked and stumbled off to the side, continuing his rather strange and awkward motions at a safe distance.

Kay smiled. "And this is why they call it a witch's dance."

"They don't fear magic here?" Chinelo asked, watching the crowds respond with excitement instead of apprehension.

Kay shook her head. "Veld was built by the first witch. It's basically the birthplace of humanity's study of the Ancient Arts. Rothvale is the only city in Iskara where magic is restricted, and that's purely because the king is a coward."

The music reached a crescendo. Kay tapped Chinelo's shoulder, pointing at Isobel. Her feet became a blur, tapping a rhythm that matched that of the beating drums, sparking, flashing brighter and brighter until her whole body appeared to glow. The music ceased, and Joanne and Isobel stood, bending one leg behind them and balancing on their toes with arms raised high.

It was a brilliant finale, one that was met with applause as the musicians commenced another upbeat song. Isobel wiped the sweat from her brow and began talking with Joanne. Partners paired up, dancing around the two.

"Oh! This is a partner song. Now is your chance!" Kay said. "Get out there!"

"I—don't know if that's..."

"Just go! Talk to her."

"You're not coming?"

"I am content to watch. Go, enjoy yourself."

Chinelo walked carefully through the dancing throng. He moved around the twirling couples, weaving through a forest of swishing skirts and fluttering coats. The crowd was dense, but in a moment, he burst into a small clearing, empty like a tranquil meadow with Isobel and Joanne at the center.

Isobel stood with her back to him, her wavy copper hair reflecting the light of the fire. Joanne saw him and smiled, nudging Isobel before vanishing into the crowd. Isobel turned to face him. She looked down, her cheeks flushing. She fidgeted with her hands, twisting the hem of her loose shirt into wrinkles and knots.

"Chinelo."

"Isobel."

Chinelo stood before her, the two of them alone in the small opening before the fire, a sea of dancers flowing around them. He scratched the back of his neck. Nervously, he cleared his throat. "Would you like to dance?"

Isobel nodded but did not meet his eyes. He stepped forward, taking her hand in his and resting his other on her shoulder blade. She brought hers to his upper arm, and they swayed stiffly to the music.

"I—" Chinelo started.

"I'm sorry, Chinelo!" Isobel interrupted, cutting off his apology. "I am so sorry. I said so many awful things. It was so... so... awful of me. I'm so sorry. Even suggesting that we should give up... that was horrible. Horrible! I don't want that. I promise I don't want that. We'll get your family back. I promise. And then I compared you to my sister and you don't deserve that. I don't know what I was thinking."

"No, you were right to be mad. I should have told you about what Joanne said about Iva. I shouldn't have kept that from you."

"But still, I behaved totally unreasonably."

"So did I."

Isobel looked up at him, not smiling, but not frowning either. "Well, I guess we are quite the pair, then."

Chinelo nodded and smiled slightly.

Isobel's eyes brightened. "Will you forgive me? I promise, I didn't mean what I said. I was angry, and I didn't think... Gah! I'm sorry." She looked down and pressed her head against his chest.

"I forgive you, Isobel."

She let out a long sigh.

"And I need to apologize, too," Chinelo continued. "I shouldn't have kept things from you."

Isobel didn't answer at first. She swayed with him, barely keeping time with the music. Then, after turning her head back and forth, she spoke. "Can I... can I ask you something about that?"

"Anything," Chinelo said.

"Do you... do you trust me?"

Chinelo's brow furrowed. "Of course I do!"

Isobel met his gaze, then looked away. "It's just... How do I put this? When I left the coven, Iva said she had been trying to protect me." Isobel's hand trembled on his shoulder. "She said..." her voice trailed off.

The two moved back and forth, turning slowly. The firelight reflected off her spectacles, causing them to sparkle. Isobel shook her head. "My mother and Priscila, they didn't tell me about her illness until she was already past the point of hope." She paused. "It just... it makes me feel like... it makes me feel like you don't trust me. You say you do, but then..."

"I'm sorry, Isobel. I was wrong."

"But, why? Why didn't you tell me?" She closed the hand on his shoulder, bunching up the sleeve of his tunic in her fingers.

Chinelo heard the pain in her voice. His stomach twisted.

"I—I was afraid of what it would do to you. I was afraid it would make things harder for you."

She looked up at him. "Maybe it would have. But, even so, I can handle it. Please, trust me like I trust you."

"I will. I promise," he said. "I'm sorry, Isobel."

She stared at him for a moment, then smiled. "All is forgiven."

Chinelo felt the weight lift from his chest.

"Now," she chimed, attempting to move with the music. "How do we do this properly?"

"Follow my lead."

Chinelo turned to the only training he had and adopted the position for an Eshgarian Ga-Shide. He guided her right hand to his just above her elbow before placing his hand on her hip.

"My, my! Getting right to business, are we?" Isobel said with a twinkle in her eye.

Chinelo chuckled. "This is the only dance I know. The tempo isn't quite right, but we can make it work. Watch my feet. Mirror them."

He began the sliding steps that formed the backbone of the Ga-Shide. Isobel quickly followed suit, picking up the rhythm incredibly quickly, though she occasionally nicked his foot with her toe.

"Sorry, I really hope I'm not making a fool of myself," she said timidly.

Chinelo chuckled. "If things get out of hand, I'll be sure to tumble down quite spectacularly so you look like a prodigy by comparison."

Isobel giggled. "I appreciate your sacrifice."

They picked up speed, repeating the motions until they had fully circled the fire.

"Earlier, by the way," Chinelo said, "you were amazing! Your dance... well, it was captivating."

Isobel looked up from his feet. "Oh nonsense! I'm terribly out of practice."

"Regardless," Chinelo said while guiding Isobel clear of Valyx and Joanne's rampaging waltz across the square, "I was thoroughly impressed. I never knew you were so talented."

"My good knight," Isobel responded slyly, "have I not already impressed you with my many skills and talents? We've been together for more than a year now. Surely, you've seen something of me that you thought was at least a little noteworthy."

Chinelo's eyes widened in shock. "I'm sorry. I suppose that didn't come out how I intended."

"Oh stop! I'm only teasing, silly."

"Right, of course."

"So, tell me, master dancer, how does one transition into more complicated movements? I assume I follow your lead?"

"Oh! That's simple!" Chinelo pushed against her side lightly, and she twirled out while still gripping his hand. He tugged her fingers gently, and she spun back into his arms. "Something like that!"

"Oh! Let's do that again!"

Chinelo complied, sending her spinning away before drawing her back in a spiral.

"Try this one!" He raised his arms and prodded her to move under it. She twisted behind him, and with a twirl on his toe he spun and caught her free hand, standing at arm's length.

They pulled closer, and continued experimenting with different movements, circling around the fire as the many strings sung their cheerful tunes. The fiddle grew louder, and the fiddler began a musical duel with another musician, one that drew a bow across long strings that produced a rich hum.

They sparred back and forth, with the high tones of the fiddle playfully gamboling above the contemplative lower tones until they joined together in a beautiful frolicking melody. The drums beat heavier, building and building to another crescendo, until the fiddler burst forth in an ardent solo, lifting the spirits of those around to the very heavens.

Isobel and Chinelo ceased their more complex movements and simply swayed back and forth in time to the music. A red whirlwind spun by, and a blonde figure let out a cry from within. Valyx had finally drawn Kay from her seat, and Joanne was scampering after with a devilish grin.

Isobel laughed as the tornado made another revolution around the fire. Kay burst forth, flying outwards until Joanne caught her arm in the crook of her own. They hopped on one foot around each other, spinning faster. Valyx bounced over, and with a rather silly smile pulled Isobel from Chinelo's arms, moving in a circle with her arm in his. Joanne sent Kay in Chinelo's direction, and he continued the chain, passing partner to partner until they had all danced arm in arm. They smiled, they laughed, they clapped, and they cheered, except for Mort, of course, who had fallen fast asleep.

Chinelo felt a push from behind, and he suddenly found himself face to face again with Isobel. They spun faster and faster. The colors around them grew blurry. Yellow from the fire. Red from Joanne's dress. Orange and crimson from the colorful banners. Green and gold from fluttering robes.

They twirled, losing sight of the world around them. Yellow and red, orange and crimson, green and gold. The music reached a climax, and Chinelo looked down at the beautiful woman before him. His heart felt as if was going to explode, tearing from his chest in a joyous eruption. Her eyes were so deep. Her lips were so gentle. Her hair was so captivating. Any pain their argument had instilled in him was long gone. He loved her, adored her more than he thought was imaginable.

She looked up at him, and her smile faded into an expression of tender longing. The city turned. Orange and crimson, green and gold.

Chinelo drew Isobel close, wrapping his arms below her shoulders. She in turn draped hers around his neck, and they swayed side to side. His eyes were like a welcoming wilderness. The slight upturn of his lips, the subtle smile that was almost always present on his face was enchanting. The gentle strength of his touch was overwhelming. Her lungs felt as if they had suddenly been filled with winter air. In his arms she was safe. In his arms she was home. The music ceased. Everything was a blur. Green and gold.

Isobel did not know how long the silence lasted. Seconds, minutes, hours, all seemed equivalent. She did not care. She stood on her toes and kissed him, closing her eyes. The world went dark, but her soul sang in a thousand colors.

Isobel's eyes flew open as something sharp poked her back directly between her shoulder blades. She dropped to her heels. The square had grown so quiet. She heard Chinelo draw in a sudden breath. He tensed, and she felt his heart pounding against her chest. She turned her head slowly and saw the source of Chinelo's fear.

They were completely surrounded by the Interior Guard.

CHAPTER 45

ISOBEL'S HEART POUNDED IN HER CHEST. A bead of sweat trickled down her temple. She glanced to her side, eyeing the legion of rapiers that were pointed in her direction. Her mind flew into action. She surged esht, applying her protection to Chinelo and herself. She shifted the flow, enhancing her strength. The sharp point on her back pressed harder.

"Lower your hands, witch," a deep voice commanded.

Isobel unlaced her fingers from around Chinelo's neck and slowly moved her arms down, passing her hands over his shoulders. In that moment, she sent a rush of esht into his back, activating his strength enhancement tattoo. She looked up into his eyes. He gave her a knowing nod. Her hands fell to her sides, and she mouthed a single phrase.

"I love you."

It began.

She surged esht into her chest, activating a tattoo she had inscribed mere weeks before. She vanished and reappeared behind Chinelo. Two of the green-robed guards were beside her, and they gasped as she appeared out of thin air.

She pushed her arms outwards and slammed her hands into their shoulders.

"Belekt fai!"

Lightning sparked from her fingertips. The guardsmen convulsed and collapsed. Small puffs of smoke rose from the points where Isobel had contacted their shoulders, bringing with them the faint smell of singed flesh. Two were down, but how many remained?

Chinelo instinctively reached for his sword, but his hand grasped at air. He had left it at the house before coming to the festival, and unlike

Isobel, he had no means of calling his weapon. He looked up, staring into the bewildered eyes of the man who had threatened Isobel. He was tall with dark skin, and his head was topped with a thin layer of blonde hair.

The man shook himself as he processed what had just happened. His arm tensed, and he took a step forward to plunge his rapier into Chinelo's chest. Chinelo sidestepped and grabbed the man's wrist before spinning and hurling him into the crowd of guards around him. A loud collective cry broke out as they crashed and fell in a groaning heap.

Chinelo took a breath. Without his sword and its accompanying spell-core, he only had what little of the language of the gods he had memorized and the few tattoos Isobel had given him. He clenched his fists and raised his arms, steadying himself in a low stance. His esht, now empowered by the core he had consumed in Kahi, swelled within him. It rushed in a cascading torrent into his fingers, and he whispered an incantation.

"Icht vasht'ra."

Isobel ducked under a stabbing rapier. She pointed her hand at the guard's side and let forth a storm of cyan bolts. They crashed into his body and enormous shining crystals erupted, tearing his clothes and draining his energy. He collapsed and writhed in agony as the fatigue set in, fatigue that Isobel was aware would be acutely painful. Three had fallen by her hand.

"Ice!" a voice cried out.

A light flashed from her side and collided with her left foot. She felt no pain, but a hideous chill washed over her leg. She tried to take a step, but her foot refused to move. A column of ice was crawling up her calf, encasing her knee in a frozen prison. She shifted her esht and muttered an incantation through gritted teeth.

"Belekt ba'vasht!"

Her leg radiated heat, rapidly melting the ice and freeing her from its frigid grasp. She whirled around and summoned her nullification barrier just as countless spells hurtled towards her. They fizzled out on impact, fading inertly. Loud ringing sounds pierced the air behind her, and she expanded her barrier, protecting herself from the magical volley that had been launched by her opponents.

Her position was hardly advantageous. The square was crowded, and with so many opponents, she barely had room to move or think. She needed space. She needed her spells. She needed her staff.

Isobel crouched and surged esht into her back. In an instant, she felt gravity's pull release her from its grasp. She was weightless. With a forceful push she leapt into the sky, flying high above the city as countless spells spiraled after her in a rainbow of deadly colors. She opened her right hand and surged esht into the tattoo on her wrist, calling forth her staff from where it rested in Joanne's house. In a moment it appeared.

Down below, there were at least thirty members of the Interior Guard in the plaza, and the few remaining locals were huddled at the outskirts, craning their necks to watch the fight. Isobel's eyes widened. Where were Joanne and Kay? Where was Valyx? Where was Chinelo?"

A flash of fire caught her eye. She saw him fighting far below. His arms were blazing with orange flames, and he was engaged in a visceral, burning brawl.

Chinelo's body moved in flow. A lifetime of training in both armed and unarmed combat had forged him into a living weapon that acted more on instinct than thought. Shining silver cut through the air, a rapier poised to strike. Chinelo arched his spine, ducking under the attack and smashing his fiery fist into the body of his attacker. The resounding crash of the impact shook the square, and the mage flew back. Chinelo dodged another, listening to the sounds of the singing steel and the hastened breaths of his attackers. He vaulted into the air, propelled by his enhanced strength, and sent a cascade of flames down at one of the many mages that tried to suppress him.

He landed and rammed his shoulder into the mage, sending him reeling. A light flashed and Chinelo ducked under a glowing purple hand. He pummeled his attacker with a series of rapid blows before pushing her away with a forceful kick. Voices shouted commands and incantations behind him, and he whirled around to face his opponents.

Chinelo slammed his boot into the ground and pressed his flaming fist forward, increasing the esht flow rate in the process. A column of fire erupted and rushed past the guards. They howled and screamed, trying to flee the intense heat. Chinelo opened his fists and waved his arms in a circle. Fire shot forth from his hands like flames from a dragon's maw, creating a burning ring around him. He had a moment of reprieve before a figure leapt through the flames with the hems of his robes charred black. He pointed his sword at Chinelo and uttered a command.

"Bind!"

Light pulsed from the rapier's hilt, and a cord of radiant green shot forth. It wrapped around Chinelo, binding his brawny arms to his side. At first it did not hurt, but in a moment, it tightened, constricting his body. Chinelo gasped. He could not move. Try as he might, the cord would neither budge nor break. Even his enhanced strength was not enough.

The guard smirked. "Men! Shackle!"

Chinelo heard steps behind him. He had no time to look, but based on the sounds, they were close. He had to move. He had to free himself. His blood coursed within him. His heart pounded. He surged his esht into his core and whispered the spell that Isobel had ingrained in his mind through countless hours of repetition.

"Homvelcht tor vrefden solstari!"

Chinelo vanished and reappeared a few steps forward. The man uttered a cry in surprise as Chinelo's clenched fist collided with his chest, sending him flying back over the wall of fire. Chinelo heard the steps pounding behind him.

He twisted, but a sharp pain cut through his side. A rapier's razor edge grazed him. Chinelo grunted, and with lightning speed he grasped his attacker's arm before slamming the back of his hand across the man's face.

His attacker collapsed and grabbed his head. Chinelo's hand darted down, attempting to claim the man's dropped rapier, but before he could, something heavy impacted his side, sending him stumbling back. He turned and stabilized himself on his foot, feeling the rough pavement tearing away at the sole of his boot. He panted as sweat trickled down his face.

Another robed guard approached him. Chinelo recognized her. Talia, the mage he first saw in Dawngale, twirled her rapier and stabbed it into the ground.

"Rise."

The ground beneath Chinelo's feet shook. The paving stones flew upwards, propelled by columns of thick clay and rock. Chinelo launched into the air.

Isobel twisted and weaved around the effervescent projectiles that flew after her. In the air, she had space to move, but she was horribly exposed. She suddenly halted and summoned her barrier, defending herself from the relentless onslaught. She glanced down, confirming that neither her allies nor the townsfolk were beneath her. Then, with a slight flourish, she pointed her staff towards the earth.

"Barrage!"

Hundreds of steel spikes formed in the air below her and rained down on the square. She heard overlapping cries of fear and pain as her spell struck her many targets.

She hastily searched the ground below. She needed to find the others. She needed to escape with them, but where were they? Her side of the square was littered with numerous groaning bodies. The south end was mostly empty. The north end was crowded with onlookers who gazed up at her with expressions that were both awestruck and terrified. She shook her head. None of that mattered. Where were the others?

A sound. It cracked like a whip. Something coiled around her ankles and brought her hurtling down. She channeled esht into a different position on her back, and she felt gravity's pull slowing her descent. However, it was not enough. She collided with the ground. Her arms shook. Her entire body ached. She coughed and gasped for air.

Chinelo tumbled through the air as a hundred small rocks flew after him. The mage he fought used stone and earth, controlling them as if they were mere extensions of her body. Chinelo fell and hit the ground hard. He tumbled across the pavement, and the countless tiny edges and points of the stone's rough texture dug into his skin. He rolled to his feet and extended his hands, beginning an incantation.

"Icht vasht'ra va ogo—"

He was cut off by another shift in the ground below him. The paving stone rose, and he was thrown off his feet again. He gritted his teeth, focusing on the sensation in his hands, forcing the esht to stay poised to fly once he completed the incantation. As he tumbled through the air, he shouted the final words.

"—iv fet!"

Spheres of fire formed in his hands and flew towards his opponent. He was too far to hear, but Chinelo saw Talia's mouth move. A wall of stone rose from the ground and the two fireballs splashed into it. Chinelo's attack had failed, and he plummeted, landing heavily on his arm. The pain in his rib returned, ambushing him like a long-forgotten foe.

Isobel clawed at the ground, dragging herself forward. Her gloves caught and tore on the pavement, ripping holes at her fingertips. She rolled and channeled esht into her chest, and, in an instant, she traveled upwards, freeing herself from the cord around her legs. She shifted her gravity towards her feet, causing her to fall sideways and land on a nearby wall. It was disorienting, standing sideways with the sky behind her and the ground rising like a stone wall in front of her. Her world had shifted, her entire reference frame for what was up and down contradicted that which was before her eyes.

She shook herself and looked at the guards ahead of her. So many had fallen, yet so many remained. She panted, trying to catch her breath. The roaring bonfire reflected off the light of swinging rapiers, and a voice called out a familiar spell.

"Volley."

Isobel dashed forward, running along the building's wall as a shower of magically conjured rapiers riddled the stonework behind her. Glass shattered, sending a thousand razor-sharp pieces shimmering in the air. They sparkled like diamonds, reflecting a rainbow of lights around the plaza. She leapt across an alleyway and landed on another building's wall. With a grunt, she opened her hand. Her staff reappeared. Her feet pounded against the rough stonework as she accelerated her sprint around the square. Behind her, she heard the endless crashing of more ethereal rapiers tearing the building apart. If she stopped, even for a moment, she would be impaled.

She looked up. Chinelo was lying on the ground above her, desperately trying to push himself up. A mage approached him, holding a pair of shackles in her hands. Isobel's heart seized. She sprinted faster and shot herself away from the wall, flying parallel to the ground.

"Form: Hammer!"

Her staff sparked to life, obeying her command. She clenched its shaft in both hands and with all her might slammed the weapon into the mage's back, resulting in a thunderous impact. With a loud crunch, the mage was thrown to the side. She screamed, and her braids fluttered behind her as she careened across the ground. The shackles skidded over the cobblestones. Isobel twisted, landing on the pavement once more and sliding to a stop beside Chinelo.

"Are you hurt?" Isobel panted. She clutched her hammer and held it threateningly between her and the guards that had chased her around the plaza.

Chinelo groaned and forced himself to his feet. A stream of blood ran down his side, soaking the hem of his trousers an ominous crimson.

"Marginally."

Isobel spun and pressed her hand into his side, activating her healing touch. The wound closed.

Chinelo sent a blast of fire towards the approaching guards. They shied back, forming a circle around the pair.

"Chinelo! Where are the others?"

"I don't know!"

Isobel frowned. "We need to find them! I can get us out of here if we do. I should have enough esht to transport us out of the city." She deflected a rapier strike with her staff.

"Understood," Chinelo replied.

Isobel pressed her back against his and spun, pointing her staff at her foes. She inhaled, preparing to shout a command, when something large and heavy hit her in the side, sending her tumbling into a nearby table.

"Isobel!" Chinelo shouted. He took a step to follow her, but a glowing cord wrapped around his body. He fell face-first on the ground and let out a pained grunt. A weight pressed on his back, a boot holding him down. One arm was pulled back so hard that he felt that it would be torn from its socket. Words spun through his head. He began to utter a travel incantation but stopped. Isobel had warned him about using the word *'homvelcht'* carelessly. With his body pressed against the pavement, the only direction Chinelo could send himself was downwards. He would need a different solution. His mind raced.

His other arm was wrenched behind him. Cold steel shackles closed over his wrists, bringing with them a noticeable heaviness that spread across his body. He tugged at his arms, but they still refused to budge. He attempted to move his esht, but suddenly he felt a familiar pain stabbing into his skin. His energy was being siphoned, and even with his expanded reserves, within seconds he was powerless.

Squirming helplessly on the ground, he caught a glimpse of Isobel lying in a heap of shattered wood. She moved slowly and listlessly, attempting to regain her bearings. His view was quickly obscured by the green and gold robes of the Interior Guard.

Isobel opened her eyes. Her head ached, throbbing like it had so many months before. A blur of green and gold moved before her. She felt a prick against her throat. A rapier pressed against her neck, and at the other end stood one of the many mages. He scowled down at her and barked to his comrades.

"Shackles! Now!"

Two of the men grabbed Isobel's arms and pulled her to her feet. She twisted and thrashed, but without any prior enhancement her arms barely moved in the guardsmen's iron grip. Isobel's brow furrowed in determination. She would not be caught like this. She shifted her esht forwards, preparing to vanish from their hands.

"I wouldn't try it," the man snarled in her direction. "I see that look in your eye, witch."

She glared back at him. He had no way of knowing what she could do. The magic she wielded had been long forgotten by man. Even the most scholarly of sages would be unable to recall the words and phrases that fueled her power.

Isobel expelled her esht, reappearing behind the man. She opened her mouth to begin an incantation, but a forceful kick from behind sent her down onto the ground. She was only down for a moment. Rolling forward, she twisted to a half standing position on one foot and one knee. She slammed her palm into the ground and began an incantation, a command to increase gravity for all that surrounded her.

"Jovachte gariasheq—"

A blade swung downwards. She jumped back, narrowly evading the strike.

"—py gra—"

A crunching noise sounded from behind her. A chill ran down her spine. She ducked underneath a large reflective shard of ice that cut through the air.

"—rengen'ra gest!"

The world shook. A loud, shared groan sounded from the soldiers that surrounded her. They fell to their knees, seemingly crushed beneath their own weight.

Isobel panted. Had she only thought of the incantation earlier, she could have ended the fight much sooner. She intensified her spell. The many men and women collapsed. She stood and surveyed the scene, turning around to look over the sea of pinned bodies around her.

A cry pierced the air. The voice was familiar. It was one Isobel had heard many times, for across her entire journey, it had never been far from her side.

Chinelo.

Isobel whirled around to see him lying on the ground. He was bound in shackles, and the veins in his face bulged outwards as if they were going to explode. In her rush to defeat her foes, she had not considered that her spell might reach her own allies.

He turned his head and looked at her. His eyes were bloodshot. Without even a second thought, Isobel released her spell and ran to his side.

"Chinelo! I'm sorry! I didn't mean to. I didn't—I'm sorry!"

Chinelo gasped, but his eyes suddenly widened in horror. Isobel saw a slight motion in her peripheral vision. A boot hit the side of her head, and she fell. Her head throbbed with dizziness. Footsteps pounded from behind her, and she was tackled and pressed face first against the ground.

Her scalp burned. She felt her hair being pulled cruelly from behind, tilting her head upwards. She screamed, and before she could even finish, a soft strip of fabric was stuffed into her mouth. Her scream became a gagged cry as the cloth strip was fastened firmly behind her head. Her arms were twisted back, and cold steel clamped on her wrists. Like an ocean wave, a dull fatigue washed over her, intensifying until it stabbed into her from all sides. She felt her gloves being removed, and something cold and wet brushed over her skin.

Isobel tried to surge her esht, but it all was pulled into the shackles. Without it, she was powerless. She kicked, but her legs were soon shackled just like her arms.

"Slippery little thing, that one," one of the men panted.

Another mage grunted and cracked her neck. "She's certainly more conniving than the last few. What's the damage?"

A voice called from across the plaza. "Fifteen, Lady Hestra."

The woman frowned. "The Archmage won't like this."

She squatted in front of Isobel and pulled her chin upwards. "You really made this difficult, witch. I've half a mind to kill you here myself. Consider yourself lucky. You'll at least get a few days to think about what you've done."

She waved one of the guards to her side.

"Quellor, this one is probably pretty light," Hestra said. "You shouldn't have any trouble. Freigan! You take the other one."

Quellor gruffly hoisted Isobel over his shoulder and began walking. She tried to squeal and thrash, but she could barely move. Her voice only formed a muffled whimper. As she was carried from the square, she watched in dismay as Chinelo was dragged after her, scraping along the ground.

Isobel's vision blurred. Hot tears ran down her cheeks and soaked into the gag. She closed her eyes tightly. It wasn't supposed to go like this. Mere minutes before, all had seemed right in the world. She had her friends. She had her family. She had Chinelo.

A croak pierced the air.

Isobel opened her eyes and looked up. Far behind them, against the waning bonfire, she saw the silhouette of a bullfrog staring after them. Mort watched with sad eyes as Isobel was carried through the streets towards unknown destinations. The guard turned a corner, and she saw the frog no longer.

CHAPTER 46

A METALLIC CLATTER RANG THROUGH THE stone halls. Isobel opened her eyes to see a set of heavy boots walking away from the iron bars, disappearing past the right wall of her prison. As had happened the previous mornings, a tray of food had been slid through a small slit at the base of the door, and, as always, much of that food had spilled on the ground. She groaned. Food had little value with a gag jammed in her mouth. She would have to wait for her two assigned guards to remove the gag before she could suffer through the meal.

The previous several days had been long. Afflicted by constant esht-drain, Isobel's body endlessly cried out in pain, though she had slowly become accustomed to that pain. She had even managed to sleep the night before, even if it was only for a few hours.

She had other problems besides the esht-drain. She had not been allowed to change clothes or bathe since she was thrown in her cell on the night of the harvest festival, and her entire body felt disgusting, as if her skin was coated in a half-dry layer of grime and sweat. She had tried numerous times to muster enough esht to either break the chains or travel out of them, but her reserves were constantly sapped dry.

She thought back to the night that had gone so horribly wrong. What had happened? The guards had appeared with little warning, and they had singled out Chinelo and her. Why? She and Joanne had used magic in their dance, so perhaps that had alerted someone to their presence, but even so, magic was not prohibited in Veld. Also, Joanne had presumably not been captured.

She closed her eyes. She could ponder such things later. After all, she had no shortage of time. Perhaps inspiration would come to her. For now, she would wait until she was allowed to eat the food that had been haphazardly tossed in her direction. Footsteps echoed through the halls, but she did not open her eyes.

She was tired, so very tired.

A familiar voice spoke. "I warned you, Isobel."

Her eyes flew open. She looked up. Standing outside of her cell was Iva. The dark-haired woman reached up and removed the cloth on her face, revealing her green eyes.

"I told you to leave Iskara, yet here you are. I told you to abandon your quest, yet what did we find in a remote village in Nesa?" She frowned sternly at Isobel. "A broken obelisk and reports of a red-haired sorceress with a dark-skinned man."

Isobel whimpered into her gag.

Iva raised her voice. "Svidar, Isobel! I told you to go to Svidar! You could have been safe there. But no! You just refused to listen! You just had to make things difficult!"

Isobel squirmed back. Iva's stern face softened.

"Why did it have to be you? This would have been so much easier if it was anyone else."

Iva glanced over at the food on the ground. Her nose wrinkled in disgust. "They don't even allow you to eat properly?"

Iva unlocked the cell and crouched down, dragging the tray beside Isobel. She circled behind her. Isobel felt Iva's gloved fingers lifting her arms, pulling her up to a sitting position. The gag tugged back, dragging against her cheeks, but it suddenly fell away. Isobel gasped and coughed.

Iva circled back around her and pressed a cup of water to her parched lips. "Drink!"

Isobel complied. The cool water flowed down her throat and spread through her stomach. Iva crossed her legs and sat on the floor before Isobel. She pulled one of the few morsels of bread that had not been soiled by the dirty floor and held it in front of Isobel's face. Isobel glared back at her.

Iva sighed. "Eat, love. I could hear your stomach rumbling before I even entered the building."

Isobel shot her another incensed glare and bit the food, tearing at it ravenously. Iva was right. She had been starving.

Iva's face fell. She continued speaking. "I apologize for how they treated you the other day. I sent word to the local garrison to bring you in peacefully if you appeared here, but those cowards passed the work off to Harlyle's men. Though, it sounds like you made quite a mess of things yourself. The report I read was... impressive to say the least."

Isobel gulped down the last scrap of bread from Iva's hand. "Where is Chinelo?"

Iva raised an eyebrow.

"Is he hurt?" Isobel demanded.

"Aside from a few scrapes, no."

Isobel let out a relieved sigh. "Good. So, why are you here?"

"I'm here to talk."

"Fine." Isobel scowled. "Why did you kill all those people?"

"I already told you."

"You told me a heap of nonsense."

"Give it time. You'll understand."

"I doubt that," Isobel retorted. "Even if you did explain it, I'm sure it would be more nonsense."

Iva leaned forward and stared deep into Isobel's eyes. "You really think so? You really think I would do this without reason? You really think that I would cause such violence and death if I didn't have some purpose for it?"

"Enlighten me."

"I'm doing this for you."

"Don't give me that trash!" Isobel snapped. "You think that will suddenly change my mind? You slaughtered half of the continent, Iva!"

Iva frowned. "Isobel, I really don't want us to fight. I've missed—"

"You've missed me? You've *missed* me? Maybe you should have thought about missing me before you vaporized everyone I love," Isobel yelled, unleashing the anger that had been brewing for several months. Her cheeks burned hot. "Of course we're going to fight! How could you expect anything different?"

"I'm sorry things must be this way." Iva looked down.

"Iva, do you know what one of the most difficult things I've come to realize is?"

Iva shook her head.

"It's not the endless nights of crying myself to sleep. It's not the stabbing loneliness that cuts that sleep short. It's not the visions of Umfrey and Clair's burning faces that appear when I look into fires. It's not seeing the man I love suffer because his entire world was stolen from him. It's not even the guilt of not being able to save any of them, no matter how much I might want to. No!"

"It's realizing that the person I loved most in the world, the person I looked up to for my whole life, the person I always dreamed would come and find me is responsible for all of it. Do you know what that's like Iva? Do you know what it's like knowing you've been raised by a monster? Do you?" Her voice began to crack. Her vision blurred. "You're vile, Iva. You're despicable. You're..." she trailed off. She looked down and closed her eyes tightly.

"I'm sorry. You are not wrong for hating me."

Isobel shook her head. "That's the thing. I don't even hate you. It doesn't make sense! I should, but I—but I..."

Iva sighed and placed a hand on her shoulder. "Isobel, why did you come back? What is your goal?"

Isobel sniffled and looked up. "Aside from stopping you? It's undoing everything you've done."

Iva's eyes narrowed. "Interesting. Then our need for the Source is the same."

Isobel cocked her head. The Source? Both Joanne and Iva had mentioned it before.

Iva rested her chin on one hand and looked over Isobel's shoulder. "Honestly, I'm not all that surprised that you would try to find it. No, I'm more surprised that you know about it in the first place. Did Joanne tell you? No, they wouldn't have shared that information with her. Esther certainly wouldn't know, either. So then, how?" She shifted her gaze to stare at Isobel. "How do you know about it?"

Isobel looked back at her with a bewildered expression.

"Isobel," Iva leaned forward and laced her fingers. "What if I told you that our goals were aligned?"

Isobel stared at Iva with a resolute gaze. "I don't see how that is possible. You're destroying entire countries. I'm trying to reverse that."

"That's because you're not thinking big enough. You wish to undo what I've done. I wish to correct what I did, what you did, what Cleo, Esther and my mother did. See? It's compatible. If I succeed, you won't need to."

Isobel tilted her head and leaned back slightly, adjusting her hands in her shackles. "I don't understand what I ever did to you, Iva."

Iva frowned. "And that is why I wish to fix things. This world hasn't been fair to us. It shaped you into who you were then. It forced me to become the person I am now. I will change that. I'll give the two of us the lives we should have had."

"How? With a few magical words and phrases?"

Iva's eyes widened. "You think this is all for the lost words?"

Isobel stared back at her blankly.

"Surely you *know* about the Source?"

Isobel blinked.

Iva ran her fingers through her hair and exhaled. "Unbelievable. Really? All this time you've been scurrying around the continent chasing a few middling runes?"

"What else am I supposed to do? Isn't that what you're doing?"

Iva leaned back on her hands, supporting herself on the ground behind her. She looked up at the ceiling for several long moments. "So, it's still out there..."

Isobel cocked her head.

"Do you know how this world was made?" Iva asked.

"I only know what you taught me."

"Then you know it was spoken. Everything in the world was spoken by the Creator. Every law, every pattern, every force, and every matter were all spoken into existence. They were given form by his words. He spoke without ambiguity, and so it was. He wrote the laws of physics. He wrote biology. He wrote all manners of sciences and mathematics. All things were described with his words. They were collected, forming the code that the world obeys, forming the Source of all things." She pushed off her hands and leaned forward. "Do you understand what that is?"

"Magic?"

"It's so much more than magic, Isobel. So, so much more. Magic is just a shadow of the Source's nature. It's an interface with it, a crude way of influencing it, but it is ultimately restricted. The gods made sure of that."

Isobel looked down. Her mind raced. "How is what you're describing in any way worth the lives of so many people?"

"Listen! Think!" Iva crossed her arms. "You're not looking at this right. Lives are irrelevant compared to what I'm working towards."

"And what is that? What are you trying to accomplish?"

Iva smiled proudly. "I'm going to rewrite the world, and in doing so, I will give us the lives we should have had."

Isobel's brow furrowed. She looked away, attempting to comprehend Iva's declaration. She looked back and forth, guiding her gaze from one grimy flooring stone to another. She opened her mouth to ask a question, but she was interrupted by a loud slam as the prison hall door flew open.

The Archmage appeared outside the cell. Iva turned and scowled over her shoulder.

"I thought I told you not to remove your veil," the Archmage grumbled.

"And I thought I told you not to interrupt us," Iva retorted.

He waved a hand. "You said it wouldn't take long. I'm merely keeping you accountable."

He glanced at Isobel with a burning glare. Isobel shied back, shrinking away from his gaze.

"Why is she still alive?" he asked.

"As I said, I'm not killing her."

The Archmage's eyes narrowed below his bushy eyebrows. "Her interference has become an intolerable. We can't let it continue."

Iva stood and looked back at him through the bars. "I know this may be difficult for you to understand, Harlyle, but some of us have people we care about. She lives. Besides, I'm confident that she does not have what we are looking for."

The Archmage's mustache twitched. He glanced between Iva and Isobel. "I suggest you get back to work, then." A subtle grin appeared beneath his beard. "We found something to the east."

Iva inhaled sharply. "The obelisk?"

"Possibly. Investigate it. Bring Talia. She should be recovered enough from her injuries to make the trip." He glared at Isobel for a moment. "No thanks to that wretch."

Iva tensed. The Archmage looked away.

"I must attend to some other matters here. And for gods' sakes cover your eyes!"

"Speak about Isobel that way again, and I'll remind you why I wear that blindfold in the first place," Iva growled.

The Archmage huffed, and with a flick of his robe he stormed out of the chamber.

Isobel let out a relieved breath. "Why are you working with him, Iva?"

"He is a convenience, a temporary one. I imagine he thinks the same of me." Iva sighed. "I have to go. I'll leave you with this. You have two options. You can help me by joining me or at least not interfering with my work. Do that and I will release you and your companion."

"And the other option?"

Iva's eyes twitched. "You can stay here in this cell until my work is completed. Think on it."

Iva circled around Isobel and moved the gag over Isobel's mouth. Isobel thrashed and squirmed, squealing against the fabric strip.

"I'm sorry, but I know how clever you are. I can't risk you using any incantations until you've had time to consider my proposal." Iva pulled the gag tight. She made a small noise, an inquisitive grunt, and touched Isobel's wrist.

"I see you finally got those tattoos you always wanted. Interesting symbol here. I don't think I recognize it."

With that, Iva exited the cell and locked it behind her. "I'll encourage the guards to bring some better food. After I have the next rune, I'll return for you." She stepped away and hesitated. The lines of her face moved slightly, and her mouth straightened. She turned her head back. "I love you. I always will."

Isobel slumped to the ground. Iva left, and as her footsteps faded into silence, Isobel lay there, closing her eyes tightly. She was once again alone with only the echo of Iva's words to keep her company.

CHAPTER 47

HOURS PASSED, AND ISOBEL REMAINED IN the cell, gradually growing more and more angry. She lay on the ground, waiting for her next paltry meal to come. She needed to process what Iva had described to her. If she could put the pieces together, perhaps she could determine her next move, assuming she could get out of her cell. Words and thoughts filled her mind, recollections both recent and distant, combining to form a myriad of questions.

Words were missing from the Ancient Tongue, and they could be restored by slaying the creatures sealed within the obelisks. But what even were the monsters? They were horrific, unnatural, unnerving amalgamations of rock and flesh that refused to die unless their spell-core was pierced. Why? What were they?

Isobel's forehead wrinkled as she concentrated. The people of Ata, Eshgar, and Nellborough knew nothing of the strange obelisks, but the people of Kahi used one as a sort of shrine or temple. What was different?

Isobel's eyes widened. The murals in Kahi! They depicted a winged goddess descending from the mountaintops and communing with the townsfolk. Winged, just like the creature Chinelo had slain, a creature that she awoke from its slumber on the mountaintops.

She thought back to the murals at the Red Coven. They chronicled the origins of mankind's use of magic and the events that led to the coven's creation. First, Minera was taught by the god Yvvusta. Then she shared her knowledge with the world. The gods attacked and killed her, culling what mages they could find.

What next?

Isobel's mind raced. The murals depicted the dark, gaunt gods spreading across the continent and then vanishing without a trace. She had always assumed that they had left for the heavens, ascending beyond the world, but what if some had remained?

Even if that were true, why would words be missing? Why would they be sealed? How did they relate to Iva's goal of finding the Source? And most importantly, what even was the Source? Iva said that it was the accumulation of the Creator's words, but how would that help Iva in her goal? Was it accessible? Could it be changed?

She closed her eyes. Nothing made sense. She needed more information, and she wasn't going to get any locked away in a prison cell.

She took a deep breath, focusing all her senses on the tattoo on her chest. The guardsmen had painted over the tattoos on her extremities, so those would likely not be useful. The tattoos on her body had thankfully been left untouched.

Her esht refused to accumulate. It was still being drained into the shackles she wore. Isobel groaned. It was a clever trick, enchanting shackles so that they absorbed esht. Clever and very effective.

"Croak."

Isobel's eyes flew open. She looked around her cell. She scanned the floor, but all she saw was the same grimy stone she had laid on for the past several days.

"Croak."

It was above her! Isobel looked up to the small window that was near the ceiling. A thin strip of blue sky was visible, and against it was the shape of a very fat bullfrog.

Mort.

Isobel let out an ecstatic squeal into her gag. The frog leapt from the window and landed with a resounding splat. He waddled forward, cringing at the dank environment. Isobel squirmed across the ground.

This was her chance!

She rolled on her back, and the metal shackles pressed into her hips rather uncomfortably. With a slight noise she nodded to her abdomen.

Mort cocked his head.

Isobel sighed and nodded again, but with much more intensity.

The frog blinked.

Isobel grunted louder and moved her neck in a bobbing motion.

Mort finally moved. He hopped onto her, dragging his flabbiness across her stomach. Yes! Just a little further! If he could channel his esht into her tattoos, then there was a chance she could escape.

Mort crawled around her stomach before moving to her chest. Isobel inhaled through her nose and let out an elated squeak. He was in the correct position. He only needed to channel a little of his esht into her. The frog stared directly into her eyes, frowned, and settled down. Isobel nodded and attempted to encourage him through her gag. She rolled slightly to the side.

Mort blinked. Suddenly, the cell collapsed around her, converging into a tiny point. The travel spell! Mort activated it! Isobel reappeared across the cell and tumbled to the ground. She moved her arms. They were finally free!

With a rush of energy, she tore at the knot that fixed the gag in her mouth. Without the drain on her esht, the incessant pain she experienced faded to a lingering fatigue. She tossed the gag aside and gasped for air.

"Mort!" She scooped up the frog and pressed him against her cheek. "You are such a good boy!"

A satisfied ribbit sounded from below her ear.

She held the frog in front of her face with both hands. "Listen. We need to get out while we can." She glanced at the set of shackles that lay empty on the floor.

"Can you help me? I'm completely drained."

Mort blinked at her and glanced at her shoulder. A tingling flow of esht rushed into her hands.

"I'll take that as a yes. First things first, I'll get out and you squeeze through the bars after me."

Isobel deposited Mort beside the bars and then vanished, reappearing on the other side. Mort wriggled through the gap. She placed the frog on her shoulder.

"Perfect! All right! I need you to give me everything you've got. Once we've found Chinelo, we will be home free."

Mort scowled. He had not factored the usurper into his plan.

Isobel smiled. "Let's go!"

She ran to the hall door on bare feet and cracked it open. The chamber, a large curving room, was dark and dreary, and numerous other doors lined the stone walls. After taking a deep breath, Isobel tiptoed out of her room and peaked into one of the others.

Empty.

She stepped to the next.

Empty.

She sidled along the wall to another.

All were empty.

The hall wrapped around a central circular wall, and a heavy door was set in the stone surface. That was her route to the other floors, and hopefully Chinelo.

Isobel flung the door open only to find herself face-to-face with an armored guard. Her heart lurched. The man stared at her with a baffled expression on his face. Aside from his uncovered head, he was fully garbed in plate armor, though it was significantly heavier than Chinelo's Eshgarian armor. He gasped and frantically reached for his sword. With a quick lunge, Isobel slammed the door. A loud clink rang through the hall. The door had only partially shut. It rested ajar, blocked by the guard's sabaton.

Isobel pushed hard against the door. It shook with a loud thud. She grunted. The man was pushing it open, sticking his knee through the gap.

Thud.

Isobel dug her toes into the floor. With every push against it, they scraped along the rough stone.

Thud.

She pressed harder, feeling every fiber of the door's wooden surface against her skin.

Thud.

The door opened further. The man was almost through the opening.

"Mort! Esht!"

The door flew open, and Isobel staggered back. Steel swished through the air. She dropped to her knee, and her hair moved, pushed aside by the blade's slipstream. Above her, the man raised his sword and gritted his teeth. The blade fell. Isobel inhaled a quick breath and forced the stream of esht she received from Mort into her left side, raising an arm to block the strike.

The sword rang and vibrated loudly. She felt the impact against her arm, but it didn't hurt or pierce her skin. Her protection spell repelled the blade as if her skin was stone.

Isobel leapt back and opened her hand to call her staff.

Nothing happened.

Painted over with a thick black tar, the tattoos on her arms were completely useless. She clenched her fists and raised them in front of her, holding them in the defensive stance Chinelo had taught her.

The guard pounced forward, thrusting his blade towards her and following up with several rapid swings. Isobel retreated, bouncing from toe to toe away from the glimmering blade. She surged esht into her fists and whispered an incantation between the man's sweeping swings.

"Jovachte gariasheq."

She held the esht, priming herself to release the spell as soon as she could make contact with the man's body.

"Hold still!" The man yelled. He stomped forward, slashing his sword at her viciously. Mort let out a frightened squawk.

With nimble steps, Isobel twirled behind the man and delivered a forceful, magically charged punch directly between the shoulder blades. The man may have been armored, but the heavy metal did little for his agility.

The man crumpled to the floor, crying out as his gravity multiplied. He pressed his hands against the ground, quivering beneath his own weight. Isobel forced more esht from her hand. The man collapsed, breathing heavily.

Isobel did not wait. She knew the consequences of increasing gravity too much. Impaired vision, dizziness, intense pain, then finally, unconsciousness. She had first experienced such sensations in her battle in the eastern plains, and she'd experienced them again while practicing her flight technique.

She sprinted away, ducking through the central door and descending a winding spiral staircase. She needed to find Chinelo. She needed to rescue him.

She burst through the door on the next floor and dashed down the hallway, checking each cell on the outer edges of the floor. None, however, contained Chinelo.

A loud clamoring sounded from above. Isobel looked up. Based on the volume, there was a large group descending the stairs. Isobel looked left and right. There was nowhere in the hall to hide. She ducked into one of the vacant side rooms and slammed the door behind her.

Her mind raced. She had to buy some time to think. She had been lucky before, but if Mort's esht ran out, they both would be trapped at the mercy of the garrison. She looked around and glanced at the back wall. A thin strip of light shone through a hole in the wall, one that was far too small for even Mort to climb through.

Her eyes widened. They were against an exterior wall! What could she use? What spell could she craft to conserve esht and get both her and Mort outside? What materials were present?

The walls were stone. The bars were iron. Iron was metal. Metal could break stone. She merely had to mold it into a useable form and encourage it with enough force.

She extended her hand. Metal could be shaped. With enough heat, she could forge it into something heavy, like a battering ram or a hammer. What could she craft that didn't require a detailed explanation?

She closed her eyes and spoke. "Icht ba'vasht diaa gra ferga gest, axxave va ogo, natte, iv fet."

The metal responded to her command, heating until it glowed orange. It flowed from the cell bars, accumulating in a sphere before her. It grew larger and larger, shining like the sun. Isobel squinted. The heat was intense. She turned, shielding Mort from the blinding light. Clattering and slamming boomed from the hall. The guards were making their way to her position.

She released Mort's esht. The metal suddenly solidified, forming a massive ball of dark iron. It blasted into the wall, shaking the entire building. Isobel opened her eyes. The sphere's deafening impact left a gaping hole in the side of the building.

The sounds of footsteps and voices grew louder. She hurried to the crack she had created and peered nervously over the edge. The curved walls of the prison extended far, far below. In a courtyard at its base, she saw people swarming around the pile of stone blocks she had shattered from the wall. She took a deep breath.

"Anything you have left, I need now, Mort."

The stream of esht increased, filling her body. She took one more step and stood precariously on the ledge. A loud thud sounded from the door.

"Hold on tight!" Isobel said. She extended her arms, lifted her bare foot from the edge, and fell.

Her heart floated. The wind howled past her ears, whistling through her hair. She plummeted, and her loose clothing fluttered around her, tickling her skin with every movement. She surged what esht she had into her back, and she halted mid-air, hovering high above the ground. She rotated and flew around the enormous tower from which she had escaped.

It was incredibly tall, overshadowing many of the other buildings and spires in Veld. As she made a revolution of the tower, Isobel recognized where she was. The tower was situated at the western edge of Veld's central castle. Rows and rows of holes encircled the outside of the tower, more of the narrow cell windows. She flew closer and slowed, floating beside the rising stone wall.

A trumpet bugled from far below, and it was followed by loud whistling and swishing. Arrows! A barrage collided with the wall below her, pinging and bouncing off before tumbling back to the courtyard.

Isobel accelerated, circling behind the rise to protect herself from the volleys. Another trumpet sounded. She twisted, only to see a flock of pointed arrow heads flying directly for her. She shifted her esht, triggering a dive to the side.

She screamed as a sharp, burning line of pain sliced through her thigh, running at an angle up from her knee. Her trousers had been slashed, and a dark red streak was visible within. Distracted by the pain, her concentration broke, if only for a moment. Her esht dispersed. She tumbled, spinning and hurtling towards the ground with Mort falling not far behind.

Isobel tried to ignore the pain, focusing her senses on her back. The little energy she had flowed, reactivating her flight glyph. She stopped, and Mort landed on her stomach.

Another trumpet blew.

Isobel spiraled around the tower and caught onto the bars of one of the windows.

"Mort! Inside!"

Mort crawled down her arm and squeezed his flabby self through the bars, landing on the other side with a loud splat. Isobel released her flight spell, and she hung from the bars, bracing herself against the wall with her feet. As her fatigue returned, she surged esht into her chest, vanishing just as another volley of arrows bombarded the tower. She rolled across the cell floor.

A loud commotion rang from the interior hall, the sound of yells and grunts, of clangs and thuds, of armor against stone. Isobel winced and grabbed her leg. She was bleeding, and the stream of red trickled down to her knee. She clenched her teeth and pressed her hand against the wound. The pain was intense, and it spread up and down her leg like wildfire. After taking a deep breath, she recited her healing spell from memory. The pain of esht-drain stabbed into her, but the wound closed, leaving behind only a dull ache.

"Mort," Isobel said through her teeth. "I need you."

Mort croaked and hopped on her foot, trying to climb up her leg. With a grunt, Isobel returned him back on her shoulder. She limped out of the cell, pressing her bloody hand against the wall.

Something slammed against the door, triggering a surprised yelp from Isobel. After waiting for the hall to grow silent, she gingerly pushed open the door, peaking through the gap. Bodies littered the floor. Bodies?

Isobel squeezed through the opening. The hall was like the one in which she had been imprisoned but strewn across the ground were numerous groaning soldiers. Their armor was bent and misshapen, as if they had been hit by countless hammers.

Isobel's brow furrowed. How had they fallen? She shook her head. Their current state was to her benefit, regardless of the cause. She hobbled to the central stairwell, hopping between the few empty patches of floor. She flung open the doors and descended the stairs. The sound of her bare feet tapping on the floor, one after the other, reverberated up and down the spiral staircase. She descended two floors and stopped.

Footsteps and voices echoed from below, getting progressively louder and louder.

"Oh, come on!" she said in exasperation.

Slamming her hand against the door, she ducked into the next round hall.

"Hey!" A figure ran towards her, raising a sword to cut her down.

She gasped and instinctively pushed off the ground while surging esht into her back. She somersaulted and landed on her feet, standing upside down on the ceiling. Mort fell below her, and with a slight push she caught him in her hand. The guard staggered, recovered, and swung the blade up at her head.

Isobel twirled over the blade, dancing on the ceiling as if it were a stage. The guard jumped and slashed at her. She rolled and pushed herself to the wall, gripping Mort tightly. He let out a displeased croak.

Standing sideways, she could completely evade the guard's swings. He jumped, flailing his sword in her direction.

"Garf! Get over here!" The man shouted. Another guard rounded the bend wielding a long spear.

Isobel gasped. With a weapon such as that, the guards could reach her easily. She turned and ran around the side of the room, directing her gravity into its outer wall. Footsteps crashed behind her. The guard ran beside the inner wall, gradually gaining ground on her.

She heard a yell, and she looked back just as the spear pierced the wall next to her. Chunks of stone bounced to the floor. The spear shook, sending the vibration of the impact recoiling down its steel shaft and into the arms of the man below.

Isobel turned her head sharply. The shaft was steel, and she could use steel. She tossed Mort from one hand to the other, grabbed the spear, and shouted.

"Belekt fai!"

Lightning sparked from her palm and arced down the weapon, chaining through the man's body. He tensed and collapsed.

Isobel leapt from the wall and returned to the ground, delivering a flurry of kicks to the first guard that had attacked. Her bare foot collided with his head, and he stumbled back. She reached down, grabbed the spear, and slammed its blunt end into the man's breast plate, sending him reeling. The man circled her warily, pointing his sword in her direction. She returned Mort to his perch on her shoulder. With a quick flourish, she grasped the spear with both hands and pointed it at her opponent. This was what she needed. This was a weapon she knew.

Their blades touched for only a moment. The man lunged, slashing upwards. Their weapons rang as they collided, pinging loudly as metal struck metal.

Isobel wielded the spear a bit awkwardly. Being composed purely of steel, its weight was distributed differently than that of her staff. She swung towards the man, but without the heavy concentrated weight of the glaive head with which she was most familiar, the strikes did not carry the same force.

They fought in a storm of blows and deflections, with neither gaining nor losing ground. Isobel was reminded of her sparring sessions with Chinelo. With limited magic, every choice was so much more deliberate. Every move carried so much gravity. Her muscle memory kicked in, and she continued to ward off the man's progression, though finding an opening was proving difficult. His foot shifted for just a second, and she lunged.

With a deft twist of his hand, the guard struck the spearhead down. The impact ricocheted up her arms, shaking every bone. With her weapon sent down, she would be unable to defend. The man spun and slashed towards her knees. The blade drew closer, closer.

Isobel surged esht and lifted her feet from the ground, floating in the air. The man's blade collided with the spear. Isobel twisted herself around its shaft and pressed her feet against the wall. She accumulated strength and swung the spear upwards, smashing it into the man's side. He was sent staggering. She jumped and slammed her feet against him. With a slight push, she sent him reeling against a wall as she flew in the opposite direction. Isobel twisted and landed on the ceiling. Tiny frog feet wrapped around her arm as Mort clung for dear life.

Continuing her assault, she leapt and rotated around the room. Every time the man recovered, she slammed the spearhead into his armor, sending him off balance again and again. She vaulted, stabbed the spear into the ground, and twisted about it to land on the wall. The weapon flowed around her, swinging upwards and striking the man across the face. He flailed his sword, but Isobel pushed off the wall, using the spear's momentum to spin her to the other wall. Mort squawked with every move.

Isobel pushed off the ceiling and gripped the spear with both hands. She released her spell, bringing the full force of her weight down upon her opponent's skull.

A horrific *thunk* echoed between the stone walls. The man crumpled in a heap.

Isobel panted heavily and glanced at the man's slouched form.

"Sorry," she whispered before taking off down the hall. She needed to find Chinelo. Fighting was wasting her time and energy.

A loud crash echoed from around the central wall of the circular chamber. It was followed by a series of grunts and cries. Footsteps approached, a rapid rhythm of feet against stone.

Isobel wiped her sweat from her brow and lifted the spear, pointing it in the direction of the sound. A shadow moved across the wall, the shadow of a tall, brawny man. He was running, drawing closer. Isobel tensed, arching her back abd holding her spear in front of her. The man rounded the bend and stumbled, slowing to a stop.

"Isobel?" It was Chinelo. His fists were scraped and bloody, his shoulders were scratched with slight abrasions, and he, like her, was without shoes.

"Chinelo?"

CHAPTER 48

ISOBEL LEAPT INTO HIS ARMS. MORT croaked in displeasure, though it was notably less displeasure than usual. Even usurpers could be welcomed from time to time.

"You're here!" She ran her fingers through his hair, pulling him closer.

"So are you!"

Isobel leaned back. "How did you break free?"

Chinelo shrugged. "Same way you did, I assume."

She cocked her head. "I don't think that's possible."

"You didn't break the shackles?"

"Break them? No! How did you manage to do that?"

Chinelo looked over her shoulder. "It was pretty simple, actually. I assumed they would be like those enchanted lanterns you used to make, so I figured they had an inscription somewhere. I just rubbed them against the wall until the inscription scraped off and they stopped draining me." He squeezed her hands lightly and whirled around, scanning the hall for any pursuers. He dropped to the ground and picked up a fallen sword, testing its weight. "After that I just waited until I had enough esht to break them."

Isobel stood dumbfounded. "Have I ever mentioned how much I love you?"

Chinelo smiled. "Maybe once or twice. I'm sure a few more times wouldn't hurt." He winked and began walking down the hall, picking his way over a sea of fallen soldiers. Isobel kicked up her spear and followed behind.

"Wait!" Chinelo stopped. "How did you escape?"

"Mort," Isobel chimed.

"Mort?" Chinelo turned his head in surprise.

"Yes! He let me out."

Chinelo blinked. "How?"

"Using his esht, of course. It's a bit odd that they didn't paint over the tattoos on our bodies. Not that I'm complaining. Just seems like an oversight."

"Wait. Wait. You had Mort with you the whole time?"

"No, of course not!" Isobel twirled her spear and rested it on her shoulder. "He came through the window."

"The window?" Chinelo's eyes widened. "We're in a tower! How did he get up that high?"

Isobel shrugged disinterestedly. "I don't know. Didn't stop to think about it."

Chinelo locked eyes with Mort, staring into the immense abysses embedded in the frog's skull. Mort stared back at him, hiding a wealth of secrets behind his big black eyes.

Chinelo shook his head. "Anyways, I suppose that commotion earlier was your doing?"

"Probably. Oh! Watch out!"."

One of the soldiers leapt to his feet, only to be met with a focused kick from Chinelo.

"Thanks! Behind you!"

A hand grabbed Isobel's leg. She twirled her spear and slammed its butt down against the man's head. He quickly let go.

"Let's continue down." Chinelo rammed open the central door. Above them, they heard the overlapping voices of arguing men. Chinelo froze, craning his neck to listen for approaching footsteps, but none were present. "Hurry!" Chinelo whispered.

They descended the torchlit stairs, running in a tight circle down the spiraling steps. Noise clattered below, footsteps rising to meet them.

 Chinelo raised a hand. "Back up! Back up!"

They hurried up the stairs, climbing carefully to avoid stubbing their bare toes. Isobel pushed open the next door and dashed into one of the side rooms, closing the door behind the two of them.

Chinelo looked around. "Any ideas?"

Isobel nodded. "I have one, but you might not like it. It involves a bit of a jump. Stand back." She stood between him and the cell and extended her arm, muttering an incantation beneath her breath. The iron cell bars melted and flowed into her hand, forming an enormous sphere. With a quick turn, she blasted the hardened sphere through the wall, breaching the stone. A strong gust of wind blew in and rustled their clothes.

"Isobel, what are we doing? I don't have your flight spell."

Isobel surged esht into her side and tapped Chinelo's forehead. A loud bang rang from the hall.

"Seems they've caught up to us. Time to go!"

"Isobel! What are we doing?" Chinelo shouted.

She pressed her hand onto his back. "Homvelcht solstari!"

Chinelo vanished, reappearing outside the tower before plummeting toward the ground. Isobel heard his scream gradually get quieter and quieter.

She picked up her spear and ran, not stopping to look over her shoulder. She leapt from the building, spreading her arms and falling to the courtyard far, far below. Mort croaked in surprise. He had no desire to become accustomed to such frequent long hops.

The wind buffeted her face, pulling tears from her eyes in a steady stream. She quickly tapped Mort's forehead, applying her protective spell to him. Then, she somersaulted and pushed her feet below her before landing on the ground with a loud thud. She bent her knees, absorbing the impact. However, her protective spell prevented the shock from doing any harm to her.

Chinelo panted behind her. "Never again!"

Isobel stood. "Oh stop! That wasn't so—" she froze.

They had landed in the courtyard, and before them a red-robed figure was slowly turning. His robes swished around him, sparkling with their silver filigree. The Archmage glared across the courtyard, glowering behind his combed beard. Two accompanying guardsmen stood at his side.

Isobel gripped her spear tightly. A bead of sweat dripped across her spectacles. Beside her Chinelo brandished his stolen sword, grasping its hilt with both hands. The Archmage blinked, and his amber eyes flashed above the hard lines of his face.

Isobel gulped.

Her heart pounded. His presence was oppressive. The world seemed to shy away from him, as if it feared his very existence. She felt her breaths hasten. She felt her stomach turn. One of the guards stepped forward and drew her rapier. Isobel recognized her as the woman who had captured her.

"Forgive me, Archmage," Lady Hestra said. "I entrusted the local garrison with their imprisonment. It seems that—"

The Archmage raised his hand, silencing her. Isobel tensed at its movement. She felt them, his iron fingers clamping around her throat.

He clenched his hand into a fist and pointed it at the pair. One of his five rings pulsed slightly, overflowing with his channeled esht. Isobel's eyes widened. She grabbed Chinelo's shoulder, digging her fingers into his threadbare shirt.

"Homvelcht tor vrefden iv gra—"

The Archmage spoke. "End."

His spell-core flashed, and a glowing black void appeared in front of him, bubbling and expanding rapidly. The air distorted around it, as if it were spoiling at the void's touch.

Isobel continued, surging her esht harder and harder to increase the range of her spell, "—tor vrefden hasa—"

The void collapsed, shooting forward in a hideous dark beam.

Isobel screamed the final word, "—SOLSTARI!"

The beam filled her vision, shadowing the world in darkness. It converged into a single point as all she saw imploded into her.

An explosion of green dazzled her eyes. She, Mort, and Chinelo had vanished and reappeared in a grassy field. In the distance, Veld's tall walls blocked the setting sun, sending a long shadow across the farmlands.

Isobel collapsed and panted. Her heart hammered, pounding so loudly she feared it would rupture. Her breath was short and shaky. Her hands quivered.

She felt a trembling hand on her shoulder.

"Hey!" Chinelo said. "You got us out of there. We're safe."

Isobel's whole body quaked. Her heart refused to slow. It pounded, louder, louder, louder!

Chinelo dropped his sword. "Hey! I've got you. You're safe, Isobel!"

His arms wrapped around her. Everything was a blur. She still saw it, the outlandish, spreading blackness the Archmage had conjured. She still felt his hands on her throat. She still saw his eyes burning into her.

She closed her eyes tightly and listened. The birds flitted through the trees, chirping in a playful tune. Isobel let out a long breath. Gradually, her soul felt at ease. Chinelo's embrace tightened. She took a deep breath and exhaled slowly. Inhale. Exhale. Inhale. Exhale.

"Sorry," she whispered. A faint croak sounded from the ground. Mort looked up at her with a look of amphibious concern.

Chinelo released her. He bent to pick up his sword but stopped, hovering his battered hand over its hilt.

"That was too close," he said in a low voice.

Isobel looked down. The blade of his sword was missing. In its place, there was only a corroded stump, a decayed remnant of the single edged blade. Isobel glanced at her spear. It was in a similar state, having been reduced to a blackened shaft with streaks of oxidation running down the sides.

She shuddered.

Chinelo crossed his arms. "What should we do now?"

"I don't know," Isobel said quietly.

Chinelo placed his hand on her shoulder. "May I make a suggestion?"

She shrugged.

"The Archmage is probably here for the obelisk," Chinelo observed. "We need to find it before he does. Joanne said it wasn't in the city, so if we can collect your staff and my sword, then we can make a run to find it."

Isobel looked up. "Wait! Iva and the Archmage visited my cell. They said the obelisk was to the east."

Chinelo touched his chin. "East? That can't be right. Your map had it to the west."

"It did? Sorry, I don't remember." Isobel twisted a lock of her hair around her finger. "You know how it is..."

He nodded. "I don't remember exactly where it was. We'd need to look at the map to confirm."

"That settles our next step."

Chinelo smiled. "Sneak back into the city and get your book?"

"Right! Though I think we have a couple other things we should do before that."

"Oh?"

Isobel stepped in front of him. "First!" She stood on her toes and kissed him quickly before turning and hurrying away.

Chinelo didn't move. He merely stood frozen with wide eyes. After a moment he shook his head and looked after Isobel.

"Wait! What's second?"

Isobel looked over her shoulder. "I need to scrub all this tar off!"

Isobel and Chinelo crouched on the side of the wall, huddling in its dark shadow. They made no sound, having magically muted any noise with a spell from Isobel's staff. Isobel pointed at a humble house built onto the side of the wall, Joanne and Kay's house. Chinelo nodded and looked down at the street below, tracking the movements of a patrol of green-robed guardsmen.

Mort sat on Isobel's horizontal back, sulking about how he had not been allowed to use such gravity defying magic. Why did the interloper receive special treatment when the king was neglected? Such matters must be fixed.

Isobel signed with her hands. The guards had rounded a bend and were out of sight. Chinelo nodded and dashed down the side of the wall, running towards the street ahead. He leapt and released the spell on his ankles, returning his gravity to its natural direction. The sensation was always disorienting for him. The sudden shift of weight, the movement of fluid in his head, the lurching of his blood always made him queasy.

He landed and rolled silently. Isobel floated to the ground after him, with Mort in one hand and her staff in the other. They tiptoed up the crude wooden stairs until they stood in front of the door. Chinelo rapped against it, but no sound was produced. He shot Isobel a look.

She raised an apologetic finger and exhaled.

"Sorry," she whispered. "Forgot to release it."

Chinelo knocked on the door again. The handle clattered and turned, and a gold stream of light streaked across the street, blinding Isobel and Chinelo in the process. He squinted and shaded his eyes.

Joanne stood frozen in the doorway. She made a slight noise of surprise.

"Sorry for showing up so late," Isobel started. "We—Oh!"

Joanne wrapped her in a tight embrace, lifting her up from the ground. "You're both all right! I was so worried!" She set Isobel back down and jumped to Chinelo next, crushing him in a strong bear hug and lifting him off the ground as well.

"We've been appealing your imprisonment for the last three days now, but they wouldn't let us visit. Come inside! Come inside!" Joanne waved them into her living room. "My! You two look awful. Did they not let you clean up when they let you go?"

Chinelo frowned. "They didn't let us go."

"I beg your pardon?"

"We escaped."

"Oh!" Joanne said. *"Chetsh!"*

Chinelo raised an eyebrow.

Kay's voice called from the hallway. "Joanne? What's all that noise? I'm trying to think in here." She poked her head around the corner. At the sight of the two travelers, she let out a relieved sigh. "Oh, good you're not hurt." She repeated Joanne's series of embraces, albeit in a much gentler fashion. "You two look like you had to fight your way out."

"We did." Isobel chuckled.

Kay's face went white. "Well. *Chetsh!"*

"Sorry to barge in like this," Isobel said. "We needed to pick up a couple things, then we'll be on our way."

"Oh, don't even start with that." Kay crossed her arms. "I already said we'd help you. There's no way I'm leaving you out on the streets while you're being hunted."

"Kay, we can't stay. The Interior Guard is after us—"

Kay put a finger to Isobel's lips. "Which is why you two need our help even more now. Let's put together a plan. I know you just want to rush out, but that's not going to work this time. Chinelo!" She looked over Isobel's shoulder. "What do you two need?"

"Shoes, a bath, probably some gloves for Isobel, her spell-book, a good night's rest, some food."

Kay snapped her fingers. "Joanne! Get both baths ready."

Joanne nodded and disappeared down the hall.

Kay threw open the pantry and dug out some bread and vegetables.

"We're running low on food, but this should at least get you two started."

"Kay, you really don't have—" Isobel stopped. Kay raised her finger and pointed it at her menacingly. Isobel's cheeks flushed red.

"I won't hear it from you, Isobel! Not a word of resistance. We're helping you and that's all there is to it." She looked back at Chinelo. "We have your shoes from the other night. All your other things are here as well. What's your plan for tomorrow?"

Chinelo leaned against the counter and crossed his arms. "We need to find Veld's obelisk before the Archmage and Iva do. If they are here, that means they are looking for it, and that means the city is in danger."

Kay nodded. "Where do you think it is?"

"Isobel drew a map of the locations a year ago," Chinelo continued.

"Right! I'll go find it!" Isobel jumped up. Mort grunted at the sudden movement. With a slight scowl he hopped to the counter beside Chinelo and began eyeing the knife Kay used to chop the vegetables.

After Isobel had disappeared around the corner, Chinelo leaned forward.

"Kay," he said in a low voice, "what happened to you three the other night? Where did you go?"

Kay frowned and continued cutting the vegetables at blinding speed, sliding them off the counter into a large metal pot. "We were on the other side of the pyre when the guards showed up. They forced us out of the square. By the time we realized what was happening, you two had already begun... whatever it was you were doing."

"I see."

"We couldn't get through the crowds until after the fight ended, and by that point you two were gone."

Chinelo nodded. "So, you two appealed the imprisonment?"

Kay set her knife down and placed the pot over the stove, adding a quick drizzle of oil before it started cooking. "Joanne and I have done some work for the duke, so it should have been easy to get an audience with him. For some reason he wouldn't see us."

Chinelo scratched his arm. "Probably the Archmage's doing."

"Probably."

"I have another question."

"Ask away." Kay flicked her wrist.

"What does '*chetsh*' mean?"

Kay looked at him in surprise. The corners of her mouth twitched. "Well, how do I put this?"

"Got the baths ready," Joanne said, returning from down the hall with Isobel a few steps behind. "Hmmm? Did something happen?"

Kay waved a hand. "No, no. He wants to know what '*chetsh*' means."

Joanne sputtered and laughed. She clapped Isobel on the back. "I'll let her explain it."

Isobel's cheeks flushed slightly. Not much, but just a little hint of rose bloomed beneath her eyes. "I'd... rather not."

Joanne chuckled. "Wait. Wait. Chinelo? Would you say you are a visual learner?"

Chinelo shrugged. "I suppose."

Isobel's face turned a deep red. "You two are awful. I hope you know that."

She slammed her book onto the counter and opened it to the final page, tapping a point on the map.

"That is where the obelisk should be."

Kay composed herself and hunched over the page. "Interesting. That's out by the battlefield. Joanne, you didn't see anything suspicious when you searched the area, did you?"

Joanne shook her head.

Chinelo stroked his chin. "Isobel, what did you say earlier?"

"The Archmage said he found it east of the city. He sent Iva that way."

Chinelo's brow furrowed. "That doesn't make sense. They can't move, right Joanne?"

Joanne shook her head. "No. Ginn made that very clear. Obelisks are essentially permanent until awakened."

"So why would he send her out there?" Isobel crossed her arms.

"Did they say anything else?" Chinelo asked.

"Iva said a lot of things. She's looking for something called the Source."

Joanne looked up. "Right! I remember her mentioning that."

Isobel nodded. "From what I gathered, it's some kind of collection of the Creator's words. She claims she's trying to find it to 'rewrite the world.' Though, I am not sure how exactly that would work, if we're being honest."

"What else?" Kay asked as she stirred the cooking vegetables.

Isobel closed her eyes tightly and touched her temples. "The sealed words play some kind of role in it. I'm assuming that the Source is one of the words they're looking for."

Kay touched her chin. "I'm perplexed about what those monsters you described have to do with it. It's so bizarre."

Isobel looked down and pursed her lips. "I may have a theory on that, actually."

Chinelo tilted his head.

"Do tell," Kay responded with a flick of her spoon.

Isobel looked over toward the table where Joanne had seated herself. "I've been thinking about it over the past few days. Joanne, do you remember those murals in the temple of the Elder Mothers?"

Joanne nodded. "Of course! I was in charge of maintaining those."

"Do you recall what was on the seventh and eighth murals?"

Joanne touched her chin. "Hmmm. I think those were the ones where the gods spread out over the continent and ascended. That would have been after the Culling War, and right before the Cataclysm."

"Right. Right." Isobel crossed her arms. "So, what if some of them didn't ascend? What if they never left?"

Kay looked up in surprise. "So, you think... that those monsters... *are* the gods?"

Isobel snapped her fingers. "Exactly. Think about it. It lines up with some of the things Iva has said. It makes sense with the villagers in Kahi worshiping the obelisk. The obelisks are all spread across the continent, just like the gods were when they vanished. And, what's more, the gods are always depicted as dark and spindly, and the creatures we've killed are exactly that. Of course there are differences. I don't recall seeing any depictions of the gods being headless, but it is something."

Kay looked down and studied the bubbling soup. "So, you two have just been going around slaughtering the pantheon?"

Isobel held her hands in front of her. "Something along those lines. Oops?"

The room fell silent.

After several moments, Kay spoke. "I'm still confused how the sealed words tie into that."

Isobel sighed. "I am, as well."

Kay gave the soup another stir. "I suppose it doesn't matter that much right now. We know Iva wants them, and we have a rough idea of why."

"So, Iva wants this Source thing to rewrite the world, right?" Chinelo stroked his beard. "What about the Archmage? What is his angle?"

"Probably something similar," Isobel responded. "He and Iva were pretty cold to each other, so I feel there is some misalignment in their goals. As to why they thought the obelisk was to the east..." She rubbed her head. "I don't know! Everything is so muddled right now. It's hard to think."

Kay snapped her fingers. "What if their map is flawed and that's why they send out investigation parties? This would be our chance to get it for ourselves!"

"That's possible, but it likely won't take long for Iva to realize," Chinelo said. "They've been able to find the others very quickly."

"We should leave first thing in the morning," Isobel said. "Chinelo should be able to find the obelisk if we get close enough. He has that weird resonance thing that happens each time we are nearby."

There was a tap against the door. All four whirled around and stared anxiously at it. Kay motioned toward the hall, ushering Chinelo and Isobel into the back of their house. She picked up a vial of a thick liquid from the table and opened it, holding it in front of her mouth.

Joanne tore her gauntlets from a hook beside the door and strapped them on quickly. She gave a knowing nod to Kay and unlocked the door.

Chinelo and Isobel pressed their backs against the wall. Isobel closed her eyes. Chinelo reached down and laced his fingers through hers, squeezing her hand gently.

The door opened. A booming voice called out.

"Joanne! Kay! I have cider! Want any?"

All four called out in response. "Valyx?"

CHAPTER 49

"YOU'RE NOT COMING WITH US VALYX!" Kay shouted.

Chinelo looked up from the saddlebag he was fastening to his mount. Valyx and Kay had been bickering all morning, and it seemed that things had finally come to a breaking point.

"I won't hear of it!" Kay scowled from atop the white horse she rode. Her bobbed blonde hair flowed around her cheeks in the cool morning wind. She wore light leather armor over her tight blue shirt and faded trousers, and several belts were wrapped around her waist and legs with small pouches for potions and elixirs.

"Oh, don't give me that, Kay!" Valyx retorted, climbing onto his steed. "I'm letting you use my horses. You could at least let me come along to make sure you bring them back safely. Besides, you need my help, and I want to help."

"Do you even know how to fight? We're talking about slaying a god. That's not something you just casually do!"

"Isobel said it was easy. Just stab them in the glowing weak point. I'm coming with you and that's the end of it. If you want my horses, then you're getting the cheese as a side dish, too."

Kay let out an exasperated huff and looked away. "If things get bad, I'm shoving one of my elixirs down your throat so you can scurry back to the city."

Valyx grinned.

"Unbelievable." Kay rode her horse to the edge of the fence around Valyx's family stable.

Joanne tapped Chinelo on the shoulder. "How much do you want to bet those two end up smooching by the time we finish?"

"I thought you said Kay wasn't interested?"

Joanne shrugged and adjusted her cuirass. "Then it should be an easy wager for you."

Chinelo's eyes narrowed. "Two crescents against."

"Twenty."

"Five."

"Ten!" Joanne smirked.

"Ten," Chinelo assented before pulling himself up onto the brown steed Valyx had offered him. "You all right over their Isobel?"

"He keeps grinning at me!" she shouted beside Kay. Her horse's dappled golden coat shone in the warm sun. "It's worrying."

Mort croaked in agreement.

Chinelo guided his horse to her side. "Just remember what Valyx and I explained. Squeeze to go. Pull to stop. Tug to turn."

"Worst case scenario I can just fly after you." She eyed the beast apprehensively. He turned his head and flashed her another one of his bizarre equine grins.

"Let's go!" Valyx yelled. He urged his horse forward with his calves, and the creature trotted a short distance before breaking into a lively canter.

The other four followed, riding their horses across the grassy fields on Veld's southern edge. Valyx crossed the main road and skirted the wall to head towards the west. Chinelo held onto the reigns tightly, watching the grass and trees fly by. His heart pounded. It was exhilarating.

They crested a hill and guided their horses to a trail that cut through the orchards. Farm hands waved at them as they flew by. Chinelo inhaled deeply, smelling the damp scent of dew and the sweet aroma of freshly picked apple-berries. In the distance, the tips of many swords and spears embedded in the earth grew larger and more defined, though they still had much ground to cover. Valyx had said that it would take them over half an hour at a good pace to reach the battlefield.

Valyx veered his horse to enter the main road leading from Veld's western gate. The others quickly followed. The horses' hooves kicked up a cloud of dust behind them, a plume of brown and tan.

Chinelo's pack bounced against his shoulders. He and Isobel had packed most of their belongings, preparing to flee Veld after they found the obelisk. After a full night's rest and a hearty morning meal, he felt he could surmount any obstacle.

They neared the battlefield. Chinelo suddenly halted his horse.

Kay steered hers around his and spun to a stop. "What's wrong?"

Chinelo raised his finger and closed his eyes, craning his neck to listen. Birds. Wind. Trees. Chinelo gasped. He felt it. The shaking. The thumping. The breathing. It resonated through his core, calling him to join it beneath the earth.

"Chinelo?" Isobel turned with an expression of concern.

"It's near!" Chinelo said. "Somewhere past that hill."

Isobel dismounted and dropped her pack beside the road, setting Mort on top of it.

"What are you doing?" Kay asked.

"Trying to scope out what we're dealing with," Isobel replied. She opened her hand and her staff appeared. "Remember what we planned. Once we awaken it, I'll transport it further from the city so we can take it down without risk of it crossing the farms."

Kay dismounted. "I see but..."

The ground shook.

A flock of birds rose from the battlefield, cawing and squawking as they fled the rumbling tremors. The horses whinnied and stamped their feet.

Isobel steadied herself on her staff.

"Impossible," she whispered. "How?"

"What is it?" Joanne shouted, trying to keep her horse under control.

Suddenly, the resonance Chinelo felt in his core ceased, and a loud, mouthless screech pierced the air.

Isobel's face went pale.

Chinelo followed her terrified gaze, ending on an enormous sword. Glowing streaks of orange moved up its surface in a grid-like pattern, disappearing around the diamond shaped hole in its center. A radiant orb of orange mist hovered in the hole, swirling and tumbling like a turbulent stream.

"The sword," Chinelo gasped. "It's the obelisk."

A gaunt hand of colossal proportions shot up from beyond the hill, supported by a bony arm that cast a long shadow beneath it. It slammed into the earth on the hilltop, causing a ripple to propagate across the black shimmering skin that coated its emaciated arm. It pushed, digging claws into the dirt until a massive figure rose.

It stood, higher, higher, higher, pushing up on two lean legs coated in bands of crimson muscle and tissue. It stretched beyond what Chinelo imagined could be possible, standing so tall that the trees were mere weeds compared to its titanic stature. Its whole body seemed to wrinkle and shift, as if the very tissue that clung to the sharp black bones were made of living oil. A stream of bile poured from the entrails that hung loosely below its ribcage, sending up clouds of steam as it splashed to the ground. Still, it stood higher.

Its arms straightened, cracking and breaking before mending in a horrific, twisting pattern. Its veins and sinew snaked over bone, wriggling and writhing until they reached their preferred positions where they embedded themselves below the skittering skin.

Its arms were frightfully long, dangling all the way to its knees. Even its legs were uncannily lengthy, being over twice as long as the creature's hunched body. As with the others, it had no face, and instead of a head its neck was fused to a stone symbol of two angled lines piercing a long vertical rectangle. Its lungs swelled, pressing against its ribs, drawing in a howling wind.

It screamed.

Chinelo covered his ears. His head throbbed. His blood ran cold. Every fiber of his being cried out with a single urgent command to run.

The horses bucked and scattered, sending the remaining riders flying.

Valyx raised a shaking hand and pointed it at the monster. "What... what is that?"

Joanne pushed herself to her feet and lowered her mask. Her hands shook.

Kay's mouth hung open. "It's so... big..."

The ground rumbled again. The god took a step forward, and it reached one of its gaunt arms to the hilt of the massive stone sword before it. Its knuckles cracked as it wrapped its gnarled fingers around the handle, and its skin bulged as muscle fibers grew around the bones. With a horrific shake, the creature lifted the sword from the ground. It took another step, dragging the blade behind it. It took a third step, moving towards the city.

Chinelo clenched his teeth. "Isobel!" he shouted. "Can you move that thing away from here?"

"It's... it's too big..."

Chinelo shook her shoulder. "Can you do it?"

She looked up at him. "I've never moved something that large... it's not supposed to be that way..."

"Can you do it?"

"I—I can try," she mumbled. "I may not be able to get it very far, though."

"Understood!" Chinelo nodded. "Then our priority is stopping that thing before it reaches the city. At the rate it's moving..." he watched the creature take another step. "It will reach the farms in a matter of minutes."

Isobel gasped and leapt to her feet. "We have to warn them."

"Valyx, can you catch your horse?" Chinelo called.

"I can try," Valyx replied.

"Good. Do it! Tell anyone you can to flee."

Valyx nodded and glanced at Kay. He smiled and ran off, chasing the fleeing steeds.

The ground continued to shake.

Chinelo turned and drew his sword. "Let's go!"

They ran up the hill, trampling down the short grass which suddenly became sparse as they entered the barren battlefield. They weaved through the ancient broken armaments strewn across the ground. Axes like redwoods, swords like battlements, and clubs larger than houses were lodged in the red dirt, casting long shadows to the west. They neared the monster's feet. There was only a short rise ahead of them.

A lone figure appeared at the hill's apex. Tall and bulky, he was clad in a billowing robe of red and silver. Chinelo halted. The Archmage turned and laced his fingers.

"You," the Archmage growled, glaring at Isobel. "Iva's little pet."

Chinelo gripped his sword with both hands. Sweat ran down his back. Joanne and Kay stopped by his side.

"Predictable, predictable," the Archmage continued. "I was certain you would show yourself. Though, you moved faster than expected."

Kay pulled a vial from her belt and gulped down its contents.

The Archmage scowled. He unlaced his fingers and clenched his right fist, pointing it in their direction. One of his rings began to glow.

"You are a pestilence." His lips curled into a cruel smile. "End!"

A swirling sphere of black appeared before the Archmage, expanding into a hideous void.

Isobel shoved Chinelo aside. She stepped in front of the three, opening her hand and holding it outwards. The Archmage's sphere collapsed, shooting forth a murky black beam of glowing destruction. It screamed towards Chinelo, threatening to consume him in its howling darkness.

A light flashed. It grew and spread, forming a shield that the beam splashed into. Isobel's barrier protected them from the danger.

The beam suddenly vanished, leaving behind only a streak of blackened earth and decayed brush. A red blur raced forward. Chinelo blinked, just as the Archmage's fist collided with Isobel's chest, sending her flying back and tumbling down the hill.

The Archmage snapped his fingers, and Chinelo was thrown back by an invisible force. He collided against a nearby armament and crumpled, gasping for breath to reclaim the air that had left his lungs. He was dazed and dizzy. He coughed and slowly recovered his senses. Beside him, Joanne groaned. She too had been sent flying.

Blue lights flashed from the bottom of the hill. A nimble figure streaked around the Archmage, leaving behind a trail of frozen shards and frigid mist. A bob of blonde hair fluttered in the wind as the figure pummeled the mage with a series of icy blasts. Kay had struck.

The Archmage shielded his face and yelled.

"Ruin!"

A dark pulse radiated out from him, covering the ground and leaving behind only a ring of ashen gray dust. Kay jumped. Spikes of ice burst from her feet and lifted her. She moved her arms in a circle and clapped her hands. Behind her, an array of icicles appeared and shot downwards, puncturing the arid earth.

Chinelo gripped his sword. The Archmage glanced his direction and muttered something into one of his rings.

"No, you don't!" Kay shouted, slamming the Archmage across the face with her ice-coated fist.

The ground shook and cracked. Chinelo took a step but was stopped by a tug from his arm.

Joanne was at his side. She pulled him away as the soil opened into a treacherous crevasse.

"Run!" Kay shouted. "I will handle him!" She gestured with her hands, and the earth around her froze solid.

Joanne pulled Chinelo's arm, fleeing from the dueling figures.

"Stop!" Chinelo shouted, ripping his arm free. "We can't leave them!"

"Chinelo! We need to stop that monster. You know how to do it. Kay can handle herself."

Chinelo looked over his shoulder at the wintry spectacle unfolding, a snowstorm of cold and decay. The battle was fierce. Kay's blizzard of strikes was punctuated by dark eruptions from the Archmage, hideous spells that rotted all they touched. She darted around the mage, moving at speeds that were barely traceable to the human eye. Beyond the fray lay Isobel, slowly moving and rubbing her head. He clenched his teeth. He felt empty, as if a part of him had been torn from his core. "I can't leave Isobel!"

Joanne grabbed his shoulders. "Listen to me! People are going to die. That thing is marching towards Veld, and I can't stop it alone. I need you to trust me. Trust Kay. Trust Isobel. They won't go down."

He closed his eyes and shook his head. His soul was burdened by a massive weight. He longed to protect her. He longed to keep her safe. He longed to be her knight.

"You do not need to protect me. Remember that, all right?"

Her words reverberated through his head, words she had spoken in his arms so many months before.

If he stayed, others would die.

He let out a pained yell, opened his eyes, and continued his pursuit of the monstrous titan. He would slay the god. He would return for Isobel.

Joanne followed close behind. They rushed over the fields, following the trench carved by the creature's massive sword. The beast rumbled forward, trampling trees and boulders as if they were twigs and pebbles beneath its skeletal feet.

"We need to move faster!" Chinelo panted. A farmhouse was directly in the creature's path. He channeled esht into his back, enhancing his strength. With a grunt he sprinted ahead, pressing forward as if each step were a massive leap.

"Speed!" Joanne yelled into her gauntlets. Their spell-cores pulsed, and she accelerated, matching Chinelo's breakneck pace.

Trees and bushes, crops and fields flew by in an instant, becoming a blur behind the pair. They vaulted from hill to hill, hurdling over the shallow valleys below.

A high-pitched ringing pierced the air. A light flew and fragmented the ground beneath them, sending Joanne and Chinelo flying. Chinelo twisted as he fell, orienting himself feet-first. He landed and skidded to a stop, searching for the source of the explosion. Joanne landed a short distance away.

A flash of silver caught Chinelo's eye. Several robed figures rode on horseback, with shining rapiers held high.

"Go, Chinelo! I'll catch up." Joanne cracked her neck and punched her fists together. "I know how to deal with mages."

Chinelo nodded and continued onwards, chasing after the beast. Crashes came from behind him, their sound like that of water bursting from a dam. He did not turn back. He charged forward.

After several minutes he finally managed to pass the monster's gigantic skeletal feet. He whirled around, gripped his sword with both hands, and shouted.

"Extend!"

His sword cut through the air, and its phantom blade sliced through the beast's skin until...

It stopped.

Chinelo gasped and released his spell. The wound he had inflicted on the monster's ankle immediately closed. The ground shook, tremoring as the creature dragged its sword to its side and pushed its stone tip into the dirt.

Chinelo looked up. High above him, partially obscured by a light morning haze, the creature had turned its head to look down on him. It had felt his blow, and it was not pleased.

Chinelo felt hollow. He stood alone, face-to-face with a living colossus. He was a mouse before a titan, an ant before a giant, a mite before a god.

The core floated within the god's blade, glowing orange like the dawn. Chinelo gritted his teeth and adjusted his grip on his own blade.

Chinelo was not a complicated man. He saw the world as it was, not as it could be. And as he saw it, any opponent, either man or monster, could be slain by his sword. At that moment, his friends, his family, his love, and his life all depended on him felling the god before him. His sword would not fail him, and he would not fail her.

The beast reached across its body, gripping its sword with both hands. It lifted it high above its head, sending fibers of muscle up its arms to support the weapon. Then, with a loud groan, the god swung it down, slamming it into the fragile earth below.

CHAPTER 50

KAY BARRAGED THE ARCHMAGE WITH A continuous assault of chilling wind and frigid ice. Her potion tingled within her. Fueled by its effects, she would only have a few minutes to conclude their battle. She clapped her hands in front of her, sending another torrent of icicles in the Archmage's direction.

He snapped his fingers and the icy javelins fell to the ground, bouncing off some invisible obstacle. He watched her closely, eyeing her every move with shrewd interest. She dashed forward, moving at speeds far exceeding what could be considered natural, and pummeled her opponent with several freezing punches before leaping away. Conserving energy was not to her advantage.

Most mages moderated their esht consumption, focusing on efficiency and precision instead of sheer unbridled displays of force. Kay was not like most mages. Born with only a middling capacity for esht, her spell-casting capabilities had always been limited. She knew all the words and incantations that her sisters did, but with only a paltry supply of energy to fuel them, using even one spell could sap an entire day from her. She had turned to other solutions. She had turned to potions.

Many considered potions to be useful situational tools. Imbue one with a healing spell, and wounds would close with just a small dose. Infuse one with a vision spell, and even the most distant objects would seem close and detailed. However, most mages dismissed any use beyond that. Kay was not like most mages. Her potions and elixirs had much more extensive effects.

Even just one vial was costly. Kay had dedicated her entire twenty-five years of life to researching chemicals and solvents that would metabolize quickly without harming the user and would bind well to enchantments without leaking esht. Weeks went into designing and drafting the spells that she infused into her elixirs, meticulously calculated instructions and conditional effects that would activate when the potion was consumed. With help from Joanne or Valyx, it would only take a few exhausting sessions to imbue the spells into the potions. Without their assistance, Kay would spend weeks or even months repeatedly draining herself for just one vial.

The results of all her hours of study and work were unlike anything the world had seen. Her own energy was limited, but once she consumed a potion, she did not need esht. The imbued spell activated, giving her access to the abilities she had prepared in advance. Her strength was enhanced. Her speed was multiplied. Her senses and reflexes were sharpened. And, with a few pre-selected gestures, she could activate spells in quick succession.

Kay vaulted and clapped her hands again, sending down a rain of spears that fell on the mage below. He sneered and deflected them. She landed and held her fists in front of her, watching her target circle around her slowly.

"Intriguing," the Archmage mused. "You use gestures to activate your spells, not sound. That would imply that you use tattoos or specialized spell-cores, but it seems that you don't." He waved his hand in her direction. "Please continue, witch. You have my attention. I will let you divert me for a couple moments."

Kay scoffed and opened her hands, sending a blizzard of frigid wind in the Archmage's direction. His breath puffed in the air.

"You've chosen an advantageous specialty," the Archmage continued. "Without that flame magic your cult likes to keep secret, most people wouldn't be able to resist ice magic. Still, there are ways around it."

He moved, suddenly accelerating towards Kay with hands like talons. Kay gasped and sidestepped, delivering a chilling punch towards his back. The Archmage counterattacked, hooking from the right into Kay's raised forearm. He jabbed and swiped, leaving a trail of light behind his glowing rings.

Kay's jaw throbbed. An intense dull pain spread from the point of the punch's impact, sending her reeling back. Her vision blurred.

"Come now! More! Show me more!" the Archmage shouted, repeatedly slamming his fist into Kay's gut. "Surely you have more!"

Kay staggered back.

Her vision focused. He stood before her, grinning behind his raised fists. She frowned. Hand-to-hand combat was Joanne's specialty, not hers. She stepped back and clapped her hands, sending another volley of frozen armaments to her opponent.

He raised his hand and batted the projectiles away as if they were mere flies. The Archmage smiled and snapped his fingers. One of the spell-cores on his hand pulsed. Kay's hair stood on end. He leapt forward, opening his hand in a vicious palm strike that sparked with lightning. Kay flexed her toes, one of her many predetermined gestures, and she shot up into the air, propelled by a growing icy pillar. It shattered below her, demolished by the Archmage's strike. She landed and backed away.

The Archmage raised an eyebrow. "Oh? You didn't move your hands that time. So, either you used a tattoo or your feet. Interesting."

Kay opened her hand, another predetermined gesture. A frozen pike formed, one of a simple shape and structure.

The Archmage chuckled. "Conjuring. I see. So, pugilism is not your preference. Very well."

He snapped his fingers. The ring on his pinky pulsed. He opened his hand as a long, slender scimitar appeared beside him. He grasped its handle, flourishing the curved blade before inviting Kay with a taunting gesture.

Kay grunted. She had barely managed to land any blows, and they had done little good. She needed to end their battle quickly before her potion's effects dissipated. She gripped her weapon tightly. Its cold surface was painful against her skin, but she would not need to hold it long.

The Archmage stepped forward, pointing his blade in her direction. He tapped its tip against her spear.

"Come now. You have the range advantage. Surely you are not afraid, witch."

Kay yelled and thrust her pike, retracting it rapidly before unleashing a second vicious swing. Vapor emanated from its shaft, leaving behind a thin cloud of mist. The Archmage swiftly stepped back, easily avoiding the strike.

She shifted her grip and followed up with an additional swing. With impressive dexterity, the Archmage blocked the strike.

His blade rang. Her spear cracked.

Kay retreated and hurled the spear at her opponent. He once again stepped to the side and watched nonchalantly as Kay's pike rammed into the earth.

"You are beginning to bore me, witch," he chided. "Enough of this!"

Kay blinked. He had moved, crossing the gap between them in an instant. His hand gripped her throat and slammed her into the earth. She let out a rasping cry and tore at his hand. Her vision blurred. Her head throbbed.

"Do you think I have not witnessed your tricks before?" he sneered. "Do you think I have not learned of your secrets? I was raised in your ways and taught their intricacies."

He lifted her up and slammed her back down. Her head stung from the impact.

"I've been immersed in your customs. I have hunted your sisters down and painted their coven halls with their blood. You are nothing unique."

Kay weakly clapped her hands. Spikes flew up into the sky but missed her target.

"Know this, witch. I have killed you before. I will kill you again. And..." he whispered into her ear, sending shivers down her spine. "I will savor every second of it."

Kay's eyes widened. She felt something beneath her. A vibration, pounding closer and closer.

A light swung above her, sending the Archmage flying. Released from his grasp, she coughed and panted. She rolled over and retched.

Noises. Thuds. Grunts. Crashes.

She looked up. A figure moved in her blurred vision, swinging a glowing hammer at a smudge of crimson. The figure vanished, reappearing on the other side. Kay's sight sharpened. The Archmage ducked under a swing and sent out a blast of lightning. His target floated above him, twirling in the air and slamming his back with the glowing weapon in her hands. He stumbled. The figure landed and delivered another earthshaking strike. The mage was thrown away, tumbling across the dirt in a spiral of red and silver until he collided with a nearby stone spear.

Isobel's hammer dissipated as she looked over her shoulder at Kay, her short red hair flowing in the wind.

"Are you hurt?"

Kay stood. "Only a little."

Isobel frowned. "Sorry. Can you fight?"

Kay joined her and downed another vial. The thick orange liquid inside slid down her throat, burning as it flowed into her stomach.

"If it means tearing that snake apart then I'll fight as long as I need to." Her feet and hands lit aflame, cloaking themselves in a flickering shroud. She would make this man burn.

Isobel nodded and gripped her staff with both hands. "Let's finish this."

Joanne sailed through the air and slammed her fist into the mage's forehead. He flew off the horse with a horrific cry and tumbled to the ground where he was promptly trampled beneath the next horse. Joanne pushed off the horse's back, receiving a displeased whinny in response. She landed on the ground with a thud.

She'd managed to surprise the first several mages, sending them flying with a sudden onslaught of spells. The others had proven more difficult. Two mages circled around her, pointing their blades threateningly. One, Joanne noted, had a ghastly brand on his cheek.

Light flashed. A cord shot through the air at Joanne. She sidestepped and caught it on her arm. With a quick tug, she pulled the mage at the other end from his horse. The third leapt to the ground and rushed at her.

She smiled. This was what she wanted. At range, she was at a disadvantage. Up close was her ideal.

She surged esht into her shoulders, forcing it through a pair of tattoos. Clouds of steam erupted from her arms, blanketing the area in a shroud of thick mist, one so dense that the sunlight could not reach the ground.

Joanne closed her eyes and listened. The footsteps grew closer.

She shifted her focus to her face, forcing esht into the carved wooden mask she wore. An overwhelming rush of senses inundated her. She felt everything. Breath moving vapor. Feet pushing aside mist as they pounded against the earth. Hearts beating in terror. The mask showed her all that was in the vapor, as if every hovering particle of water was part of her, as if she was the cloud itself. She sensed every movement, every breeze, every shift in the airborne water.

Behind her there was stillness. The mist was undisturbed. To her right she felt the vapor eddying, shifting around a shaking body. Ahead of her she felt movement. A man-shaped void approached. The vapor separated, flowing around something long and thin. A blade, cutting through the fog. She stepped forward, trusting the mask to guide her. The line of separating mist swung towards her. She ducked and heard the blade swish over her head, leaving behind a turbulent vortex that agitated her senses through the mask. She clenched her fists and punched at the void.

Her fist collided with something heavy. Robes fluttered around her knuckles, and through her thick gauntlets she felt chainmail bend and shift.

The void staggered back. Joanne followed, delivering another punch. And another. And another. The robes muddled her senses. It was difficult to feel where the vapor flowed around the legs and arms. She aimed for what was clear, the void's center, the man's chest.

The mage twisted, dodging underneath her punch. She felt his blade cut blindly through the mist. Robbed of his sight, the man's aim was poor. He merely flailed his blade around wildly hoping to hit his opponent. Joanne blocked the slash with the metal plate on her gauntlet and delivered another blow. She could feel his intentions before he even moved. Slight shifts in the air indicated tensing fingers. Small rushes in the mist indicated breaths before strikes.

She felt his arms move, tugging a paper talisman from his belt. The vapor was disturbed, rushing away from him radially.

Joanne backed away, stepping deeper into the mist. She sent another blast of vapor from her shoulders, expanding the cloud and with it, her senses. Something shot past her. It felt hard and bulky, pushing aside the mist in turbulent flows.

A voice called out from behind her. She felt the inhalation of vapor. She felt the water clinging to his throat and lungs. She felt it puff out with every syllable.

"Blade Dance."

Joanne gasped. The vapor was cut in six different locations, swirling around the mage. It slowly formed a vortex, swirling and tingling around him. His void was consumed by a much larger one, the eye of a fearsome tornado.

The ring of whirling blades moved, drawing closer to her. The mage began running, and the ring of swords progressed, clearing away Joanne's senses. Behind her, she felt the Branded Mage fiddling with talismans, bringing them close to his eyes and tossing them aside. They floated and soaked up the vapor, and it faded as it drenched the fluttering papers. He had not moved.

With a puff of steam Joanne turned and ran towards the Branded Mage. She whispered into her gauntlets.

"Strength."

Her muscles coursed with power. The Branded Mage cowered back, pointing his blade at her. She ducked, feeling the separation fly over her head. With a grunt she grabbed him by the belt, planted her feet, and hurled him over her shoulder at the approaching maelstrom of steam and steel.

The void flew, hurtling through the air and leaving a billowing trail of mist behind. It disappeared in the maelstrom, and a loud cry and crash reached Joanne's keen ears. The whirling ceased.

She concentrated, searching for her targets. The cloud drifted and swirled. She searched. The edges of the fog became blurry and unclear. The vapors rushed around the location where she heard the crash. She tensed. She felt it.

A breath.

Joanne sprinted towards its location and burst from the wall of vapor. She opened her eyes and fell upon the bloody heap below, pounding it into the dirt.

The god's blade cut through the earth, sending chunks of red clay flying past Chinelo. He leapt over the massive trench and sprinted towards the monster's legs, circling the creature's ankle, a bony mass covered in rippling black skin and writhing tissue. Chinelo gripped his blade with both hands. He needed to halt the beast's movements, otherwise he stood no chance of reaching the glowing core in its sword. He landed and shouted.

"Project!"

A slicing crescent of rippling air burst from his swinging blade and careened into the beast's heel. Dark blood spurted and coagulated on the ground. High above him, he heard the monster groan. Chinelo slashed his sword in the opposite direction, sending another wave at the creature's other heel. A wound tore open then immediately wove itself back together, sprouting tiny wriggling appendages and tendrils.

Chinelo let out a frustrated huff. A shadow moved across his. He looked up, only to see the bottom of the monster's foot above him, poised to crush him like some troublesome insect.

Chinelo dug his boot into the dirt and pushed, scrambling away as the monster's foot slammed into the ground. The earth shook. A cloud of dust rushed over him. He closed his eyes and covered his face.

Another slam. The monster stamped furiously. Chinelo stumbled out of the dust and looked up. If the heels would not yield and the bones were too thick to cut, the next places to strike were the creature's knees.

He frowned. How could he reach them? Isobel had urged him to try her flight spell, but the constant shift in gravity nauseated him every time he tried to use it, and he had ultimately refused. However, he did have an alternative.

"Xastra gariasheq py tor vrefden!"

Chinelo became weightless. He pushed off the ground and floated towards his target. As he neared it, he released his esht, and he felt gravity's pull return. His trajectory arced, and he stabbed his blade into the monster's leg, pulling it down to tear a hideous gash. The creature screeched. Chinelo slid down its thigh, leaving a bloody wake behind him until he reached the creature's knee. With a grunt he pushed his feet into the monster's calf and forced esht into the tattoos on his ankles, setting his gravity direction perpendicular to his legs.

Black tendrils sprouted, squirming and licking at the sides of his boots. Chinelo grasped his sword's hilt with both hands, accumulated strength, and forced his shining blade through the two tendons on the edges of the creature's knee. They snapped and tore apart as Chinelo was splattered with an inky black stream.

The creature's leg buckled, collapsing beneath its massive weight. Chinelo shielded his face from the stream with his hand, bracing for the impending impact. The creature's knee slammed into the earth, and its entire body shook from the thunderous crash. Chinelo shifted his gravity again. His world rotated. His stomach lurched.

He thrust his sword into the crimson sinew beneath him and ran. His feet pounded against the muscle, driving straight forward towards the sky above. He ran vertically, drawing his sword like a pen across a scroll of flesh, leaving a calligraphy of carnage behind. The beast let out a deafening screech.

Chinelo's blade caught, ringing as if it had collided with stone. The muscle hardened, crusting over with a shell of thick chitinous plates. He tugged at his sword, tearing it from the layer of living armor.

Chinelo's hair stood on end. A shadow moved in his peripheral vision, growing larger with each fleeting moment. He turned to see the god's gnarled hand swinging towards him, moving to squash him like a mosquito.

Esht cascaded from Chinelo's heart through his shoulder, spiraling down his arm and pooling in his sword. His words reached into his spell-core, calling forth a spell etched within.

"Blink." Chinelo vanished.

He reappeared above the creature's hand and fell on top of it. Chinelo crouched and sprinted up the creature's arm. He wound around it in a helix, bounding over chunks of bone and masses of muscle until he crested the creature's shoulder.

Its back stretched out like a field before him, covered in taut black skin with protruding vertebra and snaking blood vessels. Chinelo pressed on, running down the trapezius to cross to the opposite arm.

The skin quivered. It bunched up into bulging, writhing clusters, growing tighter and tighter. With a hideous tear, the masses burst, sprouting towering dark tendrils as tall as buildings.

Chinelo gasped. The creature's back was a den of headless snakes, a web of squirming fingers that flailed with erratic violence. One batted in his direction, meeting the cold steel of his blade. He ducked behind it, running and weaving through the throng. Over, under, around, behind. Slash and dive. Duck and slice. He leapt over the spine.

It split, sending forth a tongue of deep crimson flesh with Chinelo at its tip. It launched him through the air at breakneck speed.

Chinelo somersaulted. The sky and ground whirled around him, spinning round and round in a dizzying blur of blue and green. He forced a small amount of esht into his sword.

"Blink!"

Chinelo reappeared, resetting his movement and momentum in the process.

"Xastra gariasheq py tor vrefden."

He floated in the air, unbound by the pull of the celestial bodies. Far below him, the writhing knot of serpentine appendages bloomed like a flower. Chinelo had witnessed such adaptations before. The monsters' flesh was malleable and ever evolving. It could be supple or impenetrable. It could be strong or sleek. The cataract of metamorphoses, the skittering shifts in dermal composition, the contracting of muscles into stone—he had witnessed them. He had become familiar with them. Somehow, each evolution was more horrific. Each growth was more abominable. The one that blossomed before him chilled him to his core.

A ring of tendrils framed a gaping maw. The vertebra had split, tearing in jagged, sharp edges to form rows of pointed teeth, and from within the jaws was a bloodshot eye. Its iris shone like an eclipsed sun, blazing gold around the pupil.

It *saw* him.

The tendrils shot forth, stretching and thinning until they formed a spiral of scaled tissue. Chinelo twirled his blade and pointed it toward the amalgamation of flesh and bone.

"Fireball!"

Flame curled into a raging sun and plummeted. The mouth clamped shut, sending out a bone-shaking crunch. Flame splashed against skin, charring it into a gruesome patina. The tendrils converged and twisted, continuing their flight towards Chinelo. He released his esht and fell.

The ground grew larger, larger, larger. At the moment before impact, at the breath before collision, Chinelo uttered a command.

"Blink!"

The world collapsed before opening around him a flash of green and blue. He stood on the ground, unharmed by his fall. Above him, shading him from the ascending sun was the quickly descending stone blade of the defiled god he had dared to challenge. Chinelo raised his sword and shouted a command, calling forth a spell of his own design, a redirection of gravity for all that drew near.

"Repel!"

The monster's sword flew back, pulled upwards by an inversion of weight. Stones rolled from him, and even buzzing insects became projectiles forced away by his magic.

The creature reeled. It stared down at him, looking on with its eyeless face. Its arm rotated around its shoulder, sending the sword plunging into a cluster of trees nearby.

The ground rumbled. Chinelo looked down from the titan above. It had redirected its momentum, using the force of the falling blade to propel its swing in a full circle. It plowed its blade through the clay, driving an avalanche of red dirt towards Chinelo with the heavy stone edge close behind.

He heard a yell.

Something hit him. Someone wrapped their arms around him and tumbled with him down the side of the hill. They rolled, knocking knees against legs, elbows against chest until they finally separated. Chinelo jumped to his feet and looked around, locating the figure who had tackled him.

"Sorry about that, friend," Joanne said. She lifted her mask. "You looked—hey! Don't point that thing at me!"

"Sorry, Joanne. Thanks for the assistance." Chinelo lowered his sword marched up the hill.

Joanne followed. "What are we dealing with? What's the plan?"

Chinelo shook his head. "Ground it so we can get a decent shot at the core."

"Any ideas?"

"A few. Its ankles are too sturdy, and it's hardened the skin around its knees. My sword won't pierce it."

Joanne grinned and rammed her gauntlets together. "I might be able to help with that."

CHAPTER 51

ISOBEL FLEW, WEAVING AROUND THE DARK eruptions from the Archmage below. A streak of flame crashed into him. He batted it away, momentarily diverting his attention from Isobel. She took the opportunity.

"Form: Blade!"

Isobel dove, thrusting her glaive towards the mage's side. It struck something hard, an invisible force between her weapon and his hand. She twirled and released her blade before unleashing another command.

"Drop!"

The Archmage grunted as his weight increased. He braced himself, slowly bending lower and lower to the ground. The earth cracked. His feet sank into the dirt.

Kay raced by Isobel's side, leaving flaming footsteps behind. She motioned her hands in a complicated gesture, and a fiery great sword appeared above her, swinging down upon the Archmage.

He raised his hand, and the blade once again splashed against an invisible barrier.

"Kay! Behind!" Isobel signaled. Kay nodded and raced away.

The Archmage suddenly tensed his hand. His fingers sparked. Almost completely by instinct, Isobel summoned her barrier, defending herself from a thunderous lightning strike that flashed from the mage's outstretched arm.

"You think you know magic?" the Archmage growled. "You think you know anything about the Ancient Arts?"

Kay pounced from behind, sending a torrent of flaming darts at him with quick flicks of her fingers. Isobel canceled her gravity and leapt above. She summoned her staff's spearhead.

The Archmage defended once more and whirled around with a powerful kick.

Isobel fell, plunging her ever changing weapon towards the Archmage. He stepped aside and made a swift motion with his arm.

His hand was on her throat. It tightened, sending a pulse of pain into her head. He pulled her close. His eyes burned gold with rage.

"You know nothing!" he roared.

Isobel pointed her left hand at his stomach and fired a salvo of cyan lights into his belly. Crystals erupted from his body, formed from his own esht. He released her and thrashed his arms, tearing the crystals from his tattered and singed robe.

Kay sent another blast of flame from the side. Isobel floated above, summoning showers of blades and torrents of fire. Rocks burst forth from the fray, hurled at great speed into the sky. Isobel dove and weaved but was brought down by a heavy impact to her shoulder. She tumbled and rolled across the ground, digging her fingers into the dirt as she scrambled to her feet.

The Archmage strolled menacingly from the blaze. The hems and edges of his robe were blackened with soot. His eyes were like embers. With every heavy step, a cloud of dust puffed from the ground. Isobel rubbed her shoulder and pointed her staff at him.

"Inferno!"

A spiral of flame erupted with a flash, enveloping the mage in its raging vortex. Then, with barely so much as a sputter, it vanished.

The mage drew closer. His fingers tensed, bending like talons. A bead of sweat rolled down Isobel's cheek.

A streak of flame cut across the battlefield. Kay attacked from behind, summoning fireballs from her clenched fists.

The Archmage whirled and pointed his ring at Kay. Isobel's heart seized.

"End!"

With a rush of esht to the tattoo on her chest, Isobel vanished, pulling herself to the space between Kay and the Archmage. She summoned her barrier, and the black flood of decay hammered against it before dissipating.

"Thank you," Kay panted.

Isobel nodded. "I have an idea," she whispered. "He's defending from most of our attacks but—"

"But what?" The Archmage outstretched his arms, his previously combed beard wild and singed. "You'll what? Come up with some clever trick? Devise some ingenious spell? You are nothing, witch! You throw sparks and flames at me as if I was some animal. Allow me to show you how real mages fight. Allow me to show you what true mastery of the Ancient Arts is."

Isobel tensed, tightening her grip on her staff.

The Archmage clenched his fist, bringing his rings close to his lips.

Kay rushed forward.

"Kay! Wait!" Isobel screamed.

The Archmage snarled. "Rend Earth!"

Cracks formed before him, widening and splitting the barren ground like torn paper. An abyssal canyon opened beneath Kay and Isobel's feet. They fell. The expansive sky became a thin streak of blue, bordered by two endless walls of red earth. The darkness was lit only by the flames from Kay's hands and feet.

They plummeted deeper, descending into the bottomless chasm. The walls raced past, two smudges of brown and crimson. The crack above them began to close. The walls drew near.

Isobel surged esht into her back. She released her staff and dove for Kay. She flew closer and closer, pulling herself with double the earth's gravity. Kay screamed and flailed her arms, reaching for something, anything she could grasp.

Isobel crashed into Kay and wrapped her in a tight embrace. She felt the heat of Kay's flames around her, burning her clothes, singeing holes in the billowing fabric.

Isobel spun and faced directly upwards. The sky was barely visible above, a thin filament of blue against an endless void of black.

She shouted. "Homvelcht tor vrefden iv gra tor vrefden hasa solstari!"

Everything went dark. There was no sky. No light. Only silence and void.

The world bloomed around them as they reappeared on the surface. They tumbled on the ground and gasped. Isobel rolled to her back and opened her hand above her, summoning her staff.

"Extinguish!" The flames that ate at her shirt and trousers puffed out.

She groaned and dropped her staff. Patches of her skin along her arms and sides stung. They stuck to her clothes, scratching and scraping against the tattered threads. She touched one of the wounds, triggering a wave of intense agony.

Tears welled in her eyes. The pain was overwhelming, screaming, deluging her senses with incessant heat. Her breaths became short and shallow. She closed her eyes tightly.

"Isobel!"

Isobel shook. Something cold pressed against her lips.

"Isobel!" Kay's voice called. "You're burned! Drink! Now!"

Isobel opened her mouth, and a thick liquid poured down her throat. It was viscous and sweet, with a slightly bitter aftertaste. The burning sensation subsided. She opened her eyes.

Kay knelt beside her, holding an empty potion flask in her hand. She smiled softly.

A shadow loomed behind, the dark silhouette of muscular shoulders and tattered robes.

"Kay!" Isobel reached out her hand.

Fingers wrapped around Kay's throat. She was plucked from the ground, hurled to the side like a doll in a child's hand. She hit the dirt and screamed. The Archmage loomed above Isobel and glowered down at her. His hands opened like gnarled claws as he prepared to strike.

Chinelo ran alongside Joanne. The beast had lost interest in their assault, ambling towards the city, crushing anything in its way beneath its heavy feet. Chinelo looked ahead at the thin strip of field that remained between them and the city wall. They were running out of time.

"Chinelo! How do we distract this thing?" Joanne panted.

Chinelo shook his head. "I don't know! From what I've learned, their vision is based on esht flow, but with all the people in that city, I don't see how we can pull it away."

"Bah! We're never going to topple it in time at this rate."

Chinelo heard a faint thudding, the sound of hooves on grass.

"Joanne! Chinelo!" Valyx called from behind them, riding atop his horse with another following close. "Hop on!"

Chinelo sheathed his sword and leapt into the horse's empty saddle. He caught Joanne's outstretched hand and pulled her up behind him. She wrapped her arms around him and pressed against his back. With a quick kick, he spurred the horse into a gallop.

They cut through the fields, moving like the wind. The god lumbered ahead, dragging its stone sword through the ground behind it.

"Hold on tight, friend!" Joanne shouted.

Chinelo glanced down. The spell-cores in her gauntlets glowed.

"Rally!" Joanne said from behind.

Chinelo's body grew light. His aching muscles felt limber and fresh. The horse lurched forward, covering more and more ground with each stride. It moved faster than a cheetah, puffing smoke from its nostrils with every breath. Valyx's steed fell back. They circled in front of the monster, running through rows of crops and leaping over irrigation trenches.

"Joanne!" Chinelo turned his head. "Is that spell Isobel painted on your legs still intact?"

"Should be!" Joanne shouted.

"Get ready to use it!"

Chinelo veered the horse around the beast's side, leaving a wide gap between them and the massive sword. He pulled back on the reigns and the horse dug its hooves into the ground, grinding to a halt.

"Off!" Chinelo jumped down. Joanne landed behind him.

"Sorry to do this without warning."

"What?" Joanne cocked her head.

Chinelo swept her off her feet, supporting her back and legs in his arms.

"Ah!" Joanne flailed and grabbed onto his shoulders.

Chinelo gritted his teeth and crouched, channeling strength.

"Xastra gariasheq tor vrefden iv py tor vrefden hasa."

Chinelo became weightless and pushed. They launched, soaring over the monster's sword. As his feet crossed the blade, Chinelo released his esht and diverted it into his ankles, pointing them directly at the chitinous shell on the beast's calf. He plummeted and landed with a crash.

"Now!" Chinelo shouted, releasing Joanne.

She stood beside him, looking around in wonder as they stood sideways on the monster's leg.

"Well. This is certainly something," she chuckled and cracked her knuckles.

Chinelo ran up the beast's leg, stopping below the knee. He drew his sword and held it above the tendon's hardened exterior, nodding towards the carapace that coated the creature's tendons.

Joanne's fist slammed into the thick shell, cracking it. She punched it again and again, sending chunks of the exoskeleton flying.

Joanne dug her fingers into the growing crack and yelled, tearing the shell asunder. "Got it!" She moved out of the way and Chinelo slashed, cutting the tendon.

The creature roared from its mouthless throat. Its leg buckled. The beast fell.

"Keep it busy!" Chinelo shouted. He leapt from the creature's leg to the ground and sprinted to the sword, racing toward its glowing core.

"You got it, boss!" Joanne vaulted and ran up the creature's leg until she reached its back.

Chinelo bounded over clay chunks and stone shards. He reached the blade's edge. It had been driven into the ground at an angle, and with the spell on his ankles, he could run up the flat surface.

Chinelo pressed his feet against the sword. His gravity shifted. He ran, pounding his feet against the weathered blade. The core burned ahead. It was almost within reach. He twirled his blade and prepared to strike.

Far ahead, the monster's hand gripped the sword handle tighter. Its arm lurched, shaking the blade on which Chinelo stood. He continued, regaining his balance.

The sword lifted. Chinelo crouched. The sword raised. Chinelo crawled. The sword swung. Chinelo slammed into the earth.

He rolled across the red dirt until he stopped in a limp heap. The creature rose again, towering above him. It moved its head and stared down at him with its eyeless gaze. The tendrils on its back moved behind it, bending like seaweed in the tides.

Chinelo coughed. Everything hurt. His back. His sides. His arms. His head. He clenched his fist and forced himself to stand.

The Archmage stomped on Isobel's chest, forcing the air from her lungs. She surged esht into her side, activating her protection spell. She stretched her fingers toward her staff, brushing them along its wooden shaft, but it refused to budge. The Archmage crouched down, with one knee on the ground and one boot pushing down on her.

"Look at you," he sneered. "Completely helpless in the face of true mastery of magecraft."

He snapped his fingers. His hand shot down and clamped around her throat, driving the edges of his many metal rings into her skin. Isobel felt her esht drain, siphoned into his iron grip. He grinned, flashing his crooked teeth beneath his thick silver mustache.

"Here we are again, little witch," Harlyle chuckled. "Your dear big sister isn't here to interfere this time."

Isobel's eyes widened.

"She's so troublesome," the Archmage continued and adjusted his grip. "Always ruining things. Always so temperamental. I can see she passed some of that to you. It's a shame you didn't inherit those lovely dark tresses of hers, though I suppose you may not be blood. The Red Coven has such barbaric traditions when it comes to rearing children."

Pressure filled Isobel's head. The edges of her vision distorted and blurred. Something moved in her peripheral vision, a swish of golden locks. Kay pounded her fists against the Archmage's shoulder.

"Let her go!"

He swatted her away with a flick of his hand. He opened it, and Kay suddenly stopped moving. She froze in place, with one arm raised in front of her. Her eyes darted around wildly.

"Quiet! I'll have you watch this." He glared at Kay then turned his gaze back to Isobel. "I'll admit I am moderately impressed by both of you. Using potions as improvised spell-cores was clever, though ultimately limited. I tried that myself many decades ago but never could hone it as you have."

Isobel slammed her fists into his arm. Her head pounded. It was the same as before. She was weak. She was helpless. Her esht refused to muster. Her soul refused to obey.

"Oh! Your eyes are going bloodshot," the Archmage cackled. "This is my favorite part. I like to make this last. It's an art, like magic. It requires the proper balance of pressure and finesse. Watch closely, Kay. I believe that's the name she called you. See how the color of her cheeks has changed? See how her lips quiver so delicately? See how the veins grow more defined? See how—oh?"

The Archmage looked up, gazing past Isobel's head. His grip loosened slightly. She rasped a small, shallow breath as a noise sounded from behind her.

"Croak."

The Archmage raised an eyebrow.

Mort!

Isobel reached her hand above her. She felt a fleshy, bulbous mass land in her palm. She squeezed it and forced it into the Archmage's chest. Mort wrapped his frog feet around her fingers, scowling at the mage above him. Esht flowed into her hand. With what little air she had, she whispered two words.

"Awge... gariasheq..."

The Archmage's eyes grew wide. He hurtled upwards, falling into the sky above. He grew smaller and smaller, plummeting towards an endless blue abyss.

Isobel gasped. She crawled to her feet and placed Mort on her shoulder. His esht flowed into Isobel's body, alleviating the fatigue that plagued her. She snatched her staff and slammed it against the ground, shouting a command.

"Bloom!"

The ground cracked. A garden of metal spikes sprouted, pointing to the sky with their sharpened tips. She stumbled back and released her esht. Her leg buckled, but she was caught by a hand under her arm, Kay's hand.

A speck appeared above her. It tumbled and spun, plummeting towards the spikes below. The descending figure of the Archmage accelerated, falling faster, faster, faster. He became a line of red, a crimson meteor, and with a horrific tearing crash, his body was impaled on the spikes below.

Isobel fell to her knees, breathing heavily.

Mort nestled against her cheek, caressing her with his slimy frog face.

"Thank you, my friend." She stroked his back. "Thank you so much."

Kay panted beside her. She shoved her arms under Isobel's and hugged her tightly.

"It's over," Kay exhaled. "It's finally over."

Isobel nodded. "Are you hurt?"

Kay squeezed tighter and shook her head. "Not much. And you?"

Isobel's throat ached, a reminder of her defeat so many months before. "It's nothing I haven't had before."

Kay released her and began pulling vials from the belts around her legs. "Well, I have some elixirs that should fix you right up, though the burns may leave some scars."

Isobel nodded and breathed heavily. She turned her head towards the spikes she had summoned. They were stained red, splattered with the Archmage's blood. His body slumped around one of the spikes, driven halfway down the metal shaft by the force of his fall. His head lolled to the side, staring with lifeless amber eyes.

CHAPTER 52

JOANNE HELD ONTO THE CREATURE'S BACK, digging her fingers into the sunken clefts of the skin that clung to its ribs. Black tendrils writhed beside her. She had managed to tear several from their roots before the monster stood, but they had quickly regrown.

Her legs stung. The creature had slashed at her feet, rather inconveniently damaging the gravity tattoos about her ankles and tearing her boots to shreds. She looked up. The shoulder was just out of reach. If she could climb to that point, she might be able to help Chinelo in some way, wherever he might be.

The creature's skin bulged above her. Another tendril sprouted, wriggling as it grew to match the others' lengths. Joanne gritted her teeth. If she could get to the base of it, she might have enough footing to reach the shoulder.

She tensed her arms and legs. Her muscles grew taut. With a determined yell, she pushed off the creature's ribs and jumped. Her chest slammed into the base of the tendril, and she flung her arms over it. Her feet dangled in the open air. She pushed, hauling herself onto the mass of moving flesh. Kicking her leg over the side, she hoisted herself to a crouching position.

The tendril lurched. It had sensed her. It curled back on itself, reaching for her, erupting with small spikes. Joanne surged esht into her gauntlets.

"Strength!"

She jumped, leaping high over the squirming appendage. The creature's oily skin rippled below, reflecting the light of the sun in a ring of distorted colors. Joanne landed and steadied herself on the monster's shoulder. To her right, the monster's enormous stone face moved, scanning the ground below.

Joanne looked down. A tiny figure scurried before the monster's feet, shooting fire from a sparkling sword. Chinelo still lived.

Her gaze shifted. They were nearing Veld's wall, and members of the city garrison were lining the battlements. The monster twisted as it reached across its body to grip its sword with both hands. Its muscles grew, and it lifted the heavy blade above its head. Joanne gasped. It was going to swing at the wall.

She whispered a command.

"Geyser."

She clenched her fist, forcing esht through it to fuel the spell. Air rushed before her fist, accumulating vapor in a dense cloud. Joanne felt the humidity drain from around her, focusing into a single point just beyond her knuckles.

The defiled god groaned and turned its head.

"Hey! Ugly!" Joanne yelled. She ran towards the monster's head, pulling back her arm to strike. The focused mass of vapor grew, accumulating more pressurized steam.

The monster roared, blasting its putrid breath at her. Joanne coughed but continued running. She dug her boots into its skin, then jumped, soaring towards the creature's faceless stone head.

She opened her mouth and let out a vicious, piercing yell. She swung, putting her entire being behind a single, cataclysmic punch. Her knuckles collided with the creature's head, and she released her esht.

The accumulated vapor erupted, exploding like a raging volcano. It cut through the stone, bursting in a jet of steam on the other side of the creature's head. Jagged cracks spread from the point of impact up and down the monster's face. Shattered stone shards and chunks flew as the monster screamed, unleashing a mass of tendrils from its neck to catch the falling fragments. It stumbled back, staggering away from the city.

Joanne plummeted, looking up at the sky above. So, that was it. It had not been much, but perhaps she had accomplished something. Perhaps Chinelo could slay the beast. Or perhaps it had all been futile.

As the wind rushed past her ears, a thought crossed her mind. She had not hugged Kay that morning. She had not told her she loved her. In their rush to find the obelisk, she had completely forgotten.

She wasn't ready. Not yet. Not yet! She had more she wanted to do. She had more she wanted to say. She had to see her one last time. She had to...

Something struck Joanne's side. Slender arms wrapped around her, and the direction of her motion shifted.

"I've got you!" Isobel shouted, ascending to the wall.

"Isobel?"

They landed on the top of the battlement, collapsing in a small heap. Isobel pulled Joanne to her feet.

"Are you hurt?" Isobel asked, scanning Joanne's body for any injuries.

Joanne scratched her head. "Only a little. I'm fine, thanks to you. Kind of thought I was done for back there."

Isobel turned. "Not yet. Sorry, I have to go finish that thing. It's gotten too close to the city."

"Wait!" Joanne called.

Isobel looked over her shoulder.

"Where is Kay? Is she all right?"

Isobel smiled. "She's a bit tired, but otherwise fine."

Joanne sighed. "Good. Now go! I'll make myself useful here."

Isobel nodded and shot off towards the staggered titan. Joanne leaned over the wall. The beast regained its footing and pulled its sword up from the crater created by its fall. Its stone head was shattered on the left side, and the fallen shards were loosely held in place by a web of inky black tendrils. Two specks raced across the ground, one with a shining sword and another flashing with lightning.

Joanne smiled. Kay continued to fight.

She let out a deep breath and turned. Several guards leaned over the parapets, shaking in their armor. She cracked her neck and searched for any indication of commanding rank. A purple plume caught her attention, the plume of a captain's helmet. *Time to get to work.*

Chinelo ran in a limping gait. He had hit the ground hard, and his left knee ached and grinded with every move.

A bolt of lightning rushed past, stopping beneath the monsters' feet. Kay's hands sparked and crackled, and with a few short gestures, she sent out a storm of thunderbolts that chained up the beast's legs. She evaded its stomps, continuing her assault from the other side.

Chinelo muttered an incantation and canceled his gravity. With a groan he jumped, floating up towards the monster's torso with his sword outstretched. It batted him away with its arm, sending him hurtling to the ground where he landed with a loud thud. His shoulder cracked and popped, adding another dull pain to the growing collection.

Chinelo groaned and rolled to his stomach. He pushed off the ground to a kneeling position and looked up. The monster was stomping its feet, trying to snuff out Kay's lightning.

He heard a swish beside him. A hand touched his shoulder.

"Hey," Isobel said. "Are you all right?"

Chinelo let out a relieved sigh and stood. "Oh, thank the Creator you're not hurt."

Isobel smiled. "What are we dealing with here?"

Chinelo rubbed his knee. "It's much more adaptable than the others. It heals too quick, and its core is difficult to reach."

"I should be able to help there," Isobel said. "Has it used any spells?"

Chinelo shook his head. "No—at least—I don't think so."

Isobel nodded. "That's a bit worrying. I'll try to get to its core before it can."

"I'll back you up from the ground. Go. Stay safe!"

Isobel kissed his cheek then sprung into the sky. Chinelo watched as she flew toward the creature. Its head jerked up, tracking her movements. It clawed at her, trying to catch her. Lights shot from her, flying towards the sword but ultimately missing the core.

Chinelo sighed. He really should have agreed to using her flight spell, despite the accompanying motion sickness. He grunted and ran to join Kay at the monster's feet. If he could topple it one more time, that would likely be enough of an opportunity for Isobel to strike. And, if he was unable to bring it down, then he could at least distract it, just as he had for the god of Ata.

Isobel weaved around the monster's swiping hand. Every time she approached its sword, it reached for her. She needed to do something about that arm. She changed directions and dove for its shoulder.

Isobel swung her sword from over her head and cleaved through the monster's shoulder with enhanced strength. The flesh tore. The bone shattered. Sinew and fiber snapped. However, the work was not done. The arm still dangled from a few remaining strands of tissue. Isobel dispelled her blade and pointed her staff at the arm.

"Drop!"

The creature's arm lurched downwards. It plummeted, tearing the final strands asunder and crashing into the earth far below. The monster let out a deafening bellow, and dozens of tendrils sprung from its wound and raced towards her. Isobel shifted her gravity, falling sideways and twisting to face the sword. Without its arm, she would be able to reach the core!

It roared. Isobel halted. Something was different about its voice. She squinted. The sword was glowing, lit by a grid of orange lines that flowed from its pulsing core. Her eyes widened. It was using a spell. But what was it? Where was it?

A shadow spread over the ground, growing larger and larger. She looked up and gasped.

A falling star, a massive blazing stone, broke through the clouds. The meteor, poised to destroy all that was below, plummeted in a cloud of black smoke that mixed with the puffy white clouds.

Isobel's heart siezed. If that meteor struck, Veld would not survive. Her mind raced. She had to stop it. If she couldn't, she at least needed to redirect it or disperse it. But how?

She surged her esht and flew towards the falling star, passing through a layer of clouds. The air grew thin. The ground grew faint below. The city looked so tiny. The meteor looked so oppressively massive.

She pointed her staff ahead and drew near to the meteor, shouting a command.

"Nullify!"

Her staff sent out a shockwave that washed over the enormous ember. Nothing happened.

Isobel felt lightheaded. It hadn't worked. She had felt the esht drain, but the spell did nothing. Why? If it was conjured by magic, the meteor would have vanished. It *should* have vanished.

Unless...

It was not conjured by magic. If it had been summoned or re-positioned from the heavens, her spell would have done nothing. Isobel descended beside the dark comet. The air was hot, almost unbearably so. She looked around, surveying the land below. Could she redirect the meteor? Was there anywhere it could land without causing harm?

The sun reflected off the lake to the north. There! She could send it there!

Isobel circled around the stone and moved closer, extending her hand to it. She focused her senses on the heat in her palm and shouted an incantation.

"Homvelcht solstari!"

She pushed her esht through her palm. She had to give it enough. Too much esht and the meteor would overshoot the lake. Too little and it would hit the farmlands. She expelled her esht.

The meteor vanished and reappeared over the lake. She had done it. Isobel looked down. The ground was rushing towards her. She surged esht into her chest, vanishing and reappearing a short distance below. She had lost all of her momentum, and she hovered above the city.

The beast charged towards the wall, dragging its blade behind it with its one remaining arm. It whirled around, slamming the blade into the battlements, sending entire sections of the buildings crashing into the town.

She prepared to dive but hesitated. The core pulsed again, and three more meteors appeared in the atmosphere above her.

"Oh, come on!" she shouted. With an exasperated groan, she flew high into the sky to stop the blazing stones.

The earth shattered. Masses of grassy clay and shards of dull stone flew as the beast's blade cut through the ground before slamming into the Veld's wall. A jagged crack ran from the top of the wall down into a pile of broken stone blocks. The monster had breached Veld's outer defense.

Chinelo ran from the avalanche. He looked over his shoulder. The beast raised its sword over its head and sprouted another arm from the wound on its shoulder, forming muscles around the newly coalesced bone. Then, with an enraged roar, the monster brought its sword down upon the wall again, breaking off more of the stone structure.

Chinelo stopped and panted. His entire body ached, with more concentrated pains burning in his legs, shoulder, and ribs. He wiped the sweat from his brow and looked up. A small figure darted across the sky, flying from falling star to falling star before making them vanish. Isobel defended the city from above, though, without her assistance, they were no closer to landing a killing blow on the core.

Kay ran beside him and stopped, bending over to catch her breath. Mort clung onto her shoulder, scowling at the massive beast.

"How are we supposed to stop this thing?" Kay said between heavy breaths.

Chinelo frowned grimly. "I—I don't know. I'm so... tired."

Kay shoved a potion into his hand. "Drink. It's not much, but it should help. Just don't waste it."

Chinelo nodded and downed the vial's contents. He felt his esht-fatigue fade as a wellspring of energy accumulated beneath his heart. He squinted and watched the monster closely. Armored soldiers began to pour from the crack in the wall, poking and prodding at the beast's feet with their swords and spears.

The monster raised its sword again and slammed it down, shaking the earth. Chinelo squinted. Those movements. So forceful, so focused. It was like...

He gasped. It was like god was angry. The first creature they awakened was wild and feral. The second was cold and deliberate. The third was cowardly and cunning. This one was a being of wrath, a being of hatred.

"We have to pull it away somehow," Kay said. "How do we get its attention?"

Chinelo shook his head. "We would need a large esht source, one that's more concentrated than what's in the city."

"That's going to be difficult," Kay frowned.

The ground shook again, droning in a deep rumble. A low growl sounded from behind them, growing into a roar of a multitude of shouting voices. Kay and Chinelo whirled around. Far behind them, an army of soldiers charged on horseback, and at their head rode a ruddy, red-haired figure and an imposing man in golden armor.

"Valyx!" Kay said. "He rallied the duke's garrison!"

The garrison split and followed behind the duke's regal lead, flowing around them towards the monster. Valyx stopped his horse and looked down at them, grinning proudly.

"Thought you could use a few extra hands," Valyx said.

"You could say that," Kay said with a fond smile.

Chinelo's mind raced. How could they distract it? How could they amass enough esht to attract its gaze? He gasped.

"Kay! Can you siphon esht?" Chinelo looked up.

"Of course," Kay raised an eyebrow. "It will leak out of me pretty quickly, though. I don't have the reserves that you do."

"Could you accumulate it in some kind of object?"

"Probably. Why?"

Chinelo touched his chin. "There are hundreds of soldiers here. That should hopefully be enough. It has to be."

The shadow of a meteor appeared above them but quickly vanished.

"Siphon the esht from those soldiers and amass it into... something."

"I understand, but that will be very painful for them."

"Do it! This is our chance! Valyx!" Chinelo ordered. "Take Kay with you. Once she's got enough esht gathered, ride west as fast as you can! Don't stop until it falls."

"Got it!"

Chinelo gripped his sword. "I'll handle the rest. Go!"

Valyx pulled Kay up behind him. As they rode off, Mort leapt from Kay's shoulder and landed before Chinelo, looking up at him with pleading eyes.

"Let's finish this, my friend," Chinelo said, scooping the frog up and placing him on his shoulder. He turned to face the monster one final time.

Kay clung to Valyx, bouncing on the horse's back as it galloped over the fields. She clutched a stone in her hand, pressing its rough surface into her palm. The soldiers raged around them, riding towards the monster with outstretched spears. It turned to face them and swung its sword across the ground, sending riders and steeds flying. Kay winced.

"I'm sorry, but this will hurt!"

She began an incantation, muttering beneath her breath. She stitched the words together, building the spell as Chinelo directed.

"Klashadde esht vo gra gest iv axxave diaa dagas."

Valyx groaned. His horse whinnied. The army roared. Kay felt it, the esht flowing into her. It moved through her body, overwhelming her senses as it focused into the stone she held. She pushed more, more, more!

The beast looked up. It screeched and lurched for them, raising its sword above its head.

"Valyx! West!" Kay shouted. Their work was done. All that was left was for them to survive.

Chinelo ran. The beast's blade was poised above, clenched in its gnarled fist at the end of its outstretched arm. He sprang over the raging tumult and landed on a shard of the fallen wall. He gripped his sword's handle tightly, focusing all his esht into it. A steady stream flowed from Mort's perch on his shoulder, mixing with his own energy to empower his strike.

The world seemed to halt, waiting with bated breath for his next move. The sun shone above. The wind rippled along the grass. Water flooded from the lake, overflowing as more meteors filled it. Hooves pounded. Soldiers roared. Swords slashed.

Chinelo yelled.

"Project!"

His sword flashed forth, swinging in a blinding slice that sent a wave of distorted air flying up until it cleaved through the monster's arm.

The cut was incomplete, but the sheer weight of the enormous blade tore the limb in half. The sword fell and stabbed into the ground, rocking the earth beneath Chinelo's feet.

The monster screeched. It stumbled forward, reaching for its weapon.

A figure shot from the top of the wall. Long brown hair streamed behind it. Joanne had reappeared.

She punched the beast's face, cracking the right half of the stone symbol that was its head. It fell back, landing with a splash in the flood of water from the lake. The army tore it apart.

Joanne landed and shouted to Chinelo. "Go!"

Chinelo nodded and leapt for the fallen blade. He forced esht into his ankles, running up the side until he reached the core. It lay before him, swirling and churning with radiant orange mist. He adjusted his grip on his broadsword, holding it with both hands. Then, with a deep breath, he plunged his blade into the core.

It exploded, wrapping him in an eruption of orange vapor. Words and symbols flowed into his mind, knowledge of space and stars, of celestial bodies and crashing comets, of meteors and matter.

As he fell, losing connection with the world, a word echoed through him, reverberating through every bone.

"OZH!"

CHAPTER 53

ISOBEL WATCHED THE FINAL METEOR SHATTER as it collided with the growing pile in Veld's northern lake, now overflowing. The fields shone, reflecting the golden sun with a flood of water that spread across the land.

Far below, she heard a piercing shriek. The beast was down, and its body was covered in a swarm of soldiers picking it apart like ants. She saw a puff of orange mist, and the god suddenly shriveled, melting and disintegrating until only its shattered head remained. Isobel let out a relieved sigh. They had won. The god was slain.

She was exhausted. The strain of constant magic plagued her muscles, and though she had recovered much of her esht with the help of Kay's elixirs, little remained.

She floated down, descending towards the city to finally rest. She felt heavy. Even with her control of gravity, something seemed to pull her towards the earth. Something seemed to tug at every member of her body. A growing weight or an overwhelming weariness—either felt possible.

She was tired. Maybe if she just sat down for a moment...

Chinelo exhaled. Everything was so dark, so peaceful. He could stay there forever, finally resting in gentle slumber. He could remain, dreaming of wind and starlight.

Something hard dug into his back. His legs and feet were wet. A strong light tried to filter through his closed eyelids. His shoulders and hips ached. Noises. Rattling armor. Splashing footsteps. Murmuring voices.

A shout.

"Chinelo!" Kay's voice reached his ears. His eyes flew open.

Kay pulled Chinelo to his feet, supporting his arm with Mort on her shoulder. Valyx slipped under his other arm.

Chinelo groaned. His legs throbbed with dull pains that lingered at numerous points along his thighs and hips.

"What's happening?" Chinelo asked.

Kay dragged him toward the wall. Her face was as white as snow and her eyes were wild, bearing the ferocious terror of a fleeing animal. "We have to run. She's here!" The timber of her voice shook in a petrified vibrato.

"What? Who?" Chinelo hobbled up the pile of shattered stone, stubbing his toes against the rough, jagged edges.

"Iva," Joanne exhaled, following close behind. While her inflections lacked the intense dread present in Kay's, her tension was unmistakable.

Chinelo looked over his shoulder. Iva stood in the shimmering flooded field. Her faded green cloak and thick dark hair rippled in the wind, matching the motions of the grass behind her. The small army of soldiers separated her from the wall.

"I need you to hand that man over to me, Duke Kashta," Iva asserted. "I believe I detailed the threat he poses to your city in my letter."

The sun sparkled from the duke's gilded gauntlet as he waved his hand in dismissal.

"You will have to forgive me, Lady Iva, if I do not fully accept the veracity of your message. With my own eyes I witnessed him defending my city. I will not disgrace him by denying him the honor he deserves."

Iva frowned. "The Archmage has ordered his arrest and execution."

"Do not act under the delusion that I accept the Archmage's word as law," the duke responded. "I have allowed him to advise me, on occasion, but he is neither king nor of royal blood. His rank has been earned, but his influence means little in Veld. We are our own city."

Iva clenched her fist.

"Make no mistake," the duke continued, "I recognize his authority, but I know its proper place. You are not the Archmage. Your counsel means even less to me than his does. As far as I am concerned you are merely his attendant, and an attendant to an honorary noble is nothing to me."

The duke motioned with his hand. Two of the armored warriors pointed their spears at Iva.

"If you wish to continue staying in my city," the duke rumbled, "then do not disrespect me again."

Iva tensed. Her muscles grew taut. The veins in her forearms bulged as her blood coursed through her.

"Make no mistake, duke," Iva growled, "I am not offering you counsel. I am not offering you advice. That man is leaving with me. I will make no threats. I will only state the truth. If you impede me..." Iva removed her blindfold and tossed it aside. "Then you are merely an obstacle." She touched her left middle finger to her thumb.

"Run," Joanne exhaled.

"Such insolence." The duke reached for his sword. "I will not tol—"

Crunching! Cracking!

The duke's armor collapsed, compressing in on itself with him inside, pulling his arms and legs within the rapidly shrinking mass of gilded steel. The bones in his limbs shattered as they were drawn inwards. With a horrific pop, his neck broke, and his head flattened. He folded into a tiny sphere, compressed by an invisible pressure. Then, the sphere exploded into a horrendous eruption of red, leaving no skeleton behind. It happened in an instant. One moment he stood, leading his company of soldiers. The next he was gone, vanishing into an eruption of gore and a shower of blood.

Chinelo recoiled in pure horror. Iva exhaled then turned her head, glaring directly at him. A hush fell. Chinelo, his companions, and the army all stood in silence, petrified at the carnage that Iva had wrought.

With a sudden roar, the company of knights rushed upon Iva.

Joanne shoved Chinelo, Kay, and Valyx through the crack in the wall. "Get out of here! I'll handle this."

"Joanne!" Kay pleaded. "Don't—"

"Find Isobel! Leave Veld!" Joanne shouted. "Go!"

Chinelo shook free from Valyx and reached for his sword. He stumbled. His legs gave out.

"RUN!" Joanne yelled. "You don't stand a chance against her."

"And you do?" Kay stepped forward.

"Those soldiers are going to die, Kay. I—I can't let that happen."

Joanne reached for her mask and smiled. "I love you, Kay. Valyx, keep her safe. Chinelo, give Isobel my regards." She pulled her mask over her face and leapt from the crack, disappearing to the other side and leaving a cloud of thick mist behind.

Joanne cracked her neck. The battlefield ahead of her was grisly. It was just like two years before. Iva's merciless ferocity was unstoppable.

The witch struck with spell and blade, effortlessly avoiding the many sword swings of the enraged soldiers before stabbing her curved dagger between the plates of their armor. One fell, then another, then another.

She thrust her blade into an unfortunate soldier's neck, then slung him into the crowd. Another leapt with a descending slash. Iva flowed like wind around the blade before shooting the man a blood-chilling glare. He exploded into a fountain of crimson, just as the duke had.

Iva's gaze darted around the crowd, and one by one the closest line of combatants vanished, replaced only by a sickening flood of red that mixed with the water at their feet. Her opponents hesitated, shocked by the sight they had witnessed. Iva did not allow them time to breathe.

She motioned with her left hand, and a hole tore through the bodies of the soldiers in front of her, as if some great lance had pierced them. A man screamed and rushed at her. She raised her arm in defense, and the sword rang as it collided with it, singing with the sound of steel against iron.

She gestured again, and the soldier split into four pieces, sliced horizontally and vertically by an invisible force. Iva jumped over a thrusting spear from behind and spun in the air before cleaving her attacker's head from his body with single swing from her dagger.

Joanne leapt into the ankle-deep red water, splashing it against her boots. She needed to act. She needed to stop the massacre. Within seconds, scores of men had fallen against the storm of destruction that was the Red Coven's last Blade. She needed to strike. However, she first had to shroud herself from Iva's gaze.

"Scatter!" Joanne bellowed.

The men in front of her obeyed, responding to her command as if she was their new leader. Joanne sprinted, moving towards the ring of fallen corpses that surrounded Iva. She leapt and raised her fist, punching the ground as she landed.

"Mist!" Joanne shouted.

A fleeting moment of stillness passed. The water rippled around her knuckles. The men watched in fearful curiosity. Iva glared down at Joanne in surprise.

The entire field burst into a thick cloud of vapor. The water rose to the heavens in ephemeral wisps, eddying before Joanne's eyes. The sun reflected off the steam, creating a dazzling, blinding glow. Joanne closed her eyes and surged her esht into her mask.

Her senses screamed. So much information flooded into her mind. She felt everything. Breath flowing into the soldiers' lungs and releasing in terrified yells. Thundering footsteps of retreat. A playful breeze dispersing the northern reaches of the cloud. And ahead of her, Joanne felt Iva.

She was calm. Neither her breath nor her heart rate was elevated. Her left hand moved. The water clung to her fingers, alerting Joanne to their subtle motion. Iva's middle finger pressed against her thumb, forming a small circle. Her muscles tensed. Then, the mist in front of her rushed into a single point before exploding. Joanne winced. The motion was so quick, the sensation of it was almost overwhelming. She felt a scoff escape Iva's throat.

Joanne inhaled slowly, calming herself. She had a hunch, and it seemed she had been right. She was safe as long as she was within the mist. She rushed forward and whispered into her gauntlets.

"Strength."

Her muscles tensed, overflowing with vigor. She clenched her fist and slammed it into Iva's chest. Iva gasped and reeled. Joanne pushed forward and swung again, crashing her gauntlet into Iva's face.

The hair on Joanne's neck stood on end. She felt something moving towards her, a separation in the mist, a slipstream flowing around a curved blade that left vortices behind. Joanne stepped back as Iva's dagger slashed for her gut.

Joanne countered with another attack, pummeling Iva's side. The blade moved again, swinging diagonally downwards. Joanne raised her fist and deflected the blow with her plated gauntlet.

Joanne surged her esht, increasing the force behind her blows. Her fists sent shockwaves through the mist as they collided with Iva's unyielding body, creating wispy rings of fog that sharpened her senses.

She frowned. One of her enhanced punches was normally enough to incapacitate even the hardiest of men. But somehow, Iva managed to take them without faltering. Her bones did not break. Her body did not stagger. Her blood did not spill.

Iva's fingers moved. She directed her gaze in Joanne's direction, and she contorted her hand into a new gesture. Her index finger formed a loop with her thumb, and her muscles tensed.

Joanne ducked. The vapor above her tore apart, separating around a circular void. It was as if Iva had summoned an enormous spike that pierced the mist, violently tearing through anything ahead of her. Joanne delivered a powerful uppercut, lifting Iva off her feet, then scurried away.

Iva rose from the ground and shook the blood from her gloves. Joanne felt it splatter across the ground, catching and mixing with the tiny droplets of suspended moisture as it fell. Iva inhaled a deep breath. Her throat formed syllables that flowed into her words.

"I'm impressed, Joanne. I always wondered why my mother picked you as her aide. I always wondered why she fawned over you while she hated me. I think I understand now."

Joanne circled around her warily. Shrouded by the brilliant mist, Iva would not be able to predict her attacks if she was quiet enough.

Iva whirled around and repeated her previous gesture. Joanne gasped and ducked. The mist was once again pierced above her.

How? Had she made a noise? The mist was still thick. Iva should not have been able to see her. Joanne gritted her teeth and pounced forward. She needed to end things quickly. Iva was adapting to her typical methods quickly. Far too quickly.

Chinelo's feet pounded against the pavement as he hobbled alongside Valyx with Mort clinging onto his shoulder. Valyx pulled Kay behind him, guiding her through the streets. She tore her hand away.

"Kay!" Valyx shouted. "We need to go!"

"Shut up!" Kay snapped. "I can't leave her."

She reached for one of her pouches, pulling out empty vial after empty vial. She tossed them aside, shattering them against the cobblestones.

"There's got to be something left..." Kay continued searching. "Something... anything..."

"Kay!" Valyx placed both hands on her shoulders. "You heard what she said. Remember what happened at your coven? Remember Iva did?"

Kay clutched one final vial in her hand. The thick elixir inside faintly glowed. She pulled off the stopper and looked at Valyx defiantly.

"Please, Kay. We can't fight her." Valyx pleaded.

"You can't. *I* can!"

"Kay! You can't even use magic properly. What happens when that potion runs out? What happens when your esht runs out? What happens when—"

"Valyx!" Chinelo placed his hand on Valyx's shoulder. "Enough."

Valyx closed his mouth. He sighed. "Kay, please. I just want you to be safe."

Kay glared at him. Her eyes darted back and forth between him and Chinelo. She lowered the vial and returned the stopper to its place. "Once we find Isobel, we're going back."

Valyx nodded. "I saw her above the southwest gate before the beast fell. Let's head there."

Joanne drove her fist into Iva's gut. Iva's body was like iron. Her skin was like steel. Joanne felt the vibration of the impact ricochet up her arm into her shoulder. Her knuckles ached. Her fingers hurt to move. She had pummeled Iva again and again, but she showed no signs of injury. Not a drop of Iva's blood could be felt in the mist, and the haze itself had gone fuzzy, slowly spreading and thinning in the midday sun.

Joanne dashed towards Iva's position, pulling her arm back to deliver another devastating punch. Iva looked her direction and gestured with her hand. Joanne's body moved on its own, driven by pure fear and instinct to survive. She weaved to the side as another void appeared in the mist, tearing a shaft of empty space that grazed Joanne's arm. She screamed.

The pain radiated from the wound, a grisly laceration just below her elbow. It burned, branding itself into her senses. Joanne felt lightheaded. Her stomach twisted within.

"Belekt fulrech!" Iva shouted. The mist retreated, rushing away from her like the falling tide. Joanne's senses went silent. Without vapor in the air, her mask would no longer guide her. She was exposed.

Joanne opened her eyes to see Iva raising her hand, pressing her middle finger into her thumb. Joanne opened her hand and shouted.

"Steam!"

A cloud of steam burst from her gauntlet, jetting in a highly pressurized stream toward Iva. The senses in Joanne's mask returned, though they were limited to the stream in front of her. She felt it crash into Iva, tearing at her skin and armor before spreading behind her in a billowing cone. Then, Iva vanished.

Joanne heart lurched. She hadn't even felt her move. How could she vanish so suddenly? She looked up. Iva descended upon her from high off the ground, swinging her blade towards Joanne's throat.

Joanne blocked, then punched. Iva landed on her toes, twisting and swinging her blade to the other side. Joanne countered. Her fist struck Iva's steel skin once again. She had to be using some kind of spell. Nobody was that resilient. That would explain her light armor. What use were heavy plates when her whole body could be reinforced? Still, if she was using a spell, she would eventually run out of esht.

Joanne tensed, raising her fists in front of her. She was in the open, yet Iva had abruptly shifted to using her curved dagger to attack. Joanne eyed her opponent. If she was running low on energy, then she would have to limit her spell usage, focusing on defense over offense. She was either getting close to breaking, or she was trying to trick Joanne into thinking she was. That uncertainty, that unpredictability, made her dangerous.

Joanne continued her assault, pummeling the air as Iva danced around her punches. Iva leapt back and slammed her foot into the ground. The earth shook, rumbling beneath Joanne's feet. Cracks formed around her, spouting clouds of dust as the ground tore.

Joanne felt a flicker in her lungs, a chill across her heart. She stumbled, and Iva capitalized on the opportunity, moving with cold efficiency. She stabbed Joanne's side, piercing through her leather armor. Her eyes flashed, and she tore her knife out in a bloody spray, swiping it through the side of Joanne's thigh. Joanne winced, gritting her teeth to focus. She could not waver. She could not falter.

She surged her esht and delivered a crashing punch into Iva's abdomen, sending her flying. Joanne clutched her side, pressing her hand over the wound to keep the hot blood from spilling forth. She rushed esht into her shoulders, sending out a cloud of dense vapor. She had to flee. She only hoped that she had bought the others enough time to find Isobel and escape.

Chinelo stumbled and fell as the street rocked beneath him. Stones cracked. Carts and stands around them clattered and crashed. Trees shook. Houses collapsed. Then, it stopped.

He pushed himself to stand, pressing his palms against the rough stone.

"What was that?" Valyx asked, pulling Kay back to her feet.

"An earthquake, I think," Kay panted.

Chinelo continued towards the southwest gate. Where was she? Where was Isobel? He looked overhead. She should have flown back by that point. She should have seen them. So, where was she? He shuddered. Had something happened?

He broke into a limping run, clamoring through the empty streets. They rounded a bend. In the distance, he saw green fields shining through openings in the southwest gate, though the portcullis was closed. In front of it, two silhouettes moved, one of which was quickly approaching.

Isobel crashed into Chinelo with a pained cry. They tumbled and rolled into a nearby fruit stand, shattering it and stopping in a shower of apple-berries.

Chinelo pressed his hand into Isobel's back, pushing her to a sitting position. Something hot and wet ran through his fingers. Blood. Her blood, spilling from a hideous gash across her back. Chinelo grabbed his sword hilt, surging esht into his spell-core.

"Heal!" he shouted. The wound closed.

Isobel groaned and wiped blood and sweat from her brow.

"He's still alive…" she whimpered.

Chinelo looked up. A man approached them, menacingly clutching a curved black scimitar. He wore no shirt, and his broad, muscular torso was inked with a complex network of tattoos that ran down his left arm and ended on his fingers. A large jagged scar marked his skin, starting just below his sternum and ending midway down his abdomen. His gray beard and hair were matted and ragged.

The Archmage's murderous eyes gleamed a deep amber.

CHAPTER 54

ISOBEL'S HANDS SHOOK. HOW WAS HE alive? She had killed him. She had seen him die, right in front of her. He had been impaled on a spike. There was even the scar to prove it. So how did he still live?

Kay muttered beneath her breath beside her. She fumbled with an elixir vial, dribbling some of the thick orange contents down her chin.

The Archmage raised his arms, holding them wide in a taunting gesture as he crossed the cracked street. "Are you not pleased to see me, witch? Are you frightened to see a dead man walking?"

Kay charged forwards, leaving behind flames with every step. Fire flashed from her feet and danced between her fingers. She became a blazing streak, zigzagging to her target until she pounced.

The Archmage swatted her away with a single swipe of his arm.

"Did you think I would die in this cave? Did you think I would perish before I saw the true sun?"

Isobel summoned her staff and pointed it at him. She forced her esht into her staff, and her fatigue intensified, growing stronger as her energy continued to deplete.

"Volley!"

Her conjured torrent of spikes diverted around the Archmage, flying away from him in a wide fan. He lumbered closer, stomping his heavy boots with every terrifying step.

"I will see it," he hissed. "I will witness its rise with my own eyes."

A loud yell rang from Isobel's side. Valyx rushed ahead, swinging a chunk of broken wood as a club. The Archmage sent him careening with another flick of his tattooed arm.

The Archmage scoffed. "Scum. Dross. Prisoners, blind to their shackles."

Chinelo stepped between Isobel and the Archmage, clutching his sword tightly. The Archmage stopped and sneered. Mort leapt from

Chinelo's shoulder and scurried behind Isobel, peering from the safety of her shadow.

"I am ill of this captivity," Harlyle snarled. "Yet you two would keep me bound. Scampering across the continent, stealing the lost runes, slaughtering my men, breaking my laws, denying my will, taking what is not rightfully yours! And worst of all, you've done it so, so slowly. You're like an itch, a rash. You disappear from one place and reappear somewhere else. Then just when I think I have you, you vanish, only to show up again, and again, and again!"

"You're a blight! You're a plague! And you, especially!" He pointed at Isobel. "Iva is obsessed with you! It's infuriating. Why she cares so much for you is beyond me. You distract her, and she isn't useful when she is distracted."

Kay charged again, clapping her hands to send raging spheres of fire towards the Archmage. They splashed to the ground, charring the cobblestones at his feet. He hit her with the flat of his sword, and she stumbled away into a nearby storefront. Her flames spread, lighting the fallen awning on fire.

"Extend!" Chinelo shouted as he swung his sword. A line cut through the wood of the surrounding buildings.

The Archmage jumped high then dove, propelled by burst of wind from behind him. He brought his sword down, and it collided with Chinelo's raised blade. They dueled, thrusting and parrying as Isobel watched. In her mind a plan came together. It was a simple one, but it had worked to incapacitate so many of the Archmage's men before. She circled around the storm of clashing blades.

Summoning what energy she had left, she uttered a command, just as the Archmage glanced in her direction.

"Shock!"

Her staff crackled. She gripped her weapon with both hands and planted her feet, driving all her strength into its swing.

The Archmage grinned and grabbed Chinelo's wrist, forcing him between them. Isobel's staff slammed into Chinelo's chest.

"NO!" Isobel screamed.

Chinelo's face contorted. His body convulsed, seizing from the spark of lightning Isobel had delivered. He fell limply to the ground.

The Archmage cackled. He twirled his blade and held it over Chinelo's back. His fingers tensed. His muscles formed lines along his shoulder and forearm, and with a cruel sneer, he drove the blade downwards. Isobel's world stopped.

Steel thudded against wood. She deflected the Archmage's blow, shattering the blade in the process. Her muscles tensed, moving on their own. She tried to stop her swing. She tried to regain her balance, but she stumbled and fell. Her arms and legs held their positions.

She couldn't move! Why couldn't she move? She focused, desperately trying to regain control as she lay on her back.

Move!

Her arms did not obey.

MOVE!

Her legs remained stiff.

The only things that would relent were her eyes. Her heart pounded. The Archmage stood above her, sneering down as he held his tattooed hand towards her.

"Lightning is a funny thing, isn't it, witch?" He crouched. "It's actually a specialty of my family, something I've tried to share with my fellow mages."

She trembled, but her arms and legs still refused to obey her screaming instincts to fight back.

"In Rothvale we have another name for lightning, or rather the contained version of it." The Archmage's crooked smile flashed above her. "We call it electricity, and you can do amazing things with it, if you have enough power. It's truly astounding."

He stooped closer. Isobel felt his hot breath against her cheeks. She shuddered. "The development is in its infancy, of course. I only recently discovered some of its uses. This one, however, has always been my favorite," he smirked. "Did you know that the human body is powered by lightning? Yes! Little, tiny sparks move your muscles. Think of it. Thousands of adorable little lightning strikes occur in your body every second, commanding your muscles to move. It's truly magnificent, and very easy to control with the right spell."

Isobel's eyes darted around. Her muscles could not move, but perhaps her esht could. She focused her attention on her chest, trying to drive her energy into the tattoo. Her muscles spasmed. Her entire body tingled.

Ignore it!

Her back ached from the wound she had received, a dull pain running from her right hip to just below her left shoulder blade.

Ignore it!

The pavement was rough against her skin.

Ignore it! Focus only on your chest! Drive the esht into it!

Her energy flowed. She winced, as the accompanying pain of overuse afflicted her.

The Archmage frowned. He moved his right hand, opening it.

Isobel expelled her esht, and she vanished, reappearing high above the street. She was free. Now, she only needed to activate her flight spell and she would be able to—

Her spell did not activate.

Her esht expelled through her back, but nothing happened. She plummeted. Her stomach rose, resisting the fall. She flailed her arms. Her back hit the ground. The wind left her lungs.

"Pathetic," the Archmage growled and kicked her in the side, rolling her onto her stomach. His heavy boot pressed down on her, digging into the scars on her back.

Why? Why didn't it activate? The tattoo was there. It always worked. The only reason it wouldn't was if it was broken.

The realization hit her.

The wound. It had broken the sigil.

Joanne limped over the cobblestone. She had been fortunate that Isobel had transferred her healing spell into her gauntlets. The stab wounds Iva had inflicted would have been troublesome if she had left them untended, but they had been reduced to barely a faint sting. The bruising and sore muscles, though, did not seem to yield to the spell.

The streets were empty. The captain of the garrison had heeded her instructions, evacuating all of the citizens in the western district. That thought gave her some relief. At least she had accomplished a few useful things that day.

She moved towards the south, following the streets that led to the gate. The northern thoroughfares were blocked with rubble, so this was the only direction the others could have gone.

Once this was over, she needed to remember to give Kay the biggest hug she had ever experienced. Chinelo and Isobel, too. Maybe Valyx, though she still wasn't quite sure how she felt about him.

Something crashed from behind. Joanne looked over her shoulder. A hole had been torn through the city wall, and through it she saw a figure. It leapt, slowly floating to the ground. Thick black hair billowed behind. Iva had found her.

"Oh, go away..." Joanne muttered.

Chinelo rose behind Archmage Harlyle, shaking himself off. Isobel lay on the other side of the mage, coughing on the ground. Chinelo gripped his sword. He had to stop him. He had to protect her!

He raised his hand and thrust the blade, pushing off his legs to add force to the blow. The Archmage whirled around and pressed his tattooed hand forward. Chinelo's motion ceased. It was like before. He could not move.

"Kneel!" The Archmage flicked his fingers, and Chinelo fell to the ground, moving against his will.

He could not resist.

"Let them go, you snake!" Kay shouted.

Something moved in his peripheral vision. A spark and blaze. Kay stumbled towards them, singeing the ground with flaming steps. The Archmage grinned.

Isobel looked up. Kay was approaching, clenching her fists. She limped, favoring her left leg. With a yell she staggered forward.

Harlyle's voice rumbled from above. "Watch closely, Isobel. I learned this from you."

Isobel gasped. She squirmed, trying to force herself to her feet.

"Kay! No!"

The Archmage swung his hand forward and caught Kay by her belt. He snarled an incantation.

"Awge gariasheq." He released his grip.

Kay's face went white, twisting into a look of pure terror. She lurched upwards, plummeting and screaming towards the dark clouds above.

"Kay!" Isobel shrieked. She dug her fingers into the ground, clawing at the stone. The Archmage's boot pressed down harder.

Kay became a tiny burning speck in the sky, growing smaller and smaller as she flew higher.

Isobel's heart hammered in her chest. She had to save her! She surged her esht into her back and gasped.

"Belekt fai!"

The Archmage winced and recoiled from the spark. Isobel scrambled to her feet and ran. She pushed esht into her back, but again, her spell would not activate. And with that hurried push, the last of her esht faded. Her skin burned. It felt as if it was tearing itself apart. She collapsed and shouted.

"Mort!"

She turned her head. Her frog hopped towards her, drawing closer, moving from cobblestone to cobblestone.

He was snatched up in the Archmage's hand.

"Disgusting little creature, this." He turned Mort over, inspecting the squirming frog with interest. "I'm impressed it knows how to use esht. Perhaps I should keep it. I'm sure I could learn a lot from it once you're dead. Now, I think she's flown enough. Sit and watch the show."

Chinelo's muscles still refused to obey. His lips would not move. He could utter no commands. He could form no incantations. And so, he did the only thing he could. He accumulated strength.

He glanced up. A blazing dot was approaching, piercing the clouds and tumbling down.

He focused, burning through the strength he had accumulated. His arm twitched. He accumulated strength, then spent it. His sword moved.

He accumulated and spent. The sword's tip hovered behind the Archmage's back, pointing towards his heart.

The dot grew larger.

He accumulated and spent. His lips moved.

Kay's form was discernable. Her cries were audible.

He accumulated and spent. He rasped out a single word.

"Extend."

A spurt of blood erupted from the Archmage's back as Chinelo's blade pierced his skin. He roared and fell, clutching his bleeding chest. Chinelo was free. He looked up and prepared to jump. The cries grew louder.

Kay crashed into the ground.

CHAPTER 55

ISOBEL'S GLASSES WERE CURTAINED WITH CRIMSON. With trembling hands, she removed them and looked at the blurry mass that lay in front of her, a mass of red and blue, a mass of something that had fallen from the sky. Someone.

Kay.

The outline was barely recognizable as human. Limbs were vaguely discernable, but they were splayed and twisted in grotesque, unnatural shapes. A faint smear of gold marked where Kay's head had been.

The sound still echoed in her ears. The horrific cracking, splattering, crunching sound refused to quiet. Instead, it got louder, overtaking everything else.

The numbness came first. Her senses dulled. It was as if she was floating in an oppressive, cold void. The world fell still, dead, except for the sound. It screamed in her mind. It taunted her, tore at her, gnawed at her ears, reminding her of the sight she had witnessed. She knelt there, quaking on the cobblestones, waiting for Kay to stand up again. But she didn't.

Healing! She needed healing. Injuries could be healed. This would be no different. Isobel crawled forward and hovered her hand over the blurry shapes and colors that were painted across the ground. She concentrated, trying to push esht into her healing tattoo.

The pain hit, and her senses returned. She recoiled. She had no esht. Magic demanded a price, and she lacked its usual currency. If she wished to use a spell, the price would be more substantial.

Isobel gritted her teeth and pushed through the pain. Her hand began to burn, starting at her palm and spreading in a ring from there. So, this was what it felt like. Iva had always told her never to push past her esht limits. She had repeated the warning, drilling it into Isobel's young mind. And now, Isobel ignored that warning. Her body was being consumed, starting with her flesh. It would progress deeper, claiming her muscles, her bones, even her soul. Such was magecraft's one forbidden rite, that of Darkburning.

It did not matter. She would sacrifice anything she needed to, as long as Kay could stand again.

A voice pierced the echoing sound. "Isobel!"

She ignored it, closing her eyes as the burning spread towards her fingers. Pain, unspeakable pain. It was unlike anything she had ever felt before. She gave herself to it, letting her body rip itself apart.

"Isobel! Stop!"

Firm hands shook her shoulders, breaking her concentration.

Chinelo's face drew close. She could faintly discern his features. He pulled her to her feet. Her trousers were damp, and they stuck to her knees. Why was he pulling her away? She wasn't finished.

"Stop! I'm not done yet." Isobel tried to shake him off, but Chinelo's grip tightened. "Let me go! I need to heal her!"

"Isobel..." Chinelo responded in a low voice. "She's... that won't... it's too late."

"Too late? No. No! I can fix her. You know? Like I've fixed you before."

"Isobel... she's gone..."

"No. That's not right. She's..." Isobel sentence went unfinished.

It hit next. A sickening realization. A hideous truth. An unyielding emptiness. She turned and looked down at the splatter, though it was still vague in her poor vision.

"That's... not..." Isobel whispered.

Seconds passed, or were they hours?

"Where are my glasses?" she mumbled.

Chinelo bent over and picked something from the ground, wiping it on his shirt. He placed her spectacles on her face, and she finally could discern his. He looked sick. His expression was dark, and the corner of his mouth quivered. A lump formed in her throat. Was he right? Was Kay dead?

She began to turn to look at the strange shapes on the ground, but Chinelo pulled her away.

"Don't... don't look at it. It's too much. You can't unsee it."

Isobel ignored the warning, glancing at Kay's body for only a second.

She looked away. It was unbearable.

Valyx stumbled towards them, supporting himself on a wooden board. His face was as white as snow. He staggered past them and collapsed in a loud thud behind Isobel.

"Kay?" he asked.

"Valyx," Chinelo said. "We need to run."

Valyx gave no answer.

"Valyx!"

"Shut... up!" Valyx growled.

Chinelo gasped.

"You did this. Everything was fine until you two showed up."

Isobel felt Chinelo's hand release from her arm.

A sound. A snap. The impact of fist against flesh. Valyx struck Chinelo across the face. Chinelo groaned. Isobel winced.

"Leave! Leave!" Valyx roared. "Get out! Run! I'm not leaving her. Go! Get away from me, you trash!"

"Valyx..." Isobel exhaled.

"Shut up, you coward! You won't even look at her. You won't even face what you did."

Valyx stepped forward raising the board he held. Chinelo grabbed his arm.

"That's enough, Valyx," Chinelo said sternly.

"Don't touch me," Valyx hissed. His face grew red. The veins on his neck bulged.

Isobel closed her eyes tightly. Her lashes moistened. She felt her face contorting into a pained frown. She held her hand over her mouth.

"Valyx," she whispered. "I—"

"Say another word, Isobel," Valyx snarled, "and I will kill you myself."

Isobel staggered back, nausea rising. Chinelo frowned, then rested his hand on her arm.

"Let's go," he whispered.

Isobel stifled a sob and nodded, placing Mort on her shoulder. With sword and staff in hand, Chinelo walked away. Isobel looked back. Valyx had collapsed on his knees, holding Kay's hand in his. Isobel squeezed her eyes shut and hurried after Chinelo. As she rounded a bend, she heard Valyx's dreadful wail echoing through the streets.

Chinelo hobbled, supporting himself on Isobel's staff. She followed close behind, staring at the ground. She was quiet. She didn't cry. She didn't speak. She merely followed.

Where was an exit route? The west gate was blocked. The southwest gate was blocked. They could perhaps cross over the wall using one of the lifts, but how would they get down? If only he had thought to bring some travel stones.

A cloud of steam rushed into the street. From within he heard clattering and clanging. A figure shot from the mist, tearing a cracked mask from her face. They had found Joanne.

⚊

Joanne tossed her mask aside. Iva had managed to land a blow on it, breaking the inscription and rendering it useless. Without it, her vapor sense was inaccessible.

Iva burst from the cloud with dagger in hand. She issued a command into the gleaming spell-core on its hilt.

"Radial Siphon."

Joanne felt a weight afflict her. So, Iva was finally running out of esht, and she had chosen to replenish with hers. Joanne scoffed. A dirty trick, one mages tended to avoid in duels. Though Joanne had some of those of her own, and with Iva's spell core locked into the siphoning spell, she no longer had to worry about Iva casting another.

"Strength!" Joanne shouted, surging esht into her gauntlets. She pulled back her right fist, preparing to strike.

Iva's eyes darted to her fist, and she braced for the impact. In an instant Joanne diverted her esht and released a cloud of steam from the tattoo on her opposite shoulder. Iva's eyes moved again, tracking the sudden eruption, exactly as Joanne had hoped.

Joanne's fist collided with Iva's face, sending her reeling. Joanne's eyes widened. She had struck flesh, not steel. Whatever methods Iva had been using for defense had faded, likely due to her depleted esht. This was her chance.

"Geyser!" Joanne exhaled. The puff of steam accumulated in front of her left fist, forming a tight, compressed sphere. It grew, drawing in water from the air.

"Mist!" Joanne shouted, funneling esht into her other gauntlet. Her sweat evaporated, joining the growing maelstrom.

Iva wiped blood from her lips and scowled. Her green eyes flashed in rage, but something behind Joanne drew her attention away momentarily. Joanne did not wait to find out what it was.

She *punched*, releasing her esht. The sphere crashed into Iva's abdomen, tearing her apart with its quick, hyper-pressurized release. The force was enough to rip through solid stone. Iva's body was paper against it. Her face twisted in shock, and she fell in a grisly heap.

Joanne panted as the weight faded. Iva lay still on the ground before her. She looked down at her motionless body.

Dead. Iva was dead. Her face was still. Her eyes were dull. Her breath was gone. Joanne sighed. Finally, it was over.

A scream rang from behind her. Joanne whirled around to see Isobel and Chinelo racing towards her.

Strange. Where was Kay?

Isobel ran ahead of Chinelo. His uneven footsteps clattered behind her, but she did not stop. Joanne staggered towards them, rubbing her head. She was alive, and behind her lay Iva's lifeless corpse. Iva was dead. The woman who had raised her was dead.

"Hey, you two," Joanne said in a tired voice. "Glad to see you're all right! Where are Kay and Valyx? Chinelo, is it time for me to collect our wager?"

Something moved behind Joanne. Isobel stopped and gasped. A light flashed from Iva's body. The torn limbs and shattered bone reconnected, weaving together like the wounds of the dark gods. She rose, first her legs, then her hips, then her back. It arched unnaturally, popping and cracking as she stood. She opened her eyes and closed her left hand into a gesture, a finger pressing against her thumb.

Isobel's heart seized. "Joanne! Behind—"

Joanne's body collapsed, folding in on itself before exploding in a shower of crimson. Only a few tattered strips of fabric and leather were left behind.

Isobel stood, frozen in shock. She had heard rumors of Iva's magic. Twice she'd seen her threaten to unleash it. But she had never actually witnessed the unbridled brutality of her sister's spells.

Joanne was gone, crushed, erased from existence. Her blood coated the pavement. Her last expression, her smiling face lingered in Isobel's mind.

Before Isobel had been silent. Before she had been numb. But now, she was neither. It hit her like a flood, a tidal wave of rage. Her sisters were gone. Her sisters were dead, and nothing would stop her wrath.

She tore her staff from Chinelo's hand and ran towards Iva. She burned what little esht Mort had transferred to her and shouted.

"Form: Blade!"

She would tear her apart. She would rip her to pieces. Her feet splashed in the red pool on the ground and she swung her staff for Iva's neck. Iva looked up in surprise and ducked under Isobel's swinging glaive. Isobel swung again. Iva dodged. She swung again. Iva evaded. Isobel shrieked from her dry throat. Her vision blurred as tears streamed down her face. She hated her! She would pay for what she'd done!

She whirled around and slashed for Iva's side. Iva twisted and caught the shaft of the staff. She wrenched it from Isobel's hands and tossed it aside. Isobel gasped. She was unarmed, and Iva's dagger gleamed.

Chinelo's sword slashed between them, clanging as it struck Iva's weapon. She staggered back, glancing between the two figures. Chinelo stood between them, defending Isobel with his silver blade.

Iva moved like lightning, slamming her shoulder into Chinelo's gut and launching him over Isobel. He thudded as he hit the wall and fell limply to the ground.

"Chinelo!" Isobel screamed. "How much more will you take?" she roared. "How many more will you slaughter?"

"I'm sorry..." Iva mumbled.

"Give them back!" Isobel shrieked. "Give them back!"

She tackled Iva, rolling in a heap across the street. Isobel balled her hands into tight fists and slammed them down, trying to hit Iva's face.

She moved, evading the feeble blows. Isobel's fingers hit the pavement, throbbing with every impact.

"Why?" Isobel whimpered as her blows weakened. The edges of her fists began to bleed. "Why did you take them from me?"

"I'm sorry," Iva said before kicking Isobel off her. She stood and dusted herself off.

Isobel's stomach hurt, aching from the impact of Iva's boot. She wiped her eyes. She could not stop the tears.

"This is not how I wanted things to go," Iva muttered.

Isobel sobbed, her strength gone.

"Why couldn't you just stay in your cell?" Iva yelled. "I wanted you to be safe."

Isobel gasped and sniffled. "Shut up!" She screamed as she scrambled to her feet, swinging madly with her battered fists.

"Why did it have to be you?" Iva shouted, knocking Isobel off her feet with a sweep of her leg. "Why, Isobel? Why did it have to be you?"

Isobel coughed. She felt dizzy, nauseated, and disoriented.

Iva let out a guttural yell and tossed her dagger aside, pressing her hands against her head. "I wanted to avoid this." She exhaled long, heavy breaths. "I did everything I could to avoid this. You weren't supposed to be in that town. You weren't supposed to be here!" Her fingers clawed at her hair as she hunched forward. Her breaths became rapid, erratic, panicked.

After a moment, Iva clenched her fists, bringing them down to her sides. She let out a long exhalation. "I will mend this world. I will find the Source, no matter the cost."

Isobel looked up. Iva raised her hand, pressing her middle finger against her thumb. She closed her eyes briefly. Her cheeks glistened in streaks, and the muscles along her neck spasmed.

Iva opened her eyes. Her face grew cold. "Goodbye, love. I will bring you back once I am finished. I'm sorry."

Isobel's eyes widened. Her heart pounded. Then, something moved.

Chinelo slammed into Iva with his shoulder. He picked up his sword and slashed it, cutting Iva's arm. She staggered back and clutched the wound, yelling in pain. Chinelo dove and wrapped Isobel in his arms. He faced the wall, clutching Mort in one hand and his sword in the other.

"Homvelcht tor vrefden iv gra tor vrefden hasa solstari!"

Everything vanished. The world exploded in a brilliant flood of color. They collapsed on the ground, lying in the fields outside Veld. Chinelo knelt and dropped his sword. He let out a deep, pained yell. Isobel lay on her back. Raindrops splashed against her spectacles, curtaining them in a blurry shroud before rolling down her cheeks.

She felt cold. The rain washed over her, soaking into her shirt.

She felt sick. Her stomach ached and seemed to tie itself in knots.

Most of all, she felt empty.

She stared at the dark clouds above. Strange. She had not noticed that it was going to storm.

THE END OF PART 6

PART 7

THE EYE OF THE STORM

CHAPTER 56

422nd year, 3rd month, 22nd day
13 years before present day

THE BONFIRE ROARED, SENDING CRACKLING SPARKS and wispy ashes up in a twisting column of smoke. Isobel wrapped herself in a thick blanket, standing in front of the many logs occupied by her chattering sisters as she basked in the wavering light. The leaves had fallen, leaving only the jagged forms of trees over the outer walls of the compound.

The smoke shifted directions, billowing directly in her face and burning her eyes. She coughed and walked to the other side, finding one of the few empty logs. She grunted as she sat. Her legs were exceedingly sore from her long dance the previous night. She shifted until she found a comfortable position, wondering if Joanne was equally sore.

Where are they?

Kay had said they had something special for the last of the autumn bonfires. Isobel looked over her shoulder. The other fires shimmered, and the shadows of her siblings moved back and forth around them.

The log shook. Isobel yelped.

"Sorry, love. Didn't mean to startle you." Iva seated herself beside Isobel. Her hands poked from her cloak, and she rubbed them together to warm them.

"Oh! Iva," Isobel said quietly, then turned back to the fire.

Iva squinted down at her. "You're oddly melancholy tonight. "

Isobel pulled her blanket tighter.

"Hey, now." Iva leaned forward. "I know you want to tell me. Out with it."

Isobel sighed. "Joanne and Kay said they were going to meet me, but they aren't here."

Iva wrapped her arm around Isobel.

"Give them time. I'm sure Joanne got distracted or something. You know how she is."

Isobel nodded and nestled against Iva's side.

"Hey," Iva said. "Your performance last night was excellent. I'm so proud of you. You're far better than I ever was, and I was pretty good, myself."

Isobel shook her head. "I made so many mistakes. I skewed the flame's release pattern, and it got all muddled."

"Well, to my very trained eyes, you looked perfect. And—now don't tell Joanne I said this," Iva leaned close and whispered, "I heard the Elder Mothers had you picked as their favorite."

Isobel looked up. "Really?"

Iva nodded. "Oh, you would not believe the lovely things Saiya had to say about you."

Isobel grinned. Her heart fluttered for a moment. Perhaps, if they thought she was skilled enough, they would let her join the Blades, just as Iva had.

Two more thuds shook the log.

"Guess who's here!" Joanne proclaimed.

"And louder than ever," Kay added with a toss of her hair.

"Honestly, I was afraid you two had forgotten," Isobel said.

"Me? Forget? I would never," Joanne said.

"She would," Kay quipped.

Joanne glared at her briefly. "It wasn't actually my fault this time, believe it or not. Kay just took forever with these—what did you call them, Kay?"

"Mallow-root puffs."

Joanne snapped her fingers. "Right! The whole kitchen smells sticky now."

Kay opened her pouch and pulled out a white, spongey ball. "Sorry, Isobel. They took a lot longer to shape than I thought."

Isobel eyed the strange object cautiously. It squished and stuck to her fingertips.

"What is it?"

"This is the surprise I told you about." Kay beamed.

Iva leaned over, inspecting the strange puff. "What do you do with it?"

"You eat it," Kay replied.

Isobel shrugged and stuffed the puff into her mouth, filling it with its sweet taste. She gulped down the sticky mass. "Kay! That was amazing! How did you figure that one out?"

Kay ran her fingers through her hair with an air of self-importance. "Gladsa was trying honey and mallow-root as possible binding agents and got this as an accident. It doesn't hold esht well, but it is tasty."

"Fascinating," Iva said, trying one of the puffs for herself.

Joanne's eyes gleamed. "Kay! I have an idea! What if we..." she grabbed a stick from the ground. "Cooked it again?" She snatched one of the puffs from the bag and stabbed the stick into it. She held it over the fire, browning it before it ignited in a blue-gold flame, much to Kay's horror. Joanne withdrew the blackened puff and blew out the flame before taking a small bite.

"Definitely better with a light char."

"I see your lack of taste persists," Kay groaned.

Isobel smiled and stared into the dancing flames. They flickered and flashed, crackling and popping as the dried wood burned brilliantly.

CHAPTER 57

435th year, 2nd month, 13th day
Present Day

THE EMBERS OF THE DYING FIRE glowed a dull orange, and one of the few remaining twigs collapsed into a puff of ash. Isobel stared into it, remembering days long past. She shivered within her cloak. The fire's fading light provided little heat to stave off the night's chill.

She rubbed the palm of her left hand. Though she had tried to mend the wound, the burning she experienced from exceeding her esht limit still lingered behind a rough black scar. Darkburning had that effect. The wounds it created never truly healed.

Her head throbbed. Her eyes felt heavy. How long had she sat there? She finally heard the sounds of the wilds: the chirping insects, the whistling breeze, the distant drumming of thunder. She shifted on the rock upon which she sat, trying unsuccessfully to find a more comfortable position. Her legs and feet ached. They had run for so long, finally exiting the steppe and crossing into the Acronus Badlands in their flight.

She closed her eyes and returned to the dilemma that had plagued her mind for hours. What had gone wrong that day? They had slain the monster, just as planned. They had bested the Archmage, something she had feared was impossible. Joanne had even defeated Iva. So, how had they returned from the dead? Such magic didn't even exist in legends. How could such a thing be possible?

Something touched her shoulder. She squealed and jumped to her feet, whirling around and summoning her staff in a single motion. Chinelo backed away with his hands raised.

"I'm sorry. I didn't mean to startle you."

Isobel's heart pounded. She exhaled and relaxed.

"I apologize. I... I suppose I'm a bit jumpy tonight."

Chinelo cocked his head. "Tonight? It's morning."

Isobel looked up. The sky faintly glowed in the east. She rubbed her forehead. Had it really been that long?

Chinelo studied her face. "Isobel, did you sleep last night?"

"I... no. I suppose I didn't."

Chinelo sighed and sat on the stone, patting a space beside him. Isobel joined him and leaned against his shoulder, lacing her fingers through his.

"Do you want to talk about it?" Chinelo asked.

"I can't figure it out Chinelo. They shouldn't have been able to come back. Unless that's one of the words they've recovered. I suppose that's the most logical explanation. Still, I've never heard of the gods ever using resurrection magic. Though, I guess they were supposedly immortal. Maybe that was just a trick or something.

"Also, I've been trying to figure out how the Archmage was able to open up the earth like he did. Something like that would have had significant seismic ramifications and would have been exceedingly complicated to do. Maybe that's related to another rune of theirs. That could also explain that decay magic he used. I at least understand how his compulsion ability works, so if we ever face that again I should be able to make an effective counter."

She continued. "I've been thinking about your sword techniques and something we could use to augment them. I've got my summoning spell on my staff. Maybe we could do something like that for your sword. Oh! I could have the handle extend if you wanted to be able to use it like a polearm or something. It wouldn't be too hard. I would just need—"

"Isobel," Chinelo interrupted in a soft voice.

"Hmmm?" Isobel looked at his face. His eyes were clouded, and a look of weariness hung about them. His characteristic resting smile was absent.

"That's not what I'm asking about."

"I don't understand."

Chinelo squeezed her hand. "Do you want talk about them?"

"Them?"

Chinelo quivered and squeezed his eyes shut. His mouth twitched.

"Joanne and Kay."

The words stabbed into Isobel's heart like daggers. They were gone. One, slaughtered by the person Isobel had idolized for entire life. The other, killed using Isobel's own spell. She had tried to avoid thinking about them. She had tried to force herself to contemplate other, more technical, more mechanical matters. She had tried to reminisce about pleasant times, remembering the good instead of the horrific. But she could only delay the inevitable for so long.

It rushed over her like water from a hurricane, an unstoppable torrent, an undeniable flood. Her exhausted will was unable to hold it back any longer. She shook her head.

"I—I don't want to—" she sobbed.

Chinelo wrapped his arms around her, holding her as she cried.

"Why would you make me think about them?" she asked. "That's so cruel."

Chinelo stroked her hair. "I'm sorry."

"Why, Chinelo?" she wept. "Why?"

"Because I love you," he whispered in a breaking voice, "and I know you're hurting."

"Why did they have to die? They weren't supposed to. We were supposed to save everyone together. They were supposed to come with us."

Chinelo gave no answer. His body shook and he inhaled in intermittent breaths.

She buried her face in his chest, squeezing her spectacles into the bridge of her nose. "What am I supposed to do? How are we supposed to carry their memories back if they aren't here?"

Chinelo was silent.

Isobel leaned back. "Say something! You always say the right thing. That's what you do. That's why I love you. Say something! Please!"

Chinelo looked down. His tears soaked into his beard. His eyes were red. "I'm sorry. There's nothing I could say that could make this better."

Isobel closed her eyes and leaned into his chest again. They were gone. The sisters she loved were gone. The people they had become in the past eleven years, the lives they had built, the friendships they had made had all vanished.

They had been stolen. They had been robbed, torn away, like faded leaves in the winter breeze.

It wasn't fair.

She wasn't sure how long she cried. Frankly, her perception of time was completely inaccurate that morning. However, eventually she stopped shaking. As they sat there, her eyes barely staying open, another emotion rose within her.

Rage.

It *wasn't* fair. Things weren't supposed to go like this. She had to do something about it. She had to. She suddenly pushed away and stood.

"I can't accept this."

Chinelo frowned. "Isobel?"

She paced around the charred sticks and logs. She ran her fingers through her hair. There had to be a way. Surely, there was some spell she could use, some trick she could exploit to bend the world to her will. "I can't. I can't! It's not right. It's not how things ought to be."

She stopped. Her eyes widened. There *was* a way. There was someone who knew how to bring them back. She looked at Chinelo.

"I'm going back."

Chinelo blinked. "What?"

"I'm going back, Chinelo! Iva knows how to resurrect people. We saw her do it. We saw the Archmage after he came back. If they can do it, then I can bring back Joanne and Kay."

Chinelo slowly stood. "So, you're going to...?"

"I'm going to fly over there, and then I'll steal Iva's memories so I can learn how."

"How?"

"I don't know!" Isobel felt her cheeks grow hot. "I'll figure something out. I know the word for memory. I'll improvise something."

Chinelo stepped forward. "Isobel. You haven't slept."

She waved her hand. "I'm fine."

"You also can't fly anymore."

"I can make something work."

Chinelo touched her shoulder. "Iva almost killed you."

"Well then I won't give her the chance," Isobel retorted. Why wouldn't he listen? "I'll make her pay for what she's done!"

Chinelo sighed. "Isobel, I think you should rest."

"Oh! Shut up! I'm going, and you're coming with me!"

Chinelo withdrew his arm. He gave her an odd, piercing look, as if he didn't even recognize her.

"No," he whispered.

"What?" Isobel snapped.

"I said, 'no.' I can't agree to this."

"But you said you would come with me..." she responded. "You said we'd be together. You said you would stay with me."

"I'm sorry, Isobel. I cannot agree to this plan. You are going to get yourself killed."

"So, you're just leaving me?"

Chinelo tensed. "Absolutely not."

"Then... why...?" Isobel wiped her eye. "We're supposed to be a team."

Chinelo clenched his fists. "Because I can't lose you, Isobel!" he shouted. His voice echoed between the arid foothills, startling her. "I can't lose you. If we go back, we're going back exhausted, unprepared, and injured. We'll be facing an army of mages, Iva, and the Archmage, all of whom want us dead. There are just two of us! It's just you, and it's just me. And I need you to understand something. You are all I have left. My family is dead. My comrades are dead. Anyone else I had hoped to call a friend is dead. Not you, though." He pointed at her. "You're here, and I will *not* agree to something that results in you dying."

"But... Joanne..."

Chinelo sighed. "We'll bring her back, Isobel. And Kay. But we'll do it like we planned. We'll find the rune for time, we'll reverse their deaths, and we'll save them."

"But... if they can't come back with us... then the people they became are dead." Isobel trembled. "They won't be who they were."

"Then we'll guide them to become who they were."

Isobel looked down at the ground. She pressed her lips together in a line, contemplating his words.

"You can't stop me, you know?" she said defiantly.

"Isobel, I wouldn't dream of trying to force you to stay. Your stubbornness, your confounding stubbornness is one of the many things I admire about you. I love how you never give up. I love how you can't be stopped." Chinelo reached for her hand. "That's why I'm begging you, because I love every fiber of who you are, please, don't go. I don't want to lose anyone else, especially not you."

Isobel stared at his hand, clasping her palm in his. "But... I... why would you just give up on them?"

He squeezed her hand. "I'm sorry, Isobel. I'm sorry I'm asking you this. I just can't anymore. Every time we go into battle, I have to brace myself for the possibility that you will die. And I... I can't face that possibility anymore. You've come close to death so, so many times, and—" He hesitated. "Isobel, it's so, so hard. If we go back, our deaths are not possibilities. They are inevitabilities. And that future, a future without you, that is one *I* refuse to accept."

He looked up, staring into her eyes. "Please, Isobel. Please, don't leave me. Let's keep pushing forward. We'll find a way to save them, and if we have to fight Iva in the process, then I will stand by you to the very end, but let's not rush towards our deaths. Let's heal. Let's recover. Let's rest, so that when the time comes when we have to fight, we'll be able to win, you and I, together."

Isobel withdrew her hand and crouched, covering her eyes with her hands. His words shook her to her core. It was too much for her. She was overwhelmed, not even able to identify what emotions she was feeling. She felt his strong hand resting gently on her shoulder as he dropped to the ground beside her.

"Hey," he said. "I love you."

She nodded and sniffled. "I love you, too."

She moved and held him tightly. He was right. She didn't want to admit it, but he was right. She and Chinelo had been bested by the Interior Guard. They had been defeated by the Archmage. And they had fallen before Iva. Without a plan, without rest, she would be marching to her end, an end without Chinelo, and she couldn't accept that, even if she did want to bring her sisters back.

She pondered his words. If she left, not only would she be against impossible odds, but she would be hurting him, the man she loved more than anything. She would be abandoning him, leaving him in a hostile world. He would be alone like she was when her mother died. He would be alone like she was when she left the coven. He would be alone like he was when his kingdom fell. She would be betraying him and breaking the promises they had made to stay together for a miniscule chance at victory.

She squeezed him tighter. She would not leave him alone.

A thought entered her mind, rising like mist from a cold lake at dawn. It grew and lingered, haunting her. Had Iva felt that way when she left the coven? Had Joanne felt that way when they awoke to find her gone? Had Kay felt that way when they thought she had died?

Had her choices caused others to feel that way? Had her choices isolated those she cared about?

Chinelo rested his forehead against hers.

"So, will you stay with me?" he asked.

She nodded. She would, because despite it all, despite her pain, despite her guilt, despite her rage, she knew one thing.

She knew that she loved him.

CHAPTER 58

CHINELO WARILY SCANNED THE ARID HILLS to the east, searching for any signs of pursuers. On his shoulder, Mort inspected the landscape as well, surveying the expansion to his vast domain of influence. After a few moments, Chinelo slid down the small rise and made his way back to their camp, stepping over the thick brush that blanketed the ground.

The Acronus Badlands were rough and harsh, but the many hills and jagged rock formations would hide the two of them well. The slopes were extraordinarily dry, and finding water had been difficult, even with the recent storm.

He bent over the cooking pot and sniffed the humble soup that bubbled from within. It was hardly a glorious meal, but it would suffice. A minty, slightly bitter aroma wafted to his nose, the scent of the sagebrush and rich pulse-roots he scrounged that morning. He set Mort on a rock by the fire and moved to the tent, opening the flap to peek inside. She was there, sleeping peacefully under her blankets. Chinelo looked longingly at her face for a moment, then closed the tent, returning to the fire with his froggy companion.

She had slept since early morning, and it was nearly midday. Chinelo glanced at the sky. He would let her rest a little longer before waking her. She had looked completely drained when she collapsed on her bedding, and she would need her strength once they began moving.

He stared at the ground and kicked the dirt into small trenches. They really were gone. They had perished, just like the others. He had been unable to save them, just like the others. He crossed his arms and rested his elbows on his knees. Why couldn't he save them? He had tried to. He had done everything he could. Why was it never enough? Why wasn't he ever enough?

He glanced at his sword, which was propped against the rock on which he sat. He drew it from its scabbard and studied the straight, double-edged blade. The edges were nicked, and the flat was scratched.

It was in desperate need of sharpening. He sighed. How had he let it get into such a sorry state? Had he truly forgotten the routines and habits from his younger years? Azuka would be horrified.

Chinelo frowned. How long had it been since his brother died? Almost two years?

He still remembered that horrific sight, that towering, colossal column of flame spreading from Eshgar's heart into the surrounding countryside. It had been insatiable, consuming all in a blinding blaze of orange until it finally stopped beyond the outer walls. How many other cities had fallen to such a fate?

Chinelo glanced at the space where he found Isobel that morning. She had left her spell-book on the stone. He leaned forward and grabbed it, opening it to the map Isobel had drawn on the final page. Where could they go next? What had Joanne said? There had been other cities that had fallen, at least five of them since Eshgar. One in Veshda, two in Mervos, and two in Iskara.

He traced his finger along the map, moving north from the Red Coven, crossing east of Nellborough, and finally stopping at one of the marks indicating an obelisk. It was southwest of Veld, and if Joanne had gone the most direct route, she must have passed through it. That was the next closest obelisk, and if Joanne's report was true, it had already been awakened.

What other obelisks remained? They had found each of the four in the eastern half of the mainland. Iva had claimed five in addition to Nellborough and Eshgar, and those seemed to be in the western half of the continent. Only five remained.

One was likely in Rothvale, the capital of Iskara. If that had fallen, he would certainly have heard. One was in Veshda, the neighboring nation in the Northwest Peninsula. Though, he did not know which one Iva had claimed in her first journey there. One was in Yzdal, far beyond the eastern coast. One was in Trelldas, an island southwest of Eshgar. And finally, one was in the icy waves of the Northern Ocean, at the very edge of the map with no known landmass beneath it. Where was the next best option?

Mort began one of his signature frog songs, a melancholy droning.

"Mort! Shhh!" Chinelo whispered. "You'll wake her."

Mort immediately quieted with an apologetic blink.

Chinelo looked down at the frog. Isobel always stroked him along his back, running her finger between the two lines that ran parallel to his spine. Chinelo slowly and cautiously extended his finger and reached toward the frog. He paused, then gently ran it down Mort's back.

The frog squawked and whirled around, moving his neck in a way that seemed physically impossible. He opened his wide mouth and chomped down on Chinelo's finger. It did not hurt, but it was very startling.

"Sorry," Chinelo whispered. "I thought you liked that."

Mort scowled. He would only accept such treatment from his queen, as tempting as it was to experience the sensation from multiple sources.

Chinelo shrugged and stirred the pot of soup. It had reached the proper consistency. He grunted and stood before returning to the tent. He pushed his way through the opening and crawled to Isobel's side. She looked so serene, so tranquil. He lightly placed his hand on her shoulder.

"Isobel?"

She stirred and groaned.

"Isobel, dear? It's time to wake up."

She squirmed under the blanket. Her eyes suddenly flew open with a wild, fearful expression. She looked in Chinelo's direction, and in a single motion, knocked his hand away, kicked off her blanket, and retreated into the corner of the tent. She extended her left hand, pointing it at him and concentrating, preparing to fire a volley of spells into him.

Chinelo crawled backwards and raised his hands. "Isobel! It's me."

Isobel lowered her hand and sighed in relief. "I'm sorry. I—I don't know what I was thinking there."

Chinelo picked her spectacles from beside her bedding.

"Thank you." She slid them onto her face. "I'm really sorry, Chinelo. I didn't mean to…"

"It's fine. I understand. Are you all right now?"

She looked down and nodded.

"Well, I have some food prepared if you're hungry."

She nodded again but didn't move.

Chinelo gazed at her. Was that a subtle trembling he saw?

"How about this? I'll fix your bowl and bring it in here. We can just eat in the tent today."

Isobel hesitated and gave one final, quick nod.

"All right." Chinelo smiled. "I'll be back in a moment."

He spooned generous servings into two clay bowls and stuck two spoons in the thick soup. Mort was preoccupied with an insect that had dared to enter his presence.

"Mort! Watch the fire. Croak if you need anything. Mom and Dad need to talk for a bit."

Mort shot Chinelo a short glare but quickly turned attention back to the insect.

Chinelo balanced the bowls precariously on his arm and returned to the tent. Isobel had shrunk into the corner, wrapping herself in her blanket. Chinelo sat beside her and held one of the bowls in front of her, letting the cool scent fill the tent.

Isobel's hands appeared from beneath the blanket, and she took the bowl, shaking it slightly to swish the thin flecks of sage in a wide circle. She held her nose over the steam, inhaling it as it clung to her spectacles.

"Chinelo?" she said after a long pause.

Chinelo slurped the soup from his spoon and gulped it down. "Yes, dear?"

"Can you tell me about your family?"

Chinelo set his bowl on the floor. "I—I suppose. Anything in particular?"

"Can you tell me more about what your mother was like?"

Chinelo crossed his arms and looked at the ceiling. "Hmmm. She is tough to describe concisely." He moved his gaze along the seams of the fabric canopy. How *would* he describe her?

"Well, I suppose she was very... put together. She always behaved in a way that was proper or polite. Always controlled in her motions and gestures, you know? She was surgical with her word choices as well. Everything was in order about her."

Isobel began to eat her soup, watching him intently as he spoke.

"She always made sure my brother and I held to proper Eshgarian tradition, naturally. We had to learn the right introductions. We always had to bow at the right points. We had to say all the right pleasantries. She was very strict about it."

Isobel nodded.

"Really, she was strict about everything. We always had to be in bed an hour after sundown. Always awake at sunrise. It didn't matter what day it was. Rules were rules." Chinelo raised his finger. "She used to say, 'Chinelo, an agreeable man is a man that sleeps.' My father had sleeping fits so obviously their marriage was very strong."

A cough from Chinelo's side. He looked over as Isobel wiped soup from her lips.

"Sorry," she said. "I wasn't expecting that."

"We never did either. He would just be cooking away, then down he goes."

Isobel giggled. "I—I really shouldn't laugh at that, should I?"

Chinelo shrugged. "Probably not, but that never stopped him. He was a sleep-laugher. A bit horrifying when you're sharing a room."

"I'm sure." Her somber expression returned.

"Right. So, anyways, Mother was very strict, and honestly a bit cold, but she just did the nicest things. She really showed love through her actions. I remember after I was rejected by this one girl I fancied, she stayed up with me the entire night. Barely said a word, just sat with me the whole night until I fell asleep."

"She sounds lovely," Isobel said, moving her spoon in a circle in her quickly disappearing soup.

"She was."

"And your father? Can you tell me more about him?"

Chinelo scratched his head. "Well, he worshiped the ground my mother tread upon. He absolutely doted on her. She was living a life that rivaled that of the queen, let me tell you."

Isobel smiled weakly.

Chinelo continued. "If I had to use one word to describe him, I would say that he was boisterous. He was always so bouncy and jovial. A very pleasant person to have at parties if my mother's stories could be believed. I used to help him cook when I was young, and I think you've seen the result of that."

Isobel leaned forward. "He sounds very pleasant, indeed."

Chinelo smiled wistfully.

"If it's all right with you," Isobel began, "after we've found the rune for time and turned things around, could I perhaps meet them?"

Chinelo smiled. "I would like that, yes."

She placed her bowl on the ground and slid closer, leaning against his shoulder. "You should probably eat your soup before it gets cold."

"Probably," Chinelo continued his meal.

It was not the most appetizing thing he had eaten, but it was incredibly refreshing. If he had had a few additional ingredients to compliment the sage's strong flavor, it would certainly have been rather delicious. He chewed one of the pieces of root, one which proved exceedingly difficult.

"Hmmm, maybe I should have given this more time out there. I apologize if the roots were too tough, dear."

Isobel shook her head. "It was excellent."

Chinelo finished his meal and set his bowl beside Isobel's.

"I've been thinking," Chinelo said.

Isobel nodded.

"If the Interior Guard is going to come after us, they are probably going to search the towns closest to Veld first."

"Makes sense," Isobel murmured.

"So, I'm going to propose we hide out in the badlands for at least a few days until we can get our bearings. We have enough supplies to last us for a while, and the wild scale-sheep we've seen should cover anything we are lacking."

Isobel nodded.

"Good. Good. Then we should probably push a little bit deeper so there's less risk of our smoke columns being spotted."

"That sounds like a good plan. We'll need to determine where to go after that, but I'd rather not think about that for the time being."

Chinelo touched Isobel's hand. "Then let's take it slow."

"Right," Isobel said. Her mouth twitched.

"Right," Chinelo repeated.

He got up to move, but Isobel tugged on his hand gently.

"Chinelo?" she asked in a brittle voice. She looked up it him. Her eyes glistened.

"Isobel?" He sat back down.

"Could you stay?" she said. "Just a little longer?"

"Of course. Anything for you."

CHAPTER 59

ISOBEL'S FEET WERE SORE. SHE HAD proposed using her travel spells to transport them deeper into the badlands, but the uneven terrain and many jagged rock formations made aiming those spells difficult, and she certainly was not eager to experience appearing inside an obstacle. As a result, they had walked, and her feet were sore.

They had not spoken much, only exchanging a few words in the mornings and during their rest breaks. Chinelo was hurting. She could see it in his dark eyes, that sorrowful weariness that returned in spite of her many efforts to ward it off. However, she was afraid to ask him to speak on the matter, for such a conversation would likely bring back what she wished to forget.

Instead, she pondered a mystery that had eluded her for their entire journey. Why were the words they found missing from all ancient texts? For so long, she had just accepted that the words were missing and that activating the obelisks and claiming their runes from their hideous guardians would restore them. But why?

Their absence manifested in gaps in the texts, as if the words had been skipped over or erased somehow. But that didn't make sense. In the myths and legends, the gods wielded all manners of forces of nature. They shaped the constellations. They molded the land to their will. They lived eternally. And most notably to her, they commanded fire, a word that had been recovered by Mother Ginn. Even the images of Minera, the first human to learn magic, depicted her using fire. So, at some point in history, long before the Cataclysm, mankind was able to harness the full might of the gods.

She was left with a confusing conclusion that didn't seem plausible. The language of the gods, the Ancient Tongue, had been altered. But how and why would that have happened?

She absentmindedly walked straight into a bush.

"Ow."

Chinelo turned around. "You good back there?"

"I am. Just a little distracted."

"Ah. What's on your mind?"

Isobel dug her staff into the dirt. "Have you ever wondered why the missing words are sealed up the way they are?"

Chinelo crossed his arms. "Sure. Though, I feel I lack the cultural context to really make a judgement on the matter."

"It just doesn't make sense to me."

Chinelo touched his chin and looked at the cloudy sky. "What words have we identified?"

"First, there's '*Homvelcht*,' which sort of means travel in an instant. Then there's '*Gariasheq*'—gravity. After that, there's '*Chanavoshta*'—memory. Most recently, you've found '*Ozh*.' Remind me what that means."

"I don't think there is a direct translation, but the closest word I can think of is star. So '*ba'ozh*' sort of means little star. If you follow it with '*ath*,' you essentially have described a meteor. Then, of course there's '*tra'ozh*,' which means big star or sun. There are other modifiers for it, too. It can mean planet or comet depending on which one you use." Chinelo scratched his head. "It's still strange how I just know that now. Same with '*Chanavoshta*.'"

Isobel nodded. "I had the same experience. It's very jarring. Breaking spell-cores has a comparable effect. I suppose that makes sense. The monsters' cores are very similar based on my assessment."

Chinelo snapped his fingers. "There's also '*Vasht*.' Fire."

"Right. And presumably Iva and the Archmage have words that allow for resurrection, decay, and something related to earthquakes or seismic activity."

Chinelo nodded. "All right. So, we have travel, gravity, memory, stars, fire, resurrection, decay, quakes, and—I assume—time. Notice any trends there?"

Mort shifted on Isobel's shoulder. She glanced at him for a moment, then spoke.

"I suppose each of those could be considered dangerous. If you used gravity magic the wrong way, you could have essentially world ending consequences. Imagine reversing gravity's direction on a wide scale or generating an object with extremely high pull. Memory could erase humanity if you used that the wrong way, too. Stars could throw things off at a cosmic level. Decay and fire are both pretty obvious in their danger."

Chinelo nodded and continued walking with Isobel following close behind. They climbed a large hill dotted with tufts of brush.

"Could it be some kind of limitation that the gods imposed on magic?" he said.

"Maybe. I've been thinking it's something of that nature. Iva did say that the gods stole magic from us. I'm not sure how that makes sense considering they—or more specifically—the god Yvvusta was the one that taught us in the first place."

"Could it be that they taught magic then 'stole' it back?"

"It's possible."

"Then let's go with that."

Isobel frowned. The answer was not satisfying.

"Perhaps those journals Joanne gave us will help," Chinelo said.

Isobel looked up. "What did you say?"

Chinelo looked over his shoulder. "The logbooks Joanne had from Mother Ginn. I've got them in my pack."

Isobel's heart raced. "I—I didn't know she had any."

Chinelo snapped his fingers. "Oh, right! She brought them when you and Kay were talking that first night. I suppose with all the commotion, I forgot to mention them."

Isobel looked down, watching the soft dirt shift around her boots with every step. If there were any hints or clues to what they were facing, it would certainly be in Ginn's logbooks.

"How soon can we set up camp?" she asked.

"We normally set up once the sun is a bit lower. Maybe in an—"

"Want to stop early?" Isobel interjected.

Chinelo shrugged. "I suppose we can." He looked out over the landscape and pointed. "There are some trees or bushes or something over there. That's probably a good place to stop."

"Let's do it." Isobel ran down the hill, heading towards their destination. She needed to know what was in those books.

"Isobel! Wait!" Chinelo shouted.

She didn't slow. He would catch up.

Isobel turned the page of the oldest journal, quickly scanning it for anything that would be of value. The first several pages contained little of interest. They recorded the early details of Ginn's journey to Veshda, something Isobel had read about in the tattered book she found in the burned Red Coven library. She read the records, squinting to decipher the faded ink that had been scribbled on the pages over sixty years before.

... as such the day has been uneventful. Mara has been exceedingly disagreeable, likely due to her fitful rest last night, but I have already grown accustomed to her temperament. It is almost welcome to hear one of her snide remarks. Almost.

We should reach Fellgrove tomorrow. I hope to visit the ruins and excavations there. May Yvvusta guide me.

Ginn, 365, 6, 20

Another useless entry. Isobel was growing tired of Ginn's comments about Mara's mood. Such information was irrelevant to her. She sighed and turned the page. Its entry was equally short and equally informative. She flipped to the following one and perked up. The page was filled with a longer body of text. Finally! She had found something different.

I am noticing an odd trend in the ruins we visited today. It is common knowledge that the gods inscribed their wisdom into stone, carving their words into the many structures and monoliths they built.

Strangely, there are gaps in the texts on the monoliths. Such a thing should not be necessary. In most cases, I have noticed the gaps exist where there should be nouns or verbs. It is as if the gods did not complete their carvings, instead opting to inscribe them partially and leave the actual meaning to the reader's interpretation. Perhaps this was some game of theirs. It is most curious.

With this town's rich connection to the gods, there is a chance that the monoliths have been translated or interpreted. I shall investigate.

Mara's temperament is its typical flavor of sour. I would describe her somewhere between a fermented orange and an underripe lemon.

We will be here for several more days, and then we shall continue onto Veshda. All of my transcriptions from the monoliths shall be transferred to the archives when I return. May Yvvusta guide me.

Ginn, 365, 6, 22

Isobel frowned. More confirmation of what she already knew, but nothing much beyond that. She skimmed the short entries of the next several pages before stopping at another longer chunk of text.

I have discovered another oddity. In my search for a translation or interpretation of the monoliths, I have found several that have the gaps filled with words flagrantly chosen at random. These are of no concern to me. They are false doctrines peddled by the Temple of Belekshiel. It seems that they wish to expand their influence from the east into this portion of Iskara. Pests, all of them. Our allies in the Obsidian Order will be informed of this.

No, the thing that confounds me is a translation I discovered at one of the excavations here. Mara and I stumbled across partially exhumed remains near the monoliths, likely some kind of ritual burial site. We found the translation within the bones, carved on a stone tablet.

It is written in a dialect I have never heard myself, so it is likely very old. Based on the condition of the tomb, the weathering on the tablet, and the language, I can only surmise that it is at least three hundred years old. It is possible that it is even older, predating the Culling War.

Regardless of the archaic nature of the translation, I have been able to parse most of the text. All the gaps have been filled with words that are not present in our codices of the Ancient Tongue, something that sets this translation apart from the others we have seen. I am not sure what this in combination with the tablet's age implies.

The one added word that intrigues me most is "life." If we could somehow learn the rune for it, our magical capabilities would be expanded beyond what the Elder Mothers could ever imagine.

Mara has finally aimed her sharp tongue elsewhere. A certain cultist seems to be wavering between trying to proselytize her and trying to seduce her, neither of which has been successful. For once, I can enjoy the full display of her wit. It is a sight to behold.

We leave for Veshda tomorrow. We shall continue our search for answers regarding the Red Coven's altar. May Yvvusta guide me.

Ginn, 365, 6, 29

Isobel's brow furrowed. Intriguing. She glanced at the stack of books beside her. This was going to take a lot longer than she had expected, but at least she finally had something to keep her mind off things.

Days passed, and they continued pushing deeper in the badlands, veering south. Their mornings were quiet, and their evenings were even more so. Isobel spent most of her time reading from Ginn's journals, and Chinelo kept himself occupied with gathering and preparing their food. On one afternoon, he'd managed to hunt down a goat, and he prepared the meat in the typical Eshgarian method with much enthusiasm. It was a pleasant departure from the mutton he carved from the scale-sheep. Their hide was frustratingly tough, and while their meat was nutritious, it had this odd tangy flavor that was difficult to mask.

The moon had risen. The scent of warming meat tickled Chinelo's nose as he sat beside the campfire. He yawned.

A twig snapped.

Isobel!

He jumped and drew his sword. Something was wrong. She was in danger!

He saw the source of the noise. Mort was crawling through the base of a nearby bush, chasing a scurrying insect. Chinelo glanced at the tent. A light flickered from within, casting Isobel's vague shadow against the fabric.

Chinelo exhaled. He closed his eyes. His heart pounded, and he felt its beat manifesting as a rhythmic pressure in his head. He still felt the urge to run, to chase after whatever was threatening her safety. But it wasn't real. It never was. At least, not this time.

Sitting back down, he stabbed his sword into the dirt. This wasn't the first time this had happened. Every sudden noise, every shift in the wind, every movement in his periphery unsettled him. They raised fears in his mind, questions and doubts that only faded during the few hours he managed to sleep each night.

Would he be able to protect her if something *did* happen?

He had been unable to protect Kay. He had been unable to save Joanne. He had barely been able to escape with Isobel. Would he be able to again?

He could still clearly see them, as if they were inverted images that the sun had burned into his eyes. He could see Kay's body, plummeting and shattering in a crimson sprawl across the cobblestones. He saw Joanne, smiling then compressing into a horrific implosion.

He clenched his fists. He couldn't let her see him like this. She needed to think he was fine, so that if she needed someone, he could be there for her. He took a deep breath. This moment of fear would pass. It always did. He would be better in the morning. He was always better in the morning. He just needed to hold out a little longer. He just needed to forget the truth.

He just needed to forget that he didn't deserve the people he loved.

He heard a rustle of fabric. He reached for his sword but stopped as he saw Isobel crawling from the tent. Her face was sullen, and she walked slowly, lacking that characteristic spring in her step.

She sat beside him.

"Any luck?" Chinelo asked.

Isobel shrugged. "I'm not sure what happened, but her handwriting sharply declined in legibility. It's taking a lot longer for me to get through than before."

"Ah." He leaned forward and flipped the sizzling meat.

"How are things out here?"

Chinelo pursed his lips. He didn't want to burden her. She was dealing with her own grief. So, for the moment, he buried his doubts deep inside.

"I think the goat meat will be a nice change for us." He forced a smile.

"It does look good. For half-cooked meat, of course."

They sat in silence. Isobel crossed her arms and rested them on her knees. She sighed.

"How are you managing today?" Chinelo asked.

"I—I'm just trying not to think about things. The books are helping. It—it's hard."

He nodded.

She leaned forward and stared at his face intently. Her gaze was piercing.

"Are you... all right?" she asked.

Chinelo started to nod his head. He stopped. No. No more hiding. He sighed. "Honestly, no."

She slid closer and leaned against his shoulder. "If it will help, I can listen."

"Thank you. That means—that means a lot."

She nodded, though he did not say anything further.

"You know it's not your fault, right?" she asked.

Chinelo nodded. "I keep trying to tell myself that, but still, I'm not sure if I believe it."

"Chinelo..." she said. There was no reproach in her voice. No implication or suggestion, only deep, deep tenderness.

"I—I just wish I could have done more."

She nodded. "I know. I do to."

"I wish..." he looked up. Isobel pressed closer.

"I wish I could have stopped Joanne from going. Maybe then..."

"Please," Isobel whispered. "Please don't say it. Please don't do this to yourself."

Chinelo tensed. "I'm just so tired, Isobel. I'm tired of it, all of it. I feel that no matter what, everything that I want to cling to gets ripped away. My people. My country. My family. Nellborough. Joanne. Kay."

Isobel touched his hand.

He blinked, holding back the force he felt welling within him. "I took an oath, Isobel. Back when I became a knight, I took an oath to protect my kingdom, my people, my friends, and my family. I—I failed to uphold that oath."

He blinked again. The force had dissipated, if only slightly. "Knights are supposed to protect people. *I* was supposed to. And when I couldn't protect my homeland, I swore I would protect you, because then maybe just one thing I love would be safe. I couldn't even do that."

Isobel shifted. "Chinelo, you keep putting this weight on yourself, as if what Iva and the Archmage did is somehow your burden to bear. It's not, at least, not alone."

"See, I want to believe that, but... but I'm a knight—no! I'm *your* knight, so shouldn't I be able to bear that weight?"

She leaned back. "But you don't have to be a knight."

Chinelo looked at her. "What?"

"Chinelo, no one is asking you to be a knight anymore. Not me, not anyone. You can just be you, as you are."

He rubbed his forehead. "But what even is that? If I'm not a knight, then who am I supposed to be? How am I supposed to deserve the people I care about? How am I supposed to deserve you?"

"It's not about deserving or worthiness or anything like that. You keep asking what you are, as if you have to be something or someone specific," Isobel moved in front of him, grabbing both his hands in hers. "Maybe you're just Chinelo. And maybe that's enough."

"But I'm weak, Isobel. I can't save anyone."

"Maybe that's all right."

"But—but—"

"Maybe that's all you ever needed to be." She drew closer.

He fell silent.

"Maybe 'just Chinelo' is who you always were to me." She embraced him. "Not Chinelo the knight. Just Chinelo."

"Is that really enough?"

She kissed his cheek. "It always was."

They sat together in silence, feeling each other's warmth. In those quiet moments, no words were exchanged. With her by his side, the weight finally lifted. He would no longer be her knight. They would stand together, as equals, and that would be enough, for him and for her.

The smell of smoke reached Chinelo's nostrils.

"Oh! The meat!"

Isobel moved aside. Chinelo lifted the pan from the fire and set it on the ground. The meat was charred and blackened.

He put his hands on his hips. "Well, it's going to be extra crispy tonight."

Isobel laughed. "Is this the Eshgarian style?"

Chinelo shook his head. "No. I think it's just Chinelo style."

CHAPTER 60

IT HAD BEEN OVER A WEEK, and Isobel continued to read through the journals while they rested. She flipped another page. The daylight was waning, and if she hoped to finish the book before bed, she would have to read incredibly quickly. She focused on the page in front of her, skimming the text and stopping at a point that sounded interesting.

I grow tired of this lost puppy that has decided to follow us. It seems he somehow enjoys the verbal flogging that Mara administers, as if her constant insults are pleasurable. It's unnerving. I wish we had left him with his cult, but no, Mara insisted that he be allowed to come with us.

On a more favorable note, I never have to pack the tents myself anymore. The man does almost anything at the slightest order from Mara. I suppose I should call him by his name. Albrek is not a name I like, though. It is like a sneeze.

On to more important matters. We reached the repository in Trava today. It is enormous, a towering citadel that dwarfs any of the structures I've seen. The gods undoubtedly were ambitious in the scope of their constructions. Getting inside was not difficult. It seems the mechanisms to open the doors still function, unlike many of the other such devices I have seen in my travels.

The inside was astounding. There were rows and rows of monoliths, many of which were written in a dialect of our language. I have unfortunately not had time to study them all, but I will after I have attended to more pressing matters.

We discovered something unexpected. Within the citadel is an altar similar to the one at the Red Coven. Its shape is not identical, but the construction, composition, and curious angular hole are all striking in their resemblance. It seems whatever ritual was performed at the Coven was done here as well. I wonder why an altar was built in what is essentially a library. It hardly seems the venue for religious practices.

Could it be for some other purpose? Perhaps the monoliths hold the answers. May Yvvusta guide me.

Ginn, 365, 10, 10

Isobel's eyes widened. Finally! She was close to getting some proper answers. She only had to read more. She continued reading Ginn's account until one passage caught her attention.

I have made a grave mistake. Something slept beneath the altar, and I awakened it. It wanted me to. I could feel it calling to me from beneath the earth. I do not know how to describe it, so I shall not even try. Its grotesque form cannot be properly captured by words, but I can truly say that all the world's horrors were made trivial by that which I witnessed that day.

Mara has been seriously injured. The creature took her arm, and she resorted to Darkburning in her desperation. I have done what I can, but I fear she shall perish. Albrek intends to take her to Rothvale. Perhaps the mages there can help her condition beyond what I can, assuming she survives the journey.

She has not awakened since she felled the monster. In her delirium, she has only said one word, one that I do not know.

'Fai.'

May Yvvusta protect us.

Ginn, 365, 10, 30

Isobel whispered a word in shock.

"*Fai.*" The ancient word for lightning.

She turned the page, nearly tearing it out of the spine before reading the next entry as fast as she could.

I write these words alone in my tent. It is so quiet. I am left only with the conclusions we have reached from reviewing the monoliths, and they haunt me.

The world is not the world.

It is unfathomable. The world we live in is nothing more than a spell cast by the Creator, one that is governed by an inscription known as the Source.

I cannot share this with the Elder Mothers until I fully comprehend what I have learned. For now, I shall return to the Red Coven and attempt to awaken the god that sleeps beneath the obelisk at its center.

After that, I shall seek the others.

They want to be awakened. I can feel it. They want to walk the earth again. They want their punishment to end. They want to restore their language, just like the one here did when Mara slayed it. They want to break the curse, the final protection against true, unbridled magic. If that is what their wish, then I shall grant it.

The magic we know is limited. The curse made it so. It need not be. Why should we accept such restrictions? The gods may have been forbidden from altering the Source, but it seems that our souls have no such limitations. Minera is proof of that. She touched it and thus became Ushereh'va.

The map I found indicates the rough locations of the others. I have copied it and shall carry it with me to the Red Coven.

Mara has left. She and Albrek departed for Rothvale, and I have decided to inform the Elder Mothers that she has perished. They need not know of her decision. I hope that they can have a happy life together. May Yvvusta guide them.

Ginn, 365, 11, 7

Isobel dropped the book.

"Son of a motherless boarbat!" Isobel shouted from within the tent.

Chinelo and Mort both turned their heads toward the sound. She had been in there for hours, long after the sun went down, leaving the two of them to tend to the fire themselves.

"Dear? Is something the matter?"

Isobel responded with a loud groan. Chinelo looked at Mort, who responded with an extremely confused expression of his own. Isobel burst out of the tent and stamped on the ground angrily.

"It just ends, Chinelo! It just ends!"

"I beg your pardon?"

Isobel opened the book she held in her hand, the last of Mother Ginn's journals.

"She was getting somewhere, Chinelo! She was so close to spelling it out. But no! She just *had* to quit writing about it! Bah! Unbelievable!"

She tossed the book onto the ground and sat by the fire with a loud huff.

Chinelo picked up the book from where it had landed and opened it to the final written page. He read through the entry, lingering on one of the quotes.

The world is not the world.

He looked up. "What does all that mean?"

Isobel wrung her hands in exasperation. "Exactly!"

"Did you learn anything from the rest of it?"

"A couple things stand out. First, both obelisks in Veshda have been awakened, so we can cross those off our list of possibilities."

Chinelo nodded. "Good to know."

"Second, Ginn reached mostly the same conclusion we did. The gods placed a restriction on magic before they vanished."

Chinelo crossed his arms. "Well, that's something at least."

Isobel waved her hand. "Beyond that... without the transcriptions she referenced, it is difficult to really make a proper judgement. All it does is support what we already suspected. Oh, and *'fai'* was once sealed up as well. That's new."

"Interesting. So, what's next?"

Isobel leaned back and landed in the dirt. She spread her arms out and lay on her back, looking at the sky. Her eyes sparkled with twinkling starlight.

"I don't know..."

Chinelo stroked his chin. If both obelisks in Veshda had been claimed, then there were only four left. One in Rothvale and three on the islands around the continent.

Isobel rubbed her forehead. *"Ushereh'va,"* she muttered.

"What was that?"

Isobel sat up. "It's a compound word in the Ancient Tongue. I guess it's a title the gods gave Minera before they killed her. I've certainly never heard it before today."

"Hmm." Chinelo stroked his chin. "What does it mean?"

"Well, it's composed of two words, *ushe* and *reh*. So, it means..." her voice trailed off. She touched her lips, and her eyes darted down.

Chinelo's brow furrowed. "Isobel?"

"Shh!" Isobel commanded.

She leaned forward, pressing her fingers against her temples. Something was churning in that mind of hers. Her lips moved silently. After several moments, she leapt to her feet. "I know what Iva's plan is."

Chinelo straightened. "Do tell."

Isobel clapped her hands. "So! Iva described the Source as the accumulation of the Creator's words, but Ginn described it as an inscription, an inscription that was alterable. Now, Iva mentioned that she wanted to access the Source and use it to change the world. So! If it is in fact some sort of inscription, then she's trying to change it so it behaves how she wants."

Chinelo cocked his head. "I follow, but how would she do that?"

Isobel bent over and scribbled in the dirt, marking an inscription on the ground. "Think of it like this, Chinelo. What if the Source was malleable, like this dirt is?"

She held her hand over the string of runes she had drawn. A glowing orb of deep violet formed over them.

"All right! So, this light is the world, and the inscription is the Source. It makes the world purple. Now, if I'm Iva, and I don't like that the world is purple, I could just come along and change it." She filled one of the symbols with dirt, drawing over it with another. "Now! Watch!"

The glowing orb reappeared, this time radiating a bright green.

Chinelo nodded. "I see! So, if we extrapolate that idea to a universe-sized scale, then she could essentially change anything she wanted."

Isobel snapped her fingers. "Exactly! But there's a problem."

"Oh?"

Isobel grabbed his hand and pulled him to her side. "Chinelo, I want you to change the spell I wrote. Replace any of the characters, then see what happens."

"I still can't read all of that, Isobel."

"Doesn't matter!" She shook her head emphatically. "Do it anyways."

Chinelo crouched and studied the inscription. "This isn't going to go well."

"Just try."

He picked one of the symbols, a circular rune broken by a crisscross of lines. He brushed his hand over it and replaced it with one of the few symbols he knew, the wavy rune for water.

Isobel scanned the new inscription. "That should be... yes. Good. Now activate it."

Chinelo concentrated, channeling esht into the newly revised inscription. Nothing happened.

"I'm sorry, Isobel. I think I broke it."

Isobel crouched beside him and tapped the drawing. "That is exactly the point I wanted to make. Mages, witches especially, have this sort of understood rule—maybe you remember it: Never alter a spell that you do not fully understand."

"Right. Because if you get it wrong, it might break?"

"Yes! And breaking can either be a loss or a complete distortion of function."

Chinelo looked down. "So, if the Source is a spell that governs how the world operates, if someone changed that spell in the wrong way, then the Source would break. Which would mean that..."

"The entire world would break!" Isobel exclaimed. "With even the smallest mistake, everything would be over. The whole universe would come to an end. And there would be no going back."

Chinelo shuddered. "By the queen."

Isobel ran her fingers through her hair. "It makes so much sense now, though. We're talking reality altering, world changing power here. For Iva, any sacrifice would be justified, because she could just undo that sacrifice by altering the Source. She could kill without regret. She could level cities without a second thought, all to achieve her goals. Not only that, if she had already done those things, then the only way she could undo them would be to rewrite the world, so they never happened. So, it would be sort of a snowball effect. The more she did to achieve her goal, the more she would need to achieve it to right the wrongs she had done. It makes sense! It finally makes sense!"

"But how would she even be able to change the Source?" Chinelo asked.

Isobel stood and began pacing. "Well, Iva already indicated that it was linked to the obelisks somehow. So, it must be accessible with one of the sealed words. She probably doesn't know which one it is, so she has been trying all of them, kind of like what we are doing. That also explains why she was trying to get to you back in Veld. She knew you learned whatever the sealed word was there, so she would have to confirm it was not the Source, just like she tried with me."

"Ah," Chinelo said. "So, we need to either find the Source first, or we need to find the word for time first."

Isobel snapped her fingers again. "Exactly. It's a race."

"Well, if we want to go for the most accessible one, then Rothvale is the obvious choice."

"Are we sure Rothvale is left?" Isobel said. "Why would she leave that one unclaimed?"

Chinelo stood. "Think about it. Any time Iva and the Archmage have found an obelisk, they have destroyed the entire city it's in. We would definitely have heard of that happening in Rothvale. Also, the Interior Guard is based in Rothvale. They wouldn't just destroy their personal army unless that was the only option."

"I see," Isobel nodded.

"So, if we go to Rothvale, we should be able to claim its obelisk for ourselves. We don't have enough money to charter a voyage to the north, and it will take too long to reach the others. If we're lucky, Iva won't even be in Rothvale. She'll likely still be searching for us out here."

Isobel nodded again. "It would be risky, though. The Interior Guard will be looking for us, and we'd be walking into their nest."

"Then let's make a plan. Let's expand our arsenal. We have new words we haven't used yet. Let's use those. We know the word for memory. If any of them spot us, just make them forget. We know the word for meteor. If things get hectic, I can just summon one to scare everyone off."

Isobel grinned. "I like it. Let's do it. I have some ideas for ways we can counter Iva and the Archmage's spells. And I know where I want to start."

"Where is that?"

Isobel tapped her back. "My flight tattoo."

Chinelo held the needle over one of the missing sections of Isobel's flight tattoo, checking the schematic she had drawn for reference. The guidelines he had painted on her scarred back looked correct, but he was still hesitant. One of the runes just below her shoulder blades had its corner severed by the gash running to her hip. That would be where he started. He channeled esht into the inscription on the handle of her tattooing needle which triggered its buzzing reciprocation.

"You ready?" he asked.

Isobel was lying on her stomach. She rested her head on her crossed arms, the upper portions of which were mottled with several recently healed burns, burns that also appeared on her sides.

"Go for it."

Chinelo nodded and took a deep breath. Despite her insistence that he was the one who made the tattoo initially, having no memory of it did not instill much confidence within him. He glanced at Mort, who sprawled in a blobby heap across the tent from him, glowering disapprovingly.

Chinelo let out another breath and leaned forward, using his fingers to hold her skin beneath the needle. He ran it lightly over the guideline, and the trail of black ink flowed and embedded. He closed off the corner of the rune and lifted the needle.

"There! That wasn't so bad," she chimed.

Chinelo nodded and looked at the rest of the tattoo. It was a daunting task. He sighed, moving onto one of the more complex sections.

"You know," Isobel said, "I can't see what you're doing, but it feels like you are doing it correctly. So good job."

Chinelo paused. "It doesn't hurt?"

"Of course it hurts. It hurts a lot. You've had one before. You should know."

Chinelo continued, repairing the broken ring of symbols at the center of her back. It was a slow process, one that was marked by an occasional wince from Isobel.

"Once we've finished things and reset the timeline, I'm going to have to take you to this one tavern in Nellborough," Isobel said. "It's called The Fat Caterpillar. They have this dog there, Meaters—"

"Meaters?" Chinelo looked up, finishing one of the angled edges of another rune. "That's... certainly a name for a dog."

"Hey, now. I named that dog," Isobel said indignantly.

"Why would you name him that?" Chinelo cracked his neck and stretched his shoulders.

"Listen, I was fifteen and he kept stealing meat off the tables, so it stuck. And I'll have you know, everyone loved Meaters and his meat stealing tendencies."

"I'm sure they did, dear."

"What?" she replied, her voice rising. "You never came up with any stupid names as a child?"

"Well, I was already in Primary Knight's Academy when I was that age, so I didn't exactly have too many opportunities."

Isobel huffed quietly.

"I suppose," Chinelo said, "I did think it was a good idea to call my sword 'Legend Breaker' when I was thirteen or fourteen."

Isobel giggled. "Legend Breaker?"

"That's correct."

"Why?"

"I thought it sounded intimidating. Something about it being the sword to slay all evil or something."

"What do you call it now?"

Chinelo shrugged. "I call it 'my sword.'"

"No! That's boring."

He shrugged again. "You're the magic spewing, runaway, god-slaying, fire-dancing witch here, not me."

"Well, we can work on it," she said. "After you finish up back there."

"Right."

Chinelo mended more runes, bringing the tattoo closer and closer to its original form. He set the needle down and shook out his hands. His fingers were on the verge of cramping, but he was making good progress.

"Hey, Chinelo?"

"Yes, love?"

"When you were young, did you have an image of who you thought you might be as an adult?"

"Well, sure." Chinelo picked up the needle again, supplying it with esht to resume its oscillation.

"What did that look like?"

Chinelo hesitated before bringing the needle to her skin. "I think you know a lot of it already, but I saw myself being a knight, basically since I was old enough to start think about what I wanted to be when I grew up.

My brother really inspired me in that area, and my parents were very encouraging, too." He leaned over, repairing another rune. "Of course, there were the usual things like settling down after a while, raising family. And you?"

Her head moved slightly. "I wanted to be like Iva, or at least who I thought she was. Traveling the world, growing as a witch, seeing all kinds of amazing people and places along the way—that's why I hoped to be one of the Red Coven's Blades."

Chinelo resumed work, glancing up at her occasionally.

"I guess..." Isobel started, letting her words hang for a moment. "In a way, I got to live out that dream." Her eyes grew distant.

Chinelo pursed his lips, trying to focus on a particularly intricate rune. Some of the angles and shapes were remarkably complex.

"So!" Isobel said, shaking her head. "You want to stay in Eshgar? Once we fix everything?"

Chinelo finished the last rune. The many lines and angles of the runes were finally closed, leaving a recompleted tattoo on Isobel's slightly raw skin. "I mean, I'd like to spend some time there. But that doesn't necessarily mean I need to stay there forever."

"I suppose being a knight would require it, though," she said with an oddly melancholy tone to her voice.

Chinelo wiped the excess ink off her skin with a damp rag. "Actually, I think I'm going to quit my position as a knight."

"Wait! Really?"

He nodded, then shimmied around her, sitting with his legs crossed. "I'm sure Azuka will have some words about it, but he'll come around to my way of thinking. Plus, it would allow me to have some more flexibility for something else I'd like to do."

"That's so exciting!" she beamed. "How are you going to spend all your time?"

"Well, I can think of a one way I'd like to start." He looked down for a moment. He needed to ask her. It was time. Yet somehow, he was nervous. Somehow, he was afraid.

"All done back there?" Isobel said.

Chinelo glanced up. She tapped her shoulder lightly.

"Oh! Yes. Sorry."

"Excellent," Isobel said. "All right! I need to get decent."

Chinelo nodded and left the tent, closing the entryway so that she could dress herself. The sun had already crossed most of the sky, and it had bashfully hidden itself behind a gossamer shroud of thin clouds, diffusing its light over the valley in which they had camped.

Isobel scampered from the tent, clad in her typical attire of a loose, deep red shirt and flowing faded trousers. She radiated an aura of cheer and joviality that he found completely enchanting. She skipped to his side and smiled before kissing him on the cheek.

"Bye," she said with a slight wave.

"Bye?"

She crouched and jumped, flying straight up into the sky. Chinelo watched her flit about, soaring in wide circles and diving in tight spirals. Faintly, during some of her lower passes, he thought he heard her shouting and screaming in a joyous exultation at her reclaimed freedom. After several minutes, she floated down and landed beside him.

"How I've missed that!" she said with a satisfied sigh. "Excellent work! I've returned to the ground safely and with all my body parts intact."

"I do what I can."

"Well," she clapped her hands. "Tonight, I will do what I can! Sit, sit."

Chinelo sat on the rock she had indicated. "What's going on, Isobel?"

"Just you rest, good sir. Tonight, you are my guest, for I will be preparing the best meal you've ever had... in north Iskara."

He pushed himself off the rock. "Oh! Isobel, you don't have to. I am happy—"

"No!" She raised her finger and shoved it in his face. "You always cook, and you always set up the camp. It's my turn now! You are resting tonight, and that's final!"

CHAPTER 61

ISOBEL SAT HIGH ABOVE THE GROUND on a rocky spire, watching Chinelo in the field below. He swung his sword, cleaving wide slices in the tall grass around him. In their journey towards the capital, they had covered significant ground. Having access to her flight capabilities and her travel stones made crossing the continent so much faster than it had been initially. It would not be long now. They were close.

She held her hands to her mouth and shouted. "All right! Do it!"

Chinelo pointed his sword skyward. From where she sat, Isobel was unable to hear the incantation, but she could see his lips move.

A shadow appeared in the sky, an enormous blazing stone. Chinelo swung his sword down and it fell, crashing into the earth. The spire shook, and Isobel slipped off, hovering in midair with her legs crossed.

"Again! From a different angle!" she yelled.

Chinelo nodded and held his sword over his shoulder, pointing it diagonally upwards. His lips moved again, and another meteor appeared, one that crashed into the ground at an angle when he sliced his sword through the air.

Isobel clapped with glee. The spell worked! Now all they needed was to etch it into his spell-core. She floated down and alighted in the grass beside him. "How much esht did you use?"

Chinelo rubbed his shoulder. "Not as much as I would have thought for something of that size. I could probably do that ten or fifteen times before I ran out."

"That's the benefit of knowing the exact word. It really helps the spell efficiency when you don't have to describe something as much."

Chinelo nodded. "Thank you for figuring out the incantation."

"Ah, it was nothing. How about that other one you asked me to make? Have you gotten the hang of it? That meteor you dropped would be a good target for it."

Chinelo held his sword in front of him and faced the meteor. He closed his eyes and tightened his grip on the handle. Isobel watched eagerly for his strike. She waited, holding her breath as he focused his esht into his sword.

"Transcend."

He swung his sword, and Isobel heard a sound like the rushing wind. The air distorted in front of him, churning in tight curves that tore the grass to bits. The whirlwind progressed towards the meteor, slicing it into several large chunks of stone.

Isobel gasped. "That is still striking every time I see it."

"Honestly, I am a little scared to use it," Chinelo said. "That would be brutal to be caught in."

Isobel nodded. "Well, if you get desperate, meteors and whirlwinds are at your disposal."

"How are your spells coming along?"

"Well, one of them should work, but I'm not really willing to test it. Removing memories is not something I want to try."

"I appreciate that," he said slyly.

"What? I would never use it on you."

"Of course, dear."

She scowled in his direction. "Let's head back to camp. I've got a lot of spell-coding to do tonight. I've thought of a nullification technique for your sword, and I want to get it right."

Chinelo laughed. "Of course, dear."

"Oh, stop!"

She crossed her arms and legs and floated beside him, moving weightlessly through the air in a sitting position.

"You know, you look rather silly doing that." Chinelo said, grinning with that knowing expression she loved so much.

Isobel shifted her esht flow, rotating her so that she floated upside down. "Chinelo, you would not believe how comfortable this is. If you would just allow me to give you the spell, you could experience it for yourself."

Chinelo raised his hand. "I'm not eager to vomit again, but I appreciate the offer. I just don't have the stomach for it, as much as I might want to."

"Well, you have no idea what you are missing." She extended her arms and somersaulted, landing on her feet.

Chinelo touched his chin. "How about this? Could you give me one that cancels gravity? I could probably manage that, and it would definitely help my mobility."

"Certainly!" Isobel pranced ahead of him with a smile on her face. "I'll get my needle and ink ready once we are back."

They continued through the field, making their way back to their campsite which was nestled at the base of a small hill.

"Hey, Isobel. About Iva..."

Isobel felt a flicker of anger at the mention of her name. She stopped. "What about her?"

"Assuming we can reverse time, how are we going to stop her?"

Isobel frowned. "I—I'm not sure yet. I have a few ideas, but really the only person that knows how to stop Iva is Iva herself. We can't exactly ask her. My best guess is that we will have to find her before she destroys Eshgar and convince her not to." She looked down. Her lips formed a tight line. There was another option, one she found herself considering. She shook her head. "The only time I can pin her to is the night she destroyed the Red Coven, and that is somewhere in the second month of 433."

"So, we're going back at least two years, then," Chinelo said.

"I'll try to send us back further, just so we have more time. Let's make a plan. Where should we meet?"

Chinelo scratched his head. "I would say let's meet in Skyview. That's midway between our homes, and it's along the trade route. I can join one of the caravans out there. We can talk more about it when we get back to the tent and have a proper map."

She smiled. "Sounds good. We'll definitely want some kind of signal."

"I'll be sure to run around screaming your name, so you'll have no trouble finding me," Chinelo said.

"Oh! Magnificent! I'll set a building on fire or something. That will be my signal."

"I'll hurry then," Chinelo smirked.

"You'd better. I am, after all," she flourished her hands and bowed, "the famous arsonist of Nellborough."

Chinelo grimaced.

"I mean—umm, that is to say—uhhh," Isobel stammered. "Hmmm. That really wasn't a tasteful joke, was it?"

"It's not your best work. I know what you were shooting for, though."

"I suppose that is good enough then."

Isobel dropped her staff on the ground. They had arrived. She stretched and approached their tent. She began thinking through the list of items she needed to do that evening. She would need to draft Chinelo's gravity spell, help him load his meteor spell into his core, make a few final changes to her own arsenal, feed Mort...

She looked over her shoulder. Chinelo remained a few steps behind. He stood still, clenching his fists and staring at the ground. She cocked her head. He looked like he was turning something over in his mind. An idea... or a question, perhaps? Maybe he was like her, thinking through the preparations for the next few days.

"Isobel?" Chinelo said.

"That's my name."

"There's something I wanted to ask you."

"Oh?"

Chinelo remained silent for a moment. His face became slightly pallid. Isobel's brow furrowed.

"I—I mean..." he cleared his throat and took a deep breath.

"Want to talk about it while I finish up all those spells? I have a lot of work I need to do before sundown." She pulled open the tent flap.

Chinelo looked up. "Oh. Right. No—no. I don't want to distract you. We can talk about it later."

Isobel smiled. "All right! I'll let you know once I'm ready to apply your tattoo. Give me a few hours."

Chinelo nodded. "Of course..."

She crawled into the tent and began her many, many tasks of preparations.

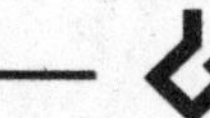

Isobel concluded her daily entry in her diary and closed the book. What a productive few days it had been. She let out a satisfied sigh.

The tent door flew open and Chinelo crawled inside, placing his boots in their usual spot in the corner. "All right. Things should be set for the morning. We'll just need to make breakfast and then we can cross the final stretch to Rothvale. We should be in the city by nightfall."

Isobel shuddered. The prospect of entering the capital was daunting. They would have to avoid the Interior Guard in the outskirts, infiltrate the city without being spotted, locate the obelisk, awaken it, hope it was in fact the correct one, and, assuming it was, try to find out how to use the rune within to turn back time.

Chinelo crawled beside her. "We can do this. Iva probably wouldn't expect us to go towards the capital."

"I mean, it is a bit bold. It's crazy that it was your idea. Such things are normally my specialty."

Chinelo stroked his beard. "It is a little reckless, but it's our best shot at getting a rune quickly. We don't have the time or money to spend on the three in the ocean, and if Iva is going by what is closest, she'll probably go to the one in the north or the one Ginn found in Veshda. That is if she doesn't already know Ginn claimed it."

"Right. Well, I am with you to the end. Whatever that end may be."

"And I you."

Isobel smiled and leaned on her elbow, watching Chinelo settle himself for the night. How had she gotten so lucky? In a way, Iva was to thank for their meeting. She wasn't sure she was ready to consider the more complicated implications of that, but she was grateful for the fact that they had met, regardless of how it happened.

"What's something you want to do once we've finished?" Chinelo asked.

Isobel extended her arm, reaching towards him. Chinelo grasped her hand in his.

"Well, for starters, I'd love to give you a more complete tour of Nellborough. After that…" she looked up at the ceiling.

"Yes?"

"Well, we already talked about going to Eshgar. That will be next! What about you?"

Chinelo looked at the ceiling. There was something odd about his expression, something Isobel could not read. Was it apprehension for their descent into Rothvale, or anxiety about something else? He looked slightly pale, and his eyes moved as if he was contemplating something deeply. He had been doing that a lot lately. She nestled into her pillow and closed her eyes, running her thumb over the veins on the back of his hand. It did not matter. He was still dashing as always, even when she had trouble reading him.

"Do you want to get married?" Chinelo asked.

"Absolutely." Isobel replied without even a moment's thought.

She lay there, pondering the idea. That would be nice—just the two of them for the rest of their lives. She could inherit his last name as was the Eshgarian custom and move her surname to the middle. She would be Isobel Valeria Ide.

Of course, they would need to decide where they would live. His entire family was in Eshgar, but her home was near Nellborough. Perhaps they could alternate between the two. Eshgar would be much more pleasant in the winters, while Nellborough had lovely summers. Given the general sentiment Eshgarians had about witches and mages, she probably wouldn't be able to practice her usual profession there. Maybe Nellborough would really be the better of the two options. They could make that decision after they had set things right.

Her eyes flew open. She shot up on her bed. "Wait! What?"

"I love you, Isobel. We've talked about our future and... well, I can't imagine my life without you. I'd like to make things official, so I'd like to marry you, if you'll have me," he said.

Wait. That was real? She released his hand and ran her fingers through her hair. Her heart pounded. Her lungs swelled, filling with an untamable fire that burned within her.

"Isobel?"

"Yes! I mean—I mean please—I mean—that is to say..." the words somehow streamed out like a raging river, but she could not string them together in a way that was coherent. "Bah! I don't know what to say. What should I say?"

Chinelo sat up and moved his blanket aside, crossing his legs. "A 'yes' will do, if that's how you feel," he said in a low voice. "If it's not..."

"Obviously my answer is 'yes!'" she declared, almost shouting for joy.

Chinelo let out a sigh of relief. He ran his hand over his brow. His face brightened, as if a heavy weight had been lifted. "I'm sorry. I know that was rather sudden, but I had to know, in case something happened."

"Wait! Was this what you've been trying to ask me?" Isobel asked.

Chinelo nodded.

Isobel covered her face. "Ah! I'm so sorry! I—I didn't know that—oh, you must have been mortified."

Chinelo smirked. "I was certainly a little anxious."

"Anxious? Did you think I would say 'no'?"

"I mean, I hoped you wouldn't," he said with a bashful grin.

Isobel tapped her chin. "Do they kiss much after proposals in Eshgar?"

"I—I think that is customary."

"Good." She pounced, flinging herself across the tent into Chinelo's arms. She kissed him passionately, running her hand down his muscular back and pulling him close. His strong arms wrapped around her, drawing her into his tender embrace.

She leaned back and giggled. "I'm going to be your wife."

"You are!" Chinelo beamed.

"So, how are proposals commemorated in Eshgar?"

"Well, to celebrate the engagement, we typically move this..." Chinelo slid Isobel's bracelet off her right wrist. "And we put it on this side." He moved the bracelet to the left side.

"Is there a significance to wearing one on your right arm?" she asked.

"In a way. Usually, the women wear them on their right if they are unmarried but have chosen a suitor, thought that is a dying tradition. None of the women I've ever pursued did that."

She giggled. "So, you've been plotting this for a while."

Chinelo twisted one of her longer locks of hair around his index finger. "You could say that."

Isobel squirmed. She could not contain her excitement.

"Do witches have wedding customs?" Chinelo asked. "I know that that is probably a complicated subject."

Isobel looked at the ceiling. "Well, witches of the Red Coven typically don't marry, or they marry for pragmatic purposes. So, we have no customs there, and my mother never told me how her wedding was handled. How are weddings conducted in Eshgar?"

Chinelo smiled and looked down. "Weddings were pretty understated in Eshgar unless you were royalty. The ones I went to were very limited in their attendance. There is a traditional vow that both parties agree to, and a witness confirms that vow. The ceremonies have some traditional rituals, nothing too complicated. It's not really anything extravagant."

"So, what I'm hearing is that we could get married as soon as we find someone to witness the deed?" Isobel cocked her head playfully.

"That is correct."

"Oh. Won't reversing time mean that our vows would be undone?" She tapped her cheek. "So, we would have to get married twice."

Chinelo laughed. "I suppose. I'm sure my family would have some questions if I acted like we were already wed without an explanation."

"Hmmm. How about this? Since we are in a hurry to find the next rune, let's hold off until we reverse time so that the vows will be binding. We can get married in Eshgar with your family there. Would you mind waiting that long?"

"Isobel, I will wait as long as you like," Chinelo replied. "The two of us together—that's what matters."

"That's what matters." She leaned forward, touching her forehead against his. "Just you and me."

A faint croak came from the foot of Isobel's bed. Isobel rolled her eyes. Chinelo grinned. "And Mort?"

"And Mort..." She shook her head. Such a menace.

Rothvale sprawled before Isobel, an enormous metropolis of towering spires and citadels, an ancient city of the gods. Golden sunlight shone through silver clouds, bathing the expansive city in its gentle glow. From the hill upon which she stood, Isobel took it all in. The city seemed endless. Though it was too far to reach before sundown, the city was so large that it looked close. Over a million people lived down there, coursing through the streets like the blood in her body.

At the far north, she saw the ivory palace of King Wendd, the ruler of Iskara. It was divided into a series of inner walls, each rising higher than the last, ending with the colossal central tower that stood like a great tree over the city. The palace was magnificent in its symmetry, and a perfect copy of it was reflected in the clear water surrounding it.

The city itself looked compact and cramped, with buildings arranged in tight clusters. In contrast to the pure white castle, the other buildings were much drabber, but their rooftops were a rainbow of colors. The many citadels and towers that were scattered throughout Rothvale were of course the typical pale gray of the gods' stonework, but within their shadows bloomed a vibrant display of life.

Chinelo stood by her side, scanning the walls for entry points. There were eight gates, one for each cardinal direction, and four placed evenly between. Beyond the walls lay many much smaller villages, farming towns that ordinarily would have tilled the many fields around Rothvale, though they were strangely filled with throngs of people exiting the city that day.

Chinelo shaded his eyes from the sun and pointed. "Is that smoke?"

Isobel squinted. A plume of dark gray climbed from the city towards the sky. Another appeared in the far east of the city. Another sprouted from the south.

"Something is happening," she said.

Chinelo pointed to the north. "By the queen. Is that...?"

Isobel turned her gaze to the boulder fields beyond Rothvale. A silver shadow crept across the land, an army marching towards the Capital.

Isobel gasped. Was there an invasion? Who would dare challenge the legendary might of the king's army of mages? Who would dare besiege Rothvale?

"You wouldn't happen to know any spells to enhance vision, would you?" Chinelo said.

Isobel glanced down at the spell-book dangling from her hip. Iva once taught her such a spell. "I do, it just doesn't work well for me, given my poor eyesight. It gives me headaches."

"Mind if I try?"

Isobel dropped her staff and unfastened the book, flipping from page to page to find the spell she sought. Where was it? It would have been one she transcribed early after her mother made the book for her. Ten pages in, she found the inscription.

"Here!" She held the book in front of Chinelo. "Try this."

Chinelo held his hand over the text and tensed. His eyes widened and he stepped back.

"Oh, my," he said. "That... that is rather disorienting."

He rubbed his eyes and turned his gaze towards the army in the distance.

"What do you see?" Isobel asked.

Chinelo squinted. "I'm looking for a flag. Ah!"

"Do you recognize it?"

Chinelo nodded solemnly. "It's Veld. The colors and armor match the garrison we encountered. I guess they aren't pleased about Iva's murder of the duke."

Isobel grimaced. Somehow, even after knowing all she did, it was still hard for her to believe Iva would do something like that. She had to let go. The woman she once knew had changed, even if Isobel still wanted to hold to her childhood image of her.

"Can you tell what is causing that smoke in the city?" Isobel asked.

Chinelo shook his head and closed his eyes. "I'm afraid not. I saw quite a bit of movement, though."

Perhaps the chaos would present an opportunity to find what they sought. Somewhere in that city lay an obelisk. Would it have what they were looking for? Would it even be there? She did not know, but with Mort on her shoulder and Chinelo by her side, she was ready to find out. She reached for his hand and laced her fingers between his before looking once more at the city.

A flash.

An overwhelming gold light burst from beyond the northern wall of Rothvale. It grew, swelling until it erupted into a swirling column of orange flames. Isobel's heart pounded. It was like before. It was the same light that had consumed Nellborough. The same blazing tornado spread, growing wider and wider. She heard Chinelo inhale sharply. Without even thinking, she summoned her barrier. The infernal maelstrom expanded, approaching the wall in its blinding fury. Isobel shook.

Then, the light vanished, leaving the city untouched.

Isobel stood there, still holding Chinelo's hand in hers. They panted, trembling as one. Chinelo gasped and pointed to where the light had been. Moments before there had been an army in those hills. Now, there was only a great black scar across the land, a perfect circle of burning carnage.

"She's here," Isobel exhaled.

CHAPTER 62

CHINELO'S HEART HAMMERED IN HIS EARS. His head spun. The sight of the blazing column hauled memories from the deep recesses of his mind. They returned, overtaking every one of his senses, and filling him with an urge, no, an order to run. He clenched his fist.

"She's not supposed to be here," Isobel said.

"We knew it was a risk." Chinelo shook his head. "We need to move."

Isobel nodded and pulled her hood over her head with Mort tucked inside. Chinelo followed suit, and they began their plunge from the hills on which they stood to the final stretch of road to Rothvale.

The highway was densely packed with travelers fleeing from Iskara's capital, and Chinelo and Isobel seemed to be the only pair that was approaching the city. Numerous camps were set up along the roadside, and as Chinelo led the way, he observed a general expression of somber bewilderment that hung over the crowds that congregated around campfires.

He stopped and looked at one of the camps. A family sat on the ground, staring blankly into the fire. He could imagine the thoughts that must be racing through their heads. Seeing such mass death, even at a distance, changed one's spirit. Such horror could not be ignored.

He continued forward, and Isobel followed behind him, having left her staff hidden in a tree to avoid drawing attention. Chinelo had concealed his sword under his cloak in the event that they were suddenly accosted, though there were none from the Interior Guard present in the traffic that evening.

The sky was dark, and the road was lit by the many torches and lanterns carried by the mass exodus. Chinelo's stomach growled.

"We're not going to make it to the city before it gets too late," he said.

"Want to find a place to camp? Maybe the roads will have cleared up by dawn."

"Maybe. Let's find somewhere away from the road."

Isobel sat in her tent in the morning sunlight, having just awoken in a bit of a sorry state. She rubbed her eyes. She was tired, grimy, and hungry. Her stomach roared at her to provide sustenance, and its persistent voice roused Chinelo from his rest as well. He seemed much more willing to begin the day than she did.

She sat with her legs still buried beneath her blankets, staring ahead blankly as her stomach continued its tantrum. They had walked the entirety of the day before. Everything hurt. Her feet were sore. Her calves were tight. Her legs ached. For some reason she could not explain, her shoulders were exceedingly stiff.

They were going to enter Rothvale that day, and she would have to walk even more if they hoped to fully scour the city. She groaned and lay back down, pulling her blanket over her head.

She felt something moving on top of her bedding. She peaked out and saw a very blurry Mort-shaped mass staring sadly up at her. She sighed. Mort needed to eat, and for that she would need to find some food.

She crawled out of bed and located her spectacles.

"Chinelo," she said.

"Yes, dear?"

"I'm going to change clothes then go find Mort some food."

"Understood. I'll do the same for us while you are gone. We should have enough crescents to last us today, though I think this will be the end of it."

She rubbed her eyes behind her spectacles. Acquiring money would definitely be a problem, one that she did not want to think about solving.

After changing into a warm tunic and donning her cloak, Isobel stowed a travel stone in her pocket to make the return trip easier. With Mort on her shoulder, she stepped out from the tent. The morning was bright. The birds sang. The fields twinkled with dew, and the road nearby was already bustling with activity. She turned and searched the hills to the west. Where would be a good location to find Mort a meal? A small cluster of trees caught her eye. There! She uttered an incantation that transported them above the peaceful oaks. She floated down, landing on the soft grass. Now, to begin.

She listened intently for any sounds that indicated life. After a moment, she heard a faint chirping. The crickets were still out. She smiled, and she was certain that Mort was doing the same, or at least the amphibian equivalent.

She crept towards the sound and crouched, placing Mort on the ground to begin his hunt. He immediately flew into motion, hoping into the tufts of grass and consuming all that hid within. It was a horrific display, a feral performance of pure bloodshed.

Isobel leaned back on her hands and looked to the sky. The clouds were arranged in long slender streaks, pressed together like several mountain ridges. Above them were even more clouds, thin wisps of frozen cotton at the upper reaches of the sky.

She closed her eyes. The previous day had been chaotic, but within the shadow of these oaks she felt peace. It was so tranquil. It was so quiet. The wind suddenly gusted, tearing her hood from her head and whistling through her slightly tangled hair.

It used to be like this every morning. She would rise from her house and draw water in the quiet forest. She would gather worms for Mort and listen to the stillness of the dawn. She would read beneath the golden trees, surrounded by the rustling leaves and bathed in the gentle wind.

It would not be long. Somehow, deep within her soul, she could feel it. It was a strange apprehension, an undeniable certainty. The eye had passed over, and the storm was resuming. Their journey would soon end.

The stillness was broken by a crunching leaf. Isobel jumped and whirled around, surging esht into her left arm.

An old man stumbled back at the edge of the grove, raising his hand defensively. He was short, a feature that was further amplified by his bent spine. He was almost completely bald, and though he had no beard, the amount of hair that comprised his white mustache rivaled that of even the most fabulous displays of facial hair Isobel had witnessed.

"Stay back!" she said, preparing to expel her esht through the tattoo on her left wrist.

The man leaned against his cane. "My, my. Jumpy little thing, aren't you?"

Isobel's eyes narrowed warily. The man poked his cane into the dirt. He looked off to the north, gazing over the charred boulder fields.

"It seems you've also found my favorite field gazing spot. Might I join you, young lady?"

Isobel stepped back a couple paces. The man did not seem threatening. His attire was simple, a shirt and trousers of homespun fabric. His cane bore no spell-core, and his wrinkled hands did not have any tattoos or marks.

She lowered her hand but kept the esht ready to fly should he decide to make any sudden moves.

"Sit, if you like." Isobel nodded to a nearby rock.

"Ah. Excellent. You looked like a reasonable lady." The man shambled to the stone and with many groans and creaks he sat himself down and let out a long sigh.

"It really is a lovely morning, don't you think?"

Isobel sat on the ground opposite him, watching him closely. She gave no answer.

"It's been an eventful few days here," the man continued, looking up at the sky as Isobel had before. "The city is really all wound up. Riots, protests, and a mass exodus. I've never seen it this agitated in all my years here."

Isobel remained quiet.

"Not much for conversation, are you? Though I suppose I cannot blame you for being on edge. Seeing a war begin and end in a day does that to people."

"What's your name?" Isobel asked after a long pause.

The man looked down at her. He smiled a crooked grin that was barely visible from underneath the cascade of white hair that adorned his upper lip. "Greebus. What may I call you?"

Isobel looked down briefly. "E—Esther."

"Ah! We don't get a lot of Esthers around here. Not a very common name these days. Very popular a few decades ago."

Isobel nodded.

"What do you think of our new queen, Esther?" the man said with a slight smirk.

"Queen?" Isobel cried. "King Wendd has married?"

Greebus cocked his head. "You haven't heard?"

"I'm sorry, I'm not from here."

"King Wendd is dead." Greebus's mustache twitched. "Keeled over a few days ago. The queen was crowned immediately after."

Isobel looked down, pulling at a strand of her hair. King Wendd was dead? Had that been the work of Veld?

"It's mighty strange if you ask me. She just appeared ehhh..." Greebus scratched his head, "a year and a half ago. Now she's queen."

Isobel fidgeted with a leaf on the ground. She had heard that King Wendd had taken no wife. So where was this queen coming from?

"I suppose having a mage as ruler would have its benefits," Greebus continued. "What do you think, Esther?"

Isobel tensed, still reeling from the revelation. "I'm not sure how I would know."

"Well, you're a mage, aren't you? That's esht I heard flowing within you."

Isobel looked up. "You can hear it? How?"

The man laughed. "No, no, dear. It was just a bluff. I know that stance you adopted. You were about to use some incantation or spell on me, weren't you?"

Isobel let out a huff. Such an obvious trick. She should have known better. Iva would not approve of her naivete.

She looked up. Why had she thought of Iva?

"What's the matter, young lady?" The man adjusted his position on his cane.

"I—sorry, it's nothing. Just thinking about a warning my sister gave me about slippery old men."

"Slippery?" the man said. "I have a horrible case of psoriasis. Nothing slippery about me."

Isobel cringed.

The man bellowed a hearty laugh. "You really are too funny, Esther. Pardon that second deceit of mine. I could not resist." His eyes twinkled.

Isobel pressed her lips together into something between a frown and a smile, for her face could not decide which was the proper response.

"Tell me more about this queen," Isobel said with a slight hint of exasperation in her voice. "What is she like?"

"Hmmm," Greebus twirled half of his mustache around his finger. Isobel was almost impressed, for it was the top half, something that didn't seem twirlable, yet there he twirled. "Well, she's a warrior, that's for sure. Not a feckless coward like old Wendd was, gods grant him rest. She's clearly rather skilled with magic, judging by how fast she rose through the ranks of the Interior Guard. Though, I suppose she was already accompanying the old Archmage a year ago. It only makes sense that she would take the title after he died."

Isobel looked up. That was also news to her. She had assumed he had just resurrected again.

"If you ask me, she's rather frightening. Something about her chills my bones. Though, I will admit she *is* pretty. Dark hair always made me swoon when my heart fluttering wasn't a threat to my health. A bit too young for me, though. You won't be seeing old Greebus be king any time soon, that's for sure."

Isobe stifled a giggle. He would certainly make a strange king.

"I'm not sure I buy this whole 'Immortal Queen' thing she's got going on," Greebus waved his hand. "I would have seen magic like that by now if it was possible."

"Immortal Queen?" Isobel asked with interest.

"Ridiculous, isn't it? Some of the Interior Guard opposed her taking the throne, so she let them try to kill her. Even when she was run through, she wouldn't stay dead. At least, that's the story they tell. Didn't see it myself."

Isobel looked down. Resurrection magic. Had she shared its secrets with the monarchy? Or...?

She jumped to her feet. "What is her name?"

"Ehhh?"

Isobel dashed forward and clasped Greebus's hand in her glove. "The queen? What is her name?"

"My, my, you're awful close." His mustache twitched.

"Just tell me, please."

"All right! All right! It's something short. Irene? No. Eva? No that's not it either."

Isobel's eyes grew wide. "Iva?"

"Yes! That's the one! Immortal Queen Iva. That's what that attendant of hers called her."

Isobel stumbled back.

Impossible!

Iva was queen? How? Why? How did that help her plan? Surely, being Archmage would be enough.

She needed to find Chinelo.

"I—I need to go."

"Ehhh? But I just got here. I don't know a thing about you," Greebus said.

Isobel dug her hand into her pocket and clutched a travel stone. "Thank you, Greebus. I hope to meet you again, in another time."

Greebus waved his hand. "Of course. Of course. Just don't forget your friend down there."

Isobel looked down. Mort was at her feet, staring up at her. She scooped him in her hand and returned him to her shoulder.

Greebus pointed his cane at her head. "Keep that hood on, Esther, and keep clear of the Interior Guard. Your hair is a dead giveaway," he said with a wink.

Isobel halted and gave him a look. He really had been toying with her the whole time. She surged esht into the stone, leaving the old man chuckling to himself in the clearing. She reappeared at their camp, and Chinelo bolted upright.

"Oh, you're safe. I was getting worried," he said.

"Chinelo, the king is dead, and Iva is queen!" Isobel exclaimed.

"What?"

"I don't know how, and I don't know why, but somehow she claimed the throne."

Chinelo stroked his chin. "She's taking control over the entire Iskaran military."

"Hmmm?"

"Think about it. The Archmage commands the Interior Guard, but the garrison is subject to the king. As queen, she would control both. She could spread out over the entire country. She's either trying to find us or planning to claim the last few obelisks with a full army."

"It also explains the fire from yesterday," Isobel said. "If she's queen, any attack on Rothvale is an attack on her. Son of a mantis! Of course she would do something like this! She probably had something to do with the king's death!"

Chinelo paced. "We do have an advantage in this situation. She might be here, but she doesn't know we're here. If we hurry, we can beat her to the obelisk."

Isobel nodded and looked over the city. "Let's finish this."

THE END OF PART 7

PART 8

SISTERS

CHAPTER 63

403rd year, 4th month, 15th day
32 years before present day

IVA AWOKE TO A CRASH OUTSIDE her window and bolted upright. Lights flashed, and she heard muffled shouts and screams, the sounds of a fight. She rolled from her bed, the lower of several bunks, and rushed to the door, not even bothering to grab her shoes. Her sisters stirred. A few sat up in their bunks and rubbed their eyes, though none of them left their beds, likely afraid of the punishment for disobeying their strict curfew.

Iva pushed open the door and ran down the dark hallways of the Red Coven. She did not care about the rules. If there was a fight, she wanted to see it. But first, she had to find Esther.

She crossed over to the adult's wing and stopped at the third door. It was ajar. She peered into the dark room. The bed was vacant, and all the familiar belongings and furnishings were absent.

"Esther?" Iva whispered. There was no response.

That was strange. Esther loved her sleep, and she had been exhausted from her return trip from Nellborough. Why would she be gone? Iva changed directions, heading for the exit of the dorm building.

Iva chewed her lip. Esther had only just arrived that afternoon on one of her few permitted visits from her assignment in west Iskara. It had been nearly six months since her last visit. Iva had expected Esther to be her usual cheery self, but Esther was oddly melancholy that day.

She burst through the door and into the courtyard. The fine gravel scraped at Iva's bare feet as she ran towards the sound. She stopped. Something else was strange.

The gravel was disturbed, scattered in irregular patterns with deep divots and indentations. Sister Jessa would not be pleased. Iva glanced at the large temple at the far end of the courtyard, the Temple of the Elder

Mothers. The heavy doors were thrown open, and one hung loosely off its hinges. Another oddity.

She turned towards the sounds. Lights flashed through the trees near the exit of the compound. Iva pulled in a deep breath and continued picking her way over the gravel. She neared the gates and finally saw the source of the commotion.

Esther stood at the gate, clutching her long crescent staff in her hand. Her auburn hair flowed as she moved. She was engaged in combat with the Blades, the Red Coven's most fearsome warriors, and miraculously, she was winning.

She dodged under a sweep from a long, slender dirk, the signature weapon of Sister Joya. Esther snapped her fingers and Joya fell, crumpling to the ground. The heavy battleaxe of Sister Violet came next. Ester caught the blade, tensed, and shattered it with her bare hand.

Iva glanced around the clearing before the gate. She gasped. The Elder Mothers were there, and they had fallen like the Blades. Impossible! No one had dared to challenge them for decades. Their mastery of magic was renowned. People trembled at the mere mention of their sorceries. Had Esther really managed to defeat them?

A flash drew her attention. A circle of purple flames erupted around Esther, warding off any final attacks.

"I did not come to fight!" Esther shouted. The entire courtyard shook at her voice. "This is pointless."

A cloaked figure leapt over the flames with thick dark hair flowing behind. Iva's eyes widened. It was her mother, the Tenth Blade. Her curved dagger flashed.

"You traitor!" Verris roared. She slashed at Esther, but once again, Esther easily evaded the attacks, bending against the tempest of strikes like grass in a storm.

Esther muttered something, and a shockwave emitted from a bracelet on her wrist. Verris flew away and skidded across the ground until she stopped at Iva's feet. Iva crouched down and shook her.

"Mother! Mother!" Iva said. "Are you all right? Are you hurt? I can heal you if—"

"Silence, child!" Verris swatted away Iva's hands and stood, picking up her dropped dagger and twirling it. "I'll kill you, Esther! You, traitor!"

She crouched, preparing to pounce like a tiger. The shadows moved around her, growing and racing towards Esther's position. Iva grabbed her arm and tugged on it. "Mother! Please! Don't!"

Verris tore free and pushed her away. "Away from me, Iva!"

"Enough!" Mother Ginn's voice echoed through the night. She supported herself with one hand against a tree.

"She's betrayed us, Mother Ginn," Verris responded. "She's supposed to die!"

"That's enough, Verris!" Ginn said. "I will have no further bloodshed in my coven tonight."

Verris's face went pale. She looked shocked, appalled at the Elder's proclamation.

"Esther, you are no longer welcome here," Ginn continued. "For your betrayal, you are banished from the Red Coven."

It hit like an avalanche. Iva's heart fell. Banished? Esther was banished?

Esther relaxed and planted the end of her staff on the ground. The flames faded. "If I may make one request, I will leave without argument."

Iva's mind raced. If Esther was leaving, she wouldn't be able to see her again. She wouldn't be able to talk to her again. They wouldn't play together anymore. They wouldn't hug anymore. There would be no more bedtime stories, no more paintings, no more trips into the forest, nothing.

Ginn waved her hand. "Speak."

If Esther was leaving, Iva would be alone, neglected by a mother that didn't love her and shunned by siblings who despised her.

Esther glanced over at Iva. Her eyes clouded. "I wish to say one final goodbye."

Ginn crossed her arms. "Very well."

Esther stepped forward and knelt, bringing herself down to Iva's eye level. "Iva?"

Iva looked up at her. She felt numb. A lump formed in her throat.

"I have to go, Iva. I—I'm afraid I won't be able to come visit anymore."

"Why? I don't want you to go."

Esther looked down. Her mouth quivered. "I know. I—I wish I could take you with me, but I cannot. Try as I might."

"Why not?"

Esther looked over Iva's shoulder at Verris. She frowned. "I made a request, Iva, one that likely was unreasonable. Your mother... your mother is right to hate me."

The lump in Iva's throat grew larger. "When are you coming back?"

Esther winced and closed her eyes tightly. She shook her head. "I'm sorry, Iva, but I can't come back. This is goodbye."

Iva sniffled. She felt her eyes watering. What would she do without Esther? Who would she be without Esther? They had always been together, from as far back as she could remember. When her mother was absent, Esther had stepped in, raising Iva as her own. But if she was gone, who would Iva have?

Iva balled her hands into fists. "I don't want you to go!"

Esther sniffled and opened her arms as she always did when she returned home. Iva leapt into her embrace, bawling as Esther held her close.

"Forgive me, Iva. I'm sorry."

Iva sobbed into Esther's cloak.

"When you are older, if you can find a way, look for me in Nellborough."

Iva nodded.

Someone tore apart the embrace and ripped Iva from Esther's arms.

"Get your hands off my daughter!" Verris barked.

Esther stood and wiped her eyes. "I have to go now, Iva. I made someone a promise."

She turned and walked towards the gate, stopping for a moment to look over her shoulder. "I love you, Iva. I always will."

With those final words, she exited the gates, walking into the forest. A man joined her, a tall, thin one with a large pack on his back.

"Disgraceful," Verris scoffed. She turned her attention to her daughter. "Iva, why aren't you in bed? You know the rules."

Iva sniffled and brushed a tear from her cheek. "Mother, why is Esther leaving?"

Verris scowled down at her. "Because she's a traitor and a liar. She's abandoning us for a man, a lowborn piece of trash. And she has the nerve to pretend to love you."

Iva sniffled and reached for her mother's hand, trying to hold in her sobs. Verris slapped her hand away.

"Go back to bed, child. I'm not in the mood to deal with you right now."

Iva nodded. It was the same as always. Without Esther, she was alone. She watched the lantern's golden glow disappear into the forest, growing fainter until it vanished. She sniffled again and whispered a final call to Esther.

"Please... please don't leave me."

CHAPTER 64

405th year, 4th month, 24th day
30 years before present day

CANDLES LIT THE DARK ROOM. THE wooden walls were painted with dozens of runes and symbols, and a thick scent of sweat and blood hung in the air. Iva hated this room. She'd been dragged here many times before, and each time was a nightmare far worse than the last. She'd done things in this room, horrific things. Today, on her tenth birthday, she'd been ordered to do the worst of them all.

Two years had passed since Esther left, two wretched, lightless years. Every month she came to this room. Sometimes her mother forced her to come more often, depending on how angry she was. Iva always protested, always begged not to come. It never worked. What she wanted didn't matter. It never had.

Esther's presence had been a lie, the cruelest of lies. She'd made Iva believe that her life could have joy in it. She'd made her believe that someone could love her. Then, she left, with only the awful, empty truth remaining in her place.

Iva clutched a dagger in her hand. It was too big for her, and its cold curved steel frightened her. She didn't want to do it. She didn't!

The boy before her whimpered into his gag, struggling against his restraints. He shook his head, his long dark hair sticking to his brown skin. Her mother stood beside her, crossing her arms and glaring down at her with her typical animosity.

"Get on with it."

Iva sniffled. Her body was sore. Her face hurt. They'd been there for hours, and her mother's patience was running thin.

"I—I don't want to."

Her mother crouched, grabbing her chin and forcing her to look her in the eye. "I don't care. Now do it."

She let Iva go. Iva stepped forward, clutching her knife tighter. She closed her eyes. She didn't want to! She didn't! She shook her head. Tears trickled down her face. She heard her mother's heavy footsteps drawing closer. She tensed, bracing herself for what was coming, what always came when she resisted.

A sharp pain spread across her face. Iva staggered and fell. Her knife slid across the stone floor.

"Worthless!" her mother shouted. "Why are you so worthless? Just for once do as you're told!"

Iva whimpered. She thought of Esther. Esther didn't hate her. She thought of their good memories together. She remembered walking in the forest with her, hiding behind trees while Esther chased after her. Esther made things bearable. Esther made things right. As long as Iva thought about her, she could ignore the rest. That was how she endured. That was how she survived.

Iva forced herself up, only to be struck once more. She sobbed.

Esther! Think of Esther! Think of—

Her mother kicked her in the side.

Why? Why did Esther leave? Why did Esther abandon her? Why did things have to change? Why was she born to a mother who hated her?

Verris pulled her up by her collar. "Are you going to behave now?"

Iva nodded. She was alone, just as she always was. Esther wasn't there to help her anymore. She'd never loved her. If she had, she wouldn't have left. Daydreaming about her was pointless.

"Good." Her mother forced her knife back into her hands. "Now. Get on with it. You can go back to bed once you're finished."

Iva walked over to the boy. His eyes widened. He shook his head. Iva's heart pounded. Then, without further hesitation, she slit his throat in a single swift motion.

Blood spattered across the floor. The boy slumped forward.

"There. That wasn't so bad, was it?" Her mother asked.

Iva dropped the dagger. Her hands shook. She felt sick.

Her mother knelt beside her, running her hand through Iva's hair. "That was your first kill, Iva. You did well. Congratulations. Your life as a Blade has begun."

Iva collapsed and burst into tears, wailing at the top of her lungs.

Her mother rolled her eyes. "Clean yourself up once you've finished your tantrum. And try to be quiet. You'll wake the others." She turned and exited the chamber, leaving Iva alone in the darkness.

Iva curled into a ball. She'd *killed* someone, a boy, the first she'd ever seen up close. She didn't even know him. He probably hadn't even done anything wrong. But now, he lay dead. It hadn't even been hard. One swift motion, one smooth cut, and it was over. It was easy.

Iva tore at her scalp. It was *easy*. Why was it easy? It shouldn't have been easy. Taking a life, severing someone's soul, that should be difficult. No! Her fingers clawed at her hair. What... was she?

She knew. She was a monster, a vile, miserable monster.

Iva had learned to hate. She hated this room. She hated the coven. She hated her mother. However, there was one person she hated most, one person she loathed beyond all others.

She hated herself.

CHAPTER 65

432ⁿᵈ year, 12ᵗʰ month, 15ᵗʰ day
2 years before present day

IVA'S HANDS TREMBLED AT THE HORRIFIC sight before her. The city of Yarvore burned, and she was the one who lit the flame. Her dagger fell from her fingers and rang as it hit the stone pavement.

Beside her, she heard a light thud. Talia, one of the few remaining mages that accompanied Archmage Harlyle had fallen to her knees, quivering and covering her mouth with her hand.

"Witch," Harlyle said, "what have you done?"

Iva remained silent. In mere moments, thousands had perished, burned to ash. She knew her error. She had not restricted her spell's esht drain radius. She had intended it to fuel itself off the creature's esht, only burning her target. Instead, the fire had grown unfettered, and the smoking bed of cinders that lay before them was the result. What was done could not be undone.

"Sir," Hestra said, drawing her rapier from its sheath. "The beast still lives."

The creature climbed from the ashes, screeching and clawing at the ground around it as its charred skin mended itself and its shattered limbs repaired. Its vaguely humanoid form was barely recognizable, yet it still moved. Even after that spell, even after a blast that had decimated an entire city, it would not die. A pulse of gold light caught Iva's attention. The glowing orb in the monster's back, though formerly hidden, was now exposed.

"How do we kill this, witch?" the Archmage asked. "You awakened it, surely you know."

Iva frowned. They had tried everything: severing the stone symbol from its neck, impaling it with thousands of conjured spikes, electrocuting it with lightning. Iva's flame, her improvised modification to her Inferno spell, was supposed to stop it. With every human it consumed, the god had grown. With every guardsman that fell, it had become more cunning. With every sleeping child it devoured, it grew more vicious. She had hoped the flames would stop it. They did not.

Ginn never told her how the gods could be killed. She insisted that Iva not awaken them until the coven was ready, warning her that she would be unable to kill the deities. Harlyle, in their initial encounter, had shared his knowledge of the slumbering gods, but he, too did not know how to rouse or slay them. In truth, it had been a stroke of luck that Iva managed to summon her current foe.

The orb pulsed again, and the beast's legs twitched, cracking and straightening as the bones reformed. Iva's eyes widened. She understood. It was a core, just like the one in her dagger.

She picked up her blade and stepped forward, exiting the safety of Hestra's barrier. She would end this. She would atone for the lives that she had snuffed out. She would undo every tragedy she had ever witnessed. She would build a world for her, for Esther, and for Isobel, a world she would not hate. What was done would be undone. She could do it. She only needed to access the Source, that forbidden inscription that the gods once protected.

This creature, this so-called god was an obstacle. Obstacles would be dealt with.

Iva touched her thumb with her left middle finger, connecting the runes of the spell tattooed on her hand. She focused her gaze on the creature's glowing core and sent a rush of esht into the sigil.

I will mend this world. I will find the Source, no matter the cost.

CHAPTER 66

435th year, 2nd month, 12th day
1 month before present day

IVA STOOD IN THE RAIN-SOAKED STREETS, listening to the drops pattering around her. Her drenched hair stuck to her skin. Her ragged cloak was heavy on her shoulders. Blood flowed past her feet, a diluted stream trickling from what she could only assume was once a body. A man, stocky and ruddy, knelt over the corpse, weeping as the rain fell around him. She recognized him. He had been with Isobel's companion, the Eshgarian.

She frowned. So much suffering. So much death. When would it end?

Something rolled across the cobblestones, clinking at every rut until it stopped at her boot. She looked down. It was glass vial, one with its neck broken and jagged. She let out a long sigh. So, that was who the body was. The poor thing. She hadn't deserved such a fate. Her life had been hard enough. Iva crushed the vial beneath her foot. Another reason to press on.

Footsteps splashed behind her. She looked over her shoulder. A robed figure approached her, a young woman with braided blonde hair. Water rolled off her green battle gown, dripping to the crimson pavement.

"Did you find them?" Iva said.

Talia shook her head. "No. I'm sorry, Lady Iva."

Iva clicked her tongue. She was almost glad they had escaped. Almost. She knew what she had to do, should Isobel return. However, she would welcome any delay to that inevitability.

She'd almost broken that day. She'd almost faltered. Seeing Isobel again, witnessing her pain had pushed Iva to the brink. Iva clenched her fist. She couldn't give up. Not yet. This was how things had to be. This was the burden she carried. She knew what it was like to hate. It was only fitting that she was hated by the one person she still cared about.

"I can find my horse and keep searching," Talia said, adjusting her hood over her head. "They couldn't have run far."

"No. There are too few of us remaining, and the city has turned on us." The sounds of battle rang faintly in Iva's ears. Beyond the walls, the other guardsmen fought the Veldian army. They were outnumbered but far better prepared in terms of training in the Ancient Arts.

Iva set her jaw, staring at the other body that lay before her. "We have to get back to Rothvale."

Talia walked to her side. She gasped and stepped forward. Iva raised her hand, stopping her.

"He's alive."

The Archmage sprawled face-down on the ground, shirtless with a bloody wound below his left shoulder. His breaths were short and weak, barely audible over the rain.

"What do we do?" Talia said. "He'll know that I—"

"Wait," Iva interjected. She drew her dagger.

The Archmage let out a final grating gasp, then fell still. Iva eyed the core at her dagger's hilt. The pale pink mist within swirled and glowed. For the third time that day, it pulsed.

Five.

The Archmage's wounds glowed faintly, closing on their own. Then, after several quiet seconds, he lurched, coughing and gasping. He pushed off the ground and rose to one knee.

The redheaded man kneeling over Kay's body suddenly looked up. He scrambled to his feet. Iva met his gaze. His legs shook. His fists clenched tightly. After a look of intense abhorrence, he ran, disappearing into a nearby alley. Behind her, Iva heard Talia's blade being drawn from its sheath. Iva again motioned with her hand, a warning for the young mage to stay back.

Harlyle took several breaths, then stood, tousling his silver hair. "They got away, didn't they?"

Iva did not answer.

Water ran down Harlyle's bare muscular chest. A horrific scar spread across his abdomen. He looked up at the cloudy sky, his wrinkled face twitching and grimacing.

"Again, they impede us," he snarled through his teeth.

Iva glared at the Archmage, clenching her dagger tightly. After a moment, he stiffened and rubbed his shoulder.

"I've used two resurrections today, witch," he said. "I expect those to be replenished by nightfall."

"You know I can't do that," Iva said.

Harlyle shot her a glare. "Why not?"

"City is too small. Not enough esht."

"Then start accumulating it in a vessel. Do a prolonged siphon."

Talia stepped forward. "But, sir! That will—"

Iva lifted her hand again. Talia fell silent.

"You lied to me, Harlyle," Iva said, her voice low and deliberate.

The Archmage turned and crossed his arms. "I did nothing of the—"

Iva sent a rush of esht into her hand.

A line of red cut cleanly through Harlyle's torso, running perfectly horizontal from just above his hips. His eyes opened wide. A surprised groan escaped his lips. His legs collapsed underneath him, and he fell in two pieces. Blood poured from his body's severed halves.

Talia screamed. Iva glanced down. After a moment, her dagger pulsed again.

Four.

The Archmage's body glowed. His two halves pulled themselves together, mending like the flesh of the dark gods. He gasped and scrambled back, supporting himself with one hand and pushing with his legs.

"Wait! Wait!" he said. "I can explain."

Iva stepped forward, standing over him. Never had she reviled another human being as she did him. Never had she loathed a creature as much as this man.

"There was nothing to the east," Iva hissed. "You told me the seal was there."

"I—I thought it was!" he said. "I swear I didn't know until your sister found the one—"

She sent another surge of esht into her hand. A gaping hole tore through his chest. With a gargled cry he slumped to the ground. Iva's dagger pulsed again.

Three.

The hole in his chest closed on itself. Harlyle resurrected again. He rolled onto his stomach and clawed at the ground.

"You were going to kill her," Iva said.

"Woman! Let me explain," he pleaded.

"I told you that she lives!" Iva yelled. Behind her, she heard Talia whimper.

"She was going to take it for herself!" Harlyle said. "I had to—"

A vertical slice cut through his body, cleaving it in half. Iva's dagger glowed.

Two.

Harlyle lept to his feet as soon as the light returned to his eyes. He snapped his fingers, and a scimitar appeared in his hand. With a shout, he pounced on Iva, swinging his blade towards her neck.

He was dead in an instant, falling to the ground in four pieces.

The dagger pulsed.

One.

His body reformed. His tattooed hand twitched. Iva knew what was coming. Compulsion magic, one of the vilest inventions of any mage. She had witnessed him use it before. He'd used it on Isobel. He had even used it on Iva the day they met. She never forgot that feeling of helplessness, that realization that her body was no longer hers to command. She glared at his hand and sent esht down her arm. Never again would he control anybody. His arm vanished, along with the entire left half of his torso. He shrieked and fell.

The dagger pulsed.

Zero.

Harlyle sat up, his amber eyes flashing. He directed his gaze at Talia.

"You!" he growled. "You traitor. How dare you turn against me?"

Talia retreated.

"I'll make you suffer! I'll cut your tongue from your mouth. I'll rip the skin from your bones. I'll squeeze the life from your throat. I'll—"

Iva's blood boiled within her. Fire filled her veins. Her heart pounded within, burning like a furnace in her chest. She stepped forward, and with a single swift motion, she slit his throat.

His body thudded as it landed at her feet.

Iva let out a long, relieved breath. He would not rise again.

Resurrections only worked if applied before death, and that had been his last. She was rid of him. Finally, she was rid of him.

"Find our horses," Iva said. "I'll gather what I can from our quarters."

Talia didn't answer. She stared at the Archmage's corpse, her rapier shaking in her hand. Her eyes were wide.

"He's dead, Talia," Iva said. "He won't be coming back."

Talia didn't move

Iva stepped forward, placing her hand on the girl's shoulder. "He won't hurt you anymore. I promise."

Talia met her gaze. "You're—you're certain?"

Iva nodded.

Talia's hand slowly stopped quivering. She sheathed her rapier, bowed, then departed, racing towards the city's heart. Iva sighed, closing her eyes and tilting her head back. The rain was cold on her skin. It was gentle, soothing, peaceful. It was a glimpse of what she longed for, a taste of that serene world. When all was mended, it would be like this quiet, gentle rain.

CHAPTER 67

435th year, 3rd month, 10th day
3 days before present day

IVA REACHED FOR THE ENORMOUS DOOR, trying to touch its ornately carved surface. The strange force still repelled her hand. She groaned. It was in there. It had to be. She channeled esht down her arm, letting it focus in her palm. She uttered a single word.

"Je."

Her voice echoed through the dark cavernous hall in which she stood, reverberating off the carved stone walls and reaching the vaulted ceiling with its many inverted statues. She reached for the door again, but her hand still could not touch it.

Why did nothing work? None of the other obelisks were so difficult. Why was this one different? Could it be the one she had been seeking? Could it be the one that housed the Source?

She knew what she had to do. Minera had once used the Source, though what exactly the first witch had altered within the Source remained a mystery. Whatever it was, it had drawn the wrath of the gods and triggered the Culling War, the massacre of the first mages. *Ushereh'va.* That was what the gods had called her. In the moments preceding her slaughter, they had granted Minera that name. It was a curious name with a curious meaning, a warning to those who might dare to seek the Source.

Though Minera's actions were secrets lost to time, Ginn's records described the spell the first witch had used to access the Source before her death. It was simple, only two words, and Iva already knew the first.

Je. Open.

She was close. Still, that one most important word eluded her. Was it here in Rothvale, or did it lie somewhere else? There were only so many places it could be.

Footsteps tapped behind her. Iva turned.

"Ah, Talia," Iva said. "It is good to see you."

"G—Greetings, Lady Iva," Talia bowed. "Forgive me for disturbing you, but the king requested your presence."

"I suppose it would be time," Iva muttered. She squinted. Talia had ornamented her braids with silver rings at the ends, rings that were almost identical to the ones Iva wore. Curious.

Talia trembled. She seemed on edge, almost afraid. She'd been like that since Iva first met her, though her anxious nature had grown far more pronounced in the months following her father's death that fateful day in Veshda. It had reached its current extreme in Veld when Iva killed the Archmage.

"Do you still feel it?" Iva asked as she walked past where Talia stood.

"Y—yes," Talia said. "It's frightening. It—it wants me to join it."

"Does it speak?"

"Not in words. I cannot describe it fully. I just know. It yearns to be free of the curse."

Iva nodded and began the long ascent up the stairs that would bring them to the citadel's ground floor. At least she knew that the seal was still intact. "It won't be long, now," she said. "I'll make it fall silent."

"It will be angry," Talia said. "It knows we are coming for it. It wants its freedom. It is not ready to depart."

Iva scoffed. She cared little for the desires of a dying god. She climbed the steep steps, and her shadow danced ominously on the torchlit stone.

"How are your injuries?" Iva asked.

"Better, thank you. I am truly grateful for your healing. The bruising has faded finally, and I'm able to sleep on my back again."

"Good. I'm glad. I've said it before, but I apologize for what Isobel did in your fight. She's certainly become quite the handful."

Talia did not respond.

"Have you finished absorbing Harlyle's spell-cores?" Iva asked.

"I—I have. The spells they contained—they're horrific."

"They certainly are. I trust you will be discreet about what you know. I don't want his sorceries spreading across the lower ranks."

"Of course," Talia said. After several seconds of silence, she spoke again. "What is going to happen now?"

"I intend to take on his mantel," Iva said. "I am already well acquainted with the inner workings of the Interior Guard. Besides, as I told you in Veld, control of the Guard is vital."

Talia glanced up at her but shied away from Iva's gaze. "D—don't you think Lady Hestra will oppose that? She's next in line for the title, being First Mage. She still suspects you, too. Of course, I will support you, but…"

Iva frowned. So, many questions. She continued climbing the stairs. "I care little for Hestra's opinions. She's hardly competent. The events in Veld prove that."

Talia did not respond. Perhaps her doubts had been quelled.

Yes. Talia had certainly changed since Veld. She was perpetually uneasy, always on edge, jumping at every sound and shrinking at loud noises. She eyed her peers with suspicion and fear, and though she remained loyal to Iva, she avoided looking her in the eye.

They finally reached the end of the stairs, stepping out from the passageway's hidden entrance behind a stone altar. The tapping of Iva's boots on the cold stone floor resounded through the enormous structure. She continued walking, crossing through the shadows of the massive columns that supported the ceiling high above them.

"Talia, something has perplexed me since Veld."

"What is it, Lady Iva?"

"Why did you betray Harlyle?" Iva said. "You didn't have to inform me of his deception. I always suspected him. He would have killed you."

The footsteps behind Iva stopped. She turned. Talia trembled, looking away from her at one of the murals on the wall.

"The Archmage was a cruel man, Lady Iva. He was always so brutal, so eager to cause violence. I—I saw what he did to your sister. I know what he planned to do to you."

Iva raised an eyebrow. "And you still followed him until Veld."

Talia flinched, as if pricked by a needle. "I—I saw what he did to those who opposed him. It was terrifying. But…"

Iva frowned. "Yes?"

"You have only shown me kindness," Talia whispered. "For the Archmage, kindness was a weakness to be avoided. I would rather support someone kind like you than someone as cruel as him."

Iva's eyes widened. Kindness? Talia thought she was kind? Ridiculous. Iva knew what she was. She was a monster, deserving of any hatred the world had to offer.

Still, the young woman's words moved her.

"Talia, I am not worthy of such praise. I can offer you one final act of goodwill, though. If you wish to leave the Interior Guard, say the word. Things will get worse from here."

Talia's quivering ceased. "I—I am honored you would do such a thing. Though, your offer merely strengthens my convictions. I will support you in your goals, Lady Iva."

"Oh? I've done far worse than Harlyle."

"But he ordered you to do what you did."

"No. I made my own choices."

"Nevertheless, I know you take no pleasure in slaughter. I know what you strive for. For that, I will support you, no matter the outcome. I have been at your side since the beginning, and it's too late for me to turn back, not if I want to atone for what we've done."

Iva sighed. So, they were of the same mind. That took less effort than she thought. She wondered, would Isobel and Talia be friends when they were younger? Perhaps she would have to include Talia in her revisions to the Source, or at least structure them so that the two would meet properly.

Iva had to admit, she was growing fond of the girl. She'd been a constant since the beginning, someone she could almost trust. Though, she would not let that cloud her judgement. She had work to do, and she could not afford to be distracted.

Iva pulled a thin strip of cloth from a pouch on her belt and tied it over her eyes. Once she entered the streets of Rothvale, she would be under scrutiny from the Royal Garrison and the Interior Guard, and though Harlyle was no longer alive to enforce his rules, she had no desire to create any needless obstacles.

"You are a good woman, Talia," Iva said before stepping into the sunlight. "You deserve better than this path. I am grateful for your support. I cannot repay it now, but I promise you this. I will atone. For both of us."

Iva knelt on the plush green carpet that blanketed the throne room of King Wendd. Banners of a deep forest green hung from the ceiling, emblazoned with the golden crescent of Iskara, the symbol of the waxing moon. Tall windows stretched around the circular room, giving the king a clear view of the capital below.

Such needless extravagance.

She was not alone. Talia knelt behind her. Beside each window stood a guard. Their silver armor was decorated with curving ornamentation, a series of crescent moons layered over their shoulders and thighs. They held heavy halberds, and their blades were sharpened crescents of polished steel. The weapons were suspiciously pristine, likely having never seen combat.

"Explain yourself, witch!" squeaked a shrill voice from atop the golden throne at the center of the room.

Iva looked up. King Wendd was a revolting figure that was exceedingly thin, like a fruit that had been on the vine so long that it had shriveled. His hair was long and unkempt, a mat of frayed gray and tangled silver. Iva had heard rumors that he refused to cut it for fear that a barber would slit his throat. Based on her experiences, such rumors were beyond plausible.

His regal robe of pale pink was barely visible under his long beard, though from what few strips of fabric Iva could see, she guessed it had not been washed in ages. The circlet on his head had no sharp edges; it was a simple band of pure gold.

The king slammed his hand on the arm of his throne. "Well? I haven't got all day."

Iva sighed. She was growing tired of putting up with such fools—a temporary inconvenience, but an exceedingly annoying one. "Forgive me, my king. My actions in Veld were well intentioned. We were dealing with a notorious witch whose mastery of the Ancient Arts rivals my own. Sacrifices were deemed necessary."

The king scoffed and rested his head on his clenched, wrinkled fist. "Sacrifices? Sacrifices? Archmage Harlyle's death is not a sacrifice. It is a loss. It is a blow to our kingdom. How can I hope to defend our borders from our enemies without his guidance? His experience cannot be replaced. That is not what I call a sacrifice!"

Iva suppressed a scowl. Iskara was at peace with its neighbors. Having been to most of the countries on the continent, she knew that war was unlikely to come from beyond the kingdom's edge.

"And then there's the other matter!" the king continued shouting. "You killed my nephew. Loathsome and crafty as he may have been, he was the only blood heir to the throne."

"Then your throne shall not be threatened, my king," Iva said. "Is that not to your—"

"Silence!" Wendd shrieked. "The Veldian Army is going to be at our doorsteps tomorrow. You started a war, a war I have prevented for almost fifty years."

"Forgive me, my king."

The king scoffed. "I will withhold my forgiveness until I have heard what you plan to do to make up for your actions."

Iva exhaled. "The venture shall continue. We are close to recovering what we need to make you immortal, my king. Just a little longer."

The king frowned. "I am growing older and older by the day, witch. I do not have a little longer, especially with rebels marching upon our city and that disgusting witch scurrying across my kingdom. She'll be here any day. She'll come for my head. I know it. I can feel it."

Iva's blood boiled. Speaking that way of Isobel was not something she could forgive. However, she could ignore it a little longer. "Forgive me, my king. If you would grant me authorization to take on the Archmage's responsibility, I shall complete the mission you gave to him."

The king ran his long fingernails down the length of the arm of his throne. His eyes burned with rage. "You are hardly in the position to make demands, witch. That would put you in line for the throne. I should have expected as much from your kind. Witches are deceitful, foul creatures. Harlyle was wrong to trust you."

Iva looked up. So, he would be another obstacle. No matter. Obstacles could be dealt with. Perhaps her endurance of his rudeness would be shorter than she had thought.

The king looked at Talia. "Guard, seize this wicked woman. Inform the First Mage that her presence is required."

The king waved his withered hand. Iva's heart pounded. How many had she used? Three? That left her with seventeen, more than enough to overcome her current situation. She glanced over her shoulder. Talia did not move, only giving her a subtle nod.

Iva stood and tore off her blindfold. She had come this far. It was too late to turn back. No obstacle would stand in her way, not when she was so close. She pressed her left middle finger and thumb together, closing the inscription that was tattooed on them. She surged esht into her fingers and fixed her gaze on the king.

It happened in an instant. The king's body crunched and cracked as it compressed into a tiny sphere. It exploded and splattered across the throne in a shower of crimson.

Talia screamed from behind her. The guards recoiled in horror and dropped their halberds. Iva turned and looked over her shoulder.

"Talia, this is my path. I will not yield to any obstacle. Do you still wish to follow?"

Talia shrunk back in terror, her rapier shaking in its sheath.

"Answer me," Iva ordered.

"I—I—yes. I do, Iva. I will not leave your side."

Iva tilted her head slightly. Talia had dropped the "Lady" when addressing her. Perhaps it was a slip. Perhaps not. No matter. The title would not be appropriate for long. Perhaps Talia realized that.

She strode up the stairs and stopped at the throne. "Tell me. Is it true that, in the absence of heirs, the Archmage has claim to the throne?

"It is as you say." Talia joined Iva, standing at the opposite side of the throne.

Iva ran her fingers across the arm of the throne, leaving streaks in the blood. "Well, it is fortunate that he just announced I would be Archmage, isn't it?"

"It is, Iva." Talia's face became like steel.

Clanking armor echoed through the room. Iva turned to see one of the guards rushing at her, halberd raised above his head. She rolled her eyes and sent another torrent of esht into her hand.

The man collapsed, imploding within his blood-soaked armor.

Iva looked around the room.

"Anyone else?"

One of the guards ran, descending the stairs that led to the ground floor.

"It seems some might oppose my ascension," Iva said, eyeing the remaining guards.

"They are foolish," Talia said, brandishing her rapier.

"If only you could demonstrate how foolish."

Talia nodded and raised her weapon. Without a moment's hesitation, she plunged it into Iva's chest, piercing her heart.

Iva collapsed. This part was always the worst. First, there was the overwhelming surge of pain. Then, there was the chill as her blood ceased to flow. Then, there was the darkness, that seeping darkness. It would be over soon. It never took long.

Sixteen resurrections left.

Iva felt warm. The pain vanished. She felt an intense drumming in her chest as her heart beat again, restoring life to her body. She opened her eyes and stood. With a muttered incantation and a flourish of her wrist, she cleared the blood from the throne. She sat, crossing her legs and leaning on one elbow.

There were matters to attend to. The Veldian army would be dealt with swiftly. They could not interfere with her work. Then, she would find Isobel, wherever she was hiding. There were only so many places she could run. Finally, Iva would find the Source, for there were few obstacles that remained.

A group of Interior Guardsmen entered the throne room, led by Lady Hestra.

"Talia, if you would," Iva said.

"Kneel!" Talia shouted. "For you stand in the presence of Iskara's immortal queen."

Iva smiled. Immortal queen? No. That wasn't what she was. She was something beyond that. Like Minera before her, she would command the Source. The gods had called the first witch *Ushereh'va*. A curious name with a curious meaning. Yes, *that* was what she would be. To mend, she must first break.

Ushereh'va.

Worldbreaker.

CHAPTER 68

435th year, 3rd month, 13th day
Present Day

ISOBEL ADJUSTED THE HOOD OVER HER head, hiding her red hair from the watchful eyes of the Interior Guard as she and Chinelo shoved past the crowd to reach Rothvale's gates. They pushed through a flood of travelers, a mass departure from the city.

Isobel ducked past the guard post and moved into the wall's shadow, waiting for Chinelo to appear from the crowd. She did not have to wait long. With a swish of his cloak, he joined her in the dark corner.

"Sorry for the delay," he said. "I was talking with someone."

"Oh?" Isobel cocked her head.

"It's about the king. He died three days ago. Iva took the throne with the backing of some of the Interior Guard, but evidently there's an entire splinter faction that opposed her."

Isobel touched her chin. "Well, I guess she'll have her hands full for a while. That could be good for us."

"Indeed. Where do you want to start?"

Isobel looked up at the sky. Their movements would be much freer at night when the shadow of the new moon would hide them, but it was early in the day, and they could not afford to wait.

"Let's explore this district," Isobel said. "If you feel anything like that resonance that you did earlier, let me know."

"Understood."

Isobel led the way as they began their exploration of Rothvale's westmost ward. The smell of bonfires drifted through the air. The plazas were filled with rioting citizens and watchful guardsmen, and the streets were densely packed with those fleeing the city. The architecture and layout of the city was cramped. There were so many buildings packed together around the narrow thoroughfares. In many places, buildings had been constructed in layers on top of each other, rising high above the streets for several stories.

They searched until the sky gradually darkened, but the noise never stopped. Exploring during the night would not be as easy as they had expected. The columns of smoke continued to rise, merging into a thick cloud over the city. Flying would not be ideal with all the haze.

Isobel shoved through a particularly crowded strip of the streets and stepped into an alleyway. She grabbed Chinelo's hand and pulled him in behind her.

"Have you felt anything yet?"

Chinelo shook his head. "Nothing. It's a big city, though. Once we've covered more ground, we might have better luck."

"Right. I'm thinking it may be better for us to rest for the night instead of trying to stay up late. We can start early in the morning instead once all the crowds have died down."

"Good plan, though where are we going to sleep? We don't have much money left, not after the food we bought this morning."

Isobel looked around. Sleeping in an alley would be risky, especially with all the commotion. Inns were notoriously expensive in Rothvale, and they needed to conserve what few crescents they had for food.

She looked up above the rooftops of the street in which they stood. The enormous dome of one of the ancient citadels blocked out the glowing smoke cloud above, and its many buttresses spread out like the legs of a spider around it. She pointed.

"There's a flat section on that citadel's roof. We should be secluded enough up there. It looks like there are clefts between those arch things."

"That ought to work," he said.

They crossed the streets and pushed through the shouting crowds. Isobel shivered as they passed more of the guardsmen. Memories of her past defeats gripped her, and she felt her heart rate accelerate. Chinelo gently squeezed her hand. He was there, and that was all she needed.

They finally reached the citadel, and it loomed above them. Its walls were carved in tight columns of runes and symbols, with noticeable gaps in select places. Isobel scanned one of the supporting columns, quickly reading the text inscribed in its weathered stone surface.

"What does it say?" Chinelo asked.

"Hmmm, a rough translation would be, '*To any who linger, heed my warning. Harm not those beneath us, lest you invite his wrath. Our kinds are separated, now and forever.*'"

"That's... ominous," Chinelo said cheerily.

Isobel nodded. "Ancient texts often are. Though, I'm not sure who 'he' is."

Chinelo shrugged. "One of the gods, I assume."

"Probably."

Chinelo looked up at the overhanging roof. "So how do you plan to get us up there?"

"The usual." Isobel pulled a pair of travel stones from her pocket. She tossed one to the rooftop and surged her esht into the other, pulling them to their destination.

She dropped her pack and walked to the back of a cleft at the base of the citadel's gargantuan dome. The roof was flat and large with a surprising amount of space to stand and walk about. There would be little risk of tumbling off the edge. Before anything else, though, she had to free a certain someone from her pack.

She opened the flap. Mort leapt from within and clamped himself directly onto her face. She let out a surprised squeak. She tried to remove him, but he was surprisingly strong for a frog. She tugged at his fat, globular bag of a body, but he refused to budge.

"Chinelo?" she said in a slightly muffled voice. "I require assistance."

Chinelo laughed and peeled the creature from her face. "What, you're not happy to see your dear friend, Mort?"

Mort glowered in his direction. Mort did not approve of being manhandled. Being womanhandled was only acceptable if it was Isobel doing it.

Isobel wiped the slime from her face. "Such a menace."

"Well, you honestly can't blame him. He must have been so bored locked up in there."

"I know, but there were so many people I was afraid he would fall and get trampled. It was for his own good."

Mort waddled to the edge of the roof and peered over. He would judge what his own good was. Leaping to the ground below was not it.

They quickly set up a makeshift camp, depositing their sleeping pads inside of their tent to protect them from the wind. Soon, the voices of the city fell silent, and they fell into slumber on their first night in the capital.

Isobel stood on the citadel's edge, staff in hand. Her rest had ended early, though in this case that was actually what she wanted. The moonless sky was dark, and the morning was still. It would be the perfect time to survey Rothvale.

With a slight push, she leapt off the building and began her flight over the sleeping city. The streets were almost completely empty of occupants, though a few guards and vagrants lingered. Heaps of rubbish and burned fabric were scattered across the cobblestones, traces of the commotion from the previous day. She stopped and hovered over one of the plazas. The embers of a fire glowed a faint orange. She shook her head and continued.

The air was cold as it whistled past her. It was so calm that morning. It was so peaceful. Nevertheless, she was on edge. They would have to fight another of the gods soon, and they would have to do so without harming any of the citizens. In a city as large as this, that would be exceedingly difficult, assuming she could even find the obelisk.

Her map indicated it was within the city, but she was uncertain of the exact location. She started with each of the major squares, hoping it would be obvious like the one in Nellborough. She found nothing. She turned and saw what appeared to be some sort of temple in the distance, a few districts over. She accelerated towards the destination. The rooftops flew past underneath her, becoming a blur of pointed eaves and vibrant shingles. She spun and swooped, diving between the temple's columns and landing inside.

"Light!" she whispered into her staff. It responded, generating a glowing orb that lit the temple's interior.

Hundreds of carved monoliths were arranged in columns running the full length of the temple. Oh, what she could learn from these if she only had the time! This city was ancient, and as such it was a treasure trove of knowledge and history.

She searched through the monoliths quickly. Sadly, none bore the signature diamond shaped cleft. She stopped. One of the monoliths had only two lines of text. She read it, mentally translating the runes.

The Construct must remain intact. We leave it in the hands of those beneath us, those that remain, those untouched by our Arts.

Should the Construct be threatened, we will finish what we started. This writes Ydross, First of the Ten.

Isobel shuddered. Her light vanished, and she turned and exited the temple. She would have to return once the work was done.

The sky glowed from the east. The sun was drawing near. Soon it would rise, returning from its nightly exile. She would not have much time to sweep the remainder of the city.

She flew from the ground and soared over Rothvale. Every plaza was the same. They were always flat with no apparent monuments that might be what she sought. She groaned. She had hoped this would be quick. After a moment of reflection, she turned and shot off towards the citadel where they had camped.

Beneath her she saw activity. People wandered the streets, scrubbing the pavement in front of stores and taverns to make them more welcoming.

She circled around the citadel's dome and dropped beside their packs. The tent was already packed up. Chinelo sat a few paces from the edge of the roof, wrapped in a cloak while he looked over the streets below.

"I was wondering when you would be back."

Isobel twisted a strand of her hair. "Sorry. I was hoping I'd find something, but nothing stood out to me. All the plazas I saw were empty."

"Thank you for trying. We'll just have to keep searching. I was thinking, if it's not in one of the plazas, maybe it's in one of these ancient buildings? Not this one, of course. The one in Kahi was in a ruined palace, and supposedly the one Ginn found was in some sort of library. If we start with those, we could clear out large sections of the city without having to search every street."

"Let's do it!"

Chinelo brushed himself off and stood, stretching his arms and back with a slight groan. He rubbed his shoulder, moving it in a circle until it popped in a couple places.

"That was a good one," Isobel said.

Chinelo cracked his neck.

"Oh, even better." Isobel chimed. She twisted a couple times, and a loud pop came from her lower spine.

"That's the winner there," he said.

Isobel giggled.

"We can probably leave our packs here," Chinelo said. "It's not like anyone could reach them."

Isobel put on her cloak and placed Mort on her shoulder. "I'll leave my staff as well to be more discreet. It's more difficult to hide than your sword. Mort comes with us, this time. I'm not leaving him to his own devices for an entire day."

Mort blinked deviously.

"Well, let's be off, then," Chinelo said. "You ready?"

Isobel looked over the city. Dome after dome appeared ahead, and they would have to check each and every one of them until they found what they sought.

"Ready."

CHAPTER 69

ISOBEL FELT A CONSTANT TENSION, AS if she was standing on the edge of a precipice. As they made their way to the next citadel, she felt the eyes of the Interior Guard watching their every step. However, they never made a move. They simply stood gazing over the crowded streets, their regal green and gold robes shimmering in the morning light. And with every guardsman she saw two knights of the Royal Garrison, garbed in their silver armor. If she and Chinelo were discovered, the ensuing battle would not be one that they could win. There were too many.

They continued to prowl the streets, gliding in hooded cloaks on the fringes of the crowds. On a normal day, she would want to take time to enjoy the sights and sounds of the city. But not that day, not with Iva's influence hovering over the city.

Chinelo walked ahead of her, moving his head subtly as if he were constantly listening for something. They neared one of the citadels, and its grand dome poked above the streetside rooftops, casting its shadow across the pavement and the many wheeled carts that clattered through the city.

"Do you feel anything?" Isobel asked.

Chinelo shook his head. "Not that I've noticed."

"What's roughly the range you can feel them from?"

Chinelo's mustache twitched. "It varies. I could feel the one in Eshgar from far beyond the walls, but the one in Nellborough I only noticed when I was directly beside it. The one in Veld was somewhere in between."

Isobel sighed. "I suppose we should move on."

They continued, picking their way through more of the side streets to reach the northern section of the city. Though the city was large, Isobel had hoped that they could locate the obelisk quickly. The longer they stayed, the more at risk they were. However, despite their efforts, their search was not fruitful, resulting in only increased exhaustion and frustration by the time they had returned to their makeshift rooftop camp. As such, few words were exchanged as the day drew to a close.

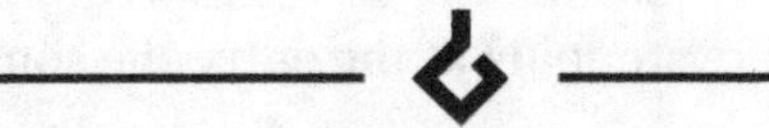

Sunlight filled the tent. Isobel sat up and looked to her right. Chinelo was gone, though a note was left on his bedding, one that was held down by a travel stone.

Good morning, dear. I'm sorry for disappearing like this, but I didn't want to wake you. I'm going to get some food for us. I'll be back soon. I've taken a travel stone, so if you get tired of waiting, feel free to use the one I left to come find me.

I love you.

Chinelo

Isobel yawned and stretched. She felt some squirming at the base of her bedding. Mort had crawled on her toes, and he was giving her an intense pleading look.

"All right my friend. I'll feed you, but if Chinelo doesn't come back soon, then we're going to have to go find him."

Mort blinked at her, but curiously, the scowl that normally appeared after mentioning Chinelo was absent that morning. She crawled to her pack and withdrew a jar of grasshoppers. She let them loose, and Mort devoured them ruthlessly.

Isobel crawled to her pack and pulled out her last set of clean clothes. After changing, she exited the tent and sat on the edge of the citadel roof, letting her feet hang over the edge. The morning air was crisp, and light reflected off the many rooftops before her. There were no smoke plumes that morning. It seemed that some of the tension in Rothvale had eased, even if that came at the cost of half the population leaving.

Isobel peered over the edge at the rooftops below. One directly next to the citadel had a small observation deck, and whoever occupied that building had planted flowers in clay pots lining the railings.

Isobel's gaze caught on a blossom of a familiar color. One of the flowerpots was filled with blooms of a distinct purple hue that was unique to the undying flowers in the Ashen Plains near her cottage. She sighed. So much time had passed since she last saw those blossoms. How long had it been? Well over a year, at least.

She hopped to her feet and reentered the tent, sitting with her legs crossed. She pulled her diary from her pack and opened it, flipping back to the earlier pages before stopping at the entry she sought.

433, 12, 15

Something exciting happened today! I went to visit town to buy some food and sell a few trinkets, and on my way back home I met a man. He said his name is Chinelo, and he is such a friendly person. We talked for hours tonight. It was lovely!

When I encountered him in the woods, he was wearing a full suit of Eshgarian armor. Honestly, I was a bit wary at first. Something seemed off about the forest, and I thought he might have been following me. It seems I was wrong. He is very pleasant, so I hope that he will forgive me for almost setting him on fire.

He actually agreed to repair that hole I burned the other day, so naturally I offered him a place to stay. Iva might say I'm being reckless, but if he tries to steal anything, then I can just use one of the spells I have for bandits. Oddly enough, he said he slayed an ash dragon, but I don't know if I believe that. Mother is the only person I know who could ever do that.

I must admit I am confused why he is so far from home. He said something happened to his family, but he did not fully elaborate on the details.

At any rate, it will be nice to have someone around for a little while. I think that I can set him up with a good job in Nellborough. Tomorrow I will have to introduce him to a few potential employers. I feel he and Valk would get along nicely.

She smiled and turned a couple pages ahead.

433, 12, 21

Chinelo has been here about a week now, and he is so very kind. He's been working as much as he can to repair the hole, and he is making some decent progress.

He did the nicest thing tonight! He cooked his favorite meal for me! It was such a wonderful experience. I felt like a princess, or I assume that is what princesses must feel like. I, of course, don't know any. But anyways, he made this magnificent dish with these little potato dumplings in this thick sauce made from sheep's milk. It was amazing.

With the Interior Guard preventing me from visiting town, he's been running errands and communicating with Umfrey. Hopefully I'll be able to return soon, but this isolation has given me some time to work out some spells I've been tinkering with. I've made some for him to try whenever he lets me teach him magic.

I've learned a few new things about Chinelo's homeland. He said Eshgar was destroyed by some kind of disaster, but I think it is still too much for him to discuss it right now. All he said was that it involved fire.

Mort has been very grumpy lately. I don't think he likes sharing the house, but he will have to get over it.

She closed her eyes and hugged the book to her chest. It was a simpler time back then, at least for her. She remembered how her affection for him had silently formed, creeping and overtaking her heart in those quiet days spent at her cottage. She remembered how she longed for him to stay, how she had hastily proposed traveling the country so that she could remain near him. She recalled how throughout their journey, in spite of everything that happened, her love had never stopped growing.

She sighed. Mort looked up at her.

"Mort, I am going to marry that man."

Mort blinked. If a union between the usurper and his empress would make her happy, perhaps he could tolerate it, if begrudgingly.

A light flashed and Chinelo appeared beside Isobel. She squealed and tossed the diary up into the air.

"Oh! Sorry," Chinelo said.

"You're fine!" Isobel snatched the diary from where it landed and slammed it shut. "I was just... reminiscing a little bit. I—I'm going to put this away." She felt her cheeks growing hot, and Chinelo seemed to notice.

"How did it go?" Isobel asked.

"I found it."

"Oh? Breakfast?"

Chinelo shook his head. "No. The obelisk. I think I know where it is."

CHAPTER 70

ISOBEL RAN BEHIND CHINELO, CUTTING THROUGH the streets at breakneck speed, much to the displeasure of many passersby. They had been so close the whole time. He felt the resonance as soon as he ventured towards the southeast portion of the city, and it would not be long until they homed in on its location.

Chinelo turned sharply to the left, heading down a wide thoroughfare. Isobel followed, and then immediately collided with someone.

"Oh!" she said. "I'm so sorry."

The man she encountered looked at her with a gaze that was somehow simultaneously bored, offended, and supercilious. Isobel was struck by his uncanny resemblance to a very unhappy rat. There was something unnerving about him, something almost familiar.

Isobel fidgeted with the strings of her cloak. "I'm sorry, sir. Please pardon me."

The man remained silent, but he squinted at her face intently, studying it. Isobel shrunk back. Why was he staring? She looked down, and his lavish tunic and billowing trousers caught her attention. She remembered those clothes. She had seen them before. But where?

"I know you," the man said, squeaking out the words in a voice that matched his appearance.

Isobel shuddered. Merchants typically wore such attire, merchants from Rothvale.

"You... you're from Nellborough," the man continued.

Chinelo rested his hand on Isobel's shoulder. "I'm sorry, sir. I think you must be confusing her with someone else. Let's go, dear."

Isobel nodded and followed Chinelo.

"And you," the man muttered, eyeing Chinelo up and down.

Chinelo tensed. Isobel trembled.

"I—I have to go," the man squeaked before turning.

"Isobel!" Chinelo said. He grabbed for the man's robe. "Make him forget!"

"Oh!" Isobel flung her arm forward. "Xastra chanavoshta!"

The man yelped and ran, tearing the corner of his robe in the process. Several people stopped moving ahead of her, staring blankly around.

Chinelo grabbed Isobel's hand. "Run."

They pushed through the crowds, weaving until they ducked into an alleyway. Chinelo stood behind a large crate and pulled Isobel into its shadow.

"Who was that man?" Chinelo asked.

"I—I don't remember his name," Isobel stammered, "but he's from the Rothvale Trade Guild that was stationed in Nellborough. Bah! My spell must have missed."

Chinelo frowned. "This isn't good. We need to hurry. If he alerts the Interior Guard, which, based on that reaction, he certainly will…"

"I understand."

"Then let's go. The resonance is getting louder. I can feel it. We are not far."

They continued, picking their way through the alley until they reached the other side. Ahead of them rose the pointed dome of another citadel, one like the others they had seen the previous day.

Chinelo crossed the bustling street, stepping around several playing children. After pushing through another narrow alley, they reached the steps at the entrance to the citadel. It towered above them, supported by its many columns and buttresses with their usual runic etchings.

"Is it here?" Isobel asked.

Chinelo nodded solemnly. "It's close."

They took a step forward and he stopped, rubbing his head.

"Chinelo? What's wrong?" Isobel dropped to his side.

"It's so loud. It's like we're right on top of it. I feel it calling me down."

Isobel looked around frantically. Though the space was far less crowded than the streets, they were beginning to gather some very judgmental stares from onlookers.

"Let's get inside," she whispered.

Chinelo nodded and stood, climbing the stairs with shaky footsteps as he attempted to regain his composure. As they entered the dark interior, he once again stopped. He whirled around, grimacing and grunting as he moved. "It's behind us, Isobel."

"Hmmm?"

"It's gotten fainter. It was more intense back out there."

Isobel looked over her shoulder. The plaza courtyard at the citadel's entrance was empty. "There's nothing out there, Chinelo. Are you sure?"

Chinelo nodded. "Very. We're definitely further from it here than out there."

Isobel touched her chin. Why would that be the case? There was nothing apparent that would be the source. How could they find it?

She gasped. The solution was obvious. With a flick of her wrist, she summoned her staff to her hand, pulling it across the space that separated it from her. It appeared in an instant, and she transferred her esht into its glowing core.

"Coarse Douse: Esht," she ordered, and the staff pulsed to life, sending out three glowing steaks of light. One pointed directly to her chest, toward the pool of her own esht. Another pointed to Chinelo. The other pierced the floor.

Isobel and Chinelo's eyes met.

"Down," she said.

"Right. But how do we get there?" Chinelo looked around the expansive hall. "I don't see any obvious stairways."

Isobel waved her hand. "Just a minute. I should be able to work out the distance."

She stood, holding the end of her staff at the level of her head. She knew how tall she was, and she could work out the angle of the beam visually. She just needed to estimate how much the angle changed when she moved to determine the vertical distance toward the esht source below.

She moved until the angle of the beam was directly between vertical and horizontal. Then she walked, counting her paces until the angle was a quarter of the way between vertical and horizontal. Twenty paces. She dropped her staff and pulled her spell-book from beneath her cloak. She scribbled on the pages, drawing triangles and marking the angles she had estimated.

"You're drawing... triangles?" Chinelo asked.

Isobel nodded and scratched her head. It had been a long time since Umfrey had taught her about triangles and their relationships to angles. With a few more scribbles, she arrived at a number.

"I've got it, Chinelo."

"Hmmm?"

She stood and slammed her book shut. "The distance we need to travel. I have it."

She grabbed his hand and closed her eyes.

"Homvelcht wavesh, iv gra tor vrefden hasa wavesh."

She surged her esht, expelling enough to transport them slightly less than the calculated distance. She felt a rush of air as they vanished and reappeared before falling into the darkness.

Chinelo shouted and landed with a loud thud.

"Isobel?"

"I'm here." She reached out and found his shoulder.

"Please. You have to start warning me about these things."

"Oh. Right. Sorry."

She felt him move and stand to his feet.

"Where are we?" he asked.

"Somewhere below the citadel. From the sound of it, we're somewhere very large."

"Hmmm. We might as well see what we are working with here. Icht vasht."

A flame appeared in the blackness, illuminating Chinelo and casting its light across the vast space in which they stood. They were in a cavernous expanse, and the flickering light caused unsettling shadows to scurry across the ceiling above them.

"Wow." Chinelo pointed up.

Isobel's eyes followed. An army of inverted statues hung from the ceiling. They were carved into twisting, uncanny forms.

"I don't think I like those," she said.

"Agreed."

Mort let out a quiet croak from beside Isobel's neck. It seemed he was displeased by the figures as well. Isobel looked around. In the pitch darkness, Chinelo's tiny flame was like the sun. Behind them was an entrance to what appeared to be a staircase. Judging by its position, it would take them back up into the citadel. At the opposite end was a door, one that climbed almost all the way to the ceiling, standing well over twenty times Isobel's height.

"Chinelo, do you still feel it?"

Chinelo nodded. "I do. It's coming from that direction." He pointed at the door.

"Well. Shall we?

They approached the door. It was carved from two slabs of stone with patterns that resembled trees and vines running its entire height. Isobel extended her hand to touch it and stepped forward. Something repelled her touch. It was a powerful force, growing stronger the further she pushed. Try as she might she could not reach the rough surface. She gave one final push and was forced back by the staggering repulsion.

"That's strange," she said.

"Hmmm?" Chinelo answered. "Let me try."

He attempted to reach the door, but with the same result.

"It's definitely on the other side?" Isobel asked.

"As best I can tell."

She removed her hood and scratched her head. "Well, this isn't a natural sensation. We should be able to force our way in if it's magic."

She summoned her staff and pointed its ornamental head at the door. "Nullify."

A shockwave spread from the staff, washing across the door's surface and climbing up to the inverted forest of statues on the ceiling. Something shook the ground.

She reached out for the door again but felt the same repulsive force as before.

"That is very strange. I guess it's not a single cast type spell."

"So, what do we do?"

"Simple!" She grabbed his hand and drew him to her side. "You hold my staff, and I'll use my barrier to create a space that is constantly being nullified."

Chinelo did as ordered, and Isobel surged her esht into her tattoo on her left hand, forcing her barrier outwards so that it completely enveloped them. She stepped forward, drawing closer to the door. She felt an odd tingling or a strange, almost tearing sensation as she moved.

First, she felt resistance, then progress was much more rapid, until her fingers rested on the cold stone.

She increased gravity at her feet. With a sudden surge of strength, she pushed with both hands against the door. She groaned. It refused to budge.

Chinelo rested his hands on the door beside hers. He pushed with her, and his hands grew tense. The skin over his tendons became taut, and his veins bulged as he strained against the massive weight. Together they struggled, and together they were finally able to persuade the door to move.

At first it only budged a little, then it scraped across the floor. Bright light burst from within. Sweat dripped down Isobel's forehead and stuck to her spectacles. The door opened wide enough so that they could pass through, and they stepped into the light. Isobel squinted and shaded her eyes, waiting for them to acclimate to the overwhelming radiance. The air was eerily still.

"Isobel," Chinelo gasped. "Where are we?"

Isobel blinked and was finally able to focus on her surroundings. She staggered back. There were no walls. There was no ceiling. They stood in what appeared to be a wide field, one that was filled with thousands of pale blue flowers, almost as white as snow, but with a faint reflection of the cerulean sky above. They were beautiful and captivating, but in the stagnant air they were as still as statues. Nothing moved. The clouds above were static. The grass and flowers were glass. The air was dead.

Isobel whirled around. The door was indeed behind them, and she could see the dark hall through the gap, but its hinges were not set in a frame. Instead, it stood there, surrounded by flowers on all sides, with hills in the distance beyond.

She scanned the horizon until her eyes caught on something that she judged to be in the north. Great boulders dotted the endless sea of blue, lying exactly where the boulder fields north of Rothvale should be. She turned, and to the west lay the hills on which they had looked down into the city, though they were somehow very different.

Chinelo gestured ahead. There was something else in the still field. A stone structure poked above the flowers. It was an almost perfect rectangle, with a familiar diamond shaped hole at its center.

Isobel stepped forward, expecting to feel the soft rustle as her feet parted the flowers, but her boot fell on something hard. She looked down. In a perfect circle around her, terminating at the ring where her barrier contacted the ground, was a floor of smooth stone. The flowers ended at her barrier, fading and withering into emptiness at its touch.

Chinelo moved, and she caught his hand.

"Wait," she said. "Something isn't right here."

"Hmmm?"

"It's too still, and the flowers disappear when they touch my barrier." She snapped her fingers. "Do you have anything in your pocket? Something small I could throw?"

Chinelo dug his hands into his pocket and produced an Iskaran crescent. "This?"

"Perfect!" Isobel snatched it and hurled it forward.

The coin exited her shield and froze in place, hanging static in midair.

Chinelo's brow furrowed. "Wait. What?"

Isobel leaned forward, allowing her barrier to pass back over the coin. It continued along its trajectory, freezing once again once it left the barrier.

"Chinelo, whatever you do, don't leave my barrier, or if you do, activate your own. There is magic here, and I don't think we'll be able to break its spell if we get caught in it."

Chinelo nodded.

They continued walking forward, and the flowers withered in their path, vanishing as they touched the barrier. Behind them they reappeared, closing over their path.

"It's strange. The landscape looks like the outskirts of Rothvale, but obviously without the city itself," Isobel said.

"It looks different though," Chinelo replied. "All the trees and things are missing, and everything is shaped differently. It's like... it's like the hills are fuller or less eroded."

"I suppose it's a result of the spell we are in."

"Any idea what the origin of it is? That obelisk doesn't look active. I can still feel it as well."

Isobel shook her head. They neared the obelisk. It stood on a floor of smooth stone, with the flowers ending in a radius a short distance from it. Chinelo tossed another crescent forward, and it clattered to the ground. With a wary look, he stepped outside of Isobel's barrier, and he walked across the stone.

"It seems we are safe here," he said. "For now, at least."

Isobel relaxed and released her esht. "This isn't going to be much room to fight. We'll need to be ready to pierce the core as soon as it appears."

Chinelo cracked his neck and drew his sword. Isobel rubbed her shoulder and grabbed her staff before setting Mort on the ground.

"Just sit and watch, friend." She pointed her finger at the frog. "Don't touch those flowers."

Mort grunted.

Isobel took that as an agreement. "Form: Spear."

Her staff sparked to life, shaping a glowing spearhead at its tip. She pushed off the ground, floating through the air until she hovered at the level of the diamond shaped hole where the core would form. She twirled her weapon and held it over the opening.

"Do it! I'm ready."

Chinelo nodded and touched the obelisk. He inhaled deeply and began speaking in a low voice, uttering the incantation they had created in Ata just over a year before.

"Gra ter o diaa, troshte!"

The ground rumbled. The stones cracked. Above her, Isobel heard a deep creaking and crumbling. She looked up. Stone blocks hovered high above the ground, suspended in midair. Lines formed across the obelisk, glowing lines that shone a deep pink. They converged into a radiant orb, a swirling mist just beyond her staff's tip. She was ready. She tensed and prepared to drive her spear into the mist as soon as it fully formed.

A shadow appeared above the obelisk, a dense vapor as black as pitch. It morphed and stretched, then exploded, releasing a deafening screech. Isobel grimaced. Her head felt like it was going to split. She had to maintain focus. If she let her esht shift, she would fall. She opened her eyes and saw it.

The god.

Like the others before, it was gaunt and emaciated, a frail skeleton covered in scraps of tissue. However, it kept growing. The bones in its arms and legs extended, growing longer and longer. Its spine hunched, and rows of spikes appeared along its back. It wailed, and the flowers flickered. They vanished, briefly throwing the space into darkness as walls and a ceiling appeared around them. She heard the crashing of stones on the ground around her. And then, in a flash, the field reappeared.

The monster's head loomed above her, a square diamond with two smaller protrusions near its lower edges. It shrieked at her, gripping the obelisk with long fingers. Isobel tensed, and without another moment's hesitation, she plunged her spear into the core.

It erupted, casting thick mist around her, completely filling her vision and wrapping her in a chilling embrace. She felt it rush into her, passing through her nostrils and open mouth, filling her entire being, causing her esht to swell and boil.

Words flooded her mind, knowledge of the temporal, visions of a world changing with the seasons. She saw the universe age in an instant. Trees grew and withered. Mountains rose then crumbled. Volcanoes formed from the depths of the seas and islands were swallowed by the ocean. With every change a single word echoed. It pounded into her soul, engraving itself on her mind. It was a word she had longed to know. It was a word she had searched for over the many, many months since she left home. It was a word that would bring her journey to its conclusion.

Time.

"ENVASH."

CHAPTER 71

ISOBEL WAS WARM. SHE FELT SAFE, held in a gentle embrace. It was dark, though she felt a light tempting her eyes to open. She sighed. She didn't want to wake up. It was pleasant here. Maybe she could sleep a little longer. She shifted and took a deep breath, inhaling a familiar scent that was oh so comforting. So that's who held her. Well, perhaps he wouldn't mind if she rested and enjoyed the moment.

How long had it been since they first met? She smiled. One year and three months. Fifteen bittersweet months. Would their journey end soon? Would they finally learn the word they needed?

Once they did, how would she craft her spell? She would need to ensure that they kept their memories, so she would have to pair *"chanavoshta"* with *"envash"* somehow.

Her eyes flew open.

Envash. That was it! That was the word! She knew it. The knowledge had been grafted into her, growing and flourishing into a bloom of ideas as if she had always known the word. She could do it. She could turn back time!

"Hey," Chinelo said. His eyes twinkled above his soft smile as he touched her cheek.

"Hey," she smiled back.

"You feeling all right?"

"It's time, Chinelo. It's time."

Chinelo's eyes widened. She sat up from where she lay. A gold light emanated from a glowing orb that she assumed Chinelo summoned while she slept.

"It's time?"

She grinned and hugged him. "Yes! This was the one we were looking for! This was the one!"

Chinelo held her and quivered. "We... we can go back?"

She laughed. "We can! We can, Chinelo!"

He wiped his eyes.

Isobel sprung to her feet and pulled him up in front of her, clasping his hands in hers. "Come on! We have work to do! I think I have most of it worked out in my head. I just need to put it down on paper now to really solidify it."

Mort croaked.

Isobel crouched over him. "Are you ready to go back home my little friend? I bet you are. I bet you are." She rubbed his back with her thumb.

They had done it. She could hardly believe it, but they had found what they sought for their entire journey. She stood and let out a long, satisfied sigh of relief. Her heart was full. Her spirits soared. Only one thing remained.

"All right!" She clapped her hands. "Let's—"

She stumbled. Something had hit her. She felt her esht drain. Her stomach turned.

"Isobel?" Chinelo said.

She rubbed her head. "Sorry. I just felt my esht deplete. Strange. Maybe I got excited and accidentally released some when I clapped. Haven't had that happen in a while."

She frowned. She didn't even notice her esht flowing. Normally there was a slight resistance if she was being siphoned, or there was a slight tingle if she accidentally channeled it. An entire chunk of it had just vanished.

Chinelo moved in front of her. "Do you want to rest?"

Isobel shook her head. "No, no. I'm fine, really. There's plenty more where that came from."

He smiled and kissed her forehead. "Well, what do you need me to do, dear?"

Her heart fluttered. She gazed into his eyes, those deep brown eyes that she loved so dearly. She opened her mouth to speak.

A sound.

Chinelo's face changed slightly, contorting in sudden terror.

A crunch. A crack. Then both repeated a million times.

Before her eyes, she saw him twist. His arms folded, snapping as they moved into his torso. His legs were drawn upwards, lifting off the ground as the bones shattered. His body compressed, and that single, horrified look lingered before he erupted into a shower of deep, hideous red, leaving nothing but a few scraps of cloth and bone behind.

In a moment he was there. Then, he was gone.

CHAPTER 72

THE CAVERNOUS CHAMBER WAS SILENT, AS still as the night. In the dim light, Isobel saw only what lay before her, a dark stain across the floor and a warped sword protruding from its bent sheath.

"Chinelo?"

Silence.

"Chinelo?"

There was no answer.

Her hands began to shake.

"Chinelo?" she screamed.

Nothing. He was gone.

Isobel covered her mouth. Gone? That wasn't right. He couldn't be gone. They were supposed to go back. She was supposed to meet his family. They were supposed to get married. She dropped to her knees. Her hands hit the ground, scraping their knuckles against the stone as her arms hung limply at her sides.

She stared at his sword. The dull blue spell-core hovered on its pommel, glowing faintly in her shadow. They had made that core together. She had formed it around a drop of his blood, and she had healed the wound from which it fell with a touch of her hand. She remembered how it felt. She remembered his warm, gentle touch. She remembered the comfort of being in his arms.

She closed her eyes and turned away. She felt her tears coming. She wanted to stop them. She wanted him to hold her, just like he always did when she cried. However, once again, even after all this time, she was alone.

The first tear trickled down her cheek. She hunched over and sobbed, letting out a wail that echoed in the darkness.

"Why?" she whimpered, striking her fist against the ground. "Please... please don't leave me..."

She wept, pressing her hands on the cold stone floor. Any strength, any will to move forward, left her. Without him, what was even the point? Her tears fell on her spectacles, completely covering the lenses.

Mort nuzzled her hand, staring up at her with sad eyes. However, the gesture brought no comfort. For the first time since Isobel met Chinelo, her mind went completely blank. There was nothing left to plan, nothing left to do, nothing left to feel. She cried in silence.

A voice broke the stillness.

"He's gone, Isobel."

Isobel turned. Iva stood a few steps away, dressed in her leather armor with a fresh dark green cloak draped over her shoulders. Mort hopped between the two of them and puffed out his belly, attempting to appear larger as he glared at Iva.

Isobel stared at her. Iva. Why was she here? Now, of all times, why was she here?

The realization hit.

Chinelo had been crushed, ground into oblivion, just as Joanne had been. This was no act of the gods. This was no cruel twist of fate. Isobel's sorrow boiled into rage.

Chinelo had been taken from her. He had been taken just like Umfrey had been. He had been taken just like Clair had been. He had been taken just like Joanne and Kay had been. The same person had been responsible every time.

The same person.

Iva.

"You!" Isobel hissed. She summoned a dagger from the tattoo on her shoulder and pointed it towards her sister. She rushed forward, driving her knife towards Iva's heart. She would kill her. She would make her pay.

Iva moved faster than Isobel could see. Before she even realized it, Iva wrenched the knife free and sent her tumbling to the ground.

Isobel scrambled to her feet, summoning her staff to her hand. She turned, but again, Iva moved like the wind. Her knee slammed into Isobel's gut, and she crumpled to the floor.

"Why?" Isobel rasped. "Why would you take him from me?"

Iva crouched, resting her forearms on her knees. "I'm sorry, love."

Her voice was somber, regretful, and somehow tender.

Isobel felt her tears returning.

"Sometimes," Iva said, "to make the world right, we must do the most horrible, wretched things. Even when we don't want to, we must hurt the ones we love most."

Isobel slammed her fist into the ground. "Shut up," she sobbed. "What do you know about love? I need him, Iva! I need him!"

"I know, love. I know."

"I'm going to kill you," Isobel said, her voice breaking as she tried to stifle a sob.

"You won't," Iva said, leaning closer. She touched Isobel's shoulder. "Because I can bring him back."

Isobel looked up. "What?"

"I know how to bring him back. There is a way. If we work together, then he'll live again."

Isobel shook away from Iva's hand. Iva stood and crossed her arms, staring down at her sternly. "The words, Isobel, tell me the words you know."

Isobel's brow furrowed. Her mind raced.

Iva made a subtle motion with her hand. Isobel heard footsteps. She caught a glimpse of several shimmering green robes flowing behind Iva, spreading in a circle around her.

Her heart pounded. She had to bring him back. Her fist clenched.

Iva's gaze darted down. "Isobel, don't make things difficult. Tell me what you know, and I will make it so that this never happened."

Isobel gasped. *So that this never happened.* She could do it. She knew the words. The spell would be simple. Just two words to reverse time. With no more than a breath she would return things to as they were. She surged her esht, then hesitated.

Her esht had drained earlier. If she reversed time without care, would she even remember doing so? No! She needed more. Time. Memory. They must weave together in unison for her to bring him back.

Iva crouched again and brought her face close to Isobel's. She stared at her with a piercing, stern gaze.

"The words, Isobel," Iva said in a low, controlled voice. "Last chance before this gets ugly."

Isobel glared at Iva. Her audacity sickened her, enraged her. That anger burned within her, and her esht flowed, charging to expel from her body as she began her incantation, the incantation she had sought for her entire journey. Reverse time. Maintain memory.

"Awge envash—" Isobel said.

Iva gasped.

"Iv stala chanavoshta—"

Iva's arm shot down to the sheath on her hip.

"Py tor vrefden!"

Iva moved like lightning, drawing her dagger in the time between breaths. The blade gleamed as it swung, slowing until it barely touched Isobel's neck.

Isobel felt a rush crashing over her. Iva's blade withdrew, following its swing in reverse. Isobel's body moved on its own. Her feeble attempts at striking Iva repeated. She felt every tear, every quiver, every rasped word, moving faster until they became a blur. She pushed, expelling more and more esht, propelling the world's inverted turn.

Further! She needed to push further. The swirling vision of moments past became a raging storm, a dancing vortex, a maelstrom of sound and sight.

Her body shot upwards, returning to a standing position. Then before her eyes, the stain rose from the ground, coalescing into a solid shape. It quickly grew, forming arms and legs and a face. It was a face she knew. It was a face she loved. It was Chinelo.

But it wasn't enough! She couldn't stop at the moment of his death. She had to go further! She channeled more, and her esht quickly drained.

The world stopped. Isobel stumbled as it lurched to a halt. Her stomach turned. Her hands tingled, as if she had just clapped them.

"Isobel?" Chinelo said.

She looked up. He was alive! He was standing in front of her, looking at her with his tender gaze. She didn't have time to enjoy the moment. She had to prepare for what she knew was coming. She summoned her staff.

"Store: Incantation: Recall!" Isobel said. Her staff pulsed as her esht rooted itself in the spell-core, waiting for words that would soon be etched within.

She repeated the incantation, "Awge envash iv stala chanavoshta py tor vrefden!"

With a sudden shake, her staff responded, flashing brightly before returning to its usual dim glow. She turned, hastily scanning the space for the source of the attack.

"Isobel?" Chinelo touched her shoulder. "What's wrong?"

A light caught Isobel's eye. It shone across the floor, spreading from the colossal door through which they had entered. More lights appeared, and behind them moved shadows, flowing shadows that shimmered a deep green. They glided silently, a quiet procession of gold trimmed guardsmen.

She squinted and recognized a figure at the front.

Iva.

Her dark hair billowed behind her, and her green eyes flashed in the dim light. Iva stopped, and her face changed, adopting a determined if slightly wary expression. Her hand twitched. Her fingers curled, closing in on each other. Her gaze shifted to Chinelo.

"No!" Isobel shouted, surging her esht into her hand, drawing forth her golden barrier. She heard a rush of air, and she felt her energy drain. Something had hit her barrier, something very powerful.

 Isobel's grip on her staff tightened. Her pulse pounded in her head. With a sudden shift of her esht, she vanished, reappearing directly in front of Iva.

"Repel!" Isobel shouted. Her staff responded, sending out a blast that threw the guardsmen off their feet. They careened into the hard stone walls, shaking the chamber.

Iva rolled, quickly regaining her footing before pouncing forward, drawing her curved dagger in a single motion. The sharpened steel flashed as it cut through the air, sweeping towards Isobel's abdomen. Isobel twirled her staff and blocked the strike. Her feet scraped across the ground at the force of Iva's blow. Iva's wrist flicked, maneuvering the dagger faster than Isobel could track.

She felt a sharp pain in her side. She screamed and glanced down. Blood poured from a wound, and Iva's swinging blade launched a splatter of red across the ground.

Isobel fell and gritted her teeth, barely forcing a word from her lips.

"Recall!"

The previous moments played out in reverse. The pain faded. She saw the dagger move, twisting beneath her staff at the point where she had blocked it. That was her error: not anticipating the follow-up strike. Iva was no novice, and simple defensive tactics would not be effective against her.

Isobel released her esht and the world returned to its forward motion. Iva's dagger rang as it collided with her staff, just as before, but this time Isobel shifted her flow to her chest, transporting her behind Iva.

"Form: Blade!" Isobel commanded, and her staff obeyed, shaping itself into her preferred glaive head.

She drove all of her strength into its shaft, slamming it into Iva's back. Isobel felt the impact through her whole body, bouncing from bone to bone, rattling every ligament, shaking every muscle fiber. It was as if she had struck hardened steel. Iva whirled around.

Another sharp pain erupted in her back. Isobel struggled to look to her side, and she saw the tip of a gleaming sliver blade protruding from just beneath her shoulder.

"Recall!"

Time reversed, and the pain once again faded. She was being careless. She had ignored her surroundings. She was outnumbered, and she needed to start adapting to that situation. She stopped, just as the hit from her blade colliding with Iva's back began to shake her arms.

Iva whirled around. Isobel shifted her gravity, pulling herself directly upwards as a blade passed beneath her. She flew above the guards and scanned their numbers. Ten. There were ten, many of whom were still recovering from her initial attack. Below her, a woman with golden braids stared up at her with wide eyes. Closer to the obelisk, she saw Chinelo charging towards the guardsmen with sword raised.

Isobel gasped. Where was Iva?

Something slammed into Isobel's back, driving her down. The ground flashed before her, and the impact knocked the breath from her lungs. She tried to move, but the only thing she could accomplish was a breathless groan.

"Impressive," Iva said, floating down to the ground beside her. "You caught me off guard there."

Isobel let out an agonized cry, trying to regain her breath.

Iva crouched. "I'd hoped we could talk things out, but I suppose you aren't going to listen, are you?"

Isobel coughed. She needed to move. She needed to keep Iva from Chinelo.

Iva sighed. "All right, well—oh?"

Footsteps echoed through the chamber. A deep voice let out a piercing roar. Iva leapt to her feet and clutched her dagger as Chinelo thundered into her, slashing his sword.

"You, again!" Iva scoffed, parrying Chinelo's strikes with her curved blade. Suddenly, Iva jumped back, opening her arms invitingly. A smile flashed across her face.

What little breath Isobel had managed to recover escaped her lips in a horrified gasp. It was a trick. Isobel scrambled to her feet. Then she saw it, the slight movement of Iva's hand, the gesture that brought Joanne's death. Chinelo's muscles tensed as he prepared to strike.

"No!" Isobel shrieked.

At the sound of her voice, Chinelo hesitated. Iva did not. Isobel watched in unbridled horror as Chinelo was once again crushed by Iva's invisible spell.

Isobel screamed, drawing a surprised look from Iva.

"Recall!" Isobel commanded, and the previous moments reversed. Chinelo reformed in front of her, then ran backwards away from Iva. Isobel lifted from the ground, returning to her flight in the air. Iva had managed to strike her from above somehow, but this time she would be ready. She released the spell and twisted, facing the ceiling instead of the ground.

A light flashed and Iva appeared above Isobel. Appeared? That was a technique of Isobel's invention. How would Iva know how to do that?

Iva dove, delivering a kick downwards. Isobel evaded, spinning and catching Iva by her cloak. With a sudden accumulation of strength, Isobel used the momentum of Iva's attack to pivot and hurl Iva back into the ceiling before launching after her. She pulled back her arm, and with a yell she surged esht into her balled fist.

She had to separate Iva from Chinelo. He was a master combatant, and he'd already proven himself against mages. He could handle the

Interior Guard. Iva was not his fight. No, Isobel would deal with her sister herself.

"Homvelcht feyrarch!" Isobel shouted, driving all the strength she could muster into a single punch. As her knuckles crunched against Iva's armor, she released her esht, activating the spell she had charged.

Iva vanished, sent away by the travel spell Isobel had delivered.

Isobel panted, hovering at the roof of the chamber. She looked down at Chinelo. At that moment, he was safe. Around the periphery of the room, the guardsmen had begun to stand.

Chinelo nodded to her. "Go!" he shouted.

Isobel nodded back. He could handle himself, just as she could. Without each other in the way, they could unleash the magic they had prepared without hesitation. She surged esht into her chest and followed after Iva, appearing high above the streets of Rothvale. Iva hovered before her with dagger in hand and regal cloak moving behind her in gentle waves.

"That's three times you've surprised me, Isobel," Iva said. She twirled her dagger. "You've grown since you were young. You make me proud."

Isobel scoffed. "So, you can fly, too."

"Of course! It seems you also developed your own method." She squinted. "Though your control array is different from mine."

Isobel shuddered. Could she somehow see the sigil on her back?

Iva floated in a wide circle around Isobel, eyeing her closely. "I am surprised you abandoned that man so quickly. I suppose that was always your specialty, though. I wonder how he'll fare down there. Perhaps we should go back."

"Chinelo is strong. He can defeat your men," Isobel retorted.

"But can he defeat me?"

Isobel felt her cheeks grow hot. "He won't have to."

Iva's head tilted slightly. "If you're so dead set on protecting him, then just tell me the words you know. Right now, you are an obstacle. If you could be more reasonable, perhaps we could come to an understanding."

"And what would that accomplish? Our friends and family would still be dead."

Iva shook her head. "No, no, no! Isobel, think! You're not thinking. If you help me, I can fix all of that."

"With the Source?" Isobel asked.

"That's right. Imagine being able to change the code that defines the world." Iva outstretched her arms. "There's so much good we could do. There's so much evil we could prevent."

Isobel frowned. "And what happens if you make a mistake Iva? You taught me that spells break in the hands of a careless mage. Remember?"

"I do not intend to make any mistakes," Iva said in a low voice. "Besides, it is the only way. That is a risk I am willing to bear."

"So, you would break the world?" Isobel shouted.

"That's the thing you don't get, Isobel." Iva tossed her hair. "My world broke long ago, eleven years ago."

Isobel adjusted her grip on her staff. A sudden gust caused her loose trousers to flutter. Her world had shattered, like porcelain, eleven years earlier as well. However, it had been rebuilt, repaired by the loving care of her mother, reinforced by the tender support of her friends, and polished to a glorious shine by the man she loved.

"What happened that night doesn't give you the right to cause meaningless deaths," Isobel said.

Iva scowled. "Will you help me or not?"

Isobel tensed. "Helping you would be abandoning those that I love, and I'm not doing that. Never again!"

Iva's eyes narrowed. "Such hypocrisy. Very well. If you won't help me, I'm sure the promise of resurrecting your corpse will be enough for that man you pretend to love."

Iva's hand moved. Isobel gasped and dove to the right. She felt a rush of air, and a hideous, all-consuming pain erupted from her shoulder. Her esht dispersed, and she fell screaming. From above, Iva looked on in disgust, growing smaller as Isobel descended further.

The ground was near. She needed to act if she was going to survive. She tried to focus, attempting to ignore the pain that overwhelmed her senses, struggling to regain control of her esht. At first it barely trickled, then it lurched, crashing in a torrent into her side, activating so that her body was protected in the instant she contacted the cobblestone pavement. The impact shook her, but she lived.

Her entire left arm was an ocean of agony. She reached out to touch it, trying to find the wound that had been inflicted. She found nothing.

Her arm was gone.

Isobel shrieked. Where her shoulder had been there was only the frayed threads of her tunic. Her breath hastened. Her hand shook, clawing erratically at the air. She grew light-headed.

She looked around and saw her staff, barely a step away. With a grunt she extended her arm, reaching for it until her fingers touched its shaft.

"Recall," Isobel rasped out.

The world stopped. She flew backwards, rising from the pavement along the trajectory in which she had fallen. Suddenly the pain faded. Her arm had been restored, and she was again floating in the sky above Rothvale.

Isobel's mind flew into action. Iva's spells did not miss. Typical projectile or beam-based magic could be tracked if one's eyes were sharp enough. This was something entirely different. She was using some other form of a casting channel. What was it? Proximity based scanning? Conal projection? The attacks seemed to always occur in front of Iva.

Isobel released her spell. She would not dodge this time. She would face the attack head on.

Iva squinted. "Such hypocrisy. Very well. If you won't help me, I'm sure the promise of resurrecting your corpse will be enough for that man you claim to love."

Isobel waited for the subtle movement of Iva's hand. There it was! She had touched her index finger and thumb together. The attack was coming. Isobel surged her esht into her hand, summoning her barrier. She felt the drain intensify for a moment, a single instance.

Iva grimaced and moved her fingers, creating a loop with her middle and thumb. Isobel once again felt her esht drain as something connected with the barrier. Interesting. Whatever spell Iva was using only acted in a short moment of time. Isobel surged esht into her right shoulder, activating a new tattoo, a copy of her magic protection spell from Kahi. With that, she could fight more freely.

"I suppose that wouldn't work," Iva said as she shook out her hand. "You've predicted it each time, though I'm not sure how."

Isobel twirled her staff. She whispered a command. "Vanguard."

Blades formed from thin air around her, pointing forward, primed to strike anything that approached.

Iva glared back and uttered a command of her own into her dagger's hilt. "Skyfire."

The clouds above glowed a deep, horrid red. They grew brighter, until spots of orange and yellow appeared.

Isobel and Iva circled each other one final time, and their battle began. They dove forwards between the barrage of spells and magically formed armaments as they clashed and separated. Beneath them, the capital shook, for battles raged both above and below the streets of Rothvale.

CHAPTER 73

FIRST THERE WERE TEN. THEY MOVED in the dim light, gliding with razor steel and billowing robes, spreading like midnight shadows to surround their target. A flash of lightning, a breath of ice, a shower of blades, a volley of stones. Together they struck. Chinelo ran with Mort clinging to his shoulder, leaping over flying rocks and deflecting the falling blades with focused swings of his broadsword.

The mages struck in pairs, darting in with swift thrusts as their comrades covered their approach with endless volleys of spells. They moved like the wind, and the sound of their fluttering green robes and rustling chainmail filled the air. It was a spectacle, a dance, a rhythm that resounded from different directions with each assault.

Chinelo felt alive in such a way that he rarely experienced. It was an undeniable, almost primal excitement that he felt, narrowly balancing on the border between life and death. Blades fell, and he flowed around them, responding to the maelstrom like a reed in the wind. His sword clanged as it parried the striking rapiers, and his heart pounded as the spells riddled the ground around him. There were few experiences that could evoke such a feeling within. Yet he remained focused. He had trusted Isobel. She had trusted him, and without the weight he used to feel, he could finally be the warrior he always was.

The pattern broke. One of the mages hesitated, and instead attacking from two directions, there was a slight delay in the approaching thrusts. Chinelo side-stepped around his opponent, delivering a thunderous strike with the flat of his blade to his opponent's knee. He heard a hideous crack, and the man fell, clutching his leg as he hit the ground. One was down. Nine more remained.

The second mage struck, but Chinelo was prepared. His sword swung upwards, diverting his opponent's momentum as the rapier was thrown above his head. That was the opening he needed. Chinelo burned through the strength he had accumulated and leapt, catching his attacker's belt as he shot from the ground. He spun and hurled the mage down, where he was promptly hit by the volley of spells intended for Chinelo. Eight more remained.

"Fire!" Chinelo shouted as he swung his sword in a flurry of slashes, sending flaming arcs towards his foes around him. He landed on his feet and crouched. He was exposed, and his opponents would take advantage of that fact.

His esht coursed within, filling the tattoos Isobel applied along their journey. His skin sprouted goosebumps as a ghostly chill buffeted his body. He pushed and canceled gravity, allowing him to fly from the icy wind until he hit one of the high chamber walls feet first. In an instant, he forced esht into his ankles, and the wall was his ground. Mort, in turn scurried up his shoulder and onto his back.

A hailstorm of summoned spikes pummeled the stone wall. He conjured his barrier, a perfect copy of Isobel's, and the blades faded into quiet breaths.

He steadied himself and moved his sword across his body, focusing his strength and will.

"Project!"

His sword flashed, a line of bright silver, and from it a blurry crescent rushed to the ground below. He heard a cry that was punctuated by the ringing of a blade hitting the ground. Seven remained.

Chinelo snatched Mort from his back then pushed, flying from the wall towards his next opponent. He landed and rolled, delivering a slash to the surprised mage's legs. The wound would not be fatal, but it would buy him enough time to return to the surface for Isobel. Six.

A shadow darted in front of him. Mort squawked and leapt from his hand, latching onto the face of an attacking mage and slathering it in a layer of his thick mucus. The man garbled out a what sounded like a scream, albeit a very wet one. With a quick sweep of his boot, Chinelo brought the man down to the ground. The crack of his head hitting the floor echoed through the chamber. Five.

The ground became slick, coating over with a sheet of ice that reflected the pale light the guards had brought. The ice crept up Chinelo's boots, stiffening his trousers and bringing with it a frosty burn.

"Heat!" Chinelo shouted.

His spell-core pulsed, and his skin steamed, radiating an intense heat the melted the frost.

Mort croaked loudly from his perch on the downed mage's face. Chinelo's hair stood on end. He turned just as an enormous sphere of ice struck him squarely in the abdomen, sending him careening across the ground. He hit the stone floor again and again. It slammed against his shoulder, then his back, then his elbow, then his face until he finally came to a stop.

The ground was rough, and though he had used a protection spell, his arms stung from the many scrapes he had received. He groaned and pushed, rising to his knees. He opened his hand and surged esht into his wrist. In a flash, his sword appeared in his hand.

He felt a sharp pain in his neck. He opened his eyes to see the shining blade of a rapier poised to pierce his throat. Beyond it stood a familiar golden-haired woman, Talia. Her shimmering locks fell in ornamented braids, and with her icy eyes she glared at Chinelo. She was shorter than him, but not by much.

"Fall still, Eshgarian," Talia said. "Until Queen Iva's battle concludes, you will remain here."

Chinelo gripped his sword tighter. "I've been trying not to kill your men. Let me go. Tend to your wounded."

"If we let you go, will you interfere with the queen?"

Chinelo frowned. "I will help Isobel. I have no desire to hurt your queen. Not anymore."

The other four remaining mages circled around him.

Talia spoke. "I—we cannot allow you to interfere. You are an enemy of Iskara. Please, drop your weapon, and we will not harm you."

"And what happens to Isobel?"

Talia's gaze fell. "If—if she does not cooperate, then she will be an obstacle."

"And what then?"

"She—she will be dealt with, as all obstacles are."

"I see. Then I am truly sorry for what I must do."

The woman looked up.

"Blink!" Chinelo said.

Before his eyes, the world converged.

He reappeared at the far side of the chamber and pivoted on his toe. He had no desire to hurt them. He had no desire to hurt anyone, but this was his fight. He would do what he must, for him and for her.

Chinelo forced esht into his sword hilt, adding it to the torrent within its spell core. His sword swished as it cut through the air.

"Transcend!"

A whirlwind shot forth, flying across the chamber where it collided with the mages that had formerly surrounded him. Four blades fell. Only one remained.

The sky burned red as smoldering darts fell around Isobel. Iva commanded a storm of flames, a shower of blazing tongues that fell upon her city. In her wingless flight, Isobel was a hummingbird before a hurricane, a wren fleeing a wildfire. She dove and alighted on the ground before breaking into a terrified sprint. Burning shingles tumbled around her. She heard a crash behind her, and several screams indicated that she had not escaped Iva's onslaught.

She ran, tripping and stumbling over broken cobblestones and rubbish. The thudding of her heels against the pavement resonated through her worn boots. She took another step, but her foot did not hit the pavement.

The street tore apart, opening into a wide crevasse, an earthen maw that hungered for her. She surged esht and flew, narrowly escaping the earth's snapping jaws. She floated to a nearby rooftop. Sweat dripped down her forehead, stinging her eyes. She wiped her brow and glanced over the skyline.

Iva fell from above, wielding her curved dagger in her hand. She yelled, swinging her blade downwards in a furious strike, one that Isobel avoided by a mere hair's breadth. The dagger sliced cleanly through the shingles. Isobel ran. She was too close. She needed room to think. The edge of the rooftop was just ahead. She could jump from there and hide in the streets.

A light flashed before her eyes. Iva appeared a few steps away, and she swung her dagger directly for Isobel's throat.

She remembered what Chinelo had taught her. The muscle memory of her training compelled her to move. She gripped her staff with both hands and held it vertically, blocking the swing with the shaft.

The blade quivered as it sunk into the wood between Isobel's hands. Iva's eyes darted to the staff's end, glancing over the inscription Isobel had carved to summon it to her hand. Isobel gasped and twisted, knocking the blade down before floating back.

"I expected more from you, Isobel," Iva said. "You were off to such a promising start. You slayed five gods and now all you do is run and hide?" With a swift motion, she tore off her cloak, and it floated away in a passing breeze. Her thick black hair moved in the wind.

"Make up your mind!" Isobel exhaled. "Either be proud of me or disappointed."

Iva frowned. "I know you're tired," she said. "So, I'll ask you once again, what are the words you know?"

Isobel closed her mouth tightly.

"So be it. I can always pull them from your spell-core." Iva brandished her weapon. Her legs tensed. Her feet pressed against the worn shingles.

Isobel swung her staff downwards. "Drop!"

Iva's face went pale. The roof creaked beneath her as her weight was multiplied tenfold, then twentyfold, then more. The timbers within the building shattered, and Iva plummeted down, screaming as she crashed through story after story until she hit the lowest level of the structure.

Isobel pushed off the pulverized roof and hovered a short distance away, panting heavily. A chill ran down her spine. She felt a heaviness in the air, a stagnation, a faint scent of decay that she had only experienced a few times before. The walls of the house collapsed, and a sickening black light tore through them, coalescing into a ray of darkness that shot in wild directions. It cut through the surrounding buildings, leaving behind a trail of rotted wood and corroded metal.

Isobel summoned her barrier and defended against the beam as it flashed in her direction. Then it vanished, leaving only a pile of rubble and a cloud of dust behind.

Isobel searched the haze. A shadow moved within the dust, the shape of a tall, muscular woman. She burst forth, landing on the street and glaring up at Isobel with burning green eyes.

She moved her hand, closing the middle finger over her thumb. Isobel gulped and again activated her protection. She felt the impact of Iva's spell, but once again she was safe. However, how much longer could she maintain that defense?

Iva grunted. "I see what you're doing, Isobel. You protect yourself with those spells on your hand and shoulder."

Isobel gasped. She had to finish this. Whatever Iva was doing activated quickly, leaving little window to react. But how did it work? It always happened after Iva gestured with her hand, but the position of her hand didn't seem to affect her aim. So how was she aiming it?

Isobel tensed. Her eyes! The Archmage had forced Iva to cover her eyes! If that was the case, then Isobel would be able to prove it. There was a tall building behind her, one that would be sufficient for her needs.

"Recall!"

She only needed a few seconds. The events played out in reverse, right up until Iva had just landed on the street.

The world resumed its forward spin. Iva's hand moved exactly as before. It would not be long, a mere fraction of a second, the time it took her to expel esht. Instead of protecting herself, Isobel surged her esht into her chest, pulling her forward in an instant. She reappeared and spun around to see the wall directly behind her torn apart, collapsing in on itself as it was ground to a fine powder by an invisible force.

So, she had been right. The position of the damage was where she predicted it would be. The spell worked along Iva's line of sight, and it was activated by her gesture. If she could deal with that, she might have a chance.

The chamber shook, and stones fell from the ceiling, crashing around Chinelo and his opponent as their blades clashed. One by one the lights summoned by Talia's fellow mages flickered out, until only one remained. Its gold light shimmered and reflected off Chinelo's broadsword, and it danced in erratic lines as Talia's rapier vibrated with every parry. She fought well, and she quickly adapted to Chinelo's fighting style, barely giving him a moment to breathe and focus his esht.

She, however, did not seem to have any trouble finding time to cast spells of her own.

"Freeze!" she shouted, sending a blast of frosty wind at Chinelo.

"Heat!" Chinelo commanded, and his body once again let off a wave of hot air.

"Rot!" She pointed her rapier at him as a blast of dark energy erupted from its tip. It tore through the ground, and Chinelo leapt to the side, narrowly avoiding the erosion.

"Fire!" Chinelo yelled, launching a blazing wave at his opponent.

Her robe caught aflame, and she tore off the top layer, exposing her chainmail armor beneath. She vaulted backwards, pirouetting on her toe and thrusting her blade into the ground.

"Rend Earth!" she shouted.

The ground shook. The stone beneath Chinelo's feet tore apart, and he stumbled, kicking off the edge of the crack and running along the jagged rim of the expanding chasm. He sprinted, scampering over the cracking floor like a mountain goat, keeping his eyes on his target as he narrowly avoided falling into the opening abyss. Talia's mouth moved, and she pointed her rapier at him, sending chunks of rockwork flying past. He pushed, canceling gravity and flying over Talia until solid ground was once again below him.

Chinelo twisted in midair and landed on his feet, immediately breaking into a ferocious charge towards his opponent.

"Restrain," Talia said, pointing her rapier at the ground beneath Chinelo.

The stone floor shook, cracking and sending up columns of rock that encased Chinelo's legs. Stone hands burst from the ground and clutched his arms. He was bound, held in place by Talia's magic. She clutched her blade with both hands, pointing it directly at his now exposed heart.

"Pummel." Stones appeared in the air. They shot forward, flying at Chinelo and bombarding him relentlessly.

Chinelo groaned. The rocks tore at his clothes, stinging as they impacted his skin. He tried to surge his esht, but every wound that Talia inflicted disrupted his focus. Talia drew closer, bringing her weapon toward Chinelo's chest. Chinelo's skin burned, covered in bruises and scrapes from Talia's unending onslaught. He had to escape!

"I'm sorry," Talia said, preparing to strike with her shining blade.

She stepped forward before letting out a surprised yelp as a bloodcurdling croak echoed from her feet. Mort latched onto her boot and bit it with a wrath Chinelo had never before seen.

The stones stopped. That disruption was all Chinelo needed.

Chinelo multiplied his strength and shattered the stone restraints. With a swift sweep of his leg, he knocked her off her feet. She pushed off the ground but stopped as her neck touched the edge of Chinelo's sword.

"Give up," Chinelo said. "It's not worth it."

"If I give up…" she said.

Chinelo raised an eyebrow.

"If I give up, then how will I atone?"

"Atone?"

She slammed her fist against the ground. "Everything I've done, every life I've helped end, every death I watched happen, how will I atone for those?"

She looked up at him. Her two golden braids had unwound, and their tattered twists framed her face.

"How? How will Iva atone?"

Chinelo cocked his head. "Your name is Talia, correct?"

"Y—yes."

Chinelo squatted down, lowering himself to just above her eye level.

"You know Iva's plan, don't you?"

"I—I'm not supposed to say."

Chinelo sighed. Mort hopped to his side and looked up at him, clearly pleased at his contributions to the battle.

"The thing she wants endangers everything," Chinelo said. "Not just her own life. Everything. Do you understand?"

Talia shook her head. "She—she said that she was going to fix things. She said that she was going to undo our mistakes."

"And she very well might be able to. But let me ask you this," Chinelo said. "Is that worth risking the lives of every person that currently lives? Is that worth it, Talia?"

Her face went pale. "You—you don't know what we had to do! We killed so many. We had to. She had to! There was no other option. There… it was all we could do…"

Chinelo's hands shook. Memories returned, flashes of charred faces and scents of singed flesh. He took a deep breath.

"There is always another option."

"You don't understand," Talia said. "I didn't want this."

"She murdered thousands," Chinelo said in a low voice.

"You think I don't know that?" Talia shouted. "I was there! I was there every time! I watched her do it. Over and over and over again. I watched Yarvore burn. I watched Eshgar burn. I watched Nellborough, Sellbrook, Mervaia, Stellest, and Bastil burn! I—I can still remember the smell."

Chinelo frowned. "She destroyed my home. She destroyed Isobel's home. It was no accident. Do you expect me to believe that can be justified?"

"She didn't want to. The gods... they wouldn't die..." Talia buried her face in her hands. "They consumed so many... we had to..."

Chinelo did not respond. He looked down at the floor briefly, searching for the words to say, trying to suppress his anger.

"My family is dead, Talia. My mother, father, and brother are all dead."

Talia's face went pale. "I—I—," she stammered.

Chinelo lowered his sword. "Do you think slaughtering millions can be justified, Talia? Do you? Do you think the Source is worth all of that?"

"Don't you get it?" Talia snapped. "I'm the same as her. I knew we were wrong. From the very start, I knew, but I didn't say anything. I could have protested, but I didn't! I'm just as guilty as she is. What else am I supposed to do? How else can I atone? I need the Source. I need it to make things right! I need it to bring my father back! It's the only way!"

The chamber shook again, and the ceiling above them cracked, sending down a shower of dirt and rubble that was lit by a ray of sunlight shining through the jagged opening. Talia gasped and looked up. One of the buttresses that supported the vaulted ceiling crumbled and fell, descending for her fallen comrades.

She scrambled to her feet and screamed.

"No!"

Chinelo swung his sword and shouted. "Transcend!"

The shard fell and suddenly stopped. A flurry of invisible cuts slashed and ground it to dust and pebbles. The guardsmen covered their eyes as the cloud descended, but they remained unharmed by the debris. They looked up in disbelief.

"There is another way," Chinelo said. He wiped his sword on his sleeve and sheathed it. "If you truly want to atone, then help Isobel and me. We're going to undo what's been done, and we're going to do it without the Source."

Talia 's head jerked in disbelief. "How?"

Chinelo scooped Mort into his hand and placed him on his shoulder.

"Time and memory. Those words are all we need. We're going back to when this all started to stop Iva."

Talia's eyes widened.

"You were there. How far do we need to go?"

Talia looked up. "I—I think it was the end of summer in 432. That is when Iva and Archmage Harlyle met. That was when she awakened the first monster."

Chinelo exhaled. So, at minimum they would have to reverse over two and a half years.

"Thank you. I won't forget this. Tend to your wounded. We'll set things right."

Chinelo crouched, preparing himself to exit the chamber through the crack in the ceiling.

"Wait!" Talia said, extending her hand.

Chinelo looked up.

"Save her! Please! She's—she's hurting."

Chinelo nodded and pushed off the ground, canceling gravity so that he flew through the crack in the ceiling. He had to find Isobel. Knowing what he did, they could finally go back and put an end to things.

He burst through the crack and into the open air above. He coughed. The faint scent of smoke filled the air, stinging his eyes and scratching at his throat. He landed on the ground and steadied himself.

Black columns of smoke reached for the sky beyond the rooftops. Rothvale was burning. In the distance, Chinelo heard faint rumblings and peals of thunder. He turned and began navigating the ruined streets. Wherever Isobel was, he would find her.

CHAPTER 74

AS THEIR BLADES CLASHED AND THEIR spells flew, Isobel remembered what Iva taught her so many years before. She recalled her training for defeating mages.

"Separate them from their spell-cores."

Isobel deflected Iva's dagger and watched the core on its handle glow.

"Damage their tattoos."

Isobel searched Iva's exposed skin for any sign of a glyph. Nothing was visible. She kept most of her tattoos in areas that were clothed. However, one location was very obvious. Iva's left hand had some kind of tattoo on it, one that changed functions depending on which finger touched her thumb.

Countering that was almost impossible. Iva was relentless, sending wave after wave of lightning, fire, and stone hurtling towards Isobel. Whenever Isobel's feet touched the ground, the earth shook and opened to swallow her. Whenever she found cover, it was immediately vaporized. No matter where she ran, Iva always seemed to find her.

Isobel heard the rush of fire falling around her. The streets below burned, and though much of the population had fled during the previous days, they were still packed with panicked citizens and screaming children. Such chaos. Such carnage. All of it was unnecessary.

Isobel spiraled and flew towards one of the many citadels, she surged esht into her chest, traveling to the other side in an instant. She dissipated her esht and stopped to breathe. She was drenched in sweat. Her muscles ached. Her face was raw from the constant wind. How long would this go on? How long could she endure? Already, she could feel her esht dwindling. The final swell from the core she consumed had fully restored it, but even she had limits.

The roof shook. Isobel let out a faint cry of surprise and pushed off, continuing her flight. A deafening crash sounded from behind her. She whirled around, only to see an explosion of dust and stone flying in all directions.

"Jorech envash!" Isobel shouted.

Time slowed to a crawl. It was an improvised spell, one that affected her movements and the world's equally. Given enough time, she would have added a condition to allow her to move freely, but this would do for the moment. Her perception remained sharp. She could see everything. Every shard of carved rock. Every chunk of flying debris. She could see it and predict its movement. And beyond the explosion was Iva.

Isobel altered her flight, rolling around one moving chunk of stone before vanishing and reappearing at a safe distance. Time restored.

Iva turned her head, looking up at Isobel with a piercing glare, gesturing with her left hand. Isobel summoned her barrier once more, and once again she was protected. Iva grimaced and twirled her dagger, mouthing something Isobel could not discern into its hilt.

She knew what was coming. Iva alternated attacks, activating one of her vision-based spells before switching to traditional ranged options in an effort to wear Isobel down. It was working. Isobel panted as her muscles grew heavier. Regardless of what happened next, she needed to remove one of Iva's offensive options. And so, she added the modification to her earlier incantation.

"Jorech envash py gra zho tor vrefden!"

Time slowed as the air around Iva lit up, forming a thousand tiny suns that orbited her. They flew, one after the other, homing in on Isobel's position. However, they were sluggish and slow, and with her added change to her spell, Isobel was no longer hampered by the slowdown that affected everything else. She dove, spiraling around the blazing stars, descending into the brilliant galaxy of lights with Iva at its center.

Closer. She was almost there. Iva was in range!

"Form: Blade!"

Isobel's staff flashed. With all the strength she could muster, she drove the blade toward Iva's wrist. It sank into her armor, cutting until it reached the skin. Already, Isobel could see Iva reacting to her accelerated movement, swinging her dagger towards her.

Isobel's weapon hit what felt like bedrock. She gasped. Somehow, Iva managed to maintain her ironclad defense. Was it constant channeling?

Would she have the capacity for that? Or was it like Haru's protection, a single or multi-use protection that she could activate only when she needed it?

Isobel gritted her teeth. She could try nullifying it, but they were both incredibly high above the ground. Any spell she had active would be canceled as well. She could try something else. If blades and impacts had no effect, perhaps fire would work.

Isobel glanced at Iva's face. Her expression was surprised, enraged, and determined. Even with the decreased time flow, already her dagger had almost reached Isobel's arm.

Isobel accelerated, spinning rapidly so that she faced Iva's back. She surged esht into her left wrist, sending out volley after volley of cyan lights that slowed as they left her fingers. Then, she reached out her hand and grabbed Iva's before releasing her time dilation spell.

"Icht vasht'ra!" Isobel shouted.

Flame erupted from her palm, engulfing Iva's glove in an orange blaze. Isobel's spells collided with Iva's back, sprouting a garden of bright crystals, brilliant lattices that formed from Iva's esht.

Iva roared and bent over her burning hand, falling to the streets below in the process. She landed with a loud crunch.

Isobel warily descended to the pavement, landing softly and clutching her staff in front of her. Iva lay in a bloody heap with limbs contorted around her and crystalline shards piercing her torso from behind. Isobel squinted. She wasn't breathing.

Iva's body glowed. The limbs reformed, crunching as they returned to their original shape. She let out a loud gasp and shot to her feet, gripping her dagger tightly in her right hand. Her back arched backwards. Popping and cracking, it straightened. Her shoulders moved, flinging her left arm forward with the thumb and middle finger closed in a loop. Her eyes flew open, and she let out an angry yell.

Isobel's heart seized. She wouldn't have time to activate her barrier. If Iva's spell connected, she was dead. She wouldn't be able to go back. She wouldn't be able to see him again.

Nothing happened.

Iva looked at her hand confusedly and tore off the tattered glove with her teeth. The skin had been healed, but it bore scars of a burn with the faded remnants of a complex tattoo on the sides of her fingers. She scoffed.

"Clever. I suppose I didn't account for burns in my resurrection spell. Not being able to have a time condition for restoration is tricky. I'm sure you understand. Though, it seems you might know how to work around that."

Isobel flinched.

"What? Do you think I haven't noticed?" Iva said with a sneer. "You avoid my attacks even when you can't see them coming, and each time your esht depletes in chunks. It's almost like—" she touched her chin. "It's almost like you can sacrifice your esht to undo a mistake."

Isobel's hands trembled.

Iva laughed. "It's not like I can do much about it. Still—" she held her dagger in front of her. "I *can* make you use all your esht."

Isobel accumulated strength. Something wasn't right. Iva was planning something.

"I'll survive this," Iva said, a chilling gleam in her eye. "Will you?"

Isobel traveled forward, swinging her glaive as she reappeared. Her blade vibrated as it hit Iva's iron skin. Then, Iva vanished.

"Perfect Inferno," Iva's voice shouted from behind Isobel.

Isobel felt heavy. Her esht drained. She spun to see Iva holding her dagger above her head, pointing it to the sky. A light flashed, a familiar gold light. It suddenly expanded, forming a raging vortex of flame that rushed towards her.

It was the same column. Just like in Nellborough, it had flashed before engulfing the town in its ravenous blaze. And now, Rothvale was to burn.

A wave of hot air hit Isobel's face, drawing tears from her eyes.

"Recall!"

The flames retreated, returning to the column from which they had spread. Isobel pushed further, reversing time until Iva's glove rose from the ground and returned to her hand.

Isobel sent herself to Iva's position. Iva let out a surprised gasp then blocked Isobel's slash with her arm. She vanished, just as before, and Isobel spun around, sending herself to Iva's new position, delivering a vertical strike. Iva deflected her blade.

"Form: Blade!" Iva shouted. Her spell-core flashed, sending out curving pink threads that weaved into a slender, single edged sword. She slashed and Isobel defended.

"So! I was right!" Iva said between swings. "You *can* influence time."

Isobel ducked under her sword and slammed her blade against Iva's body. It once again bounced off her skin with no apparent effect.

Iva's sword swung upwards, colliding with a quickly summoned barrier from Isobel's left hand. It shattered and disintegrated, returning it to its dagger form.

Iva gritted her teeth. "That is getting annoying, love."

"Shut up!"

Isobel stepped and swung her weapon towards Iva's knee. If she couldn't break the skin perhaps she could at least knock her off her—

Feet?

Isobel's body lurched from the ground. The street spun around her. Her legs flailed above her. She channeled esht into her protection spell, and she hit the pavement. She tumbled. Rolling to a stop, she pushed off the ground and attempted to regain her bearings.

Wait. Where was her staff?

She looked up. Iva held her staff in one hand, and with a swift cut of her dagger, she cleaved the shaft in two. Isobel opened her hand to summon it.

Nothing happened.

The two broken halves fell, bouncing along the pavement.

"Form: Blade!" Iva said. Her sword returned, and she twirled it, pointing it directly at Isobel. She pounced forward, driving a speedy thrust towards her heart.

Isobel summoned her barrier. That attack hadn't worked before. Why would Iva think it would work this time? Iva wasn't the kind to attack recklessly unless—

Isobel screamed. Her entire left hand cried out in pain. She glanced frantically, hesitantly at her hand and shuddered. Iva's dagger protruded through the back of her glove, a stream of blood trickling from around the curved blade. It had been thrust cleanly through Isobel's palm and was lodged between the bones.

Chinelo followed the sounds, running through the winding streets. Lights flashed above him, a stream of glowing stars that flew to the heavens. He was close.

Mort croaked quietly on his shoulder.

"I know, friend. We always seem to end up in situations like this," Chinelo said.

Chinelo rounded a bend and stopped. An entire tower had collapsed into the street, completely blocking his path forward. Over was the only option.

He canceled his gravity and jumped. He landed on a rooftop and continued running, drawing closer to the sound. Just another step. Just another leap. He was almost there.

Isobel's eyes welled with tears. The pain was overwhelming. It was all she could focus on, all she could think about.

"Foolish," Iva said with disgust. "Your barrier only defends against magic."

Isobel clenched her teeth. She could endure. She had to. There was no other option. The dagger was still lodged in her palm, and if she could somehow force Iva to release her grip, then she too would be disarmed.

"Xastra chanavoshta!" Isobel rasped. She grabbed Iva's arm and expelled her esht, erasing a piece of Iva's memory. It wouldn't be much. Isobel had barely any esht left, but maybe, just maybe, it would be enough.

Iva's face went blank. Her hands fell to her sides. She blinked several times. Isobel collapsed. Her stomach turned. She once again shot a hasty look at her wounded hand and gasped. The dagger was still there. It had worked! She had canceled out Iva's two primary means of attack.

She only had a moment of reprieve. Iva, having regained her bearings, kicked her in the side, sending her careening across the street. Isobel slammed into a nearby wall and stopped, laying dazed for a moment. Iva stomped in her direction with every vein in her arms bulging.

"Why, Isobel?" Iva shouted. "Why are you making this so difficult? Why are you standing in my way?"

Isobel groaned and pushed herself to a sitting position. She had to move. She had to run. She was so tired. She was so heavy. Her esht was gone. Her body was covered in scrapes and bruises. She just wanted to be done.

Iva glared down at her.

"I just wanted to go back to how things were!" Iva shouted. "Is that not enough? Is that not enough, Isobel?"

Isobel backed away. What could she do? She could no longer use magic. What was she supposed to do?

Something moved in her peripheral vision. She turned. A muscular silhouette descended from high above, falling with drawn sword upon Iva. As it drew closer, she recognized it. It was a figure she knew and loved.

Chinelo.

Iva's eyes widened. She spun and raised her arm as Chinelo's sword cut through the air. It clanged as it hit her skin.

"Chinelo!" Isobel shouted. "She's using a spell to make her invulnerable."

Chinelo landed with bent knees. He shot Isobel a quick look of understanding. He knew what to do. Those eyes told her everything. He twisted his wrist and yelled.

"Null!"

His spell-core pulsed. His sword flashed, moving faster than Isobel could perceive. A stream of blood shot vertically from the blade.

"I won't let you hurt her!" Chinelo roared, grabbing Iva by her armor and launching her a considerable distance away. He pointed his sword to the sky and issued one final command.

"Starfall."

Iva was not down for long. She coughed and pressed her hand over the gash Chinelo had inflicted on her torso. A shadow fell over her. Her face went pale.

The sky darkened. A great ember, a blazing meteor, pierced the clouds. It burned hotter, hotter, igniting in a raging storm, breaking apart in a shower of smoldering ashes.

Iva froze, watching the fireball fall upon her.

Impact.

Chinelo dropped, shielding Isobel with his body as a cloud of dust and ash swept over them. Isobel closed her eyes. She felt his hand pressing her face into his chest. Then, silence.

Isobel coughed and opened her eyes. Chinelo relaxed and sighed.

"Hey," he said. "Are you all right?"

Isobel nodded. "I think so."

Chinelo looked over his shoulder. "Do you think she's dead?"

"Probably," Isobel said with a sigh. "You nullified her magic. She... she couldn't have survived."

He turned back and froze. His eyes opened wide. "Isobel! Your hand!"

Isobel looked down at the dagger that protruded from her skin. She shuddered as the pain suddenly returned. In a moment of panic, she clutched the dagger's hilt and began pulling it from her palm.

"No, no!" Chinelo implored. "Don't do that!"

Isobel grimaced and tore the dagger out. She dropped it beside her and bent over her hand, clenching her teeth to endure the pain. She clasped her hands to her chest.

"Isobel!" Chinelo pleaded.

"Esht!" Isobel said through her teeth. "Please."

Chinelo placed his hand on her shoulder. In a moment, she felt his energy flow into her, like a brook cascading from the mountains into a shimmering lake below. She activated her healing spell, and the pain faded.

Isobel exhaled and removed her glove. "See? Good as new!"

Chinelo sighed. "Please don't do anything like that again."

A loud squawk came from within Chinelo's shirt. Mort wriggled from beneath his neckline and crawled onto his shoulder, staring down at Isobel with a look of concern.

"I'm glad you're well, my friend," Isobel said.

Chinelo smiled and helped her to her feet, supporting her arm on his shoulder. They stood for a moment, the two of them together. Isobel wrapped her arms around him and held him close. It was over. It was finally over. She leaned her head against his chest and stared at the slowly settling dust cloud where Iva once stood. She took a deep breath.

There was still one thing they still needed to do. However, based on her currently dwindling esht, it seemed that it would not be as easy as she had hoped.

"Chinelo, I'm afraid we have a problem."

"Oh?"

"I used the time reversal spell," she said. "It works."

Chinelo looked down. "Really? That—that doesn't sound like a problem."

"Well, I *only* was able to turn back maybe five minutes. If we worked together, we might be able to go back ten minutes or so..."

"But not two years," Chinelo added. "Well. I suppose we'll have to figure something else out."

"It's frustrating. Iva would have probably known. That spell she used to burn Nellborough was essentially the same as my Inferno spell. She just made some modification that let it adopt a much greater scale."

Chinelo reached down and picked up the dagger, twirling it in his fingers. The hilt suddenly pulsed.

"Chinelo! The dagger!"

Chinelo gasped and looked into the cloud of dust. A shadow moved within. Iva burst through the haze and staggered into the open air. Her armor was bent and singed, and she was covered in dirt and recently healed burns.

"Why, Isobel?" Iva lamented. "Why are you trying to stop me? I'm doing all of this for you."

"Chinelo," Isobel whispered. "Hand it to me."

Chinelo nodded and passed the dagger to Isobel. With a determined breath, he drew his sword and stood beside her.

Isobel looked at the spell-core on the dagger's hilt. Spell-cores were repositories of a mage's mastery and understanding of magic. They were collections of spells, but they were also collections of knowledge, in a way. She did not know how Iva's resurrection magic worked, but it had not been nullified when Chinelo attacked her, meaning that it had a different source, the dagger itself.

Isobel frowned. Spell-cores could be broken.

She opened her mouth and crushed the core between her teeth.

"No!" Iva shouted.

A cloud of vapor erupted. It rushed into Isobel, filling her mind with words and spells she had never known. Spells of momentum. Spells of resurrection. Spells to control the earth, sky, and sea. Spells to command decay and rot. Countless spells, all swirling through her head as if they had always been there. One stood out, one that resembled her Inferno with a single modification, a modification to draw esht from the surroundings and not the caster. That was the spell. That was how Iva destroyed Nellborough.

Everything went dark.

CHAPTER 75

ISOBEL FELT SOMETHING COLD AND WET against her face. Her eyes fluttered open. Directly in front of her, so close that she could smell his pungent aroma, sat Mort.

She bolted upright. Chinelo stood before her, holding his sword warily, and beyond him Iva was sitting on the ground, resting one arm on her knee. She was just sitting there, not moving, not looking, just staring at the pavement in front of her. In a moment Isobel understood. From the knowledge she had absorbed from Iva's core, she had learned her resurrection spell. It was conditionally activated from the dagger, using esht she had accumulated previously from the entire population of Rothvale. Without the core, she was just as vulnerable as any other person.

"Isobel," Iva said. "Do you not want to go back to how things were? Before all of this. Before everything went wrong."

Chinelo glanced over his shoulder at her as she stood and brushed herself off. Within her, the rage she felt still smoldered. It was difficult to ignore. Iva had tried to kill Chinelo. Iva had killed Joanne. She had destroyed Nellborough. She had destroyed Eshgar. And now, Isobel understood how.

Isobel summoned a dagger from her shoulder. Iva was unarmed, weakened, burned, and exposed. She could kill her. She wanted to. That was what she deserved, right? She clutched the knife tightly. If she killed her, this would all be over.

Isobel looked at Chinelo. He had refrained from striking, and his eyes were clouded with concern. She saw no anger in his face. No hatred, no wrath. She remembered what he had once said. He had learned to let go of his anger long ago. She sighed.

Maybe it was time she did as well.

Isobel dropped the knife.

She stepped to Chinelo's side and brushed her hand against his shoulder. He nodded.

"Iva," Isobel said. "I want more than anything for things to go back to how they were."

"Then... then why won't you help me?" Iva pleaded in a low voice. "We can do this together. We can find the Source and rewrite reality. I'll set things right, and we can go back to when you were young. You can have the childhood that you should have. You can finally have a happy life! I can even make it so that we can see the world like you wanted to. Don't you see? With the Source, anything is possible."

Isobel looked down. "But Iva, I *did* have a happy life. I met my mother. She loved me. She loved me even before she met me. I made so many friends. Umfrey and Priscila, Oros and Valk, Clair and Mort! They all loved me, too, each in their own ways. I built a life for myself, and it was a life I hoped that you would be proud of one day."

Iva ran her hand through her hair and stared at the sky.

"Are you trying to take that away from me?" Isobel asked.

Iva blinked. "I just thought... I just thought that if I changed things I could give you something better. I could build an environment for you to be the person you always wanted to be. Not... not whatever you've become."

Isobel stiffened. "Iva. I don't want to be a different person. I am me... and I like me. I'm the culmination of every choice I've made, every experience I've had, every person I've loved, every joy I've tasted, every loss I've felt. I am all of those things. This person is who I want to be. This person is who I chose to be."

Iva looked down.

Isobel sat a short distance away, crossing her legs. Chinelo stood behind her with sword still drawn.

"Iva," Isobel said. "What happened to you? You were always so strong. Why did you do all this?"

Iva sighed. "I was never strong Isobel. I did what my mother made me do. I killed people. That was my job. Even when I didn't want to, that is what I did. That was what it meant to be a Blade. And... it was easy. It was just something I did. That was my place in the coven."

"You could have left," Isobel said. "Why didn't you?"

Iva's face twitched. "When you've done the things I've done, where could you possibly go that would accept you? Where could you be who you were aside from the place you've always been?"

"I wanted to change things," Iva continued. "I've always wanted to change things. I wanted to..." Her voice trailed off.

"Atone?" Chinelo asked.

Iva looked up. "The Source was the only way I could do that. How I got it didn't matter. Any act could just be reversed. After what happened in Veshda, it really was the only way."

Isobel rested her chin on her hand.

"But that's not the only reason why," Iva said. "That was just the excuse I made to convince myself that I was justified."

"Then why?" Isobel asked.

Iva leaned back, supporting herself on her hands. "It's because... it's because I wanted to build a world where we had what I always wanted. I wanted to build a world with you and Esther. No more pain. No more abandonment. No more hate. I wanted to give you the life you deserved. I—I wanted you both to love me again."

Isobel jerked back. "What?"

"It's ridiculous, I know," Iva said. "Back when I was younger, I was always... alone. My mother hated me. The others hated me. Except Esther. She—she did love me. And for a few years, it wasn't so bad."

Iva wiped her eyes. "But then she abandoned me, and it was the same as it always was. Then you came along. You were the one thing that kept me going. Every morning, seeing those pretty blue eyes of yours and that adorable smile... it was my whole world. I kept doing what they made me do because it meant I could be with you. Knowing that you loved me made it all worth it."

"But you left, too." Iva pushed off her hands and leaned forward. "Just like your mother did. I wanted to be who you needed. I wanted to be the mother you deserved. I failed. I wasn't enough, just like I wasn't enough for her to stay. And just like her, you decided you no longer loved me."

"Iva," Isobel said. "That's not right."

Iva looked up.

"I was fifteen, Iva. They were going to use me like some kind of animal. They were going to make me do things that I refused to do."

"But—"

Isobel raised her finger. "I'm not done! I left because it was horrible there. I left because Cleo..."

She paused. She wanted to explain, but those days were difficult to revisit.

A hand rested on her shoulder. Chinelo knelt beside her.

Isobel let out a determined huff. "I left because Cleo hurt me. I left because I wanted a different life. And you know what? I don't regret leaving."

Iva's face fell.

"However," Isobel continued, "if there's one thing I do regret, it's not asking you to come with me. I was mad. I was confused. But I should have asked you to join me. *That* is my biggest regret, Iva. It's because I love you. It's because I've always loved you. I thought about you every day for ten years. I missed you every day for ten years. Even after everything you've done, I still love you. Because you're my sister. I'm sorry I hurt you back then."

Iva's cold expression broke. Tears streamed down her face.

"My mother also loved you," Isobel said. "She always loved you. We talked about you all the time. She wanted to go back for you, but then her illness... her illness made that impossible."

"You mean... all this time..." Iva said," everything I've been doing... was all for nothing?"

Isobel stood. Her hands trembled. She closed her eyes. The rage had sputtered out, growing colder and colder.

Iva chuckled. "This life really is a cruel joke."

"I don't excuse your actions, Iva," Isobel said. "I can't. You've done horrible, horrible things to me, to Chinelo, and to everyone you killed. I will never, ever pretend to excuse that. It disgusts me. It enrages me."

Isobel stepped forward. "However, I do understand you. I should have come back for you. I should have told you the truth. I'm sorry that I didn't, and I'm sorry I hurt you."

Chinelo stepped beside her.

"What am I supposed to do? Everything I've ever done to find the Source—" Iva said. "If it was all meaningless... then... then..."

Isobel extended her hand.

"Then let me help you."

Iva looked up and wiped her eyes.

Isobel smiled. "If I had come for you Iva, would you have left the coven?"

Iva nodded slowly.

"Then, I promise I will. I'll tell you how I truly felt."

Chinelo sheathed his sword. "If you really do want to atone, then let us go back and stop you from making the choices you've made."

"So, with that, do I have your permission to change your past?" Isobel asked.

Iva blinked. "You—you can do that?"

"Of course I can do that!" Isobel said, putting her hands on her hips. "You said it yourself. I can influence time."

Iva squinted. "You're out of esht, Isobel. If you're planning on doing what I think you are, then you're going to need more."

Isobel grinned. "See that's the thing, Iva. I know your tricks now. I know the modifications you made to the Inferno spell you taught me. How many people are in Rothvale?"

Iva took Isobel's hand and stood. "Normally at least one and a half million, though with the mass exodus, it's difficult to say."

Isobel looked up and tapped her cheek. "Interesting. If we assume a typical esht capacity, then the average person could probably sustain a time reversal of at least a minute, based on my experience. How far back are we aiming, Chinelo?"

Chinelo laced his fingers in hers and held Mort in his free hand. "Over two and a half years, if we can."

Isobel touched her chin. "Hmmm. If we factor in animals and plants, then we should have enough. I think. We'll do the best we can. We'll set things right, and we'll stop you from going down this path."

"You'd do that?" Iva asked. "Even after all I've done, you would do that? I—I don't even have the right to ask for such forgiveness."

"That's the funny thing about forgiveness, Iva" Isobel said. She locked eyes with Chinelo briefly, then continued with a smile. "It's not about worthiness."

Iva chuckled, then laughed. "It really is a cruel joke. Very well! Do what you must! Change our past!"

"First, one question," Isobel said. "If we're able to go back as far as we want, where should we go to find you?"

Iva crossed her arms and tapped her foot. Her forehead wrinkled. "I was at the coven until the ninth month of 432. I was sent to Yarvore after that."

"Then we will look for you there." Isobel looked up at Chinelo. "You ready?"

He nodded. "Ready."

Mort croaked.

Iva looked on and smiled. "For what it's worth, Isobel, I truly am proud of you. You're a better witch than I."

Isobel let out a satisfied sigh and turned, resting Chinelo's hand in hers so that her fingers touched Mort. She commenced her incantation. She began with the basics: a command to reverse time.

"Awge envash—"

She added the targets: herself and anyone she touched.

"Py tor vrefden iv gra tor vrefden hasa—"

She concluded with the modifiers: a command to draw esht from her surroundings.

"Yor klashadde'de iv frithe'de esht vo gra gest!"

She accumulated her sliver of energy, and with one last wistful look, she watched Iva smile.

"Goodbye, Iva. I love you. When I see you next, you won't remember this."

Isobel expelled her esht, and time grinded to a halt. It suddenly reversed, flowing backwards faster and faster. Isobel felt a surge of esht flowing through her, the siphoned energy of all who remained in Rothvale. It was unlike anything she had experienced before, an overwhelming inundation of power that threatened to overflow. Then it was used, adding to the world's reversed spin. The events of that day played out before her eyes. She saw them moving.

Faster.

She saw her fight with Iva.

Faster.

She saw their struggle beneath the capital.

Faster.

She saw when she woke up that morning.

Faster!

It became a blur, moving so quickly that she could not process the swirl of colors and shapes. And so, she did not even try. She just kept pushing. She felt the faint touch of Chinelo's hand in hers. Though she could no longer see him, she knew he was there, holding onto her as he had for so, so long.

She pushed. Her esht drained. She watched their journey flow in reverse. Every happy moment was a reminder of her joy, and every defeat was an encouragement to press forward. For Joanne. For Kay. For Valyx. For Haru. For Umfrey. For Clair. For Oros. For Valk. For those she did not know. For those she did not remember. For Iva.

But most of all, for Chinelo.

CHAPTER 76

THE PEN FELL FROM ISOBEL'S HAND and bounced from her desk to the floor. She sat there for a moment, staring. Everything seemed blurry. She squinted. Vague shapes were visible, but the colors and textures were so muddled. It was like a sketch that was unfinished, a painting that was smudged. She blinked, and everything quickly came into focus.

She was in her house, seated at her work desk. The familiar aroma of musty books and pungent chemicals hung in the air. Isobel shot to her feet. The chair tumbled behind her.

She was home.

Had it worked?

She scrambled through her kitchen, running past a smoldering pile of embers in her fireplace. She scurried up the stairs, habitually stepping to avoid the hole she had blasted in the floor, only the hole wasn't there. Down the hall, her bedroom door was shut. She hurried and flung it open, stepping into the bright gold light that shone through her window. She saw what she sought.

Her diary.

She snatched it and opened it, thumbing through the many blank pages with trembling fingers until she found the most recent entry.

432, 2, 25

Isobel covered her mouth. They had done it. They had gone back three years. She fell to her knees and laughed. A tear ran down her cheek. She wiped it away and continued reading.

Today was not particularly interesting. I went to see Umfrey and Priscila. They seem to be doing well. Clair is getting rather big, too, the little scamp. She did seem rather disappointed that I cut my hair. It's much harder for her to tangle now."

Isobel reached up and touched her hair. It really was short, hanging just below her chin. She had not worn it like this in a long time.

She looked up. Clair! Umfrey! Priscila! She could go see them. She dropped her journal and ran back downstairs, descending the steps so quickly that she collided with the back wall. She hopped the last two and landed with a loud thud, one that was followed by an equally loud croak.

"Mort!"

Isobel plucked him from the floor and held him in her hands.

"We did it! We did it, Mort!"

Mort looked oddly pleased, for once.

"Come on! Let's go! We must go see the town!"

She placed Mort on his customary perch on her shoulder and opened her hand to summon her staff.

It did not move. She looked down at her hands. The tattoos on her wrists were gone, leaving only her barrier and healing glyphs. Even the Darkburn scar on her right hand was absent.

"Silly me. That is going to take some getting used to."

She slid on her boots, grabbed her staff from beside the door, and with a deep breath stepped out into the forest.

It was the same as it had always been. She took in the scents, the smells of leaves and dirt, the hint of perfume from the Ashen Plains, the touch of rotting wood. And the sounds, oh, the sounds! The birds sang their familiar songs. How she had missed those songs! They were friends of hers, family almost, and they greeted her soul just as long separated comrades would.

She ran. The forest raced by as she leapt over fallen log and cracked stone alike. The leaves crunched beneath her feet. The wind rushed through her hair. She burst from the forest, entering the wide rolling hills of radiant green. The sky shone a brilliant azure, and woolly clouds were scattered across the blue expanse like the many sheep on the distant hills around her. She hurried down the trail, running faster, faster, faster, until she crested the final hill. There it was. Nellborough.

It was nestled between the hills just like it always was. Those familiar rooftops with their wisps of smoke rested happily in those hills. The city sang, with gentle overlapping melodies drifting in the breeze. It was too much for her. She collapsed in a heap, weeping for joy. She tried to stifle the tears, but they just kept flowing. Did it matter, though? This was how things should have been. Over a year had passed for her since she first wept for Nellborough. If she had to weep a second time for it to return, then maybe that was not so bad.

"Bel?" a voice called.

Isobel looked up to see that familiar, gangly figure she had missed so much. She sobbed and forced a smile.

"Umfrey."

Umfrey ran forward and stopped, dropping the basket he carried and placing his hand on her shoulder. "My, my Bel. What's wrong?"

Isobel sniffled and tackled him, wrapping her arms around him. In the process, Mort let out a terrified squawk and leapt from her shoulder.

"I—I missed you, Umfrey."

"Woah, now, Bel. I—I missed you, too, but it's only been since yesterday."

Isobel smiled and nestled her head in his chest. "Just let me have this, just for a moment."

Umfrey returned her embrace. "Of—of course. Whatever you say, Bel. Are you sure you're well?"

Isobel nodded. "Never better."

"Umfrey!" another voice called. "If you're going to walk ahead, would you at least do it at a pace that I can match?"

Isobel's eyes flew open. She knew that voice.

"Priscila!"

Isobel looked up. There she was, dressed in that plain white dress that she always wore. And beside her, holding her hand with tiny fingers, was a small child with short blonde hair. Clair.

Isobel sat back and let out a long sigh of relief. At last, they had set the world right.

Chinelo blinked as the world slowly came into focus. The sun was bright, almost blinding as it lit the sandstone streets of Eshgar. Something hit his shoulder, creating a loud clang.

"Watch it, Chinelo," a voice said.

"Azuka?" Chinelo turned his head to see his brother, clad in his suit of Eshgarian armor that matched Chinelo's.

"Yes, did you see that, too?" Azuka said, rubbing his eyes. "Was that a heat mirage or something?"

Chinelo stepped forward and hugged him with shaking hands.

"That's not—what are you doing?"

"Sorry." Chinelo backed away. He wiped a tear from his eye. He was back in Eshgar. He fell to his knees and laughed as tears flowed down his cheeks. He was home!

Azuka adjusted his helmet. "Chinelo? Is something wrong?"

Chinelo looked up at him with a wide grin. "No. Not a thing, brother."

He looked around the bustling street and saw a familiar restaurant sign. He was only a few streets over from his family's apartment.

Chinelo pushed to his feet.

"Where are you going?" Azuka called. "We haven't finished our patrol!"

Chinelo ran, weaving through the crowds until he reached the steps that lead up to his family's home. He bounded up them, three at a time, and burst through the door.

He was greeted by the scent of crimson potato stew. His father and mother peaked out of the kitchen.

"Chinelo? You're here early," his father said, smiling from above his white beard.

"Finally listening to his mother, I see," his mother poked her husband in the ribs.

Chinelo walked into the kitchen and hugged them both, sobbing as Azuka entered the door behind him.

"I'm back," Chinelo said. "I'm finally back."

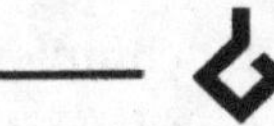

Umfrey set a steaming mug of tea in front of Isobel. She eyed it with slight apprehension, then cautiously took a sip. She wrinkled her nose.

"Sorry," Umfrey said. "I forgot you don't like tea."

"No, no!" Isobel took another difficult sip. "I really should like it by now. It was very kind of you. It's just that—how do I put this?" She waved her hand in a circle before snapping her fingers. "It's just that dirty flavor, yes!"

Umfrey laughed and sipped from a mug of his own. "It doesn't taste like dirt."

"Have you ever eaten dirt?"

"Well, no."

"Then how do you know?" Isobel asked.

Umfrey gave her a suspicious look.

"I've got something that should make it better!" Priscila said. She slammed a large jar of honey on the table and began dumping spoonful after spoonful of the golden syrup into Isobel's mug.

Isobel's eyes widened.

"Oh, stop that, dear," Umfrey said. "Surely that much can't be good for her."

"Are you the doctor, here?" Priscila asked with a grin. "Besides, Isobel is twenty-three now. She's perfectly capable of telling me to stop. Is this enough, honey?" Priscila winked.

"Maybe two more," Isobel said. "Just to be safe."

Umfrey opened his mouth to respond, then quickly took another sip of his tea. "I just think that with that many repetitions, Isobel will be just drinking honey. There's no point to the tea."

Isobel gulped down the significantly thicker liquid. "You're correct and it's magnificent."

A loud croak sounded from the corner of the room. Clair was madly chasing a very displeased Mort in circles, and he was ensuring his displeasure was known.

"So, about this journey you're taking," Priscila said as she sat beside her husband. She wrapped her arm around him and scooted her chair closer.

Isobel smiled. They made an odd if complementary pair. Umfrey was tall and boney. Priscila was shorter and a bit imposing, and her frizzy brown hair was certainly a sight to behold.

"You said you're going to Eshgar?" Priscila cocked her head.

Isobel nodded. "Skyview actually. So right between here and Eshgar. I'm supposed to meet Chinelo there."

Umfrey shook his head. "It really is a wild story. It's hard to believe that you've finally found yourself a man, Bel. Especially when you've never mentioned him to us before now."

Priscila elbowed him in the stomach. "Oh, be quiet, honey. You saw how happy she looked when she talked about him. I'm sure he's lovely, Isobel. Though, before you two get too serious, I expect the opportunity to give him a proper Fellen welcome."

"Oh, of course. I'm sure Chinelo would love one of your interrogations." Isobel giggled.

"Just trying to keep my baby safe," Priscila said. She let out a long sigh. "Look at you. Esther and Bartoss would be so proud of you."

Isobel frowned and looked down. "I really hope so."

Umfrey fidgeted nervously. "So! When are you planning on leaving?"

"Well, I had planned to just fly there, but it seems that none of the words I recovered work anymore." She took a sip of her honey tea. "So, I'm hoping to catch a ride on the next caravan down that way."

"Ah, well Blithe leaves for Eshgar tomorrow," Umfrey said. "You should check with him. He still owes you a favor so I'm sure he would let you tag along."

Isobel nodded. "Good idea! Thank you!"

"You will come back and visit, won't you, honey?" Priscila asked with a concerned expression.

"Oh! Of course!" Isobel waved her hand. "It may be several months, though. Would you mind keeping an eye on the house for me? It shouldn't be too hard."

"It would be our pleasure," Umfrey said.

"We'll make sure it's nice and clean for when you two get back," Priscila winked.

Isobel blushed. "I appreciate that. Thank you, both. For everything. You both were like the parents I—well I suppose I did have parents, but you know, it's complicated."

Priscila smiled and rested her hand on Umfrey's. "And you truly are a daughter to us. You'll always be welcome here. You and this mysterious man of yours."

The wagon bounced over a rough stretch of road, waking Isobel from her nap. She rubbed her eyes and looked out the back. The terrain had changed. No longer were they in the green foothills of Iskara. Instead, they were crossing the rocky sandstone fields that signaled their proximity to Eshgar's mountainous border. The trees were strange. Their trunks spiraled in long, winding patterns before ending in wide canopies that stretched far further than what seemed physically possible. Though it was already winter, they still held all of their foliage, likely due to the much warmer climate. That day in particular was unusually hot.

Isobel stretched and rubbed her bare shoulders. She was glad she had brought some lighter clothing, though she had not accounted for the intensity of the sun when she packed. It was fortunate that Blithe's wagon was one of the few that was covered.

"Skyview is up ahead, Miss Valeria," Blithe shouted from the front.

Isobel donned her wide hat and glanced at Mort, who was himself sleeping rather soundly. She shrugged. He could sleep for a bit longer. She crawled forward and joined Blithe on his seat behind the horses.

Blithe twirled his curly dark mustache. "So, what's next for you, Miss Valeria?"

Isobel cracked her neck. "I'm meeting my partner here, and then we're traveling east together. I have some... family matters to attend to out towards Dawngale."

"Ah! Is your partner from this area?"

"He's from Eshgar, yes."

Blithe grinned. "Well fancy that! My mother lives in Eshgar. I'm actually going to see her myself!"

Isobel adjusted her hat to better shade her eyes and looked to her side. "Is that why you take this route so frequently?"

"It is, yes! My grandparents from my father's side live north of Nellborough, and of course my mother is from Eshgar, so it's the perfect excuse to see both and make some coin along the way."

Isobel nodded and hugged her knees to her chest. Would she and Chinelo have to adopt some kind of arrangement like that? Regardless of where they settled, there would be traveling involved, and that really wasn't so bad. She just needed to find him first. Once they stopped Iva, they could make their plans properly.

"There she is! Skyview in all her glory!" Blithe pointed ahead. "The pride of and joy of southwest Iskara."

Skyview was like many of the towns she and Chinelo had visited. It was tight and crowded, but it looked inviting. Most of the buildings were made of sandstone blocks, so it had a much brighter color palette than some of the towns like Ata or Kahi. She wondered what she would find there.

"Oh! Look! There's someone waving underneath that tree over there," Blithe shaded his eyes and squinted.

Isobel turned her head. In the distance, a lone figure stood at the top of a small rise. It was difficult to see, but he was tall, and his silhouette was full and defined.

Isobel gasped. No! It couldn't be.

She turned her head and listened. Faintly, carried by the wind, she heard a soft call. She couldn't make out the words, but she kept listening. Again, the call came, slightly louder. Then, a third time.

"Isobel!"

She gasped. "I'll—I'll catch up, Blithe!"

She jumped from the wagon and tumbled across the ground.

"Wait! Your frog!" Blithe shouted.

Isobel looked over her shoulder. "I'll be back!"

She ran, climbing up the arid rise towards the shadow at its summit. It was him. She knew it was him. As she drew closer, his features became clearer, more defined. He stood there, smiling at her with those gorgeous eyes, opening his welcoming arms towards her.

She ran faster, and her hat caught the warm breeze and flew away. She kept going, not looking back for even a moment. Then, atop the hill outside of Skyview, beneath the hot sun, she leapt into his arms.

"I missed you," Chinelo said.

"I missed you, too."

"You look gorgeous, by the way," he added.

"Oh, stop. I woke up like this."

She leaned back and looked into his eyes. He looked so refreshed, so bright. All the weariness, the sorrow, the pain had vanished from his face. It was like meeting him again for the first time, a version of him unburdened by loss, untouched by regret. She could stare at his beautiful face all day, and she would have, had he not pressed his lips against hers. He kissed her, gently, softly, tenderly.

They separated, and Isobel's heart fluttered. She exhaled, feeling slightly overwhelmed.

"Your hair is so short," Chinelo said, twisting a strand around his finger.

"D—do you like it?"

"Of course, I like it!"

"You're clean shaven, now, too," Isobel said.

Chinelo chuckled nervously. "I was concerned that the beard wouldn't fill in fast enough. I didn't want it to look bad on our first meeting. I know you generally prefer it, though."

"Well, you know, it does make kissing you less scratchy, so there are benefits," Isobel said with a playful toss of her hair. "And, you do look rather dashing."

Chinelo smiled. "I love you, Isobel."

"Well, that's convenient, because I love you!"

She kissed him again, and they lingered for a moment, enjoying being with each other once more. Isobel sighed and rested her head on his chest. This is what she had dreamed of. She was safe. She was home.

CHINELO ADJUSTED THE BUCKLE ON HIS pack's left strap. It had come loose, and with the substantial weight he was carrying, the imbalance made navigating the steep terrain difficult. Isobel hopped from rock to rock in front of him, looking as cheery and carefree as ever.

Their short journey from Skyview was a pleasant one, owing to the mild climate Eshgar had in winter. Though, as soon as they began their climb into the forest that surrounded the Red Coven, the weather took a dramatic shift towards the frigid. He remembered this winter. It was the final one before Eshgar fell, and it had been incredibly inconsistent, something that Azuka complained about many times during their patrols.

Returning to Eshgar had been strange, after all that time. His family thought he was hysterical with how emotional he had been. He tried to explain the story to his family, but for them, magic was such an alien concept that just accepting it as a reality had proven difficult. Still, his father supported his decision to leave the Royal Guard and the capital. His mother would likely take time to be convinced that it was the right decision, but he was confident she would come around.

His final meeting with Azuka, however, had been incredibly heated. Chinelo only hoped that he could smooth things over between them when he returned.

"Chinelo, I'm worried," Isobel said.

"Oh? What's wrong, dear?"

"What if your mother doesn't like me?" she asked, stepping carefully over a rather sharp rock.

"Well, sometimes people are wrong. She's a reasonable person. I'm sure she will in time."

Isobel ducked under large spiderweb, maneuvering her staff so that it did not get caught. "I just don't want it to be too difficult for her. I'm sure it was confusing when you told them."

Chinelo chuckled. "Well, my father wasn't too hard to sway. Though I think he was convinced that you'd fallen madly in love with me after only a few days, given they had never heard of you."

"Oh, yes. Wouldn't that have been something?" The back of Isobel's neck turned red, and she walked faster.

"Wait a minute," Chinelo said. "Isobel, how long did it take you?"

Isobel stopped and stiffened. "Don't ask me that. It's embarrassing."

Chinelo scampered to her side and leaned over her shoulder. "Isobel. What are you hiding from me?"

Isobel looked away. "A week," she whispered.

"A week?" Chinelo teased.

"Yes, now leave me alone!" she said. "It's your fault anyways. If you hadn't been so nice and attractive and funny, I could have kept my wits about me. But no! You just had to crash in and be perfect! You with your hair and your eyes and your everything. How dare you?"

Chinelo laughed. "Well, I'm hardly perfect, you know."

Isobel looked over her shoulder. "Name one thing wrong with you."

"I snore, really, really loudly."

Isobel frowned. "I'll give you that." She continued walking onwards, using her staff to help her up the rougher sections of the steep path.

She stopped. "Wait a second!"

"Hmmm?"

"How long was it for you?"

"Oh! For me?"

She stepped in front of him and looked up at him, poking his chest with her finger. "Yes, for you! How long?"

Chinelo scratched his head nervously. "Man, I really set myself up for that one, didn't I?"

"You did. Now answer or I shall be very cross."

Chinelo chuckled nervously. "Maybe..."

"Yes?" She leaned closer.

"If we're being honest..."

"Hmmm?" She poked him again.

"Three days?"

Isobel's face turned beet red, though it had already been working its way in that direction.

"Three days?" she shrieked.

"It's hard to say, really. I mean it took me a month to actually acknowledge it, and I wasn't really in a place to do anything about it at first, but yes. Those first few days were enough for me."

Isobel blinked. "Why?"

"Why?"

"Yes, Chinelo! Why?"

"I mean. You know." He vaguely gestured in her direction with his hand.

"Be more specific."

"I thought I told you already. Remember back in Kahi?" Chinelo scratched the stubble on his cheek.

"I was concussed, my memory was erased, and I reversed time. You'll have to forgive me if I'm a bit fuzzy on the details," she chimed.

"Fair enough. Fine. You're witty. You're smart. You're kind. And you're the most beautiful person I've ever seen. Adequate?"

Isobel tapped her chin. "More."

"You're gentle. You're fun. You're caring. You encourage growth in others, and you don't judge them for their shortcomings. You're stubborn, but in a good way."

"More!"

"You're adorable when you get lost in your work."

"More!"

Chinelo took in a deep breath. "Fine, I'd journey across the entire world and face a thousand gods just to see you smile. Good enough?"

She smiled. "Good enough. Now! Let's go! We should be close."

Chinelo breathed out a sigh of relief.

"Don't get too comfortable yet, dear," Isobel said. "When you meet Priscila, you'll have a lot more questions to answer, and she's much more persistent than I am."

Chinelo laughed. "What makes you think I haven't experienced that?"

"What?"

"Isobel, I've met Priscila. And believe me, she already grilled me about you. I just didn't say much, and I didn't tell you. Don't think I don't know what she'll ask, though."

"Sneaky," Isobel muttered.

They continued their trek through the forest, finally reaching the point where the terrain leveled off. The wind howled as it whipped through the trees, buffeting them with gust after gust. Chinelo picked his way over a few fallen logs and stubbed his toe on something hard.

"That got you last time, too," Isobel said.

Chinelo looked down. It was the strange grotesque statue he had tripped over on their first journey to the Red Coven. He glanced up. The path was lined with more of the hideous carved statues. They were close.

The path wound and curved through the trees, and they finally reached the wooden walls. They were high and built from cut timber, with small watch towers spaced at regular intervals. The gates, however, were tightly shut.

Isobel gripped her staff and stepped forward. Chinelo touched his sheath and followed behind. Her ominous warnings still rang in his head. If they entered, what would happen?

Isobel drew a deep breath and shouted. "Open the gate!"

From the watch post above the gate, Chinelo heard a frantic scuffling. A head peered over the edge, looking down with surprised eyes.

"Who goes there?" the woman called.

"A witch, returning from a long journey."

The woman squinted at Chinelo. "Outsiders are not permitted. Men, are most definitely forbidden."

Isobel shouted back. "I am no outsider. I was raised in the Red Coven, and I have returned to see Iva."

Another face appeared, that of a second, much older woman.

"State your name, stranger," the older woman shouted. "I will decide if you live or die."

"Isobel Valeria!" Isobel shouted. "Daughter of Esther Valeria!"

The woman's face went white, and she whispered something to her companion before disappearing. Several minutes passed. Chinelo glanced at Isobel. She seemed unconcerned. After an exceedingly long pause Chinelo heard a loud creaking and clanging from behind the gates.

"See, I knew they would let me in," Isobel said.

The gates gradually opened, revealing a lone figure in leather armor. Her shoulders were covered by a tattered green cloak, and her dark hair was tied and ornamented with silver rings.

"Isobel?" Iva stepped forward. "Is it—is it really you?"

Isobel handed Chinelo her staff and walked to where Iva stood.

"Hello, Iva. It's been a while," Isobel said.

"It has." Iva eyed her with a look of astonishment. "You—you've grown."

Isobel leapt forward and wrapped Iva in a tight embrace. "I missed you. I missed you so much, Iva!"

"I—I missed you, too, love," Iva said softly.

They separated, and Isobel held Iva's hands in hers.

"You came back," Iva said. "After all this time, you came back."

"Yes," Isobel said. "I wanted to tell you something, something I should have told you long ago, on the day we parted."

"All right. I'm listening."

Isobel smiled. "I love you."

THE END OF PART 8

EPILOGUE

432nd year, 9th month, 1st day
Present Day

CHINELO SAT WITH HIS BACK TO the wall, resting on one of the fur pads Isobel had set in her living room. He turned the page of the tome, trying to understand the accounts of ancient history that were recorded within. It was honestly quite confusing. So many words and names and battles that the gods waged against each other and mankind. He remembered Minera, the first witch, and Yvvusta, the god who bestowed magic upon mankind. Beyond those two, things got confusing.

Many things perplexed him. The history books described a desperate war that preceded the gods' ascension. Based on what he and Isobel had discovered on their journey, the gods had sealed away their magic, protecting it from mankind's untethered ambition. He supposed that given what Iva had done that was probably a wise choice.

None of the books he had studied described how or why exactly the gods sealed up their language. So, what had truly happened to the other gods? What did it truly mean to ascend? And what did Ginn's words mean? They unsettled him, haunted him.

"The world is not the world."

Haunting words indeed.

He looked down. Isobel had fallen asleep resting her head in his lap. She breathed softly, rhythmically, peacefully. He brushed a strand of hair away from her face and admired it for several moments. If she was there, maybe those mysteries didn't matter. He really had been lucky to meet her. Even the few weeks he spent without her seemed strangely empty. Having her close to him again truly felt right, so right that he never wanted it to end. Maybe one day soon he could show her the nation he had called home before he met her.

Things had been busy in the two months since they returned from the Red Coven. Isobel had convinced Joanne and Kay to join them in Nellborough, and their lodging had taken time to arrange. Oros offered Chinelo temporary employment at the forge, so his arms had a mild soreness that refused to fade.

Isobel twitched, drawing his attention back down.

How she managed to get so comfortable on the floor was beyond him, but he supposed she had had a long day the previous day. Negotiating with merchants, visiting Iva at the village inn, and catching up with Joanne and Kay would all have been tiring, even for her. She would probably want to eat soon, since the sun was already climbing rather high. Maybe he could wait a few more minutes.

Her stomach roared. She jerked, and her eyes flew open.

"Oh, son of a dead goose!" Isobel said. "I was just getting comfortable."

Chinelo chuckled. "I thought you were asleep."

"I was! And it was an amazing sleep, I'll have you know. Curse this stomach of mine, always causing problems."

She sat up and ran her fingers through her hair a few times. "I guess it's time for breakfast."

Chinelo closed the book and set it on the center table before standing and stretching. "I can cook today. You can resume your nap for a little longer."

Isobel frowned. "It's not quite the same if you're not there."

Chinelo shrugged. "Suit yourself. I'm still happy to cook, though. It is your birthday, after all."

"Well, I am happy to accept that offer. Though I will help you a little and you can't stop me."

She dug through her cupboards and pulled out a bundle of food she had purchased the previous day.

"What are we working with today?" Chinelo asked.

"I've got sausage, a couple of crya eggs, and the usual assortment of oils and spices."

"Perfect! I can work with that."

Chinelo rolled up his sleeves and began cutting up the meat. Isobel lit the fire and prepared a couple pans in which to cook their breakfast.

"How were Joanne and Kay yesterday?" Chinelo asked. "I forgot to ask you last night when you got back."

Isobel stiffened. "They seem to be managing, though life outside the coven is quite the adjustment. Joanne is doing rather well, though Kay is taking a bit longer to acclimate. Though, that's to be expected."

"Are you two getting along?" Chinelo asked.

"Oh, Kay and I?" Isobel said. "Well, I suppose you could say that. It's difficult. She still seems hesitant to open up. It makes sense. She's only had a few months to process things, and when we met in Veld she had had well over a year. She is at least cordial if a bit cold."

"Well, keep trying. I'm sure she appreciates the effort."

"I got lunch with Iva, too. She said she might be traveling for a bit."

"I see." Chinelo tensed. That thought of her still sent shivers down his spine.

Isobel looked over her shoulder. "Do you want to see her before she leaves? She really seemed to like you the last time. I—I know it's been awkward."

Chinelo set the knife down and sighed. "I—I'm not sure if I'm ready yet, Isobel. I know she hasn't done it yet but knowing that she killed my family—well let's just say that I cannot understate my ambivalence. I know she hasn't done that here, though. It's just complicated, and I need to work some things out before I'm ready to trust her like you have."

Isobel kissed his cheek. "I understand. I'm sorry for pushing it."

"I'll get there, Isobel. I promise. I just need a little more time."

She smiled. "Take the time you need. When she gets back we can talk about it again."

Chinelo resumed cutting up the meat. He scraped the slices into one of the pans, splashing them in the thin drizzle of oil Isobel had prepared.

"I did have an idea, though," Isobel said with a twinkle in her eye.

"Oh? What's that?"

"Since Iva won't be around for a while, and we've had time to settle and rest, would you like to go visit your family now? I think it's time!"

"Absolutely. Let's go!"

Isobel laughed. "I thought as much. I might be able to convince Joanne and Kay to come, too! They said they wanted to go sightseeing, so maybe this will be their chance."

Chinelo smiled. "Sounds like a dream."

"I am going to get them up to Veld at some point. Mark my words," Isobel waved her finger.

"When do you want to leave?" Chinelo asked as he slid the pans into the fireplace.

"Hmmm. Now?"

Chinelo shot her a look. "Never change, Isobel. Never change."

"So, in a couple days is good?" she placed her hands on the counter and hopped up and down excitedly.

"Do you even have to ask? Though, there are maybe one or two stops I would like to make."

Isobel tilted her head.

Isobel smiled broadly as she stepped into the clearing, one that they had passed every day on their way to Nellborough. Ruin fragments poked through the ground, and tufts of grass rustled as small animals skittered through the brush. Chinelo stopped walking.

"This is where you want to stop?" she asked.

"Of course! For old time's sake," Chinelo replied.

She'd been standing here on that day, clutching her staff in her hands with her satchel hastily dropped on the ground. She remembered the moment he burst from the trees, his armor shining and clanking with every step. How lucky she had been that day. She hadn't known it at the time, but that single moment had changed both her future and her past.

"This is where we met," she said wistfully.

Chinelo held his new sword in front of him, attempting to imitate her catlike posture. "Don't make another move," he said in a fast, high-pitched voice.

"Hey, now! You were big and scary," she said.

"And you were both adorable and terrifying."

"Well, yes, of course. Such is the way of the witch." She batted her eyes. "Also, I do *not* sound like that, dear."

"No? I'll have to work on my mimicry, then. Maybe you could put together a spell to help." Chinelo joined her and kissed her.

"Oh! Speaking of terrifying, don't think I've forgotten that bluff you pulled at the Red Coven. I thought we were going to die."

"Bah! Verris is a coward." Isobel waved her hand. "I knew she'd fall for it. That bit about slaying the gods did the trick rather nicely, I think."

"Well, it's a good thing she did. I've had enough fighting to last me a long time."

She rested her hands on his shoulder and looked up at him. "But not enough adventures, right?"

"Obviously not. We've only seen three of the eight kingdoms so far."

Isobel sighed and looked into his eyes. Yes, she had been very lucky that day. Chinelo suddenly clapped his hands.

"All right! Next stop!"

"What? That's it?" Isobel cried.

"I've got something planned!" He jogged ahead, waving for her to follow him. "It's a surprise. A birthday surprise!" He hurried down the path with her chasing close behind. They reached a fork in the road. One path led to Nellborough, and the other led to...

Chinelo turned to the right.

"This isn't the way to Nellborough, Chinelo," Isobel said.

"I know! I know! There's something I want to see with you."

Isobel caught up to him and placed her hand in his. "I'll have you know, I am very excited for this surprise. You are quite good at those."

Chinelo scratched his neck. "Well, I don't know about all that."

She patted his arm. "You *are*. I won't be convinced otherwise."

They reached the edge of the forest. The air was filled with the sweet scent of flowers, so, so many flowers. They stretched beyond the horizon, creating a sea of purple on their slender gray stems. The blooms danced in the wind. Wave after wave flowed off into the distance. Like always, the beauty of this Ashen Plains took her breath away.

Chinelo released Isobel's hand and began running, trampling down the slim shoots.

"Chinelo! Wait!" Isobel shouted. He was very excited that day. Did he... was he planning to...?

Chinelo stopped and turned as Isobel jogged behind him. She let Mort off her shoulder, allowing him to search the ground for any unsuspecting insects that might serve as a snack.

"All right! So, what's your surprise?" Isobel asked, bouncing on her toes. She clasped her hands in front of her, quivering with anticipation. Was this what she thought it was?

"Well, there are three pieces to it. This is the first." He waved his hand over the field. "I've wanted to see this with you since the moment I knew I loved you."

"It is a very romantic place to take your partner. You really are good at crafting excellent itineraries. We've already been to the place we met, and the most beautiful landscape in all Iskara and it isn't even lunchtime, yet."

Chinelo reached into his pocket. "The second piece is this." He produced a bracelet from his pocket, a loop decorated with singing birds.

Isobel let out a short squeal. "Oh! You remade it! Chinelo! This is so sweet."

"Since today is your birthday, I thought it would be appropriate to give you the present you lost when we reversed time." He slid the bracelet on her right arm, but he did not let go of it just yet.

She looked down. The *right* arm? That wasn't correct.

"And now for the third part!" Chinelo continued. "Since it technically hasn't happened yet, given our meddling with history, I wanted to ask you something properly."

Chinelo inhaled a deep breath. He clasped her left hand in his.

"Isobel Valeria, will you marry me?"

Isobel smiled softly. "Do you even need to ask?"

————— **THE END** —————

ACKNOWLEDGEMENTS

What a journey this has been. When I started writing *The Witch and the Worldbreaker*, I could barely even imagine what it would become. I've had the idea for this story for several years, and finally getting to set it free from its cage in my head has been one of the most fulfilling things I have ever done.

Of course, none of this would have been possible without the support and encouragement of my friends and family. When I first said that I was trying to write a novel, I did so with hesitation. I think many of us have met someone who said they were writing a book only to never hear about it ever again. I was naturally a little afraid of being one of those cases. However, after two years and a lot of help from several different people, I can proudly acknowledge that yes, I did write a book. So, to all those who joined me on this adventure, I offer my thanks. You all mean the world to me, each in your own unique ways.

To Mary and Jonathan, who were the first to read my opening chapter and who gave me the push that I needed to actually commit to this project. I was scared that anything I wrote would be dreadful, but your detailed praise and critique set a fire in me, and it has refused to fade. It has been fun ironing out the wrinkles of this first novel, and I can't wait for more brainstorming sessions in your living room about our various different writing ventures. Also, thank you especially for being the ones to say how awful that one line in Part 5 about giraffes was. You have spared the world from the horrors I wrote while jetlagged.

To Gurden, who finally encouraged me to stop saying that I was *trying* to write a novel and to say that I *was* writing a novel. Your creativity and kindness has always been an inspiration, and I hope that this story could live up to how many times I talked about it. I'm grateful to have you as a friend after so many years.

To Kelsey, who was always willing to lend an ear to my crazy story ideas. Sorry I spoiled the whole thing for you two years before I wrote it (also for spoiling the ending of several books I haven't started yet). We should go climbing on Monday.

To my sisters Jessica and Kathryn, who beta read the earlier drafts and who did not hold back on their feedback. It was very much needed.

Thank you also for your constant encouragement and interest in my writing journey. Having you as siblings is truly a blessing. You both make me proud to be your brother.

To Abby, who threatened to write W&W fanfiction. I hope you got what you needed.

To Alison, who let me cheat off her indie book publishing homework. Watching you publish *Shadowless* was so inspiring. Thank you for always being willing to offer advice because it was very much needed!

To my father David, who doesn't often read fiction or fantasy, but was still willing to read this book. You've always supported my many creative endeavors, even when they were a bit weird. That is something I will always appreciate.

And, of course, the biggest thank you I can give goes to my mother Michelle. This project could not have happened without you. Thank you for beta and proofreading, helping me edit when I had to fire my editor, letting me rant about my ideas, reading through an entire fantasy series just so we could talk about it, and always pushing me forward on this and in all areas of life.

Last of all, thank you to you, the reader, for reading my book. I hope you enjoyed reading it as much as I did writing it. Isobel and Chinelo's journey has been such a major component of my life for so long, and having someone to share it with is just magical (even if I don't know you personally).

As an indie author, I don't expect to be picked often in this industry of constant major releases and floods of fantasy epics. So, thank you for giving my work a chance. I hope our paths will cross again in the future!

If you enjoyed *The Witch and the Worldbreaker*, please consider reviewing it on Goodreads®, Amazon®, or any of your preferred book-buying sites.

Thank you all! I can't wait for our next adventure!

ABOUT THE AUTHOR

Jonathan Wurst is the debut author of the *Ashes of Iskara* series. Jonathan grew up near Atlanta, Georgia and currently lives in North Alabama.

When he isn't writing epic fantasy or working at his day job as an engineer, Jonathan enjoys rock climbing, cooking, and spending time with friends and family.

www.jonathanwurst.com

www.ingramcontent.com/pod-product-compliance
Lightning Source LLC
Chambersburg PA
CBHW011154010826
48971CB00015B/2726